SIX GOTHIC TALES

SIX
GOTHIC
TALES

SELECTED
AND CONDENSED BY
THE EDITORS OF
THE READER'S DIGEST

THE READER'S DIGEST ASSOCIATION
Pleasantville, New York
Montreal, Sydney, Cape Town, Hong Kong

Contents

Jamaica Inn

by Daphne du Maurier

ILLUSTRATED BY BEN WOHLBERG

On a desolate Cornish moor stood Jamaica Inn. Once warmly hospitable, it was now avoided by decent folk. To this forbidding place came young Mary Yellan, seeking the protection of her uncle and aunt, the inn's proprietors. She found instead an atmosphere of harsh brutality, and became frighteningly aware of stealthy nighttime visitors to the crumbling edifice. Then into her strange new life came an albino preacher and a wickedly charming horse thief. A classic of romantic suspense by the author of *Rebecca*.

CHAPTER ONE

I T WAS A COLD gray day in late November. The weather had changed overnight, when a backing wind brought a granite sky and a mizzling rain with it, and although it was now only a little after two o'clock in the afternoon, the pallor of a winter evening seemed to have closed upon the hills, cloaking them in mist. It would be dark by four. The air was clammy cold, and for all the tightly closed windows it penetrated the interior of the coach. The leather seats felt damp to the hands, and there must have been a small crack in the roof, because now and again little drips of rain fell softly through, smudging the leather and leaving a dark blue stain like a splotch of ink. The wind came in gusts, and in the exposed places it blew with such force that the whole body of the coach trembled and swayed, rocking between the high wheels like a drunken man.

The driver, muffled in a greatcoat to his ears, bent almost double in his seat in an endeavor to gain shelter from his own shoulders, while the horses plodded sullenly to his command. The few passengers huddled together for warmth, exclaiming in unison when the coach sank into a heavier rut than usual. And one old fellow, who had kept up a constant complaint ever since he had joined the coach at Truro, rose from his seat in a fury, and fumbling with the window, let it down with a crash; then he thrust his head out, and shouted up to the driver that they would all be dead before they reached Bodmin if he persisted in driving at breakneck speed. He put up the window again, having thoroughly chilled the interior of the coach, and settling himself once more in his corner, wrapped his blanket about his knees, and muttered in his beard.

His nearest neighbor, a jovial red-faced woman in a blue cloak, sighed heavily in sympathy and remarked for at least the twentieth time that it

9

was the dirtiest night she ever remembered. Then, burrowing into the depths of a large basket, she brought out a great hunk of cake and plunged into it with strong white teeth.

Mary Yellan sat in the opposite corner, where the trickle of rain oozed through the crack in the roof. Sometimes a cold drip fell upon her shoulder, which she brushed away with impatient fingers. She sat with her chin cupped in her hands, her eyes fixed on the window splashed with mud and rain, hoping that some ray of light would break the heavy blanket of sky, and but a momentary trace of that lost blue heaven that had mantled Helford yesterday shine for an instant as a forerunner of fortune.

Already, though barely forty miles by road from what had been her home for three-and-twenty years, that rather gallant courage which was so large a part of her, and had stood her in such stead during the long agony of her mother's illness and death, was now shaken by this driving rain and the nagging wind. This country was alien to her, which was a defeat in itself. How remote now were the green hills and sloping valleys of Helford, the white cluster of cottages at the water's edge. It was a gentle rain that fell at Helford, pattered in the many trees, and sank into the grateful soil, which gave back flowers in payment. This was a lashing, pitiless rain that soaked into a hard and barren soil. No trees here, save one or two bent, twisted, and blackened from centuries of storm—a land without hedgerow or meadow; a country of stones, black heather, and stunted broom.

So many childish memories clung about Helston, where Mary had taken the first coach. The weekly drive to market with her father and, when he was taken from them, the fortitude with which her mother held his place, winter and summer, as he had done, with her hens and her eggs and her butter at the back of the cart, while Mary sat at her side. The name of Yellan was respected in the town, for there were not many women who would have lived alone as the widow did, with never a thought of taking another man. There was a farmer at Manaccan who would have asked her had he dared, and another up the river at Gweek, but they could tell from her eyes she belonged in body and mind to the man who had gone.

It was the hard work of the farm that told upon her in the end. Little by little her stock had decreased; then a sickness attacked the ground and killed the livestock in the villages around Helford. The chickens and the ducklings sickened and died, and the young calf fell in the meadow where he stood. The most pitiful was the old mare upon whose sturdy back Mary had first straddled her young legs. She died in the stall one morning, her faithful head in Mary's lap; and when a pit was dug for her under the apple tree in the orchard, Mary's mother turned to her and said, "There's something of me gone in the grave with poor Nell, Mary. My heart feels tired and I can't go on anymore."

She went into the house and sat down in the kitchen, listless, pale as a sheet, and she began to cry softly, who had never cried before. Mary fetched the old doctor who lived at Mawgan and who had brought her into the world, and he drove her back in his trap along the twisting lane to the farmhouse at the top of the village. A neighbor met them at the gate. "Your mother came out of the door just now, staring like a ghost, and she fell down in the path; they've lifted her inside, poor soul."

Firmly the doctor pushed the little gaping crowd away from the door. Together he and Will Searle lifted the still figure from the floor and carried her upstairs. "It's a stroke," said the doctor. "This is what I've been afraid of—that she'd snap suddenly."

For six long months Mary nursed her mother in this her first and last illness. But it was not the widow's will to recover, as though she longed for release. She said to Mary, "I don't want you to struggle as I have done. It's a breaking of the body and of the spirit. There's no call for you to stay on at Helford after I am gone. It's best for you to go to your aunt Patience up to Bodmin."

There was no use in Mary telling her mother that she would not die. It was fixed there in her mind, and there was no fighting it.

"I'd be no use in a town," said Mary. "I've never known anything but this life by the river. Going into Helston is town enough for me. I'm best here, with the few chickens that's left to us, and the green stuff in the garden, and the old pig, and a bit of a boat on the river. What would I do up to Bodmin?"

"A girl can't live alone, Mary, without she goes queer in the head or comes to evil. I'd not rest in my grave, nor your father neither, if we didn't leave you safe. You'll like your aunt Patience; she was always a great one for games and laughing, with a heart as large as life. You remember when she came here, twelve years back? She had ribbons in her bonnet and a silk petticoat."

Yes, Mary remembered Aunt Patience, with her curled fringe and large blue eyes, and how she laughed and chatted, and how she picked up her skirts and tiptoed through the mud in the yard. She was as pretty as a fairy.

"What sort of a man your uncle Joshua is I cannot say," said her mother, "for I've never set eyes on him. But when your aunt married him ten years ago last Michaelmas she wrote a pack of giddy nonsense you'd not expect from a woman over thirty."

"They'd think me rough," said Mary slowly. "I haven't the pretty manners they'd expect."

"They'll love you for yourself. I want you to promise me this, child, that when I'm gone you'll write to your aunt Patience and tell her that it was my last and dearest wish that you should go to her."

"I promise," said Mary, but her heart was heavy and distressed at the thought of a future so insecure and changed. Her mother lingered through harvest-time, but when the frosts settled on the ground, and the swollen river ran to meet the boisterous sea, the widow turned restlessly in her bed, plucking at the sheets. She called Mary by her dead husband's name, and spoke of people Mary had never known. For three days she lived in her own world, and on the fourth day she died.

One by one Mary saw the things she had loved and understood pass into other hands. The livestock went at Helston market. The furniture was bought by neighbors, stick by stick. A man from Coverack took a fancy to the house and purchased it; with pipe in mouth he straddled the yard and pointed out the changes he would make, while Mary watched him in dumb loathing from her window as she packed her small belongings.

Once more she read the letter from her aunt, written in a cramped hand, on plain paper. The writer said she was shocked at the blow that had befallen her niece; and she went on: "I no longer live in Bodmin, but nearly twelve miles outside, on the road to Launceston. It's a wild and lonely spot, and if you were to come to us, I should be glad of your company, wintertime. Your uncle does not object, he says, if you are quiet-spoken and not a talker. He will expect your help in the bar, in return for your board and lodging. You see, your uncle is the landlord of Jamaica Inn." A cold, empty letter, giving no word of comfort. Aunt Patience, with her silk petticoat and delicate ways, the wife of an innkeeper! The letter was very different from the one penned by a happy bride ten years ago.

However, Mary had promised, and there was no returning on her word. Her aunt was her own mother's sister, and that was the one thing to remember. The old life lay behind—the dear familiar farm and the shining Helford waters. Before her lay—Jamaica Inn.

AND SO IT WAS that Mary Yellan found herself northward bound from Helston in the creaking, swaying coach. It rumbled into Bodmin, gray and forbidding like the hills that cradled it, and one by one the passengers gathered up their things—all save Mary, who sat still in her corner. The driver, his face a stream of rain, looked in at the window.

"Are you going on to Launceston?" he said. "It'll be a wild drive to-night across the moors. You can stay in Bodmin and go on by coach in the morning. There'll be none in this coach going on but you."

"My friends will be expecting me," said Mary. "And I don't want to go as far as Launceston; will you please put me down at Jamaica Inn?"

The man looked at her curiously. "Jamaica Inn?" he said. "That's no place for a girl. You must have made a mistake, surely. Here, wait a minute." He called over his shoulder to a woman who stood in the doorway of the Royal, lighting the lamp above the porch.

"Missus," he said, "come here an' reason with this young girl. She's asked me to put her down at Jamaica."

The woman came down the steps and peered into the coach. "It's a wild, rough place up there," she said, "and if it's work you are looking for, you won't find it on the farms. They don't like strangers on the moors. You'd do better here in Bodmin."

Mary smiled at her. "I shall be all right," she said. "I'm going to relatives. My uncle is landlord of Jamaica Inn."

There was a long silence. In the gray light of the coach Mary could see that the woman and the man were staring at her. She felt chilled suddenly; she wanted some word of reassurance from the woman, but the woman drew back from the window. "It's none of my business, of course," she said. "Good night."

The driver began to whistle, rather red in the face, as one who wishes to rid himself of an awkward situation. Mary leaned forward impulsively and touched his arm. "Is my uncle not liked? Is something the matter?"

The man looked very uncomfortable. He avoided her eyes. "Jamaica's got a bad name," he said. "Respectable folk don't go there anymore. Queer tales get about; but I don't want to make any trouble. Maybe they're not true."

"What sort of tales?" asked Mary. "Do you mean there's much drunkenness there? Does my uncle encourage bad company?"

The man hesitated; then he shook his head. "We'd best be going. You are the only traveler on the road tonight. I'll whip the horses on when we've climbed the hill out of Bodmin, for it's no night for the road. I shan't be easy until I reach my bed in Launceston." He slammed the door and climbed to his seat.

The coach rumbled away down the street, past the safe and solid houses. Through the shuttered windows Mary could see chinks of friendly candlelight; there would be a fire within the grate, and a cloth spread on the table, a woman and children sitting down to their meal, while the man warmed his hands before the cheerful blaze. Then the horses were climbing the steep hill out of the town, and looking through the window at the back of the coach, Mary could see the lights of Bodmin fast disappearing, until the last glimmer winked and flickered and was gone. She was alone with the wind and the rain, and twelve long miles of barren moor between her and her destination. She sat huddled in her corner, swaying from side to side as the coach was shaken, and it seemed to her that never before had she known there was malevolence in solitude. The very coach, which all the day had rocked her like a cradle, held a note of menace in its creaks and groans. The wind tore at the roof, and the showers of rain, increasing in violence now there was no shelter from the hills, spat against the windows with new venom.

On either side of the road the country stretched interminably, mile upon mile of dark moorland, with never a light to waver for an instant as a message of hope to the traveler. Mary lost count of time and space; the miles might have been a hundred and the hour midnight, for all she knew. At last she lowered the window and looked out. She was met with a blast of wind and rain that blinded her for the moment, and then, shaking her hair from her eyes, she saw that ahead of her, on the crest of a hill, was some sort of a building, standing back from the road. She could see tall chimneys, murky dim in the darkness. There was no other house, no other cottage. If this was Jamaica, it stood alone, foursquare to the winds. Mary gathered her cloak around her. The horses had been pulled to a standstill, the steam coming from them in a cloud. The driver climbed from his seat, pulling her box down with him. He seemed hurried, and kept glancing toward the house.

"Here you are," he said; "across the yard there yonder. I must be getting on or I'll not reach Launceston tonight." Then he was up on his seat again, whipping the horses in a fever of anxiety. In a moment the coach was away and down the road, swallowed up in the darkness.

Mary stood alone, with the trunk at her feet. She heard a sound of bolts being drawn in the dark house behind her, and the door was flung open. A great figure strode into the yard, swinging a lantern.

"Who is it?" came the shout. "What do you want here?"

Mary stepped forward and peered up into the man's face. The light shone in her eyes, and she could see nothing. He swung the lantern to and fro before her, and suddenly he laughed and took hold of her arm, pulling her roughly inside the porch.

"Oh, it's you, is it?" he said. "So you've come to us after all? I'm your uncle, Joss Merlyn, and I bid you welcome to Jamaica Inn." He drew her into the shelter of the house, laughing again, and shut the door, and stood the lantern upon a table in the passage. And they looked upon each other face to face.

CHAPTER TWO

HE WAS A GREAT husk of a man, nearly seven feet high, with a creased black brow and a skin the color of a Gypsy's. His thick dark hair fell over his eyes in a fringe and hung about his ears. He looked as if he had the strength of a horse, with immense powerful shoulders, long arms that reached almost to his knees, and large fists like hams. His frame was so big that in a sense his head was dwarfed, and sunk between his shoulders, giving that half-stooping impression of a giant gorilla. But there was nothing of the ape about his features, for his nose was hooked, curving to a mouth that might have been perfect once but was now sunken, and there was still something fine about his great dark eyes, in spite of the pouches and the red blood flecks.

The best things left to him were his teeth, which were white, so that when he smiled they showed up against the tan of his face, giving him the hungry appearance of a wolf. And, though there should be a world of difference between the smile of a man and the bared fangs of a wolf, with Joss Merlyn they were one and the same. "So you are Mary Yellan," he said at length, his head bent to observe her more closely, "and you've come all this way to look after your uncle Joss. I call it very handsome of you." He laughed again, mocking her, his laugh bellowing through the house, acting like a lash on her strung nerves.

"Where is my aunt Patience?" she asked, glancing around her in the dimly lit passage, cheerless with its cold flagstones and narrow rickety staircase. "Is she not expecting me?"

" 'Where's my aunt Patience?' " he mimicked. "Can't you wait for an instant without running to her? Haven't you a kiss for Uncle Joss?"

Mary drew back. The thought of kissing him revolted her. He was either mad or drunk, probably both. "Oh no," he said, "I'm not going to touch you; I've better things to do than to play cat's cradle with me own niece." He jeered down at her contemptuously; then he lifted his head to the stairs. "Patience," he roared, "what in hell are you doing? Here's the girl arrived, whimpering for you."

There was a little flutter at the head of the stairs, then the flicker of a candle and an exclamation. Down the narrow stairs came a woman, shielding the light from her eyes. She wore a dingy mobcap on her thin gray hair, which hung in elflocks to her shoulders. Her face had fallen away, and the skin was stretched tight across her cheekbones. Her eyes were large and staring, as though they perpetually asked a question, and she had a little nervous trick of working her mouth, now pursing the lips and now relaxing them. She wore a faded striped petticoat, and over her shoulders was flung a much-mended shawl. She had obviously just strung a new scarlet ribbon in her cap in some small attempt to brighten her dress, and it showed up in horrible contrast to the pallor of her face. Mary stared at her, stricken with sorrow. Was this poor tattered creature the bewitching Aunt Patience of her dreams?

The little woman took Mary's hands in hers and peered into her face. "Have you really come?" she whispered. "It is my niece, Mary Yellan, isn't it? My dead sister's child?"

Mary nodded. "Dear Aunt Patience," she said gently, "I'm so glad to see you again."

The woman kept pawing her with her hands, stroking her clothes, feeling her, and suddenly she clung to her, burying her head against her shoulder, and began to cry, drawing her breath in loud gasps.

"What have you got to squark about, you damned fool?" growled her husband. He bent down and shouldered Mary's box as though it weighed less than a paper packet. "I'll take this to her room," he said, "and if you've not got a bite of supper on the table by the time I'm down again, I'll give you something to cry about; and you too, if you like," he added, laying one great finger across Mary's mouth. "Are you tame, or do you bite?" he said, and then he laughed once more, and thundered up the narrow stairs with the box swaying on his shoulders.

"You mustn't mind your uncle Joss," Aunt Patience said, her manner changing suddenly, fawning like a whimpering dog that has been trained by constant cruelty to implicit obedience, and who, in spite of kicks and curses, will fight like a tiger for its master. "Your uncle must be humored, you know. He's a very good husband to me." Working her mouth, she led the way to yet another murky passage, and so into the kitchen, which was lit by three candles, while a low turf fire smoldered on the hearth.

She pattered on mechanically, taking bread, cheese, and dripping from the big cupboard behind the paneling, while Mary crouched beside the fire in a hopeless attempt to warm her chilled fingers. The kitchen was heavy with peat smoke. It stung Mary's eyes and nostrils, and lay upon her tongue.

"You'll soon come to like your uncle Joss and fit into his ways," continued her aunt. "He has a great name hereabouts and is much respected. The gentry are most civil to us, most civil. Even the squire himself—that's Squire Bassat from North Hill; he owns all the land hereabouts—he passed me on the road the other day and he took off his hat. 'Good morning, madam,' he said, and he bowed to me from his horse. Then out comes Joss from the stable. 'How's life, Mr. Bassat?' he says. 'As large as yourself, Joss,' answers the squire, and they both fell to laughing."

There was a footfall outside the door, and with a sinking heart Mary realized that Joss had come downstairs again and had in all probability listened to his wife's conversation. Aunt Patience heard him too, for she turned pale. He came into the room and looked from one to the other.

"So the hens are clacking already?" he said, the smile and the laugh gone, his eyes narrow. He pulled a chair from the wall, crashed it against the table, and reaching for the loaf, cut himself off a great hunk of bread, which he slabbed with dripping. He crammed it into his mouth, the grease running down his chin, and beckoned Mary to the table. He proceeded to cut carefully a thin slice from the loaf, which he quartered in pieces and buttered for her, the whole business very delicately done and in striking contrast to his manner in serving himself. Had he cut her a chunk of bread and hurled it at her, she would not have minded so much. But this sudden coming to grace, this quick and exquisite moving of his hands, was a swift and rather sinister revelation, sinister because it was not true to type. She thanked him quietly and began to eat. No one spoke. Mary was aware of Joss Merlyn watching her across the table. "What'll you drink?" he asked her. "Brandy, wine, or ale? You may starve here, but you won't go thirsty. We don't get sore throats at Jamaica." And he winked at her.

"I'll have a cup of tea if I may. I'm not used to drinking spirits."

"Oh, you're not? Well, you can have your tea tonight, but you'll want something stronger in a month or two. Patience, my dear, here's the key. Go and fetch me a bottle of brandy. I've a thirst on me that all the waters of Dozmary would not slake."

Mary's eyes watered from the peat smoke, but she watched her uncle, for already she had caught something of the nervousness of her aunt Patience and felt that in some sense they were here like mice in a trap, with him playing with them like a monstrous cat. In a few minutes his wife returned with the brandy, which she put in front of her husband, and while she fried some bacon and served Mary and herself, he fell to drinking, staring moodily before him. Suddenly he thumped the table.

"I tell you what it is, Mary Yellan," he shouted. "I'm master in this house. You'll do as you're told and serve my customers, and I'll not lay a finger on you. But, by God, if you open your mouth and squark, I'll break you until you eat out of my hand the same as your aunt yonder."

Mary faced him across the table. She held her hands in her lap so that he should not see them tremble. "I understand you," she said, turning pale. "I'm not curious by nature, and I've never gossiped in my life. It doesn't matter to me what you do in the inn or what company you keep. I'll do my work about the house and you'll have no cause to grumble. But if you hurt my aunt Patience in any way, I'll find the magistrate, and bring him here, and have the law on you; then try and break me if you like."

The torrent of words had come from Mary in spite of herself, wrung with pity for the poor broken thing that was her aunt. Had she but known it, she had saved herself, for her little show of spirit impressed the man.

"That's very pretty," he said. "Now we know just what sort of lodger we have. Scratch her, and she shows her claws. All right, my dear; you and I are more akin than I thought. I may have work for you at Jamaica one day, work that you've never done before. Man's work, Mary Yellan, where you play with life and death." Mary heard her aunt Patience give a little gasp.

"Oh, Joss," she whispered. "Oh, Joss, please!"

There was so much urgency in her voice that Mary stared at her in surprise. She saw her aunt lean forward and motion her husband to be silent, and the agony in her eyes frightened Mary more than anything that had happened that night. She felt chilled suddenly, and rather sick.

What had Joss Merlyn been about to say? Her uncle waved his hand impatiently. "Get up to bed, Patience," he said. "I'm tired of your death's-head at my supper table. This girl and I understand one another."

The woman rose at once and went to the door, with a last ineffectual glance of despair over her shoulder. Joss Merlyn and Mary were alone. He pushed the empty brandy glass away.

"There's been one weakness in my life," he said. "It's drink. I'll feel the thirst come on me and I'll soak for hours. It's power, and glory, and women, all rolled into one. I feel a king then, Mary. I talk—talk until every damned thing I've ever done is spilled to the four winds. I shut myself in my room and shout my secrets in my pillow. Your aunt turns the key on me, and when I'm sober I hammer on the door and she lets me out. But I'm not drunk enough to tell you why I live in this God-forgotten spot, and why I'm the landlord of Jamaica Inn." Now he scarcely spoke above a whisper. The turf fire had sunk low in the hearth, the candles too had burned down and cast a monstrous shadow of Joss Merlyn on the ceiling. With a foolish drunken gesture he laid his finger against his nose.

"If you want to know any more, you can ask your aunt. I heard her blathering tonight, telling you the squire takes off his hat to her. It's lies, all lies. Squire Bassat's too mortal scared to shove his nose in here. The coaches don't stop now, nor the mails neither. I don't worry; I've customers enough. There's drinking here all right. On Saturday night, when every cottage on the moors is dark and silent, the only lights for miles are the blazing windows of Jamaica Inn. They say the shouting and the singing can be heard as far down as the farms below Rough Tor. You'll be in the bar those nights and you'll see what company I keep."

Mary sat very still, gripping the sides of her chair. She dared not move for fear of that swift changing of his mood which would turn him from this sudden intimate tone of confidence to a coarse brutality.

"They're all afraid of me," he went on, "the whole damned lot of 'em. If I'd had learning, I'd have walked the breadth of England beside King George himself. It's drink that's been the curse of all of us, Mary. There's never been a Merlyn yet that died peaceful in his bed.

"My father was hanged at Exeter—he had a brawl with a fellow and killed him. My granddad had his ears cut for thieving; he was sent out to a convict settlement and died raving mad from a snakebite. I'm the eldest of three brothers, all of us born under the shadow of Kilmar Tor, away yonder above Twelve Men's Moor. You walk out over there across the East Moor till you come to Rushyford, and you'll see a great crag of granite like a devil's hand sticking up into the sky. That's Kilmar. My brother Matthew, he was drowned in Trewartha Marsh. We thought he'd gone for a sailor, and then in the summer there was a drought, and no rain fell for seven months, and there was Matthew sticking up in the bog,

with his hands above his head and the curlews flying round him. My brother Jem, damn him, he was the baby. Hanging on to Mother's skirts when Matt and I were grown men. Too smart Jem is, too sharp with his tongue. Oh, they'll catch him in time and hang him, same as they did my father."

He fell silent a moment, gazing at his empty glass. "I've said enough. I'll have no more tonight. Go up to bed, Mary, before I wring your neck. Here's your candle. You'll find your room over the porch."

Mary took the candlestick without speaking and was about to pass him when he seized her shoulder and twisted her around.

"There'll be nights sometimes when you'll hear wheels on the road," he said, "and those wheels will stop outside Jamaica Inn. And you'll hear footsteps in the yard and voices beneath your window. When that happens, you'll stay in your bed and cover your head with the blankets. Do you understand?"

"Yes, Uncle."

"Very well. Now get out, and if you ever ask me a question, I'll break every bone in your body."

She went out into the dark passage, and so upstairs, feeling her way with her hands, judging her whereabouts by turning around and facing the stairs again. Her uncle had told her the room over the porch, and she crept across the unlit landing, past two doors on either side—guest rooms, she imagined, waiting for those travelers who never sought shelter nowadays beneath the roof of Jamaica Inn—and then stumbled against another door and turned the handle, and saw by the flickering flame of her candle that this was her room, for her trunk lay on the floor.

The walls were rough and unpapered, and the floorboards bare. The bed creaked when she leaned upon it, and the two thin blankets felt damp to her hand. For a long while Mary sat huddled on the bed, a prey to despair. She wondered whether it was possible to break from the house and find her way back the twelve long miles to Bodmin. She felt caught here, like a bird in a net, and however much she struggled, she would never escape. If she wished to be free, she must go now, climb from her window, and run like a mad thing along the white road that stretched like a snake across the moors. Tomorrow it would be too late.

She waited until she heard her uncle's footsteps on the stairs. He went along the other passage, to the left of the staircase. In the distance a door closed, and there was silence. She decided that she would wait no longer. If she stayed even one night in this house that reeked of evil, her nerve would go from her and she would be lost, mad, and broken, like Aunt Patience. She opened the door and tiptoed to the head of the stairs. Her hand was on the banister when she heard a sound from the other passage, somebody crying. It was someone whose breath came in little gasps and who tried to muffle the sound in a pillow. It was Aunt Patience. Mary turned back and threw herself on her bed and closed her eyes. However frightened she would be, she would not leave Jamaica Inn now. She must stay with Aunt Patience. It might be that in some way which she was now too tired to plan, Mary could act as a protector to Aunt Patience and stand between her and Joss Merlyn. Mary's mother would have had the courage to fight her enemies. Yes, and conquer them in the end.

And so Mary counted the minutes and the hours of an eternal night, and when the first cock crowed in a field behind the house she counted no more, but sighed, and slept like a dead thing.

CHAPTER THREE

MARY WOKE TO a high wind from the west and a thin watery sun. Looking out across the yard, she saw that the stable door was open, and there were fresh hoofmarks in the mud outside. With a great sense of relief she realized that the landlord must have gone from home, and she would have Aunt Patience to herself. Hurriedly she unpacked her trunk, pulling out her thick skirt and colored apron and the heavy shoes she had worn at the farm, and in ten minutes she was down in the kitchen and washing in the scullery at the back.

Aunt Patience came in from the chicken run behind the house with some new-laid eggs in her apron, which she produced with a little smile of mystery. "I thought you'd like one for your breakfast," she said, obviously making an effort to be cheerful. "I saw you were too tired to eat much last night."

They both avoided any reference to Joss. Mary could see that her aunt was eager to speak of things unconnected with her present life; she seemed afraid of any questions, so Mary plunged into a description of the last years at Helford, the strain of the bad times, and her mother's illness and death. Whether Aunt Patience took it in or not she could not tell; it seemed to Mary that years of fear and anxiety had taken away her powers of concentration, and that some underlying terror prevented her from giving her whole interest to any conversation.

During the morning there was the usual work of the house, and Mary was thus able to explore the inn more thoroughly. It was a dark, rambling place, with long passages and unexpected rooms. There was a separate entrance to the bar, at the side of the house, and there was something heavy in the atmosphere reminiscent of the last time the room was full: the sour smell of drink, and an impression of warm, unclean humanity packed one against the other on the stained benches.

The other rooms appeared unused; even the parlor by the entrance porch had a solitary air, as though it were many months since an honest traveler had stepped upon the threshold and warmed his back before a glowing fire. One of the guest rooms upstairs was used for lumber, and old horse blankets chewed by families of rats. In the room opposite, potatoes and turnips had been stored upon a broken-down bed. Downstairs, along a passage that ran parallel to the one above, and in the opposite direction from the kitchen, was another room, the door of which was locked. Mary went out into the yard to look at it through the window, but there was a board nailed up against the frame.

The house and outbuildings formed three sides of the little square that was the yard, in the center of which was a grass bank and a drinking trough. Beyond this lay the road, a thin white ribbon that stretched on either hand to the horizon, surrounded on each side by moorland, brown and sodden from the heavy rains. Mary went out onto the road and looked about her, and as far as her eyes could see there was nothing but the black hills and the moors. The gray slate inn, with its tall chimneys, was the only dwelling place on the landscape. To the west of Jamaica high tors reared their heads; some were smooth like downland, and the grass shone yellow under the fitful winter sun; but others were sinister, their peaks crowned with great slabs of stone. Now and again the sun was obscured by clouds, and long shadows fled over the moors like fingers. Color came in patches; sometimes the hills were mottled purple, and then a feeble ray of sun would come from a wisp of cloud, and one hill would be golden brown while its neighbor still languished in the dark. The scene was never once the same, for it would be the glory of high noon to the east, and away to the westward arctic winter fell upon the hills, brought by a jagged cloud, shaped like a highwayman's cloak, that scattered hail and snow and a sharp spittle rain onto the granite tors. The air was strong and sweet smelling, and strangely pure.

However grim was this new country, however barren and untilled, there was a challenge in the air that spurred Mary Yellan to adventure. It stung her, bringing color to her cheeks and playing with her hair. She went to the water trough and put her hands under the spring. The water ran clear and icy cold. She drank some, and it was bitter, queer, with a lingering peat taste like the smoke from the turf fire in the kitchen.

It was satisfying, for her thirst went from her. She felt strong in body and emboldened in spirit, and she went back into the house to find Aunt Patience, her appetite sharp for the stewed mutton and turnips she knew awaited her. Then, her hunger appeased, she felt her courage return, and she was ready to question her aunt and risk the consequences. "Aunt Patience," she began, "why is my uncle the landlord of Jamaica Inn?"

The sudden direct attack took the woman by surprise, and for a moment she stared at Mary without reply. Then she flushed scarlet and began to work her mouth. "Why," she faltered, "it's—it's a very prominent place here, the main road from the south. There's always travelers, and private gentlemen, and sometimes sailors from Falmouth. There's men come in from the farms and cottages scattered over these moors for miles around."

"Yes, Aunt Patience. But why don't the travelers stop at Jamaica? The parlor is never used, and the guest rooms are stored with lumber."

Her aunt twisted her fingers in her lap. "Your uncle Joss doesn't encourage folk to stay," she said at length. "Why, in a lonely spot like this we might be murdered in our beds. There's all sorts on a road like this."

"Aunt Patience, you're talking nonsense. What is the use of an inn that cannot give an honest traveler a bed for the night?"

Her aunt was silent and sat stubborn as a mule. Mary tried another question. "Why did you come here in the first place? My mother knew nothing of this; we believed you to be in Bodmin."

"I met your uncle in Bodmin, but we never lived there," replied Aunt Patience slowly. "Your uncle bought the inn from Mr. Bassat. It had stood empty a number of years, and your uncle decided it would suit him. He wanted to settle down."

"It seems a funny thing to come to this place to settle," said Mary. "He couldn't have chosen much worse, could he?"

"It's near his old home," said her aunt. "Your uncle was born only a few miles away, over on Twelve Men's Moor. His brother Jem lives there now in a bit of a cottage, when he's not roaming the country. Your uncle Joss does not care for him much." She leaned back in her chair, exhausted from her cross-examination.

"Aunt Patience," Mary said, "I want you to answer me this, and then I won't worry you again. What has the barred room at the end of the passage to do with the wheels that stop outside Jamaica Inn by night?"

A strange expression crept upon the woman's face. Her mouth trembled, and her hand wandered to her throat.

Mary pushed back her chair and went over to her aunt. She put her arms around her and held her close. "I'm sorry," she said. "I've no right to question you. Please forget what I said."

Aunt Patience took Mary's hands in hers and gazed into her face. "Mary," she said, and her voice was hushed and low, "Mary, I can't answer your questions, for there's many I don't know the answer of myself. But because you are my own sister's child, I must give you a word of warning." She glanced over her shoulder, as though she were afraid that Joss himself stood in the shadows behind the door.

"There's things that happen here, Mary, that I've never dared to breathe. Evil things. I dare not even admit them to myself. Some of it in time you'll come to know. Your uncle Joss mixes with men who follow

23

a strange trade. Sometimes they come by night, and your uncle takes them along that passage to the room with the locked door. From my bedroom above I can hear the mutter of their voices through the long hours. Before dawn they are away, and no sign left that they have ever been. When they come, Mary, you must lie in bed and put your fingers to your ears. You must never question me, nor your uncle Joss, for if you came to guess but half of what I know, your hair would go gray, Mary, as mine has done, and you would tremble in your speech and weep by night, and all that lovely careless youth of yours would die, Mary, as mine has died."

Then she rose from the table, and Mary heard her climb the staircase with heavy, faltering feet, and so along the landing to her room.

JOSS MERLYN WAS away from home for nearly a week, and during that time Mary came to know something of the country. Her presence was not required in the bar, for no one came to it when the landlord was from home, and after giving her aunt a hand with the housework, she was free to wander where she pleased.

The moors, like an immense desert, rolled from east to west, with tracks here and there across the surface and great hills breaking the skyline. Where was their final boundary Mary could not tell, except that once, away to the westward, after climbing the highest tor behind Jamaica, she caught the silver shimmer of the sea. On the high tors the slabs of stone leaned against one another in strange forms. Some were shaped like giant furniture, with monstrous chairs and twisted tables. There were long stones that stood on end, balancing themselves in a queer miraculous way, as though they leaned against the wind; and there were flat altar stones whose polished faces stared up toward the sky, awaiting a sacrifice that never came. Wild sheep dwelt on the high tors, and there were ravens and buzzards; the hills were homing places for all solitary things.

Black cattle grazed on the moors beneath, their careful feet avoiding the tufted, tempting grass that was not grass at all, but soggy marsh. Strange winds blew from nowhere; they crept along the surface of the grass; they breathed upon the little pools of rain in the hollowed stones. Sometimes the wind shouted and cried, and the cry echoed in the crevices and was lost again. There was a silence on the tors that belonged to an age when pagan footsteps trod upon the hills. There was a stillness in the air, and a stranger, older peace that was not the peace of God.

One day Mary Yellan crossed the East Moor, in the direction Joss Merlyn had given her that first evening; and when she had gone some way she saw that the land descended to a deep and treacherous marsh, through which a brook burbled and sang. And rising beyond the marsh was a crag like a great split hand coming sheer out of the moor, its surface molded in granite as though sculptured.

So this was Kilmar Tor; and somewhere among that mass of stone, where the ridges hid the sun, Joss Merlyn had been born and his brother lived today. Below her in the marsh, Matthew Merlyn had been drowned. In her fancy she saw him flounder helplessly, beating the weeds with his hands. She heard him scream in terror, and a curlew rose from the marsh in front of him, flapping his wings and whistling his mournful cry.

Mary turned her back upon Kilmar and began to run across the moor, stumbling among the heather and the stones. It seemed an eternity before the tall chimneys of Jamaica Inn stood out above the winding road. As she crossed the yard she noticed with sinking heart that the stable door was open and the pony was inside. Joss Merlyn had returned.

She opened the door as silently as possible, but in a minute the landlord appeared from the back, bending his head under the beam. He had a glass in his hand and was, it seemed, in high good humor, for he shouted boisterously at Mary. "Well," he roared, "don't drop your face a mile at the sight of me." She made an effort to smile and asked him if he had had a pleasant journey. "Pleasant be damned," he answered. "There was money in it, and that's all I care." He shouted with laughter at his joke, and his wife appeared behind his shoulder, simpering in harmony. As soon as his laughter died away the smile faded from Aunt Patience's face, and the strained, haunted expression returned again.

Mary turned to go up the stairs to her room, when Joss called her. "Here," he said, "no skulking up there this evening. There'll be work for you in the bar. Don't you know what day of the week it is?" She paused to think. Was it Monday's coach she had taken? That made today Saturday. At once she realized what Joss Merlyn meant. Tonight there would be company at Jamaica Inn.

THEY CAME SINGLY, the people of the moors, crossing the yard swiftly and silently. They seemed no more than shadows as they passed under the shelter of the porch to knock upon the door of the bar. One or two rode into the yard on ponies, whose hoofs clattered on the stones, the sound strange in the still night; this was followed by the creaking of the stable door and the furtive mutter of voices as the men led their ponies to the stalls. The reason for stealth was not apparent, for any passing traveler upon the road could see that tonight Jamaica Inn gave hospitality. The light streamed from the windows, usually so shuttered and barred, and the sound of voices rose upon the air, singing and shouting.

They were a strange assortment gathered there, grouped around Joss Merlyn. Securely separated by the counter, and half screened by a barrier of bottles, Mary could look down upon the company and remain unobserved. They straddled stools, sprawled upon the benches, slouched against the walls and beside the tables, ragged, with matted hair and broken nails;

tramps, vagrants, poachers, thieves, cattle stealers, and Gypsies. One, a poor half-witted fellow from Dozmary, had a birthmark that blazed his face purple, and he kept plucking at it with his hands, so that Mary turned sick at the sight of him. Luckily she did not have to move among them; her duty was to do what washing of glasses was required, refilling them from tap or bottle, while Joss Merlyn handed them to his customers or lifted the flap of the bar and strode out into the room, laughing at one, flinging a coarse word at another. After the first hilarious outburst, the company accepted Mary as niece of the landlord, fearing that any familiarity on their part might anger him, as he had probably brought her to Jamaica for his own amusement.

Those who remained sufficiently sober to stand had crowded now around a dirty little blackguard from Redruth, who had established himself wit of the assembly. He was a tinker, peddler, salesman, and had stored up a string of loathsome songs, and with these he now provided entertainment to the company at Jamaica Inn. His sallies nearly shook the roof, and to Mary there was something appalling in this ugly, screaming laughter which in some strange way held not a note of mirth. The peddler was making bait of the wretched idiot from Dozmary. He made him repeat the words of his songs, complete with actions, amid the frenzy of laughter from the crowd; and the poor beast jigged up and down on a table, whinnying delight. Mary could bear it no longer. She touched her uncle on the shoulder, and he turned to her, his face blotched with the smoke and heat of the room. "I can't stand this," she said. "You'll have to attend to your friends yourself."

He stared down at her. "Think yourself too good for such as we?" he said. "I'll tell you this, Mary. You've had an easy time behind the bar because you're my niece, but if you hadn't had that honor—by God, there wouldn't be much left of you now!" He shouted with laughter and pinched her cheek between his finger and thumb. "Get out, then," he said. "You'll lock your door tonight and pull down your blind. Your aunt's been in bed an hour with the blanket over her head." Seizing her wrist, he doubled it behind her back, until she cried out in pain. "All right," he said. "That's like a foretaste of punishment, and you know what to expect. It doesn't do to be curious at Jamaica Inn." He frowned. "You're not a fool like your aunt; that's the curse of it. You've got a clever little monkey face, and a ferreting monkey mind. But I'll break that mind of yours if you let it go astray, and I'll break your body too."

He turned away from her, frowning still. "Strip that damned idiot of his clothes," he thundered. "Maybe the November air will cool that purple face of his and cure his dog tricks."

The peddler and his group yelled in delight and began to tear off the half-wit's coat and breeches. Mary ran out of the room, up the rickety stairs, her hands over her ears, and threw herself on her bed. There was a babel of noise in the yard below, while a stream of light from a tossing lantern cast a beam up to her window. She got up and drew the blind, but not before she had seen a naked form bound across the yard with great loping strides, screaming like a hare and pursued by hooting men, with Joss Merlyn in the lead cracking a horsewhip above his head.

Mary undressed and crept into bed, pulling the blanket over her head, stuffing her fingers in her ears, her only thought to be deaf to the horror and the revelry below; she lay in that half-conscious state on the border of sleep. There had been voices, and now there were none; somewhere far away on the highroad a horse galloped and wheels rumbled.

She slept; and then, without warning, she was awake suddenly. She was aware of the little path of light made by the moon on the floor. There came from beneath her room the sound of heavy things being dragged along the flagstones in the passage, bumping against the walls. She got out of bed and went to the window, pulling aside an inch of blind. Five wagons were in the yard. Three were covered, each drawn by a pair of horses, and the remaining two were open farm carts.

Gathered around the wagons were some of the men who had been drinking in the bar earlier in the evening; the peddler who had tortured the poor idiot was climbing into one of the open carts and lifting something from the floor. And there were strangers in the yard. Mary could see their faces clearly because of the moonlight, the very brightness of which seemed to worry the men, for one of them pointed upward and shook his head, while another man, who had an air of authority about him, waved his arm impatiently, as though urging them to make haste. Meanwhile the heavy dragging sound continued. Something was being taken along the passage to the room at the end, the room with the barred windows and the bolted door.

Mary began to understand. Packages were brought by the wagons and stored in the locked room. Because the horses were steaming, she knew they had come over a great distance—from the coast, perhaps. The men in the yard worked quickly, against time. The contents of one covered wagon were not carried into the inn, but were transferred to one of the open farm carts. Some were large parcels, some were small, and others were long rolls wrapped round about in straw and paper. When the cart was filled, the driver climbed into the seat and drove away. All was done in silence. Even the horses stood motionless.

Joss Merlyn came out of the porch, the peddler at his side. "Is that the lot?" the landlord called softly, and the driver of the last wagon nodded and held up his hand. The men began to climb into the carts. They did not leave unrewarded; all carried boxes strapped over their shoulders, bundles under the arm. So the wagons and the carts departed from Jamaica, creaking out of the yard, one after the other, in a strange funereal procession, until there was no one left but one man Mary had not seen before, the peddler, and the landlord of Jamaica Inn himself. Then they too turned and went back into the house, and she heard their footsteps die away along the passage in the direction of the bar.

Mary came away from the window and sat down upon the bed. The thought of sleep now was impossible. She was too alive in every nerve, and although the dislike and fear of her uncle was as strong as ever within her, curiosity held the mastery. She understood something of his business now. What she had witnessed tonight was smuggling on the grand scale. Jamaica Inn stood alone on the great highroad that ran north and south, and Mary could see that it must be easy enough for anyone with a capacity for organization to work a team of wagons from the coast to the Tamar River, with the inn itself as halting place and general store on the way to Devon. Spies were needed about the countryside to make a success of the trade; hence the Gypsies, the tramps, the vile little peddler.

And yet, allowing for his personality, his energy, the very fear which his enormous physical strength must engender in his companions, had Joss Merlyn the necessary brain and subtlety to lead such an enterprise? It must be so; and although Mary's loathing for the landlord increased, she allowed herself a grudging respect for his management.

The whole business must be controlled and the agents picked, for all their rough manners and wild appearance, otherwise the law could never have been evaded for so long. A magistrate who suspected smuggling would surely have suspected the inn before now, unless he were an agent himself. Mary frowned, her chin in her hand. If it were not for Aunt Patience, she would find her way to the nearest town and inform against Joss Merlyn, and there would be an ending of the traffic. However, the fact that Aunt Patience still held a doglike devotion for her husband made this course at the moment impossible.

But had Mary seen only part of the game? She remembered the terror in Aunt Patience's eyes, and those words spoken that first afternoon, when the shadows of early twilight crept across the kitchen floor: "There's things that happen here, Mary, that I've never dared to breathe. Evil things. I dare not even admit them to myself."

Smuggling was forbidden by the law of the land; but was it evil? Mary needed advice, and there was no one she could ask. Had she been a man, she would have gone downstairs and challenged Joss Merlyn to his face, and his friends with him. But she was a girl of three-and-twenty, with no weapons but her own brain to oppose a fellow twice her age and eight times her strength. Then Mary swore; a thing she had done only once before in her life, when chased by a bull, and then it had been for the same purpose as now—to give herself a certain bold pretense.

"I'll not show fear before Joss Merlyn or any man," she said, "and to prove it I will go down now, in the dark passage, and take a look at them in the bar, and if he kills me it will be my own fault."

She dressed hurriedly and crept out into the passage and down the stairs to the dim hall by the entrance door, empty except for one unsteady chair and the shadowed outline of a grandfather clock. Its husky breathing jarred upon the silence like a living thing. The hall was as black as a pit, and although she knew she stood alone there, the very solitude was threatening, the closed door to the unused parlor pregnant with suggestion. As she hesitated, a sudden beam of light shone into the passage that ran at the back of the hall, and she heard voices. The door of the bar must have swung open. There was a demon of curiosity within her that carried her through to the passage beyond, and so to crouch against the wall a few paces from the door of the bar. The men must be sitting on the benches against the farther wall, for she could not see them. Suddenly a strange voice rang out, quavering and high.

"I tell you for the final time, I'll not be a party to it. I'll put an end to the agreement. That's murder you'd have me do, Mr. Merlyn, it's common murder." The voice trembled on the final note, as though the speaker were carried away by the force of his feelings. Someone—the landlord himself, no doubt—made reply in a low tone, and his speech was broken by a coarse cackle of laughter that Mary recognized as belonging to the peddler.

He must have hinted a question, for the stranger spoke swiftly in self-defense. "Swinging, is it?" he said. "I'm not afraid of my neck. No, I'm thinking of my conscience and of Almighty God. When it comes to the killing of innocent folk, maybe women and children, that's going straight to hell."

Mary's uncle lifted his voice for the first time. "Not so fast, my friend," he said. "I've been doubtful of you from the first, with your gentleman's airs, and I've proved myself right. Harry, bolt the door over there."

There was a sudden scuffle and a cry, and the door to the yard was slammed. Once more the peddler laughed, odious and obscene, and he began to whistle one of his songs. "Shall we tickle him up like Silly Sam?" he said, breaking off in the middle. "Tickle him up with the whip, Joss, and let's see the color of his skin."

"Shut your mouth, Harry," answered the landlord. "Stand where you are by the door and prick him with your knife if he tries to pass you. Now, look here, Mr. lawyer-clerk or whatever you are in Truro town, you've made a fool of yourself tonight, but you're not going to make a fool of me. You'd like to be away to Bodmin, wouldn't you? Yes, and by nine in the morning you'd have every magistrate in the country at Jamaica Inn, and a regiment of soldiers into the bargain."

The stranger must have been hurt in the scuffle, for when his voice came it was contracted, as though he were in pain. "Do your devil's work if you must," he muttered. "I give you my word I'll not inform against you. But join you I will not."

There was a silence, and then Joss Merlyn spoke again. "Have a care," he said softly. "I heard another man say that once, and five minutes later he was treading the air on the end of a rope. They said afterward he had taken seven and three-quarter minutes to die."

Outside in the passage Mary felt her neck and her forehead go clammy with sweat, and with a growing sense of horror she realized that she was probably going to faint. Her uncle's voice came from very far away, as though he spoke with his hands against his mouth. "Leave me alone with him, Harry," he said. "Take his horse and cast him loose the other side of Camelford. I'll settle this business by myself."

Somehow Mary found her way to the hall, turned the handle of the parlor door, and stumbled inside. Then she crumpled in a heap on the floor, her head between her knees. Her world went black; but the position in which she had fallen brought her to herself and in a moment she was sitting up, listening to the clatter of a pony's hoofs in the yard outside. The sound of the hoofs drew away and disappeared in the distance down the highroad. Her uncle was alone now in the bar with his victim, and Mary wondered whether it would be possible for her to find her way to the nearest dwelling place on the road to Dozmary and summon help. But it meant a walk of two or three miles across a moorland track before the first shepherd's cottage was reached, and possibly the inhabitants of the cottage belonged to her uncle's company.

Mary began to feel desperate. If only there were a gun somewhere, or a knife, she might be able to wound her uncle or at least disarm him while the wretched man made his escape from the bar. She was about to step out into the hall once more and creep past the stairs to the farther passage, when a sound from above made her lift her head. It was the creaking of a board: quiet footsteps pacing gently overhead. Someone was in the empty guest room on the floor above.

Mary's heart began to thump in her side. Whoever was in hiding up above must have lain in waiting there since the early evening; stood behind the door when she had gone to bed. She had been separated from him by a thin partition of wall, and he must have heard her every movement—the falling onto her bed, and later her opening of her door. Had he been one of the company in the bar, surely he would have questioned her movements. Who had admitted him? He must have hidden there so that he should remain unseen by the smugglers. Therefore he was not one of them; he was enemy to her uncle. An ally perhaps was hiding in the guest room and could help her save the stranger in the bar. She had her foot on the lowest step of the stairs when the beam of light shone forth once more from the back passage, and she heard the door of the bar swing open. Her uncle was coming out into the hall. Mary stepped quickly back into the parlor and stood with her hand against the door, still open a crack, trembling with excitement and fear. She heard the landlord's footsteps cross the hall, climb the stairs, and come to a halt above her head, outside the guest room. He waited, then tapped twice, very softly, on the door.

Once more the board creaked, and the door was opened. Mary's first despair returned. This could be no enemy to her uncle, after all. Her uncle had known him to be there all the time, and that was why he had sent the peddler away. He did not wish the peddler to see his friend. She thanked God then that she had not knocked on the door. Now they were coming down the stairs; they stopped for an instant outside the parlor door. They were so close to Mary that she could have touched her uncle on the shoulder through the crack of the door. His voice whispered right against her ear.

"It's for you to say," he breathed. "I'll do it, or we'll do it between us. It's for you to say the word."

Screened as Mary was by the door, whatever gesture or sign her uncle's new companion made in return escaped her. They turned back along the hall to the farther passage, and so down it to the bar beyond. Then the door closed, and she heard them no more.

Mary must have stood still for ten minutes. Once she fancied she heard a cry; but it was gone and lost in an instant, and was so faint that it might have been her imagination. Then she went out into the hall, and so through to the dark passage. No crack of light came under the skirting of the door to the bar. She ventured as far as the door and laid her ear against the panel. There was not even the murmur of a voice. The old fusty drink smell had cleared, and through the keyhole came a steady draft of air. Mary gave way to a sudden uncontrollable impulse, and lifting the latch, she stepped into the room.

There was nobody there. The door leading to the yard was open. The men must have turned to the left and walked straight onto the moor, for she would have heard them had they crossed the road. The air felt cold and sweet upon her face, and now that her uncle and the strangers had left it, the room seemed harmless and impersonal once more. The horror was spent.

A last little ray of moonlight made a white circle on the floor, and into the circle moved a dark shadow like a finger. Mary looked up to the ceiling and saw that a rope had been slung through a hook in the beam. It was the rope's end that made the blob in the white circle; and it kept moving backward and forward, blown by the draft from the open door.

CHAPTER FOUR

As THE DAYS passed, Mary Yellan settled down to life at Jamaica Inn with a sense of stubborn resolution. Perhaps, with the coming of spring, Patience Merlyn could be persuaded to see reason, and the pair of them would leave the moors for the peace of Helford Valley. Meanwhile she was determined, if possible, to expose her uncle and his confederates to the law. The events of that first Saturday night were never far from her mind, and Mary had not a doubt that a stranger had been killed by her uncle and another man, and his body buried somewhere on the moors.

Considered in the light of day, however, the very story seemed fantastic. She had returned to her room that night after the discovery of the rope, for the open door of the bar suggested that her uncle would be back at any moment. Exhausted with all she had seen, she fell asleep. When she awoke, the sun was high, and she could hear Aunt Patience pattering about in the hall below.

No sign remained of the evening's work; the bar had been swept and tidied, and there was no rope hanging from the beam. The landlord himself spent the morning in the cowhouse, pitchforking filth into the yard. When he came into the kitchen at midday to wolf an enormous meal, he questioned Mary about the farm stock at Helford and asked for her opinion on a calf that had fallen sick. Mary had seen him with her own eyes lash the naked idiot boy across the yard, and heard him threaten the stranger who opposed his will; and here he sat before her now, his mouth full of hot stew, shaking his head over a sick calf.

And she answered yes and no in reply to her uncle, and drank down her tea, watching him over the brim of her cup, her eyes traveling from his great plate of steaming stew to his long powerful fingers, hideous in their strength and grace.

Two weeks went by, and there was no repetition of Saturday night. Mary's uncle appeared to have no objection to her wandering on the moors, and day by day she came to know more of the surrounding country, stumbling upon tracks she had not noticed at first and which kept her to the high ground, leading ultimately to the tors, while she learned to avoid the low soggy grass with tufted tops, the border line of treacherous marsh. Companionship there was none, and no one came to the inn for rest or nourishment. She would watch the coaches pass twice in the week, and they were gone by in a moment, rumbling down the hill without drawing rein. Once, Mary waved to a driver, but he took no notice of her, and she realized with a rather helpless sense of futility that so far as other people were concerned she must be considered in the same light as her uncle. Even if she tried to walk to Bodmin or Launceston, the doors would be shut in her face.

It was in a mood of truculence, following upon a day of wind and rain that had made it impracticable to venture out of doors, that Mary one morning set herself to clean down the long stone passage that ran the full width of the back of the house. The hard work did not improve her temper, and the sight of her aunt in the kitchen defeated her.

She was about to start on the flagstones of the entrance hall when she heard a clatter of hoofs in the yard, and in a moment someone thundered on the closed door of the bar. Mary went back to the kitchen to warn her aunt, but she had left the room, and looking out of the window, Mary could see her pattering across the garden to her husband. They were both out of earshot and could not have heard the sound of this new arrival.

Mary wiped her hands on her apron and went into the bar. The door must have been unlocked, for to her surprise there was a man sitting straddle-legged across a chair, with a glass in his hand filled to the brim with ale, which he had calmly poured out from the tap himself. For a few minutes they considered one another in silence.

Mary wondered where she had seen him before. The rather drooping lids, the curve of his mouth, and the outline of his jaw, even the insolent stare with which he favored her, were things known to her and definitely disliked. The sight of him looking her up and down and drinking his ale at the same time irritated her beyond measure.

"You haven't any right to walk in here and help yourself," she said sharply. "Besides, the landlord doesn't encourage strangers." The man finished his ale, and feeling in his pocket for a pipe, he lit it, puffing a great cloud of smoke into her face. His manner infuriated Mary, and she pulled the pipe out of his hand, throwing it onto the floor, where it smashed. He shrugged his shoulders and began to whistle.

"Do you want to speak to the landlord or not?" Mary asked. "Because I can't stand here all day awaiting your pleasure. If you don't want to see him, and you've finished your drink, you can put down your money on the counter and go away."

The man laughed, and his smile and the flash of his teeth struck a chord in her memory, but still she could not name the resemblance. "Do you order Joss about in that way?" he said. "What a creature of contradictions he is. I never thought he'd run a young woman alongside his other activities. What do you do with poor Patience of an evening? Do you turn her out on the floor, or do you sleep all three abreast?"

Mary flushed scarlet. "Joss Merlyn is my uncle by marriage," she said. "Aunt Patience was my mother's only sister. My name is Mary Yellan.

Good morning. There's the door behind you." She left the bar and walked into the kitchen, straight into the arms of the landlord himself.

"Who in hell's name were you talking to?" he thundered. Pushing Mary aside, he stepped into the bar.

"Oh, it's you, Jem, is it?" he said. "What do you want at Jamaica to-day? I can't buy a horse from you. Things are going badly, and I'm as poor as a field mouse after a wet harvest." He closed the door, leaving Mary in the passage outside.

She went back to her bucket of water in the front hall. So that was Jem Merlyn, her uncle's younger brother. He had reminded her of her uncle throughout the conversation, and she had not realized it. He had Joss Merlyn's eyes, without the blood-flecked lines and without the pouches, and he had Joss Merlyn's mouth—firm, though, where the landlord's was weak, and narrow where his lower lip sagged. He was what Joss Merlyn might have been eighteen, twenty years ago, but smaller in build and neater in person.

Mary splashed the water onto the flagstones and began to scrub furiously, her lips pressed tight together.

What a vile breed they were, these Merlyns, with their studied insolence and coarseness, their rough brutality of manner. This Jem had the same streak of cruelty as his brother; she could see it in the shape of his mouth. Although he was a head and shoulders smaller than Joss, and half the breadth, he looked hard and keen. "There's no going against bad blood," her mother used to say. "It always comes out in the end." What a waste it all was. Here was poor Aunt Patience dragged in the current with the Merlyns, and she might have been a farmer's wife at Gweek, with sons of her own, and a house and land. Why were women such fools? wondered Mary; and she scrubbed the last flagstone of the hall with venom, as though she might blot out the indiscretions of her kind.

She had worked up her energy to a frenzy, and turning from the hall, proceeded to sweep the gloomy, dim parlor that had not seen a broom for years, so absorbed she did not hear the stone flung at the window. It was not until a shower of pebbles made a crack in the glass that her concentration was disturbed, and looking out, she saw Jem Merlyn standing in the yard beside his pony. Mary unbolted the heavy entrance door and went out into the porch. "What do you want now?" she asked him, conscious suddenly of her loose hair and rumpled dirty apron.

He still looked down at her with curiosity, but the insolence had gone, and he had the grace to appear the smallest bit ashamed of himself.

"I know I deserve black looks for speaking to you as I did," he said. "But if you knew my brother as well as I do, you'd understand me making the mistake. It looks strange, having a maid at Jamaica Inn. Why did you come here in the first place?"

Mary considered him from the shadow of the porch. He looked serious now, and his likeness to Joss had fled for the moment. She wished he were not a Merlyn. "I came here from Helford to be with my aunt Patience," she said. "My mother died some weeks ago, and I have no other relative. I'll tell you one thing, Mr. Merlyn—I'm thankful my mother isn't alive to see her sister now. My uncle is a brute, and many worse things besides. He's turned my aunt from a laughing, happy woman into a miserable drudge, and I'll never forgive him for that."

Jem whistled tunelessly and patted his horse's neck. "We Merlyns have never been good to our women," he said. "I can remember my father beating my mother till she couldn't stand. I can't remember my grandmother, but they say she fought side by side with Granddad once near Callington. What she had to love in Granddad I can't say, for he left all his savings with another woman the other side of the Tamar."

Mary was silent. The indifference in his voice appalled her. He spoke entirely without shame or regret, and she supposed that he had been born, like the rest of his family, lacking the quality of tenderness.

"What have you learned here in your short time?" he asked abruptly.

Mary was not easily led. "I helped my uncle in the bar one Saturday night," she said, "and I did not think much of the company he kept."

"I don't suppose you did," said Jem. "You'll have Joss throwing dice for you next time, I daresay, and when he loses you'll find yourself riding pillion behind a dirty poacher from the other side of Rough Tor."

"They'd have to knock me senseless before I rode pillion with anyone," said Mary.

"Senseless or conscious, women are pretty much the same when you come down to it," said Jem. "The poachers on Bodmin Moor would never know the difference, anyway." And he laughed again and looked exactly like his brother.

"What do you do for a livelihood?" asked Mary in sudden curiosity, for she had become aware that he spoke better than his brother.

"I'm a horse thief," he said pleasantly, "but there's not much money in it, really. You ought to ride here. I've got a little pony that would suit you handsomely. He's over at Trewartha now. Why don't you come back with me and look at him?"

"Aren't you afraid of being caught?" said Mary.

"Thieving is an awkward thing to prove," he told her. "Say the pony had a long mane, and one white foot, and a diamond mark in his ear— that narrows the field down a bit, doesn't it? And off goes the owner to Launceston fair with his eyes wide open. The pony is there, right enough, and he's bought by some dealer and sold away upcountry. Only his mane is clipped, his four feet are all the same color, and the mark in his ear is a slit, not a diamond. That's simple enough, isn't it?"

"So simple that I can't understand why you don't ride past Jamaica in your own coach, with a powdered footman on the step."

"Ah, well," he said, shaking his head, "I've never had the brain for figures. Do you know, I had ten pounds in my pocket last week. I've only a shilling piece today. That's why I want you to buy that little pony."

Mary laughed. He was so frank in his dishonesty that she had not the heart to be angry with him. "I can't spend my small savings on horses," she said. "If I ever get away from Jamaica, I shall need every penny, you may depend on that."

Jem Merlyn looked at her gravely, and then, on a sudden impulse, he bent toward her, first glancing over her head into the porch. "Look here," he said, "I'm serious now. Jamaica Inn is no place for a maid. My brother and I have never been friends; we go our own ways. And there's no reason why you should be caught up in his dirty schemes. Why don't you run away? I'd see you on the road to Bodmin all right."

His tone was persuasive, and Mary could almost have trusted him. But she could not forget he was Joss Merlyn's brother, and she dared not make a confidant of him. "I can look after myself," she said.

Jem threw his leg over the pony's back and stuck his feet into the leathers. "All right," he said, "I won't worry you. My cottage is across the Withy Brook, if you ever want me. The other side of Trewartha Marsh, at the foot of Twelve Men's Moor. Good day to you." And he was off down the road before she had time to say a word in return.

Mary went slowly back into the house. She was in urgent need of a friend, but the landlord's brother was no more than a common horse thief, a dishonest scoundrel, when all was said and done. Because he had a disarming smile and his voice was not unpleasing, she had been ready to believe in him, and he all the time perhaps laughing at her the other side of his face. No, whatever happened, she must stand alone in this business and trust no one.

The sky became overcast, the black heather bowed before the wind, and the stinging rain blurred the glass of the parlor window. As Mary sat there, alone, with her chin in her hand, the tears ran down her cheeks in company with the rain. She turned away from the window; and the cold, dead atmosphere of Jamaica Inn closed in upon her.

THAT NIGHT THE wagons came again. There were only two carts this time, with one horse in harness, and less than half a dozen men standing in the yard. The wagons looked ghostly in the dim light, like hearses, and the men themselves were phantom figures, moving silently about the yard as some weird pattern in a nightmare fantasy. The scene held a fatal fascination, and Mary could not leave the window. This time the wagons had arrived empty and were loaded with the remainder of the cargo deposited at the inn the time before. Mary guessed that the inn served as a storehouse for a few weeks and then, when opportunity occurred, the cargo was carried to the Tamar River bank and so distributed.

It was with a sting of disappointment that she wondered whether the visit of Jem Merlyn to the Jamaica Inn this morning had significance. A strange coincidence that the wagons should follow in his train. He had come from Launceston, he said, and Launceston stood on the Tamar bank. Mary was angry with him and with herself. In spite of everything, her last thought before sleeping had been the possibility of his friendship. She would be a fool if she had hopes of it now. Jem might disagree with his brother, but they were in the same trade. He had ridden to Jamaica to warn Joss that he might expect the convoy in the evening.

Now the two wagons were loaded, and the drivers climbed into the seats with their companions. Mary could see the great head and shoulders of her uncle on a level with the porch; he held a lantern in his hand, dimmed by a shutter. Then the carts rumbled out of the yard and turned in the direction of Launceston. She came away from the window and climbed back into bed. Presently she heard her uncle's footsteps on the stairs, and he went along the farther passage to his bedroom. There was no one hiding in the guest room tonight.

THE NEXT FEW days passed without incident. There came a fine crisp morning with frost on the ground, and for once the sun shone in a cloudless sky. Mary, whose spirits always rose at the sight of the sun, had turned her morning into washing day, and with sleeves rolled well above the elbows, plunged her arms into the tub of hot, soapy water she had set up in the yard. She sang as she worked. Her uncle had ridden away on the moors somewhere, and a sense of freedom possessed her. An urgent tapping on the window made her look up, and she saw Aunt Patience beckon to her, very white in the face. She wiped her hands on her apron and ran to the back door of the house. No sooner had she entered the kitchen than her aunt seized upon her with trembling hands.

"It's Mr. Bassat from North Hill," she whispered. "He's come on horseback, and another gentleman with him. He's never been before. He's heard something, I know he has. Oh, Mary, what are we going to do?" There was a loud knock at the entrance door and then a pause, followed by a thunder of blows. Aunt Patience took her niece's hand and held it to her heart. "You'll not tell him of the wagons? If any danger came to Joss, I'd kill myself, Mary."

There was no argument after that. "Come with me to the door," Mary said. "You needn't be afraid; I shall say nothing."

They went into the hall together, and Mary unbolted the heavy door. There were two men outside the porch. One had dismounted. The other was a burly fellow, in a cape, seated on a fine chestnut horse. His hat was pulled over his eyes, but Mary could see that his face was heavily lined and weather-beaten, and she judged him to be somewhere about fifty years of age.

"There doesn't seem to be much of a welcome for travelers here," he called. "Is the landlord at home?"

Patience Merlyn poked at her niece with her hand, and Mary made answer. "Mr. Merlyn is from home, sir," she said.

"H'mph," growled the squire, "that's a damned nuisance. I wanted a word or two with Mr. Joss Merlyn. Now look here, my good woman, I've had my eyes on this place for a long while. A house doesn't get a bad name without reason, Mrs. Merlyn, and Jamaica Inn stinks from here to the coast. Richards, hold my confounded horse."

The other man, who by his dress appeared to be a servant, held the bridle, and Mr. Bassat climbed heavily to the ground. "While I'm here I may as well look round," he said. "I'm a magistrate, and I have a warrant." He pushed his way past the two women, and so through to the little entrance hall and looked about him in disgust. "Good God!" he exclaimed. "What in the world have you done to the place? Jamaica Inn was always roughcast and plain, and the fare homely, but this is a positive disgrace." He had thrown open the door of the parlor and pointed to the damp walls with his crop. "Go on, Mrs. Merlyn, lead the way upstairs."

The rooms on the landing were thoroughly explored. The squire peered into the dusty corners, all the while uttering exclamations of anger. "Call this an inn, do you?" he said. "Why, you haven't even a bed fit to sleep a cat. The place is rotten, rotten right through. Well, there's nothing more to see up here, so you'll kindly take me downstairs again and show me the room that has the boarded-up window. I noticed it from the yard."

Aunt Patience passed her tongue over her lips and looked at Mary. She was incapable of speech.

"I'm very sorry, sir," Mary replied, "but if you mean the old lumber room at the end of the passage, I'm afraid the door is locked. My uncle always keeps the key, and where he puts it I don't know."

The squire looked from one to the other in suspicion. "What about you, Mrs. Merlyn? Don't you know where your husband keeps his keys?"

Aunt Patience shook her head. The squire snorted and turned on his heel. "Well, that's easily settled," he said. "We'll have the door down." And he went out into the yard to fetch his servant. In a few minutes he returned with the man Richards, who had taken the horses to the stable and now carried an old bar he had found there. They seized the bar between them and rammed it against the lock of the door. There was a splitting of wood and a crash, and the door gave way. Aunt Patience uttered a little cry of distress, and the squire pushed past her into the room.

"Get me a candle, one of you," shouted the squire. "It's as black as a pit in here." The servant produced a stump of candle from his pocket, and a light was kindled. He handed the candle to the squire, who lifted it high above his head. For a moment there was silence as the squire turned, letting the light shine in every corner. Except for a pile of sacks, the room was empty. On the top of the sacks lay a length of twisted rope. Clicking his tongue in annoyance and disappointment, the squire faced the little group behind him. "Nothing," he said. "The landlord has made a fool of me again." He flicked his boot with his whip and stared moodily in front of him. "You've been lucky, Mrs. Merlyn," he said. "If I'd found what I expected to find, this time tomorrow your husband would be in the county jail. Now listen to me"—Mr. Bassat pointed his crop at Mary— "this aunt of yours may have lost her tongue, but you can understand plain English, I hope. Does anybody ever call here, by day or by night?"

"I've never seen anyone," Mary said, looking him straight in the eyes.

"Have you ever heard wheels in the yard by night?"

"I'm a very heavy sleeper. Nothing ever wakes me."

"Don't you think yourself it's very peculiar to keep an inn on the king's highway, and then bolt and bar your house to every passerby?"

"My uncle is a very peculiar man."

"He is indeed. In fact, he's so damned peculiar that half the people in the countryside won't sleep easy in their beds until he's been hanged, like his father before him. You can tell him that from me. Well, I don't envy you your relatives. I'd rather see any daughter of mine in her grave than living at Jamaica Inn with a man like Joss Merlyn."

He turned away and the two women followed him to the porch. The servant brought the horses, and Mr. Bassat climbed onto his, gathering the reins in his hands. "One other thing," he called from his saddle. "Have you seen anything of your uncle's younger brother, Jem Merlyn?"

"No," said Mary steadily, "he never comes here."

"Oh, he doesn't? Well, that's all I want from you this morning." And away they clattered from the yard.

Aunt Patience had already preceded Mary to the kitchen and was moaning and whimpering before the fire. Mary was in no mood to comfort her. She had lied to save her uncle's skin, when every inch of her longed to proclaim his guilt. Because of her aunt she had to stand still and say nothing. It was damnable, there was no other word for it. For better, for worse, she had become one of the company at Jamaica Inn. In the end she would probably hang beside her uncle. Not only had she lied to save him, she thought with rising anger, but she had lied to help his brother Jem. Why she had lied about him she did not know.

When Joss returned just before noon, he was met with a babble of words from his wife. Mary stayed where she was by the washtub. In a little while her uncle beckoned her from the window and she went inside. He was standing on the hearth, his legs straddled wide, his face as black as thunder. "What's your side of the story?" he shouted. "A magpie makes better sense than your aunt. What's been going on here?"

Mary told him calmly what had taken place during the morning, and ended with Mr. Bassat's own words—that people would not sleep easy in their beds until Joss Merlyn was hanged, like his father before him.

"The damned skulking bastard!" the landlord roared. "He'd no more right to walk into my house than any other man. His talk of a magistrate's warrant was all bluff, you blithering fools; there's no such thing. I'll burn his house round his ears if he plays his tricks again."

For all his thunder Joss Merlyn was frightened, Mary could see that; and his confidence was rudely shaken.

"Get me something to eat," he said. "I must go out again, and there's no time to lose."

As soon as he had finished his meal, the landlord rose, and leaving the kitchen, he went down to the end of the garden and climbed the stile in the field. Mary watched him strike across the moor and ascend the steep incline that led to Tolborough Tor and Codda. For a moment she hesitated, but the sound of her aunt's footsteps overhead decided her. She waited until she heard the door of the bedroom close; seizing her thick shawl from its peg on the wall, she ran down the field after her uncle. She crouched beside the stone wall until his figure crossed the skyline and disappeared, and then she leaped up again and followed in his tracks, picking her way among the rough grass and stones. Her idea was to keep Joss Merlyn in view, remaining unseen, and in this way perhaps she would learn something of his secret mission. She had no doubt that the squire's visit to Jamaica had altered the landlord's plans, and that this sudden departure on foot across the heart of the West Moor was connected with it. It was a mad and senseless venture, no doubt, but her mood was a reckless one.

She kept to the high ground as much as possible, following as best she could the tracks taken by her uncle. She was forced to keep a good length between them in order to remain unseen, and the landlord took such tremendous strides that before long Mary saw she would be left behind. Codda Tor was passed, and he turned west now toward the low ground at the foot of Brown Willy, looking, for all his height, like a little black dot against the brown stretch of moor.

The prospect of climbing some thirteen hundred feet came as something of a shock to Mary, and she paused for a moment and wiped her streaming face. She let down her hair for greater comfort, and let it blow about her face. Why had the landlord of Jamaica Inn thought it necessary to climb the highest point on Bodmin Moor on a December afternoon?

She set off again at a sharper pace, but her uncle had already traversed the worst of the bog with uncanny quickness, and she could just make out his figure among the great boulders at the foot of Brown Willy. Then he was hidden by a jutting crag of granite. Ignorant of the whereabouts of the track that had carried her uncle dry-shod over the bog, Mary made a wide circuit to avoid the treacherous ground. But she was now hopelessly left without a prospect of finding her uncle again. Nevertheless, she set herself to climb Brown Willy, scrambling up the great peaks of jagged granite, while now and again a startled hill sheep ran out from behind a boulder to gaze at her and stamp its feet. When Mary reached the summit, the evening clouds were banked high above her head and the world was gray. Her escapade had been to little purpose, for as far as her eyes could see, there was no living thing within their range.

Discouraged and depressed, and all excitement gone from her, Mary scrambled down the steep face of the tor, one eye on the marshes below and the other for the darkness that swiftly overtook her. There was no danger from the boggy ground if she kept to the high moors, so, trussing up her skirt and wrapping her shawl firmly around her shoulders, she walked steadily, feeling the ground with some care. That the direction she was taking was unknown to her was soon obvious, for her way was barred suddenly by a stream that she had not passed on the outward journey. She plunged through it recklessly, soaking herself above the knee. The ground now seemed to rise in front of her, and she struck boldly across the high downland, coming at length to a rough track bearing ahead and slightly to the right. It was then that she heard the sound of a horse, his hoofs thudding dully on the turf, and blowing as though he had been ridden hard, coming out of the darkness to the left of her.

Mary waited in the middle of the track, her nerves ajingle with the suddenness of the approach, and presently the horse appeared out of the mist in front of her, a rider on his back, the pair of ghostly figures lacking reality in the dim light. The horseman swerved as he saw Mary and pulled up his horse to avoid her. He peered down at her and exclaimed in surprise, "A woman! What in the world are you doing out here?"

"Can you put me on the road?" Mary asked. "I'm miles from home and hopelessly lost."

"Steady there," he said to the horse. "Where have you come from? Of course I will help you if I can." His voice was low and gentle, and Mary could see he must be a person of quality.

"I live at Jamaica Inn," she said, and no sooner were the words out of her mouth than she regretted them. The very name was enough to make him whip on his horse and leave her to find her own way.

For a moment the man was silent. When he spoke again his voice had not changed, but was quiet and gentle as before. "Jamaica Inn," he said.

"You've come a long way out of your road, I'm afraid. You're the other side of Hendra Downs here."

"That means nothing to me," she told him. "I'd be grateful if you could show me to the right path, and once on the highroad, it won't take me long to get home."

He swung himself off the saddle to the ground. "You're exhausted," he said. "We are not far from the village, and you shall ride there. Will you give me your foot, and I'll help you to mount." In a minute she was up in the saddle, and he stood below her, the bridle in his hand. "Your shoes are soaking wet, and so is the hem of your gown. You shall dry those things and rest awhile, and have some supper, before I take you back myself to Jamaica Inn." He arranged the reins to her satisfaction, and she saw his eyes for the first time looking up at her from beneath the brim of his hat. They were strange eyes, transparent like glass, and so pale in color that they seemed near to white. They fastened upon her and searched her, as though her very thoughts could not be hidden. His hair was white too, under his black shovel hat, and Mary stared back at him in some perplexity, for his face was unlined and his voice was not that of an elderly man.

Then, with a little rush of embarrassment, she understood the reason for his abnormality, and she turned away her eyes. He was an albino.

He took off his hat and bared his head before her. "Perhaps I had better introduce myself," he said with a smile. "My name is Francis Davey, and I am the vicar of Altarnun."

CHAPTER FIVE

THERE WAS SOMETHING strangely peaceful about the house, something very rare and difficult to define. It was like a house in an old tale, discovered by the hero one evening in midsummer; there should be a barrier of thorns about it through which he must cut his way with a knife, and then a galaxy of flowers growing in profusion, monstrous blooms untended by human hand. Giant ferns would mass themselves beneath the windows, and white lilies on tall stems. In the tale there would be strands of ivy clustering the walls, barring the entrance, and the house itself would have slept for a thousand years.

Mary smiled at her fancy and spread her hands once more to the log fire. The silence was pleasing to her; it soothed her weariness and took away her fear. This was a different world from Jamaica Inn. There the silence was oppressive and heavy with malice; the unused rooms stank of neglect. Here the room in which she was sitting had the quiet impersonality of a drawing room visited by night. The furniture, the table in the center, the pictures on the walls, were without that look of solid familiarity belonging to the day. They were like sleeping things, stumbled upon at midnight by surprise.

Mary watched the vicar as he laid the table for supper, and she thought how wisely he had allowed himself to become submerged in the atmosphere of the house; for another man would have chatted, perhaps, or made some clatter with the cups, feeling the silence a constraint. Her eyes wandered about the room, the walls bare of the usual Biblical themes, the polished desk empty of papers and books that in her mind were associated with the living room of a rectory. Standing in the corner was an easel, and on it a half-finished canvas of the pool at Dozmary. It had been painted on a gray day, with the rain clouds overhead, and the water was slate-colored, without wind. The scene held Mary's eyes and fascinated her. She knew nothing of painting, but the picture had power, and she could almost feel the rain in her face. He must have watched the direction of her eyes, for he went to the easel and turned the painting with its back toward her. "Don't look at that," he said. "It was done in a hurry. If you like pictures, you shall see something better. But first of all I'm going to give you your supper. Don't move from the chair. I'll bring the table to you."

It was a novelty to be waited upon, but he made such little show that it seemed natural. "Hannah lives in the village," he said. "She leaves every afternoon at four. I like getting my own supper, then I can choose my own time. Luckily she made apple tart today."

He poured her out a steaming cup of tea, heaping into it a spoonful of cream. She could not yet accustom herself to his white hair and his eyes; they were such a direct contrast to his voice, and his black clerical dress made them the more remarkable. Mary swallowed her supper, and now and again she stole a look at him from behind her cup of tea, but he seemed to sense her glance at once, for he would turn his eyes upon her with their cold white stare—like the impersonal stare of a blind man.

"It was providential that I should come upon you on the moor tonight," he said at length, when she had pushed away her plate. The warmth of the room had made her drowsy, and his gentle voice came to her from far away. "My work sometimes takes me to the outlying farms. This afternoon I helped to bring a child into the world."

Mary had nothing to say in reply. She wondered what was the scent of roses that filled the air, and she noticed for the first time the bowl of dried petals on the small table behind her chair. Then he spoke again, his voice gentle as ever, but with a new insistence.

"Why did you wander on the moor tonight?" he said.

Mary roused herself. His eyes stared down at her in infinite compassion, and she longed to trespass on their mercy. Scarcely aware of how it happened, she heard her voice reply to his.

"I'm in terrible trouble," she said. "I've not been at Jamaica Inn much over a month, but it seems like twenty years. It's my aunt that worries me; if only I could get her away. But she won't leave Uncle Joss, for all his treatment of her. Every night I go to bed wondering if I shall wake up and hear the wagons. The first time they came, there were six or seven of them, and they brought great boxes that the men stored in the locked room at the end of the passage. A man was killed that night; I saw the rope hanging from the beam downstairs—" She broke off, the warm color flooding her face. "I've never told anyone before," she said. "I shouldn't have said it. I've done something terrible." For a little while he did not answer; then he spoke gently, like a father reassuring a frightened child.

"Don't be afraid," he said; "your secret is safe; no one shall know of this but me. But isn't your imagination running away with you a little? I know I must seem unsympathetic, but this is the nineteenth century, you know, and men don't murder one another without reason. Don't you think you had better let me hear the rest of your story? What is your name, and how long have you been living at Jamaica Inn?"

Mary looked up at the pale eyes, the halo of cropped white hair, and she thought again how strange a freak of nature was this man, who might be twenty-one, who might be sixty, and who with his soft, persuasive voice would compel her to admit every secret her heart possessed. She hesitated, turning the words over in her mind.

"Come," he said with a tense smile, "I have heard confession in my time. Not here in Altarnun, but in Ireland and in Spain. Your story will not sound as strange to me as you think. There are other worlds besides Jamaica Inn."

She plunged headlong into her story with jerky, ill-framed sentences, beginning with that first Saturday night in the bar, and then working backward to her arrival at the inn. He heard her to the end without question, but all the while she felt his white eyes watching her, and he had a little trick of swallowing at intervals which she came instinctively to recognize and wait for. The fear she had sustained, the agony and the doubt, sounded to her ears, as she listened, like the worked-up invention of an overstimulated mind, and the conversation in the bar between her uncle and the stranger had developed into an elaborate piece of nonsense. She sensed, rather than saw, the vicar's unbelief; and in a desperate attempt to tone down her now ridiculous story, her uncle, who had been the villain of it, became the usual hard-drinking bully of a countryman who beat his wife once a week, and the wagons themselves had no more menace than carriers' carts, traveling by night to expedite delivery.

The visit of the squire of North Hill early that day had some conviction, but the empty room struck another note of anticlimax, and the only part of the story that rang with any sense of reality was Mary's losing herself on the moors during the afternoon.

When she had finished, the vicar got up from his chair and began to pace about the room. He whistled softly under his breath and kept playing with a loose button on his coat that was hanging by a thread. Then he came to a standstill on the hearth, with his back to the fire, and looked down upon her—but Mary could read nothing from his eyes.

"I believe you, of course," he said after a moment or so. "You haven't the face of a liar, and I doubt if you know the meaning of hysteria. It's a scandal and an outrage, we all know that, but smuggling is rife all over the county, and half the magistrates do very well out of it. If the law were stricter, there would be greater supervision, and your uncle's little nest at Jamaica Inn would have been blotted out long ago. I have met Mr. Bassat once or twice, and between ourselves, he is a bit of a fool. Actually he had no business to walk into the inn and search the rooms, and if it becomes known that he did so and found nothing for his pains, he'll become the laughingstock of the countryside. Unless he can catch your uncle at work, as it were, with the wagons in the yard, there's little chance of convicting him. And then again, you don't want your aunt to be implicated in the business, but I don't see how it can be avoided, if it comes to an arrest."

"What do you suggest I should do, then?" said Mary helplessly.

"If I were you I should keep a close watch on your uncle, and when the wagons do come again you can report at once to me. We can then decide together what is best to be done."

"What about the stranger who disappeared?" said Mary. "He was murdered. Can nothing ever be done about it?"

"I'm afraid not, unless his body is found, which is extremely unlikely," said the vicar. "Forgive me, but I think you allowed your imagination to run away with you over that. All you saw was a piece of rope, remember. Now I am your friend, and you can trust me. If you ever become worried or distressed, I want you to come and tell me about it. If you come at any time and I'm not in, Hannah will be here, and she will look after you. That's a bargain between us, isn't it?"

"Thank you very much."

"Put on your stockings again, and your shoes, while I go to the stable and get the dogcart. I'm going to drive you back to Jamaica Inn."

The night was fine; the dark clouds of the early evening had passed away, and the sky was ablaze with stars. Mary sat beside Francis Davey on the high seat of the dogcart, wrapped in a greatcoat with a top collar of velvet. This was not the same horse that he had been riding when she met him on the moor; this was a big gray cob who, fresh from his

45

sojourn in the stable, went like the wind. It was a strange, exhilarating drive. The vicar pricked the cob with his whip, so that he laid his ears flat to his head and galloped like a mad thing, and Mary was flung against her companion. He made no effort to rein in his horse, and glancing up at him, Mary saw that he was smiling. "Go on," he said, "you can go faster than this"; and his voice was low and excited, as though he were talking to himself.

He looked like a bird. Crouched in his seat, with his black cape coat blown out by the wind, his arms were like wings, and Mary was aware of a feeling of discomfiture, as though he had betaken himself to another world and had forgotten her existence. Then he smiled down at her and was human again. "I love these moors," he said. "They have a fascination unlike any other part of the county. The moors were the first things to be created; afterward came the forests, and the valleys, and the sea. Climb Rough Tor before sunrise and listen to the wind in the stones. You'll know what I mean then."

They had come to the dip in the road now. Already Mary could see the tall chimneys of Jamaica Inn outlined against the sky. The vicar stopped his horse just short of the yard, under the lee of the grass bank.

"It's like a house of the dead," he said quietly. "Would you like me to try the door?"

"The door of the bar will be bolted, and the kitchen too," said Mary. "We can slip round, if you like, and make certain."

"Very well," her companion said, "I will take care the landlord does not see me. I am going to look in at the window."

She watched him go to the side of the window, and he stood there for a few minutes gazing into the kitchen. Then he beckoned to her to follow, that same tense smile on his face she had noticed before. Mary pressed forward to the window. The kitchen was lit by a single candle, stuck into a bottle. Joss Merlyn sprawled at the table in a drunken stupor, his great legs stretched out on either side of him. He stared before him at the guttering candle, his eyes glazed like a dead man's. A bottle lay with its neck smashed on the table, and beside it an empty glass.

Francis Davey pointed to the open door. "You can walk inside and go upstairs to bed," he said. "Your uncle will not even see you. Good night to you, Mary Yellan. If you are ever in trouble, I shall be waiting for you at Altarnun."

Then he turned the corner of the house and was gone.

JOSS MERLYN WAS drunk for five days. He was insensible most of the time and lay stretched out on a bed in the kitchen that Mary and her aunt had improvised between them. About five in the evening he would wake for half an hour or so, shouting for brandy and sobbing. His wife would give him a little weak brandy and water, talking to him gently as she would to a sick child.

Aunt Patience had accepted without question her niece's explanation of losing herself on the moors. Now she became another woman, showing a calm coolness that Mary had not believed her capable of possessing. She was obliged to do everything for her husband, and Mary watched her change his blankets and his linen with a sick feeling of disgust. These were the only times when Aunt Patience had the controlling of him, and he would let her sponge his forehead without a protest. Then she would smooth his mat of hair, and in a few minutes he would be asleep again, his face purple, his tongue protruding, snoring like a bull. It was impossible to live in the kitchen, and Mary and her aunt turned the little unused parlor into a dwelling room for themselves. Aunt Patience told Mary that every two months or so Joss had had these bouts of drinking, and now they were becoming more frequent. This present one had been caused by the visit of Squire Bassat to the inn—when the landlord came back from the moors at six in the evening he went straight to the bar.

On the fifth morning after Joss Merlyn began his drinking bout, the wind dropped and the sun shone, and Mary decided to brave the moors again. She slipped out of the house, rolling a crust of bread in a handkerchief. This time she made for the East Moor, striking out toward Kilmar, and with the whole day in front of her, there was no fear of being lost. She kept thinking about Francis Davey, her strange vicar of Altarnun. She wondered what had called him to priesthood. It was nearly Christmas now, and home at Helford the little parson, wearing a festive air, would beam upon his world. Did Francis Davey decorate his church with holly at Christmas and call down a blessing upon the people?

Mary had walked for an hour or more before she stopped short, her further progress barred by a stream that lay in a valley between the hills and marshes. Looking beyond the smooth green face of the tor ahead, she saw the great split hand of Kilmar pointing his fingers to the sky. She was gazing at Trewartha Marsh once more, but this time she faced the southeast, and the hills looked different in the brave sunshine. The brook burbled merrily over the stones, and there was a fording gate across the shallow water. The marsh stretched away to the left of her.

Mary turned her back on the marsh and forded the gate over the stream. She kept to the high ground, with the stream beneath her, and followed its course along the winding valley between the hills. A solitary curlew rose into the air, calling his plaintive note and streaking for the south. Something had disturbed him, and in a few minutes Mary saw what it was. A handful of ponies had clattered down the hill beyond and splashed into the stream to drink. They must have come through a gate on the left that led to a rough farm track, heavy with mud.

Then Mary saw a man coming down the track, carrying a bucket in either hand. She was about to move when he shouted to her. It was Jem Merlyn. He wore a grimy shirt and a pair of brown breeches, covered with horsehair and filth from a stable. There was a rough stubble of beard on his jaw. He laughed at her, showing his teeth, looking for all the world like his brother must have done twenty years ago.

"So you've found your way to me, have you?" he said. He thrust one of the buckets in her hand before she had time to protest, and was down to the water after the ponies. "Come out of it!" he shouted. "Get back, will you, fouling my drinking water! Go on, you big black devil."

He hit the largest of the ponies on his hindquarters with the end of the bucket, and they stampeded up the hill. "What would you have done if you hadn't found me at home?" he said, wiping his face on his sleeve.

Mary could not help smiling. "I didn't even know you lived here. I'd have turned left if I'd known."

"I don't believe you. Well, you've come in good time to cook my dinner."

He led the way up the muddy track, and rounding the corner they came to a small gray cottage built on the side of the hill. "The fire's on, and it won't take you long to boil a scrap of mutton," he said.

Mary looked him up and down. "Do you always make use of folk this way?"

"I don't often have the chance," he told her. "Since my mother died, there's not been a woman in the cottage. Come in, won't you?"

She followed him, bending her head, as he did, under the low door. The room was half the size of the kitchen at Jamaica, with a great open fireplace in the corner. The floor was littered with rubbish; potato scrapings, cabbage stalks, crumbs of bread, and ashes from the turf fire covered everything. Mary looked about her in dismay.

"You've got this kitchen like a pigsty," she told him. "Leave me that bucket of water. I'll not eat my dinner in a place like this."

In half an hour she had the stone floor shining and all the rubbish cleared away. She had found crockery in the cupboard, and a strip of tablecloth, and meanwhile the mutton boiled in the saucepan on the fire, surrounded by potatoes and turnips.

Jem came in at the door, sniffing the air like a hungry dog. "I shall have to keep a woman," he said. "Make haste with the dinner; I'm as empty as a worm."

"You're impatient, aren't you?" said Mary. "Not a word of thanks to me that's cooked it."

She put the steaming mutton down in front of him, and he smacked his lips. "They taught you something where you came from, anyway," he said. "I always say there's two things women ought to do by instinct, and cooking's one of 'em."

Mary had filled a cup with water and passed it to him in silence.

"We were all born here," said Jem, "up in the room overhead. But Joss and Matt were grown men when I was still a little lad, clinging to Mother's skirt. We never saw much of my father, but when he was home we knew it all right. I remember him throwing a knife at Mother once—it cut her above her eye, and the blood ran down her face. Mother just bathed her eye, and then she gave my father his supper. She was a brave woman."

"How long has your mother been dead?" asked Mary.

"Seven years this Christmas," he answered, helping himself to more boiled mutton. "What with my father hanged, and Matt drowned, and Joss gone off, and me growing up as wild as a hawk, she turned religious and used to pray here by the hour. I couldn't abide that, and I shipped on a Padstow schooner, but the sea didn't suit my stomach, and I came home. I found Mother gone as thin as a skeleton. 'You ought to eat more,' I told her, but she wouldn't listen to me, so I went off again, and stayed in Plymouth, picking up a shilling or two in my own way. I came back here to have my Christmas dinner, and I found the place deserted. I went to North Hill, and they told me my mother had died. I might just as well have stayed in Plymouth for all the dinner I got that Christmas. There's a piece of cheese in the cupboard. Will you eat the half of it?"

Mary shook her head, and she let him get up and reach for it himself.

"What's the matter?" he said. "You look like a sick cow."

"It will be a good thing when there's not a Merlyn left in Cornwall," Mary said. "You and your brother were born twisted. Do you never think of what your mother must have suffered?"

Jem looked at her in surprise, the bread and cheese halfway to his mouth. "Mother was all right," he said. "She never complained. Why, she married my father at sixteen; she never had time to suffer. I was an afterthought, I was. Father got drunk at Launceston fair, after selling three cows that didn't belong to him. But for that I wouldn't be sitting here."

Mary got up and began to clear away the plates in silence.

"How's the landlord of Jamaica Inn?" said Jem, tilting back on his chair and watching her dip the plates in water.

"Drunk, like his father before him," said Mary shortly. "We had Mr. Bassat from North Hill last week."

Jem brought his chair to the ground with a crash. "The devil you did," he said. "And what had the squire to say to you?"

As Mary told her tale, Jem whistled tunelessly, his expression blank, but when she came to the mention of his name, his eyes narrowed and then he laughed. "Why did you lie to him?"

"It seemed less trouble at the time," said Mary. "You've got nothing to hide, have you?"

"Nothing much, except that black pony you saw by the brook belongs to him," said Jem carelessly. "He was dapple gray last week, and worth a small fortune to the squire, who bred him himself. I'll make a few pounds with him at Launceston, if I'm lucky. Come down and have a look at him."

They went out into the sun, and Mary stood for a few moments at the door of the cottage while Jem went off to the horses. There was a shout and a clatter of hoofs, and Jem rode up astride the black pony. "This is the fellow I wanted you to have," he said, "but you're so close with your money. I won't give you the chance again. He'll go to Launceston on Christmas Eve; the dealers there will swallow him up." He slid to the ground and clapped his hands on the hindquarters of the pony. "Get on with you, then"; and the animal made a dash for the gap in the bank.

Jem broke off a piece of grass and began to chew it, glancing sideways at his companion. "What did Squire Bassat expect to see at Jamaica Inn?" he said.

Mary shrugged her shoulders. "I didn't come here to answer questions. I had enough of that with Mr. Bassat."

"It was lucky for Joss the stuff had been shifted," said his brother quietly. "You must have a good view from that little room over the porch. Do they wake you out of your beauty sleep?"

"How do you know that's my room?" Mary asked swiftly.

He looked taken aback at her question. Then he laughed. "The window was wide open when I rode into the yard the other morning," he said. "I've never seen a window open at Jamaica Inn before."

The excuse was hardly good enough for Mary. A horrible suspicion came into her mind. Could it have been Jem who had hidden in the empty guest room that Saturday night? Something went cold inside her.

"All I think about is getting my aunt away from the place," said Mary. "As for your brother, he can drink himself to death for all I care. His life is his own, and so is his business."

Jem whistled and kicked a loose stone with his foot. "So smuggling doesn't appall you? But supposing he meddled in other things—supposing it was a question of murder—what then?" He turned around and faced her; his careless, laughing manner was gone, and his eyes were grave.

"I don't know what you mean," said Mary.

He looked at her for a long time without speaking. All his resemblance to his brother vanished. He was harder suddenly, and of a different breed. "Perhaps not," he said at length, "but you'll come to know, if you stay long enough. Why does your aunt look like a living ghost? Ask her, next time the wind blows from the northwest. There'll be trouble between Joss and myself one day, and it's he that'll be sorry for it, not I." And with that cryptic remark he went off after the pony.

Mary watched him thoughtfully. The stranger in the bar that night had talked of murder, and now Jem himself had echoed his words. She was not a fool, then, whatever she was considered by the vicar of Altarnun. And if Jem was the man who crept so stealthily down the stairs behind her uncle, there would be reason enough for all his questions. She began to walk slowly down the hill toward the Withy Brook. She had reached the gate when she heard his running footsteps behind her.

"Why are you going?" he said. "It won't be dark till after four. What's the matter?" He took her chin in his hands and looked into her face. "I believe you're frightened of me. We're a desperate lot of fellows, we Merlyns, and Jem is the worst of the pack. Is that what you're thinking?"

She smiled in spite of herself. "Something of the sort. But I'm not afraid of you. It's a long walk back to Jamaica Inn, and I don't fancy losing myself on the moors."

"Well, Mary Yellan, are you coming to Launceston with me on Christmas Eve?"

"What will you be doing over to Launceston, Jem Merlyn?"

"Only selling Mr. Bassat's black pony for him, my dear. I'll bring you home by midnight. Say you're coming, Mary."

"Supposing you are caught in Launceston with Mr. Bassat's pony? You would look a fool, then, and so would I, if they clapped me into prison alongside of you."

"Take a risk, Mary; don't you like excitement, that you're so careful of your own skin? They must breed you soft down Helford way."

She rose like a fish to his bait. "All right, then, Jem Merlyn, you needn't think I'm afraid. I'd just as soon be in prison as live at Jamaica Inn, anyway. How do we go to Launceston?"

"I'll take you there in the jingle, with Mr. Bassat's black pony behind us. Do you know your way to North Hill, across the moor?"

"No, I do not."

"Go a mile along the highroad, and you'll come to a gap in the hedge on the top of the hill. You'll have Carey Tor ahead of you, and Hawk's Tor away on your right; you can't miss your way. I'll come half of the distance to meet you. We'll keep to the moor as much as we can. There'll be some traveling on the road Christmas Eve."

"What time shall I start, then?"

"The streets will be thick enough for us by two o'clock. You can leave Jamaica at eleven, if you like."

"I'll make no promises. If you don't see me, you can go on your way. You forget Aunt Patience may need me."

"That's right. Make your excuses."

"There's the gate over the stream," said Mary. "You don't have to come any farther. Good afternoon, Jem Merlyn." And Mary leaped boldly across the running brook, with one hand on the gate to guide her. Her petticoat dipped in the water, and she lifted it up. She heard Jem laugh from his bank on the other side, and she walked away up the hill without a backward glance.

DARKNESS WAS FALLING as she crossed the highroad and into the yard of Jamaica Inn. As usual, it looked dark and uninhabited, with the door bolted and the windows barred. She tapped on the door of the kitchen. It was opened by her aunt, pale and anxious. "Your uncle has been asking for you all day," she said. "Where have you been?"

"I was walking on the moors," replied Mary. "I didn't think it mattered. Where has Uncle Joss gone?"

"He wanted to sit in the parlor," Aunt Patience said. "He's been sitting there all afternoon at the windows, looking out for you. You must humor him now, Mary. This is the bad time, when he's recovering. I'll go and tell him you're home." She left the room.

Mary crossed to the dresser and poured herself a glass of water from the pitcher. The glass trembled in her hands, and she cursed herself for a fool. She had been bold enough on the moors just now, and no sooner was she inside the inn than her courage must forsake her and leave her quaking and nervous as a child. Aunt Patience came back into the room.

"He's quiet for the moment," she whispered. "He's dozed off in the chair. He may sleep now for the evening. We'll have our supper early. There's some cold pie for you here."

The long evening passed, and still there was no call from the landlord. Mary threw some turf on the fire and crouched beside it. She nodded, her eyes closed, and in that heavy state between sleeping and waking she heard her aunt whisper in her ear, "I'm going to bed. Your uncle won't wake now; he must have settled for the night."

On the landing above, a door closed softly. Mary's head sank lower into her hands. The slow ticking of the clock made a pattern in her mind, like footsteps dragging on a road . . . one . . . two . . . one . . . two. . . . It was cold, though, much too cold. . . . Mary opened her eyes and saw that she was lying on the floor beside the white ashes of the fire. The candle had burned low. She yawned and shivered and stretched her stiff arms. When she lifted her eyes she saw the door of the kitchen open very slowly, an inch at a time.

Mary sat without moving, her hands on the cold floor. Then the door was flung wide, crashing against the wall behind it. Joss Merlyn stood on the threshold, his arms outstretched, rocking on his two feet.

At first she thought he had not noticed her; his eyes were fixed on the wall in front of him. She crouched low, her head beneath the level of the table, hearing nothing but the steady thump of her heart. Slowly he turned in her direction and stared at her a moment or two. When his voice came, it was strained and hoarse. "Who's there?" he said. "Why don't you speak?" His face was a gray mask, drained of its usual color. His bloodshot eyes fastened themselves upon her without recognition. Mary did not move.

"Put away that knife," he whispered. "Put it away."

She waited, holding her breath. He stepped forward into the room, his head bent, his two hands feeling the air, and he crept slowly along the floor toward her.

"Uncle Joss," Mary said softly, when he was within a yard of her. "Uncle Joss . . ."

He crouched where he was, staring down, and then he leaned forward and touched her hair and her lips. "Mary," he said, "is it you, Mary? Why don't you speak to me? Where have they gone? Have you seen them?"

"You've made a mistake, Uncle Joss," she said. "There is no one here, only myself. Aunt Patience is upstairs. Are you ill? Can I help you?"

He looked about him in the half-light, searching the corners of the room. "They can't scare me," he whispered. "Dead men don't harm the living. They're blotted out, like a candle. . . . That's it, isn't it, Mary?"

She nodded, watching his eyes. He pulled himself to a chair, his hands outstretched on the table. He sighed heavily and passed his tongue over his lips. "It's dreams," he said, "all dreams. The faces stand out like live things in the darkness, and I wake with the sweat pouring down my back. I'm thirsty, Mary; here's the key; go into the bar and fetch me some brandy." She took the key, her hand trembling, and slipped out of the room into the bar. When she returned to the kitchen he was sprawling at the table, his head in his hands. She put a bottle and a glass on the table in front of him. He filled the glass and held it between his hands, watching her all the while over the rim of it.

"You're a good girl," he said. "I'm fond of you, Mary; you've got sense and you've got pluck; you'd make a good companion to a man. They ought to have made you a boy." He rolled the brandy around on his tongue, smiling foolishly, and then he winked at her, and pointed his finger.

"They pay gold for this upcountry," he said. "King George himself hasn't better brandy than this in his cellar. And what do I pay? Not one damned bloody sixpence. We drink free at Jamaica Inn." He laughed and put out his tongue. "They can't catch me, Mary, I'm too cunning; I've been at the game too long. There's over a hundred of us, working inland to the border from the coast."

He beckoned Mary to his side, winking again, glancing first over his shoulder to the door. "Here," he whispered, "come close, where I can talk to you." He seized hold of her arm and pulled her onto the floor beside his chair. "It's this cursed drink that makes a fool of me," he said. "Damn it, Mary, I've killed men with my own hands, trampled them underwater, and I've slept in my bed like a child. But when I'm drunk I see them in my dreams; I see their white-green faces staring at me, with their eyes eaten by fish; and some of them are torn, with the flesh hanging on their bones in ribbons. . . . There was a woman once, Mary; she was clinging to a raft, and she had a child in her arms; her hair was streaming down her back. The ship was close in on the rocks, you see, and the sea was as flat as your hand; they were all coming in alive, the whole bunch of 'em. She cried out to me to help her, Mary, and I smashed her face in with a stone; she fell back, her hands beating the raft. She let go of the child, and I hit her again; I watched them drown in four feet of water. Then we were afraid some of them would reach the shore. We had to pelt 'em with stones; we had to break their arms and legs; they drowned because they couldn't stand. . . ."

His face was close to Mary, his red-flecked eyes staring. "Did you never hear of wreckers before?" he whispered.

Outside in the passage the clock struck one, and the single note rang in the air like a summons. Neither of them moved. The room was very cold, for the fire had sunk away to nothing, and a little current of air blew in from the open door. The yellow flame of the candle bowed and flickered.

He reached out to her and took her hand; it lay limp in his. Perhaps he saw something of the frozen horror in her face, for he let her go and turned away his eyes and jerked his head toward the ticking of the clock. "When it struck one just now, it was like the tolling of a bell buoy in a bay," he said. "One, two, one, two, backward and forward the clapper goes against the bell, as though it tolled for dead men. When you work on the coast you have to pull out to the bell buoys in a boat and wrap the tongues in flannel. There's silence then. Maybe it's a misty night, with patches of white fog on the water, and outside the bay there'll be a ship casting for scent like a hound. She listens for the buoy, and no sound comes to her. And she comes in then, driving through the fog—she comes straight in to us who are waiting for her, Mary—and we see her shudder suddenly and strike, and then the surf has her."

He reached for the bottle of brandy and let a little liquid trickle slowly into the glass. He smelled it and rolled it on his tongue. "Have you ever seen flies caught in a jar of treacle?" he said. "I've seen men like that, stuck in the rigging like a swarm of flies. They cling there for safety, shouting in terror at the sight of the surf. I've seen the ship break up beneath them, and the masts and yards snap like thread, and there they'll be flung into the sea, to swim for their lives. But when they reach the shore they're dead men, Mary."

Mary felt deadly sick. She longed only to stumble to her bed, pulling the blanket over her for greater darkness. Perhaps if she pressed her hands against her eyes she would blot out the pictures her uncle had painted for her. She looked up and saw that he had fallen forward onto the table. His mouth was wide open, and he snorted and spluttered as he slept. His arms rested on the table before him, and his hands were clasped as though in prayer.

CHAPTER SIX

ON CHRISTMAS EVE the sky was overcast and threatened rain. Mary leaned out of the window, and the soft wet wind blew upon her face. In an hour's time Jem Merlyn would be waiting for her on the moor to take her to Launceston fair, and she could not make up her mind. She had grown older in four days, and the face that looked back at her from the cracked mirror had dark rings beneath its eyes and little hollows in its cheeks. For the first time in her life she saw a resemblance between herself and her aunt Patience. They had the same pucker of the forehead, and if she pursed up her lips and worked them, it might be Aunt Patience who stood there. She began to pace up and down her cramped room.

Mary and Aunt Patience shared a secret now, a secret that must never be spoken between them. She wondered how many years Aunt Patience had kept that knowledge to herself in an agony of silence. The pain of that knowledge would never leave her alone. In her own way Aunt Patience was a murderer too. She had killed by her silence. Her guilt was as great as Joss Merlyn's himself.

In the old days at Helford, there had been whispers of these things; but not now, not in the light of the new century. Once more she saw her uncle's face pressed close to hers, and she heard his whisper in her ear: "Did you never hear of wreckers before?" Mary had lost her fear of him. There was only loathing left in her heart. He had lost all hold on humanity. He was a beast that walked by night. Now that she knew him for what he was, neither he nor the rest of his company could frighten her. They were things of evil, rotting the countryside, and she would never rest until they were blotted out.

There remained Aunt Patience—and Jem Merlyn. He broke into her thoughts against her will. There was enough on her mind without reckoning with Jem. He was too like his brother. His eyes, and his mouth, and his smile. She could see her uncle in his walk, in the turn of his head; and she knew why Aunt Patience had made a fool of herself ten years ago. And there, in spite of herself, came Jem's face again, with the growth of beard like a tramp's, and his dirty shirt, and his bold offensive stare. He was rude, and he had more than a streak of cruelty in him; he was a thief and a liar. He stood for everything she feared and hated and despised; but she knew she could love him. Something inside her responded to him; the very thought of him was an irritant and a stimulant at the same time. She knew she would have to see him again.

Once more she looked up at the gray sky and the low-flying clouds. If she was going to Launceston, then it was time to make ready and be away. And this time it was Jem Merlyn who would answer her questions; he would show some humility too when he realized she could destroy them when she chose. And tomorrow—well, tomorrow could take care of itself. There was always Francis Davey and his promise; there would be peace and shelter for her at the house in Altarnun.

This was a strange Christmastide, she pondered, as she strode across the East Moor with Hawk's Tor as her guide, and the hills rolling away from her on either side. Last year she had knelt beside her mother in church and prayed that health and peace and courage should be given to them both. For answer she was alone now, caught in a mesh of brutality and crime, and she was walking across a barren, friendless moor to meet a horse thief and, it might be, a murderer of men. She would offer no prayers to God this Christmas.

Mary waited on the high ground above Rushyford, and in the distance she saw the little cavalcade approach her: the pony, the jingle, and two horses tethered behind. The driver raised his whip in a signal of welcome. Mary felt the color flame into her face. This weakness was a thing of torment to her. She thrust her hands into her shawl, her forehead puckered in a frown. He whistled as he approached her and flung a small package at her feet. "A happy Christmas to you," he said. "I had a silver piece in my pocket yesterday and it burned a hole. There's a new handkerchief for your head."

She had meant to be curt on meeting him, but this introduction made it difficult. "That's very kind of you," she said.

He looked her up and down in the cool offensive way of his. "You were early here," he said. "Were you afraid I'd be going without you?"

She climbed into the cart beside him and gathered the reins in her hands. "I like to have the feel of them again," she said, ignoring his remark. "Mother and I, we would drive into Helston on market days."

He folded his arms and watched her handle the reins. "What's the matter with you today?" he said. "Your color is gone, and you've no light in your eyes. I fancied jogging into Launceston with a pretty girl beside me, and fellows looking up as we passed. Don't lie to me, Mary. I'm not as blind as you think. What's happened at Jamaica Inn? You've had no more visitors, have you?"

"None that I know of. Nobody's crossed the yard. You asked me last time we met if I knew why my aunt looked like a living ghost. Well, I know now, that's all."

Jem watched her with curious eyes, and then he whistled.

"Drink's a funny thing," he said. "I got drunk one night, in Amsterdam, the time I ran away to sea. I remember sitting on the floor with my arms round a pretty redhead. The next thing I knew, it was seven in the following morning, and I was lying on my back in the gutter, without any breeches. I'm damned if I can remember what I did during those hours."

"That's very fortunate for you," said Mary. "When your brother gets drunk he finds his memory instead of losing it. This time I happened to be there when he woke. And he'd been dreaming."

"And you heard one of his dreams, is that it?" said Jem. He leaned over her suddenly and took the reins out of her hands. "You don't look where you're going." She sank back in the jingle and allowed him to drive. The pony picked up his feet and broke into a trot.

"What are you going to do about it?" asked Jem.

Mary shrugged her shoulders. "I have to consider Aunt Patience. You don't expect me to tell you, do you? You're his brother. There are many gaps in the story, and you fit remarkably well into some of them."

"Do you think I'd waste my time working for my brother? Have you ever seen a moth flutter to a candle and singe his wings? A ship will do the same to a false light. It may happen once, twice, three times, perhaps; but the fourth time, a dead ship stinks to heaven, and the whole country is up in arms and wants to know the reason why. My brother has lost his own rudder by now, and he's heading for the shore himself. I've run cargoes, but I'll tell you one thing, Mary Yellan, and you can believe it or not: I've never killed a man—yet." He cracked the whip savagely over his pony's head, and the animal broke into a gallop. "There's a ford ahead of us; we cross the river and come out on the Launceston road. Then we've seven miles before we reach the town. There's bread and cheese in the basket under the seat, and an apple or two. You'll be hungry directly. So you think I wreck ships, do you, and stand on the shore and watch men drown? And then put my hands into their pockets afterward, when they're swollen with water? It makes a pretty picture."

Whether his anger was pretended or sincere she could not say, but his mouth was set firm, and there was a flaming spot of color high on his cheekbone. "You haven't denied it yet, have you?" she said.

He looked down at her, half contemptuous, half amused, as though she were a child without knowledge. With a sudden intuition she knew the question that was forming itself, and her hands grew hot.

"If you believe it of me, why do you drive with me today to Launceston?" he said.

He was ready to mock her; a stammered reply would be a triumph for him, and she steeled herself to gaiety. "For the sake of your bright eyes, Jem Merlyn," she said, and she met his glance without a tremor.

He laughed at that, and all at once there was between them a certain boyish familiarity. The very boldness of her words had disarmed him; he suspected nothing of the weakness that lay behind them, and for the moment they were companions without the strain of being man and woman.

They came now to the highroad, and the jingle rattled along behind the trotting pony, with the two stolen horses clattering in tow. The rain clouds swept across the sky, threatening and low, but as yet no drizzle fell from them. Mary thought of Francis Davey in Altarnun away to the left of her, and she wondered what he would say to her when she told him her story. He would not advise a waiting game again. The voice of Francis Davey would mean security and a forgetting of trouble. There was a strangeness about him that was disturbing and pleasant. He had not the male aggression of Jem beside her; he was without flesh and blood. He was no more than two white eyes and a voice in the darkness.

The pony shied suddenly at a gap in the hedge, and Jem's loud curse woke her with a jar from the privacy of her thoughts.

"Do you know who has the living at Altarnun, Jem Merlyn?"

"No, I do not, Mary Yellan. I've never had any truck with parsons. Get out the bread and the cheese; my belly is sinking away to nothing."

It was a hilarious cavalcade that clattered into Launceston at half past two in the afternoon. Mary, in spite of her firm resolution of the early morning, had melted to Jem's mood and given herself to gaiety. There was an infection in the air caught from the sound and bustle of the town, a sense of Christmas. Carriages, and carts, and coaches too were huddled together in the cobbled square; the cheerful crowd jostled one another before the market stalls; turkeys and geese scratched at the wooden barrier that penned them; and pastry cooks and little apprentice boys pushed in and out among the crowd with the hot pasties and sausage meat on trays. A lady in a feathered hat and a blue velvet cape stepped from her coach and went into the warmth and light of the White Hart, followed by a gentleman in a padded greatcoat of powder gray. He lifted his eyeglass to his eyes and strutted after her for all the world like a turkeycock himself. This was a happy world to Mary. The town was set on the bosom of a hill, with a castle framed in the center, like a tale from old history. There were trees clustered here, and sloping fields. The moors were forgotten.

Mary wore the handkerchief Jem had given her. She even unbent so far as to permit him to tie the ends under her chin. They had stabled the pony and jingle at the top of the town. Now Jem pushed through the crowd, leading his two stolen horses, making straight for the main square, where the booths and tents of the Christmas fair stood end to end. There was a place roped off from the fair for the buying and selling of livestock, and the ring was surrounded by farmers, and gentlemen too, and dealers from Devon and beyond. Mary's heart beat faster as they approached the ring; supposing there were someone from North Hill here, or a farmer from a neighboring village, surely they would recognize the horses? Jem looked back at her once and winked his eye. Mary saw Jem take his place among a group of men with ponies. He looked cool and unperturbed. Presently a flashy fellow with a square hat and cream breeches crossed over to the horses. His voice was loud, and he kept hitting his boot with a crop, and then pointing to the ponies. From his air of authority, Mary judged him to be a dealer. Soon he was joined by a little lynx-eyed man, who now and again jogged his elbow and whispered in his ear.

Mary saw him stare hard at the black pony that had belonged to Squire Bassat; he went up to him and felt his legs. Then he whispered something in the ear of the loud-voiced man. Mary watched him nervously.

"Where did you get this pony?" said the dealer, tapping Jem on the arm. "He was never bred on the moors, not with that head and shoulders."

"He was foaled at Callington four years ago," said Jem carelessly, his pipe in the corner of his mouth. "I bought him as a yearling from old Tim Bray; you remember Tim? The dam was Irish bred, and won prizes for him upcountry. I tell you what, I'll take eighteen guineas for him."

The two men consulted together and appeared to disagree. Mary heard the word fake, and Jem shot a glance at her over the heads of the crowd. The loud-voiced dealer looked regretfully at the black pony. "He's a good looker," he said. "What makes you so particular, Will?"

Once more the lynx-eyed man whispered in his ear. The dealer listened and pulled a face. "All right," he said aloud. "You've got an eye for trouble, haven't you? Perhaps we're better out of it. You can keep your pony," he added to Jem. The two men elbowed through the crowd and disappeared in the direction of the White Hart. Mary could make nothing of Jem's expression; his lips were framed in the inevitable whistle.

At a quarter to four Jem sold the other horse for six pounds to a cheerful, honest-looking farmer, who rode off on the back of his purchase with a grin from ear to ear. Twilight gathered and the lamps were lit. Mary was thinking of returning to the jingle when she heard a woman's voice behind her. She turned and saw the blue cloak and the plumed hat of the woman who had stepped from the coach earlier in the afternoon. "Oh, look, James," she was saying. "Did you ever see such a delicious pony in your life? He holds his head just like poor Beauty did. What a nuisance Roger isn't here. I can't disturb him from his meeting. It would be such a good Christmas present for the children. They've plagued poor Roger ever since Beauty disappeared. Ask the price, James, will you?"

The man put up his eyeglass and drawled to Jem, "Look here, my man, this lady has taken a fancy to your pony. She has just lost one, and she wants to replace him. What is your price?"

"Twenty-five guineas," said Jem promptly. "At least, that's what my friend was going to pay. I'm not anxious to sell him."

The lady in the plumed hat swept into the ring. "I'll give you thirty for him," she said. "I'm Mrs. Bassat from North Hill, and I want him as a Christmas present for my children. I want to surprise Mr. Bassat as well as my children. My groom shall fetch the pony immediately and ride him to North Hill before Mr. Bassat joins us in this square. Here's the money."

Jem swept off his hat and bowed low. "Thank you, madam," he said. "I hope Mr. Bassat will be pleased with your bargain. You will find the pony exceedingly safe with children."

"Oh, I'm certain he will be delighted. Of course the pony is nothing like the one we had stolen. Beauty was a thoroughbred." She made her way from the ring toward the coach that waited in the square, followed by her companion with the monocle.

Jem looked hastily over his shoulder and tapped a lad who stood behind him on the arm. "Here," he said, "would you like a five-shilling piece?" The lad nodded, his mouth agape. "Hang on to this pony, then, and when the groom comes for him, hand him over for me, will you? I've just had word that my wife has given birth to twins and her life is in danger."

And he was off in a moment, walking hard across the square. Mary followed, her face scarlet, the laughter bubbling up inside her, her mouth hidden in her shawl. When they reached the farther side of the square, out of sight of the group of people, she stood with her hand to her side, catching her breath. Jem's face was as grave as a judge's.

"Jem Merlyn, you deserve to be hanged," she said. "To stand there as you did and sell that stolen pony back to Mrs. Bassat herself!"

He threw back his head and laughed, and she could not resist him. Launceston itself seemed to rock in merriment as peal after peal of gaiety echoed in the street. The torches cast strange lights on the faces of people, and there was color, and shadow, and the hum of voices. They plunged into the thick of the fair, with all the warmth and the suggestion of packed humanity about them. Jem bought Mary a crimson shawl, and gold rings for her ears. They sucked oranges beneath a striped tent and had their fortunes told by a wrinkled Gypsy woman. "There's blood in your hand, young man," she told Jem. "You'll kill a man one day."

"What did I tell you in the jingle this morning?" said Jem to Mary. "I'm innocent as yet. Do you believe it now?" But she shook her head at him; she would not say. Little raindrops splashed onto their faces, and Jem dragged Mary under cover of a doorway and held her with his hands and kissed her. The soft rain came in gusts at the open doorway, and

Jem stood with his back to the weather, making a screen for Mary. He untied the handkerchief she wore and played with her hair.

She felt the tips of his fingers on her neck, traveling to her shoulders, and she put up her hands and pushed them away. "I've made a fool of myself long enough for one night, Jem Merlyn," she said. "It's time we thought of returning. Let me alone."

"You don't want to ride in an open jingle in this wind, do you?" he said. "It's coming from the coast, and we'll be blown under on the high ground. We'll have to spend the night together in Launceston."

"Very likely! Go and fetch the pony, Jem, while this shower lifts for the moment. I'll wait for you here."

"Do they make you different from other women, then, down on Helford River? Stay here with me tonight, Mary, and we can find out. You'd be like the rest by the time morning came, I'd take my oath on that."

"I haven't a doubt of it. That's why I'd rather risk a soaking in the jingle."

"I've never known a woman so perverse. All right, I'll fetch the jingle and take you home to your aunt, but I'll kiss you first, whether you like it or not." He took her face in his hands. " 'One for sorrow, two for joy,' " he said as he kissed her. "I'll give you the rest when you're in a more yielding frame of mind." He bowed his head against the rain and strode across the street, and so around the corner.

She leaned back once more within the shelter of the door. The thought of staying in Launceston with Jem Merlyn made her heart beat faster, but for all that she would not lose her head to please him. She had given too much away as it was. She thought of Aunt Patience, trailing like a ghost in the shadow of her master. That would be Mary Yellan too, but for the grace of God and her own strength of will.

Mary waited, blowing upon her hands. The long minutes passed and Jem did not come. Somewhere a clock struck eight. He had been gone over half an hour, and the place where the pony and jingle were stabled was only five minutes away. Mary was dispirited and tired. Jem had taken his gaiety with him.

At last she could stand it no longer, and she set off up the hill in search of him. In a few minutes she came to the stable where they had left the pony and jingle in the afternoon. The door was locked, and peering through a crack, she saw that the shed was empty. She knocked at the little shop next door, and it was opened by the fellow who had admitted them to the shed. "I'm looking for my companion," Mary said. "We came here together with a pony and jingle."

At first the man did not recognize her, wild as she was in her wet shawl. Then he muttered an apology. "Your friend has been gone twenty minutes or more. He seemed in a great hurry, and there was another man with him. He looked like one of the servants from the White Hart."

The man shut the door in her face, and Mary retraced her steps in the direction of the town. What would Jem want with one of the servants from the White Hart? Once more she came to the cobbled square. The White Hart looked hospitable enough, with its lighted windows, but there was no sign of the pony and jingle. Mary hesitated for a moment, and then she passed inside. The hall seemed to be full of gentlemen, talking and laughing. Among them, in the company by the fire, she recognized the horse dealer and the little lynx-eyed man, and she was aware of a sudden sense of foreboding.

Again her country clothes and wet hair caused consternation, for a servant went up to her and bade her begone. "I've come in search of a Mr. Jem Merlyn," said Mary firmly. "He came here with a pony and jingle and was seen with one of your servants."

The lynx-eyed man was there before her. "If it's the dark Gypsy fellow who tried to sell my partner a pony this afternoon, I can tell you about him," he said, smiling wide and showing a row of broken teeth. Laughter broke out from the group by the fire. "He was in the company of a gentleman barely ten minutes ago," continued the lynx-eyed man, still smiling and looking her up and down, "and with the help of some of us he was persuaded to enter a carriage that was waiting at the door. He was inclined to resist us, but a look from the gentleman appeared to decide him. His destination is unknown to me. No doubt you know what became of the black pony? The price he was asking was undoubtedly high."

Mary turned her back on him without a word. As the door closed behind her she caught the echo of his laughter.

She stood in the deserted market square with the gusty wind and scattered showers of rain for company. So the theft of the pony had been discovered. Stupidly she stared before her at the dark houses, wondering what was the punishment for theft. Did they hang men for that as well as murder? For the moment she was stunned, and hardly knowing that she did so, she began to walk aimlessly across the square toward the castle hill. If she had consented to stay in Launceston, this would never have happened. They would have gone from the shelter of the doorway and found a room in the town and they would have loved one another. And even if he had been caught in the morning, they would have had those hours alone. Mind and body cried out in bitterness and resentment, and she knew how much she had wanted him.

The castle wall frowned down upon her, and she stumbled along with the mizzling rain driving in her face, careless of the fact that eleven long miles lay between her and her bedroom at Jamaica Inn. The steep hill rose before her. They had clattered down it in the afternoon; Jem had whistled, and she had sung snatches of song. Suddenly she came to her senses and faltered in her steps. It was madness to walk any farther; two miles of the road would bring exhaustion in this wind and rain.

She turned again on the slope of the hill, with the winking lights of the town beneath her. Someone perhaps would give her a blanket on the floor. She had no money; they would have to trust her for payment. She went away down the road, driven like a leaf before the wind, and out of the darkness she saw a carriage crawling up the hill toward her, the full force of the weather against it. On an impulse she ran toward it and called to the driver, wrapped in a greatcoat on the seat. "Are you taking the Bodmin road?" she cried. "Have you a passenger inside?"

The driver shook his head and whipped on his horse, but an arm came out of the carriage window, and a hand was laid on Mary's shoulder. "What does Mary Yellan do alone in Launceston on Christmas Eve?" said a gentle voice from within. A pale face stared at her from the dark interior of the carriage: white hair and white eyes beneath the black shovel hat. It was the vicar of Altarnun.

CHAPTER SEVEN

SHE WATCHED HIS profile in the half-light; the prominent thin nose thrust downward like the curved beak of a bird. He leaned forward, with his chin resting on a long ebony cane that he held between his knees.

"So once more I have the good fortune to help you by the wayside," he said, and his voice was soft and low, like the voice of a woman. "You are wet through to the skin; you had better take off your clothes." He stared at her with cold indifference, and she struggled in some confusion with the pin that clasped her shawl. "There is a dry rug here that will serve you for the rest of the journey," he continued.

Without a word she slipped out of her soaking shawl and bodice and wrapped herself in the coarse hair blanket that he held out to her. Her hair fell from its band and hung like a curtain about her bare shoulders. She felt like a child that has been caught on an escapade, and now sat meekly, obedient to the master's word.

"Well?" he said, looking gravely upon her, and she found herself at once stumbling into an explanation of her day. As before at Altarnun, there was something about him that made her untrue to herself, for her story was poor telling, and she came out of it just another woman who had cheapened herself at Launceston fair and had been left by the man of her choice to find her way home alone. There had been some trouble in Launceston over the sale of a pony, and she feared he had been caught in some dishonesty.

Francis Davey heard her to the end in silence. "So you have not been too lonely after all?" he said at length. "Jamaica Inn was not so isolated as you supposed? What was the name of your companion?"

Mary flushed in the darkness, her sense of guilt stronger than ever. "He was my uncle's brother," she replied, aware of the reluctance in her voice. "You think ill of me, of course," she went on hurriedly. "Mistrusting and loathing my uncle as I do, it was hardly in keeping to make a confidant of his brother. He is dishonest and a thief, I know that; he told me as much at the beginning; but beyond that . . ."

"You mean the brother knows nothing of the landlord's trade by night?" continued the gentle voice at her side. "He is not of the company who bring the wagons to Jamaica Inn?"

Mary made a little gesture of despair. "I don't know," she said. "But he told me that he had never killed a man. And I believed him. He said also that my uncle was running straight into the hands of the law. He surely would not say that if he was one of the company."

Jem's innocence became suddenly of vital importance. "You told me before that you had some acquaintance with the squire," she said quickly. "Perhaps you could persuade him to deal mercifully with Jem Merlyn. After all, he is young; he could start life afresh; it would be easy enough for you in your position."

His silence was an added humiliation. He must see that she was pleading for a man who had kissed her, and that he despised her went without saying.

"My acquaintance with Mr. Bassat of North Hill is of the slightest," he told her gently. "It is hardly likely that he would spare a thief because of me, especially if the thief happens to be the brother of the landlord of Jamaica Inn." Quick as a flash of lightning he continued, "And if your new friend was guilty of conspiring with his brother against the belongings and perhaps the lives of his fellowmen, what then, Mary Yellan? Would you still seek to save him?" She felt his hand upon hers, cool and impersonal, and she broke down and began to rave like a child.

"I didn't bargain for this," she said fiercely. "I could face the brutality of my uncle and the pathetic dumb stupidity of Aunt Patience. I'd planned to take my aunt away from him and see justice done, and then to find work on a farm somewhere and live a man's life, like I used to do. I don't want to love like a woman, Mr. Davey; there's suffering, and misery that can last a lifetime. I don't want it." She leaned back, worn out by her torrent of words. The carriage had climbed away from the Launceston valley and was now upon the high ground, exposed to the full force of the wind and the rain. There was nothing but the moor on either side of the road, and above, the great black vault of the sky; and there was a scream in the wind that had not been before.

"How old are you?" he asked abruptly.

"Twenty-three," she told him.

She heard him swallow in the darkness, and taking his hand away from hers, he placed it once more upon the ebony stick and sat in silence, but she knew that he had turned and was looking down upon her, and for the first time she was aware of his proximity as a person; she could feel his breath on her forehead. She remembered that her wet shawl and bodice lay on the floor at her feet, and she was naked under her rough blanket. When he spoke again she realized how near he was to her, and his voice came as a shock, confusing suddenly, and unexpected.

"You are very young, Mary Yellan," he said softly. "You are nothing but a chicken with the broken shell still around you. Come now, dry your eyes; you are not the first to bite your nails over a lost lover."

She wondered why he had not used the conventional phrases of comfort, said something about the blessing of prayer. She remembered that last ride with him, when he had whipped his horse into a fever of speed, and how he had crouched and whispered words under his breath she had not understood. Again she felt something of the same sensation of uneasiness she had experienced then. She reached for her clothes and began to draw them on furtively under cover of the blanket.

"So I was right in my surmise, and all has been quiet at Jamaica Inn since I saw you last?" he said after a while.

Mary brought herself back to reality with an effort. She had forgotten her uncle for nearly ten hours. At once the staring bloodshot eyes swung before her again, his drunken smile, his groping hands. "Mr. Davey," she whispered, "have you ever heard of wreckers?"

She had never said the word aloud before, and now that she heard it from her own lips it sounded obscene, like a blasphemy. It was too dark in the carriage to see the effect upon his face, but she heard him swallow. "My uncle is one of them; he told me so himself," she said.

Still her companion made no reply; he sat motionless, like a stone thing, and she went on again, never raising her voice above a whisper. "They are in it, every one of them; all those men I saw that first Saturday in the bar at the inn. They've murdered women and children; they've held them under the water; they've killed them with rocks. Those are death wagons that travel the road by night. My aunt lives in mortal terror of discovery; and my uncle has only to lose himself in drink before a stranger, and his secret is spilled to the four winds. There, Mr. Davey, now you know the truth about Jamaica Inn."

The face beneath the black shovel hat turned toward her; she caught a sudden flicker of the white lashes, and the lips moved. "So the landlord talks when he is drunk?" he said, and it seemed to Mary that his voice rang sharper in tone, as though pitched on a higher note.

"He talks, yes," she answered him. "That's why I know. And that's perhaps why I've lost faith in humanity, and in God, and in myself; and why I acted like a fool today in Launceston."

The gale had increased in force, and now with the bend in the road the carriage was brought almost to a standstill. The moor was bare and unprotected, and there was a salt, wet tang in the wind that had come from the sea fifteen miles away.

Francis Davey leaned forward in his seat. "We are approaching Five Lanes and the turning to Altarnun," he said. "The driver is bound to Bodmin and will take you to Jamaica Inn. I shall leave you at Five Lanes and walk down into the village. Am I the only man you have honored with your confidence, or do I share it with the landlord's brother?"

Again Mary could not tell if there was mockery in his voice. "Jem Merlyn knows," she said unwillingly. "We spoke of it this morning."

"And suppose he could save his own skin by betraying his brother?"

Mary started, and for a moment she clutched at the straw. Glancing up at the vicar for confirmation of her hopes, she saw him smile, as though his face were a mask and the mask had cracked. She looked away, feeling like one who stumbles unawares upon a sight forbidden.

"That would be a relief to you and to him, no doubt," continued the vicar, "if he had never been involved. But there is always the doubt, isn't there? And a guilty man does not usually tie the rope around his own neck."

He laid his hand on her knee. "*The bright day is done. And we are for the dark,*" he said softly. "If it were permitted to take our text from Shakespeare, there would be strange sermons preached in Cornwall tomorrow, Mary Yellan. You shake your head at me. I speak in riddles. 'This man is no comforter,' you say. 'He is a freak with his white hair and eyes.' I will tell you one thing for consolation. A week from now will bring the new year. The false lights have flickered for the last time, and there will be no more wrecks."

"How do you know this?" said Mary.

He began to fasten his coat preparatory to departure. He lowered the window and called to the driver to rein in his horse, and the sting of frozen rain rushed into the carriage. "I return tonight from a meeting in Launceston," he said, "and those of us present were informed at last that His Majesty's government were prepared to take certain steps to patrol the coasts of His Majesty's country. There will be watchers on the cliffs instead of flares, and the paths known at present only to men like your uncle and his companions will be trodden by officers of the law."

He opened the door of the carriage and stepped out into the road. He bared his head under the rain, and she saw the thick white hair frame his face like a halo. "Your troubles are over," he said. "The wagon wheels will rust, and the barred room at the end of the passage can be turned into a parlor. Your aunt will sleep in peace, and your uncle will either drink himself to death or he will turn Methodist and preach to travelers on the highroad. As for you, you will ride south again and find a lover. Tomorrow is Christmas Day, and the bells at Altarnun will be ringing for peace and goodwill. I shall think of you." He waved his hand to the driver, turned to the right down one of the five lanes and was lost to sight.

As the carriage rattled on along the Bodmin road, Mary wished that she had gone with Francis Davey. Tomorrow she could have knelt in the church and prayed for the first time since leaving Helford. The day of the wrecker was over; he would be broken by the new law. Ships would come to England without fear; there would be no harvest with the tide. It was the dawn of a new age.

Then as Mary sat in the corner of the carriage, through the open window, traveling down upon the wind, she heard a shot ring out in the silence of the night. The voices of men came out of the darkness, and the padding of feet upon the road. She leaned out of the window, the rain blowing in her face, and she heard the driver of the carriage call out in fear as his horse shied. There in the distance were the lean chimneys of Jamaica Inn crowning the skyline like a gallows. Down the road came a company of men, led by one who leaped and tossed a lantern before him as he ran. Another shot rang out, and the driver of the carriage crumpled in his seat and fell. The horse stumbled, and the carriage swayed upon its wheels. Somebody screamed a blasphemy to the sky; somebody laughed wildly; there was a whistle and a cry.

A face was thrust in at the window of the carriage, crowned with matted hair that fell in a fringe above the bloodshot eyes. The lips parted, showing the white teeth. Joss Merlyn smiled—a crazy, delirious smile—and leveled a pistol at Mary, leaning forward into the carriage so that the barrel touched her throat.

Then he laughed, and wrenching open the door, he took her hands and pulled her out, holding the lantern above his head so that all could see her. There were ten or twelve of them standing in the road, half of them drunk as their leader, wild eyes staring out of shaggy bearded faces; one or two had pistols in their hands; some were armed with broken bottles, knives, and stones. Harry the peddler stood by the horse's head.

When they saw who she was a howl of laughter broke from the company of men, and the peddler put his two fingers to his mouth and whistled. The landlord bowed with drunken gravity; he seized her loose hair in his hand and twisted it in a rope, sniffing at it like a dog.

"So," he said, "you've come back again, like a little whining bitch, with your tail between your legs?"

Mary said nothing.

"So you're dumb, are you?" cried her uncle, and he hit her across the face with the back of his hand. "You'll come to heel if I kill you first," he said. "What do you think you do, at midnight, riding in a hired carriage, half naked, with your hair down your back? You're nothing but a common slut, after all." He jerked at her wrist, and she fell.

"Leave me alone," she cried. "You're a bloody murderer and a thief. Your reign is over, Uncle Joss. I've been to Launceston today to inform against you."

A hubbub rose among the group of men, but the landlord roared at them, waving them back. "You damned fools! Can't you see she's trying to save her skin by lies?" he thundered. "She's never walked the eleven miles to Launceston. Look at her feet. She's been with a man somewhere down the road, and he sent her back on wheels when he'd had enough of her. Get up—or do you want me to rub your nose in the mud?" He pulled her to her feet. Then he pointed to the sky, where the low clouds fled before the scurrying wind and a wet star gleamed.

"Look there," he yelled. "There's a break in the sky, and the rain's going east. There'll be more wind yet before we're through, and a wild dawn on the coast in six hours' time. Get your horse, Harry, and put him in the traces here; the carriage will carry half a dozen of us. And bring the pony and the farm cart from the stable. Come on, you lazy drunken devils, don't you want to feel gold and silver run through your hands? By God, I want the coast again. Who'll take the road with me through Camelford?"

A shout rose from a dozen voices, and the men turned with the carriage and followed it, some mounting to the driver's empty seat. Joss Merlyn stood looking down upon Mary with a foolish drunken smile; then on a sudden impulse he caught her in his arms and pulled her toward the carriage. He threw her onto the seat in the corner; then leaning out of the window, he yelled to the peddler to whip the horse up.

The animal topped the hill at a gallop, with half a dozen madmen clinging to the reins and screaming at his heels. Jamaica Inn was ablaze with light; the doors were open, and the windows were unbarred. The house gaped out of the night like a live thing.

The landlord forced Mary back against the side of the carriage. "You'd inform against me, would you?" he said. "You'd run to the law and have me swinging on a rope's end like a cat? All right, then, you shall have your chance. You shall stand on the shore and watch for the dawn and the coming in of the tide. You know what that means? You think you're not afraid of me? You sneer at me with your pretty white face and your monkey eyes. Tonight you shall come with us, Mary, to the coast."

She stared back at him in horror; the color drained from her face and she tried to speak to him, but his hands forbade her.

CHAPTER EIGHT

IT WAS A NIGHTMARE journey of two hours or more. Harry the peddler and two other men had climbed in beside her uncle, and the air became foul at once with the stink of their bodies. At first they talked at Mary and for her, Harry the peddler bursting into his lewd songs, which rang with immoderate force in such close quarters, stimulating his audience to greater excitement. They watched her face, hoping that she would show some sign of shame, but Mary heard their voices through a haze of exhaustion, caring little what became of her.

When they saw how lifeless she was, her presence lost its flavor, and Joss Merlyn fumbled in his pocket and produced a pack of cards. Closing her eyes, Mary resigned herself to the movement of the swaying, jolting carriage. Darkness came upon her like a boon from heaven. Time had nothing to do with her then. It was a sudden stillness, and the cold damp air blowing upon her face through the open carriage window, that dragged her back to the world.

She was alone in her corner. The men had gone, taking their light with them. She sat motionless at first, fearing to bring them back. Then she leaned forward to the window, and a weal of pain ran across her shoulders where the cold had numbed her. The carriage had been abandoned in a narrow gullyway with high banks, and the horse had been taken from the traces. The gully appeared to descend sharply. The night had thickened considerably, and in the gullyway it was black, as in a pit. Mary put her hand out of the window and touched the bank. Her fingers came upon loose sand and stems of grass, sodden through with the rain. She tried the handle of the door, but it was locked. Her eyes strained to pierce the darkness ahead of her, and borne up to her on the wind came a sound at once sullen and familiar, a sound that for the first time in her life she could not welcome, but must recognize with a shiver of foreboding.

It was the sound of the sea. The gully was a pathway to the shore. She heard a murmur and a sigh as the spent water gave itself to the strand and withdrew; a pause as the sea gathered itself, and then once more the crash, the roar of surf upon shingle and the screaming scatter of stones following the drag of the sea. Mary shuddered; somewhere in the darkness below, her uncle and his companions waited for the tide. This deadly quietude was sinister. Business had sobered them.

Her first fatigue cast aside, Mary considered the size of the carriage window; with straining she might squeeze her body through the narrow frame. She worked at the window, leaning backward through the gap, the effort made even more difficult because of her stiff shoulder; and then with a sickening squeeze her hips were through, the frame of the window scraping the flesh and turning her faint. She lost balance and fell backward to the ground below.

She dragged herself to her feet and began to creep up the lane, in the dark shelter of the bank. With her back turned away from the sea, she would be putting distance between herself and her late companions. There was little doubt that they had descended to the shore. The carriage must have traveled by a road; and if there was a road, there would be dwelling houses before long; there would be honest men and women who would rouse the countryside when they heard her story.

She felt her way along the narrow ditch, stumbling over the stones, her hair blowing into her eyes. She did not see the humped figure of a man kneeling in the ditch with his back toward her, his eyes watchful of the winding lane ahead. She came against him, knocking the breath from her body, and he, taken by surprise, fell with her, crying out in mingled terror and rage. They fought on the ground, but in a moment he was too strong for her, and rolling her over on her side, he leaned on her, peering closely at her, his gaping mouth showing yellow broken teeth. It was Harry the peddler.

He expected her to cry or struggle, but when she did neither he shifted his weight to his elbow and smiled at her slyly. "It's been cold and damp in the ditch," he said, "but that's no odds now," and she felt his furtive hand fasten itself upon her. She moved swiftly, lashing out at him, and her fist caught him underneath the chin, with his tongue caught between his teeth. He squealed like a rabbit and lurched sideways upon her. He was fighting now for possession, and she lay limp suddenly, to deceive him. As he grunted in triumph, relaxing his weight, she jabbed at him swiftly with the full force of her knee, at the same time thrusting her fingers in his eyes. He doubled up, rolling onto his side in agony, and in a second she had struggled from under him. She grabbed in the ditch for loose earth and sand, scattering it in his face and in his eyes. Then she began to run like a hunted thing up the twisting lane. A sense of panic swamped her reason, and she started to climb up the high bank that bordered the lane, her foot slipping at every step in the soft earth, until with an effort born in terror she reached the top and crawled, sobbing, through a gap in the thorn hedge that bordered the bank; then she ran along the cliff.

A wall of fog closed in upon her. She fell at once upon hands and knees and crawled slowly forward, following a narrow sandy track that wound in the direction she wished to take. It seemed as though she could hear the sea on every side of her and there were no escape from it. She realized that with her ignorance of the coastline she had not turned east, as she had meant to do, but was now upon a cliff path that was taking her straight to the shore. Even as she decided this, there was a gap in the mist ahead of her, showing a patch of sky. She crawled on uncertainly, the path widening and the fog clearing, and there she knelt amid driftwood and seaweed, while not fifty yards away were the high combing seas breaking upon the shore.

When her eyes had accustomed themselves to the shadows, she made out, huddled against a jagged rock that broke up the expanse of the beach, a little knot of men peering ahead of them into the darkness of the incoming sea. A jutting piece of rock stood between Mary and the bare beach. She crawled as far as the rock and lay down behind it; ahead of her, directly in her line of vision, stood her uncle and his companions, with their backs turned to her.

The mist began to lift very slowly, disclosing the narrow outline of the bay. The expanse of water widened to a bare line of shore that stretched away interminably. To the right, in the distance, where the highest part of the cliff sloped to the sea, Mary made out a faint pinprick of light. She watched it intently, and it danced and curtsied, a living flare that would not be blown. The group of men on the beach before her heeded it not; their eyes were turned to the dark sea beyond the breakers. And suddenly Mary was aware of the reason for their indifference, and the small winking light became a symbol of horror.

It was a false light placed there by her uncle and his companions. She saw a dark figure pass in front of it; then it burned clear again. The figure became a blot against the gray face of the cliff, hurrying down the slope to his companions on the beach. Mary saw him put his hands to his mouth and shout, but his words were caught up in the wind and did not come to her. They reached the little group of waiting men, who broke up at once in excitement. They ran toward the breakers, their voices topping one another above the crash of the sea. Then one of them—her uncle it was; she recognized his loping stride and massive shoulders—held up his hand for silence; and they waited, spread out in a thin line like crows. Mary watched with them, and out of the mist and darkness came another pinprick of light in answer to the first. This new light dipped low and was hidden; then it would rise again, pointing high to the sky, a hand flung into the night in a last and desperate attempt to break through the wall of mist. The new light drew nearer to the first. The one compelled the other. And still the men crouched motionless upon the narrow strand, waiting for the lights to close with one another.

Now Mary could see the shadowed outline of a hull, the black spars like fingers spreading above it, while a white surging sea combed beneath the hull. Closer drew the mast light to the flare upon the cliff, fascinated and held, like a moth coming to a candle. She could bear no more. She scrambled to her feet and ran down upon the beach, shouting and waving

her hands above her head, pitting her voice against the wind and the sea. Someone caught hold of her and forced her down upon the beach. She was trodden upon and kicked. Her cries died away, smothered by the coarse sacking that choked her mouth, and her arms were dragged behind her back and knotted together, the rough cord searing her flesh.

They left her then, the breakers sweeping toward her not twenty yards away; and as she lay there helpless, the breath knocked from her and her scream of warning strangled in her throat, she heard the cry that had been hers become the cry of others and fill the air with sound. The cry rose above the smash of the sea, and with the cry came the shuddering groan of twisting, breaking timber.

A breaker running high above its fellows flung itself with a crash of thunder upon the lurching ship. Mary saw the vessel roll slowly upon its side like a great flat turtle; the masts and spars were crumpled threads of cotton. Little black dots stuck themselves fast to the splintering wood like limpets; and when the shuddering mass beneath them broke monstrously in two, they fell one by one into the white tongues of the sea.

The men who had waited during the cold hours waded waist-deep into the breakers, all caution spent, snatching at the bobbing, sodden wreckage borne in on the surging tide. Some of them ran naked in the cold December night, the better to fight their way into the sea and plunge their hands among the spoil that the breakers tossed to them. They chattered and squabbled like monkeys, tearing things from one another, and one of them kindled a fire in the corner by the cliff. The spoils of the sea were dragged up the beach and heaped beside it. The fire cast a ghastly light where the men ran backward and forward, industrious and horrible.

When the first body was washed ashore they clustered around it, picking it clean as a bone; and when they had stripped it bare, tearing at the smashed fingers in search of rings, they abandoned it to loll upon its back in the scum where the tide had been. They robbed haphazardly, each man for himself, drunk with success—dogs snapping at the heels of their master. They followed him where he ran naked among the breakers, the water streaming from the hair on his body, a giant above them all.

The tide turned, the water receded, and a gray color came upon the water and was answered by the sky. Joss Merlyn lifted his great head, turning about him as he stood, watching the clear contour of the cliffs as the darkness slipped away; and he shouted suddenly, pointing to the sky that was leaden now and pale. The men hesitated, glancing once more at the wreckage that surged and fell in the trough of the sea, unclaimed as yet and waiting to be salvaged; and then they turned with one accord and began to run up the beach toward the entrance of the gully, silent once more, their faces scared in the broadening light. Success had made them careless. The world was waking up around them.

It was Joss Merlyn who pulled the sacking away from her mouth and jerked Mary to her feet. Seeing that she could neither stand alone nor help herself in any way, he cursed her furiously, and then he threw her over his shoulder as he would a sack. He ran with her up the strand to the entrance of the gully; and his companions. caught up already in a mesh of panic, flung the remnants of spoil they had snatched from the beach upon the backs of the three horses tethered there. They worked as though unhinged, lacking all sense of order, while the landlord, sober now, cursed and bullied them to no avail. The carriage, stuck in the bank halfway up the gully, resisted their efforts to extract it, and this sudden reverse to their fortune increased the panic and stampede. Some of them began to scatter up the lane. Those who remained finally wrenched the carriage from the bank in so rough a manner that it overturned, smashing a wheel.

There was a wild rush to the farm cart that had been left farther up the lane, and to the already overburdened horses. Someone put fire to the broken carriage, whose presence in the lane screamed danger to them all. The riot of fighting that followed for the possession of the farm cart that might yet carry them away inland was a hideous scrap of teeth smashed by stones, of eyes cut open by broken glass.

Those who carried pistols now had the advantage, and the landlord, with Harry the peddler by his side, stood with his back to the cart and let fly among the rabble. The first shot went wide and gave one of the opponents a chance to cut the landlord's eye open with a jagged flint. Joss Merlyn marked his assailant with his second shot, spattering him in mid-stomach, and the fellow doubled up screaming in the mud.

The remaining rebels turned as one man and scuttled up the twisting lane. Now that they were alone, the landlord and the peddler wasted little time. What wreckage had been salvaged and brought to the gully they threw upon the cart beside Mary. The man who had been shot sprawled in the lane beside the cart. It was Harry the peddler who dragged his body to the fire, which burned well; much of the carriage was already consumed. Joss Merlyn led the remaining horse to the traces, and without a word the two men climbed into the cart and jerked the horse to action.

Lying on her back in the cart, Mary watched the low clouds pass across the sky. She could still hear the sound of the distant sea. The wheels of the cart crunched the uneven lane, and turning right, came out upon a smoother surface of gravel that was a road running northward between low hedges. From far away came the merry peal of bells.

She remembered suddenly that it was Christmas Day.

THE SQUARE PANE of glass was familiar to her. It was larger than the carriage window and had a ledge before it, and there was a crack across the pane that she remembered well. Mary moaned and turned her head restlessly from side to side; out of the tail of her eye she saw the brown discolored wall beside her and the rusty nailhead where a text had once been hung.

She was lying in her bedroom at Jamaica Inn.

The sight of this room she hated was at least protection from the wind and the rain and from the hands of Harry the peddler. Shock had made a dummy of her and taken away her strength; tears of self-pity welled into her eyes.

Now there was a face bending down to her, and her hands were held gently, and the eyes that peered at her were red-rimmed like her own from weeping. It was Aunt Patience. They clung to one another, seeking comfort in proximity; and after Mary had wept awhile, allowing the tide of emotion to carry her to the limit, nature took command of her again, something of the old courage and force coming back to her.

"You know what has happened?" she asked, and Aunt Patience held her hands tightly, the blue eyes begging dumbly for forgiveness, like an animal punished through no fault of its own.

"How long have I lain here?" Mary questioned, and she was told that this was the second day. She was silent, considering the information; two days was a long time to one who but a few moments ago had watched the dawn break on the coast.

"You should have woken me," she said roughly, pushing away the hands that clung to her. "I'm not a child, to be pampered because of a few bruises. There's work for me to do; you don't understand."

"You could not move," Aunt Patience whimpered. "Your poor body was bleeding and broken. I thought at first they had injured you terribly, but thank the dear God no real harm has come to you."

"You know who did it, don't you? You know where they took me?" Mary began to talk about the men on the shore, but when she saw the thin mouth working she became sickened of herself and could not continue. She sat up in bed, swung her legs to the floor, her temples throbbing with the effort, and began to drag on her clothes.

"Your uncle is below," said her aunt. "He will not let you leave."

"I'm not afraid of him."

"Mary, for your sake, for my sake, do not anger him again. Ever since he returned with you he has sat below, white and terrible, a gun across his knees; the doors of the inn are barred. If you go down now, he may even kill you. . . . I beg you on my knees not to go down." She clutched at Mary's skirt, clasped at her hands, and kissed them.

"Aunt Patience, I have gone through enough out of loyalty to you. All your tears won't save Uncle Joss from justice. He's an inhuman brute, half mad with brandy and blood." Her voice rose dangerously high; hysteria was not far away.

Aunt Patience prayed too late for silence; the door opened, and the landlord of Jamaica Inn stood on the threshold. He stooped his head under the beam and stared at them. The cut above his eye was still a vivid scarlet. He was filthy, and there were black shadows beneath his eyes.

"I thought I heard voices in the yard," he said. "I went to a chink in the shutters, but I saw no one. Did you hear anything from this room?"

Nobody answered. He sat down on the bed, his restless eyes roaming from the window to the door.

"He'll come," he said. "I've cut my own throat; I've gone against him. He warned me once, and I laughed at him; I wanted to play the game on my own. We're as good as dead, all three of us sitting here—you, Patience, and Mary, and I. Why did you let me drink? Why didn't you turn the key on me? Now it's too late."

They stared at him, dumbfounded and awed at the expression on his face they had not seen before.

"What do you mean?" said Mary at length. "Who are you afraid of?"

He shook his head, the old cunning in his eyes as he glanced at Mary. "You'd like to know, wouldn't you?" he said. "You'd like to sneak out of the house with the name on your lips and betray me. But I saved you, didn't I? Have you thought what that rabble would have done to you had I not been there?" He laughed, something of his usual self returning to him. "Nobody touched you that night but myself. Why, you poor weak thing, you know as well as I do I could have had you your first week at Jamaica Inn if I'd wanted you. You'd be lying at my feet now, like your aunt Patience, crushed and contented and clinging, another bloody fool. Let's get out of here."

He shambled to his feet, dragging her after him, and when they came onto the landing he thrust her beneath the candle stuck in the bracket, so that the light fell upon her bruised, cut face. He took her chin in his hands and held her for a moment, smoothing the scratches with delicate, light fingers. She stared back at him in loathing, the graceful hands reminding her of Jem's; and when he bent his hated face lower, indifferent of Patience, and his mouth, so like his brother's, hovered an instant on hers, the illusion was horrible and complete; and she shuddered and closed her eyes. He blew out the light, and they followed him down the stairs without a word.

He led the way into the kitchen, where the door was bolted and the window barred. Two candles were on the table to light the room. Reaching for a chair, he straddled his legs across it and considered the two women. "We've got to think out a plan of campaign," he said. "We've been sitting here for nigh on two days now, waiting to be caught."

His wife stole over to him and plucked at his jacket. "Why can't we creep away now, before it's too late?" she whispered. "The trap's in the stable; we'll be in Launceston and across to Devon in a few hours. We could travel by night; we could make for the eastern counties."

"You damned idiot!" he shouted. "Don't you realize the whole country knows by now what happened on the coast on Christmas Eve? And if they see us bolting, they'll have the proof. No, we've got one single chance in a million. If we sit here tight at Jamaica Inn, they may start scratching their heads and rubbing their noses. They've got to get the sworn proof before they lay hands on us. And unless one of that blasted rabble turns informer, they won't get the proof.

"Oh yes, the ship's there, with her back broken on the rocks, and there's chunks of stuff lying on the beach—ready to take away, they'll say. They'll find a body, charred to cinders, and a heap of ashes. 'What's this?' they'll say. 'There's been a fire; there's been a scrap.' It'll look bad for many of us, but where's your proof? I spent my Christmas Eve in the bosom of my family, playing cat's cradle with my niece." He put his tongue in his cheek and winked.

"You've forgotten one thing, haven't you?" said Mary.

"No, my dear, I have not. The driver of that carriage was shot, and he fell in the ditch a quarter of a mile down the road outside. You were hoping we'd left the body there, weren't you? But it traveled with us to the coast, and it lies now beneath a ten-foot bank of sand. Of course, someone is going to miss him, but they'll never find his carriage. Maybe he was tired of his wife and has driven to Penzance. And now you can tell me what you were doing in that carriage, Mary. If you don't, I can find a way of making you talk."

Mary thought rapidly. It was easy enough to lie; time was the all-important factor. She must play upon it and give her uncle rope enough to hang himself. His confidence would go against him in the end. She had one hope of salvation, and he was not five miles away, waiting in Altarnun for a signal from her.

"I'll tell you my day," she said. "I walked to Launceston on Christmas Eve and went to the fair. When it came to rain and blow, I hired that carriage and I told the man I wanted him to take me to Bodmin. I thought if I said the Jamaica Inn he would have refused the journey."

"And in Launceston you spoke to no one?"

"I bought a handkerchief from a woman at a stall."

Joss Merlyn spat on the floor. "All right," he said. "If your story's true, then our prospects improve. They'll never trace that driver here. Damn it, I shall feel like another drink in a moment." He tilted back his chair. "You shall drive in your own coach yet, Patience," he said, "and wear a velvet cloak. You wait; we'll start afresh again, we'll live like fighting cocks."

He threw back his head and laughed; but his laugh broke short, and he stood up in the middle of the room, his face as white as a sheet. "Listen," he whispered hoarsely.

They followed the direction of his eyes, fastened as they were upon the chink of light that came through the narrow gap in the shutters. Something was scratching softly and furtively at the kitchen window, tap . . . tap . . . like the drumming of a beak; tap . . . tap . . . like the four fingers of a hand.

The landlord stood motionless, his figure shadowed monstrously on the ceiling. He bent forward, crouching on tiptoe like a cat, and his fingers fastened themselves upon his gun that stood against the farther chair, never once taking his eyes from the chink of light between the shutters. Then he sprang forward, tearing the shutters apart, the gray light of afternoon slanting at once into the room. A man stood outside the window, his livid face pressed against the pane, his broken teeth gaping in a grin.

It was Harry the peddler. . . . Joss Merlyn swore and threw open the window. "Damn you," he shouted. "Do you want a bullet in your guts? You've had me standing for five minutes with my gun trained on your belly. Unbolt the door, Mary; don't lean against the wall there like a ghost." Like all men who have been badly scared, he now blustered to reassure himself. Mary crossed slowly to the door. The sight of the peddler brought back a vivid memory of her struggle in the lane, and she could not look upon him. She opened the door, screening herself behind it, and went to the dull fire, piling the turf upon the embers. "Well, have you brought news?" questioned the landlord.

The peddler jerked his thumb over his shoulder. "The country's gone up in smoke," he said. "Every cluttering tongue in Cornwall, from the Tamar to St. Ives. I was in Bodmin this forenoon; the town was ringing with it, and they're hot mad for blood. Last night I slept at Camelford, every man jack in the place shaking his fist in the air. There'll only be one end to this storm, Joss." He made a gesture with his hands across his throat.

"We've got to run for it," he said. "It's our only chance. But it's like this, Joss; I don't see the fun in quitting empty-handed. There's a mint of stuff we dumped along in the room yonder two days ago, from the shore. And there's none of 'em left to claim it but you and I. I don't see why some of it shouldn't help us into Devon, do you?"

The landlord stared down into his face. "So you didn't come back to Jamaica Inn because of my sweet smile alone, then?" he said. "I was thinking you were fond of me, Harry, and wanted to hold my hand. And supposing I've disposed of the stuff already? I've been here kicking my heels for two days, you know, and the coaches pass my door. What then, Harry boy?"

The grin faded from the face of the peddler. "What's the joke?" he snarled. "It was your damned stupidity brought us into this mess, wasn't it? You got us mad drunk like yourself and led us to the shore, on a crazy venture that none of us had planned. We took a chance in a million, and the chance came off—too damned bloody well. Do you play a double game up here at Jamaica Inn? I've seen things I haven't understood, and heard things too. You've made a brilliant job of this trade; too brilliant, some of us thought, for the small profit we made out of it who took most of the risks. And we didn't ask you how you did it, did we? Listen here, Joss Merlyn, do you take your orders from one above you?"

The landlord was on him like a flash. He caught the peddler on the point of the chin with his clenched fist, and the man went over backward onto his head, striking the flagstones with a crash. He scrambled to his knees, but the landlord towered above him, the muzzle of his gun pointed at the peddler's throat.

"Move, and you're a dead man," he said softly. "You didn't come here tonight to warn me; you came to see what you could get out of the smash. The inn was barred, and your little mean heart rejoiced. You scraped at the window there, because you knew from experience that the hasp of the shutter is loose and easy to force. You didn't think to find me here, did you? Do you think I didn't see it in your eye when I flung back the shutter? Do you think I never heard your gasp of surprise, nor watched your sudden yellow grin?"

The peddler passed his tongue over his lips and swallowed. He threw a glance toward Mary, motionless by the fire, the round button of his eye watchful, like a cornered rat's.

"Very well," her uncle said. "We'll strike a bargain, you and I, as you suggested. I've changed my mind, and with your help we'll take the road to Devon. There's stuff in this place worth taking, as you reminded me, nor can I load alone. Tomorrow is Sunday, and not even the wrecking of fifty ships will drag the people of this country from their knees. There'll be blinds down, and sermons, and long faces, and prayers offered for poor sailormen who come by misadventure by the devil's hand; but they'll not go seeking the devil on the Sabbath.

"Twenty-four hours we have, Harry, my boy, and tomorrow night, when you've broken your back spading turf and turnips over my property in the farm cart, and kissed me good-by, and Patience too, and maybe Mary there as well—why, then you can go down on your knees and thank Joss Merlyn for letting you go free, instead of squatting on your scut in a ditch with a bullet in your black heart."

The landlord shifted his gun, and bending down, he jerked the peddler to his feet. "Come on," he said. "Open the kitchen door and walk down the passage until I tell you to stop. Your hands have been itching to explore the wreckage we brought from the shore, haven't they, Harry?

You shall spend the night in the storeroom amongst it all. Do you know, Patience, my dear, I believe this is the first time we've offered hospitality at Jamaica Inn." He laughed, his mood switched around now like a weathercock; and butting his gun into the peddler's back, he prodded him out of the kitchen and down the dark flagstone passage to the storeroom. The door that had been battered in by Squire Bassat and his servant had been reinforced with new planking and was now stronger than before.

After Joss Merlyn had turned the key on his friend, with a parting injunction not to feed the rats, the landlord returned to the kitchen, a rumble of laughter in his chest.

"I thought Harry would turn sour," he said. "He's jealous of me. They're all jealous of me. They knew I had brains and hated me for it. What are you staring at me for, Mary? You'd better get your supper and go to bed. You have a long journey before you tomorrow night."

Mary looked at him across the table, her mind seething with plans. Sometime, somehow, before tomorrow night, she must go to Altarnun. Once there, her responsibility was over; she knew nothing of the complexities of the law; but at least justice would win. It would be easy enough to clear her own name and her aunt's. The thought of her uncle powerless forever was something that afforded her exquisite pleasure. Aunt Patience would recover in time; the years would drain away from her, bringing her peace at last. Mary wondered how the capture would be effected. Perhaps they would set out upon the journey, and as they turned out upon the road, he laughing in his assurance, they would be surrounded by a band of men, and as he struggled against them, borne to the ground by force, she would lean down to him and smile. "I thought you had brains, Uncle," she would say to him, and he would know.

She dragged her eyes away from him and turned to the dresser for her candle. "I'll have no supper tonight," she said.

Aunt Patience made a little murmur of distress, but Joss Merlyn kicked at her for silence. "Let her stay sulky if she has the mind. Wait, Mary, you shall sleep sounder still if I turn the key on you. I want no prowlers in the passage."

His eyes strayed to the gun against the wall and half-consciously back to the shutter, which still gaped open before the kitchen window. "Fasten that window, Patience," he said thoughtfully, "and put the bar across the shutter. When you have finished your supper, you too can go to bed. I shall not leave the kitchen tonight."

Mary went out into the dark passage, strangely thankful that her uncle had decided to make a prisoner of her as well. The house was treacherous tonight, her very footsteps sounding hollow on the flags, and there were echoes that came unbidden from the walls. Even the kitchen, the one room in the house to possess some measure of warmth and normality, gaped back at her as she left it, sinister in the candlelight. Was her uncle going to sit there, then, the candles extinguished, his gun across his knee, waiting for something . . . for someone?

He crossed into the hall as she mounted the stairs, and he followed her along the landing to the bedroom over the porch. "Give me your key," he said. He lingered for a moment, looking down at her, and then he bent low and laid his fingers on her mouth.

"I've a soft spot for you, Mary," he said. "You've got spirit still, for all the knocks I've given you. If I'd been a younger man I'd have courted you, Mary—aye, and won you too, and ridden away with you to glory. You know that, don't you?"

She stared back at him, and her hand that held the candlestick trembled slightly without her knowledge.

He lowered his voice to a whisper. "There's danger for me ahead," he said. "Never mind the law; I can bluff my way to freedom if it comes to that. It's other game I have to watch for—footsteps, Mary, that come in the night and go again, and a hand that would strike me down."

His face looked lean and old in the half-light, and there was a flicker of meaning in his eyes that leaped like a flame to tell her, and then dulled again. "We'll put the Tamar between us and Jamaica Inn," he said; and then he smiled, the curve of his mouth painfully familiar to her, like an echo from the past. He shut the door upon her and turned the key.

She went then to her bed and sat down upon it, and for some reason forever unexplained—thrust away from her later, and forgotten, side by side with the little sins of childhood and those dreams never acknowledged to the sturdy day—she put her fingers to her lips, as he had done, and let them stray thence to her cheek and back again.

And she began to cry, softly and secretly, the tears tasting bitter as they fell upon her hand.

CHAPTER NINE

SHE HAD FALLEN asleep where she lay, without undressing, and her first conscious thought was that the storm had come again, bringing with it the rain which streamed against her window. She opened her eyes and saw that the night was still. Her senses were alert at once, and she waited for a repetition of the sound that had awakened her. It came again—a shower of earth flung against the pane of glass. She swung her legs to the floor and listened.

If this was a warning signal, someone with little idea of the geography of the inn might have mistaken her window for the landlord's. Perhaps the visitor her uncle waited for below with his gun across his knee had come. . . . She crept softly to the window. The figure of a man stood directly beneath the porch. He bent again to the ground, fumbling in the barren flower bed outside the parlor, then he raised his hand and threw a little clod of earth at her window.

This time she saw his face, and the wonder of it made her cry out in surprise. It was Jem Merlyn standing below her in the yard. She opened her window and would have called to him, but he lifted his hand for silence. He cupped his hands to his mouth and whispered, "Come down and unbolt the door."

She shook her head. "I am locked here in my room," she told him. He ran his hands along the slates; the low tiles of the porch were within his reach, but they had no gripping surface.

"Fetch me the blanket from your bed," he called softly. She guessed at once his meaning and tied one end of her blanket to the foot of her bed, throwing the other out of the window. Swinging himself to the low roof of the jutting porch, he hauled himself up on a level with her window. Mary struggled with the framework of the window, but her efforts were useless. It opened only a foot or so. She knelt, her face at the window gap, and they stared at one another. His eyes were hollow, and there were lines about his mouth she had not noticed before.

"I owe you an apology," he said at length. "I deserted you at Launceston on Christmas Eve. You can forgive me or not, but the reason for it I can't give you. I'm sorry."

She was hurt by his cool manner. When she saw him first in the yard, she thought of him only as the man she loved, but he did not even ask how she had returned that night, and his indifference stunned her.

"Why are you locked in your room?" he questioned.

She shrugged her shoulders, and her voice was flat and dull when she replied. "My uncle fears I should wander in the passage and stumble upon his secrets. You appear to have the same dislike of intrusion."

"Oh, be a man for the moment," he flashed suddenly, "and send your hurt pride to hell. I'm treading delicate ground, Mary, and one false step will finish me. Where is my brother?"

"He told us he would spend the night in the kitchen. He is afraid of someone; the windows and doors are barred, and he has his gun."

Jem laughed harshly. "He'll be more frightened before many hours are passed. I came here to see him, but if he sits there with a gun, I can postpone my visit until tomorrow, when the shadows are gone."

"He intends to leave Jamaica Inn at nightfall."

Jem was silent. The news had evidently come as a surprise to him. Mary watched him, tortured by doubt; she was thrown back now upon her old suspicion of him. He was the visitor expected by her uncle, and therefore hated by him and feared. The sneering face of the peddler returned to her, and his words: "Listen here, Joss Merlyn, do you take your orders from one above you?" The man whose wits made service of the landlord's strength, the man who had hidden in the empty room.

She thought again of the laughing, carefree Jem who had kissed her and held her. Now he was like a stranger obsessed by some grim purpose she could not understand. The idea of dual personality frightened her. Whatever Jem had done, whether he was false and treacherous and a murderer of men, she loved him.

Suddenly, leaning forward, he looked into her face and touched the scratch that ran from her forehead to her chin. "Who did this?" he said sharply, turning from the scratch to the bruise on her cheek.

She hesitated a moment, then answered, "I got them Christmas Eve."

The gleam in his eye told her at once that he understood and had knowledge of the evening, and because of it was here now at Jamaica Inn.

"You were there with them, on the shore?" he whispered.

She nodded, wary of speech, and he cursed aloud and smashed the pane of glass with his fist, careless of the splitting sound and the blood that spouted from his hand. He had climbed into the room and was beside her before she realized what he had done. He lifted her in his arms and laid her down upon the bed, and fumbling in the darkness for a candle, lit it, throwing the light upon her face. He traced the bruises with his finger down her neck, and again she heard him swear.

"God Almighty, why did you go with them?" he said.

"They were crazy with drink. I could no more have stood against them than a child. My uncle . . . he led them."

"How much have they hurt you?"

"Bruises, scratches—they bound my hands and feet down on the shore, and tied sacking over my mouth so that I could not scream. I saw the ship come through the mist, and I could do nothing—I had to watch them die." She broke off, her voice trembling.

He took her hand. "My brother shall die for this," he said.

"Don't waste your sympathy. I can revenge myself in my own way."

"Mary, you are best out of this business now. The issue lies with me."

She did not answer him, she would not hazard her plans into his keeping. He was still an unknown quantity, and above all else an enemy to justice. It came to her then that by betraying her uncle she might also betray him. "If I ask you to do something, how would you answer me?" she said.

He smiled then for the first time, mocking and indulgent, as he had done in Launceston, and her heart leaped to him at once, encouraged at the change.

"How can I tell?" he said.

"I want you to go away from the moors, away from Jamaica Inn. I can stand up against your brother. I don't want you to come here tomorrow; trust me."

"Trust you? It's you who won't trust me, you damned little fool." He laughed silently and kissed her, as he had kissed her in Launceston, but deliberately now, with anger and exasperation. "Play your own game by yourself, then, and leave me to play mine," he told her. "If you must be a boy, I can't stop you, but for the sake of your face, which I have kissed, and shall kiss again, keep away from danger. When it comes to life and death, like my business now, God knows I wish you sitting primly, your sewing in your lap, in a trim parlor somewhere."

"That's never been my life, nor ever will."

"Why not? You'll wed a farmer one day, or a small tradesman, and live respectably among your neighbors. Don't tell them you lived once at Jamaica Inn and had love made to you by a horse thief. They'd shut their doors against you."

He went toward the window, climbed through the gap he had broken in the pane, and swinging his legs over the porch, fell lightly to the ground.

She watched him from the window, then pulled up the blanket and replaced it on the bed. Morning would soon be here; she would not sleep again. She sat on her bed, waiting until her door should be unlocked, and made her plans for the evening to come. She must act as though feeling had at last been stifled in her, and she was prepared to undertake the proposed journey with the landlord and Aunt Patience. Later she would make some excuse—a desire to rest in her room before the strain of the night journey—and then she would leave Jamaica Inn secretly and run like a hare to Altarnun. This time Francis Davey would understand, and he must act accordingly. She would then return to the inn and trust that her absence had remained unnoticed. This was the gamble. If the landlord went to her room and found her gone, her life would be worth nothing. But if he believed her to be sleeping still, then the game would continue. They would make preparations for the journey; they might even climb into the cart and come out upon the road; after that their fate would be in the hands of the vicar of Altarnun.

So Mary waited for the day; and when it came, the long hours stretched interminably, the atmosphere of strain apparent among them all. Aunt Patience pottered aimlessly, making bundles of what poor clothes remained to her. She wrapped a single candlestick in a shawl and put it side by side with a cracked teapot and a faded muslin cap, only to unwrap them again and discard them for treasures more ancient.

Joss Merlyn would watch her moodily, cursing her in irritation. The very fact that his visitor had not come upon him made him if possible more restless than before. He roamed about the house, peering from the windows. No sound came from the peddler in the barred room, nor did the landlord go to him or mention him by name, and this silence was sinister in itself. Had the peddler shouted obscenities or thundered on the door, it would have been more in keeping.

At the midday meal the landlord sat wrapped in gloom. This was a mood Mary had experienced before and knew led to danger. At length she took courage. "If we are to travel tonight," she said, "would it not be better if Aunt Patience and myself rested now during the afternoon? Aunt Patience has been upon her feet since daybreak, and I too." To control her anxiety she pretended to fumble in the cupboard.

"You may rest if you will," he said. "I shall be well rid of you for the time."

Her aunt, who acted always like a dummy to suggestion, followed Mary meekly upstairs and padded along the farther passage to her own room.

Mary entered her little room and turned the key. She could walk the distance to Altarnun in an hour. If she left Jamaica Inn at four o'clock, when the light was failing, she would be back again soon after six; and the landlord would hardly come to rouse her before seven. She would climb out onto the porch and fall to the ground, as Jem had done this morning; the drop was an easy one. She put on her warmest dress, and fastening her old shawl across her shoulders with trembling, hot hands, sat by the window, looking out upon the highroad where no one ever passed, waiting for the clock in the hall below to strike four. When it sounded at last, the strokes rang in the silence like an alarm, and unlocking the door, she listened, hearing footsteps echo the strokes, and whispers in the air.

It was imagination, of course; nothing moved. The clock ticked on into the next hour. She locked the door again and went to the window. She crawled through the gap, and in a moment she was astride the porch, looking down upon the ground. The distance seemed greater, now that she crouched above it, but she shut her eyes and launched herself into the air. Her feet found the ground almost immediately—the jump was nothing. She looked up at Jamaica Inn, sinister and gray in the approaching dusk, the windows barred, and turned away from it as one turns instinctively from a house of the dead, and went out upon the road. Dusk came as she walked. Away to the left the high tors, shrouded at first in mist, were gathered to the darkness. Later there would be a moon. She wondered if her uncle had reckoned with this force of nature that would shine upon his plans.

She came at length to Five Lanes, where the roads branched, and she turned to her left, down the steep hill of Altarnun. Excitement rose high within her now as she saw the twinkling cottage lights. She passed them by and went to the vicarage beside the church. There were no lights here, and the trees closed in upon it. She hammered upon the door, and she heard the blows echo through the empty house. She looked through the windows, and her eyes met nothing but darkness.

Cursing her stupidity, she turned back again toward the church. Francis Davey would be there, of course. It was Sunday. She hesitated a moment, uncertain of her movements, and then the gate opened and a woman came out into the road, carrying flowers.

"Forgive me," Mary said. "I see you have come from the church. Can you tell me if Mr. Davey himself is there?"

The woman looked at her curiously and shook her head. "I am sorry," she said. "The vicar went away today to preach at another parish, many miles from here. He is not expected back in Altarnun tonight."

MARY WAS THINKING desperately. To come to Altarnun and then return again without help to Jamaica Inn was impossible. She must find someone in authority—someone who knew something of Joss Merlyn and Jamaica Inn. "Who is the nearest magistrate?" she asked the woman.

"Why, the nearest would be Squire Bassat over to North Hill, and that must be over four miles from here—maybe more. It's scarcely a walk for a maid like you after nightfall; you'd best stay here and wait for the vicar."

"That is impossible," said Mary. "But wait, though; if you have pen and paper, I will write him a note of explanation."

"Come into my cottage here, and you may write. I can take the note to his house and leave it where he will see it as soon as he comes home."

Mary followed the woman to the cottage, and the woman found paper and quill. Mary wrote desperately, never pausing to choose her words.

I came here to ask your help, and you were gone. By now you will have heard with horror of the wreck upon the coast on Christmas Eve. It was my uncle's doing, he and the company from Jamaica Inn. He knows that suspicion will fall on him, and because of this he plans to leave the inn tonight and cross the Tamar into Devon. Finding you absent, I go now to Mr. Bassat at North Hill, to warn him of the escape, so that he can seize my uncle before it is too late. In haste, then,

Mary Yellan

She had placed such faith in Francis Davey that it was disheartening to leave the lights of Altarnun behind her. She climbed the hill with a heavy heart and a wretched sense of isolation. At this moment, perhaps, her uncle was thundering upon her bedroom door. He would find her gone, and a smashed window. Whether this would play havoc with his plans, she could not know. Aunt Patience was her concern, and the thought of her setting out upon the journey like a shivering dog tethered to its master made Mary run along the bare white road to North Hill with fists clenched and chin thrust in the air.

She came at last to the turnpike and turned down a narrow twisting lane as the woman in Altarnun had told her. The contour of the land had changed, and hills rose away from her, forested and dark. The moorland was no more. The moon came now, topping the farther trees, leading her downward to the valley. Finally she reached lodge gates and the entrance to a drive, while beyond her the lane continued to a village.

That must be North Hill, and this the manor house belonging to the squire. She went down the avenue to the house, large and forbidding in the darkness. She swung the great bell, and the sound was met by the furious baying of hounds. The door was opened by a manservant, who called sharply at the dogs. Mary was conscious of her old dress and shawl. "I have come to see Mr. Bassat on very urgent business," she said. "He would not know my name, but the matter is of desperate importance."

"Mr. Bassat left for Launceston this morning," answered the man.

A cry of despair escaped Mary. "I have come some way," she said, in an agony of feeling, as though by her very distress she could bring the squire to her side. "If I do not see him within the hour a great criminal will escape the law. If only there were someone I could turn to . . ."

"Mrs. Bassat is at home," said the man, stung with curiosity. "Perhaps she will see you. Follow me, will you, to the library."

The wide library, with its blazing fire, seemed unreal to Mary. A woman whom she recognized immediately as the fine lady from Launceston market square was sitting in a chair before the fire, reading to two children. She looked up as the servant began his explanation in some excitement. "This young woman has very grave news for the squire, madam," he said. "I thought it best to show her in to you directly."

Mrs. Bassat rose to her feet and spoke quickly to her children, who ran from the room, followed by the manservant. "What can I do for you?" she said graciously. "You look pale and fatigued. Won't you sit down?"

Mary shook her head impatiently. "Thank you, but I must know when Mr. Bassat is returning home."

"I have no idea," replied his lady. "The squire has set out upon a highly dangerous mission. Your face is new to me, and I conclude you are not from North Hill, otherwise you would have heard of this man Merlyn who keeps an inn upon the Bodmin road. The squire has suspected him for some while of terrible crimes, but it was not until this morning that the full proof came into his hands. He departed at once for Launceston to summon help, and intends to surround the inn tonight with a large body of men and seize the inhabitants."

Something in Mary's face must have warned her, for she turned very pale and reached out for the heavy bellpull that hung on the wall. "You are the girl he spoke about," she said quickly, "the niece of the landlord. Don't move, or I will summon my servants. What do you want with me? If you have come to North Hill to plead for your uncle, it is too late."

"You misunderstand me," said Mary. "And the landlord of Jamaica Inn is a relative to me by marriage only. I fear and detest him more than anyone in the country, and with reason. I came here to warn Mr. Bassat that the landlord intended to leave the inn tonight, and so escape justice. I have definite proof of his guilt, which I did not believe Mr. Bassat to possess; but I have done a very senseless thing. I have only succeeded in making a fool of myself and of everyone else. My uncle will discover my room is empty and guess at once that I have betrayed him. He will leave Jamaica Inn before Mr. Bassat arrives. How did the squire learn the truth so suddenly?"

"I have not the slightest idea; he was sent for this morning, and he gave me only the barest details before he was gone. You have been placed in a fearful position, and I think you very brave to come here tonight. Now, won't you rest yourself? You are probably famished." She pulled the bell rope.

The servant appeared, his inquisitive nose in the air, and was told by his mistress to bring a tray of supper for Mary. She ate mechanically, forcing herself to swallow the food, then sat staring at the fire while Mrs. Bassat tried to distract her. But when the clock on the mantel chimed eight, she could bear it no longer. "Forgive me," she said, rising to her feet, "but I am desperately anxious. I can think of nothing but my poor aunt. I must know what is happening at Jamaica Inn, if I walk back there myself tonight."

Mrs. Bassat was in a flutter of distress. "Of course you are anxious. How terrible it is! I am as concerned as you are, for my husband's sake. I will order the trap. Richards shall go with you, armed in case of need." Mrs. Bassat had already pulled the bell. "Have word sent to Richards to bring the trap round immediately," she said to the astonished servant. She then fitted Mary out with a heavy cloak and hood, thick rug, and foot warmer. In a quarter of an hour the trap drove up to the door, with Richards in charge—the servant who had ridden with Mr. Bassat to Jamaica Inn—two large pistols stuck in his belt.

The drive was silent, with no other sound but the steady clopping of the horse's hoofs. The trap came out upon the Bodmin road, and once again the moor stretched out on either side. The dark tors held their sleeping faces to the sky, softened and smoothed by the moonlight that bathed them. The old gods slept undisturbed.

Briskly the horse and trap covered the weary miles that Mary had walked alone, and the wild stretch to Jamaica lay before them. Though Mary strained her ears, she could hear nothing. On such a night the slightest sound would be magnified, and the approach of Mr. Bassat's party, said Richards, would easily be heard two miles or more away. "We shall find them there before us, as likely as not," he told Mary. "It's a pity we were not here sooner; there'll have been some sport in taking the landlord."

"Little sport if Mr. Bassat finds that his bird has flown," said Mary quietly. "Joss Merlyn knows these moors like the back of his hand."

"My master was bred here, same as the landlord," said Richards. "If it comes to a chase across country, I'd lay odds on the squire every time. He's hunted here, man and boy, for nearly fifty years." The steep hill to Jamaica rose in front of them, and as the dark chimneys appeared above the crest, Mary's heart beat fast and she held tight to the side of the trap. The horse bent to the climb, his head low, and it seemed to Mary that the clop of his hoofs rang too loudly on the surface of the road; she wished they had been more silent.

As they drew near to the summit of the hill, Richards turned and whispered in her ear, "It's strange, this silence. I'd expected shouting and fighting, and my master's voice topping it all. They must have been detained in Launceston. I fancy there'd be more wisdom if we turned aside down that track and waited for them to come."

"I've waited long enough tonight, and gone half mad with it," said Mary. "I'd rather come upon my uncle face to face than lie here in the ditch, seeing and hearing nothing. It's my aunt I'm thinking of. She's as innocent as a child in all this business. Give me a pistol and let me go." She threw off the heavy cloak and hood that had protected her from the night air, and seized hold of the pistol that he handed down to her reluctantly. "Should you hear a shot fired," she said, "it would be as well to come after me. For my part, I believe my uncle to have gone."

The yard was empty. The stable door was shut. The inn was as dark and silent as when she had left it nearly seven hours before, the windows and the door barred. She looked up to her window, and the pane of glass gaped unchanged since she had climbed from it that afternoon. There were no wheel marks in the yard, no preparations for departure. She crept across to the stable and laid her ear against the door, and then she heard the pony move restlessly in his stall.

So they had not gone, and her uncle was still at Jamaica Inn. Mary hesitated; the situation had become odd now, and unreal. She ventured a little way around the corner of the house, past the entrance to the bar, and so to the patch of garden behind the kitchen, and came to where a chink of candlelight would show through the gap in the kitchen shutter. There was no light. She laid her eye against the slit. The kitchen was black as a pit. She slowly turned the knob of the door. It gave, to her astonishment, and the door opened. This easy entrance, unforeseen, shocked her, and she was afraid to enter.

Supposing her uncle sat on his chair, waiting for her, his gun across his knee?

Very slowly she put her face to the gap made by the door. No sound came to her. Out of the tail of her eye she could see the ashes of the fire. Some instinct told her that the kitchen had been empty for hours. She pushed the door wide and went inside. There was a candle on the table, and she thrust it into the feeble glow of the fire. When it burned strong enough, she held it high above her head. The kitchen was still strewn with the preparations for departure. In the corner of the room was her uncle's gun. They had decided, then, to wait for another day, and were now asleep in the room upstairs.

The door to the passage was open, and the silence became more oppressive than before, strangely and horribly still. Something was not as it had been; some sound was lacking that must account for the silence. Then Mary realized that she could not hear the clock. The ticking had stopped. She went forward slowly, carrying the candle, and turned the corner where the long dark passage branched into the hall; and she saw that the clock, which had always stood beside the parlor door, had fallen across the narrow hall. Its glass was splintered and the wood split. Not until she came to the foot of the stairs did Mary see what was beyond.

The landlord of Jamaica Inn lay on his face among the wreckage, one arm flung across the fallen clock, his legs stretched out, his great frame blocking the entrance from wall to wall. There was blood on the stone floor and blood between his shoulders, dark now and nearly dry, where the knife had found him.

When he was stabbed from behind he must have stretched out his hands, reaching for the clock, and when he fell upon his face the clock crashed with him to the ground, and he died there.

IT WAS A LONG while before Mary moved away from the stairs. It was the silence that frightened her most. The light of her candle did not reach to the top of the stairs, where the darkness gaped at her like a gulf. She knew she could never climb those stairs again, nor tread that empty landing. Whatever lay above must rest there undisturbed. Death had come upon the house tonight, and its brooding spirit still hovered in the air.

Mary dreaded panic, above all things; she was afraid that it might come to her, destroying reason. Her fingers might lose their sense of grip and the candle fall from her hands. Then she would be alone and covered by the darkness. She backed away toward the passage. When she came to the kitchen and saw the door still open to the patch of garden, her calm deserted her and she ran blindly like a thing pursued across the yard and to the open road, where the familiar stalwart figure of the squire's groom confronted her. He put out his hands to save her, and she groped at his belt, feeling for security, her teeth chattering now in the full shock of reaction. He led her back to the trap and put the cloak around her.

"He's dead," she said. "Stabbed in the back. The blood was dry, and he looked as though he had lain there for some time."

"Was your aunt gone?" whispered the man.

Mary shook her head. "I don't know. I had to come away."

He helped her up into the trap and climbed onto the seat beside her. They fell silent, watching the road for the coming of the squire. Then at last Mary spoke, her voice husky. "Something has happened to my aunt as well; I know that. She is lying there in the darkness, on the landing above. Whoever killed my uncle will have killed her too."

"Who'd have killed the landlord?" said Richards, puzzled. "There was plenty who might have had a hand in it, though, for all that."

"There was the peddler," said Mary slowly. "I'd forgotten the peddler. It must have been him, breaking out from the barred room." She fastened upon the idea, to escape from another, and retold the story of how the peddler had come to the inn the night before.

"He'll not run far before the squire catches him," said the groom.

Mary held up a warning hand. "Listen," she said sharply. "Can you hear something?"

They strained their ears to the north. The faint clop of horses came from beyond the valley, and when a minute had passed, the first horseman appeared like a black smudge against the hard white road, followed by another, and another, traveling at a gallop. Richards in his relief ran out upon the road to greet them, waving his arms.

The leader drew rein, holding up his hand to warn his followers. "What the devil do you do here?" he shouted, for it was the squire himself.

"The landlord is dead, murdered," cried the groom. "I have his niece here with me in the trap. It was Mrs. Bassat herself who sent me out here, sir. This young woman had best tell you the story in her own words."

He held the horse while his master dismounted, and the little band of men gathered around him too.

"If the fellow has been murdered, as you say, then it serves him right," said Mr. Bassat. "Go into the yard, the rest of you, while I see if I can get some sense out of the girl."

The squire heard with astonishment how Mary had walked the long miles to North Hill in the hopes of finding him. "This is altogether beyond me," he said gruffly. "I believed you to be in conspiracy with your uncle. Why did you lie to me, then, when I came here earlier in the month?"

"I lied because of my aunt," said Mary wearily. "If I tried to explain everything now, you would not understand."

"Nor have I the time to listen," replied the squire. He raised his voice and shouted for the servant. "Take the trap up to the yard and stay

beside it with the young woman while we break into the inn." And, turning to Mary, he said, "I must ask you to wait in the yard, if your courage permits you; you were the last to see your uncle alive." Mary nodded her head. She was nothing more now than a passive instrument of the law.

The squire led the way around to the back, at Mary's direction, and presently the bleak and silent house lost its shuttered air. The windows in the bar and parlor were flung open, and some of the men went upstairs and explored the empty guest rooms above, for these windows were also opened to the air. Only the heavy entrance door remained shut; and Mary knew that the landlord's body lay stretched across the threshold.

Someone called sharply from the house and was answered by a murmur of voices and a question from the squire. Richards glanced across at Mary, and he saw by the pallor of her face that she had heard. She drew her cloak farther around her shoulders and pulled the hood across her face. Presently the squire himself came out into the yard and crossed to the trap. "I'm sorry," he said. "I have bad news for you."

"Yes," said Mary.

"She must have died at once. She was lying just inside the bedroom at the end of the passage. Stabbed, like your uncle. She could have known nothing. Believe me, I wish I could have spared you this." He stood by her, awkward and distressed, then stamped back across the yard to the inn.

Mary sat shrouded in her cloak; and she prayed in her own way that Aunt Patience would find peace now, that the dragging chains of life would fall away from her. She prayed also that Aunt Patience would understand what she had tried to do; these were the only thoughts that brought her a measure of consolation.

Once again, though, there came a murmur of excitement from the house, and this time there was shouting, the sound of running feet, and a crash of splintering wood as the barricade was torn away from the window of the barred room, which no one, apparently, had entered up to now. Someone held a flare to light the room; then around the corner to the yard came six or seven of them, led by the squire, holding among them something that squirmed and fought for release, with hoarse bewildered cries. "They've got him! It's the murderer!" shouted Richards to Mary; and she turned, brushing aside the hood that covered her face, and looked down upon the group of men who came to the trap. The captive stared up at her, blinking at the light they flashed in his eyes, his clothes cobweb-covered, his face unshaven and black; it was Harry the peddler.

"What do you know of this fellow?" the squire said to Mary. "We found him in the barred room yonder and he denies all knowledge of the crime."

"He was of the company," said Mary slowly, "and he came to the inn last night and quarreled with my uncle. My uncle locked him up, threatening him with death. He had every reason to kill my uncle."

"But the door was locked upon him; it took three of us to break it down from the outside," said the squire. "This fellow had never been from the room at all. He's not your murderer."

The peddler's mean eyes darted to right and left, and Mary knew at once that what the squire had said was the truth; Harry the peddler had lain in the dark, barred room since the landlord put him there, over twenty-four hours ago. During the long hours someone had come to Jamaica Inn and gone again, his work completed in the silence of the night.

"Whoever did it knew nothing of this rascal, locked in the room yonder," continued the squire, "and he heard and saw nothing. But he shall turn king's evidence and give us the names of his companions. One of them has killed the landlord for revenge, and we'll track him down if we set every hound in Cornwall on his heels. Take this fellow to the stable, some of you, and hold him there; the rest come back to the inn with me."

As they dragged the peddler away, he turned his rat's eyes to Mary, muttering blasphemies beneath his breath. She neither heard his blasphemies nor saw his furtive eyes, for she remembered other eyes that had looked upon her in the morning, and another voice, calm and cold, saying of his brother, "He shall die for this." He had gone to Jamaica Inn, and his brother had died, as he had sworn. The whole truth stared up at her in ugliness and horror, and she wished that she had stayed, and he had killed her too. He slept now, perhaps, forgetful of his crime and caring not at all, stretched on his bed in the lonely cottage where he and his brother had been born. When morning came he would be gone, whistling, throwing his legs across a horse, and so away out of Cornwall forever, a murderer like his father before him.

In her fancy she heard the clop of his horse upon the road, beating a tempo of farewell; but fancy became reason, and reason became certainty, and the sound of the horse was not a dream thing but a live tapping on the highway, and it drew nearer still. He was trotting at a steady, even pace, and she was not alone now as she listened. The men who guarded the peddler murmured to one another in low tones and looked toward the road, and Richards went swiftly to the inn to call the squire. The beat of the horse's hoofs rang a challenge to the night, and as it rounded the wall into view, the squire came out of the inn.

"Stop!" he called. "In the name of the king. I must ask your business on the road tonight."

The horseman drew rein and turned into the yard. When he bared his head, the halo of hair shone white under the moon, and the voice that answered was gentle and sweet. "Mr. Bassat of North Hill, I believe," he said. "I have a message here from Mary Yellan of Jamaica Inn, who asks my help; but I see by the company assembled that I have come too late. We have met before. I am the vicar of Altarnun."

CHAPTER TEN

MARY SAT ALONE in the living room at the vicarage and watched the smoldering turf fire. She had slept long and was now rested, but the peace which she craved had not yet come to her.

They had been kind to her and patient; Mr. Bassat himself patted her on the shoulder as he would a hurt child and said to her in his gruff way, "Now I promise you that we shall find the man who killed your aunt very soon, and he shall hang at the next assizes. And when you are a little recovered from the shock of these last few months, you shall say what you would like to do, and where you would like to go."

When Francis Davey offered his home for shelter, she accepted, conscious that her listless word of thanks savored of ingratitude. Once more she knew the humility of being born a woman, when the breaking down of strength and spirit was taken as natural.

The vicar had roused his housekeeper from the cottage nearby and bade her come with him to the vicarage to prepare a room for his guest. She warmed a rough woolen nightdress, and Mary allowed herself to be led to the bed as a child is led to a cradle.

She would have closed her eyes but for an arm suddenly around her shoulders and a voice in her ear, "Drink this," persuasive and cool, and Francis Davey himself stood beside the bed, with a glass in his hand and his strange eyes looking into hers, pale and expressionless. She knew from the bitter taste that he had put some powder in the hot drink and that he had done this in understanding of her restless, tortured mind.

It was nearly four in the afternoon before she awoke, and the sharp grief for Aunt Patience had softened, and reason told her that she could not put the blame upon herself. There remained regret, and regret could not bring Aunt Patience back again. But when she was dressed and had gone below to the living room, to find the fire burning and the curtains drawn and the vicar abroad upon some business, the old nagging sense of insecurity returned to her, and it seemed to her that responsibility for the disaster lay on her shoulders alone. Jem's face was present with her as she had seen it last, haggard in the false gray light, and there had been a purpose in his eyes, and in the set of his mouth, that she had willfully ignored. One word to the vicar when he returned, and a message to the squire, and Aunt Patience would be avenged. Jem would die with a rope around his neck as his father had done; and she would return to Helford, seeking the threads of her old life.

She got up from the chair beside the fire and began to walk the length of the room, but even as she did so she knew that the word would never be given. Jem would ride away with a laugh at her expense, while she dragged through the years, the stain of silence marking her, coming in the end to ridicule as a soured spinster who had been kissed once in her life and could not forget it.

As Mary prowled about the room, her mind as restless as her body, she felt as though Francis Davey himself were watching her, his cold eyes probing her soul. She could imagine him standing in the corner by the easel, his brush in his hand. There were canvases with their faces to the wall close to the easel, and Mary turned them to the light in curiosity. Here was an interior of his church painted in the twilight of midsummer. There was a strange green afterglow upon the arches that cast a haunting and uncanny light upon the picture, and Mary knew that had she a home she would not care for it to hang upon her walls.

She could not have put her feeling of discomfort into words, but it was as though some spirit, having no knowledge of the church itself, had groped its way into the interior and breathed an alien atmosphere upon the shadowed nave. As she turned the paintings, one by one, she saw that they were all tainted in the same manner. She wondered, for the first time, whether by being born albino his sight was neither normal nor true. This might be the explanation, but, even so, her feeling of discomfort remained as she continued her inspection of the room. His desk was bare of correspondence. She drummed with her fingers on the polished surface, and suddenly and unpardonably she opened the narrow drawer beneath the desk. It was empty. She was about to shut it when she noticed that the paper with which the drawer was laid had one corner turned, and there was some sketch drawn upon the other side. She took hold of the paper.

This was a caricature, grotesque as it was horrible. The people of the congregation were in their best clothes as for Sunday, but he had drawn sheep's heads upon their shoulders. The animal jaws gaped at the preacher with silly vacant solemnity, and their hoofs were folded in prayer. The features of each sheep had been touched upon with care, as though representing a living soul, but the expression on every one of them was that of an idiot who neither knew nor cared. The preacher, with his black gown and halo of hair, was Francis Davey; but he had given himself a wolf's face, and the wolf was laughing at the flock beneath him.

The thing was a mockery, blasphemous and terrible. Mary quickly replaced the paper in the drawer, with the white sheet uppermost, and went and sat once more in the chair beside the fire. She had stumbled upon a secret, and she would rather that the secret stayed concealed.

When she heard the vicar's footstep on the path outside, she rose hurriedly and moved the light away from her chair, so that when he came into the room he could not read her face.

Her chair had its back to the door, and he was so long in coming that she turned at last to listen for his step, and then she saw him, standing behind her chair, having entered the room noiselessly from the hall. She started in surprise, and he came forward into the light.

"Forgive me," he said. "You did not expect me so soon, and I have blundered into your dreams."

She shook her head and stammered an excuse.

"Have you eaten today?" he said, and she told him she had not. "You have supped with me before, Mary Yellan, but this time, if you do not mind, you shall lay the table and fetch the tray from the kitchen. Hannah will have left it prepared, and I have writing to do. At a quarter to seven, then," he said, turning his back on her.

She made her way to the kitchen, wishing she had not opened the drawer. The memory of the caricature lingered with her unpleasantly. She made play of getting the supper, at home among the familiar kitchen smells, and awaited reluctantly the summons of the clock. Then she carried the tray to the living room, hoping that nothing of her inner feeling showed upon her face.

He was standing with his back to the fire, and he had pulled the table in readiness before it. Although she did not look at him, she felt his scrutiny upon her, and her movements were clumsy. Out of the tail of her eye she saw that the canvases were no longer stacked against the wall. The desk was in disorder, with papers and correspondence piled upon it, and he had been burning letters, for the blackened scraps lay among the ashes under the turf.

They sat down, and he helped her to the cold pie.

"Is curiosity dead in Mary Yellan that she does not ask me what I have done with my day?" he said, mocking her gently and bringing the flush of guilt to her face at once.

"It is no business of mine where you have been," she answered.

"You are wrong there," he said, "and it is your business. I have meddled in your affairs the livelong day. You asked for my help, did you not?"

Mary was ashamed and hardly knew what to reply. "I have not thanked you yet for coming so promptly to Jamaica Inn," she said, "nor for my bed last night and my sleep today. You think me ungrateful."

"I never said that. I wondered only at your patience. It had not struck two when I bade you sleep this morning, and it is now seven in the evening. Long hours; and things do not stand still by themselves."

"Did you not sleep, then, after you left me?"

"I slept until eight. And then I was away again. My gray horse was lame, so progress was slow with the cob. He jogged like a snail to Jamaica Inn, and from Jamaica Inn to North Hill, where Mr. Bassat entertained me to luncheon. There were eight or ten of us present, and we were all of one accord that the murderer of your uncle will not remain at liberty for long."

"Does Mr. Bassat suspect anyone?" Mary's tone was guarded, and she kept her eyes on her plate.

"Mr. Bassat has questioned every inhabitant within a radius of ten miles, and the number of strange persons who were abroad last night is legion. It will take a week to have the truth from every one of them."

"What have they done with—with my aunt?"

"They were taken, both of them, to North Hill this morning and are to be buried there."

"And the peddler? They have not let him go?"

"No, he is safe under lock and key, screaming curses to the air. I do not care for the peddler. Neither, I think, do you. I gather from Richards that you suspected the peddler of the murder and said as much to Mr. Bassat. What has the peddler done to incur your displeasure?"

"He attacked me once."

"When did this happen?"

"On Christmas Eve."

"I am beginning to understand. You fell in with the landlord and his friends upon the road, and they took you with them to the shore to add to their sport?"

"Please, Mr. Davey, do not ask me any more."

"You shall not speak of it, Mary Yellan. I blame myself for having allowed you to continue your journey alone. Looking at you now, the way you carry your head, and the set of your chin, you bear little trace of what you endured. You have shown remarkable fortitude."

She looked up at him, and then away again, and fell to crumbling a piece of bread in her hand.

"When I consider the peddler," he continued, helping himself generously to stewed damsons, "I feel it very remiss of the murderer not to have looked into the barred room. The peddler is no ornament to the world while he lives, and dead he would at least make food for worms. What is more, had the murderer known that the peddler had attacked you, he would have had a motive strong enough to kill twice over."

Mary cut herself a slice of cake and forced it between her lips. The hand shook, though, that held the knife.

"I don't see," she said, "what I have to do in the matter."

"You have too modest an opinion of yourself," he replied.

They continued to eat in silence, Mary with eyes fixed upon her plate. Instinct told her that he played her as an angler plays a fish. At last she could wait no longer, but must blurt him a question. "So Mr. Bassat and the rest of you have made little headway, and the murderer is still at large?"

"Oh, but we have not moved as slowly as that. Some progress has been made. The peddler, for instance, in a hopeless attempt to save his own skin, has turned king's evidence. He went so far as to suggest that the landlord of Jamaica Inn had his orders from one above him. The gentlemen became excited and a little disturbed; if this is so, it would seem that the unknown leader and the murderer must be one and the same person. Don't you agree?"

"Why, yes, I suppose so."

"That should narrow the field considerably. We may disregard the general rabble of the company and look for someone with a brain and a personality. Did you ever see such a person at Jamaica Inn?"

"No, never."

"He must have gone to and fro in the silence of the night when you and your aunt were abed. He would not have come by the highroad, because you would have heard the clatter of his horse's hoofs. But there is always the possibility that he came on foot, in which case the man must know the moors. One of the gentlemen suggested that he lived within walking or riding distance. And that is why Mr. Bassat intends to question every inhabitant in the radius of ten miles. So you see the net will close around the murderer if he tarries long. Did I tell you I saw an acquaintance of yours today?"

"No, you did not. I have no friends but yourself."

"Thank you. That is a pretty compliment. But you have an acquaintance; did not the landlord's brother take you to Launceston fair?"

Mary gripped her hands under the table. "The landlord's brother?" she repeated, playing for time. "I have not seen him since then. I believed him to be away."

"No, he has been in the district since Christmas. He told me so himself. It had come to his ears that I had given you shelter, and he came up to me with a message for you. 'Tell her how sorry I am.' I presume he referred to your aunt."

"Was that all he said?"

"I believe he would have said more, but Mr. Bassat interrupted us."

"Mr. Bassat? Mr. Bassat was there when he spoke to you?"

"Why, of course. There were several of the gentlemen in the room. It was just before I came away from North Hill this evening."

Mary lifted her face to him, her eyes heavy with the agony of restraint. "What will they do to him, Mr. Davey?" she said.

The pale, expressionless eyes stared back at her, and for the first time she saw a shadow pass across them, and a flicker of surprise.

"Do?" he said, obviously puzzled. "Why should they do anything? They will hardly throw old sins in his face after the service he has done them. Did you not know that it was Jem Merlyn who informed against his brother? It appears that it was the squire himself who fell in with your friend at Launceston on Christmas Eve and carried him off to North Hill as an experiment. 'You've stolen my horse,' said he. 'I've the power to clap you in jail and you wouldn't set eyes on a horse for a dozen years. But you can go free if you bring me proof that your brother at Jamaica Inn is the man I believe him to be.'

"Your young friend asked for time; and when the time was up he shook his head. 'No,' said he, 'you must catch him yourself if you want him. I'm damned if I'll have truck with the law.' But the squire pushed a proclamation under his nose. 'Look there, Jem,' he said, 'there's been the bloodiest wreck on Christmas Eve since the *Lady of Gloucester* went ashore above Padstow last winter. Now will you change your mind?' As to the rest of the story, I gather your friend slipped his chain and ran for it in the night, and then came back again yesterday morning, when they thought to have seen the last of him, and went straight to the squire as he came out of church and said, as cool as you please, 'Very well, Mr. Bassat, you shall have your proof.' "

Mary stared before her into space, her whole mind split by his information, the evidence she had so fearfully and so painfully built against the man she loved collapsing into nothing, like a house of cards. "Whatever happens," she said slowly, "I can face the future now without shame."

"I am glad of that," the vicar said.

She shook her hair back from her face and smiled for the first time since he had known her. The anxiety and the dread had gone from her at last. "What else did Jem Merlyn say and do?" she asked.

The vicar glanced at his pocket watch and replaced it with a sigh.

"I wish I had the time to tell you," he said, "but it is nearly eight already. The hours go by too fast for both of us. I think we have talked enough about Jem Merlyn for the present."

"Tell me one thing—was he at North Hill when you left?"

"He was. In fact, it was his last remark that hurried me home. He announced his intention of riding over tonight to visit the blacksmith at Warleggan."

"Mr. Davey, you are playing with me now. What has it to do with you if he visits the blacksmith?"

"He will show the nail he picked up in the heather, down in the field below Jamaica Inn. The nail comes from a horse's shoe; the job was carelessly done. The nail was a new one, and Jem Merlyn, being a stealer of horses, knows the work of every blacksmith on the moors. 'Look here,' he said to the squire. 'I found it this morning in the field behind the inn. I'll ride to Warleggan, with your leave, and throw this in Tom Jory's face as bad workmanship.' "

"Well, and what then?" said Mary.

"Yesterday was Sunday, and on Sunday no blacksmith plies his trade unless he has great respect for his customer. Only one traveler passed Tom Jory's smithy yesterday and begged a new nail for his lame horse, and the time was somewhere near seven o'clock in the evening. After which the traveler continued his journey by way of Jamaica Inn."

"How do you know this?" said Mary.

"Because the traveler was the vicar of Altarnun," he said.

A SILENCE HAD fallen upon the room. Although the fire burned steady as ever, there was a chill in the air that had not been there before. Mary heard Francis Davey swallow once. At length she looked into his face and saw the pale eyes staring at her across the table, cold no longer but burning in the white mask of his face like living things at last. She knew now what he would have her know, but still she clung to ignorance as a source of protection.

His eyes compelled her to speak, and she forced a smile. "You are pleased to be mysterious, Mr. Davey."

He leaned forward in his chair. "You lost your confidence in me today before I came," he said. "You went to my desk and found the drawing; I saw that the paper had been moved, and when you heard my footsteps on the path you crouched in your chair there, before the fire, rather than look upon my face. It frightened you. You said to yourself, 'This man is a freak of nature, and his world is not my world.' You were right there, Mary Yellan. I live in the past, when men were not so humble as they are today, when the rivers and the sea were one, and the old gods walked the hills."

He rose from his chair and stood before the fire, a lean black figure with white hair and eyes, and his voice was gentle now, as she had known it first. "Yes, I am a freak in nature and a freak in time. I was born with a grudge against the age. Peace is very hard to find in the nineteenth century. The silence is gone, even on the hills. I thought to find it in the Christian Church, but the dogma sickened me. Christ is a puppet thing created by man himself. Only the old pagan barbarism is naked and clean. However, we can talk of these things later, when the heat and turmoil of pursuit is not upon us. We have eternity before us."

Mary looked up at him, her hands gripping the sides of her chair. "I don't understand you, Mr. Davey."

"Why, yes, you understand me very well. You know by now that I killed the landlord of Jamaica Inn, and his wife too; nor would the peddler have lived had I known of his existence. You know that it was I who directed every move made by your uncle. I have sat here at night, with him in your chair there and the map of Cornwall spread out on the table. Joss Merlyn, the terror of the countryside, touching his forelock when I spoke to him. His vanity was like a bond between us, and the greater his notoriety amongst his companions the better was he pleased. No other man knew the secret of our partnership.

"You were the block, Mary Yellan, against which we stubbed our toes. With your wide inquiring eyes and your gallant inquisitive head you came amongst us. In any case, we had played the game to its limit, and the time had come to make an end. How you pestered me with your courage and your conscience, and how I admired you for it! Of course you must hear me in the empty guest room at the inn, and must creep down to the kitchen and see the rope upon the beam; that was your first challenge.

"And then you steal out upon the moor after your uncle, who had tryst with me on Rough Tor, and losing him in the darkness, stumble upon myself and make me confidant. I knew something of your determination, and that time alone would quiet your suspicions. But your uncle must drink himself to madness on Christmas Eve and set the whole country in a blaze. I knew then he had betrayed himself, and with the rope around his neck would play his last card and name me master. Therefore he had to die, Mary Yellan, and your aunt, who was his shadow; and, had you been at Jamaica Inn last night when I passed by, you too— No, you would not have died."

He leaned down to her, and taking her two hands he pulled her to her feet, so that she stood looking in his eyes. "No, you would have come with me then as you will come tonight." His grip upon her wrists was firm and held no promise of release.

"You are wrong," she said. "You would have killed me then as you will kill me now. I am not coming with you, Mr. Davey."

"Death to dishonor?" he said, smiling, the thin line breaking the mask of his face. "I face you with no such problem. You have proved yourself a dangerous opponent, and I prefer you by my side; there, that is a tribute. In time we will take up the threads of our first friendship, which has gone astray tonight. Are you ready? Your cloak hangs in the hall, and I am waiting."

She backed to the wall, her eyes upon the clock, but he still held her wrists and tightened his grip upon them.

"Understand me," he said gently. "The pitiful vulgarity of screams would be heard by no one. I am stronger than you would suppose. A poor white ferret looks frail—but your uncle knew my strength. I don't want to hurt you, Mary Yellan, or spoil that trace of beauty you possess, but that I shall have to do if you withstand me. Come, where is that spirit of adventure which you have made your own?"

She saw by the clock that he must have overstepped already his margin of time. It was half past eight, and by now Jem would have spoken with the blacksmith at Warleggan. Twelve miles lay between them, but no more. She thought rapidly, weighing her chances. If she went now with Francis Davey she would be a brake upon his speed. The chase would follow hard upon his heels, and her presence would betray him in the end. Should she refuse to go, why, then there would be a knife in her heart at best. If he were insane—and this she believed him to be—his insanity would bring about his destruction; if he were not, she would be that stumbling block she had been to him from the beginning, with her girl's wits matched against his brains. She had the right upon her side, and faith in God, and he was an outcast in a hell of his own creation.

She smiled and looked into his eyes. "I'll come with you," she said, "but you'll find me no companion in your road."

"Roads? Who spoke of roads? We go by the moors and the hills, and tread granite and heather as the druids did." He held the door open for her, and she bowed to him, mocking, as she passed into the passage. She had no fear of him, nothing mattered now, because the man she loved was free and had no stain of blood upon him. She could love him without shame, and she knew what he had done for her, and that he would come to her again. In fancy she heard him ride upon the road in their pursuit, and she heard his challenge and his triumphant cry.

She followed Francis Davey to the stable, where the horses were saddled, and this was a sight for which she was ill prepared. "Do you not mean to take the trap?" she said.

"No, Mary," he replied, "we must travel light and free. You can ride; every woman born on a farm can ride; and I shall hold your rein."

The sky was overcast with low-flying clouds, and the moon was blotted out. It seemed as though the night itself favored the vicar of Altarnun. Mary climbed into the saddle of the gray, wondering whether a wild cry for help would rouse the sleeping village, but she felt his hand upon her foot, placing it in the stirrup, and looking down, saw the gleam of steel beneath his cape. He lifted his head and smiled.

"That'd be a fool's trick, Mary," he said. "By the time they were astir in Altarnun, I should be away on the moor yonder, and you would be lying on your face, with your youth and beauty spoiled."

He mounted the cob, with the gray attached to him by a leading rein; they set out upon their fantastic journey like two pilgrims. They came to the rough track leading to the ford and then to the great black heart of the moor, where there were no tracks but only the coarse tufted grass and dead heather. The tors rose up around them and hid the world behind, and the two horses were lost between the tumbling hills. Mary's hopes began to falter; already North Hill belonged to another world.

"Where are we bound?" she said at length. Francis Davey pointed to the north. "You have heard of ships, Mary Yellan, though of late you would not speak of them; and a ship it will be that shall carry us from Cornwall. You shall see Spain, Mary, and Africa; you shall feel desert sand under your feet, if you will. I care little where we go; you shall make the choice. Why do you shake your head?"

"Mr. Davey, you know as well as I do that I shall run from you at the first village. I came with you tonight because you would have killed me otherwise, but in daylight, within sight and sound of men and women, you will be as powerless as I am now."

"Mary Yellan, I am prepared for the risk. You forget that the north coast of Cornwall is as lonely and untraveled as these moors themselves; never a man's face shall you look upon but mine until we come to the haven that I have in mind."

"Let me grant you, then," said Mary, "that the sea is reached, and we are upon your waiting ship, with the coast behind us. Name any country as you please, Africa or Spain; do you think that I should not expose you, a murderer of men?"

"You will have forgotten it by then, Mary Yellan."

"Forgotten that you killed my mother's sister?"

"Yes, and forgotten your tears on the highroad from Launceston, and the young man who caused them. I told you before, I have heard confessions in my day, and I know the dreams of women better than you do yourself. There I have the advantage of the landlord's brother."

She turned away so that she could not see the eyes that degraded her, and rode on in silence. The horses picked their way delicately, and now and again stopped in their tracks and snorted, as though uncertain of their steps. Mary knew by the feel of the yielding grass that they were encompassed by marshes.

Her companion leaned forward in his saddle, straining his eyes to the darkness. Francis Davey knew the moors, but even he was not infallible and might lose his way. Mary watched the damp mist rise from the low ground. And then in front of them rolled a great bank of fog out of the night, a white wall that stifled every scent and sound.

Francis Davey drew rein. "The gods have gone against me after all," he said. "I know these fogs of old, and this one will not lift for several hours. To continue now amongst the marshes would be madness. We must wait for the dawn."

He took her rein once more and urged the horses to the left, away from the low ground, until the yielding grass gave place to firmer heather, while the white fog moved with them step by step.

"There will be a cave for your shelter and granite for your bed, Mary Yellan," he said. "Tonight you shall sleep on Rough Tor."

The horses bent to the strain, and they climbed ponderously out of the mist to the black hills beyond.

Later Mary sat shrouded in her cloak, a phantom figure, with her back against a hollow stone. The great jagged summit of the tor lifted its face to the sky like a crown above the mist, and below them the clouds hung solid and unchanged. The air was crystal clear; there was a wind here, keen as a knife, that blew upon the surface of the altar slabs and echoed in the caves. The horses stood against a boulder for shelter. Even they were restless and uneasy, turning now and again toward their master. He sat apart, a few yards distant from his companion, and sometimes she felt his eyes upon her in consideration, weighing the chances of success. She was ever watchful, ready for attack; and when he moved suddenly or turned upon his slab of stone, her hands unclasped themselves from her knees and waited, her fists clenched. She knew that sleep might take her before she was aware; and later she would wake with the touch of his cold hands upon her throat and his pale face above her.

The wind rose, making a moan upon the stones. It sang in the hollow caves and in the crevices of rock, at first a sigh and then a lamentation. It played upon the air like a chorus from the dead. Mary pulled the hood about her ears, but even as she did so the wind increased, tugging at her hair. Below the tor the heavy fog clung to the ground, with never a breath of air to roll away the clouds. But here on the summit the wind fretted and wept, a wild, lost note that echoed in the granite high above Mary's head, on the very peak of Rough Tor, as though the gods themselves stood there with their great heads lifted to the sky. In her fancy she could hear the whisper of a thousand voices and the tramping of a thousand feet, and she could see the stones turning to men beside her. Their faces were inhuman, older than time, carved and rugged like the granite; and they spoke in a tongue she could not understand, and their hands and feet were curved like the claws of a bird. They turned their stone eyes upon her and came toward her, shoulder to shoulder, moving like blind things to her destruction; and she cried suddenly and started to her feet, every nerve in her body throbbing.

The wind dropped and was no more than a breath upon her hair; the slabs of granite stood beyond her, dark and immobile, and Francis Davey watched her, his chin upon his hands. Her brain kept falling on and off into a dream, and he walked into it, a giant figure with white hair and eyes, who touched her throat and whispered in her ear.

She woke at last to certainty, feeling his hand upon her mouth. He forced her hands behind her back and bound them, using his own belt. Then he placed a handkerchief across her mouth, knotting it behind her head. He helped her to her feet and led her to the slope of the hill. "Listen to this, Mary," he said, "and you will understand why I have bound you, and why your silence may save us yet."

She must have slept longer than she thought, for to the east a faint glow heralded the pale, reluctant sun. The fog was with them still and hid the moors below like a white blanket. She followed the direction of his hand and listened, and far away, from beneath the mist, there came a sound between a cry and a call, like a summons in the air. It was faint at first, strangely pitched, unlike a human voice, unlike the shouting of men. It came nearer, rending the air with some excitement, and Francis Davey turned to Mary.

"I had forgotten that the squire of North Hill keeps bloodhounds in his kennels. It is a pity for both of us, Mary, that I did not remember."

With a sudden comprehension of that distant eager clamor she looked up at her companion, horror in her eyes, and from him to the two horses standing patiently by the slabs of stone.

"Yes," he said, following her glance, "we must let them loose and drive them down to the moors below. They would only bring the pack upon us."

She watched him, sick at heart, as he released the horses and led them to the steep slope of the hill. Then he bent to the ground, gathering stones in his hands, and rained blow after blow upon their flanks, so that they fled, snorting with terror, down the steep slope of the tor, dislodging boulders in their descent, and so plunged out of sight into the white mist below. The baying of the hounds came nearer now, deep-pitched and persistent, and Francis Davey ran to Mary, stripping himself of his long black coat and throwing his hat into the heather.

"Come," he said. "Friend or enemy, we share a common danger now."

They scrambled up the hill, among the boulders and slabs of granite, he with his arm about her, for her bound hands made progress difficult; and they waded in and out of crevice and rock, knee-deep in soaking black heather, climbing to the great peak of Rough Tor. Here, on the very summit, the granite was monstrously tortured and twisted into the semblance of a roof, and Mary lay beneath the great stone slab breathless, and bleeding from her scratches, while he climbed above her, gaining foothold in the hollows of the stone. He reached down, and though she shook her head, he dragged her to her feet again, cutting at the belt that bound her and tearing the handkerchief from her mouth.

"Save yourself, if you can," he shouted. She clung to a table of stone rising some ten feet from the ground, panting and exhausted, while he climbed above her, his lean black figure like a leech on the smooth surface of the rock. The chorus of the hounds was joined now by the shouting of men, a turmoil of excitement that filled the air and was the more terrible because it was unseen. The clouds moved swiftly across the sky, and the yellow glow of the sun swam into view. The mist parted and rose from the ground, and the land that it had covered for so long stared up at the sky pallid and newborn.

Mary looked down upon little dots of men standing knee-deep in the heather, while the yelping hounds, crimson-brown against the gray stone, ran before them like rats among the boulders. Somebody shouted, and a man who knelt in the heather, scarcely fifty yards from Mary, lifted his gun to his shoulder and fired. The shot spat against the granite boulder, and when he rose to his feet she saw that the man was Jem, and he had not seen her. He fired again, and the shot whistled close to her ear.

The hounds were worming in and out amid the bracken, and one of them leaped at the jutting rock beneath her, his great muzzle snuffling the stone. Then Jem fired once more; and looking beyond her, Mary saw the tall black figure of Francis Davey outlined against the sky, standing upon a wide slab like an altar, high above her head. He stood for a moment poised like a statue, his hair blowing in the wind; and then he flung out his arms as a bird throws his wings for flight, and drooped suddenly and fell, down from his granite peak to the dank heather and crumbling stones.

CHAPTER ELEVEN

IT WAS A HARD, bright day in early January. The ruts and holes in the highroad were covered with a thin layer of ice. This same frost had laid a white hand upon the moors, and they stretched to the horizon indefinite in color, a poor contrast to the clear blue sky above. Mary walked alone on Twelve Men's Moor, with the keen wind in her face. She was at liberty now to go where she would, and her thoughts turned longingly to Helford and the green valleys of the south. She would concern herself with the business of her farm, and count the strain an antidote to pain. She belonged to the soil and would return to it again. Helford had given her birth, and when she died she would be part of it once more.

She would not linger as she had done during the week, faint and indecisive, but make known her project to the Bassats when she returned for the midday meal. They were kind, and full of entreaties that she should stay among them, for the winter, at least—have a care, perhaps, for the children, be companion to Mrs. Bassat herself. She thought of these things as she walked, and she knew she must go away from North Hill very soon, for these people were not her people.

There was a cart coming toward her from Kilmar, the one moving thing upon the silent plain. She watched it in suspicion, for there were no cottages on this moor except Trewartha, away in the valley by the Withy Brook; and Trewartha, she knew, stood empty. Nor had she seen its owner since he had fired at her on Rough Tor. "He's an ungrateful rascal, like the rest of his breed," said the squire. "I grant he did well and was the means of tracing you, Mary, and that black-coated scoundrel, but he's never as much as thanked me for clearing his name in the business, and has taken himself to the world's end now. There's never been a Merlyn yet that came to any good." So Trewartha stood empty, and the horses were gone wild and roamed free upon the moors, and their master had ridden away with a song on his lips, as she had known he would.

The cart came nearer to the slope of the hill, and Mary shielded her eyes from the sun to watch its progress. She saw that the horse labored beneath a strange load of pots and mattresses and sticks. Someone was making for the country with his home upon his back. It was not until the cart was below her and the driver, walking by the side, looked up to her and waved, that she recognized him. She went down toward the cart with a fine show of indifference and turned at once to the horse to pat him, while Jem kicked a stone under the wheel and wedged it there for safety.

"There was a rumor you were to be companion to Mrs. Bassat," he called from behind the cart. "Well, you'll lead a soft enough life with them, I daresay."

"They've been kinder to me than anyone else in Cornwall since my mother died. But I'm going back home to Helford. I shall try and start the farm again."

"Where will you live?"

"There's not a cottage in the village I couldn't call home."

"I've had the feeling always it would be like living in a box, to live in a village. You poke your nose over your gate into another man's garden, and you know that if you cook a rabbit for your supper he'll have the sniff of it in his kitchen. Damn it, Mary, that's no life for anyone."

She laughed at him, for his nose was wrinkled in disgust, and then she ran her eye over his laden cart.

"What are you doing with that?" she asked him.

"I want to get away from the sight of Kilmar yonder, with his ugly face frowning upon me from dusk till dawn," he said. "Here's my home, Mary, in the cart, and I'll set it up wherever my fancy takes me."

Mary went on patting the horse, the good flesh warm beneath her hand, and Jem watched her, the ghost of a smile on his lips.

"Which way will you go?" she said.

"Somewhere east of Tamar, it doesn't matter to me, maybe the midlands," he said. "I'll never come west again, not until I'm old and gray, and have forgotten a lot of things. Perhaps I'll have money in my pockets one day and buy horses for pleasure instead of stealing them."

"It's an ugly black country in the midlands," said Mary.

"Moorland peat is black, isn't it?" he answered. "And so's the rain when it falls into your pigsties down at Helford."

"There's no sense in what you say, Jem."

"How can I be sensible when you lean against my horse, with your wild daft hair entangled in his mane, and I know that in five minutes I'll be over the hill without you." He went around to the back of the cart and kicked the stone away from the wheel. "I've havered here long enough," he said. "If you were a man, I'd ask you to come with me, and you'd fling your legs over the seat and rub shoulders with me for as long as it pleased you."

"I'd do that now if you'd take me south," she said.

"Yes, but I'm bound north, and you're not a man, you're only a woman, as you'd know to your cost if you came with me. Move off from the trace there, Mary, and don't twist the rein. I'm going now." He took her face in his hands and kissed it, and she saw that he was laughing. "When you're an old maid in mittens down at Helford, you'll remember that," he said.

He climbed into the cart and looked down upon her, flicking his whip and yawning. "I'll do fifty miles before tonight," he said, "and sleep like a puppy at the end of it, in a tent by the side of the road. Will you think of me or not?"

She stood with her face toward the south, hesitating. Beyond those hills the peace and quiet of Helford waited for her beside the running water.

He drew the reins into his hands and whistled to the horse. "Wait," said Mary. "Hold him still, and give me your hand."

He reached down and swung her beside him on the driver's seat. "If you come with me it will be a hard life, and a wild one, with no biding anywhere. Men are ill companions when the mood takes them, and I, God knows, the worst of them. You'll get a poor exchange for your farm."

"I'll take the risk, Jem, and chance your moods."

"Do you love me, Mary?"

"I believe so, Jem."

"Better than Helford?"

"I can't ever answer that."

"Why are you sitting here beside me, then?"

"Because I must," said Mary.

He laughed and took her hand and gave her the reins; and she did not look back, but set her face toward the Tamar.

Mission to
Malaspiga

Mission to Malaspiga

A CONDENSATION OF THE NOVEL BY

EVELYN ANTHONY

ILLUSTRATED BY JEAN-LÉON HUENS

Katharine di Malaspiga Dexter had never thought of her middle name as anything but her mother's rather silly insistence on an aristocratic Italian ancestry. But when Katharine's brother, Peter di Malaspiga Dexter, died of an overdose of heroin, the name drew an urgent visit from Ben Harper, a federal drug-enforcement officer. There was reason to believe, he told Katharine, that at the top of an international drug ring was the present Duke of Malaspiga. Her family tie provided a unique opportunity to infiltrate the ring. Would she go to Florence?

Katharine agreed. But Ben Harper had not foreseen the force of the duke's personal magnetism—nor the agonizing dilemma into which it would plunge her. The stakes are high in this intriguing novel, set in the beautiful Renaissance city of Florence and in the forbidding mountaintop castle of the Malaspigas, by the author of such Gothic thrillers as *The Tamarind Seed* and *The Legend*.

CHAPTER ONE

I T WAS THE fifth morning, and still there was no letter. No message. She had waked early. Having slept deeply for the first time since she had arrived, she didn't immediately recognize her surroundings.

The windows showed her an unfamiliar view of red Tuscan-tile roofs and a hot blue sky. She was in Florence, in a hotel bedroom. She showered and dressed; the maid brought her coffee. Nine o'clock. It was time to go downstairs and approach the reception desk and ask the same question.

The clerk looked up and smiled. "Good morning, Signorina Dexter. Nothing has come. I'm sorry."

He assumed that she was waiting to hear from a lover. She could tell by the sympathetic look he gave her. And he had shown special interest in her since he saw the middle name on her passport when she registered. The manager himself had approached her in the restaurant and asked her if there was anything she wanted. It gave her an uneasy feeling to know that in spite of her American nationality, the Florentines regarded her as part of themselves.

"I'm going out," Katharine Dexter told the clerk. "If anyone calls, ask them to leave a telephone number."

"Certainly, signorina." The clerk had his countrymen's love of blondes, and her hair was a beautiful golden color, the eyes brown. She was unusually pretty, he thought. He wasn't deceived by the guidebooks and the tours which occupied her. She wasn't an ordinary tourist, however hard she tried to act the part. She was waiting for a letter, a telephone call. Whoever the man was, he was behaving very badly.

It was early May, and Florence languished under an unexpected heat wave. She had arrived a week ago, after an exhausting flight from New York via Rome, and landed at the Pisa airport. She had looked with indifference out of the taxi window during the long drive to Florence, dazed with travel fatigue and a deep sickness of the spirit—the aftermath of grief and anger. She had even dozed, awaking to find the taxi drawing up to the sixteenth-century *palazzo* that had been converted into a modern hotel.

It was now five days since she had made the approach, with no response. And they were not away. She had telephoned the villa the day she arrived and hung up when she was told the family was at home. She had decided it would be better if she wrote, a good excuse for cowardice. Perhaps tomorrow there would be an answer.

Now, walking down to the Via dei Fossi, she was more attuned to the atmosphere, less disoriented. She paused by the antique shops, drawn by the simplicity and elegance with which they displayed their treasures. There were times since her arrival when she had lost herself in the city, falling a victim to its beauty and the magnetism of the Florentines. They were shrewd, energetic, with a passionate enjoyment in doing business. They had invented banking; it was perhaps the least of their many gifts to the civilized world. By contrast with the tourists of all nationalities who crowded the city, the Florentines stood out, dark and sinuous as cats, gracefully sharpening their claws for the exploitation of the foreigner. She paused, seeing her own reflection in the window of a shop displaying swaths of silk. She looked like an American, slim and neat in a cool linen dress.

She turned down the Lungarno to reach the Ponte Vecchio, which crossed the ribbon of the river Arno to her right. The narrow, cobbled road across the bridge, only open to those on foot, was hemmed in on either side by jewelers' shops and silversmiths. This was the ancient center of the Florentine art of making beautiful ornaments for the women and the houses of the rich. The bridge glittered from one end to the other, but Katharine was not tempted to buy. It would have seemed frivolous under the circumstances.

On the opposite bank of the Arno, she took the sloping road up toward the Pitti Palace, that morning's destination. She had spent the two previous days exploring the enormous treasure-house of the Uffizi Gallery, forty-two rooms filled with the great paintings, sculptures, ceramics and jewels garnered by the Medici rulers of the city, which had been bequeathed to the citizens of Florence in the eighteenth century. As she walked up the cobbled surface of the Piazza Pitti toward the magnificent Renaissance building, one of a stream of enthusiastic tourists, her spirits rose. Students swarmed everywhere, eating ice cream, reading, gossiping, enjoying the sunshine. She thought suddenly that there was a gaiety about

Italian youth which was absent among Americans, a love of life which didn't have its origin in drugs or mystical religions.

She bought a ticket and began to climb the enormously wide staircase. In the first-floor gallery she paused by one of the windows. A cluster of middle-aged Germans, shepherded by a guide, came to a halt close by her. The guide explained the history of the painting immediately in front of them. Katharine had taken German at college. She understood everything the guide was saying, although it was not an easy language for her, unlike Italian, which she had learned to speak as easily as if it were her own. She had majored in Renaissance literature, a curious subject in her father's opinion. He didn't see how it could assist her in making a nice, conventional marriage, suitable for the daughter of the owner of a large department store. He had been unlucky in his children. He and her mother were affectionate parents, prepared to cope with the average disorders that might overtake their kind of family. But they hadn't a hope of understanding what had happened to their son.

The Germans moved on into the next gallery, and Katharine found herself standing alone in front of a life-size portrait of a young boy, dressed in the elegant costume of the early sixteenth century, crimson embroidered with gold. A pale face, full lips without a smile, enormous eyes. It was the most arrogant face she had ever seen, physically beautiful but coldhearted and proud.

She read from the plaque below: ALFREDO, PRINCE OF MALASPIGA, AGED NINE, 1512, and the artist's name, A. VITALI. PRESENTED TO THE PITTI PALACE BY ERNESTO, DUKE OF MALASPIGA, 1921.

Malaspiga. Confronted by the name, Katharine felt shaken. It was a threat, that name. Malaspiga. But it was the middle name on her own passport. The reason why, as she left the cemetery after her brother's funeral in New England, men like Ben Harper and Frank Carpenter had come into her life.

IT HAD BEEN a beautiful spring day, crisp and cloudless. She had granted Peter's wish to be cremated. The minister had just committed the small metal urn to a two-foot hole in the ground. She heard the closing words of the service and found no comfort in them. A single wreath of spring flowers was laid by the side of the newly cut turf. Her writing was on the card.

Peter di Malaspiga Dexter had gone out of the world as he had lived in it for the last seven years. Uncared for and unmourned by anyone except her. He had been twenty-seven when he died. She had a handkerchief in her hand; she had no tears left, and she put it away.

Two men were waiting by the cemetery gates. "Miss Dexter?" One of them took off his hat; he was going slightly bald, and he had hard brown eyes. "My name is Ben Harper. And this is my assistant, Frank Carpenter. We'd like to offer you our sympathy."

"What do you want?" she said. The man called Harper produced an identification card, and then she understood.

"I'm sorry," she said. "I made a statement to the police. There's nothing more I can tell you." He didn't stand aside.

"We'd like to talk to you," he said. "Just a few minutes of your time."

She looked at them in turn. The second man was taller, younger, but he had the same hard face and wary eyes. Men who lived in their world couldn't be expected to have pity left. Suddenly she was too tired to resist.

"All right," she said. "There's a drive-in café down the road. I'll meet you there." She got into her car and drove away.

It was a pleasant little café, decorated in cedarwood, with brass fittings and checked tablecloths. Frank Carpenter ordered coffee.

"You cared for your brother for seven years," Ben Harper said. "He must have meant a lot to you."

"Yes," Katharinè said. "And he tried. Believe me, he tried. But it was hopeless. Clinics, psychiatrists, everything. He hadn't a dollar or a friend in the world when he died."

"Except you," Ben Harper said. "I saw your face when I showed my ID, Miss Dexter. Just another cop wanting to know where he got it. Well, we know the pusher who supplied him, but we're not interested in small-time operators. We want the top men, the millionaires who run yachts on getting heroin to people like your brother. It wasn't just dope that killed him; it was organized crime. That's why we're here. I believe you can help us get to them." And that was how it had begun.

SHE TURNED AWAY from the portrait of the Malaspiga prince; even the lofty rooms of the Pitti seemed claustrophobic. She pushed her way through knots of people by the doorways, going against the stream. She made her way to the Boboli Gardens surrounding the palace and found a vacant space on the steps of the amphitheater in the brilliant sunlight.

Before Peter's condition became chronic, she had had a job in a prestigious publishing house in Manhattan. Her brother was at the Harvard business school. Life had never seemed more satisfying; she loved her job, a college romance had gently blown itself out, she felt free and excited by the future. And then one night Peter, the person she loved best, came to her apartment and told her that he was a heroin addict. During his final year at Princeton, he'd smoked pot in common with his contemporaries, and one night it had seemed like fun to try something a little stronger. First it was sniffing cocaine—then the need for stronger rushes drove him on to heroin. She had held him in her arms while he

wept and shook and told her how he had tried to stop and couldn't. Couldn't . . . that was what his parents never understood. That one word.

He went away for cures; he tried psychiatry, group therapy, a long cruise with Katharine, who'd given up her job to help him, but nothing worked. Their mother died, and from then on his home was closed against him. Katharine had never forgiven her father; he had abandoned his son.

For seven years she had lived with him, fought for him and seen the handsome, friendly, responsible person she knew transformed into an uncaring stranger, a liar, a thief, capable of stealing from her when her back was turned.

Then he had come out of a well-known clinic in upstate New York after a stay of six months. And for the first time it seemed as if there was hope of a cure. A week later she left him alone in the apartment. When she came back, he had disappeared. A few hours later she found him in Bellevue Hospital, dead of an overdose.

It had been a long, hard journey to that cemetery in New England— to the two-foot-square plot with its urn full of ashes.

Katharine left the amphitheater and began to walk up the steps to the top of the Boboli Gardens. She looked at her watch; it was almost twelve o'clock, but she didn't want to eat anything.

She had gone to the Drug Enforcement Administration center in Manhattan for a crash course before coming to Florence. Ben Harper had assigned Frank Carpenter as her instructor. He had been curt and irritable with her. "If you think penetrating an organization like the Malaspigas' is going to be easy, you'd better walk right out of here. Having a Malaspiga as a grandmother may be a great introduction, but after that you're on your own."

Malaspiga. Her mother had given her a ring with a lapis lazuli stone, carved intaglio with an armorial crest, that had belonged to her grandmother, a vague figure recalled from early childhood. The crest was a wreath of laurel surmounted by a coronet. Coming through its center was an ear of corn, ending in a sharp spike. There was something sinister in the crest. She had disliked the little ring and never worn it. She remembered being irritated by her mother's references to their noble Italian connections.

Katharine's grandmother had run away from home to marry their grandfather, the son of a poor tradesman. They had immigrated to the States, where he had ended by owning one of the biggest chains of department stores on the East Coast. Her mother had never emphasized that. Only her grandmother's aristocracy was stressed. Katharine had thought it ridiculous. She felt the same way about the name Malaspiga. Katharine di Malaspiga Dexter. Peter di Malaspiga Dexter. That was what had brought Ben Harper to the cemetery. Peter was a known addict. The notification of his death had disclosed that curious middle name. And it had a very special significance for the narcotics bureau.

She turned left at the top of the stairs. Beyond a little pink bell tower was a panoramic view of the city. Pink plaster, gray domes, slender towers. The birthplace of the Renaissance. The trading center of the medieval world. The city where the Duke of Malaspiga and his family lived during the spring. It had sounded easy. She had the means of introducing herself without suspicion. All she had to do was get to know them, and then use the training Frank Carpenter had given her.

To CARPENTER, THE idea of using women on high-risk missions was bad enough—to bring in an amateur was making certain of disaster.

"We've tried getting to them and we've failed," Harper had said. "They're too smart to let anyone penetrate their organization. This girl is our only chance."

"That's what we thought about Firelli," Carpenter pointed out. "He looked cast iron. One of our most experienced agents—right background, knowledge of antiques, judo expert, crack shot, everything. And he disappeared. I'm sorry, Ben, you want me to train this girl to take on a setup like that? It's a death sentence."

"We haven't any choice. We've got to crack this. The stuff's pouring in, and all we get is a few pushers."

The lead had come from an Interpol report. The driver of a truck that had arrived at Genoa with a shipment of antiques for New York was stopped by the customs for questioning. He was recognized as a drug smuggler who had previously operated in Naples. Nothing was found in his load or on his person, and he had to be released and his shipment cleared. The goods he was carrying came from the town of Malaspiga. The Italian narcotics authorities had carried out discreet investigations in the town and found nothing to connect it with drug smuggling. It was a sleepy Tuscan community, resentful of questions from outsiders, and feudally attached to its hereditary duke. The antiques were part of a collection sent by him to the United States. Without evidence except the coincidence of the truck driver's previous narcotics connection, the authorities declined to investigate further. But a narcotics agent named Raphael, in the Florence office of Interpol, had noticed a police report that the driver of the truck had been found strangled, Mafia-style, in Genoa within a week of his detention by the customs.

Raphael was a man of strong convictions and fierce integrity. On a visit to the States he had stayed at Harper's house. Now, unable to convince his Italian superiors that there was a connection between Malaspiga and the smuggling of drugs, he cabled his finding to Harper. In his experience the murder was evidence enough. He hoped Harper might make use of it, since the shipment, innocent though it turned out to be, was destined for New York. Harper had sent Firelli to Florence to penetrate the family and investigate the town of Malaspiga. A month after his arrival, well covered as an antique dealer, he had disappeared, leaving one garbled telephone call for Raphael: *Dangerous . . . I've found . . . Angelo.* That had been repeated before the line went dead. *Angelo.* He had apparently checked out of his hotel in Florence, again by telephone; his luggage was picked up, and he was never heard from again.

So now there was no doubt that Malaspiga was involved. And sending in an agent with a genuine connection was the best chance they'd ever have of going to the heart of the organization. The Italian authorities wouldn't move against a titled family without absolute proof, Raphael assured Harper. But Interpol would assist, and he would act as liaison.

"I want you to give this girl everything you've got," Harper had told Frank Carpenter. "I've seen you turn the rawest material into something first-rate. You can do it."

Carpenter soon had to admit that her ability was exceptional. She mastered the mechanics of simple electronic bugging and showed a rare facility for identification. At the end of three weeks he reported to Harper that she would soon be ready. One element of training she had refused, and Carpenter hadn't argued, had even felt relieved. She wouldn't learn to fire or carry a gun. "I'd never use it," she said. "No matter what happened I couldn't shoot anybody. So why carry it?"

The night before she left for Italy, he had taken her to dinner. They went to Noni's, a small restaurant on West Fifty-sixth.

"Do you come here very often?" Katharine asked.

"I come here sometimes with a friend of mine," he said. "He's a bureau man too. We have a beer together on our way home."

"Is home far away?"

"Out along Pelham Bay Parkway, beyond the golf course. I have a small apartment there and sometimes grab a weekend game."

"You're not married?"

"Not anymore." Silence developed between them.

It was obvious that his marriage had been a failure and that the experience had hurt. He was very professional, very reserved. She admired him, but after a month she knew nothing about him.

Their drinks had arrived, and he sipped his beer. "You've got to give a woman time to keep her happy," he said. "I work a sixteen-hour day; I have to fly off anyplace at a moment's notice. My wife couldn't believe it was work keeping me away from home. So she invented other women. We had a rough two years before we got divorced. So." He shrugged. "That's my life story. How about yours?"

"I should think you know it all. I know how your department checks up!" He smiled at her; he didn't usually smile, and it made him look relaxed and attractive.

"I know you're thirty-one, where you were born, educated; one boy friend who dropped out after you left college. Seven years taking care of your brother. And you've never been married. That's surprising. You're an attractive girl."

"Addicts need time too. Anyway, I'm old-fashioned. I never met anyone I really cared about. I need to be in love before I marry. Right now, I just want to get to Italy."

Carpenter leaned across the table toward her. "I've told Ben what I think of the idea. I think it stinks. I told you how Firelli got one message through which made no sense and then disappeared. I want you to think about that. He's dead. And that's what you're walking into."

"I know," Katharine said quietly. "I'm not doing it under any misconception. But my grandmother was a Malaspiga. I believe that's fate."

"It wasn't fate that killed Firelli." Carpenter's expression was grim. There seemed nothing more to say.

He brought her back to the hotel she'd moved into after Peter's death, and on the steps outside he kissed her urgently. It was the first time he had even touched her. "Be careful," he said. "Don't take any risks. Promise me."

"I promise," Katharine said.

The next morning she left Kennedy airport on the first leg of her journey to Florence. She had never felt more alone in her life.

CHAPTER TWO

EVEN BEFORE THE reception clerk signaled to her, she saw the letter in the slot below her room number. "It came by hand after you'd gone out," the clerk said, smiling. On the back of the envelope, embossed in crimson, was the crest of the dukes of Malaspiga. Katharine went up to her room and opened the letter:

Dear Signorina Dexter,
    Thank you for your kind letter and welcome to Florence. We should be pleased if you can take tea with us on Wednesday at five o'clock.
                                                        Isabella di Malaspiga

She lit a cigarette to prove to herself that her hand was steady, and then she sat quietly on the edge of the bed, smoking and thinking. Her letter had introduced her as the granddaughter of Maria Gemma di Malaspiga, niece of the twelfth duke, who had married and gone to America. When telling a lie, Frank Carpenter had said, always hide it in the middle of a truth. She had said she was making a pilgrimage to her ancestral city, recovering from the loss of her brother who had recently died, and would very much like to make the acquaintance of her cousins. She had added a hypocritical flourish, to the effect that she had dreamed of coming to Florence and seeing her grandmother's old home ever since she was a child.

She put out the cigarette and picked up the phone. She asked the switchboard to get the Villa Malaspiga. When a voice answered, Katharine asked for the Duchess di Malaspiga, and gave her own name. There was a long wait. Then a high-pitched voice sounded through the receiver. "Isabella di Malaspiga is speaking. Is that Signorina Dexter, who wrote to us?"

"Yes," Katharine said. "It is. I'd be delighted to come for tea on Wednesday. It's very kind of you."

"Not at all." The voice sounded friendly and excited. There was no suggestion of grandeur. "We are so looking forward to meeting you, my dear child. Until Wednesday then. Good-by."

She had been very welcoming, very warm. It was ridiculous to feel afraid of them one moment and then charmed by a few friendly words over the telephone.

The taxi crossed the Ponte Alla Carraia and wound upward on the Viale Galileo away from the center of Florence. Pine trees stood sentinel over the enormous houses, shielded behind ornamental gates. The road rose higher, climbing steeply; when they turned into the entrance of the Villa Malaspiga the city lay below them, sparkling in the sunshine, the roof of the great cathedral at its heart glowing red. The family crest was everywhere. On the twenty-foot-high wrought-iron gates, carved in stone above the pillared doorway. On the mosaic floor of the entrance hall. She followed a manservant through the entrance hall, past a pair of magnificent marble statues, and into a long, cool room where a musty smell intruded. A man came toward her, a tall, slim man. The best-looking man she had ever seen in her life.

"Signorina Dexter? I am Alessandro di Malaspiga." She gave him her hand, and he brought it up to his mouth, without actually touching it. His eyes were black, large, heavy-lidded.

"Please come in; my mother is waiting for you." The room was like a vast corridor, the walls covered with tapestries, a huge table standing in the center, and around a fireplace, carved and gilded with the Malaspiga coat of arms, was a group of people. Two servants stood behind a table covered with a white cloth and glittering with silver. In a long chair, her feet raised on a footrest, a woman looked up at Katharine and held out a pale hand, flashing with rings.

"How delightful this is. I am Alessandro's mother. We talked on the telephone. Do come and sit beside me; let me look at you." It was a bell-like voice, beautifully modulated. Her lovely face was impossibly white-skinned, with great glowing black eyes and a mouth which was painted bright scarlet. Delicate waves of silvery hair curved under a wide-brimmed hat, with a wisp of veil falling from the crown. On the left lapel of her black silk dress she wore a pale pink rose.

A painfully slim girl with a handsome face and coal-black eyes rose from a settee with the grace so natural to Italian women.

"My daughter-in-law, Francesca," the old duchess said. "And this is our friend, Mr. Driver."

A young man, somewhere in his early thirties, with fair hair and gray eyes, came forward and shook Katharine's hand. "Hullo," he said. "John Driver—nice to meet you, Miss Dexter." The accent was Canadian.

"Sit down," the old duchess suggested again, "close to me, my dear. I don't hear all that clearly." She gave Katharine a beautiful smile.

Then the servants began to pour tea into tiny cups. Sugar and milk were presented on a silver salver. Plates of rich pastries were passed around. Katharine wondered suddenly if Ben Harper or Frank had any idea what they were asking her to do when they suggested she get to know her family. Family! The beautiful, mummified old woman in her picture hat, the impossibly handsome Duke di Malaspiga, his elegant wife with her sad expression—only the man named Driver was real.

The duke leaned toward her. "You have a distinct resemblance to one of my aunts," he said. "She was a blonde too. I must show you her portrait. She was very beautiful."

They were all beautiful. Katharine didn't doubt that.

"I've been looking up the family records," the duke continued. "I have some papers relating to your grandmother and her marriage. I thought you'd be interested to see them."

"I would," Katharine said. "I'd love to see them. I hope you don't mind my introducing myself. It seemed such a perfect opportunity to look up my grandmother's family."

"We're very happy you wrote to us, aren't we, Mamia?" The duke turned to his mother.

She nodded. "Very happy. Tell me about yourself, my dear."

"My father's family came from Philadelphia," Katharine said calmly. "We lived there when I was a child, but then we moved to New York. My father's still there. My brother and I lived together. When he died, I decided to take this trip."

"You won't regret coming over," John Driver interposed. "I came on a short visit and I'm still here." He laughed. "I fell in love with Florence. People talk about Rome and Venice, but I found the heart of the Renais-

125

sance right here." He had an attractive face, not strictly good-looking, but likable and humorous.

"How long have you been here?" Katharine asked him.

"Four years and two months. Your cousins won't let me leave."

"We'd miss you, John." It was the first contribution Francesca di Malaspiga had made. "Sandro and I will keep you forever, if we can." She handed her empty cup to one of the servants. The old duchess gave a signal and the service was cleared away.

"If you would like to come to the library with me," the duke said, "I could show you the portrait of my aunt. The likeness is extraordinary."

One of the white-coated servants went ahead and opened the door for them. Katharine passed through first, followed by her cousin. She wondered if he ever opened anything for himself.

In the hallway he paused. "We can go to the library first," he said. "And then I could take you for a little tour. We have a lot of family portraits here. Are you in a hurry?"

Katharine looked into his smiling face. His charm was very powerful; he was using it deliberately, like someone displaying a talent. He wanted her to stay and look around the villa. For all his exquisite manners, he wouldn't have suggested it otherwise. "I'm not in a hurry," she said. "But I don't want to be a nuisance."

"That wouldn't be possible," the duke said gently. "It isn't every day one finds a beautiful cousin from America. Come, this way." He took her arm and guided her to the library.

"This is my favorite room," he said. "My mother prefers the long salon. She adores the tapestries, but I find them musty. I like the smell of wood and leather." So that was what she had noticed about the long room. The smell of tapestries woven hundreds of years before, perhaps hanging undisturbed for years.

"This is lovely," Katharine said. The room was paneled in oak, with three walls of books behind exquisite grillwork. There was another fireplace, the Malaspiga coat of arms in carved wood above it. The floor was marble, the furniture very old and dark. An enormous iron chandelier hung above their heads.

"Here," the duke said, "is your aunt. Now, isn't she like you?" It was a pastel portrait standing in an elaborate gilt frame on a side table. It showed a young woman in the fashion of twenty years ago, blond and dark-eyed.

"You're right," Katharine said. "There is a look—even I can see it. What was her name?"

"Elsabetta di Carnevale; she was a famous beauty. She married a Venetian, a prince with a fortune. That's rare for our aristocracy these days. We've begun to marry rich Americans."

"That's surely an old European habit," Katharine answered. "The English and French have been doing it for years."

He laughed. "You mustn't mind if I tease you, my dear cousin. I always tease people I like. And I like you. I adore Americans."

"Have you been to the States?"

"Yes. I went there on my honeymoon seven years ago. We went to New York first, then on to Hollywood. We stayed with friends of my father's in Beverly Hills. I was fascinated."

She could imagine he would be; equally, the people whose business was fantasy must have been fascinated by him. "Did anyone offer you a film contract?" Now the memory which Carpenter had trained was waiting to record every detail. Information was what they wanted: when he had gone to the United States, how long and where he had stayed, any contacts he might have made.

"How funny you should ask—yes, they did. I was very flattered." He took out a gold cigarette case and lit a cigarette. "I'm sorry, do you smoke? Nobody does here except me. I forget about visitors."

"Thank you." They were long, filtered, printed with a monogram.

"I have papers concerning your grandmother here," he said. "But I'm not going to show them to you today. Then you will have to come again."

"I was hoping you'd invite me." Katharine wasn't good at this kind of game, but he was a master and he made it easy for her. Women would find him irresistible.

"I'll take you upstairs now," he said. "And then we'll rejoin my family in the salon."

"Who did you stay with in California—someone connected with the film world?"

"Yes, John Julius and his wife. He was a famous star before the war. He'd met my father in Italy and they became friends." He gripped her elbow, pretending to support her up the stairs. She eased herself free of him as they walked down a wide landing.

"Portraits," he said. "All Malaspigas, but of the eighteenth and nineteenth century. The earlier pictures are at the castle in Malaspiga. Over there is your great-grandmother."

"She looks very proud," Katharine said. "I don't envy my grandmother when she wanted to marry a poor man."

"A *common* man," Alessandro corrected. "Poverty was not a disgrace in those days, but to marry a social inferior was impossible."

She didn't answer. To call him snobbish and old-fashioned was pointless. Her purpose was to ingratiate herself. She walked beside him slowly, pausing to look at the great-aunts and uncles, the cousins, the relatives by marriage who adorned the gallery walls.

He looked at his watch. "It's past six—we must go downstairs and have a drink with my mother. Fortunately, John is very good with her."

"He seems so fond of you all," Katharine said.

"It's entirely mutual. Besides which, he has a great talent. I hope the ancestors haven't bored you?"

"Of course not—it was terribly interesting. Thank you."

"Please," he said, leading her back toward the salon, "call me Alessandro. If I may call you Katharine. Miss Dexter is ridiculously formal between cousins."

The salon was full of subdued lights. Scented candles were burning on the big center table. One of the servants was offering drinks. Only the old lady and the Canadian were there, sitting close together and laughing. There were two little spots of red on the old duchess' cheeks, and her eyes sparkled. Her glance at her son was mischievous.

"There you both are," she said. "What a long time you kept Miss Dexter, Sandro. She must be sick of her ancestors by now!" Her laugh was a bright trill, with a sweet note of malice in it.

Katharine sat near her on the other side of John Driver. The duchess laid a hand as dried and thin as old paper on top of hers. On the little finger she wore a crested ring which was the twin of the one Katharine had in her hotel room and had forgotten to wear.

"John will make you a wonderful old-fashioned," the duchess continued. "Or would you prefer champagne?"

"Just whiskey, please," Katharine said.

"And another of those delicious cocktails for me," the old lady demanded. "When you get old," she said to Katharine, "life has few compensations. One lives for something as simple as an old-fashioned!"

"Come now," John Driver said gently. "You look like a girl tonight. Doesn't she, Sandro?"

"You have the secret of eternal youth, Mamia," he said. "Our cousin will think we don't look after you, if you talk like that. No more cocktails tonight; you're becoming sad."

It was said with gentleness, but the old lady put her glass down. It seemed she understood her son. "I must change my dress for dinner," she announced. The beautiful, painted face turned to Katharine. "You must visit us again, my dear."

It was a dismissal, and Katharine got up immediately.

"I'll take Miss Dexter back to her hotel," John Driver said. "My car's outside."

Alessandro bowed over her hand. This time his lips brushed the back of it. "I will collect you at one o'clock tomorrow, and we will have lunch. Then you can look at the papers."

As they crossed the Ponte Alla Carraia, Driver looked at Katharine and grinned. "Don't be overpowered," he said. "I felt just the same when I first met Sandro. He sort of takes you over. It comes naturally to him."

"So it seems," Katharine said. "It's just that I'm used to being asked."

Contrary to what Driver thought, she was not overcome by the duke's looks and charm. Now that she was out of the villa and sitting next to an ordinary human being, she felt that Alessandro di Malaspiga was the most frightening man she had ever met. She felt as if she had come out of a tomb. The smell of scented candles and faded tapestries was still with her, cloying and unhealthy. Nothing except her purpose in coming to Florence would have made her see any of them again.

JAMES NATHAN HAD worked with the old Federal Bureau of Narcotics before it was assimilated into the DEA—the Justice Department's Drug Enforcement Administration. He was a veteran of fifteen years.

He spoke to a younger colleague of Frank Carpenter's. "He always comes and has a beer on a Friday at Noni's. Last two times I asked him he was busy. What's up with him?"

The younger man shrugged. "He's training a special rookie. Pretty important mission. Something to do with Firelli's assignment."

"First I've heard of it," Nathan said. "So what's the mission? Another agent going to Italy?"

"I guess so."

Nathan looked at his watch—seven thirty-five. He went out of the office, wandered toward Noni's, and had a drink by himself. Firelli's assignment. Firelli was posted missing, presumed dead. A statistic on the ledgers of the most lucrative business in the world. The old-time gangsters had run liquor, gambling and women. But a kilo of heroin was worth half a million dollars. Millions of dollars, pounds, Deutsche marks, francs, yen. Every currency in the world for the dust that brought dreams. A lot of his old associates had thought exactly the same thoughts he was thinking, and the process had only led one way. The old bureau had contained a hard core of corrupted officers, men who stole impounded drugs and resold them on the market. Men who took bribes, suppressed evidence, gave protection. The Mafia had reached them all. He had known many of them, but he had never taken anything.

It was after eight o'clock. He went to the telephone booth in the corner of the bar. He dialed a number but there was no answer. He'd have to try again when he got home.

He took the subway to Grand Army Plaza and walked to his home on Eastern Parkway. There was a smell of roasting chicken as he opened the apartment door. He smiled.

"Marie? I'm home." His wife came to meet him. She was thin and small, with dark hair tied back in a ponytail. He kissed her, slipping his arm around her waist. "How's my girl?" he asked.

"I'm fine," she said. "Hungry?"

"Starving," Nathan said. He kissed her again. Three years; three years of being married to the only human being he had loved in his life. At thirty she had the figure of a teenage girl. He liked being seen out with her—she looked so young. She was the most vulnerable woman he had ever known, and in the course of his career Nathan had seen some pathetic specimens of humanity.

He had met her in a police raid. She had been working as a waitress in a coffee shop which was a known meeting place for addicts in the East Village. He remembered the wispy, hollow-eyed girl, trembling and mute with fear, standing against a wall while the arrests were made. Something touched a sympathy in him he didn't know existed, and he hadn't arrested her, although he'd known immediately that she wasn't clean.

The next night he was back at the coffee shop, looking for her. She had left there, but she wasn't difficult to find. She had another job, cleaning up in a seedy hotel. She worried him—it was like a toothache. He felt none of the contempt most addicts inspired in him. He bought her a meal she didn't eat, and tried to get her to talk about herself. But he was a cop, and she just sat and stared at him. She'd been seeing Nathan for two months when she confessed she was on heroin.

"You can't go on seeing me," she had said, quite without warning, when they were walking through Prospect Park on his Sunday off. "I'm hooked on the stuff. So thanks for everything and good-by." She had turned and rushed off. It took Nathan a few seconds to catch up with her. She was crying, and that was when he decided he would have to marry her. Someone had to take care of her.

He looked at her tenderly as they ate their evening meal. She was the exception, the single statistic that meant success. She had taken a cure, under Nathan's direction, and she married him clean. And she'd stayed clean. She was safe. She was house-proud, frugal, a good cook, and he loved her so much that the emotion was a pain. He helped her clear the table and dried the dishes.

It was almost ten o'clock when he went to the telephone. "Get me a cup of coffee, honey." He sent her back to the kitchen as he dialed. "This is Nathan." He lowered his voice and glanced at the door. "There's another pigeon being trained. Yeah—as soon as I know, I will. But the heat's on. Let your end know." He hung up just before the door opened and Marie came in with two cups.

In a dozen years they had never gotten to him, and they had tried many times. But it was inevitable the moment he married Marie. They had the lever and they applied it. If he didn't do as they had told him, he would come home one night and find she'd had visitors. And the visitors would have put the needle in her again.

CHAPTER THREE

KATHARINE HAD TAKEN a lot of trouble to get ready, choosing a light-weight dress in pale yellow, putting on the little signet ring she hated. She carried a large shoulder bag. Inside it was the set of tiny bugs and the recording device Carpenter had given her. She was to spend the afternoon alone in the library, looking up her family records. The duke had said it was his favorite room. There couldn't be a better place to set a recording device.

Alessandro called for her at one o'clock, driving a wicked-looking Ferrari. He was casually dressed, wearing a canary yellow sweater and a silk scarf. He kissed her hand and told her how charming she looked. They lunched at the Loggia Restaurant on the Piazzale Michelangelo, set high up in the Florentine hills overlooking the city. When they came into the restaurant, everybody stared at them; several people smiled and waved. He guided her straight to their table, preceded by the manager himself. "I have already ordered lunch," he said, smiling. She thought quite dispassionately that a woman would have to be very brave or very foolish to become involved with him.

"What are you thinking about?" he asked.

"You," Katharine answered truthfully. "You're not what I expected."

"And what was that—some effete degenerate out of a Fellini film?"

"I didn't expect you to be so friendly," she said. "I'm only a distant relative—very distant. A quick trip around the villa would have been enough for most people."

"Believe me," Alessandro said, "that's what most people would have got." He laughed out loud. "You have a delightfully expressive face. Italian women don't make faces—they're so frightened of getting wrinkles! I love people who show what they feel."

"I can't help it," she said. "Is that how your mother looks so incredibly young?"

"Eighty-two years old," he said. "She is still beautiful. I remember when I was a little boy seeing her dressed to go to a reception. She was wearing the Malaspiga diamonds and she was like a vision. Then the war came, the diamonds were sold. My father had collaborated with the Fascists, you see, and we were outcasts for a time. We lost nearly everything."

"If you're so poor," Katharine said, "I don't understand how you can keep the villa and a castle."

"I didn't say I was poor now," he replied. "With my wife's money I began a business. I've made a great success of it."

"What sort of business?"

"Antiques. Furniture, china, sculpture, objects of art. I have a thriving export business and shops in the capital cities. Paris, New York, West Berlin. Stockholm's the most recent."

Alessandro had an appointment at three, so he left her at the villa after lunch. The house was very silent. "Siesta," he said. "They are all sleeping. There is the library; everything has been left out for you on the table. Enjoy yourself."

The library was cool; the shutters had been half drawn to keep out the sun. On the center table was a small heap of letters tied with brown ribbon, an album of photographs, a large envelope full of documents. She pulled a chair to the table and sat down. She pretended to read the letters, listening for any sounds of activity outside. She heard nothing. She went to the window and looked out. The library was at the back of the villa, and it faced the elaborate gardens. They were deserted too. She made a careful examination of the room. There was a fine marble table on a carved ebony base. She took the tiny bug out of her bag. It was fitted with a magnetic surface. The recording device which taped what the bug picked up was the size of a cigarette pack.

She ran her fingers under the marble table; they were black with dust. Nobody cleaned underneath the furniture. She fitted the little recording machine under the tabletop, hidden at the back. Two suction cups held it in place. The bug, which had to be a minimum of five feet from the ground, was more difficult to conceal. She looked around. The bookcase on one side of the fireplace was covered by a delicate grille. She stood on her toes to inspect the tenth row of books. They too were dusty. She slipped the bug inside the grille and clamped it to the wall. It had been surprisingly easy.

There was a desk near the fireplace and a telephone. She went to the desk and was surprised to find that none of the drawers were locked. Inside them were writing materials and a leather address book. It read like the Almanach de Gotha. Princes, counts, dukes, English aristocracy, half a dozen Blue Book American names, and then in a separate section, a list of business addresses. Paris, Rome, London, Stockholm, Brussels, Beirut and New York. E. Taylor, 493 Park Avenue, New York, and the telephone number. Alessandro could have been making as much money as he said out of exporting antiques all over the world. Or he *could* be growing rich on a different kind of trade.

She went back to the table. She would be asked about the letters, the family documents. She began to read through them, skipping large sections, memorizing small items. The admonishments of her great-grandmother to the lovesick Maria Gemma, refusing to receive her lover and threatening to disown her. It made Katharine wince for her grandmother.

At five o'clock a servant knocked on the door and announced that the duchess was expecting her in the salon for tea.

Both women, the old and the young, were waiting for her. Francesca gave her a slight smile and relinquished the seat next to her mother-in-law. "How pretty you look today," the old lady said. She wore a hat of pale straw, a silk dress of the same neutral color, and another pink rose, fastened with a diamond pin. She trailed a brown chiffon scarf in one hand. Her daughter-in-law looked stark and austere in black, relieved by huge matched pearls around her neck and in her ears.

"Sandro won't be home till this evening," the old duchess said. "He asked us to take care of you. Bernardo, pass the signorina some tea! And John isn't here either—he always looks after me when Sandro isn't here."

"Alessandro said John was talented," Katharine said. "But he didn't say how. Is he a painter?"

"He's a sculptor," Francesca said. "I think he will be one of the world's great sculptors."

"Oh, come." The old duchess gave a little laugh. "He's good, but only centuries will determine his greatness."

"Excuse me." Francesca got up and came over to Katharine. "I have something to do for my husband; I quite forgot. I hope you will come again." She held out her hand and took Katharine's in a limp clasp. Her black eyes were empty, cold as pit water. She went out of the room.

The old duchess sighed. "Oh, dear," she said gently. "I upset her by suggesting John wasn't guaranteed greatness. Now she will be angry all evening. I'm very fond of John," the duchess went on. "He's kind, and he amuses me. But I cannot pretend to admire him as much as my son and Francesca do. I shouldn't have contradicted her."

"She'll forget it," Katharine said. "I shouldn't worry about it." For a time there was silence. "I've had a fascinating time," Katharine said then. "Reading my great-grandmother's letters. It's been so kind of Alessandro to make them available to me."

"I know it's given him pleasure," the duchess said. "His family means so much to him. All the Malaspigas are very proud. Being forced to leave the castle helped to kill his father. It was difficult for us after the war. But Sandro promised his father he would make up for all that we had lost. We owe everything to him. He's an extraordinary man."

Katharine looked at the beautiful old woman, emphasizing her remarks with graceful gestures and that constant smile, and wondered how much she had deliberately suppressed a keen intelligence in order to accommodate the conventions of her generation. Men ordered the world in which the duchess lived. If one was fortunate, they governed wisely.

Katharine recalled herself to the purpose which had brought her there. "I didn't have time to read everything," she said. "Do you think Alessandro would mind if I came back?"

"But of course not. Come whenever you like."

"Thank you for tea," Katharine said. "I'll come again in a day or two."

"I shall look forward to it," Isabella di Malaspiga said. The bright smile was still on the duchess' face when Katharine left the room, but her eyes were looking somewhere else. Katharine realized suddenly that this was the recipe for her survival. Nothing and no one came too close to Isabella di Malaspiga. The gracious manner was an impenetrable barrier against the outside world.

As she began the long walk down the Viale Galileo to the bridge, Katharine envied the duchess' barred and bolted attitude to life. She herself had never felt more vulnerable or more uncertain. The life she had lived, even the nightmare of her brother's addiction and death, seemed to have blurred around the edges. It was as if she were losing her contact with the real world and slipping into that inhabited by her cousins. Alessandro di Malaspiga had disturbed her. She had to fight consciously against his charm. It was a mistake to analyze him, to probe into the reasons why he was what he had become, to pass opinions on his mother. It was getting too close, becoming involved. That didn't make it easier to go through his desk, to record his conversations. She had to remember that none of them were what they seemed.

Back in the hotel, she took a hot bath, trying to relax. Then she dialed the Florence telephone number which was the Interpol contact with the narcotics bureau in New York. It was the same number Firelli had dialed before he disappeared. A woman answered and Katharine gave the code word. A man came on the line. "This is Cousin Rose," she said. "I've made contact and I want to report."

"Then we must meet. I will be outside the Ghiberti bronze doors in half an hour. I will carry a large sketch pad under my arm, and wear a Panama hat with a green band. Use your call sign—mine will be Raphael."

In the Piazza del Duomo, she found him on the steps of the baptistery. He was standing a little apart from a group of tourists gazing at the Ghiberti bronze doors, which were one of the wonders of the city.

"I'm Cousin Rose," she said. He took off his hat, showing a semibald scalp with a fringe of curly black hair.

"Raphael," he said. "I'm glad to meet you. Let's go to that café over there and have coffee."

They found a corner table, and he tucked himself in, apologizing for the crush of tourists. He seemed a nice, ordinary man in his mid-forties.

After he had ordered, he asked quietly, "You're afraid, aren't you? Any intelligent person would be. Tell me about it."

"I don't know how much you've been told about me," she said. "But I'm just an ordinary person who has been given some quick basic training and sent out. I had a special motive."

"Yes," Raphael said. "Your brother."

She lit a cigarette. "Nobody forced me. In fact my instructor tried to scare me off. But I was determined to stop these people. Now that I've met the Malaspiga family I'm not sure I can do it. They're not at all what I expected."

"Nicer?" he prompted.

She hesitated. "Different," she said. "It seems impossible that they could be mixed up in this."

"You expected these Malaspigas to be monsters, Mafia villains, didn't you? Instead, you meet a cultured, charming family of Italian aristocrats, and believe me, charm is the passport issued to that class at birth. They've been friendly to you, and you don't like spying on them. Also you're in Florence, and what happened to your brother in the States seems a little far away. A bad dream. Am I exaggerating?"

"No," Katharine said quietly. "I don't think you are."

"Ben Harper thought this might happen," Raphael said, "and so he prepared me for it. Before you feel guilty about betraying family trust, you should know the real reason your brother died."

"What do you mean?" she said. "The real reason. . . ."

"Your brother spent six months in that clinic in upstate New York, didn't he? They told you he was rehabilitated, that he was off heroin and there was hope."

"Yes," she whispered. Tears had come into her eyes. The memory was vivid. Peter coming back with her in the car, looking alert, able to talk about the future; he'd put on weight; he looked in possession of himself for the first time in years.

"He was going to live," Raphael persisted. "For the first few days you stayed with him day and night, watching him, not quite believing it was true—and then you went out to the theater. He stayed at home. And when you came back, he'd disappeared. You never saw him alive again, did you?"

"No." She said it very low. "No. When I got to Bellevue he was dead."

"He was murdered," Raphael said. "When the police found him, he was lying in a back street, unconscious from an overdose. But your brother didn't go out to look for drugs. As soon as he was left alone, pushers came and forced a fix on him. They gave him a lethal dose and took him out of your apartment to die. You mustn't cry—people are watching you."

"Oh, God," she whispered. "Why didn't Harper tell me?"

"Because you didn't need to know it then; you had a strong motive. You know why they killed him, don't you?"

She shook her head. She found a handkerchief and pressed it to her eyes. Raphael was leaning over the table, holding her hand. To the onlooker, it seemed as if he were comforting her.

"The police run regular checks on the roster of clinics like the place where your brother went. They ran one around the time he left. The pushers weren't taking any chances on his breaking under questioning. So they killed him. It's the mark of the Malaspiga operatives. They never lose sight of their customers." He let go of her hand. "Still feel guilty about deceiving your cousins?"

Katharine opened her bag and put the handkerchief away. "You've played your ace," she said. "What you've just told me makes the duke my brother's murderer."

"As surely as if he shot him. Policies like that are made at the top. Would you like to tell me what you've found out?"

"He took me out to lunch today," she said. She felt shaken but in command of herself. "He told me a lot about himself and about the family. They were poor after the war. He said he'd financed an antique business with his wife's money and was making a success of it."

"He's made a considerable fortune," Raphael said. "The antiques couldn't account for all of it, but they're a good cover. What else?"

"He has an antique shop in New York at 493 Park Avenue. The name of the man who runs it is E. Taylor. I saw it in his address book this afternoon. There are shops all over Europe and one in Beirut. I set a bug and a recorder in the library. I'll be going back in a day or so and I can get it."

"You've been very enterprising," he said. "Congratulations."

"I also discovered that the duke and his wife went to America seven years ago. They stayed in Beverly Hills with a film star named John Julius. Will you pass this on to New York? There could be a drug connection."

"Of course."

"But what about the antiques?" Katharine asked.

"I ran a check in the customs on one of Malaspiga's exports to Paris, but we found nothing," Raphael said. "My opinion is that they don't send drugs with every shipment. The last was three months ago."

"Then you think the next one—"

"It could be. Your job now is to find out when the next consignment of antiques is leaving for the States. Go to the villa as often as possible. Make a note of anyone who visits there."

"I'll do my best," Katharine said. "There's something I'd like to ask you. How far did Firelli get?"

"We'll never know," he answered. "When he made his last telephone call, he wasn't alone, that was obvious. And whatever he was trying to tell us had to be disguised. *Angelo*—that was the only clue. It didn't connect with anything."

"It's horrible," she said. "It's worse than knowing for certain he's dead."

"Oh, there's no doubt about that. They murdered him because he was on to something. Firelli's dead, but we will never find him. Take my advice. Don't be afraid to be afraid. Fear breeds caution, and you need to be very cautious in dealing with your family. Don't imagine that a blood tie would protect you. Be very careful." Raphael got up and they squeezed out between the tables. "I think you should leave first," he said. "I will pass on this information to New York. You've done very well."

They shook hands briefly, and Katharine went outside. It was dusk, a warm, humid evening. The Florentines were setting out for the bars and cafés before going home. Everywhere the shops were open, lights blazing. The scene had a medieval quality, with the great cathedral and the baptistery brooding over the scurrying people. High above her, a bell began to toll; a flock of pigeons rose whirring in alarm and then as quickly settled. Bells began to ring in different parts of the city. The sound was indescribably sad and beautiful. A pair of sharply dressed Italian men paused as they came by her; one of them half turned back, a smile of invitation on his face. Katharine walked quickly on and found a taxi to take her back to the hotel.

Be very careful, Raphael had said. *A blood tie won't protect you.* Her handsome cousin would kill her as pitilessly as he had Firelli. As those who worked for him had killed her brother.

In her room there was a huge parcel wrapped in cellophane and tied with a pink ribbon. A card was pinned to the front with the familiar crest in crimson on the envelope: "Thank you for lunching with me. Until tomorrow. Alessandro." Under the cellophane there was a gilded wicker basket full of pale pink flowers, heavily scented. The same out-of-season roses his mother wore.

CHAPTER FOUR

FRANK CARPENTER FLEW to the Coast for a lunchtime appointment with John Julius. It was a day of travel-poster sunshine; everything sparkled in the heat. Carpenter took a taxi out to the Julius mansion in Beverly Hills. He knew California well and had never liked its artificiality. Hollywood reminded him of a fantasy city, like the streets and houses on a film set. In spite of the busloads of sightseers crawling past the mansions of the stars, in the Hills there were elegance and space, handsome trees and beautifully laid-out avenues. At the end of a long drive they came to a mock-Spanish villa, white stuccoed and red-tile roofed, set among flowering shrubs. A Hawaiian butler appeared at the door.

"Mr. Julius is expecting you," he said.

It was cool and green inside the vast reception area leading off the hall. One wall was constructed of multicolored glass, which gave a beautiful kaleidoscopic effect. Huge sofas, single pieces of modern sculpture in aluminum and stone—a room full of soft furniture and hard surfaces.

"Sit down, please, sir. Mr. Julius will be right with you."

Carpenter recognized the face as soon as Julius came into the room. Handsome, with gray hair, blue eyes, a well-preserved body in expensive casual clothes. Julius shook hands firmly, gave a professional smile and sat down opposite Carpenter.

"What can I do for you?" he asked. The appointment had been set up as an interview with a well-known film magazine. Carpenter took out his DEA badge and passed it across. John Julius looked at it.

"What the hell is this? I thought you came for an interview!"

"In a way I have. I want to ask you some questions, Mr. Julius."

John Julius stood up, pushed his fists into his trouser pockets and glared down at Carpenter. "I don't like being taken for a fool," he said. "I've a perfect right to throw you out."

"But you won't—unless you've got something to hide."

"Hona!" The call brought the Hawaiian running. "Hona, tell Jumie this gentleman won't be staying for lunch after all." He sat down. "All right," he said. "You've come into my home under false pretenses. But I have a duty as a citizen. If you've got questions, ask them."

Carpenter lit a cigarette. "About seven years ago you entertained the Duke and Duchess of Malaspiga here, didn't you?"

"Yes. They came on their honeymoon."

"Would you mind telling me how you met them?"

"I had met Sandro's father when I was making a film in Italy. He asked if I could show his son and daughter-in-law around Hollywood. They stayed with us for ten days."

"And do you still see them?"

"No," John Julius said. "We lost touch after my wife died."

"Could you tell me anything about them? Any recollection."

"He was impressive," Julius said. He leaned a little back in his chair and crossed one leg over the other, seeming to relax. "He was a beautiful man. I mean beautiful in the aesthetic sense. He could have made a fortune on the screen. He was the only duke I've ever met who looked the part. There were half a dozen producers fighting to sign him when they were over here. As for the women—well."

"How did he take it all?"

"As his due," John Julius said. "He was amused by flattery."

"And what was the duchess like?" Carpenter asked.

The actor's face closed like a fist. "Nothing much to look at. I don't remember her all that clearly," Julius said coldly. He wasn't worried about answering questions concerned with Malaspiga, but the young duchess had the opposite effect. He looked at his watch. Carpenter knew that he was going to cut the interview short.

"Did the duke and duchess go anywhere more than once when they stayed with you—were there any social contacts that might have stuck?" he asked. "This is important, Mr. Julius."

"They didn't make any real friends," he said. "Ten days isn't very long. Now, Mr. Carpenter, I'm afraid you'll have to excuse me."

"Sure. But don't you want to know why I'm asking about the Malaspigas? Or do you know?"

Suddenly Julius looked his age. "I expect I know," he said. "You've come to dig up some dirt connected with Elise. Well, you won't get anything from me. Hona! Show the gentleman out."

Carpenter walked slowly between lines of palm trees to the avenue. Before going to interview John Julius, he had made a quick investigation of the star and his background. He was a respected member of the film community. There were no scandals in his life—his marriage to a rich socialite, Elise Bohun, had lasted fifteen years, until her death. He had no children, and was one of the few Hollywood stars to keep his money. He had admired the Duke of Malaspiga, but he hadn't been able to hide his dislike of the duchess. There was pain, as well as defiance, in the suddenly aged face when he said those last words about Elise. Until that moment, Carpenter hadn't known there was any dirt to dig for.

Before leaving for California, Carpenter had asked Jim Nathan to investigate Edward D. Taylor's background and early connections. At eight thirty the night after his return, he and Nathan met in a corner booth at Noni's for a beer.

"Well." Nathan raised his glass to Carpenter. "So how was the sunshine state—black with smog as usual?"

"No. Sun was shining. Pretty stewardess on the flight back too. What'd you get me on Taylor?"

Nathan shrugged. "Nothing much. He runs a very classy antique business. What's the angle on the place?"

"I don't know yet, but it's a link with our new drug pipeline. Where was he before he opened the shop on Park Avenue?"

Nathan paused to light his pipe; he looked down at the bowl, stuffing the tobacco in with his fingers, before he put the match to it. "He had a place in Beverly Hills," he said. "He bought it, ran it for a year or two and then sold out. There's no connection with drugs there, Frank."

"Go on digging," Carpenter said. "We'll find something."

"Tell me," Nathan said. "Where's the pipeline coming from?"

"Italy. We're sure of that."

"It's Mafia controlled, then?"

"It must be, or they'd have wiped the operation out. They don't encourage competition. My guess is it started from small beginnings and is slowly building up in New York and spreading to the Coast. But all we have is circumstantial evidence. We've got to get proof."

"How?" Nathan said. His hands were moist with sweat. Carpenter was getting close. He had to find out what was happening, give Eddy Taylor warning. Otherwise something would happen to Marie. "What's your plan of attack?"

"Penetration," Frank said. "From inside."

"Damn! That's giving somebody a one-way ticket. Was that what happened to Firelli?"

"That was Firelli," Carpenter said. "It's the only way to nail them in a hurry. Give them a couple of years more and they'll have grown too big to cut down. How about another beer, Jim?"

"No." Nathan shook his head. "I'll go home smashed and Marie'll murder me. The way that girl bullies me, it's a crime!"

"The way she spoils you, you mean. You know something—you're the only happily married people I know."

"You're getting sour," Nathan said. "You mustn't let one bum deal spoil the whole game. Look for a nice girl and try again!"

"Nice girls don't marry cops," Frank said. "They marry nice guys with regular jobs, reasonable working hours and a hefty paycheck. I'm happy single, thanks."

"Okay. What's the connection with California, Frank? Anything to do with the agent we're sending in?"

"No," Carpenter said. He had a professional dislike of direct questions, even those asked by colleagues. "It's just a lead. But I'm hopeful. Give my love to Marie."

"I'll do that," Nathan said.

They parted, Nathan on the way to his car. Carpenter stayed on in the bar. He ordered himself a chicken sandwich. By a coincidence they had been sitting in the booth where he and Katharine had eaten their first meal together. When her message was relayed from Interpol, he hadn't shown his feelings; he was sure his relief was concealed even from eyes as sharp as Harper's. *A one-way ticket*, Nathan had said. But he couldn't afford to think about her. Getting personally involved would make it too difficult to fish around in California and drink beer with Jim Nathan while she faced the menace that had destroyed Firelli. He forced her out of his mind; the effort cost him more than he realized.

He thought of Nathan with his wife, sitting together watching TV. He felt unhappy and envious. He called for coffee and the bill, angry with himself for a weakness he didn't understand.

ISABELLA DI MALASPIGA was sitting in the garden. She wore a wide-brimmed straw hat, and sheltered under a canvas umbrella. The modern woman's passion for roasting her skin was incomprehensible to her. She waved at John Driver as he crossed the lawn. "John, *caro*," she said. "Come talk to me; I'm lonely." Driver went over and kissed her cheek. She smelled of the rose pinned to her blouse. The rose was her emblem, and her countless lovers had been notified of their selection by the gift of the one she was wearing. The old duchess had always had a sense of theater.

"John," she said, "I'm worried about this Katharine Dexter."

Driver pulled up a chair beside her and took her hand. "Why are you worried about her? Tell me."

"Sandro is interested in her. I know the signs. He's been restless; I hear him and Francesca quarreling again. This girl has taken his fancy—I knew it immediately. I spoke to my florist this morning, and he said Sandro had sent a huge bouquet of my roses to her. The florist was afraid he couldn't supply me until the end of the week."

"I wouldn't worry," Driver said. "She isn't staying long."

"You don't know my son. Not when it comes to women. I want you to warn her that as far as he's concerned it's just a game. Italian men never leave their wives; having a love affair with a stranger means nothing to them. Frighten her off. Persuade her to go home. Please, *caro*. I'm too old for family dramas."

"I'll try," Driver said.

"If only Francesca had had children. Sandro is the last of the Malaspigas. And I'm responsible. I suggested Francesca for him."

"She's everything a man would want in a wife, except for that one rotten piece of luck," John said. "She's sweet and gentle." For a moment his expression tightened. Under her heavily painted lids, the old duchess saw it, as she had seen it many times before.

"Don't you worry," Driver continued. "I'll take Katharine Dexter out and talk to her."

The duchess watched him walk away across the lawns to the house. Strong and faithful, simple and kind. Her son had taken him up, playing the patron to the artist in the best Florentine tradition. He had become part of the family, and he was in love with Francesca. The old duchess didn't care what they did, provided that it was done with discretion. But she cared very much about the disruption of her life. The war had broken her privileged world. Alessandro had restored it. Now she was pampered and secure once more. And that depended upon Alessandro.

The wife of a friend, a film actress perhaps—none of these would have disturbed the duchess as the American girl had done. She was different. And her son's reaction to her was different too. His mother knew it, with her sharp survivor's instinct.

"How DID YOU like my roses?" Sandro was smiling down at Katharine.

"They're beautiful," she said. "It was very kind of you."

The duke laughed. They were walking across the lobby of her hotel.

"Don't be so formal with me," he said. "It wasn't kind at all. I wanted to send them to you. My car is over there. First we will go to the Church of San Miniato, and I shall take you down into the crypt to see your ancestors; and then we will have lunch." He took her arm as they went into the street. The Ferrari crossed the Arno and slid through the traffic up to the Viale Galileo.

"What happens to your business when you take days off like this?"

"I delegate," he said. "Isn't that the secret of all successful tycoons? I make the decisions and other people do the work. I can see by your face you don't approve. My dear cousin, that is quite untypical of your family. We never show our feelings! Now you are smiling. That's better."

Katharine made a conscious effort not to be affected by his charm. Yet there were so many contradictions about him that she felt herself swept away in confusion. He had taken her arm again, while guiding her through the dark cool Church of San Miniato al Monte, explaining the history of the superb marble pulpit made for the Urbino dukes and given by them to the church. She had known men of culture before, but nobody like him. He made the incidents of centuries alive and relevant, and the touch on her arm was as light as it was positive.

"We'll go to the crypt," he said. "That's where all our family are buried. Except for two dukes who died on the Crusades."

A sacristan in a musty green soutane guided them through a side door and down a flight of steep steps incongruously lit by bare electric bulbs in the wall. At the bottom, he opened a massive carved oak door. The walls here were yellow stone blocks, the floor marble flagstones, and down each wall were the arched recesses where the city's great families had been buried. There were eighteen Malaspiga tombs. The effigies on the earliest ones wore armor. Heraldic dogs slept at their feet; their wives and children lay beside them.

"Now," the duke said, "look at this. This is Alfredo di Malaspiga, the fourth duke, modeled by Cellini. It's one of the greatest works of art in the world." The figure was life size; it rose from a bier in colored marbles. "Isn't it superb?"

The fourth duke had died at the age of thirty-seven, having outlived three wives and fathered eleven children. He lay slightly on one side, an elbow bent, his head resting on his palm as if he were peacefully contemplating. It was an astonishing face modeled in bronze. A tracery of veins showed at the temple, the mouth was so mobile it could have moved.

"It's incredible," Katharine said. "It's you!"

"It's said to be very like me," he answered. "But that's not important. It is the quality of the work that matters. It is a shame that so few people see it; commissioning this statue and hiding it away must have been the only unobtrusive action of his life."

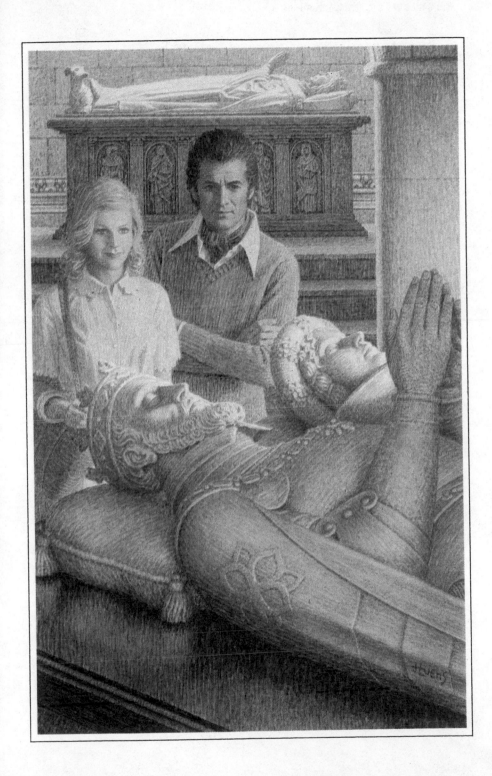

"He looks like a bad man," Katharine said quietly.

"It depends on what you mean by bad. He took, rather than gave, and no one would have insulted him by suggesting he was chaste. But he was a man of his time. A true Renaissance prince, a lover of women and the arts, a warrior, a statesman."

"And that's what you admire?" The air was colder in the crypt than when she first came in.

"My dear cousin," he said. "That's what I hope I am. In my own way. We'll go and have lunch now." When they went outside into the brilliant sunshine, she realized that she was trembling.

As if he knew she was frightened, Alessandro flung an arm casually around her shoulders, drove her off to a smart restaurant near the Piazzale Michelangiolo, where they were given a table in the garden. He set himself out to be gay. He spoke amusingly of his antique business, Italian politics and the coming American elections. She looked at him, remembering her brother, and was afraid he would see the hatred in her face.

"You've eaten very little," he said. "I think the crypt depressed you."

"It's hot today," she excused herself. "The crypt was most interesting. But I've been wondering—could I look through my grandmother's papers again?"

"Why, yes. We can go back and look at them together." He gave a slow, confident smile, as if he knew she was making an excuse to get back into the villa, to recover the tape from the little recording machine. "Are you enjoying yourself, Katharine?"

The question was so unexpected that she stammered for a moment, not knowing what to answer. When she did, it sounded clumsy and false. "Of course—I'm having a wonderful time! Why do you ask?"

"Because you look unhappy," Alessandro said quietly. "I'm an impetuous man—perhaps I've forced you into coming out with me. But if I'm impetuous, you are the sort of woman who can say no and mean it. I feel you've been unhappy. Is that true?"

She didn't want to discuss her life or expose the grief which he had inflicted, however indirectly. He reached across and took her hand. She felt her body stiffen.

"Is it your brother's death?"

"Yes," she said slowly. "He suffered very much, and I shall never be able to forget it. We were very close."

"I had a younger sister," Alessandro said. "We felt the same. We were companions as children; there was no fighting, no jealousy. After the war she caught meningitis and died. I was terribly upset. She was the only person I have ever loved."

"That's an extraordinary thing to say," Katharine said. "You must love your mother—and your father, what about him?"

"He also died after the war. He had never done anything to make me love him. He only knew how to make us all afraid. Even my mother feared him. He was an autocrat, someone you went to see to be punished. When he died I was relieved. As for my mother—she was just a beautiful visitor who came to my nursery when I was a child, kissed me and went out. She lived for her beauty and her love affairs. My sister was the only one."

"I thought Italian families were affectionate," she said. "We were all very close—my mother doted on us."

"The Malaspigas are not typical. We have a reputation for being heartless. As you will see, when you read some of the letters today. Your grandmother was very brave. I feel you've inherited this quality."

"What makes you think that?" Brave. Why should he say that?

"It's just a judgment I made when I first met you. I watched you come into that room and find us all sitting there. You were nervous, my dear cousin. Your hand trembled, and you have a trick of looking long and intently at people when you are not sure of them. As if to show that you don't care. It's charming. Cowards cannot do it."

Hours later, after a visit to his library, he took her back to the hotel. While alone in the library she had retrieved the tape, and it was safe in her handbag. "I have to go to the castle tomorrow to look at some imports," he said. "A big consignment has arrived for sorting and pricing before I send it to my shops. I will be away for two days. When I come back, will you have dinner with me?"

"Doesn't your wife mind?" It came out instinctively. She saw a flash of anger in his face.

"Francesca wouldn't mind at all. I'm not suggesting anything improper."

Katharine felt herself change color. "I never thought you were. I just thought she might object to staying behind while you had dinner with me. I know I would."

"American women object to everything their husbands do," he said softly. "Perhaps that's why there are so many divorces. I shall come at about eight thirty on Friday. John will look after you while I'm away."

CHAPTER FIVE

THE VOICE-ACTIVATED tape had run for twenty minutes. There were conversations between the duchess and Alessandro, inconsequential and rather formal, several telephone calls which didn't convey anything unusual, long gaps of silence, and then at last a call made by Alessandro himself.

"This is the Duke of Malaspiga. When can I expect the consignment of goods? On Wednesday—by the usual route. Excellent. I shall go to the castle myself and supervise the sorting. No, certainly not; this is our most important shipment so far. Arrange for Taylor to take delivery. Good. Good-by."

The most important shipment so far. This time there would be false compartments, secret places built into the furniture to carry the plastic bags filled with pure heroin. She reached for the telephone and asked for Raphael's number. A woman's voice answered, cool and brisk. Raphael was not available. "But I've got to talk to him! Where can he be reached?"

"I'll pass on your message," the woman said.

"Tell him to call me as soon as possible," Katharine said angrily. "It's urgent." She wondered if the same woman had answered Firelli's final desperate call.

She switched on the tape again and played it through. After the telephone call there was silence. Then she heard the sound of a door opening and closing and the Duchess Francesca's voice.

"Sandro, I want to talk to you."

"Not now, I'm busy." Alessandro's voice was cold and impatient.

"You're always busy when you want to avoid something. You had lunch with that American girl today, didn't you?"

"That's no concern of yours. I will not discuss Katharine with you."

"Oh, I've seen the way you look at her! You're happy, smiling—a changed man."

"I've told you, Francesca—I will not discuss her!" Now his anger came out, harsh and vibrating through the machine.

"You love to humiliate me, don't you! You've done it for years. Now it's this girl! I know you, Sandro."

"You know nothing about me." The contempt was acid. "You wouldn't understand what it means to meet a woman who's fresh and honest. You say I want her? Well, you're right. I can't think why you should mind."

The tape clicked and stopped. It had run out. Katharine had a dreadful sense of eavesdropping, as if she had been concealed in the room listening to that bitter private exchange. The references to herself, the hate and jealousy, the contempt . . . She felt sickened. She had been deluding herself that Malaspiga's interest was platonic, ignoring the way he looked at her, the sensuous touch of his hand on her bare arm. She was frightened of the desire which flickered around her like fire. He was a drug smuggler, her brother's murderer. And she knew, with horror, that in spite of everything, there had been times when she had forgotten what he really was.

She locked her tape recorder in the wardrobe and waited. At last the call came. Raphael was full of congratulations. "This is wonderful. I'll cable the message to New York immediately. They'll make arrangements to search the goods when they arrive. It'll take several weeks for them to get here."

"Would you ask them when I can come home?" She hadn't meant to say that—she was surprised when it came out.

"Yes," he said. "Good night."

She undressed and got into bed. She didn't expect to sleep, and when at last she did, it was a sleep tormented by confusing dreams.

She was awakened by the telephone. It was Raphael. "I've had an answer from New York. Go to the nine o'clock Mass at the Santa Trínita Church on the Piazza Santa Trínita. I'll be in the back row on the right of the Sassetti Chapel. Kneel beside me."

It was a bright, warm morning, although still early. The Santa Trínita Church was a beautiful old building. A mass in the Italian rite was being said in the Sassetti Chapel; there was little light except for the candles on the altar and a spotlight directed on the crucifix. Raphael was already there. She moved in and knelt beside him. He glanced at her and smiled.

"What did New York say?" she asked.

"They said to congratulate you. They believe this consignment will contain heroin, and so do I. When it reaches the States, they will examine it secretly, find the heroin and then arrest Taylor when he takes delivery. We've been tipped off that a large quantity of heroin has been processed in Naples and is on its way to a pipeline. This must be it."

"I hope you're right," she murmured. The church amplifier crackled, exhorted the Lord to be with them all, and a mutter of response came from the congregation.

"I mentioned that you'd like to go back," he said, "but New York wants you to get a look at the furniture before it's shipped and mark it for identification. That way, nobody can say the pieces were switched after they left Malaspiga Castle. I've brought something for you."

He passed a prayer book to her. A marker was hidden in the middle of it. It was the shape and size of a small pencil, only thicker.

"It's stain," he said. "And it doesn't come off without repolishing. All you have to do is make a small mark, perhaps a T, something which won't immediately be noticed. It works on marble too. Bronzes are no good—there you'll have to try and memorize what you can."

"I don't want to do it," Katharine said.

"Nobody can make you." Raphael's tone was patient. "But if you want to avenge your brother's death it will make all the difference. It's up to you."

"Lamb of God," the amplifiers invoked, "Who takest away the sins of the world . . ."

"Have mercy on us," the scattered worshippers replied.

"All right," Katharine said quietly. "I'll do it." She bent her head, her eyes closed. It was a thought, not a prayer, a groping in the darkness of doubt. Help me. I'm frightened.

They stood up to receive the blessing, and Raphael crossed himself. "You're being very brave," he said. "But you will have to be careful. Malaspiga is a little town; you will have nobody to help you if anything goes wrong."

"I know," she said. "I hope you said a prayer for me just now."

"As a matter of fact, I did. Call me in an emergency and I'll come. But don't do it unless you have to. Good luck."

He hung back, and she went out ahead of him, shielding her eyes against the sun. The inside of the church had been cold and musty with the smell of age. She walked slowly across the Piazza Santa Trínita. Back at her hotel, she found John Driver waiting for her in the lobby.

"Hi, there," he said. "I've come to take you on a tour of the city. Then we can have lunch, if you'd like?"

"I'd love it," Katharine said. "How very nice of you."

"I hate to admit it," he said, "but it was just as much Sandro's idea. He was afraid you'd be lonely."

"Yes," she said, suddenly chilled. "He told me you'd be around." Out in the busy street, she took his arm.

"I have a car around the corner," he said. "I thought you might like a tour of the galleries. Do you like modern art?"

"Why, yes," Katharine said. "I do."

"I hate it," he said. "But it has something to teach me, so I go along and study."

"You sculpt, don't you? The old duchess was talking about you. I'd love to see some of your work."

"You'd have to come to Malaspiga Castle to see that," Driver said. "And I don't think you'd like the castle." He took a corner with surprising speed. "It's a very gloomy, medieval place." He found a parking space on the Piazza Santa Croce, and they went into the famous Lanzarrotti Gallery to see an exhibition of abstracts by an avant-garde English sculptor. She found Driver a knowledgeable and relaxed companion.

They ate lunch in a simple *trattoria*, quite unlike the smart restaurants frequented by the duke. Driver asked her about herself, and she gave him the story invented for the Malaspigas.

"How about you?" she asked. "Are you going to stay here indefinitely?"

Driver shrugged. "Alessandro wants me to," he said. "And it's a big temptation."

"Do you like having a patron?" Katharine asked him. "Isn't it a little old-fashioned?"

"Of course it is." He smiled. "But then Alessandro is a Renaissance prince, born into the wrong century. He believes in my work. He'll support me for as long as I'll let him. His ancestors did the same. Your ancestors, I should say."

"That's a very good description of him," Katharine said slowly.

"How much do you like him?" She looked up in surprise to find Driver watching her. His gray eyes were worried.

"Very much. He's been so kind to me."

"Don't fall in love with him. You'd only get hurt."

"You needn't worry," she said quietly. "In the first place I don't go for married men; in the second, Alessandro's not my type. I'm not likely to take him seriously."

"Okay." He smiled at her. "And we're still friends?"

"Of course. It was nice of you to warn me."

"I was thinking of Francesca too," he admitted.

"She looks unhappy," Katharine said.

"She's miserable," John said simply. "She hasn't had children, and you know what that means to an Italian family. And Alessandro's the last of the line. He's never forgiven her for it. And she can't forgive herself."

"Francesca said you were a genius," Katharine remarked. She watched his face and saw a sudden change in the expression.

"She shouldn't say that," he said. "I have talent, but I don't have the immortal gift. Francesca just likes me because I'm nice to her. That's why she talks about my being a genius."

"I hope I'll see your work," she said, and she meant it. She felt he was a man on whom one could rely. She wondered what he would say if he knew what his patron was doing. They lingered over coffee, and her resolution returned. She leaned toward him. "Tell me," she said, "about Malaspiga Castle."

"THIS IS GREAT news," Ben Harper said. "When that consignment comes over here, we'll have them cold."

"Then why don't you bring her home?" Frank Carpenter said. "The job's finished."

Harper looked at him, making a bridge of his fingers. He had suspected Carpenter's attitude toward Katharine Dexter very soon after he undertook her training. It wasn't as impersonal as he pretended. "Frank," he said slowly. "I want her to get to that stuff and mark some of it, if she can. *Then* I'll recall her. How is your end of the investigation going?"

"I'm flying out to the Coast again tomorrow," Frank said. "I want to check on Eddy Taylor's connections, and I want a few questions answered about Mrs. John Julius. There's an old gossip item I want to look into. A piece in Harriet Harrison's column. I brought a Xerox copy with me."

Harper took the copy from him. A blurred inset picture of one of Hollywood's most feared gossip columnists was set on the top right-hand corner, surrounded by a halo of stars. The section mentioning Elise Bohun Julius had been ringed in red pencil.

All is not right between the lovebirds in John Julius' luxury nest up on Honeymoon Hill. In between entertaining our ducal couple, there's been quite a lot of angry squawking. The reason? Well, watch little Harriet's column to find out whether the lovebirds have got a cuckoo in their nest.

Harper gave it back to Frank. "So what was the scandal?"

"Harriet never made the revelation. If you look at the date, it was written around the time the Malaspigas were visiting. There's a later item mentioning a big party given for them, full of bitch and bite about the guests but nothing against the John Juliuses. Whatever Harriet Harrison was going to say about them, she thought better of it. But she might have something to tell me."

"Nathan hasn't made any progress on Edward Taylor," Harper said. "He says he can't find anything."

"I know," Frank said. "Maybe I'll do better in Hollywood."

The following morning he flew to the Coast, and spent the first part of the afternoon checking on Taylor's former antique business. The shop now sold Spanish rugs and ironwork, and was owned by an arty little woman with long hair, yards of colored beads and an Indian dress. She talked openly and at length. The shop had been selling antiques, she said, but it hadn't done well, and the owner had sold out to her. There was nothing, in spite of her middle-aged hippie appearance, to connect her with drug smuggling. He had to check on her as a routine, but he didn't feel it would yield anything.

Then he took a cab to the Bel Air Sanatorium, high up in the hills above Hollywood. The sanatorium was a smart, mock-colonial mansion, surrounded by beautifully kept grounds. When he asked for Miss Harrison at the reception desk, a bright, pretty nurse directed him to the first floor. "Room eighteen, sir. She's expecting you."

Harriet Harrison was sitting up in a chair beside a window, a blanket over her knees. Her hair was nicely dressed and still faintly blond; her eyes were blue and must have been her best feature. It was a petite face, lined with pain and bitterness. He introduced himself.

"Sit down, Mr. Carpenter. I've ordered tea," she said. "Now what can I do for you?"

"I'm grateful for the appointment," he said. "I promise not to tire you."

"Oh, you won't do that!" She laughed. "I'm so bored I could scream! I suppose you want information."

"Yes," Carpenter said. "Do you mind if I smoke?"

"Go ahead," she said. "And light one for me."

Carpenter took out the copy of the clipping. "You never followed this up. You were pretty tough on everyone else, but you left the Juliuses alone. Why, Miss Harrison?"

She was watching him with her beautiful, embittered eyes. They were carefully shadowed and mascaraed. "Are you investigating me—or them?"

"Them," he said. "And some friends of theirs. The Duke and Duchess of Malaspiga. They paid a visit to the Juliuses about seven years ago; do you remember them?"

"Of course I do. Newly married, on their honeymoon. *That* was a laugh. Why are you asking about them?"

"There's a big drug smuggling organization," he said quietly, "and we believe that the Malaspiga family are tied up with it. Please tell me anything you can."

"It was the only time in my life I suppressed news," she said. "And all the while I was sitting on dynamite." There was tension in the room; her long association with the film world had given her a sense of theater. She had a big scene coming up, and she was going to play it. "You want to know about Elise Julius and the Malaspigas?" She blew out smoke. "Okay, Mr. Carpenter. I'll tell you."

EDWARD TAYLOR'S APARTMENT was beautifully decorated and furnished with seventeenth-century French and Spanish pieces. Taylor held a drink in his hand, and it was trembling. He was facing Jim Nathan.

"You say you've taken the heat off me," he said. "How do I know that? And what about this agent they're planting?"

"I'm doing all I can," Nathan snarled. "I've given you a clean bill. And I'll get the agent's name—it takes time!"

"Well, time is what we *haven't* got," Taylor said. "I've got goods coming in—while they're sniffing around me I don't dare touch them! You've got to get me the details on this agent—if they penetrate the other end, we're in real trouble. I told Lars Svenson we'd have the details before he left."

"I'll get them," Nathan said. "Stop leaning on me!"

"We won't lean on *you*," Taylor said. His round face was dull and cruel. "It's your wife who'll be getting the visitors."

Nathan swung around, his fists clenched. Sweat shone on his forehead. "I tipped you off about Firelli," he said. "I'll find this one. But just don't talk about hurting Marie."

In the last two years Nathan had often thought of killing Taylor. But it wouldn't have protected Marie from the forcible fix that would start the whole nightmare over again. Even if he moved her away somewhere, and busted the whole organization to the bureau, he could never be sure that sometime, somewhere, the hoodlums known as rent collectors wouldn't find her alone one day. Dealers in narcotics had long memories. There was nothing he could do but work for them.

"Svenson leaves on Saturday morning," Taylor said. "You get me the name of the agent by next Friday. Or else."

CHAPTER SIX

DINNER AT THE villa was at nine. The old duchess sat at the head of the long marble table in her son's absence, with John and her daughter-in-law on either side. It was a long low room, paneled in rose-colored marble and lit by a superb Venetian chandelier. The furniture was painted in the soft colors of eighteenth-century lacquer, pale yellow and gold with touches of green and blue. The duchess looked at Francesca and at Driver and smiled.

"It always seems strange without Alessandro, doesn't it?"

"He'll be back soon," Driver said.

"I don't know why he ever goes near that horrible place," the old duchess said. "I hated it, but his father always spent the summer months there, and Sandro is just the same. He says his uncle Alfredo gets lonely staying there by himself." She patted her lips to hide a yawn. "I'm tired tonight." She smiled affectionately at John Driver and put out a hand to him. It was a gesture that had brought men running to her all her life. "Help me upstairs, please, caro."

John Driver took her arm. Over his shoulder he signaled to Francesca: wait for me. Then, supporting the duchess, he climbed the staircase to the first floor.

When he returned, Francesca was sitting waiting for him in the library. He came toward her and their hands reached out and gripped. He knelt by the chair and put his arms around her.

"Why were you so long?" she whispered. "What were you doing?"

"She wanted to talk. I'm sorry you were waiting."

"I spend my life waiting," she said. "Waiting for her to go to bed and for Sandro to be out of the house. So we can be together. I love you so much."

"I know," he said. "I know."

"What happened with the cousin today?" she asked. "Did you fall in love with her?"

"No," Driver said gently. "There's only one woman for me. You ought to know that. I took her around the galleries, and then I gave her lunch."

"And what did you talk about?"

"About Sandro," he said. "I told her to be careful, I told her not to take him seriously."

"I hate him as much as I love you," she whispered. "I hate them all."

"Shush, sweetheart," he said. "When the moment comes, I'll take you away. We'll have the rest of our lives together."

She reached up and kissed him passionately. "You are my life."

"Come upstairs then. Let's not waste time talking about him."

THE ASHTRAY WAS FULL OF cigarette butts, and the room at the sanatorium was stuffy with smoke.

"Why did you keep this quiet so long?" Carpenter asked.

"Because they had a habit of throwing acid at people who crossed them," Harriet Harrison answered. "Now, I don't give a damn. Nobody sees me anyway." She held out her hand. "I hope I've been some help."

"You'll never know how much. I think you've just saved someone's life. Could I come and see you again sometime?"

"Sure." She shrugged. "Anytime you want."

He took a cab back to the city and booked into a hotel. The next morning he had an appointment with one of the smart lawyers who looked after the affairs of the rich. Then he telephoned John Julius and asked to see him urgently.

The same Hawaiian manservant showed him into the reception lounge, but John Julius kept him waiting. When he came in and Carpenter saw the look on his face, he knew the delay was due to fear. He had been nerving himself for the interview—his breath smelled of whiskey. "Why have you come back here? What do you want?"

"The truth," Carpenter said. "I went to see Harriet Harrison yesterday."

"Oh, God." Julius sat down, his body sagging.

"She told me about Elise," Carpenter said quietly. "I'm very sorry. It must have been tough on you."

"Tough?" He gave a bark of laughter. "You've no idea! Living with it was bad enough, but keeping it quiet— Then Harriet dug it up. That woman—if you knew the lives she's ruined . . ."

"I can imagine. But you shut her up, didn't you?"

"I went to Elise's uncle. He said to leave it with him. I never asked how he stopped her."

"Harriet Harrison told me she had visitors," Carpenter said. "They promised her a face full of acid if she printed anything."

"Too good for her," he snapped. "Two of my best friends committed suicide because of what she wrote about them."

"When did you find out your wife was an addict?" Carpenter lit a cigarette. Julius' haggard face turned slowly toward him.

"Three months after I married her," he said. "I was very much in love. She was a lovely girl. I found the works in her bedroom. It nearly broke me. I wanted her to take a cure. She wouldn't. She said she could cope with the problem so long as she got the heroin."

"And she wouldn't have had any difficulty with that," Carpenter said.

"No," Julius agreed. "It was all laid on for her."

"Harrison told me about the young Duchess of Malaspiga," Carpenter said. "That was true too?"

"Yes." He covered his face with his hands for a moment. "They change," he muttered. "The drug changes them. Elise wasn't that way when I married her. . . ." Suddenly he looked like an old man; the façade of middle-aged charm had cracked.

"Tell me about Eddy Taylor," Frank said.

"How did you find out about him?"

"I went to see your wife's lawyer this morning. He told me about her business affairs. She owned the antique shop Taylor operated over on Sunset and she set him up in business. It didn't take much to find that out. But I want you to tell me how it happened."

"Elise met him when we had an apartment in New York and she was furnishing it," Julius said. "They got on well, and she staked him in a business out here. I thought he was a creep. But tell me, Mr. Carpenter—why are you digging all this up? Elise is dead."

"I want the people she was connected with," Frank said. "I want the racketeers who sell the drug and the smugglers who bring it in. And don't worry, none of this will be made public."

"That's good to know," he said. "We built up a life together. Maybe it was partly a lie, but some of what we had was good. I don't want to see it exposed now. I did care for her."

"I want to know about her family. Not the Bohuns, the others."

"Ah, yes." Julius smiled a wry smile. "The grandfather, the uncles, the cousins. I can tell you a bit about them. But you'll have to be careful. They were very proud of Elise. Just don't let any of them know you're snooping."

TWO HOURS LATER Frank Carpenter was on the 747 back to New York. He telephoned Ben Harper's office from the airport. His secretary said he had gone to Washington. "Jim Nathan's here," the girl added. "He wants to see Ben too."

"Put Jim on, will you?" Frank said.

Nathan sounded cheerful. "Hi, Frank. You get anything?"

"No," Carpenter said. "Nothing. Any luck with Taylor?"

"I've checked and double-checked. He's absolutely clean."

"Too bad," Carpenter said. He was ashamed to feel in clichés, but the small hairs at the back of his neck were on end. "I'll be seeing you, Jim."

Clean. Checked and double-checked. He'd known Jim Nathan for twelve years, ever since he joined the bureau. He was a straight man; he hated crime and he hated drugs. But he was lying. Carpenter had known about Nathan as soon as he learned that Elise Julius owned the Beverly Hills shop. Nathan would have discovered that in a routine inquiry. Instead he'd pretended that it belonged to Taylor. Carpenter had needed time to accept the fact that his friend was lying to him. Now there was no doubt, no chance of mere carelessness. Nathan had told lies, deliberate lies to keep Taylor clear of the investigation. And that meant he was on Taylor's payroll.

Carpenter got his car out of the airport parking lot and drove toward the city. Ben Harper was keeping a special file on the Malaspiga case—it included the plan for using Katharine Dexter as an undercover agent, her reports, Raphael's messages. Everything.

If Nathan was taking money from Taylor, then he was also working for the Malaspiga organization. If he got into Harper's office, he would look in that file. Nathan had been friends with Firelli too.

Carpenter's foot flattened on the accelerator. There was a siren fixed to his car, to be used only in an emergency. He stabbed at the button and it began to scream as he cut through the traffic.

BEN HARPER'S SECRETARY was a talkative girl. She gave Jim Nathan coffee from the machine and settled down to entertain him. For twenty minutes he kept on smiling and let the flow run over him. Then he made up his mind. There was only one way to do it. Otherwise she'd sit there talking till it was time to close the office.

"Betty." He leaned over the desk. "How about coming out for a drink?"

She stared at him in delight. "Why, that would be lovely! You mean right now? It's not six o'clock yet—but I guess I could lock up and go."

"I'll go inside and leave a message on Harper's dictaphone," Nathan said. "I won't be long."

"You can use my machine—nobody's supposed to be in there."

"Too confidential," Nathan said as he turned Harper's door handle. "I can't record in front of anyone." He went inside and shut the door.

"YOU KNOW"—SANDRO di Malaspiga leaned across the table toward Katharine—"I missed Florence while I was at home. That's strange, because I prefer the castle. I grew up there."

They were dining in a restaurant high in the hills at Fiesole, seated in the garden with a beautiful view over the city. "Perhaps I was missing you," he continued, "and that's why I wanted to come back." There was an expression in his dark eyes which was intense and frightening.

"Perhaps," Katharine said. She looked away from him. His hand, lying across the table, the gold signet ring gleaming on the little finger, moved toward hers.

"You don't like me to say things like that, do you?"

"No," she said. "It makes me uncomfortable."

"You talked about my wife last time—is that the reason?"

"Yes, of course it is."

He laid his hand over hers. "You're making a mistake, Katharine," he said. "There is nothing between us anymore—there hasn't been for years."

"Is that her fault?"

"Yes," he said quietly. "I don't owe Francesca anything."

"We're cousins," Katharine said. "Can't we just leave it like that? I don't want complications. I've very little time left before I have to go home."

"I know," he said. "That's why I can't afford to be patient. Normally I'm more subtle."

"Normally?" Katharine asked. Her tone was cool—the word irritated her with its arrogant assumptions.

"I don't live with Francesca," he answered. "And I certainly don't live like a monk. Does that answer your question?"

"I don't think I asked one," she said.

Suddenly he laughed. "Do you realize we are nearly quarreling? Maybe that's a hopeful sign. Come, drink your coffee, Katerina, and don't be angry with me."

It was the first time he had Italianized her name. She felt herself change color. She smiled, with a tremendous effort, thinking of Raphael and what she had to do. "You must make allowance for my American prudery. We take things a little more slowly at home than you do here."

"When are you leaving?" He thought how clear her profile was against the garden lights. She had a beautiful chin and neckline, a natural grace in the way she moved and sat still.

"I should go at the end of next week," she said. "But there's something I wanted to ask you—as a favor—before I leave."

"Please," he said. "I would be happy to do something for you."

"Can I go to Malaspiga Castle?"

"But of course! We will go tomorrow. All of us, so you will feel chaperoned—and you'll meet Uncle Alfredo."

"You've never mentioned him—does he live there?"

"Yes," Alessandro said. "Now he does. But when things were difficult for us after the war, he was put in a home outside Massa that was run by monks. I brought him back to Malaspiga. I think you'll like him. He's very eccentric, but quite harmless. He's known as the Prince of the Hats by everyone in Malaspiga. You'll see why when you meet him. I know he will love you."

"Is he your father's brother?"

"Yes. He was always a little strange—childlike. The war upset him. He hated the Germans. My mother was always terrified he would do something to provoke them. Before we married, Francesca suggested we send him back to the monastery. I wouldn't hear of it. But he knew, and he never forgave her."

"He must be very grateful to you for what you did for him."

"He is," Alessandro said. "He told me he'd be happy to die for me, and I believe he meant it. Even in senility, we're a passionate family." He smiled and squeezed her hand. "You'll love the castle. I have so many things to show you. Some beautiful treasures. My father sold everything, but I have bought most of it back. Bronzino, a Giorgione . . ."

"What about the antiques you went home to sort out?" Katharine said casually. "I'm fascinated to see what you sell."

It seemed to her he hesitated.

"Yes, you can see them. They are ready for packing, but that won't be done yet. They're going to the States. I have a magnificent Louis XV *poudreuse* which was discovered in a private house in Siena. That's the prize piece. And you'll love Malaspiga. The little town is almost untouched by the present day."

"You like that, don't you? John said you were born centuries too late."

"Perhaps," he said. "I find you very beautiful, Katerina. But not in the modern way. Bronzino could have painted you, with your hair in a gold net, and a dress embroidered with pearls. The more I look at you, the more I see what a true Malaspiga you are. When you come home with me, you'll see for yourself."

Home. *Firelli had gone to Malaspiga Castle and disappeared. They murdered him. We'll never find his body.*

"Are you cold? I thought you shivered." He was pushing back the chair, calling for their bill.

"A little cold. We should go anyway, it's getting late."

He drove her back to her hotel, and took her arm as they walked up to the entrance. He was taller than she was and she had to look up. "I loved Fiesole," she said. "It was a perfect evening."

"Then you should look happier than you do," he said. "I think a change will be good for you. I'm glad I'm taking you to Malaspiga. The car will collect you tomorrow at five. Good night."

He took her hand and kissed it; before she could stop him he had turned it over and pressed her palm against his mouth. She ran upstairs to her room, not waiting for the elevator. When she got into bed she began to cry.

CARPENTER CAME OUT of the elevator and down the corridor at a run. Outside the door of Ben Harper's offices he unbuttoned his coat, so that he could reach the gun in his shoulder holster. He didn't stop to answer Harper's secretary. The door of the inner office was locked. The light was on and he could see a shadow behind it. He knew Nathan was inside.

"Jim!" he yelled, wrenching at the locked door. "Jim—open up!"

On the other side, Nathan slammed the file drawer shut. Katharine Dexter. And she had been in Florence almost two weeks. He moved very quickly, grabbed the mike from the dictaphone and switched it on. Then he unlatched the door and came face to face with Carpenter. He gave his usual friendly grin. "Hi, Frank—what's the panic?"

Carpenter walked past him. "What the hell are you doing in Ben's office? Nobody's supposed to come in here."

Nathan looked pained, as any innocent man would at the suggestion he was doing anything irregular. "I wanted to leave a message on his tape. It's highly confidential. But I didn't have time. You were trying to bust the door down. What's this all about, Frank?"

Suddenly Carpenter felt at a disadvantage. He had accused, tried and judged his friend on evidence that was only circumstantial. "I'm sorry. Maybe I just got uptight after a long day. But Ben gets very edgy about anybody coming in here. He's liable to fire Betty for letting you in."

"Forget it." Nathan relaxed.

He felt in his pocket for his pipe. The movement turned him slightly, and Carpenter looked past him to the filing cabinets against the wall. He slid his hand toward his holster. "Jim," he said. Nathan looked up from lighting his pipe and saw the gun. "What were you doing in the Malaspiga file? You know that's got a highly confidential sticker on it."

"I've never touched anything in this room," Nathan exploded. "You've gone nuts! Pulling a gun on me—"

"You didn't quite shut the drawer," Carpenter said. "The edge of the file is sticking up. You were looking for something, weren't you? Something Eddy Taylor wanted to know."

"Now listen, you crazy bastard—"

"Keep your hands where I can see them," Carpenter told him. "I'm arresting you on suspicion. Go on into Betty's office. And don't try anything."

Nathan walked ahead of him. Outside, the secretary saw them both and opened her mouth in amazement.

"Get me Security," Carpenter said. He didn't look at her. He knew Nathan. All he would need was a second's inattention. "This is Carpenter here. I have a suspect in Ben Harper's office. Send up two men immediately."

"You're making a mistake," Nathan said. He looked white and grim. "He's nuts," he said to the secretary.

"If you're clean," Frank Carpenter said, "you can prove it. And Ben Harper will bust me for what I'm doing. Keep your hands out from your sides, Jim. If you try anything, I'll shoot."

Betty cringed back behind her desk. The two security men came in and Carpenter spoke to the senior officer. "I'm booking Jim Nathan on suspicion. He's to be kept in close custody until Ben Harper gets back."

"I want a lawyer!" Nathan snarled. "What about my wife—"

"Betty will telephone her and say you've been called away on a case. You can have a lawyer when Ben says so." Nathan looked from Carpenter to the two burly security men and knew he didn't have a chance. Fear made him cautious. Fear for Marie, not for himself. If he couldn't find a way, some way, of getting that message to Taylor . . . He went out with the two men and down to the security section under the building.

Carpenter turned to the secretary. "How long was he in there?"

"Oh, just a few minutes, Mr. Carpenter."

"Did he make any phone calls?"

"I'll ask the switchboard. You can't dial direct."

The answer was negative. So whatever Nathan had found out, he hadn't been able to pass it on. Carpenter went back into Harper's office. The file drawer was jammed open by the right-hand corner of the Malaspiga file, where it had been hurriedly shoved back. He didn't touch it. Ben Harper would need to see what had made him arrest one of the most senior agents in the bureau.

LARS SVENSON WAS a respected member of the rich industrial circle of Stockholm. He was an importer of antiques and works of art, owned a chain of retail furniture stores where cheap reproductions were sold, and was the head of a heroin smuggling ring. He had operated on a modest scale years ago, after a dubious career with the Swedish Red Cross during the war, where he discovered the purchasing power of stolen morphine. The profits from his activities during those years had set him up in legitimate business. His connection with the Malaspiga organization had begun two years before, through an introduction to Eddy Taylor. He had since made personal contact with the organization in Italy, and was about to go there now for his annual visit.

He stretched out on Eddy Taylor's sofa and his blue eyes went narrow. "You realize it's Friday night," he said. "What's this Nathan think he's doing?"

"He should have called today," Taylor said. "I told him you were leaving Saturday morning."

"One thing's sure," Svenson said. "I'm not taking any shipment at my end if there's a bureau agent on their track. And I shall tell them so when I get there! They won't be pleased with you. You're responsible for the New York end."

"I know that," Taylor snapped back at him. Svenson didn't frighten him; he was only a middleman like himself. But at Malaspiga there was someone of whom he was very frightened indeed. "I'm going to call his home," he said. "Right now." He went to the telephone and dialed the number.

"Could I speak to Jim Nathan? Oh, he's not? I see. I'll try next week." He banged the receiver down. His face was contorted. "That was his wife— he's been sent away on an assignment, and she doesn't know where he is, or when he'll be back!"

"He can't get the information and he's run out on you," Svenson remarked. "Maybe you should have paid him."

"I'll pay him," Taylor almost spat. "I'll pay him exactly what I promised!" He swung on one foot, and went for the phone again.

Svenson heard Taylor's voice, rising with anger. "You get over there tomorrow. And you fix her good, understand! No rough stuff, just fix her!" He hung up and turned to Svenson. "Nobody crosses me and gets away with it," he said. "Tell them at Malaspiga there's going to be a replacement for Firelli, to be on their guard against strangers. Anyone turning up unexpectedly, no matter what the cover story. Tell them I'll find out what I can, but my contact inside has gone sour on me." Taylor's plump face was pinched and spiteful. "The bastard," he said, not really speaking to Svenson. "That'll teach him."

"Okay. I'll pass on your messages." Svenson grasped Taylor's hand in his big fist. "Good-by," he said. "If anything does come through, call me at the hotel."

Taylor saw him to the door. He went to his bedroom and undressed and crawled into bed. He felt sick and tense. Everything he had built up for himself was in jeopardy—a big bank account in Switzerland, a thriving business, and a beautiful apartment, full of the treasures he loved. Whoever the bureau was sending out to investigate at Malaspiga must inevitably lead to him if they succeeded. He had already been screened once, but then it was Nathan asking the questions and telling the lies. Taylor disliked taking anything, but he knew he'd lie awake, worrying all night, so he took a mild barbiturate. A few minutes later he was asleep, his mouth ajar, his hands folded meekly under his cheek like a small boy.

"I WANT A lawyer," Nathan said. "And I want to talk to my wife!"

"You're not talking to anybody, Jim," Carpenter said.

There was a small wooden table between them, and Nathan faced him, snarling defiance. "I know my rights," he shouted. "You can't hold me like this!"

"I'm holding you till Ben gets back," Carpenter said. "Why are you covering up for Eddy Taylor?"

"I'm not covering for anyone. You're out of your mind! And how do you think my wife feels? Haven't you any decency?"

"Your wife was sent a message yesterday," Carpenter said. "You're the one that's worried, Jim. Why?"

Nathan covered his face with one hand. His skin was dry and hot; his eyes felt as if they were hot coals. All he had to do was get a message out to Taylor. Fear gripped him so tightly it became a physical pain. He looked up. "Okay," he said. "I'll make a deal. You let me talk to my wife, and I'll give you everything you need."

"You'd spill everything just to talk to Marie? Why?"

Nathan was calm now. It was a desperate gamble, but he had to take it. "She's pregnant," he said slowly. "That's why. The doctor says she's due to have the kid at any moment."

"Why didn't you say so before?" Carpenter said. "You stupid clown, why didn't you tell me?"

"Because I was mad," Nathan said. "Let me talk to her, Frank. . . . I want her to go to my brother. Right away. Tonight."

Carpenter got up. "Okay," he said. "You can call from my office. The regular switchboard's shut by now."

Two security men were in the office with them. Nathan took his place behind Frank's desk and picked up the phone; he pressed the switch to give him an outside line. He knew the figures by heart. It was one of the latest push-button machines. His fingers flew over the tiny buttons.

"Thanks, Frank. I appreciate this." The ringing began.

Taylor was deep in sleep. By the side of his bed the telephone shrilled. The sound screamed in his unconscious, clamoring for recognition. He turned over, fighting the noise.

In Carpenter's office, Nathan waited as the phone rang. Now he was sweating, trickles were running down his neck and under his arms.

"It's past eleven," Carpenter said. "She must be asleep."

Finally the ringing triumphed over the barbiturate Taylor had taken. Fumbling in the darkness, he unhooked the telephone. "Hello—"

Nathan could have shouted with relief. "Honey? This is Jim. How are you? Sure, fine, fine. Just for a few days. Listen, I want you to go over and stay with Bud. . . ."

Holding the receiver, Taylor dragged himself up in the bed. Nathan. It was Nathan on the line, talking gibberish. He tried to concentrate. The voice went on. "Look after you, honey. Sure. I'll be home soon."

Taylor cleared his throat. "Nathan—what the hell is this?"

"Listen, honey." Nathan went on talking. "I know it's going to be a girl. Understand that? A girl. And we'll call her Katharine."

Frank Carpenter saw that Nathan was smiling. Something in his head went off like a rocket. He reached out for the phone, but Nathan was quicker. He hung up. "Thanks," he said. "I feel a whole lot better now. She'll be okay."

Taylor clicked on his lamp. As he appreciated the significance of the last exchange in that garbled telephone call, he sat upright. *I know it's going to be a girl. Understand that. A girl. And we'll call her Katharine.* Nathan must have made the call under great difficulty. A girl. The agent was a woman, and the name was Katharine. Taylor got out of bed. He felt slightly dizzy. Damn pill. They were the weakest prescribed, but it was still confusing him. There were two things he had to do. Contact

Svenson. And something else. He looked at his watch. It was almost midnight. Svenson was staying at the Plaza. He got out the directory, found the number, and dialed.

"WHO DID YOU call?" Carpenter had Nathan up against the wall. "It was Taylor, wasn't it?"

Nathan made an obscene suggestion and Carpenter smashed his fist into his face. Nathan sagged but didn't fall. "You'll have to do better than that," he said.

Carpenter took him at his word. Before he finally lost consciousness, Nathan's last thought was that no matter what happened to him, his wife wouldn't be harmed.

TAYLOR HEARD THE doorbell ringing just as he was about to make the second phone call. Nathan had come through. Now he had to call the "rent collectors" off his wife. The doorbell rang long and stridently, and was suddenly accompanied by loud knocking. Taylor hesitated. Instinct told him what was outside. His nerves were dulled by the sleeping pill, and he stayed calm. He put on a red silk dressing gown and went to the door. "Who's there?"

"Federal agents. Open the door."

Taylor opened it. Twenty minutes later he was in Carpenter's office. He had never made the call to reprieve Marie Nathan.

CHAPTER SEVEN

MALASPIGA WAS A fifteenth-century town about a hundred miles from Florence. It clung to the skirts of a massive hill, green with olive trees and spiked by clusters of tall cypresses. The houses were pink and dusty yellow, roofed in red tile, with the church and the campanile dominating everything. The car drove through narrow rough-paved streets; the houses leaned toward each other, closing out the light. There was a little piazza with a statue of a man in armor on a stylized prancing horse. Katharine didn't need to see the inscription to know that it was a duke of Malaspiga. The Duchess Francesca was with her; John Driver drove. A second car with a uniformed chauffeur preceded them. The duke and his mother sat together in the back. It was a ritual, the procession of a feudal lord, and it moved at an appropriately slow pace. People saluted the front car, and several children waved and called after it. Whatever they were to the outside world, the Malaspigas were popular among their own. They left the town and began a steep climb up the side of the hill. The drop on their right became more precipitous as they went higher. Katharine turned to Francesca, who had been silent for most of the journey. "Is the castle at the top?"

"Yes. I hope you brought some warm clothes." Francesca's kohl-painted eyes looked at her with blank hostility. "It gets very cold in the evening."

"Thanks. I'll be all right." Katharine turned away and looked out of the window. She had never been in close proximity to her cousin's wife before. During the two-hour drive she had had an impression of coldness and bitterness, which was unpleasant, even if it was understandable. Alessandro, she thought suddenly, must have found it impossible to love such a woman. Then she reproached herself angrily for making this excuse for him.

A few moments later they rounded a sweep in the road and came upon a massive stone arch which was part of a wall, the Malaspiga arms carved above the gateway. Inside the gateway, beyond the courtyard, the castle itself rose like an illustration from a history book, huge and tall, with square turrets and cliff-high walls.

A manservant in a dusty black suit opened the car door for the duchess and Katharine. The sun was going down, staining the sky above the battlements with red. Alessandro's car was parked ahead of them. Katharine stood for a moment looking around her at the great fortress, its stones bloodied by the sunset, and a sense of cold fatality came over her.

"Katerina," Alessandro's voice said close by her side. "Welcome to Malaspiga."

Something very old woke in her heart, a sense of dignity before danger, of the contemptuous acceptance of death. It did not belong to Katharine Dexter and the New World across the ocean. She smiled into the face above her. "It's magnificent," she said. "But if I weren't a Malaspiga myself, I think I'd be afraid." Holding his arm, she went inside.

Katharine was shown to a second-floor bedroom overlooking the range of the Apuan Alps at the rear of the castle. It was filled with out-of-season roses; the hand of Alessandro was unmistakable. The room had a seventeenth-century walnut bed, massive chests and a ceiling-high cupboard, its doors painted with the coat of arms. After changing for dinner, she went down to the small salon. A tall old man was standing directly in line with the door. He had a beautiful head, crowned by thick white hair, and perched on top of it was an ancient fez with a black silk tassel. On his patrician face there was the shy expectancy of a child. Katharine came toward him and held out her hand. "Uncle Alfredo?" He nodded. "I am your cousin, Katharine. I am so glad to meet you."

His smile was like a sunburst. He took her hand and kissed it. "The pleasure is mine, my dear! Alessandro told me about you. But he didn't say how beautiful you were!"

Dinner was a long, formal meal, taken in a small stone room dating back to the fifteenth century. They ate by candlelight, and a manservant wearing white livery and gloves served the food.

Katharine looked around the table, and the faces seemed to belong to people from another age. Francesca, so pale and dark, seldom speaking and never seen to smile; her mother-in-law, beautiful as a girl in the dim light, swathed in dark green; Alessandro, in a dark blue velvet coat, seated like a medieval prince at the head of the table; the bland, senile smile of Uncle Alfredo as he chattered to John Driver; the sense of unreality was sinister. The conversation was general, and trivial—much of it referred to local people and affairs she didn't understand.

She saw the eccentric old man watching her and pretending not to. She got the impression he was much less unbalanced than he appeared. When they left the table, he came up to her, his vacant smile ready. "How do you like my hat?" he asked.

"I think it's very unusual," Katharine said. He nodded.

"It was given to me by an Englishman, years and years ago. I have over sixty different kinds of hats—what do you think of that?"

"Marvelous," she said, smiling.

"You're nice," the old man said suddenly. "I like you. Be very careful here. I'm not such a fool as people think." As she turned to join Alessandro, he repeated in a whisper, "Be very careful here."

MARIE NATHAN DIDN'T understand why Frank Carpenter had called her so late the previous night asking if she'd heard from Jim. She didn't understand why she hadn't heard, because if he was ever away from home he always telephoned her. She tried not to worry. She woke up early the next morning and cleaned the apartment carefully, comforting herself by doing Jim's laundry. She loved housework and routine. So much of her life had been spent in shiftless wandering and casual jobs—no settled home, no future, no background. Only heroin to offer an escape route. Jim had loved her and saved her. She would have died for him.

The doorbell rang at ten forty-five. In reply to her question through the door, a man said, "FBI, Mrs. Nathan. We've got a message from your husband." There were two of them—medium height, lightweight suits, soft hats.

One of them closed the front door, and the second one said quietly, "Now don't be alarmed, Mrs. Nathan," before he grabbed her around the shoulders and slapped adhesive tape across her mouth. She kicked and flailed while he pulled her into the bedroom and threw her on the bed. He sat on her legs and held her down. The other man had a leather case open on the dressing table. Behind the stifling tape she tried to scream as she saw the hypodermic. The second man grabbed her arm and tied a rubber band around it to raise a vein. Then he put the needle in. "Baby," he said, "you're going to love it." They got up and looked down at her. Her eyes were closed and tears were running down her face. The man who had injected her reached down and pulled off the tape from her mouth. "It's hit her already," he said. "Let's get the hell out of here."

Somewhere in her mind she heard the front door slam. Slowly she got off the bed. The working of the drug was familiar, terrifying in its intensity. *Jim.* She had to get to him—she had to get help. She fought her inertia as far as the front door. When she got it open and started down the short stairway to the street, she had forgotten where she was going and why.

LARS SVENSON ARRIVED in Rome at three o'clock in the morning, Italian time. He was due to fly to Pisa, and then go on to Florence by car next day. But Taylor's message couldn't wait. The agent would be a woman named Katharine. He roused a sleepy telephone operator at his hotel and placed a call to Florence, but there was no reply at the villa. He slept uneasily for a few hours and then made another call. This time the phone was answered by a servant who said the duke was not at home. He was expected at the castle later that day.

Svenson ordered a combined breakfast and lunch, and then began the difficult assault on the Tuscan telephone exchange at Massa, through which calls were passed to the town and the castle at Malaspiga. Through a storm of crackling he heard that the duke and his party had gone out. Cursing, Svenson slammed down the phone and went out into the afternoon sunshine of Rome.

KATHARINE WOKE EARLY. The mountains outside her window were snow-white in the morning sunshine; cold and dangerous, glittering with the sheen of the famous Carrara marble. Michelangelo himself had come to these mountains to choose the materials for his greatest works.

After dinner the night before, they had taken coffee in the small salon. She had listened carefully to all the conversation, noting the names of servants, hoping to hear that single clue left behind by Firelli. *Angelo.* But she had heard nothing.

She had slept unevenly. A mirror in a gilt Florentine frame showed her the reflection of a ghostly woman in a white dressing gown. She dressed in slacks and a silk shirt and went downstairs. She found Francesca waiting in the hallway.

"We are going to Mass," she said. "I think it would be better if you wore a skirt. They're very old-fashioned here."

"That won't be necessary, as I'm not going," Katharine said. "I don't go to church anymore."

"I see." The young duchess turned and picked up her gloves and a missal. "Sandro won't be pleased. He likes the family to go."

"I'm sorry about that, but he'll just have to excuse me."

"And what will I have to excuse you?" He had come up behind them and put a hand on Katharine's shoulder.

"Your cousin doesn't want to come to Mass," his wife said.

"I haven't been for years. I'd feel a terrible hypocrite," Katharine said to him.

"Then there's no problem," he said. "You shall do exactly as you like." They turned as Driver came up to them. "John isn't a Catholic," Alessandro went on, "but he can go this morning, and I shall stay and keep you company."

Katharine saw a look of hatred cross Driver's face. Then the old duchess appeared, looking frail and exquisite in misty blue, a tiny veil over the brim of her hat. The uncle followed her, seeming glum and abstracted. He wore a simple Panama hat and carried a cloth cap in his right hand.

The old duchess gave Katharine a smile and kissed her hand to her as they drove away. For a moment Katharine and the duke stood side by side in the courtyard.

"You shouldn't have stayed with me," Katharine said. "It's upsetting your wife terribly. How could you be so cruel to her?"

"I'm not cruel to Francesca," he said. "In Italy it is the custom for the women of the family to go to Mass. On all important feasts and many Sundays I go with them." He took her arm and she stiffened. "Don't be angry. Let's enjoy our morning. There are some lovely walks, if you'd like that."

She turned to face him, forcing herself to smile.

She didn't want to climb the terraced hills with him beside her, knowing that in some secret place they would stop, and he would try to take her in his arms. "I don't feel like being outside," she said. "Why don't you show me your antiques—this famous *poudreuse* you've discovered?"

For a moment he seemed reluctant. Then, "Of course," he said. "If it would amuse you."

The coolness inside the castle made her shiver after the heat outside. If they were going to the storeroom, she would need the marker. He gave her the excuse to get it. "You're cold," he said. "Go and fetch something warm." Upstairs in her room, she put on a long cardigan and hid the little marker in the pocket.

Alessandro was standing exactly where she had left him, watching the stairs for her return. They crossed the entrance hall, proceeding through a low stone archway into a long vaulted passage, its walls lined with suits of armor, and weapons arranged in geometric patterns above.

"After the war," Alessandro said, "the anti-Fascists came here and broke up the armor and scattered it. Parts of that suit over there, which is from Cellini's workshop, were found around the walls outside. This is a fine collection now. But it took a long time and a lot of money to restore it."

Katharine looked at the suits of armor and said, "They must have cost a fortune." As much as a consignment of heroin, she thought.

"Come through here," Alessandro said. "This is the old banqueting hall. We're living now in what used to be the servants' quarters. I had them modernized after I married Francesca."

The hall was a staggering size, the flagstone floor covered by a green carpet scrolled with crimson and black. A huge refectory table ran down its center, flanked by superb gilded Florentine chairs upholstered in faded crimson velvet. She stifled a wish to turn and run, to run out of the castle with its treasures and its history, to run from the man standing so close that when he turned their shoulders touched.

He reached out and opened a small paneled door. "Down here are the antiques," he said. "I'll switch the light on, but be careful. The steps down are very steep." They descended into the room below. It was a big storeroom, brilliantly lit by fluorescent lighting. Katharine slipped her hand into her pocket, gripping the marker. With her finger and thumb she eased off the cap.

There were a dozen pieces of furniture stacked neatly at the end of the room. A superb Italian chest, its front and lid painted and carved; two Florentine chairs, their arms shaped as Nubian boys; two exquisite tables, on one of which there stood a small marble bust of a child, and a Renaissance bronze inkwell in the form of a nest of serpents. The *poudreuse* was a gem of eighteenth-century French craftsmanship. It was made in tulipwood, the top, drawers and sides marquetried in a pattern of scrolls and wreaths of flowers.

"It's magnificent," Katharine said. She stepped close to it and pulled out the drawer. Alessandro was behind her; she had the marker in her palm, and she pressed the tip of it along the inside of the polished wood. Her hand was shaking as she closed the drawer again.

"Lovely things," she said. The chairs were next; she sat in both of them, again the marker slid along the edge of the seats. She went on making comments, moving among the pieces, pulling out drawers, lifting the lids of the chest.

Bronzes couldn't be marked; they had to be memorized, Raphael had said. The sinister nest of serpents wouldn't be difficult to identify. She was touching the marble bust of the child when Alessandro asked suddenly, "What do you think of that?"

"It's charming. It has such an innocent expression. But it looks modern."

"It is," he said. "It's John's work. There are a pair. I sell them for him, and he makes a little money. They don't command much, but he likes to feel he's independent."

"The more I look at it," she said, "the less I like it. It's sentimental, and after the first impression it cloys a bit."

"It's sentimental because it's commercial," Alessandro said. "John did a fine male nude last year. I sold that to Sweden, and it fetched quite a lot of money. One day he'll make a great name."

"And in the meantime you'll go on supporting him?"

"Of course." He smiled at her. "The treasures of the Renaissance only came into being because the Medicis and people like our ancestors commissioned most of them."

"Where does he work?" she asked. "He told me he spends a lot of time up here."

"He has a big ground-floor workshop on the northern side, where he can keep his marble and work in peace. He lacks confidence in himself, you know, and he won't let anyone see his work until it's ready. There's the companion to that bust." He lifted the little head and shoulders of a boy and stood it next to the girl. They made a charming pair, a study in innocence with a disturbing superficiality about them.

Katharine noticed an easel, the picture on it covered by a green cloth. "That must be something good," she said, touching the cloth. "What is it?"

This time his hesitation was unmistakable. He concealed it quickly, but he caught her arm, holding it tightly to keep her from moving the cloth. "A landscape," he said. "One of those dull Venetian views of the Grand Canal. I detest Canaletto, and I doubt this is genuine. But your Americans love that sort of picture. Let's go upstairs now and out into the sunshine. There's nothing more to see down here."

He steered her firmly toward the stairs, stepping aside to let her go ahead of him. She hadn't marked the marble children, and he had moved her away from the picture. She had seen only one corner of a massive, heavily carved Florentine frame. Hollowed out, such a frame could contain a large quantity of drugs. She must somehow get back into the storeroom and mark the statues and the picture.

NATHAN WAS DOZING in the detention room, stretched out in the chair, his head leaning against the back. He was sore and bruised from Carpenter's assault, but his mind was at peace. Marie was safe. He had kept his bargain with Taylor. The department had no proof against him. Even if Taylor had been picked up, so long as he kept his head and waited for the inevitable sharp lawyer to get him out, the worst Nathan could expect was to be fired. He could survive that. One of the less particular detective agencies would be happy to employ him.

When the door opened, Nathan was instantly awake. He saw Frank Carpenter standing there, an armed security guard behind him. "Ben Harper wants to see you," Carpenter said. "Upstairs."

They took the elevator eight floors up to Harper's office. Nathan was surprised to see a patrolman there. Harper was turning a pencil in his hands, around and around between his fingers. "This is Patrolman Regan from the Seventy-fourth Precinct," he said to Nathan. "I'm afraid we've got bad news for you."

Nathan looked from Harper to the policeman, who was young and looked uncomfortable, at Carpenter, who was stony-faced, and then back to Harper again.

"What bad news?" he asked. Now there was a lump in his throat—it was swelling up, choking him. "Marie . . ."

"Your wife's dead. She was hit by a car," the patrolman said. "Right outside your apartment. I was not more than twenty feet away when she came staggering out of the building like she was drunk or something. She just walked into the street and the car struck her."

Nathan was staring at him. A trick, his mind screamed, a lie . . . she isn't, she couldn't be . . . Regan was saying something else. "I was the first to get to her, and she was still conscious. She said, 'Tell Jim I didn't take it . . . they fixed me.' That was all. She died a couple of minutes later."

Fixed. Taylor had done it then. He hadn't phoned in time and Taylor had sent the rent collectors around to see her. Nathan was aware that he was crying. He found a handkerchief in his trouser pocket and wiped his face roughly. "Where is she?" he said. His throat was clear now, but a hammer was beating in his chest, every stroke a pain.

"In the city morgue," Ben Harper said. "There'll have to be an inquest. I'm sorry, Nathan."

"Where's Taylor? Are you holding him?"

"No," Harper said. "His lawyer came around half an hour ago, and we had to release him. But we'll get him back. You'll be glad to know he sprung you too. Considering he says he's never seen you before, that was a mighty friendly thing to do."

"Then I'm free to go?"

"Yes." Harper stood up. "Unless you want to talk to us. You're in this, and I can't believe you haven't got a reason."

"I'm not in anything," Nathan said. He blew his nose and shoved the handkerchief back in his pocket. "You've made a big mistake." He turned and walked out of the office.

Harper looked at Carpenter and shook his head. "We blew that one, Frank. I thought for a moment he was going to crack."

"You think he'll contact Taylor?"

"There's a twenty-four-hour watch on both of them from now on," Harper said. "Taylor's telephone's been tapped, and I had the apartment bugged this morning."

"And Katharine Dexter?" Frank Carpenter asked.

"Now Taylor's loose, we'll have to pull her out," Harper said. "Cable Raphael. She's to come home."

OUT IN THE STREET NATHAN stood slowly fastening his jacket. Having murdered his wife, Taylor had sprung him to freedom. So that he could be shut up before he talked. There'd already be a contract on him. He stepped forward and hailed an empty cab.

He told the driver to go to the morgue, settled back against the seat and found that he was crying again. He gave way and sobbed with his hands covering his face. His imagination kept showing him pictures. Marie opening the door, being grabbed, strong-armed inside, fighting as they put the needle in.

The cab was drawing up to a red traffic light. Harper's men would be following him. And very soon Taylor's men. Maybe just one. A contract killer—a crack shot. The light turned green, and at the same moment Nathan opened the cab door and jumped out. Within seconds he was lost in the crowds on the sidewalk. He took the subway to Fifty-ninth and Lexington and walked the rest of the way to Taylor's building. "Hello," he said to the doorman. "Mr. Taylor's expecting me."

"What name is it?"

"Mr. Lars Svenson," Nathan said.

When the name was phoned up from the hallway, Taylor panicked. Svenson should have been in Rome by now. . . . All the bureau needed was to pick him up and establish another link in the chain of coincidence. For a moment he shook with nerves; then his stubborn coolness reasserted itself. He told the doorman to send Svenson up.

Taylor was completely unprepared when he opened the door. He tried to batter at the body of the man whose hands were around his throat. He choked and writhed, groping for Nathan's face, but thumbs were pressing relentlessly into his neck and his vision grew dark. When Nathan felt Taylor go slack, he let go. He climbed off the body and stood looking at it. After a moment he spat on the dead man. Then he let himself out of the apartment. In the street, he got into an empty cab and gave the bureau headquarters address. He felt calm and numb. His wife was dead, and he had murdered the man who was responsible. His career was finished. The men who'd trusted him and worked with him were his enemies. He had put the finger on Katharine Dexter, and Frank Carpenter had heard him do it. There was no forgiveness for him, nothing to live for but revenge. Taylor was dead, but there were others. Twenty minutes later he was in Carpenter's office. "Get a stenographer in here," he said. "I want to make a full confession."

"COME, KATERINA," ALESSANDRO said. "We shall make a little tour before lunch." He took her by the arm and led her to the staircase. At the top they passed Uncle Alfredo. He was wearing a tall silk hat, which he raised to Katharine. He looked at his nephew. "You will take good care of her, won't you?"

"Very good care. I promise," Alessandro said. He pressed Katharine's arm as they walked on. "He has taken a great liking to you," he said. "You have a disturbing effect on your relations."

They passed under a narrow arch and out into a vast gallery, lit by windows high up in the wall. The light fell downward as if they were in a church. "This was where our family and their household used to walk and gossip and amuse themselves. The duke heard petitions here. I use it for my collection of pictures." He stopped. "This is the Giorgione. Isn't it beautiful?"

Katharine said simply, "Yes." Anything more would have been superfluous. The painting was of a Madonna and child with Saint Anne and the infant Saint John. The colors were as fresh and brilliant as if the artist had just finished the picture. She thought wildly, Why does he do this dreadful thing—there's more than a million dollars hanging there in front of me. "If you were so poor after the war," she said suddenly, "why didn't you sell this?"

"Because it was supposed to be a copy. It wasn't thought to be of any value. I had it authenticated afterward. Now nothing would induce me to sell such a masterpiece. I was thinking of keeping it for my son, if I had had one."

"You must be making a fortune out of your antique business," she said, "if you can afford to keep pictures like that."

He laughed. "I am. All Florentines are good at trading."

"You know the pieces you're sending to America." She tried hard to sound casual. "Perhaps I could look at them again."

"I'm afraid not," he said. "They're being crated and the men are coming in the morning. And this afternoon we're going to the Villa Romani."

She looked away, afraid to let him see her face. Tomorrow—the furniture would be packed up by tomorrow. And she had to mark that picture. It could be the biggest cache in the whole shipment. "Come and look at the view from the window," he said. "Then I'll show you the portrait of the wicked Paolo di Malaspiga."

She followed him to a wall embrasure; a little flight of steps brought them up to the level of the window. He put his arm across her shoulders. "You can see right across the plain to the coast," he said.

She stood stiffly beside him, staring ahead, hating the feel of him so close to her.

"The Malaspigas held the whole countryside around here for five hundred years," he said. She felt his face turning, moving imperceptibly downward toward hers, and with an effort she drew back.

"Show me the wicked Malaspiga," she said.

"Aren't you looking at him?" Alessandro asked.

"If you say so." Katharine hoped her voice was steady.

"He's here, in this corner. Nobody knows who painted him. I want you to look at the interior very carefully. There's an interesting story." The portrait showed a thickset man with a sallow complexion, a hooked nose and small black eyes, wearing the loose red surcoat and cap of the fifteenth century. He was standing in a stone-walled room, with a small arched window, no wider than an arrow slit, high on one wall.

"He built the eastern wall and the turret," her cousin said. "He was the second son, and tradition says he poisoned his brother. And his nephews. His wife was the daughter of a nobleman who held lands over by Bocca di Magra, and Paolo kidnapped her and married her as a hostage against her father. People who didn't pay his taxes were roasted alive. But he's really remembered for one of the rooms in the eastern turret. He was so pleased with it, he had it painted into his portrait."

"He sounds delightful." Katharine shuddered. "What was so special about the room?"

"I'm keeping that a secret," he said. "It's part of the grand tour we will make tomorrow. Now we'd better go to lunch." He caught Katharine by the hand and swung it as if he were holding a little girl. "And don't worry. I shall be discreet. This afternoon, after we've been to the Villa Romani and walked through the gardens, we will have a little talk. I can see, my dear cousin, that you are not going to accept me without an explanation."

CARPENTER WENT DOWN to the detention cells with Nathan. He went inside and waited, while Nathan sat on the cot and bent down to undo his shoes.

"Is there anything you want? Coffee—"

"No." Nathan shook his head. He straightened, kicking his shoes off, and grimaced. Under the naked light he was sickly white.

"Why don't you tell me?" Carpenter said. "Why did you do it? You were the last guy in the world to go bent."

Nathan looked up at him. "You got your confession," he said. "I murdered that bastard because I knew he was going to put a contract on me. You've got his contact in Sweden and the connection in Italy. The next assignment coming from there is going to be full of junk. I can't give you any more, and my motives are my own business. I'd like to get some sleep." Nathan lay back on the cot. The hammers were breaking down the walls of his chest. He was not going to discuss Marie with anyone.

As Carpenter went out, the lock snapped into place. Nathan lay with his eyes closed, feeling the pain in his chest increase. Blow after blow, melting into one another until it was a single agony, running like fire down his left arm. Sweat ran down his face, and he groaned once before the embolism burst through from his heart and exploded in his brain.

A few minutes later, when the guard looked through the peephole in the door, he thought the prisoner was asleep.

CHAPTER EIGHT

FRANK HAD THE Malaspiga file out in his office. He wasn't going home that night until he had confirmation from Raphael that Katharine Dexter had been safely withdrawn. Nathan's evidence would give the Italian authorities enough to justify the arrest of the Duke of Malaspiga and of his associate, Lars Svenson. In Carpenter's experience, there was no loyalty among drug smugglers. There would soon be a general roundup of all Malaspiga's business partners.

He poured some coffee from a thermos and sipped it, reading through the file. Harriet Harrison's revelation—the morbid scandal of seven years ago, hushed up by threats. Elise Bohun Julius, gliding through the society columns, giving her famous Hollywood parties, and the reality behind the pose. A drug addict, the daughter of a Blue Book Pennsylvania lawyer, whose fortune came from an obscure Italian girl he'd met in college. A fortune founded on bootlegging, prostitution and the protection racket. Elise was the granddaughter of Angelo Zappone, one of the most feared and powerful of the Mafia crime syndicate that operated in New York State. No one had connected him with his daughter. She had taken her mother's name, but his power and money had made a judge out of his son-in-law, Richard Bohun, and reestablished the couple in the old Bohun house, previously sold because of debts. It had introduced his granddaughter, Elise, as a beautiful debutante in the best society. When, after her much-publicized marriage to John Julius in Hollywood, Elise had fallen victim to heroin, Zappone moved quickly to protect her. Since they knew of no cure, the family supplied her, and in consequence they had used her to set up Eddy Taylor.

Harriet Harrison had stumbled on a part of the story and had bribed one of the Juliuses' maids to obtain a drug syringe from Elise's bedroom. An analysis of the syringe showed traces of heroin, and Harrison had in her hands one of the biggest stories in her career. As a prelude to the final revelation, she had published the hint about the Malaspigas. Apart from the hypodermic, the maid had discovered something else. Carpenter remembered Harrison's face as she looked at him, the mouth twisted in a sneer. "It must have been some honeymoon! And then the husband caught Elise and the duchess together. The maid said it was a real Grade B Hollywood scene. But I never got to print it."

Zappone's emissaries had made sure of that.

Perhaps Malaspiga had been blackmailed. There were so many pressures the Mafia could exert. The duke might have been unwilling to start with, but the young duchess had given Zappone the means to involve the head of one of Italy's great families in providing cover. Then the fantastic profits from the sale of heroin provided their own motive.

Angelo Zappone had died three years ago; Carpenter remembered the wide press coverage given the funeral. The unknown king of crime. And the usual speculations as to who would assume his crown. It was ironic that the Tuscan duke should have learned so quickly from the Neapolitan peasant. Zappone's business interests, if that was the right description, had been dissipated among rivals—the kingdom had disintegrated. Nobody imagined that it had transferred its most profitable enterprise to Italy.

There was a knock at Carpenter's door and one of the night staff secretaries came in. "Cable from Florence," he said. Carpenter grabbed it.

UNFORTUNATELY COUSIN ROSE LEFT FOR MALASPIGA CASTLE TO COMPLETE MISSION AS INSTRUCTED. IMPOSSIBLE PROCEED AGAINST FAMILY WITHOUT HIGHEST AUTHORITY. THIS CANNOT BE OBTAINED UNTIL AFTER WEEKEND. ATTEMPT TO CONTACT COUSIN ROSE WILL BE MADE. RAPHAEL.

Carpenter threw the cable on his desk. She was shut off from any kind of help but a doubtful telephone link, in exactly the same situation as Firelli. If Raphael got a message to her, she might still get out. But if Taylor had passed on his warning to Svenson, then they were already too late. He dialed Ben Harper's private number.

"This is Frank," he said. "Sorry to call you at home, but I want permission to go to Italy. Tonight."

"Sorry, Frank. It can't be done. This is an internal Italian matter, in liaison with Interpol. We have no right to interfere."

"I've had a cable from Raphael," Carpenter said. "Katharine's gone to the castle. He can't be sure of contacting her, and nothing can be done to pick the duke up till they have their authority. They'll kill her, Ben."

Harper's tone was sympathetic. "I know how you feel," he said. "But I can't break the rules. From what Nathan told me, it's probably too late anyway."

For a moment Carpenter didn't speak. *Too late*. While they were holding Taylor that morning, the Swede was in Italy carrying the message to Malaspiga. "I'm taking leave," he said, "and I'm going. On my own time and unofficially." He hung up. He dialed TWA and booked a seat on the last flight to Rome that evening.

IT TOOK AN hour to drive to the Villa Romani. The old duchess decided not to go, and at the duke's suggestion John drove Francesca separately. Katharine's murmur that they could all go in one car had been completely disregarded.

"What's so special about the Villa Romani?" she asked as they drove. "Wait and see."

"You have a passion for secrets, haven't you? First it's that horrible man's room you won't tell me about, and now it's this villa. You make me feel like a naughty child."

For a moment his hand left the wheel and pressed hers where it lay in her lap. "It's because I feel like a child myself," he said. "Free and happy and excited to be showing you the things I know and love. Bear with me, Katerina. I haven't felt like this for many years."

They stopped at the end of an avenue of cypresses, tall and dark against the brilliant blue sky, having left the autostrada behind them. The duke got out, paid the custodian and took Katharine through the door in the massive iron-studded main gates. Fronted by a green lawn, encircled by a mass of camellia trees in full bloom, the Villa Romani gleamed like a fantastic wedding cake. White and pink stucco, a façade of classical statues, pillars and arches and curves; it only lacked the figures of the bride and bridegroom. Alessandro took her arm and turned down a side path. "This way," he said. "To the gardens."

The descent into the sunken gardens was from a balustraded staircase in mellow gray stone, guarded by life-size statues, flanked by a pair of nymphs holding conch shells on each shoulder. Everywhere there were statues—centaurs, goddesses, satyrs with leering faces, nymphs with open mouths. Another custodian, dressed in the faded blue of the peasant, came toward them, and Alessandro murmured something to him. The old man laughed and shuffled away.

Alessandro slid his hand down her arm until it closed over her wrist. "Let's walk this way," he said. Katharine thought at first there had been a cloudburst. There was a sudden rushing noise, and water rained on them from all directions—from the steps, the ground, the flower beds. Every statue was a fountain—water spouted from the mouths, the eyes, the conch shells. She heard Alessandro laugh and felt him pulling her. They began to run until only the way ahead of them was clear. There was a tall archway, built under a bridge at the far end. "In here," the duke gasped. "Quickly." Under the archway there was a grotto; as they went in, Katharine couldn't see in the dim, almost green light.

"Now! How do you like the Romani gardens? Have you ever seen a *giocchi d'aqua* before?" There was water on his face and his coat—she could feel drops in her own hair. "My darling," he said, "You're wet. . . ."

She knew what was going to happen, but she couldn't move. He had his arms tightly around her, and the kisses she had been dreading were being pressed on her mouth. She saw a great double cross spray of water shoot up at each side of the grotto entrance, sealing them off completely inside. She began to struggle with him. "Stop fighting yourself," he said. Her eyes closed, and she opened her lips to him. She felt his grip tighten and then relax. Then she wrenched her head back, and the wetness on her face came from tears.

"Don't do that! Let me go—"

"I love you," he said. The fountain outside the grotto sank and stopped as suddenly as it had sprung up. A wide pool of water gleamed at the entrance. Alessandro was still holding Katharine, looking at her with an expression she had never seen before.

"I'll never let you go," he said quietly. "You belong to me. I knew it the first time I saw you."

She stepped back, pulling his hands away. "I don't want to hear any more! It's time to go home." She walked out through the puddle, pushing her damp hair away from her face. He was behind her and then alongside.

"You kissed me, Katerina," he said. "Nothing you say can change that. But I made a mistake. I should have talked to you first."

Katharine could see John Driver and the young duchess watching them from the top of the steps. "I'll ask John to let me drive home with them," she said.

He caught hold of her wrist. "You do that," he said, "and I'll throw him out. If he's in love with my wife, he's welcome to her. But don't let him try to interfere with you!"

They mounted the steps together. "Well." Driver sounded false in the attempt to be cheerful. "Quite a surprise, isn't it? Great fun—"

"You should take Francesca there," Alessandro said coldly. "I can recommend the grotto." He walked quickly away and toward the gates, pulling Katharine with him. He opened the car door for her and slammed it. He got in and started the engine. Then he swung the wheel, and the car roared back down the avenue of cypresses and onto the autostrada. It seemed to Katharine that they drove for a long time. She didn't recognize the road when they swung off the autostrada through the last tollgate. She felt very near tears.

"Where are we going?" she said. "This isn't the road we took from Malaspiga."

"We're not going to Malaspiga," he said. "We're going somewhere where we can talk."

They were now on a narrow mountain road that wound and twisted upward through the cypress-covered hills. He drove slowly through a village dominated by a little sugar-pink church with its Tuscan bell tower. A soft rose was coming into the sky at the horizon's edge. He left the village and drew up by the side of a road. He leaned over and opened her door. Reluctantly she got out; he came and stood beside her.

Below them the ground sloped away for many hundreds of feet to the valley, where the river Magra was a stretch of silver, dotted with tiny boats.

Behind them towered the great Carrara mountains that had seemed so cold and sinister when she had seen them from the castle. Now they only suggested grandeur and peace, brooding over the lovely scene at their feet. Alessandro put a hand on her shoulder and turned her toward him.

"Monte Marcello. It is the most beautiful place I know," he said. "I was planning to bring you here so we could share it. But not like this, not with anger between us."

"I'm not angry," Katharine said. "You don't understand."

"No," he admitted. "I don't. You say you don't feel anything for me; but when you kissed me, you proved that was a lie. You think I'm just a callous Italian who humiliates his wife and makes a public show of his affairs?"

"I think you treat her abominably," Katharine said. "And I'm not in love with you, whatever you say."

"Then why won't you look at me when you say it?" He held her at arm's length. "Why are you afraid of me, Katerina—it isn't just Francesca. What is the real reason you fight against me and yourself? All right," he said. "You won't answer. Very well." He let her go and turned away, facing the magnificent view. "So we will talk about Francesca first. About our relationship."

"I don't want to hear," Katharine said slowly.

"You're going to hear. You owe me that at least." She looked at him. "Please," he said. "Listen to me, and then judge. I told you we were poor after the war. I told you I married Francesca and that her money was a consideration. That offends you, because you're American, and marriages have to be made in heaven, but we're not a sentimental people. I knew my duty to my family, and I chose a girl who had the right background and a personal estate which would help restore ours. But I was also very attracted to her. She reminded me of a Giotto painting, secretive and somehow out of reach. I wanted to have children and rebuild, with her beside me."

A light breeze had sprung up, and the olive trees on the terraced slopes below were gently fluttering their feathery leaves. Katharine looked down, gripping the parapet.

"For the first few days of our honeymoon she was in tears," Alessandro said. "When we went to America, she pretended to be ill on the boat. Something was wrong, but I didn't know what it was. I didn't realize that she hated men.

"In Hollywood, she avoided me even more. There were parties given for us, a lot of interesting things to see. I hoped she'd change. But when I saw the loathing in her eyes, how she'd stiffen when I came near . . . You would never understand what such a thing can do to a man. I think I could have compromised in some way, if I hadn't found her with Julius' wife. I went into the bedroom and saw them together. They were kissing, like lovers."

"Oh, God," Katharine said. The wind was rising, the trees below were swaying in agitation.

"I took her home," he said. "There was no divorce in Italy at that time, and even if I tried to get the marriage annulled, the scandal would have killed my mother. Fate had tried to give the Malaspigas a deathblow. I wasn't going to accept that."

Looking at him, she saw the face of his ancestor, the ruthless prince of the Renaissance, cast forever by Cellini into a mask of pride.

"I went back to Florence," Alessandro continued, "determined on two things. I would have a child with this woman—and I would see my family restored to everything they had lost. No matter how I had to do it."

He pressed her close against him, and she closed her eyes, fighting with all her strength not to give in. *No matter how I had to do it.*

"I forced her," he said. "I was without pity. I made love to her and I hated it as much as she did. But there was no child. Francesca won in the end. She was barren."

His hold seemed to be tighter, as if he would never let her go. "I built up my business. I studied hard, I became an art expert, an authority on Italian furniture and bronzes. I built a reputation, became a rich man. Perhaps I have done things you wouldn't admire, my darling. But they had to be done. For seven hundred years the Malaspigas have been part of Tuscan life. They aren't going to die out with a whisper of self-pity. History can be my judge."

He turned her to him, and she made no resistance. Her arms went around his neck and her body fitted into his.

"I love you," he said at last. "And you have told me that you love me, without any words."

"Take me back," she said. "Please, Sandro."

He brushed his fingers over her cheek. "Tears," he said softly. "I'll make them tears of joy."

CARPENTER HADN'T EVEN dozed during the eight-hour flight to Rome. His mind was savaging the problem, planning a single assault, unsupported by Interpol or the Italian authorities, on Malaspiga Castle. He was not a man ruled by emotions. He seldom lost his temper or his sense of proportion. But he had made up his mind that if Katharine had disappeared from Malaspiga, he would kill the duke. He no longer pretended. He had defied Harper in order to rescue her because he had fallen in love.

At the ticket office in Rome they told him he would have to go to Milan to get a connection to Pisa. In Milan airport, a notice informed transit passengers that there was a fifty-minute delay on the connecting flight. He went to the telephone and dialed Raphael in Florence. The girl in his office said he had gone to Rome. He was expected back next morning.

"Tell him," Carpenter said, "that I've gone to Malaspiga." He hung up and went outside to wait for the plane. He could guess why Raphael had gone. It was Sunday. He couldn't get the authority necessary to force a way into Malaspiga Castle with a warrant until after the weekend. And that kind of authority came from Rome. Without question, Katharine had not been reached in time.

THEY HAD DRIVEN back from Monte Marcello in silence. Several times during the journey Alessandro had quietly pressed her hand, and once he kissed it, as they waited by the toll on the autostrada. It was the most intimate silence she had ever known. She went upstairs to her room and closed the door. She saw her reflection in the mirror and was shocked. Her face was colorless, her lipstick gone, dark shadows under her eyes. She combed her hair, her hand unsteady. She had cried in the grotto at Romani, and again on the ridge of that windswept hill. He had wiped the tears away with his fingers, not understanding what they meant.

She hated Alessandro di Malaspiga and feared him. But now she knew she also loved him. Ruthless, a murderer, enriching himself by the most evil traffic in the world, responsible for the final extinction of hope for her brother. He talked of being judged by history, but it wouldn't be history who passed sentence. It would be the woman who loved him. The modern-minded, self-sufficient American girl who had left on Harper's mission had been taken over by another self, a stranger with alien feelings and traditions that were very old. She was a Malaspiga, in love with one of her own kin, and she knew by instinct the course that must be taken. She was going back to the storeroom that night, to see the picture and to mark it and the marble busts. Through her, justice would overtake her cousin, and whatever part of her survived, it would be purged. She changed into a plain black dress, painted her pale lips and went downstairs.

Alessandro was walking in the garden. He had changed his clothes and come down early. He was exultantly happy, and yet he wanted solitude.

From the top terrace, the view stretched out over the Tuscan plain, turned golden by the setting sun. As he walked, a lizard streaked for safety along the gray stone wall and vanished down a crevice. He climbed a flight of rough stone steps, their borders crowded with graceful blue plumbago, and at the top he lit a cigarette. It was a perfect evening, warm and peaceful—the scent of flowers and shrubs was strong.

She loved him. He blew smoke into the air, his happiness enlarging like the smoke ring. There was a step behind him and he turned. John Driver stood there.

"It's a beautiful evening," the duke said. "I wanted to be alone for a few minutes."

"Sandro, I've got to talk to you. This is crazy!"

"Walking alone in my garden before I spend the evening with my family?" The duke's tone of voice should have silenced the younger man.

"Bringing that girl here is crazy," Driver said. "I don't understand why you're taking the risk."

"There is no risk," Alessandro said impatiently. "Katharine is my cousin. I brought her here because she wanted to come and because I wanted to invite her."

"All right, all right. You show your cousin the family home. But you took her to the gallery and down to the storeroom. She's not a fool—she could notice something. . . ."

"I didn't know you were so nervous," the duke said, and his smile was momentarily cruel. Then it became friendly, and he put his hand on Driver's shoulder. "Don't worry," he said. "I'm not a fool either. Just because we know what we are doing, we imagine it must suggest itself to everybody else. This is nonsense. I can assure you there is nothing to fear. But any personal matter concerning my cousin is nothing to do with you. I hope you understand?"

"We're in this thing together," Driver said. "I'm a partner, not a bloody lackey. I say you should take her back to Florence and let me get on with sending the consignment out."

Alessandro looked at Driver calmly. "You're not a partner, my dear John, although you share in the profits. I shall do exactly what I like regarding my cousin, and you will keep quiet. Otherwise it is you who will go back to Florence." He turned and walked away toward the castle.

THE DUKE AND Uncle Alfredo were drinking champagne in the salon. The old duchess came in, looking a frail, exquisite figure in pink lace, her corsage of roses nestling in a ruby and diamond spray.

Alessandro kissed her on the cheek. "You look beautiful, Mamia," he said. The duchess smiled.

"Lovely, lovely," declared Alfredo. "Bella Isabella!" He swept a low bow, at the same time removing an embroidered velvet smoking cap. The duchess took a glass of champagne. She looked at her son and wondered what had happened at the water gardens that afternoon. He was in a gay, relaxed mood. The trip must have been a success. She had always thought that Alessandro was as cold and controlled as his father, devoid of deep feelings except pride and ambition. But she had never really known him at all. She had never seen him so happy, and she knew with a sad, jealous pang that the cause was love for someone else.

When Katharine came into the room, Alessandro hurried to her and kissed her hand. "I've opened champagne for tonight," he said. "I want to celebrate." Over the glass he toasted her silently. There might have been no one else in the room.

Katharine saw John Driver come in; he took a glass from the butler and wandered across to the old duchess. Some moments later Francesca came through the door and moved quickly to a chair near the fireplace. When the champagne was offered, she shook her head and turned away.

"Katharine," the old duchess said, "how pretty you look tonight." She had never called another woman beautiful in her life. It was a word she reserved for herself. She gazed at Katharine for a moment, her head slightly on one side. "You look quite different from when you first came. You look more Italian than American. Perhaps it's the way you've done your hair."

They were all looking at her—Driver with disapproval, Francesca with blatant hatred—but Katharine wasn't aware of anyone but the duke. The magnificent black eyes, blazing their message of love and pride, the chiseled lips curved in a tender smile. For a second her hand crept to her breast and touched it. She had never believed that love could be a physical pain.

"My mother is right," Alessandro said. "Your Italian blood is coming out. You must always wear your hair brushed back like that. It makes you even more beautiful."

At that moment the telephone began to ring. John Driver moved across to answer it. He listened for a moment, then turned to Alessandro. "The call's for you," he said. "It's Lars Svenson. He's in Rome."

THE OLD DUCHESS went to bed soon after ten thirty. And all but Alessandro followed. When Katharine got to her feet with the others, the disappointment in Alessandro's eyes was quickly hidden. He gave his lazy smile and said lightly, "Stay for five minutes."

"I'm afraid I'd fall asleep," Katharine said. "It must be the air here."

She knew what had to be done and she had made her decision to do it. She couldn't trust herself to be alone with him again. Betrayal. She loved him and she was going to betray him, but being what he was, there was no other course. She turned back and came to him. "I won't stay," she said. "But it's been a lovely evening. Thank you." She reached up and kissed him on the cheek. A Judas kiss.

When she got to her own room, she changed into a skirt and sweater, with slip-on shoes. She put the marker in the skirt pocket and sat on the bed to wait. It was a brilliant, clear night, with a full moon that turned the marble mountains into snow, showing the clouds floating past on what must be a keen wind. Her room was illumined by the moonlight. It was her good luck that it should be such a perfect night; finding her way to the banqueting hall in the dark would have been very difficult.

When it was eleven forty-eight by her watch, she got up and went to the door. It was superstitious to wait for midnight. There was no magic in the hour, no guarantee that she wouldn't meet him on her way downstairs. She very carefully opened the door and looked out into the corridor. It was shadowy and silent. She walked quickly and lightly to the stairwell. A rope guideline ran down the inside of the wall. She felt for this, held tight to it and climbed downward.

Slowly she tiptoed across the entrance hall and opened the door leading into the armory. In the bright moonlight coming through the arched windows she hurried past into the banqueting hall. It was silver and gray in the light from its great central window, and the long table could have been the feasting board of ghosts. She crossed at a run and came to the storeroom door. She pulled a small iron loop, and the door opened. She felt for the switch and snapped it on. Pulling the door closed behind her, she hurried down the steep stairs to the storeroom below.

Fluorescent lighting flooded the room—for a moment she blinked at the contrast. There was the furniture, ready for packing. The picture stood on its easel, shrouded in the green cloth. Someone had been back and covered the corner of frame. The marble children stood side by side on a table; they too had been moved since morning. She took the marker out of her pocket, slipping the cap off, and lifted the girl with both hands. She made a cross on the base, and as she did so, a hand fell on her shoulder and a voice behind her said, "I thought I'd find you here. . . ."

She turned with a cry of terror, dropping the sculpture at her feet, and she was face to face with him.

PISA WAS A very small airport, but there was a Hertz office, and Frank Carpenter rented a Fiat 127, small and fast. The night outside was warm and windless, bright with moonlight.

When he reached the autostrada outside of Pisa, his foot went down on the pedal until it was slammed against the floorboards. Soon he was touching 180 kilometers, and the little car was shuddering under the strain. A glance at his watch showed that it was close to midnight on the luminous dial. A big blue and white sign said MASSA 2 KILOMETERS, with an arrow on the right, and he slowed down for the exit lane. He stopped at the tollbooth, flung a five-thousand-lire note at the duty officer, who shouted after him to collect his change as he drove on. Now it was difficult to drive fast; the country road was narrow. There was a sign saying MASSA, but no indication of where Malaspiga lay. He pulled off the road to look at a map he had bought.

ALFREDO DI MALASPIGA had undressed, putting on pajamas and dressing gown, and then began sorting through his collection of nightcaps. There were a dozen little round ones, some of linen, others of wool—plain, decorated, with tassels and without. He tried on several before he made his choice.

Alfredo had always considered the head the most important part of the

human body. The soul must surely be inside the skull, allied to the brain. His obsession seemed perfectly sensible to him. He cared for the most vital part of himself and adorned it at the same time. When the well-meaning monks had tried to regulate his changes of hats and caps, he had reacted, first with violence and then with miserable apathy. But he didn't think of the monastery, except when he saw Francesca. She had wanted to send him back there—he knew that. He had enjoyed his dinner. He felt stimulated by the company of his family. He liked the beautiful blond cousin. Hats had not been his only interest in youth. He gave a sly little grin. He had liked blond hair; there was a girl in Malaspiga . . . long, long ago. His mind flitted, restless, touching on one subject and then another. The cousin was not only beautiful to look at, but she had admired his hats.

He wandered to the door. He was not supposed to leave his room at night. Alessandro would be angry. There was a danger he might trip and fall. He opened the door. Once, some time ago, he had left his room. He had been going to the kitchen for something to eat. He had gone downstairs and he had seen . . . He stopped, one hand cupped to his mouth. He gave a little groan of fear and distress. Never mind what Alessandro said. He had to go and tell the girl with the lovely hair that it wasn't safe for her to stay at Malaspiga. He wasn't such a fool as everybody thought. He began to creep down the passageway toward the stairs.

ALESSANDRO STAYED ON for a time in the little drawing room. He felt at peace. Closing his eyes, he thought of Katharine. His mother had been right when she remarked on how much she had changed. She seemed to have grown older, not in the context of age but of the indefinable wisdom and experience that denotes a mature woman. Perhaps Francesca too had matured; perhaps the adolescent instinct which had sought pleasure and fulfillment from her own sex had grown to normality. Alessandro no longer cared. He sensed that John Driver was in love with her and that in her chilly way she was responding, but this aroused no jealousy or interest. He needed John. Until John came into their lives, his business had been profitable, but not by standards that included restoring and refurnishing Malaspiga Castle. The castle had become an obsession with him. And the need to leave it for posterity, to erase the scars of war and poverty, began after his return from Hollywood, when he took shelter there without hope for the future. He had found it a forsaken shell, the weeds from the once splendid gardens creeping up to the outside walls. By the time he met Katharine he had built a school and a pediatric clinic for the town, brought modern drainage and electricity to its people, and was enjoying the selfish, hedonistic life of a rich man with no one to love but himself. He was the master of his household and his family, and he had come to terms with Francesca by ignoring her completely.

Although he didn't want to sleep, he went upstairs to his bedroom. He had been born in its huge oak bed, hung with velvet and damask, its headboard painted with the Malaspiga arms. Tonight it looked like a dark cave, vast and uninviting for one person. He wanted Katharine Dexter. He had almost despaired, until the moment in the grotto when in spite of herself she had responded. Again she had tried to escape him, slipping out of reach at the last moment. When he told her the truth about his wife and held her in his arms again, he knew he had won. He had never been so happy in his life. Or so in need. He wanted to hear her say she loved him, he wanted to wring the promise out of her that she would never leave. . . .

CHAPTER NINE

"OH, GOD," KATHARINE said. His hand was still on her shoulder, and he was looking down at her with a slight smile on his lips. "Thank God," Katharine whispered. "It's you—I thought . . ."

"You thought it was Alessandro, didn't you?" John Driver said. "What are you doing down here?"

She saw the look in his pale gray eyes and went stiff with terror. "I lost something—this morning. I was looking for it."

"You were looking for the stuff," he chided her. "I know all about you, Miss Dexter, so you needn't try to lie. There's what you were looking for, right by your feet."

She looked down at the little sculpture of the girl. Its nose had broken off, and a stream of white dust lay on the floor.

"It's made in two halves," Driver said. "The join is in the carving of the hair. I'd say there are twenty pounds of heroin inside that one head. The other one's full of it too."

For a moment Katharine thought she was going to faint. There was a pain in her shoulder where his fingers were pressing harder and harder into the skin.

Angelo. Firelli's clue. But only half of it, misheard down a crackling telephone line. Michelangelo, the sculptor.

"Don't pass out on me," he said. With his free hand he slapped her face. She raised her arm to defend herself, and immediately he caught it, twisting it savagely up and backward. "What were you doing besides looking?"

"Nothing," she gasped, fighting the pain as he bent her arm backward. "Oh, God, you're breaking my arm!"

He let her go so suddenly she staggered. She reached out for the table to steady herself, and the marker fell out of her clenched hand. "Ah," he said, "you were identifying the pieces. But since my little children won't be

186

going now, it won't do any good. There's nothing in the other things. Only in my sculptures. They may not be great works of art, Miss Dexter, but they've made me a millionaire. That's surely something for a poor hick Canadian who learned to carve by whittling sticks on a farm."

The plain face with the frank expression had become cruel and watchful. It was like a nightmare. "Why did you work for him?" she whispered. "You could have been a great artist. . . ."

"Work for him?" He snarled. "He thinks he owns me! He figures he's some kind of twentieth-century Medici. . . . You talk about talent! I wanted genius, not talent. I wanted to create beauty. When I was a kid, I borrowed a book on Michelangelo. I saw what he sculpted, what he painted. I knew that's what I had to do. I have the vision in my head. But not in my hands. Do you have any idea what it means to spend your whole life reaching toward something and to fail?" His eyes were feverish, blazing. She thought in terror and confusion that in some way he was insane.

"No," she said. "I don't know what it means. But I don't see what it has to do with smuggling drugs and making money out of murder."

"You're brave," he said. "You don't whine when you're caught. When Lars told me on the phone about you tonight, I was shocked. I liked you. I hoped you'd go home and get out of Alessandro's hair, but I never suspected you were a narcotics agent. A spy—what am I going to do with you, Miss Dexter? I'm going to have to shut you up somewhere while I think about it."

There was a second when he looked away. Fear made her incredibly quick. She flung herself sideways, eluding his sudden grab, and ran toward the stairs. She heard him bump into something and swear fiercely as he followed. She raced up the stairs, gasping, and on a quick impulse snapped off the light in the room below. She could hear him behind her as she pushed open the door into the banqueting hall. Silhouetted clearly against the brilliant moonlight stood Francesca di Malaspiga. She held a gun in her hand, pointed at Katharine.

"Don't move," she said. "I would love to kill you."

Driver was behind her then. He spoke to Francesca. "We'll have to put this one in a safe place," he said. His hand covered Katharine's mouth, pulling her head backward. "You go ahead, my darling, and be sure there's nobody around."

Francesca lowered the gun. "Upstairs?"

"I guess so," Driver said.

ALFREDO MOVED VERY slowly, taking one cautious step down the stairs and then another. At last he came around the corner of the stairway onto the bottom step. And there, crossing the hallway, he saw the same scene as the other time. Only now it was the cousin who was being taken. . . .

With a little gurgle of alarm, he cringed against the stairwell, watching as they forced her to the same door, leading to the same place. He turned and stumbled back up the stairs.

With Francesca gliding ahead of them, Katharine was hustled through the banqueting hall, her arm wrenched up behind her back, Driver's hand tight on her mouth. He half lifted, half dragged her through the armory to a door on the right of the entrance that was partly hidden by a leather screen. It led into a long stone passageway, lit by the moonlight. He eased the pressure on her arm and pushed her to walk forward. At the end of the passage they passed through a large room filled with furniture shrouded in dust sheets; at this point Francesca switched on lights. They passed through a door, and up a small winding stair which ended on a landing.

Driver took his hand away from Katharine's mouth. "You can scream your head off now," he said. "Nobody will hear you here." He turned to Francesca. "You stay behind, darling. I'll take her up."

There was another door. Francesca opened it, dragging the heavy latch up with difficulty. She reached in and snapped on a light. Rising ahead of them was a steep and narrow spiral stair. From the shape and the angle of the curve, Katharine knew they were at the foot of one of the castle towers.

"Go on up," Driver said.

Looking at the tortured stair, Katharine felt such a sense of horror that she leaned against the gray stone wall, trembling. "I can't," she whispered. "I can't go up there."

He squeezed in front of her and took her right hand in his, gripping it tight. The next moment she was almost jerked off her feet as he started up the stairs. Pulling and dragging her, he led her higher and higher.

"Uncle Alfredo!" Alessandro caught the old man by the hands. He had flung open the door to Alessandro's bedroom and stood leaning against the lintel, gasping for breath. Even if Alessandro were angry with him for leaving his room, he had to tell what he had seen. The duke brought him inside and closed the door.

"Are you ill, Uncle . . . what's the matter?"

"They're going to kill her! Stop them—for the love of God!"

"Be calm, Uncle," Alessandro said gently. "You've just had a nightmare. I'm going to take you back to bed."

"No! I went downstairs. I wanted a biscuit! And I saw them. Taking that poor child to the east tower! Just like the other one. It wasn't my business what happened to him. But I like her—she's our cousin!"

"Katharine? Who's taking Katharine to the east tower?"

The old man grew calm. "Your wife and John—I saw them dragging her across the hall. It was a man they took there the last time, and I never saw him again. You were in Florence." He opened his mouth to explain in more detail, but his nephew brushed past him and ran down the corridor. He raced down the stairs, crossed the hall at a run, opened the door behind the screen and ran the length of the passage. He went through the room at the end, then up a short flight of stairs that ended on a landing. There he saw Francesca. She was standing with her back to him, leaning against the wall. There was a gun in her right hand. There was only one door on the landing and he knew where that led. It was open.

FRANCESCA SHIVERED. SHE wore a sweater, but it didn't protect her from the chill in the atmosphere. She hated stone, hated the bleakness and the feel of it. Her earliest memory of the castle was one of revulsion, even before she came there as Alessandro's wife. She associated it afterward with the torment of her life with him. She had spent the first part of her honeymoon frigid with fear and disgust. She remembered her stay in Beverly Hills with gratitude. To the frightened, unhappy young girl, Elise Bohun had been comforting and kind. Motherless, yearning for the sympathy of her own sex, Francesca had responded to the older woman's solicitude and affection. She had let herself be petted, soothed. When the relationship assumed a different nature, Francesca found that it was satisfying something which recoiled from Alessandro. And Elise had told her of the delights of heroin.

She hadn't taken it herself, even when Elise came out to Italy, and they met in Rome. But she saw nothing wrong with anyone who did. And then there was the money. Alessandro was poor, and her fortune was modest. She liked beautiful clothes and jewels. When John Driver came to the villa as a student of sculpture—his introduction arranged by Elise—Francesca welcomed him. She owed it to Elise to do this favor. And her husband had not been able to resist the pressure put on him.

She balanced the gun in her right hand and looked at her watch. In a few minutes it would be over. Then they had to pack, drive off in John's car, and establish an alibi on the autostrada. When paying the road toll, he would call attention to her, using Katharine's name. It could be done all along the route, making certain some of the attendants on duty would remember their passage. Once in Florence, they would buy a single railway ticket to Pisa for the early morning train, and slip back behind the barrier, driving along the old coast road to Malaspiga before dawn. Driver had worked out the story since receiving Svenson's warning. He would say that Katharine had asked him to drive her away from the castle and her cousin's distressing attentions. He had left her at the station en route for Pisa. There would be witnesses to prove he had been with a woman named Katharine. Late at night and wearing a deep-brimmed hat, who could identify her clearly afterward? Before the full repercussions came from

189

America, she and Driver would have vanished. They had enormous wealth deposited in Switzerland.

There was nothing in the world she wouldn't do for John Driver. They had come together in mutual need. He was consumed with ambitions that couldn't be satisfied, and she with the guilt of her only love relationship, convinced she was an outcast. John and she had groped toward their love. He had shown her patience and tenderness, without reproach for her past. She had given him passionate gratitude. She loved him, and soon they would be alone together for the rest of their lives. Out of the shadow of the Malaspigas forever.

When Alessandro sprang on her, she gave a shrill scream of fear; the gun was wrenched out of her hand, and she was backed against the wall. She saw Alessandro's face and cowered away from him.

"Where is she?" Alessandro said. "Has she gone up to the east turret with John?"

"Yes," she whispered. "She wanted to see it."

"At the point of a gun—" Alessandro released her. "If anything has happened to Katharine, I will kill both of you." He threw her to one side and started up the spiral stairs.

WHEN THEY REACHED the top, Driver released Katharine. She pushed the hair back from her face and looked at him. He had switched on a light and it was harsh, coming from a bare bulb in the ceiling. Sweat glittered on his forehead, and he was breathing hard.

"Come on," he said. "I'm going to shut you in here for a while." He took her arm. There was a door set in the wall. It was blackened with age, hinged with massive wrought iron, and held shut by a bolt of wood that fitted into a socket in the wall. On the wall to the right, there hung an iron ring.

"In here," John Driver said, and pulled her toward the door. Panic overwhelmed her, a terror so intense that she found herself able to fight. She kicked and struck out at him, flailing at his face with her nails. He grabbed her, cursing and struggling. She shrieked wildly as he dragged her to the door, and managed to swing the wooden bolt upright out of its socket. The door opened; inside was blackness and a gush of fetid air.

"Okay." He grunted the word. "Okay—in you go! Give my regards to Firelli!"

He gave a violent heave forward and threw her through the opening. The sound of her own horrified scream echoed back at her as the door slammed shut. In the total darkness, her senses failing, memory overcame her. Malaspiga Castle. It had always sounded sinister—the signet ring with its wreath and its spike growing out of the corn . . . Cruelty and death, a death invented by a human monster. She lay in a heap on the floor and sobbed.

She knew now why she had fought against going up the spiral stair, why the sight of that door had made her fight like an animal. She was in Duke Paolo's special room.

"DON'T TOUCH THAT!" Alessandro shouted.

With his fingers reaching for the iron ring in the wall, John Driver jerked around to see Malaspiga standing at the head of the stairs. The gun was pointed at him. "Take your hand away from that ring," Alessandro said, "or I'll shoot!"

"You can't," Driver said. "Kill me, and she goes too." He stood there, his right hand grasping the ring, with a mocking smile on his face. "You don't understand," he went on. "She can destroy us all. Me, Francesca and you. She has to die, Sandro. Put down the gun, and let me get on with it."

"Don't move!" The duke took a step toward him.

"It's not what you think, Sandro," Driver said. "She didn't come here to find out about that. She's a narcotics agent. Drugs! That's what it's all about—millions of dollars' worth of heroin, stashed away in my crummy sculptures!"

"I don't believe you," Alessandro said. "Let go of that ring!"

"You don't believe me"—Driver almost spat the words at him —"you think I spent my time here working for *you?* Wasting my time on your little racket? I'm a millionaire! You want proof? Go and look in the storeroom— one of those little busts has had an accident. That's what Katharine found. We've been running a Mafia operation for the last four years. And you try telling anyone you didn't know about it."

"We," Alessandro said slowly. "You and Francesca?"

"That's right." Driver had regained his calm. "Be sensible," he said. "The operation's just about blown anyway. But we've made millions. I'll talk to New York and they'll cut you in. We'll wind up the business here and nobody will be able to prove anything. She won't feel anything, Sandro— it's very quick."

"If you pull that ring," the duke said, "I am going to kill you."

"She isn't worth it," Driver said. "Jail for life, think of that. Think what would happen to your mother. Poor Uncle Alfredo."

"*You* can get away," Alessandro said. "Take Francesca with you. You have so much money—you can go anywhere. Just forget Katharine. I promise you, she won't say anything."

"I never thought you could be so naïve," Driver said. "You don't walk out on the Mafia. And you don't think you can open that door and expect her not to say anything? She's a trained operator for the narcotics bureau in New York. Like Firelli, that antique dealer who came down here. I had to get rid of him the same way. I'm going to pull this handle, Sandro. There's nothing like a *fait accompli* for settling an argument."

INSIDE, KATHARINE SLOWLY raised her head and lifted herself up from the floor. There was a feeble glimmer of light, and it came from a narrow slit in the wall. Numb, exhausted, she dragged herself upright. At any moment it would happen. Perhaps Driver was delaying this long out of sheer cruelty, leaving her to suffer the ultimate in terror and despair. She couldn't judge how far she had fallen into the room when he threw her inside. She could only find a wall by going to the window slit. She heard someone crying out to God to help—the voice was her own—and she began to stumble in the darkness toward that slit of light.

"STOP!" ALESSANDRO SHOUTED. "If you move it, I'll shoot—"
"You won't," John Driver said. "You won't throw everything away for one woman." His fingers gripped the ring, and with a sudden jerk he pulled the handle down. Through the thick walls and the door, Alessandro heard a single scream. He shot John Driver through the chest. He fired again, shooting repeatedly into the sagging body. Then Driver toppled over, and his hand slipped free from the ring. He lay dead at Alessandro's feet. It was a second or two before Alessandro heard the scream again and its significance sank in. He cried out, throwing the gun aside, and with all his strength he rammed the ring slowly upward into its original position.

KATHARINE HAD FOUND the wall. She felt the rough stone with her hands and flattened herself against it. Instinct kept her upright, terror kept her still. The crash came without warning, a rush of foul air blew up around her, and she began to scream. The floor had fallen away—there was a bottomless void at her feet. Now she was going to fall into the pit that lay under the room where Paolo di Malaspiga had imprisoned his victims. She gave a single cry of terror before she lost consciousness.

Alessandro found her lying face downward on the floor; the light from the corridor picked her out in the darkness. When he killed Driver, he had thought it was her death cry he heard. Even when he brought the floor back, with the second and third screams as evidence that somehow, by some miracle, the mechanism hadn't worked, he hadn't expected to find her. There was less than three feet of solid flooring around the perimeter of that awful drop into the castle bowels. He lifted her in his arms and carried her into the passage, stepping over Driver's dead body. The floor was patterned with blood. He laid her down a little distance away and knelt beside her, holding her against him. "My darling." His voice called her back. "My darling, thank God you're safe. I'm with you. . . ."

Slowly, Katharine opened her eyes. Alessandro drew her tightly into his arms and she felt his kiss on her forehead. "My darling," he repeated. "I killed him! I shot him at the very moment I thought he'd killed you—"

"Don't," Katharine whispered. "I don't want to hear."

He eased her upright, stroking her hair. He leaned forward and kissed her very gently on her cold lips. "I love you," he said. "I'm going to leave you for a moment, and while I'm gone I want you to turn your head and not look after me." He laid his hand against her cheek and gently turned her head away. She heard him walk away, and soon there was a muffled crash. It seemed a long time till he bent over her again. He helped her to stand, supporting her with his arm around her waist. He stooped and put the gun in his pocket. "I sent John the way he chose for you," he said. "I thought it was appropriate. Now we are going downstairs. I have to find Francesca."

IT WAS SOME moments before Francesca got her breath. Then the shots cracked out, echoing down the well of the narrow stair through the open door. She knew, as if she had seen it happen, that her husband had shot John. She moaned and swayed on her feet, and then began to stumble down the stairs. Out through the end room, past the passage and into the main hall. She ran to the main door, struggling with the massive bolts to open it. Weakness and despair defeated her.

She turned away and began to run up the stairs, not thinking where she could hide; instinct brought her to Driver's bedroom. She slammed the door and locked it. The sight of his coat across a chair, the objects she associated with him, induced an outburst of hysterical grief, which subsided as suddenly as it had begun. John was dead. Her husband would be looking for her. She had to get away, and the car was outside, ready to undertake the trip to Florence. She went to Driver's chest of drawers and began searching; she found a roll of money clipped together. If she could get to Switzerland, she knew the number of their bank account at Lausanne. There were millions of dollars there. . . . She could disappear where Alessandro would never find her.

She opened the door and crept down the stairs, holding her breath. Through the dining room and out, down a long cold corridor to the back door. Very carefully she slid back the bolts. Outside, the moonlight was brilliant. The walls reached up above her like cliffs; she moved along them, looking for the outline of the western tower. Beyond that, through a small gate, was the main courtyard where they had parked the car. The gate was locked from the inside; she turned the key and opened it very carefully. The car stood in the shadows, waiting.

ALESSANDRO WENT TO his mother's bedroom. The habit of his lifetime was to make sure she was unharmed. He had left Katharine in her own bedroom, wrapped up against shock, and had locked the door after him. He knocked on the old duchess' door and went inside. There was always a small light burning, in case she needed to ring for her maid, and by the light

193

of it he saw that she was awake. She pulled herself up on the pillows, her thick hair hanging loose around her shoulders.

"Sandro? What is the matter?"

"Nothing." He came to the bedside. "Did I wake you?"

"No," his mother said. "But you look strange."

It never occurred to him to tell her. He bent down to her with a smile and kissed her. "I wanted to talk to Francesca. I thought she might have come in here. She isn't in her room."

Isabella di Malaspiga shook her head. "No, I haven't seen her. Why don't you wait till morning? It must be very late."

"You go to sleep," he said. He took the key out of her door without her noticing and locked it from the outside, then started back down the corridor to look for Francesca. Chance made him glance through one of the windows as he hurried, and in the courtyard, clearly visible in the moonlight, he saw the car. He took the last flight of steps to the main hall at a run. He felt for the gun in his pocket. Francesca came out from the shelter of the gateway. She made a dash forward and dragged the car door open.

"Francesca! Come away from the car."

"No," she cried out in terror. "She's dead, and you're going to kill me!"

He took a step toward her. "Why did you do it?" he asked her. "Murder, drug smuggling—why, Francesca?"

"Because of Elise," she said. "You thought you separated us, but you didn't. We arranged everything, she and I. We deceived you. The blackmail was my idea. You thought you were being so clever, making use of John—and all the time it was you who were being used! Then *she* came, and you had to put us all in jeopardy because you wanted her! I'm glad she's dead! I don't care if you kill me—"

"Katharine is safe," Alessandro said. "This time it didn't work. It's John who is dead."

Tears crept down her face. "You shot him," she said. "I heard you. Now you think you'll save yourself by killing me. Then nobody will know. But she's a narcotics agent, a spy! So we've destroyed you, John and I. You'll go to jail for smuggling heroin, and she's the one who will convict you!"

She looked wild in the moonlight, her eyes wide and staring, her makeup smudged by crying. She wrenched the door back and sprang into the driver's seat.

Alessandro took aim at the car tire nearest him and pulled the trigger. There was a useless click. He had fired the last bullet into Driver's body. The car roared forward, heading for the main gateway. There was a screech as it turned, scattering stones, and for a second its red taillight glimmered. He stood looking after it, the useless gun hanging from his hand. She had gone. Insane with grief and hate, she was capable of anything. He turned and went back inside the castle.

When he unlocked the door of Katharine's room, he saw that she had gotten up. She was sitting in a chair and she had been crying. "You should have kept warm," he said. "You are suffering from shock!"

She looked at him. "You made a mistake," she said slowly. "You should have let them kill me."

He walked to the bedside table. There was a silver box with cigarettes. He took two and lit them. "Because of the heroin?" He crossed to her and gave her one.

"That's why I'm here," she said. "I enrolled in the narcotics bureau just to come out and get evidence against you."

"I know that," Alessandro said. "Driver told me before I shot him. My wife just taunted me with it." He stood looking down at Katharine. "Is that why you were crying—because you believe I am guilty and you'd have to give me up to the police?"

"I haven't any choice. Unless you decide not to let me go."

"Are you suggesting," he said, "that I would hurt you to save myself?"

"You killed Firelli. He died in that dreadful room."

"I see." He looked at the end of his cigarette, blew a little to make it glow red. "So I am a drug smuggler and a murderer. But I saved your life because I am in love with you. Isn't that a little silly?"

"It's what happened," she said.

"I don't think your American policemen would agree with you. The Italians might, because we're great sentimentalists. And I would be tried in an Italian court. Perhaps there's some hope for me." He played with the cigarette again. "Anyway, you don't have to do very much. Francesca will be the star witness."

Katharine looked up quickly. "She's gone?"

"Yes. I didn't kill her either. I couldn't even shoot the tires out on the car, because there weren't any bullets left. I'm not a very efficient murderer." Katharine got up—she felt weak and uneasy. He seemed to be mocking her.

"Where has she gone?"

"To the *carabinieri*. Probably at Massa. They might not listen to anything so sensational in Malaspiga itself."

"But she can't denounce you—she was in it too!"

"I don't think she cares what happens to her. She is determined to have vengeance. For John Driver. My good friend the sculptor. Before she gets back with the police, I want to show you something. Will you come and look at it?"

Katharine hesitated. The sight of him standing there, already ruined, with that smile on his lips, caused her unbearable pain. "All right," she said.

"Thank you," he said gravely. "I don't want you to think any worse of me than is deserved." He opened the bedroom door and held it for her to pass. They crossed the hall and went through the armory. He walked ahead and Katharine followed, past the sinister suits of armor, shimmering in the moonlight. In the banqueting hall he paused and looked back at her. "We're going down to the storeroom," he said.

With the light flaring above them, they descended into the big room below the banqueting hall. "Now," Alessandro said. "You wanted to look at this picture this morning. I wouldn't let you." They were standing in front of the easel, shrouded in its green cover.

"That's why I came back," she said. "To mark it for identification."

"Well, you shall look at it now." He stepped up to the picture and pulled the cover off. Katharine stared at it in disbelief. There, framed in a magnificent Florentine wood frame, was the Giorgione she had seen in the gallery upstairs. The same exquisite coloring, the same grace and tenderness. She turned to Alessandro. "You're selling this? But you said—"

"I said I'd never sell my Giorgione," he answered. "This is a forgery. That was John Driver's great talent. He was a mediocre sculptor, as you were quick enough to recognize. But he was a great forger of old masters. That picture was sold for a million and a quarter dollars to a New York collector. Through the agency of an antique dealer called Taylor. It is fully authenticated."

"But how? How could you get away with it?"

"Two art experts from Florence came here last week and saw the real Giorgione. They naturally gave it a certificate. John had spent a year in copying it. The collector believes he is buying the Malaspiga picture. As nobody will ever see my own Giorgione again, and as John's work is undetectable—he's deceived experts from all over the world—I shall never be discovered."

She said slowly, not looking at him, "And this was what you were doing? Selling fakes? Not heroin. . . ."

"Never heroin," the duke answered. He took her by the shoulders. "Look at me, Katharine. I never knew anything about the drugs. I sold fakes to rich men who thought they were getting a bargain at the expense of a poor Italian duke who was forced to sell his family treasures. I cheated, and if you like to think of it, I stole a great deal of money. But I give you my word of honor that nothing, not even the blackmail which started all this, nothing would have made me smuggle drugs. I beg you to believe that."

She gave a deep sigh, and suddenly put both hands to her face. "I do believe you," she said.

"If I were mixed up in drugs," he said, "I wouldn't have to sell anything else. Can you forgive me for being a forger?"

He held her close to him. Katherine didn't move; she rested against him for a moment with her eyes closed. She felt suddenly too drained to think or reason.

"Whatever happens," Alessandro said, "I can survive it, so long as you believe in me. Now we're going upstairs to wait for the police. And while we wait I will tell you how it started." He put his arm around her shoulder as they walked to the stairs. "I can tell that you believe me," he said calmly. "You've lost that look of misery."

AT A BEND in the road Carpenter saw the massive outline of the castle, silhouetted against the clear night sky, lights pinpointed from some of the windows. He drove fast, but carefully hugged the side of the road away from the precipice at the edge. He had no plan clear in his mind, nothing but the rescue of Katharine.

There was a sharp bend, and he had slowed, swinging slightly into the middle to negotiate it better. As he did so a double beam of dazzling light cut across the windshield from a blind corner. Carpenter wrenched the wheel to the right, slamming his foot on the brake. He felt the thud and scrape of his car as it hit the rock bank and he came to an emergency stop. And then there was a fearful shriek of tires and a shattering crash which reverberated through the darkness. He leaped out of the car and ran to the side of the road. Far below him, three hundred feet down among the pine trees, a burst of yellow flame flickered and then roared up in a cone of orange and crimson. The other car, traveling at top speed, must have gone out of control and careered over the edge. It was burning furiously—some of the surrounding trees had caught alight. There was nothing he could do for anyone who had been inside it.

He wiped his sleeve across his forehead; it was sticky with sweat. Among the tumult of crashing glass and metal, he had imagined for a second that he heard a woman screaming. He got into the car and drove on, holding close to the rock side. A few minutes later he saw the gateway of Malaspiga Castle.

CHAPTER TEN

"IT STARTED A year after I came back from the States," Alessandro said. "By that time I had established a small reputation as a dealer in Renaissance antiques and my business was growing."

They were alone in the small sitting room. He had awakened a maid and she had made them coffee. "I was in Florence when this American, Taylor, came to see me," he went on. "We spent some time talking about antiques, and he was very knowledgeable. He said he had a proposition to make to me. He had a shop in Beverly Hills, and I thought I might do a lot of business. But it wasn't that kind of proposition. Francesca was visiting her

197

sister in Rome that week. He took a photograph out of his briefcase and passed it to me.

"It showed my wife with Elise Bohun. I'll spare you the details. He informed me that it was taken at a Rome hotel only a few days earlier, and that Francesca had used her sister as an alibi to resume the relationship which had started in Hollywood. I was stunned. I knew then that I was going to be blackmailed. Taylor was very businesslike. Unless I agreed to his proposition, those photographs would be sent to the police and a formal complaint made. Also, there are several newspapers in Italy who would have welcomed a scandal about one of the old aristocratic families. There was no question of paying him off. He wanted me to front, as he put it. To pass through art forgeries and authenticate them as having come from my collection. He made it clear that there would be profit in it for me and that I need never worry about my wife being exposed after the first deal."

"Couldn't you have gone to the police?" Katharine asked him. "Why didn't you fight back?"

"There are many reasons. The first was my determination to protect my family name. No vulgar *carabiniere* in Rome or Florence was going to gloat over those photographs."

"How did John Driver come into this?" she asked him.

"He was sent out by Taylor to be the copyist. He enrolled at the Academy of Arts here, and we played out the charade of his coming to repair some of the statues at the villa and my becoming his patron. He worked on the forgeries at Malaspiga, and a year after he came, we sold a fake Domenico Ghirlandajo which was so good a collector in Canada paid half a million dollars for it. I became a rich man, working with Driver and using Taylor as my outlet. But I had no idea there was any other trade in progress. I didn't think Francesca knew any more about John than what I told her. A talented sculptor working for an exhibition and selling a few commercial pieces.

"Francesca said they had made a fool of me for years. She and that woman planned it all. Blackmail to get me involved in something illegal, and then the introduction of the smuggler. I liked John—that's ironical, isn't it? I knew he didn't have the talent he really wanted, and that forging other artists' masterpieces was some kind of revenge. I was genuinely sorry for him." He took her hand. "Do you think anyone will believe in my innocence? I can hardly believe in it myself."

"I'll tell them what happened," Katharine said.

He looked at her and smiled. "As a narcotics agent, your word will carry more weight than anything Francesca says. And I shall need your help," he said. "But the only way I can account for John Driver is by admitting that we were forging pictures. And I can never do that. It would mean certain disgrace and ruin for my family. I want you to promise me, Katerina, that even if it looks black for me, you won't think you'll help by revealing the art forgery."

"I can't promise," she said. "I can't stand by and see you go to jail for life for drug smuggling."

"The sentence would be nearly as heavy for selling fakes," he said. "Italians are very sensitive about their reputation in the art market. At least I can plead innocent to the drug charge and be telling the truth. You're disappointed in me, aren't you?"

"Yes," she admitted.

"Women are very illogical," he said gently. "When you thought I was a murderer and a drug smuggler, you still loved me. You could love the black villain, but you are upset because you find that in fact he is a little gray. I can see it in your eyes—they show all your feelings. I could have been a hypocrite and pretended I was forced to sell the pictures. But I love you, my darling, and I want to be honest. I saw the chance of doing everything I wanted for my family and for Malaspiga. The sale of the Giorgione copy will completely restore our fortune to what it was before the war. And my mother and Uncle Alfredo will have everything they want."

Before she could respond, the door opened. It was a maid. There was a car in the courtyard, she said. Somebody was ringing the bell at the entrance. Alessandro got up, drawing Katharine with him. "She has acted very quickly," he said. "I didn't expect them so soon."

He went out into the hall, still holding Katharine by the hand. They found Frank Carpenter waiting for them.

"VERY INGENIOUS," RAPHAEL and his assistant were in John Driver's studio. The evidence collected in the storeroom was already sealed up and documented. Several small pieces, two more busts of children, a classical torso, two feet high and hollowed out in the middle. "Very ingenious," Raphael repeated. He glanced over his shoulder at the duke. "Was this his idea or yours?"

"I told you," Alessandro said. "I knew nothing about it."

"I don't believe you," Raphael said. "You say you are running a legitimate antiques business, and the fact that your New York customer is a proven drug smuggler is pure coincidence. I find that difficult to accept. But your ignorance of how the heroin was brought here and smuggled out in sculptures worked by a man in your employ—I find that quite impossible!"

"It happens to be the truth," Malaspiga said. "And you have Katharine Dexter's word for what happened."

"Yes," Raphael agreed. "You shot this man Driver, and you saved her life. You say he and your wife confessed to murdering Firelli. It is perhaps a little convenient for you that both these witnesses are dead."

Raphael and a squad of special police had arrived in the early hours, and the duke was under arrest in his own house. Standing in the storeroom, he had watched Raphael and his men examining the pieces, seen the frame on the forged Giorgione split open. They had found nothing, except in the bust of the little boy, which was full of heroin, like its companion. Nobody mentioned the Giorgione. They weren't looking for art forgeries. Now, as he looked around at the work in Driver's studio, the enormity of the case against him couldn't be denied.

When the search was over, and Driver's studio was locked and sealed, Raphael demanded to see the old duchess and Prince Alfredo. "My mother is over eighty years old," Alessandro said, "and she knows nothing. My uncle is senile. In the name of common sense, if not humanity, I must ask you to leave them alone."

Raphael felt in his pocket for a cigarette. "When it comes to murder and drug smuggling, Duke Alessandro," he said, "nobody's sensibilities are sacred. I will ask your mother and your uncle to come down together. I am sending Katharine Dexter back to Florence. There is nothing more for her to do here." He was watching the duke closely, while pretending to adjust his lighter. He had the satisfaction of seeing his expression change.

"I should like to see her before she goes," Alessandro said.

Raphael shook his head; he held the little flame to his cigarette end and inhaled the smoke. "That won't be possible," he said. "I will see your mother and your uncle in the little room across the entrance hall. You will wait here. My men have orders not to let you leave the room."

"KATE"—FRANK CARPENTER had his hand on her arm—"Kate, he isn't going to hurt them. He'll just ask them a few questions." Katharine pulled away from him and went up to the duchess. The old lady was walking across the hall toward the room where Raphael was waiting. Uncle Alfredo, guided by a policeman in civilian clothes, was following behind.

Isabella di Malaspiga paused. "Something has happened," she said. "There are policemen here; that must mean there's been an accident. Where is Alessandro?" Her mouth trembled.

"He's here, he's perfectly all right," Katharine said quickly. Carpenter had come beside her. She could feel his impatience.

The duchess turned and spoke to Uncle Alfredo. "There's no need to worry," she said. "Alessandro will be with us; he will look after you. So come along, and we'll find him together." She held out her hand, and the old man hurried toward her. They looked so frail and helpless, the old lady holding her brother-in-law's hand, that Katharine's eyes filled with tears.

Carpenter put his arm around her. "You've had enough," he said. "I'm taking you out of here right now."

"I want to see my cousin," she said. "They're my family—I want to know what's going to happen to them!"

"Raphael's got a warrant for the duke," Carpenter explained. "The old couple will be all right. Don't worry about them. Come on now—it's all over for you."

He thought she slept during the drive back to Florence, until he saw her face as they stopped by a tollbooth; the lights showed that she was crying. He didn't say anything, because he felt sure a few hours' sleep would bring her down from the nervous peak which was expressing itself in tears. She was safe now and with her own kind. He had kept telling her so while Raphael listened to her account of what happened. Raphael himself had said very little, except that her part was over and she should leave the castle.

Carpenter drove to her hotel and came up to her room. She remembered the first day she arrived there, and the manager's personal attention because of the name Malaspiga on her passport. She had come to Italy to destroy the Malaspigas, and because she was one of them, she had succeeded. She opened her bedroom door and turned, blocking Carpenter's way.

"I'll rest," she said. "I'm so tired I can't think."

"I want to talk to you," he said. "But I guess it can wait." She saw how worn and tired he looked. He deserved something better than her frantic concern for someone else. But she couldn't give it.

"Raphael is bringing Malaspiga down," he said. "He'll want to see you, but I'll head him off till morning."

"No," she said quickly. "I'll see him this afternoon."

"Okay." He shrugged. "If that's how you want it. I'll come and pick you up." His tone was abrupt. He turned away without looking at her.

She lay on the bed, with an arm over her eyes, and woke hours later with the telephone shrilling beside her. It was Carpenter; he was downstairs in the foyer, waiting to take her to Raphael's office.

"YOU REALIZE," RAPHAEL said, "that you are my only witness? The contact in New York is dead; the bureau man who was spying for him had a heart attack; Svenson has vanished. The Duchess Francesca and the Canadian . . . There is no one who can testify against Malaspiga except you." He paused and looked at Carpenter. They were sitting in his top-floor office on the Via Vecchia. Below them the city was preparing for the evening. The shops were illuminated, and the cafés filling with people.

"You've had a rough time," Carpenter said. "He saved your life, and naturally you want to believe he's innocent. But look at the facts."

"He's guilty," Raphael said. "He's the head of the drug ring; everything points to it. His connection with Taylor—coincidence?" He shook his head. "I don't accept that. A smuggling ring dealing in millions of dollars' worth of drugs is being run from his home by his wife and this Canadian, and in four years he never suspects anything? Why did he play the patron to this particular artist, when Florence is full of starving young students? Why pick a criminal in the pay of the Mafia?"

Katharine didn't say anything. Raphael was walking up and down, gesticulating angrily as he argued. He stopped suddenly and came over to her. "You know he's guilty," he said. "Whatever has happened between you—I appeal to your conscience not to try to protect him. Have you forgotten what his drug ring did to your brother? This man, this cousin of yours, was responsible for that!"

"No," Katharine said, looking up at him. "He wasn't. Driver himself said he was innocent."

"What?" Raphael swung around on her. "What is this?"

She hadn't prepared the lie—it just came out. She felt very calm, and she folded her hands on her lap to steady them. No jury in the world would acquit Alessandro when Raphael had presented his case. There was too much circumstantial evidence. She had to lie, or tell the truth and break her promise. Expose him, not as a racketeer in drugs, but as a dealer in forgeries, employing a master craftsman to fake works of art.

She didn't hesitate. "When Driver found me in the storeroom, he said, 'You thought it was Alessandro, didn't you? But he knows nothing about it. We've been making millions behind his back, and he never suspected anything.' Those are his exact words."

Raphael stood over her; his face was ugly with rage and contempt. "It's a lie. Why didn't you tell us this before?"

"I thought I had," she said. "I was very shocked; I must have been confused, and forgotten."

"Kate," Carpenter pleaded. "Kate, don't do this. Malaspiga is guilty as hell. Okay, you want to protect your family"—he hesitated and then went on—"or you're in love with him. But he's a murderer. Okay, the old man said the others killed Firelli. But what about your brother—what about the addicts back home, dying of heroin? He's killed thousands of innocent people and got rich on it."

"If he were guilty, I wouldn't protect him," she said. "But he isn't. He had nothing to do with the drugs. Driver said so." It had distressed her to lie to Carpenter and see him turn away from her, bewildered and disgusted. But the lie was only an extension of the fundamental truth. She held fast to that too, and kept her courage.

Raphael stuck both hands in his pockets and rocked slightly on his heels. "You are a Malaspiga!" he spat at her. "You don't know the meaning of right or wrong— This is useless," he spoke to Carpenter. "She has been completely corrupted. It is hopeless to bring a case against him while an agent of the narcotics bureau insists on telling this pack of lies."

There was silence for some moments. Katharine didn't move. Raphael went and sat behind his desk. "Take her away," he said. "Get her out of my office." Katharine stood up, and Carpenter nodded toward the door. They went down in the elevator and got into his car. He drove through the slow traffic, looking ahead, as if she weren't there.

"Well," he said as they approached the hotel. "I wish I could say I understand what you've done, but I don't. You've got him off the hook— and that's what you wanted."

"There is a reason," Katharine said, "but I can't tell you what it is. He *is* innocent. I promise you that."

"You lied," Carpenter said. He didn't appear to have heard what she said. "I wouldn't have believed it. He got out on bail this afternoon—there was a smart lawyer waiting. As Raphael said, if he'd been an ordinary Italian citizen, he'd have been stuck in jail for months and nobody would have given a damn. But there was so much political muscle being flexed about that bastard, Raphael couldn't hold him. He's out, so you can go right to him if you feel like it. Tell him what you've done."

"I won't see him again," Katharine said. "It wouldn't work. I'm going home. I'll see if I can get a flight tomorrow."

The car stopped outside the hotel entrance.

"I was going to ask you to marry me," Carpenter said.

"That wouldn't have worked either," Katharine said. "But thank you, anyway."

"Don't thank me." He turned and looked at her. His eyes were cold. "I had a different picture of you. I'll send a full report to Ben back home. From the bureau's point of view, I suppose it's been a very successful operation. We've cleaned it up in New York, and it's finished over here. But I'm sorry, I don't feel like pinning any medals on you."

He leaned across and opened the door for her. She got out.

"Good-by, Frank." He drove away without answering.

THERE WAS A flight from Pisa to Milan that connected with Paris. From Paris she could get a seat on a 747 to New York. It was a grueling journey, but all the direct flights from Rome to the States were fully booked.

She left the ticket agency and began to walk, without purpose except to waste time. It was a magnificent morning; the sky was blue and cloudless. She looked at her hand, at the little gold signet ring on her finger, with the wreath and the spike surmounted by the Malaspiga coronet. It was a part of her which she had been unable to deny. But it had no place in the world to which she was returning. The real world, where she had been born and spent her life. The last weeks had been part of a dream regressing into the past. She came out into the Piazzale del Duomo. The great twelfth-century cathedral reared up over the buildings in the square, above the crowds that thronged around it; its multicolored marble and the rose-tile dome were brilliant in the sunshine.

For six hundred years people had been sitting on the cathedral's steps. There was a timeless quality to the scene that made her feel suspended.

This too was a dream, like the silver olive groves and the marble mountains at Carrara, the castle of her ancestors standing guard over the town of Malaspiga. She would love Alessandro for the rest of her life, but she would never see him again.

She walked back to her hotel, and as she came into the lobby the clerk looked up at her and smiled; it was like the morning she received Duchess Isabella's letter.

He leaned toward her. "This was delivered for you," he said. It was a long package wrapped in paper and sealed securely.

"Is there a message?"

"Nothing, signorina."

In the elevator she pulled at the tapes and began unwrapping the parcel. It was half undone when she reached her room and opened the door. Alessandro was sitting in the chair. He got up, but he didn't move toward her.

"They told me you were leaving today," he said.

"Yes," Katharine answered. "This afternoon. Please, Alessandro—I don't want to say good-by."

"I thought you would do something silly like this," he said. "Don't be angry with the reception clerk, I bribed him to let me in. The charge against me was formally withdrawn this morning. I understand that you were responsible. Why are you running away?"

"I can't explain it," she said. "You wouldn't understand."

"I understand everything about you," he said. "You're a part of myself. Please finish opening your parcel."

The wrapping came away and the parcel unrolled itself and hung down, the end curling over the floor. The Giorgione Madonna nursed the Christ child at her breast, serene and majestic, guarded by a kneeling Saint Anne.

There were two big slashes right across the canvas.

"I hope," he said, "that you will accept it as a wedding present. I have decided to sell the real one."

Mistress of
Mellyn

Mistress of Mellyn

A CONDENSATION OF THE NOVEL BY

VICTORIA HOLT

ILLUSTRATED BY HECTOR GARRIDO

Martha Leigh was young, proud and poor when she came to Mount Mellyn as governess. On the surface she found it a charming place: a vast Elizabethan mansion set amid lavish gardens on the coast of Cornwall. But within the great house lay a secret network of dark passageways and "peeps" from which hidden eyes watched Martha.

Within the hearts of the people, too, she sensed dark and hidden memories. What was the tragic secret behind the recent death of Alice, former mistress of Mellyn? And why did Alice still seem to be present in the brooding house? What manner of man was her enigmatic widower, Conan?

The lady whose pen name is Victoria Holt has always been fascinated by ancient and stately mansions, and resides in one of her own on the coast of Kent. There, and in a sunny London flat, she spins her tales of romance and brooding mystery, eight of which have been Reader's Digest Condensed Books selections.

CHAPTER ONE

"THERE ARE TWO courses open to a gentlewoman in penurious circumstances," my aunt Adelaide had said. "One is to marry, and the other to find a post in keeping with her gentility."

As the train carried me past hills and meadows I was taking this second course, partly because I had never had an opportunity of trying the former.

I pictured myself as I must appear to my fellow travelers if they bothered to glance my way, which was not very likely: a young woman of medium height, already past her first youth, being twenty-four years old, in a brown merino dress with cream lace collar and cuffs. My brown velvet bonnet, tied under my chin, was of the sort which was so becoming to feminine people like my sister, Phillida, but, I always felt, sat a little incongruously on heads like mine. My hair was thick, with a coppery tinge, parted in the center and drawn into a knot behind the bonnet. My eyes were large, in some lights the color of amber, and were my best feature; but they were too bold—so said Aunt Adelaide—which meant that they had learned none of the feminine graces. My nose was too short, my mouth too wide. In fact, I thought, nothing seemed to fit; and I must resign myself to journeys such as this, since for the rest of my life it would be necessary for me to earn a living, and I would never acquire a husband.

We were now deep in the moorland and wooded hills of Devon. I had been told to take good note of a masterpiece of bridgebuilding: the bridge which spanned the Tamar River at Saltash. After crossing it I would pass into the strange and picturesque duchy of Cornwall. I was becoming rather ridiculously excited about crossing the bridge.

This is absurd, I told myself. Mount Mellyn may be a magnificent house; Connan TreMellyn as romantic as his name sounds; but that will be no concern of yours. You will be confined to the nursery and some attic room, concerned only with the care of little Alvean. What strange names these people had! The family to which I was going was Cornish, and the Cornish had a language of their own. Perhaps my own name, Martha Leigh, would sound odd to them.

One of Aunt Adelaide's numerous friends had heard of "Connan Tre-Mellyn's predicament." He needed a governess—a genteel person patient enough to care for his daughter and sufficiently educated to teach her: an impoverished gentlewoman, in fact. Aunt Adelaide had decided that I fitted the bill.

When our father, a country vicar, had died, Aunt Adelaide had swooped down on us and taken us to London for a season of partygoing. Phillida had married at the end of that season, but after four years I had not. So there came a day when Aunt Adelaide pointed out the two courses to me.

I glanced out of the window. We had stopped at Plymouth. The door of the carriage opened and a man came in. He looked at me with an apologetic smile, as though hinting that he hoped I did not mind sharing the compartment with him, but I averted my eyes. When we had left Plymouth and were approaching the bridge, he noticed my interest and said, "You like our bridge, eh?"

I turned and saw a man a little under thirty, well dressed in the manner of the country gentleman, and rather dissipated-looking. His brown eyes twinkled, as though he were fully aware of the warnings I must have received about entering into conversation with strange men.

I answered, "Yes, indeed. It is very fine."

"Traveling far?" he asked as we crossed the bridge.

His brown eyes surveyed me, and I was immediately conscious of my drab appearance. "I leave the train at Liskeard," I said.

"Ah, Liskeard." He stretched his legs and turned his gaze from me to the tips of his boots. "Are you staying there?"

I was not sure that I liked this catechism, but I remembered that Phillida had once said, "You are far too gruff, Marty, with the opposite sex. You scare them off."

So I answered civilly, "No, I'm going to a little village on the coast called Mellyn."

"I see." He was silent for a few moments, and his next words startled me. "I suppose a sensible young lady like you would not believe in second sight . . . that sort of thing?"

"Why," I stammered, "what an extraordinary question!"

"May I look at your palm?"

I hesitated. Could I offer my hand to a stranger in this way?

He smiled. "I assure you that my only desire is to look into the future." He leaned forward and with a swift movement secured my hand. He held it lightly, contemplating it. "I see," he said, "that you are moving into a strange new world. You will have to exercise caution . . . the utmost caution."

I smiled cynically. "You see me taking a journey. What would you say if I told you I was visiting relatives?"

"I would say you were not a very truthful young lady." His smile was puckish. I could not help liking him. "No," he went on, "you are traveling to a new life, a new post. You are going to a strange house, a house full of shadows. You have to earn your living. I see a child there and a man. . . . There is someone else there . . . but perhaps she is already dead."

The deep sepulchral note in his voice momentarily unnerved me. I snatched my hand away. "What nonsense!"

He ignored me and half closed his eyes. "You will need to watch little Alice, but your duties will extend beyond the care of her. You must most certainly beware of Alice."

I felt a faint tingling creep up my spine. Little Alice! But her name was Alvean. Then I felt angry. Did I look the part already? The penurious gentlewoman turned governess!

He looked at his watch, for all the world as though this extraordinary conversation had not taken place. "In four minutes," he said briskly, "we shall pull into Liskeard."

He took my bags down from the rack. "Miss Martha Leigh, Mount Mellyn, Mellyn, Cornwall," was clearly written on the labels. He did not glance at them, and I felt that he had lost interest in me. When we came into the station, he alighted and set my bags on the platform. Then with a deep bow he left me.

While I was murmuring my thanks an elderly man came toward me, calling, "Miss Leigh! Be you Miss Leigh? I be Joe Tapperty."

I was facing a merry little man with a brown, wrinkled skin. "Well, miss," he said, "so I picked you out. Be these your bags?" He loaded them into a trap and I climbed in beside him.

He seemed a friendly man, and I could not resist trying to discover something about my new post. I said, "This house, Mount Mellyn, sounds as though it's on a hill."

"Well, 'tis built on a clifftop, facing the sea, and the gardens run down to the sea. Mount Mellyn and the Nansellocks' house, Mount Widden, are like twins. Two of them, standing defiantlike, daring the sea to come and take 'em."

"So we have near neighbors," I said.

"In a manner of speaking. Mount Widden, it be more than a mile away, and there's Mellyn Cove in between."

"Do they keep many servants at Mount Mellyn?" I asked.

"There be me and Mrs. Tapperty, my wife, and my girls, Daisy and Kitty, and Mrs. Soady in the gatehouse. Then there's Mrs. Polgrey, the house-keeper, and Tom Polgrey and young Gilly. Not that you'd call her a servant."

"Gilly!" I said. "That's an unusual name."

"Gillyflower. Reckon Jennifer Polgrey was a bit daft to give her a name like that. Jennifer was Mrs. Polgrey's girl. Great dark eyes and the littlest waist. Kept herself to herself until one day—she got into trouble, miss. Before we know where we are, little Gilly's arrived; as for Jennifer—her just walked into the sea one morning. There wasn't much doubt who Gilly's father was. Geoffry Nansellock left broken hearts wherever he went." He looked sideways at me. "But he can't hurt *you*, miss. He was killed in a train accident, at Plymouth."

"And is that all the servants?"

"There be odd boys and girls—some for the stables, some for the gardens. But things have changed since the mistress died."

"How long is it since she died?" I asked.

"Little more than a year, I reckon."

"And Mr. TreMellyn has just decided he needs a governess?"

"There have been three governesses so far. They don't stay. The first two, they said the place was too quiet. Then there was Miss Jansen. A real pretty creature, and she liked Mount Mellyn—loved old houses, she said. But she was sent away—took what didn't belong to her. 'Twas a pity. We all liked her."

I turned my attention to the August countryside. We passed cornfields where poppies and pimpernels grew, and an occasional gray stone cottage, grim and lonely. Then I had my first glimpse of the sea through a fold in the hills, and I felt my spirits lift. Flowers grew by the roadside; I could smell the scent of pine trees. We turned down a cliff road. Before us stretched a scene of breathtaking beauty. The cliff rose steep and straight beside the sea; deep purple heather, grasses and flowers grew along the indented coast. At length we saw the house, high on the cliff plateau. Mount Mellyn was like a castle, built of granite, grand and noble—a house which had stood for two hundred years, and would stand for hundreds more.

"All this land belongs to the master," said Tapperty with pride. "And if you look across the cove, you'll see Mount Widden." Like Mount Mellyn, it was built of gray stone, but it was smaller, and seemed of a later period.

The trap had climbed to the plateau and a pair of wrought-iron gates confronted us. "Open up there!" shouted Tapperty.

There was a small lodge beside the gates and at the door sat a woman knitting. A child standing beside her ran over to open the gates. She was an extraordinary-looking girl with long straight hair almost white in color and wide blue eyes. "Thanks, Gilly girl," said Tapperty as we went through. "This be Miss Leigh, Gilly, who's come to take care of Miss Alvean."

I looked into a pair of blank blue eyes which stared at me with an expression impossible to fathom. The old woman rose and came over. Tapperty said, "This be Mrs. Soady."

"Good-day to you," said Mrs. Soady. "I hope you'll be happy here along of us."

"Thank you," I answered.

"Well, I do hope so," added Mrs. Soady. Then she shook her head as though she feared her hopes were somewhat futile.

"Gilly didn't speak," I observed as we went on up the drive.

"No. Her don't talk much. But sing, her do."

The drive was about half a mile in length and edged with hydrangeas and fuchsias. I caught glimpses of the sea between the pine trees, and then I saw the house again. Before it was a wide lawn where peacocks strutted. The house itself was of three stories, long and L-shaped. The sun caught the mullioned windows, and I immediately had the impression that I was being watched.

When we reached the front steps the door opened, and I saw a woman standing there, with a white cap on her gray hair. She was tall, with a hooked nose and a dominating manner. I did not need to be told that she was Mrs. Polgrey, the housekeeper.

"I trust you've had a good journey, Miss Leigh," she said. "Come along in. You shall have a nice cup of tea in my room. Leave your bags. I'll have them taken up."

I felt relieved. This woman seemed to emit common sense, and she dispelled the eerie feeling which had begun, I realized, when I encountered the man in the train. Joe Tapperty had done little to disperse it, with his tales of death and suicide.

I thanked Mrs. Polgrey and she led the way into an enormous hall. The floor was of flagstones and the timbered roof was lofty. At one end were a dais and a great open fireplace. On the dais stood a refectory table.

"It's magnificent," I said, and Mrs. Polgrey was pleased.

"I superintend all the polishing of the furniture myself," she told me. "You have to watch girls nowadays. Those Tapperty wenches are a pair of flibbertigibbets, I can tell 'ee. Beeswax and turpentine, that's the mixture. All made by myself."

I followed her to the door at the end of the hall. She opened it, revealing a short flight of steps. To the left was a door which, after a moment's hesitation, she opened.

"The chapel," she said, and I caught a glimpse of flagstones, an altar, a few pews. There was a smell of dampness about the place. She shut the door quickly. "We don't use it nowadays," she said. "We go to the church down in the village."

We went up the stairs and through a vast dining room, where the walls were hung with tapestries. "This is not *your* part of the house," Mrs. Polgrey told me, "but it's as well you know the lay of the land, as they say." I thanked her, understanding that this was a tactful way of telling me that as governess I would not be expected to mingle with the family.

We mounted yet another flight of stairs, and came to what seemed like an intimate sitting room, the walls again hung with tapestries which were repeated on the chair backs and seats. "This is the punch room," Mrs. Polgrey said. "It has always been called so because it is here that the family retires to take punch. We still follow the old customs in this house."

Beyond this room we entered a gallery, the walls of which were lined with ancestral portraits, and went quickly along it to a door at the far end. As we passed through I saw that we were in a different wing of the house, the servants' quarters, I imagined. "This," said Mrs. Polgrey, "will be *your* part of the house. That staircase leads to your room and the nurseries. But first come to my sitting room and we'll have our tea."

"You're very kind."

"Well, I do want to make you happy here with us. Miss Alvean needs a sensible governess."

"I gather there have been other governesses before me."

"Yes. Not much good, any of them. Miss Jansen was the best, but it seemed she had habits. You could have knocked me down with a feather. She quite took *me* in!" Mrs. Polgrey looked as though she thought anyone who could do that must be clever indeed. "Miss Celestine was most upset when it came out."

"Miss Celestine?"

"The young lady at Widden. Miss Celestine Nansellock. She's often here. A quiet young lady and she loves the place. That's why she and Miss Jansen seemed to get on so well. Both interested in old houses, you see. You'll meet Miss Celestine. Some of us think . . . Oh, my dear life! I'm letting my tongue run away with me, and you longing for your tea."

She threw open the door of her room, and it was like stepping into another world. Gone was the atmosphere of brooding antiquity. This room was crammed with furniture. There were antimacassars on the chairs; there was a whatnot filled with ornaments, including a glass slipper and a gold pig. I felt something comfortingly normal about this room, as I did about Mrs. Polgrey. A minute later a black-haired girl with saucy eyes appeared, carrying a tea tray.

"This be Daisy, Miss Leigh," said Mrs. Polgrey. "You can tell her if you find anything is not to your liking."

Daisy dropped a little curtsy and went out.

Mrs. Polgrey unlocked a cabinet and took out the tea canister. "When you've had your tea and seen your room," she said, "I'll introduce you to Miss Alvean."

"What would she be doing at this time of day?"

"She'll be off somewhere by herself." Mrs. Polgrey frowned. "She does that, and Master don't like it. That's why 'e be anxious for her to have a governess, you see."

I began to see. I was sure now that Alvean was going to be a difficult child.

Mrs. Polgrey measured the tea into the pot as though it were gold dust, and poured boiling water on it. I gathered, as we sat together and talked, that Connan TreMellyn was away.

"He has another estate farther west," Mrs. Polgrey told me. "Penzance way." She did not know when he would return.

Soon after that she took me up to my room. It was large, with big windows, a window seat and a view of the front lawn. There was a tallboy and a chest of drawers, and my bed was a big four-poster, but it was dwarfed by the room. I noticed that there was a door in addition to the one by which I had entered.

Mrs. Polgrey followed my gaze. "The schoolroom," she said. "And beyond that is Miss Alvean's room."

I looked at the fireplace and pictured a roaring fire there on winter days. "I can see I'm going to be very comfortable."

"You'll be the first governess to have this room. The others used to sleep on the other side of Miss Alvean's. It was Miss Celestine who thought this would be more pleasant."

"Then I owe thanks to Miss Celestine."

"A very pleasant lady. She thinks the world of Miss Alvean." Mrs. Polgrey shook her head significantly, and I wondered whether she was thinking that perhaps one day the master would marry again. Who more suitable to be his wife than this neighbor who was so fond of Miss Alvean?

"Perhaps you'd like to unpack and have a little rest. Traveling is so fatiguing, I do know. Meals could be taken in the schoolroom, if you'd prefer that to your room?"

"With Miss Alvean?"

"She takes her meals nowadays with her father, except her milk and crackers in the evening. All the children have taken meals with the family from the time they were eight years old. Miss Alvean's birthday was in May."

"There are other children?"

"Oh, my dear life, no! I was talking of the children of the past. Well, I'll be leaving you. If you care for a stroll in the grounds before dinner, ring for Daisy or her sister, Kitty, to show you the back stairs. Dinner is served at eight."

As soon as she had gone I was aware of silence—the eerie silence of an ancient house. I looked at the watch pinned to my bodice and saw that it was just past six o'clock. Two hours to dinner. I opened the door to the schoolroom. It was larger than my bedroom and had red plush cushions on the window seats. There was a table in the center with scratches on it and splashes of ink; presumably this was the table where generations of Tre-Mellyns had learned their lessons. A few books lay on the table. They were children's readers, and there was an exercise book on which was scrawled "Alvean TreMellyn. Arithmetic." I opened it and saw several sums, most of them with wrong answers. Turning the pages I came to a sketch of Gilly, the child at the lodge gates.

Not bad, I thought. So our Alvean is an artist. That's something. I closed the book. I had the strange feeling, which I had had as I entered the house, that I was being watched.

"Alvean!" I called on an impulse. "Where are you hiding, Alvean?" There was no answer, and I flushed with embarrassment. Abruptly I turned and went back to my room.

By the time I had unpacked it was eight o'clock, and Daisy appeared and placed my tray on a table. I asked, "Where is Miss Alvean? It seems strange that I have not seen her yet."

"She's a bad 'un," said Daisy. "Her heard new miss was coming, and so off her goes. We don't know where her be till a boy comes over from Mount Widden to tell we that she be over there—calling on Miss Celestine and Master Peter, if you do please. Listen! That do sound like the carriage."

Daisy went to the window and beckoned me. I felt I ought not to stand at the window with a servant, spying, but the temptation was too strong. So I stood beside Daisy and saw them getting out of the carriage: a young woman whom I judged to be of my own age or perhaps a year or so older, and a child.

This then was Alvean. She was somewhat tall for her eight years. Her light brown hair had been plaited, and was wound round her head, and she was wearing a dress of brown gingham, with white stockings and black shoes with ankle straps. She looked terrifyingly precocious, like a minia-ture woman, and my spirits fell. She seemed to be conscious that she was being watched, and glanced upward. Involuntarily I stepped back, but I was sure she had seen the movement. I felt at a disadvantage before we had met.

I sat down and began my dinner. Daisy was about to go when there was a knock and Kitty entered. "Oh, miss," she said, "Mrs. Polgrey says will you go down to the punch room when you'm finished. Miss Nansellock be there and her would like to see you. Miss Alvean have come home."

"I will come when I have finished my dinner," I said.

"Then would you pull the bell when you'm ready, miss, and me or Daisy'll show you the way."

"Thank you."

I finished my meal in a leisurely fashion. I imagined that Mrs. Polgrey,

Alvean and Miss Nansellock would be impatiently awaiting my coming, but I had no intention of becoming the poor little drudge that so many governesses were. If Alvean were what I believed her to be, she needed to be shown, right at the start, that I was in charge. Finally I rang and Daisy appeared.

"They'm waiting," she said. "It's well past Miss Alvean's suppertime."

"Then it is a pity that she did not return before," I replied.

Daisy giggled, and her plump breasts shook. Daisy enjoyed laughing, I could see. She led the way to the punch room, where Celestine Nansellock was sitting in a tapestry-backed chair. Mrs. Polgrey was standing beside Alvean, who had her hands clasped behind her back. She looked, I thought, dangerously demure.

"Ah," said Mrs. Polgrey, "here is Miss Leigh. Miss Nansellock have been waiting to see you." There was a faint reproach in her voice. I, a mere governess, had kept this important lady waiting while I finished my dinner. As I bowed to Miss Nansellock, I was aware of the startlingly blue eyes of the child fixed upon me. I thought, She will be a beauty when she grows up.

Celestine Nansellock rose and laid a hand on Alvean's shoulder. "Alvean came over to see us," she said. "I trust you will not be cross with her."

Alvean bristled. I answered, looking straight into her defiant blue eyes, "I could hardly scold for what happened before my arrival, could I?"

"She looks on me—on us—as part of her own family," Celestine went on. "We've always been such close neighbors."

For the first time I gave my attention solely to Celestine. She was taller than I, and by no standards a beauty. Her hair was a nondescript brown and her eyes were hazel. There was an air of intense quietness about her.

"I do hope," she said, "that if you need my advice about anything you won't hesitate to call on me." Her mild eyes looked into mine. "We want you to be happy here, Miss Leigh."

"You are very kind," I said. "I suppose the first thing to do is to get Alvean some supper."

Celestine smiled. "Indeed, yes. But you must be weary after your journey, Miss Leigh. Tonight I will look after her."

Before I could speak Alvean cried out, "No! I want *her* to! She's my governess. She should, shouldn't she?"

A hurt look appeared in Celestine's face, and Alvean could not repress the triumph in hers. I felt I understood; the child wanted to feel her own power.

"Oh, very well," said Celestine. "Then I'll go."

"Good night," Alvean said flippantly. And turning to me: "Come on. I'm hungry."

"You've forgotten to thank Miss Nansellock for bringing you back," I told her.

"I didn't forget," she retorted. "I never forget anything."

"Then your memory is better than your manners," I said.

They were astonished—all of them. Perhaps I was a little astonished myself. But I knew that if I were going to assume control of this child, I should have to be firm.

Alvean's face flushed and her eyes grew hard. Not knowing how to retort, she ran out of the room.

"Miss Leigh," said Celestine, "you must go carefully with that child. She lost her mother . . . quite recently."

"I understand," I replied. "I shall do my best for Alvean."

In the schoolroom Alvean sat at a table with her milk and crackers. She deliberately ignored me as I went to the table.

"Alvean," I said, "we shall be happier if we come to an understanding."

Alvean shrugged. "If we don't," she told me brusquely, "you'll have to go. I'll have another governess. It's of no account to me." I felt myself shiver involuntarily. For the first time I understood the feelings of those who depend on the goodwill of others for their bread and butter.

"It should be of the greatest account," I answered, "because it is far more pleasant to live in harmony than in discord with those about us."

"What does it matter, if we can have them sent away?"

"Kindness matters more than anything in the world."

She smiled into her milk and finished it.

"Now," I said, "to bed." I rose with her.

"I go to bed by myself," she said. "I am not a baby."

"Perhaps I thought you were younger than you are because you have so much to learn."

She considered that. Then she gave that shrug of her shoulders which I was to discover was characteristic.

"I'll come and say good night when you are in bed." I went into my room feeling very depressed. I had had no experience in handling children, and here I was with a difficult child on my hands. I accepted the fact that I was frightened. Not until I had come face to face with Alvean had I realized that I might not succeed with this job. I tried not to look down the years ahead when I might slip from one post to another, never giving satisfaction. What happened to women like myself, penurious gentlewomen without those feminine attractions which were so important? I walked up and down my room, trying to control my emotions. Finally I went to the window and looked out across the lawn to the hills beyond the plateau. Such beauty! Such peace without, I thought. Such conflict within.

I turned from the window and went through the schoolroom to Alvean's room. "Alvean," I whispered. There was no answer. She lay in bed, her eyes tightly shut—too tightly.

I bent over her. "Good night, Alvean. We're going to be friends, you know," I murmured.

There was no answer. She was pretending to be asleep.

EXHAUSTED AS I WAS, my rest was broken that night. I felt that there were whispering voices about me. I had an impression that there had been tragedy in this house which still hung over it. I wondered in what circumstances Alvean's mother had died. Then I thought of Alvean, who showed such a rebellious face to the world. There must be some reason for this and I determined to discover it. I determined to make her a happy, loving child.

The coming of day comforted me. I had breakfast in the schoolroom with Alvean; and later, when we settled down to work, I discovered that she was an intelligent child. She had read more than most children of her age, and her eyes would light up with interest in her lessons almost in spite of her determination to preserve a lack of harmony between us. My spirits began to rise, and after lunch, when Alvean volunteered to take me for a walk, I felt I was getting on better with her.

There were woods on the estate, and she said she wished to show them to me. I gladly followed her through the trees. In a little opening, she cried, "Look!" and picked a crimson flower. "Do you know what this is?"

"It's betony, I believe."

She nodded. "You should keep some in your room, Miss Leigh. It keeps evil away."

I laughed. "That's an old superstition. Why should I want to keep evil away?"

"Everybody should. They grow this in graveyards because people are afraid of the dead."

"It's foolish to be afraid. Dead people can hurt no one." She was placing the flower in the buttonhole of my coat. I was rather touched. Her face looked gentle, as if she had a sudden protective feeling toward me. "Thank you, Alvean," I said.

She looked at me and the softness vanished from her face. "You can't catch me," she cried defiantly, and off she ran.

I called, "Alvean, come here." But she disappeared through the trees and I heard mocking laughter in the distance.

Instead of pursuing her I decided to return to the house, but the woods were thick and I was not sure of my direction. I turned back, but soon it seemed to me that this was not the direction from which we had come. Panic seized me, but I was not going to give Alvean the satisfaction of having brought me to the woods to lose me. So I walked purposefully through the trees, which grew thicker as I walked. My anger against Alvean was rising. Then I heard a crackle of leaves, as though I were being followed, and a strange voice singing slightly off-key.

"Alice, where art thou? . . .
One year past, this even,
And thou wert by my side,
Vowing to love me,
Alice, what e'er might betide."

"Who is there?" I called.

There was no answer, but in the distance I glimpsed a child with lint-white hair, and I knew that it was little Gilly.

I walked on and after a while I saw the lodge gates through the trees and I soon found the drive. When I reached the house I went into the schoolroom, where tea was waiting. Alvean sat at the table. She looked demure and made no reference to our afternoon's adventure, nor did I.

After tea I said to her, "I don't know what schedule your other governesses had, but we shall do our lessons in the morning, and again from five until six, when we will read together."

Alvean did not answer; she was studying me intently. Suddenly she said, "Miss Leigh, do you like my name? Have you ever known anyone else called Alvean?"

I said I liked it and had never heard it before.

"It's Cornish. My father can speak and write Cornish." She looked wistful when she spoke of her father, and I thought, He at least is one person she admires. She went on. "In Cornish, Alvean means Little Alice." She came to me and placed her hands on my knees. She looked up into my face and said solemnly, "You see, my mother was Alice. She isn't here anymore. But I was called after her. That's why I am Little Alice."

I stood up because I could no longer bear the scrutiny of the child. I went to the window.

"Look," I said, "two peacocks are on the lawn."

But I was not seeing the peacocks. I was remembering the man on the train who had warned me to beware of Alice.

CHAPTER TWO

THREE DAYS AFTER my arrival at Mount Mellyn, the master of the house returned.

I had already slipped into a routine with Alvean and I found her a good pupil. It was not that she meant to please me; it was merely that her desire for knowledge was so acute that she could not deny it.

I had been shocked when I first heard the name of Alice mentioned, and after the daylight had passed I would feel that the house was full of eerie shadows. That was pure fancy, of course. But I woke in the night to hear what seemed to be voices moaning, "Alice. Alice. Where is Alice?"

Daisy explained away my fancies the next morning. "Did 'ee hear the sea last night, miss, in the cove? Sis . . . sis . . . woa . . . woa . . . just like two old biddies having a good gossip. 'Tis like that when the wind be in a certain direction."

I laughed at myself. There was an explanation to everything.

I had grown to know the people of the household. Mrs. Tapperty called me in one day for a glass of parsnip wine, and I went to see Mrs. Soady at the lodge gates and heard about her three sons and their children, who kept her knitting because they were always putting their toes through their stockings.

I tried on occasion to talk to Gilly, but she always ran away. I was angry with these countryfolk who, because she was unlike them, believed her to be mad. Something must have happened to frighten her at some time. If I could discover what, I believed I could help her to become more like other children. I said this to Mrs. Polgrey, but she was uncommunicative and told me by her looks alone that Gilly was no concern of mine.

This was the state of affairs when Connan TreMellyn returned to Mount Mellyn. I was aware of his presence, indeed, before I saw him.

It was afternoon when he arrived. Alvean had gone off by herself and I had sent for hot water to wash. Kitty brought it and her black eyes gleamed as she said, "Master be home."

At that moment Daisy put her head round the door. There was about both sisters just then a certain expectancy which sickened me. I thought I understood the expression in the faces of these lusty girls; I had already seen them in scuffling intimacy with the boys who came in from the village to work about the place. Their excitement over the return of the master led me to one conclusion: He was *that* sort of man.

"Master came in half an hour ago," said Kitty. "He be asking for you, miss. He be waiting in the punch room."

I inclined my head and said, "I will come in a moment. You may go now." My heart was beating fast and my color was heightened. I smoothed my hair. My eyes were amber today; and they were resentful, which seemed ridiculous. As I went down to the punch room I told myself that I was building up a picture of this man because of the look I had seen on the faces of those two flighty girls. I was already sure that poor Alice had died of a broken heart because she had found herself married to a philanderer. I knocked at the door.

"Come in." His voice was strong—arrogant, I called it even before I set eyes on him. He was standing with his back to the fireplace and I was immediately conscious of his height; he was well over six feet tall, and the fact that he was thin—almost gaunt—accentuated this. His hair was black

221

but his eyes were light. He wore riding breeches and a dark blue coat with a white cravat. There was an air of careless elegance about him. He gave an impression of both strength and cruelty.

"So, Miss Leigh, at last we meet." His manner seemed insolent, as though he were reminding me that I was only a governess.

"It does not seem a long time," I answered. "I have been here only a few days."

"Mrs. Polgrey gives me good reports of you."

"That is kind of her."

"Why should it be kind of her to tell me the truth?"

"I meant that she has been kind to me and that has helped to make this good report possible."

"I see that you are a woman who does not employ the usual hollow phrases in conversation but means what she says. Good. I have a feeling that we shall get on well together."

His eyes were taking in each detail of my appearance, I knew. I thought, At least *I* shall be safe from the attentions of this man, who must be a connoisseur of beautiful women.

"Tell me," he said, "how do you find my daughter? Backward for her age?"

"By no means. Alvean is extremely intelligent, but I do find her in need of discipline."

"I am sure you will be able to supply that lack."

"I intend to try."

"Of course. That is why you are here."

"Please tell me how far I may carry that discipline."

"Short of murder, you have my permission to do what you will. If I do not approve your methods, you will hear."

"Thank you."

"I suppose," he went on, "we should make excuses for Alvean's lack of good manners. She lost her mother a year ago."

I looked into his face for a trace of sorrow. I could find none. "I had heard that," I answered.

"It was sudden." He was silent a moment, then continued. "Poor child, she has no mother. And her father . . . ?" He lifted his shoulders and did not complete his sentence.

"Even so," I said, "there are many more unfortunate than she is. All she needs is a firm hand."

He leaned forward suddenly and surveyed me ironically. "I am sure," he said, "that you possess that necessary firm hand."

I was conscious in that brief moment of the magnetism of the man. The clear-cut features, the cool light eyes, the mockery behind them—all these I felt were but a mask for something he was determined to keep hidden.

At that moment there was a knock on the door and Celestine Nansellock came in. "I heard you were here, Connan," she said.

"My dear Celestine, it is good of you to come over," he said. "I was just making the acquaintance of our new governess. She tells me that Alvean is intelligent but needs discipline."

"Of course she is intelligent!" Celestine spoke indignantly. "I hope Miss Leigh is not planning to be too harsh with her. Alvean is a *good* child."

"I don't think Miss Leigh entirely agrees with that. You see our little goose as a beautiful swan, Celeste."

"Perhaps I am overfond."

"Would you like me to leave now?" I suggested. "We have finished our talk, I believe."

"Let us say it is to be continued," Connan TreMellyn said lightly.

I bowed my head and left them together.

In the schoolroom tea was laid, ready for me, but Alvean was not there. At five o'clock she still had not put in an appearance, so I sent Daisy to find the child and to remind her that from five to six we had work to do.

Shortly I heard footsteps. The door opened and there stood Connan TreMellyn holding Alvean by the arm. She looked so unhappy that I found myself feeling sorry for her, while her father looked as though he were amused. Behind him was Celestine.

"Here she is," he announced. "Duty is duty, my daughter. When your governess summons you to your lessons, you must obey."

I could see that Alvean was hard put to restrain her sobs.

"Connan," Celestine said, "it *is* your first day back, you know, and Alvean so looked forward to your coming."

He smiled, but I thought his mouth was grim. "Discipline," he murmured. "That, Celeste, is of the utmost importance. Come, we will leave Alvean with Miss Leigh."

Alvean threw a pleading glance at him, which he ignored, and the door shut, leaving me alone with my pupil.

That incident taught me a great deal. Alvean adored her father and he was indifferent to her. My anger against him increased as my pity for the child grew. Small wonder that she was difficult!

ALVEAN WAS REBELLIOUS all evening. She told me she hated me, though there was no need for her to have mentioned a fact which was apparent. After she went to bed, I felt so disturbed that I slipped out of the house and went into the woods. There I sat on a fallen tree trunk, brooding. It had been a hot day and there was a deep stillness in the woods. I was not sure whether I could remain in this house.

I was a little afraid of Connan TreMellyn, although I could not say why. I was certain that he would leave *me* alone, but there was something magnetic about him. And I amused him in some way. Was I so unattractive in his eyes? Or was it because I belonged to that army of women obliged to earn their living and dependent on the whim of people like himself? Had he a streak of cruelty in his nature? Perhaps poor Alice, like Gillyflower's mother, had walked into the sea.

As I sat there thinking, I heard the sound of footsteps. A man was coming toward me, and there was something familiar about him which made my heart beat faster. Then he smiled and I recognized the man I had met on the train.

"Why, you look as though you have seen a ghost," he said.

"Who are you?" I asked.

"I am Peter Nansellock. I must confess to a little deception."

"You are Miss Celestine Nansellock's brother?"

He nodded. "I suspected who you were when we met in the train. I saw you sitting there, looking the part of a governess, and I guessed. Your name on the labels of your baggage confirmed my guess, for I knew they were expecting a Miss Leigh at Mount Mellyn."

"I am comforted to learn that my looks conform with the part I have been called upon to play in life."

"You really are a most untruthful young lady. You are in fact quite discomfited to have been taken for a governess."

I felt myself grow pink with indignation. "Because I am a governess, that is no reason why I should be forced to accept insults from strangers."

I rose from the tree trunk, but he said pleadingly, "Please let us talk awhile. There is much I have to say to you."

My curiosity overcame my dignity and I sat down.

"That's better, Miss Leigh. You know, you are a little like a hedgehog; one has only to mention the word governess and up come your spines."

"Since I resemble a hedgehog, at least I am not spineless."

He laughed. "I hoped you would be grateful for my interest, Miss Leigh. I was going to say, if things become intolerable at Mount Mellyn, you need only walk over to Mount Widden."

"Why should I find life intolerable at Mount Mellyn?"

"Connan is overbearing, Alvean is a menace to anyone's peace and the atmosphere since Alice's death is like a tomb."

I turned to him abruptly and said, "You told me to beware of Alice. What did you mean by that?"

"Alice is dead," he said, "but somehow she remains. Nothing was the same at Mount Mellyn after she . . . went."

"How did she die?"

"You have not heard? I should have thought Mrs. Polgrey or one of those girls would have told you. It's a very simple story. A wife finds life with her husband intolerable. She runs away with another man." He looked at the tips of his boots. "In Alice's case the man was my brother."

"Geoffry Nansellock!" I cried.

"So you have heard of him!"

I thought of Gillyflower, whose mother had walked into the sea. "Yes," I said. "He was evidently a shameless philanderer."

"It sounds a harsh term to apply to him. His great weakness was women. He found them irresistible, and women love men who love them. How can they help it? It is such a compliment, is it not? One by one they fell victim to his charm."

"Evidently he did not hesitate to misuse it."

"Spoken like a true governess! But, my dear Miss Leigh, it is true that all was not well at Mount Mellyn. Do you think Connan would be an easy man to live with?"

"It is surely not becoming for me to discuss my employer."

"Miss Leigh, anyone who is obliged to live in a house should know something of its secrets."

"What secrets?"

He bent closer. "Alice was afraid of Connan. Before she married him she had known and loved my brother. She and Geoffry were on the train which was wrecked at Plymouth . . . running away together. They identified Geoffry, although he was badly smashed up. There was a woman close to him. She was so badly burned that it was impossible to identify her, but a locket she was wearing was recognized as one Alice was known to possess . . . and, of course, there was the fact that she had disappeared."

"How dreadful! Was she so unhappy at Mount Mellyn?"

"You have met Connan. Remember, he knew that she had once been in love with Geoffry. I imagine life was hell for her."

"Well, it was very tragic," I said briskly. "But it is over. Why did you say, 'Beware of Alice,' as though she were still here?"

"They recognized her locket, not her, Miss Leigh. There are some who think that it was not Alice who was killed with Geoffry."

"Then if it was not, where is she?"

"That is what some people ask themselves. That is why there are long shadows at Mount Mellyn."

I stood up. "I must get back. It will soon be dark."

He was standing beside me—a little taller than I—and our eyes met. "I thought you should know these things," he said gently.

I began walking back in the direction from which I had come. He walked beside me. "There is no need for you to escort me back to the house," I said.

"I am forced to contradict you. I was on my way to call."

I was silent until we came to Mount Mellyn. Connan TreMellyn was coming from the stables. He looked mildly surprised to see us together. "Hello there, Con!" cried Peter Nansellock.

I hurried into the house, and went early to bed. But it was not easy to sleep that night. I could hear the waves thundering into Mellyn Cove, and it seemed that there were indeed whispering voices down there, and that the words they said to each other were, "Alice! Where is Alice? Alice, where are you?"

CHAPTER THREE

IN THE MORNING the fancies of the previous night seemed foolish. I asked myself why so many people—including myself—wanted to make a mystery of what had happened in this house. It was an ordinary enough story. Alice was killed on a train, and that was the end of Alice.

My room was filled with sunshine and I felt like a different person. I was exhilarated and I knew why. It was because of Connan TreMellyn. Not that I liked him—quite the reverse; but it was as though he had issued a challenge. I was going to make a success of this job. I was going to make of Alvean not only a model pupil but a charming, unaffected little girl. I felt so pleased that I began to hum softly under my breath. I went to the window to look out. The lawns were fresh and lovely with the early morning dew on them, so I threw open my window and leaned out.

Connan TreMellyn, emerging from the stables, saw me before I was able to draw back, and I felt myself grow scarlet with embarrassment to be seen with my hair down and in my nightgown. He called jauntily, "Good morning, Miss Leigh."

Had he been riding already, or out all night? I imagined his visiting one of the less reputable ladies of the neighborhood. "Good morning," I said curtly, still blushing.

"A beautiful morning," he cried. As I withdrew into my room I heard him shout, "Hello, Alvean! So you're up too."

I heard Alvean cry, "Hello, Papa!" Her voice was gentle, with that wistful note I had detected when she spoke of him on the previous day. I knew that it would make her extremely happy if he stopped and chatted with her, but he went on into the house.

I put on my dressing gown and on impulse crossed to Alvean's room and opened the door. She was sitting astride a chair, with her back to me, talking to herself.

"There's nothing to be afraid of. All you have to do is hold tight and not be afraid, and you won't fall off." She was so intent that she had not heard the door open.

I learned a great deal in that moment. Her father was a great horseman; he wanted her to be a good horsewoman; but Alvean, who desperately wanted to win his approval, was afraid of horses.

I started forward to tell her that I would teach her to ride; it was one thing I could do really well because we had always had horses in the country. But I hesitated because I was beginning to understand Alvean. She was an unhappy child. She had lost her mother, the biggest tragedy which could befall any child; now her father seemed indifferent to her, and she adored him.

Quietly shutting the door, I went back to my room. I looked at the sunshine on the carpet and my elation returned. I *was* going to make a success of this job. I was going to fight Connan TreMellyn. I was going to make him proud of his daughter.

AFTER LUNCHEON THAT day I decided to approach him. When I saw him leave the house and cross to the stables, I followed him. I arrived in time to hear him ordering Billy Trehay, the stableman, to saddle Royal Russet for him.

He looked surprised to see me. "Why, it's Miss Leigh."

"I had hoped to have a few words with you," I said. "Perhaps this is an inconvenient time."

"That depends," he said, "on how many words you wish us to exchange." He looked at his watch. "I can give you five minutes, Miss Leigh. Let us walk across the lawn."

I fell into step beside him. "In my youth," I said, "I was constantly in the saddle. I believe Alvean wishes to learn to ride. I am asking your permission to teach her."

"You have my permission to try, Miss Leigh," he said, "but I doubt that you will succeed."

"You mean others have failed to teach her?"

"*I* have failed. It is strange to find such fear of riding in a child. Most children take to it like breathing." His tone was clipped, his expression hard. I pictured the lessons, the lack of understanding, the expectation of miracles. No wonder the child had been frightened. He went on. "There are some people who can never learn to ride."

Before I could stop myself I burst out, "There are some people who cannot teach."

He stared at me in astonishment, and I knew that nobody in this house had ever dared to talk to him in such a way. I thought, I have failed. I shall now be told that my services are no longer required. I could see that he was fighting to control his temper. He still looked at me, but I could not read the expression in those eyes.

"You must excuse me, Miss Leigh," he said, and he left me.

I FOUND ALVEAN IN THE schoolroom and came straight to the point. "Your father says I may teach you riding. Would you like that?"

I saw the muscles of her face tighten, and my heart sank. Would it be possible to teach a child who was as frightened as that? I went on before she had time to answer. "When we were your age, my sister and I were keen riders. It's great fun."

"I can't do it," she said. "I don't like horses."

"You don't like horses!" My voice was shocked. "Why, they're the gentlest creatures in the world."

"They're not. Gray Mare ran away with me, and if Tapperty hadn't caught her rein she would have killed me."

"Gray Mare wasn't the mount for you to start with."

"Then I rode Buttercup. She was as bad in a different way. She wouldn't go when I tried to make her."

I almost laughed, but I saw the wistful look in her eyes. I wanted to put my arm about her, but I knew that was no way to approach Alvean. "There's one thing to learn before you can begin to ride," I said, "and that is to love your horse. Then you won't be afraid and your horse will begin to love you. He wants a master; but it must be a tender, loving master."

She was giving me her attention now.

"When a horse runs away as Gray Mare did, it means that she is frightened. She's as frightened as you are, and her way of showing it is to run. Now when you're frightened you should never let her know it. You just whisper to her, 'It's all right, Gray Mare . . . I'm here.' As for Buttercup— she's a mischievous old nag. She's lazy and she knows that you can't handle her, so she won't do as she's told. But once you let her know you're the master, she'll obey."

"I didn't know Gray Mare was frightened of me," she said.

"Your father wants you to ride," I told her. "Wouldn't it be fun to surprise him? Suppose you learned to jump and gallop, and he didn't know about it until he saw you do it?"

It hurt me to see the joy in her face, and I wondered how any man could be so callous as to deny a child the affection she asked.

"Alvean," I said, "let's try."

"Yes," she said, "let's try. I'll change into my things."

I gave a little cry of disappointment, remembering that I had brought no riding habit with me. I said, "I have no riding clothes."

Her face fell and then lit up. "Come with me," she said.

We went along the gallery to the main upstairs bedrooms. Alvean paused before a door, as if steeling herself to go in. Then she threw it open and stood aside for me to enter.

It was a dressing room, with a long mirror, a tallboy, a dresser and an oak chest. Beyond it, through another door, was a large bedroom, beautifully furnished, with blue velvet curtains. Alvean went to the bedroom door and shut it. "There are lots of clothes here," she said. "There's bound to be a riding habit."

She threw up the lid of the chest with an excitement I had not seen in her before. "There are a lot more clothes in the attic," she said. "Trunks of them. Grandmama's and Great-grandmama's. When there were parties, they used to dress up in them and play charades. . . ."

I was so delighted to have discovered a way to her affections that I allowed myself to be carried along. I put on a lady's black beaver hat—obviously meant for riding—and Alvean laughed with a catch in her voice. That laughter moved me deeply. It was the laughter of a child who is unaccustomed to laughter.

"You look so funny in it," she said.

I stood before the mirror. My hair looked quite copper against the black. I decided that I looked slightly less unattractive than usual, and that was what Alvean meant by "funny."

"Not the least like a governess," she explained. She was pulling out a black woolen riding habit, elegantly cut, and trimmed with braid and ball fringe.

I held it up. "I think that this would fit."

"Try it on," said Alvean. "No, not here." She suddenly seemed obsessed by the desire to get out of this room.

We went back to our rooms and I put on the habit. It was not a perfect fit, but I was prepared to forget that it was a little tight at the waist, for a new woman looked back at me from my mirror. Delighted, I set the beaver hat on my head and ran along to Alvean's room. When she saw me, her eyes lit up.

We went down to the stables and I told Billy Trehay to saddle Buttercup for Alvean and another horse for myself. He looked at me with astonishment. When we were ready I put Buttercup on a leading rein and, with Alvean on her, took her back into the paddock. We were there for an hour, and when we left I knew that Alvean and I had entered into a new relationship. She had not accepted me completely, but I was no longer an enemy.

I concentrated on giving her confidence. I made her grow accustomed to sitting her horse, to talking to her horse. I made her lean back full length on Buttercup and look up at the sky. I gave her lessons in mounting and dismounting. At the end of the hour I had done much toward making her lose her fear.

I was astonished to find that it was half past three, and Alvean was too. "We must return to the house at once," I said, "if we are to change in time for tea."

As we came out of the field a figure rose from the grass. To my surprise it was Peter Nansellock. He clapped his hands. "Here endeth the first lesson," he cried, "and an excellent one."

"Were you watching us, Uncle Peter?" demanded Alvean.

"For the last half hour. My admiration is beyond expression."

Alvean smiled slowly. "Did you really admire us?"

"The art was never so gracefully taught, never so patiently learned."

"Mr. Nansellock is a joker, Alvean," I put in.

"Yes," said Alvean almost sadly, "I know."

"And," I added, "it is time that we returned for tea."

Holding Buttercup's leading rein, I started forward. Peter Nansellock walked behind us, and when we reached the stables I saw him making for the house. Alvean and I dismounted, handed our horses to two stableboys and hurried up to our rooms.

I changed into my dress and, glancing at myself, thought how drab I looked in it. I picked up the riding habit to hang in my cupboard, and as I lifted it I saw the name "Alice TreMellyn" embossed in tiny letters on the waistband. Then I understood. My heart leaped into my throat. That room had been her dressing room, and the bedroom I had glimpsed, her bedroom. I wondered that Alvean had given me her mother's clothes. I went to my window and looked along the house, trying to locate Alice's bedroom. I thought I placed it, and in spite of myself I shivered. Then I shook myself. She would be glad I had used her habit, I told myself. Was I not trying to help her daughter?

There was a knock on my door and Mrs. Polgrey came in. I felt very fond of her in that moment; there was such an air of normality about her.

"I have been giving Miss Alvean a riding lesson," I said. "And as I had no riding habit, she found one for me. I believe it to have been her mother's." I produced the habit. Mrs. Polgrey nodded. "I wore it this once. Perhaps it was wrong of me."

"Did you have the master's permission to teach her riding?"

"Oh yes, indeed."

"Then he would have no objection to your wearing the dress."

"Thank you," I said. "You have set my mind at rest."

I could see that she was rather pleased that I had brought my little problem to her. "Mr. Peter Nansellock is downstairs," she said. "The master is not at home. And Mr. Peter has asked that you entertain him for tea—you and Miss Alvean."

"Oh, but should we . . . I mean should I?"

"Why, yes, miss, I think it is what the master would wish. I have told Mr. Nansellock that tea will be served in the punch room and that you will join him and Miss Alvean."

Mrs. Polgrey smiled graciously and sailed out, and I found myself smiling too. It was turning out to be a most enjoyable day.

WHEN I REACHED THE PUNCH room Alvean was not there, but Peter Nansellock leaped to his feet on my entrance.

"Mrs. Polgrey has told me that I am to do the honors in the absence of Mr. TreMellyn."

"How like you, to remind me that you are merely the governess!"

"I felt," I replied, "that it was necessary to do so, since you may have forgotten."

"Indeed, I never saw you look less like a governess than when you were giving Alvean her lesson."

"It was my riding habit. Borrowed plumes. A pheasant would look like a peacock if it could acquire the tail."

"My dear Miss Pheasant, I do not agree. But let me ask you this before Alvean appears. What do you think of old Connan?"

"The adjective you use is inaccurate, and it is not my place to give an opinion."

He laughed aloud. "Dear governess, you'll be the death of me."

This banter was interrupted by the appearance of Alvean.

"Dear Alvean!" cried Peter. "How good it is of you and Miss Leigh to allow me to take tea with you."

"I wonder why you want to," replied Alvean. "You never have before, except when Miss Jansen was here."

"Hush, hush! You betray me," he murmured.

Mrs. Polgrey came in with Kitty, who laid a cloth on a small table and brought in the tea tray, cakes and cucumber sandwiches. I made tea and Alvean passed the sandwiches.

"What luxury!" Peter cried. "I feel like a sultan with two beautiful ladies to wait on me."

I changed the conversation briskly. "I think Alvean will make a good horsewoman in time," I said. "What was your opinion?"

"She'll be the champion of Cornwall; you'll see!"

Alvean could not hide her pleasure, and at that moment there was only one person in the world I wanted to be: Martha Leigh, taking tea with Peter Nansellock and Alvean TreMellyn.

Alvean said, "It's to be a secret for a while."

"Yes, we're going to surprise her father."

"I'll be silent as the grave."

Alvean offered the cakes to him; it was pleasant to have her so docile and friendly.

"You have not paid a visit to Mount Widden yet, Miss Leigh," Peter said. "The house is not so ancient nor so large as this one. It has no history, but it's a pleasant place and I'm sure my sister would be delighted if you paid us a visit one day."

"I am not sure—" I began.

"That it lies within your duties? I'll tell you how we'll arrange it. You shall bring Alvean to take tea at Mount Widden."

The door opened suddenly and to my embarrassment Connan TreMellyn came in. I felt as though I had been caught playing the part of mistress of the house in his absence, but he gave me a quick smile. "Miss Leigh," he said, "is there a cup of tea for me?"

"Alvean," I said, "ring for another cup, please."

She got up immediately. Her eagerness to please her father made her clumsy, and as she rose from her chair she knocked over her cup. She flushed scarlet with mortification. I said, "Never mind. Ring the bell. Kitty will clear it up."

Kitty came and I indicated the broken cup. "And please bring another cup for Mr. TreMellyn," I added.

Kitty was smirking a little as she went out. The situation evidently amused her. As for myself, I felt it ill became me. Now that the master of the house had appeared, I felt awkward.

"Had a busy day, Connan?" asked Peter.

Connan then began to talk of complicated estate business, reminding me that my duties as an employee consisted of dispensing tea and nothing else.

It was Peter who finally drew me into the conversation. "Miss Leigh and I met on the train the day she arrived."

"Really?"

"Indeed, yes. By some strange chance I shared her compartment."

"That," said Connan, "is very interesting." He looked as though nothing could be less so.

I glanced at my watch and said, "I am going to ask you to excuse Alvean and me. It is time for our studies."

"But surely," cried Peter, "on such an occasion there could be a little relaxation of the rules."

Alvean was looking eager. "I think it would be unwise," I said, rising. "Come along, Alvean."

She threw me a look of dislike and I feared I had forfeited the advance I had made earlier. "Please, Papa . . ." she began.

He looked at her sternly. "My dear child, you heard what your governess said."

Alvean blushed and we went upstairs. In the schoolroom she glared at me. "Why do you have to spoil everything?" she demanded. "We could have done our reading anytime."

"But we do our reading between five and six, not anytime," I retorted. I wanted to say to her: You long for your father's approval. But, my dear child, you do not know how to win it. Let me help you. But I had never learned to be demonstrative.

She sat at the table scowling at the book we were reading. She had lost her habitual enthusiasm; she was not even attending, for she looked up suddenly and said, "I believe you hate him. I believe you cannot bear to be in my father's company."

"What nonsense," I murmured, but I was afraid my color would deepen. "Come," I said, "we are wasting time."

THAT NIGHT, AFTER Alvean had retired, Kitty knocked on my door. "Miss," she said, "Master be asking for 'ee in the library." And she led me to a wing of this vast house which I had as yet not visited. There she opened a door, and I saw Connan TreMellyn sitting at a table covered with papers and leather-bound books. The only light came from a rose-quartz lamp on the table.

He said, "Do sit down, Miss Leigh."

I thought, He has discovered that I wore Alice's riding habit. He is shocked. I held my head high, waiting.

"I was interested to learn this afternoon," he began, "that you had already made the acquaintance of Mr. Nansellock."

"Really?" The surprise in my voice was not assumed.

"It was inevitable," he went on, "that you would meet sooner or later. He and his sister are constant visitors here, but—"

I felt embarrassed and I interrupted. "I imagine you feel that it is unbecoming of me to be . . . on terms of apparently equal footing with a friend of your family."

"Miss Leigh, what friends you make are your own concern. But your aunt put you under my care, in a manner of speaking, when she put you under my roof; so I wish to offer you a word of advice on a subject which, I fear, you may think a little indelicate. Mr. Nansellock has a reputation for being . . . how shall I put it . . . susceptible to young ladies."

"Oh!" I cried, unable to suppress the exclamation.

"Miss Leigh." He smiled, and for a moment his face looked almost tender. "This is in the nature of a friendly warning."

"Mr. TreMellyn," I protested, recovering myself with an effort, "I do not think I am in need of such a warning."

"There was a young lady here before you," he went on, "a Miss Jansen. He often called to see her. Miss Leigh, I do beg of you not to misunderstand me. And there is another thing I would also ask: Please do not take all that Mr. Nansellock says too seriously."

I heard myself say in a high-pitched voice, "It is extremely kind of you, Mr. TreMellyn, to concern yourself with my welfare."

"But of course I do. You are here to look after my daughter. Therefore your welfare is of the utmost importance to me."

He rose and I did the same. I saw that this was dismissal.

He came swiftly to my side and placed his hand on my shoulder. "Forgive me," he said. "I'm a blunt man, lacking in those graces which are so evident in Mr. Nansellock."

For a few seconds I looked into those cool light eyes and I thought I had a fleeting glimpse of the man behind the mask. I was sobered suddenly and, in a moment of bewildering emotion, I was deeply conscious of my loneliness, of the tragedy of those alone in the world who have no one who really cares for them.

"Thank you," I said, and I escaped back to my room.

ALVEAN AND I went riding every day. As I watched the little girl on Buttercup, I knew that she would soon be giving a good account of herself. I had discovered that every November a horse show was held in Mellyn village, and I had told Alvean that she should take part. Connan TreMellyn would be one of the judges, and we both imagined his astonishment when a certain rider, who came romping home with first prize, was his daughter who he had sworn would never learn to ride. The triumph in that dream was something Alvean and I could share. Hers was, of course, the more admirable emotion. She wanted to succeed for the sake of the love she bore her father; for myself I wanted to imply: See, you arrogant man, I have succeeded where you failed!

On the day we tried her first gallop we were elated.

Afterward we returned to the house together, and because I was with her, I went in by way of the front entrance. In the hall Alvean ran ahead. As I followed her I noticed a damp, musty smell. I saw that the door leading to the chapel was ajar. Thinking that Alvean had gone in there, I went in. It was cold, and I shivered as I stood on the blue flagstones and gazed at the altar. Suddenly I heard a gasp behind me.

"No!" said a voice so horrified that I did not recognize it.

My whole body seemed to freeze. I turned sharply, but it was only Celestine Nansellock who stood looking at me. She was so white that I thought she was going to faint. She had seen me in Alice's riding habit and had believed in that second that I *was* Alice. "Miss Nansellock," I said quickly to reassure her, "Alvean and I have been having a riding lesson."

She swayed a little; her face was a grayish color. "Whatever made you come into the chapel?" she said.

"Alvean ran off and I thought she might be in here."

"Alvean! Oh no . . . no one ever comes in here."

"You look . . . unwell, Miss Nansellock. Would you like me to ring for some brandy?"

"No . . . no. I'm perfectly well."

I said boldly, "You're looking at my clothes. They're—borrowed. I have to give Alvean riding lessons. These were . . . her mother's. I'm afraid I startled you."

"Oh no, you mustn't say that. I'm quite all right. . . ."

We went back to the hall and then out of the house. She had regained her normal color. "Does Alvean enjoy her riding lessons?" she asked. "Are you getting along better now?"

"Yes, I think we are becoming friends. The riding lessons have helped considerably."

"So she is becoming your friend, Miss Leigh. I am glad of that. Now I must go. I was just on my way out when I passed the chapel and saw the door open."

I said good-by to her and went up to my room to change.

A WEEK PASSED and lessons both in the schoolroom and on the riding field progressed favorably. Peter Nansellock came over to the house on two occasions, but I eluded him. I knew Connan TreMellyn's warning to be reasonable. I faced the fact that I could easily find myself looking forward to Peter's visits.

I thought now and then of his brother, Geoffry, and I concluded that Peter must be very like him. And when I thought of Geoffry I thought also of Mrs. Polgrey's daughter of whom she had never spoken: Jennifer. I shivered to contemplate the pitfalls which lie in wait for unwary women.

My interest in Alvean had made me forget little Gillyflower temporarily. Occasionally I heard her singing in her thin reedy voice; and I would say to myself, If she can learn to sing, she can learn other things. Side by side with that picture of Connan TreMellyn handing his daughter a prize at the horse show, another picture was growing: a picture of Gilly sitting at the schoolroom table with Alvean. I imagined people whispering, This could never have happened but for Miss Leigh. She is a wonder with children. But at this time Alvean was still stubborn and Gilly elusive and, as the Tapperty girls said, "with a tile loose in the upper story."

Then into those more or less peaceful days came two disturbing events.

The first was of small moment, but it haunted me.

I was going through one of Alvean's exercise books, marking her sums while she worked; and as I turned the pages a piece of paper covered with drawings fell out. I had already discovered that she had a talent for drawing, and one day I intended to approach Connan TreMellyn about this, for I felt she was worth a qualified drawing teacher. I recognized a picture of myself. Did I really look as prim as that? Then there was her father. I turned the page and this was covered with girls' faces. Herself? No . . . Gilly, surely. And yet it had a look of herself.

Alvean snatched the page away. "That's mine," she said. "You have no right to pry."

"My dear child, that paper was in your arithmetic book."

"I'm sorry," she murmured, still defiantly.

Why was she so annoyed? Why had she drawn those faces which were part Gilly's, part her own? I said, "Alvean, why did you not wish me to see those faces? I thought some of them quite good." She did not answer. "Particularly," I went on, "those girls' faces. Who were they supposed to be—you or Gilly?"

She said almost breathlessly, "Whom did you take them for?"

"Well, let me look at them again."

She hesitated; then she brought out the paper. I studied the faces. I said, "This one could be either you or Gilly."

"You think we're alike then?"

"No, no. I hadn't thought so until this moment."

"I'm not like her! I'm not like that . . . idiot." She was shouting, trying to convince herself that there was not the slightest resemblance between herself and Gilly. What was the reason for this vehemence?

I said, calmly looking at my watch, "We have exactly ten minutes to finish your sums." I drew the arithmetic book toward me and pretended to give it my attention.

THE SECOND INCIDENT was even more upsetting.

It had been a peaceful day and I had taken a late-evening stroll. When I returned I saw two carriages drawn up in front of the house. One I recognized as from Mount Widden. The other I did not know.

I went swiftly up the back stairs to my apartment.

It was a warm night, and as I sat at my window I heard music and realized that Connan TreMellyn was entertaining guests. I pictured them in the drawing room, which I had not even seen, at the card tables or perhaps simply listening to the music. It was Mendelssohn's "A Midsummer Night's Dream," and I longed to be down there among them. Kitty or Daisy always knew what was going on. I rang the bell and Daisy answered it.

I said, "I want some hot water, please, Daisy."

"Yes, miss," she said.

"There are guests here tonight, I understand."

"Yes, miss. I reckon now the year of mourning is up, Master will be entertaining more."

"Of course. Who are the guests tonight?"

"Oh, there's Miss Celestine and Mr. Peter, of course. And Sir Thomas and Lady Treslyn." She looked conspiratorial.

"Oh?" I said encouragingly.

"Though," went on Daisy, "Mrs. Polgrey says that Sir Thomas baint fit to go gallivanting at parties. He'll never see seventy again and he's got a bad heart. Mrs. Polgrey says you can go off sudden with a heart like that, and no pushing neither. Not that—" She stopped and twinkled at me. "Well, *she's* another kettle of fish."

"Who?"

"Lady Treslyn, of course. Got a gown cut right down to *here*. She's a real beauty, and you can see she's only waiting . . ."

"I gather she is not of the same age as her husband."

"They say there's nearly forty years' difference."

And Daisy went off to get my hot water, leaving me with a clearer picture of what was happening in the drawing room.

I was still thinking of them as I made ready to retire. The musicians were playing a Chopin waltz now, and it seemed to spirit me away from my governess' bedroom and tantalize me with pleasures outside my reach. I went to the window. I could smell the sea and hear the gentle rhythm of the waves. The "voices" were starting up in Mellyn Cove.

Then suddenly I saw a light in a dark part of the house. I knew that window. It belonged to Alice's dressing room. The blind was down. I was sure it had not been like that earlier in the evening, because I had made a habit—which I regretted—of glancing at that window whenever I looked out of my own.

The blind was of thin material, and behind it I distinctly saw a faint light. I stood at my window staring out, and as I did so I saw a woman's shadow on the blind. I'm dreaming, I told myself. My hands, gripping the windowsill, were trembling. I had an impulse to go to Mrs. Polgrey, but I restrained myself, imagining how foolish I would look. So I remained staring at Alice's window, and after a while all was darkness.

I went to bed, but I could not sleep for a long time; and at last, when I did sleep, I dreamed that a woman came into my room. She was wearing a riding habit trimmed with braid and ball fringe, and she said to me, "I was not on that train, Miss Leigh. You wonder where I was. It is for you to find me."

The first thing I did on rising next morning was to go to my window and look across at the room which—little more than a year ago—had belonged to Alice.

The blinds were drawn up. I could see the rich blue velvet curtains.

CHAPTER FOUR

IT WAS ABOUT a week later that I first saw Linda Treslyn. It was just past six o'clock. Alvean and I had put away our books and had set out for a stroll through the gardens. The plateau on which Mount Mellyn stood was a mile or so wide. The slope to the sea was steep, but zigzag paths made the descent easier. Flowering shrubs grew profusely here, and several rose arbors had been set up where one could sit and gaze out to sea.

We made our way down a sweet-smelling path and were level with an arbor before we noticed that two people were there. They were sitting side by side and close. She was very dark and one of the most beautiful women I had ever seen. She wore a gauzy scarf over her hair, and her dress was made of some clinging material, caught at the throat with a diamond brooch.

"Why," Connan said, "it is my daughter and Miss Leigh. You have not met Lady Treslyn?" She nodded to me, and he added, "So, Miss Leigh, you and Alvean are taking the air."

"It is such a pleasant evening," I said. I made to take Alvean's hand, but she eluded me.

"May I sit with you and Lady Treslyn, Papa?" she asked.

"You are taking a walk with Miss Leigh," he said. "Do you not think that you should continue to do so?"

"Yes," I answered for her. "Come along, Alvean."

Connan had turned to his companion. "We are very fortunate to have found Miss Leigh. She is . . . admirable!"

"The perfect governess this time, I hope, for *your* sake, Connan," said Lady Treslyn.

I felt awkward, as if I were a mare standing by while they discussed my points. I said, "It is time we turned back, Alvean."

Alvean protested. "But I want to stay, Papa. Please!"

Lady Treslyn murmured, "I see Alvean is very determined."

Connan TreMellyn said coolly, "Miss Leigh will deal with her."

"Of course. The perfect governess." There was a note of mockery in Lady Treslyn's voice.

I seized Alvean's arm. She was half sobbing, but she did not speak again until we were in her room. Then she said, "I hate her, Miss Leigh. She wants to be my new mama."

"How could she wish to be your mama," I said, "when she has a husband of her own?"

"He will soon die. Everybody says they are only waiting."

I was shocked that she should have heard such gossip, and I thought, I will speak to Mrs. Polgrey about this. The servants must be careful what they say in front of Alvean.

"She's always here," went on Alvean. "I won't let her take my mother's place. I won't let *anybody*."

Poor little Alvean, I thought, poor lonely child!

I HAD SEEN Alvean to bed and had returned to my room, but I kept thinking of Connan TreMellyn out there in the arbor with Lady Treslyn. Of course Alvean and I had interrupted a flirtation. I felt shocked that he should indulge in such an intrigue, for the lady had a husband.

I went to the window and looked out at the scented evening. Twilight was on us. My eyes turned to Alice's window.

The blinds were up, and I could see the blue curtains. I don't know what I expected. Was it to see a beckoning hand at the window? Then I saw the curtains move, and I knew that someone was in that room.

Alice's room was not in my part of the house, but I felt reckless that evening. I did not care. I had a burning desire to discover what mystery lay behind her death.

I went along the gallery to Alice's dressing room, knocked lightly on the door and, with my heart beating like a hammer, swiftly opened it. For a second I saw no one. Then I detected a movement of·the curtains. Some-one was hiding behind them.

"Who is it?" I asked. There was no answer.

I strode across the room, drew aside the curtains and saw Gilly cower-ing there. "It's all right, Gilly," I said gently. "I won't hurt you. Tell me, what are you doing here?"

She said nothing. She began to stare about the room as though she saw something—or someone—I could not see.

"Gilly," I said, "you know you should not be in this room, do you not? I am going to take you back to my room, Gilly."

I put my arm about her; she was trembling. I drew her to the door. At the threshold she looked back over her shoulder and cried out, "Madam, come back . . . *now!*"

I led her firmly to my bedroom. There I shut the door and stood with my back against it. "Gilly," I said, "I won't hurt you." Taking a shot in the dark I went on. "I want to be your friend as Mrs. TreMellyn was."

That startled her and the blank look disappeared for a moment. I had made another discovery. Alice had been kind to this child. "You went there to look for her, did you not?"

She nodded, looking so pathetic that I knelt down and put my arms about her. "You can't find her, Gilly. She is dead. We must try to forget her, mustn't we?"

The pale lids fell over the eyes to hide them from me.

"We'll be friends," I said. "I want us to be."

She was not trembling now, and I was sure that she was no longer afraid of me. But suddenly she slipped out of my grasp and ran to the door. She opened it and turned to look back at me, with a faint smile on her lips. Then she was gone.

I thought of Alice, who had been kind to this child. I went to the window and looked across the L-shaped building to the window of the room. I thought of that night when I had seen the shadow on the blind. My dis-covery of Gilly did not explain that. It was no child I had seen silhouetted there. It was a woman.

NEXT DAY I WENT TO Mrs. Polgrey. "Mrs. Polgrey," I said, "there is something I should very much like to discuss with you."

She looked delighted. I could see that the governess who sought her advice must be, in her eyes, the ideal governess.

"I shall be delighted to give you an hour of my company and a cup of my best tea," she told me.

Over the teacups in her room she surveyed me affectionately. "Now, Miss Leigh, pray tell me what it is you would ask of me."

"I am a little disturbed," I told her, "about a remark of Alvean's. I am sure that she listens to gossip, and I think it most undesirable in a child of her age." I told her how we had met Connan TreMellyn with Lady Treslyn. "And Alvean," I went on, "said that Lady Treslyn hoped to become her mama."

Mrs. Polgrey shook her head. She said, "What about a spoonful of whiskey in your tea, Miss Leigh? There's nothing like it for keeping up the spirits."

I had no desire for it, but I could see that Mrs. Polgrey had, so I said, "A small teaspoonful, please, Mrs. Polgrey."

She unlocked the cupboard, removed a bottle and measured out the whiskey. Now we were like a pair of conspirators, and Mrs. Polgrey was clearly enjoying herself. "You may find it somewhat shocking," she began.

"I am prepared," I assured her.

"Well, Sir Thomas is a very old man, and only a few years ago he married this young lady, a playactress, some say, from London. Her set the neighborhood agog, I can tell you. They do say she's one of the handsomest women in the country. And men like the master can be foolish." Mrs. Polgrey leaned closer. "There's some as say that they'm not the sort to wait for blessing of clergy."

"So you think . . ."

She continued gravely. "When Sir Thomas dies there'll be a new mistress in this house." Then she added piously, "And I'd sooner see the master of the house I serve living in wedlock than in sin, I do assure you. All they have to wait for now is for Sir Thomas to go. Mrs. TreMellyn, her . . . her's already gone."

"Was this so . . . when Mrs. TreMellyn was alive?"

Mrs. Polgrey nodded slowly. "He visited Lady Treslyn often. It started almost as soon as she came. Sometimes he rides out at night and we don't see him till morning."

"Could we warn the girls not to gossip before Alvean?"

"As well try to keep a cuckoo from singing in the spring. I could wallop them two till I dropped with exhaustion and still they'd chatter."

I nodded, thinking of poor Alice. No wonder she had run away with Geoffry Nansellock!

Mrs. Polgrey was now in such an expansive mood that I felt I might ask about other matters. I said, "Have you ever thought of teaching Gilly her letters?"

"Gilly! Why, you must know, miss, that Gilly is not as she should be." Mrs. Polgrey tapped her forehead.

"If she could learn songs, could she not learn other things?"

"She's a queer little thing. Sometimes I think she be a cursed child. Us didn't want her; and she was only a little thing in a cradle . . . two months old . . . when Jennifer went."

"When did you notice that she was not like other children?"

"Some four years ago, it would be. She were born a few months after Miss Alvean. They'd play together now and then. Then there was an accident. Gilly were playing near the drive and the mistress were riding along to the house. Gilly, her darted out from the bushes and caught a blow from the horse."

"Poor Gilly," I said.

"The mistress were distressed. Blamed herself, although 'twas no blame to her. She made much of Gilly after that. Gilly used to follow her about and fret when she was away."

Mrs. Polgrey poured more tea. I marveled that she had not connected Gilly's strangeness with the accident.

I longed to understand Gilly, to soothe Alvean. I was discovering a fondness for children in myself which I had not known I possessed.

THERE WAS EXCITEMENT throughout the house next day because there was to be a ball—the first since Alice's death. Invitations were being sent out all over the countryside. Kitty and Daisy were hysterical with delight, and I found it difficult to keep Alvean's attention on her lessons.

"When my mother was alive," she said dreamily, "there were lots of balls. She loved them. She used to come show me how she looked. Then she would let me sit in the solarium and watch the ball through the peep."

"The peep?" I asked.

"Ah, you don't know what peeps are?" She regarded me triumphantly. "There are several in this house. A lot of big houses have them. My mother told me the ladies used to sit there when the men were feasting. They could look down and watch, but they must not *be* there. There's one in the chapel—we call it the lepers' squint. Lepers couldn't come into the chapel, so they looked through the squint. Come to the solarium with me and watch the ball through the peep! Please do."

"We'll see," I said.

On the day of the ball Alvean and I took our riding lesson as usual, only instead of riding Buttercup, Alvean was mounted on Black Prince. Prince was behaving admirably and Alvean's confidence was growing.

We had done rather well for the first few lessons. But this day we were not so fortunate. I suspect that Alvean's thoughts were on the ball rather than on her riding. As we began to gallop she gave a little cry, and her fear was communicated at once to Black Prince. In a flash he was off, racing toward the hedge, and I saw Alvean swaying to one side. I was after her immediately. I had to grasp Prince's bridle before he reached the hedge, for if he jumped it, Alvean would have a nasty fall. Fear gave me strength and I got his rein and brought him to a standstill while a white-faced, trembling Alvean slid unharmed to the ground.

Shaken as she was, I made her remount. She obeyed me, although reluctantly. But when our lesson ended she was well over her fright, and I knew that she would want to ride next day.

As we were leaving the field she suddenly burst out laughing. "Oh, Miss Leigh!" she cried. "You've split!"

"What *do* you mean?"

"Your dress has split under the armhole. And it's getting worse and worse!" I must have shown my dismay, for she added, "Never mind, I'll find you another habit. There *are* more."

Alvean was in high spirits as we went back to the house. It was disconcerting to discover that my discomfiture could give her so much pleasure she could forget the danger through which she had so recently passed.

THE BALL WAS being held in the great hall. Kitty had urged me to take a peek, and I thought I had rarely seen a setting so beautiful. The beams had been decorated with leaves. "An old Cornish custom," Kitty told me. Pots of hothouse blooms had been brought in from the greenhouses; great wax candles were in the sconces. I pictured how it would look when those candles were lighted and the guests danced in their colorful gowns, their pearls and diamonds.

How I wanted to be one of those guests! I turned away and there was a foolish lump in my throat.

At supper that evening Alvean said, "I've put a new riding habit for you in your cupboard."

"Thank you," I said. "That was thoughtful of you."

"Hurry and finish now," she said, "so we can watch the ball."

"I suppose you have permission . . ." I began.

"I always peep from the solarium. My mother used to look up and wave to me." Her face puckered a little. "Tonight I'm going to imagine that she's down there . . . dancing. Miss Leigh, do you think people come back after they're dead?"

"What an extraordinary question! Of course not."

"Still," she went on dreamily, "if she *were* coming back, she would come to the ball."

THE VASTNESS OF THE HOUSE continued to astonish me as I followed Alvean up yet another stone staircase to the glass-roofed solarium. "There are two peeps up here," said Alvean. She disappeared behind one of the heavy brocade curtains hung on the walls, and when I followed her I found myself in an alcove. In its inside wall was a star-shaped opening, decorated so that one would hardly have noticed it. I gazed through it and looked down into the chapel.

"They sat up here to watch the service if they were too ill to go downstairs. They had a priest in the house in the old days. Miss Jansen told me that. She knew a lot about the house."

"You were sorry when she went, Alvean, I believe."

"Yes, I was. The second peep's on the other side." We went across the room into another alcove with a similar star-shaped opening.

I found myself looking down on the great hall and it was a magnificent sight. Musicians were on the dais. The guests stood about talking. I saw Connan TreMellyn in conversation with Celestine Nansellock; Peter was there too. Then I saw Lady Treslyn in a gown composed of yards and yards of flame-colored chiffon. Her dark hair looked almost black against the flame, and she wore a tiara of diamonds in it.

Alvean saw her and frowned. "*She* is there," she said.

"Is her husband present?"

"Yes." She pointed out to me a bent old man, white-haired and wrinkled. It seemed incredible that he should be the husband of that flamboyant creature.

"Look!" whispered Alvean. "My father is going to open the ball. He used to open it with Aunt Celestine, and Mother with Uncle Geoffry. The first tune is always the 'Furry Dance.' "

The musicians began to play, and I saw Connan lead Celestine into the center of the hall; Peter Nansellock followed, with Lady Treslyn as his partner. I watched them start the traditional dance, and I thought, Poor Celestine! Even gowned as she was in blue satin she looked ill at ease with that elegant trio.

An hour passed as we stood looking at the ball, and I fancied that Connan glanced up once or twice. Alvean watched the dancers breathlessly. It was now dark, but a great gibbous moon had risen. I looked up at it through the glass roof. . . . You are banished from the gaiety and the glitter, it seemed to say, but I will give you my soft and tender light instead. The room, touched by moonlight, took on an almost supernatural quality. I felt that in such a room anything might happen.

I turned my attention back to the dancers. They were waltzing now and I found myself swaying to the rhythm.

When I felt a hand touch mine, I was so startled that I gave an audible gasp. I looked down. Standing beside me was Gillyflower. "You have come to see the dancers?" I said. She nodded and I moved a stool over so she could reach the peep.

Alvean did not seem to want to look now that Gilly had come. She moved away, and as the musicians began the opening bars of "The Blue Danube," she began to dance across the solarium.

The music affected my feet too. I danced toward Alvean, waltzing as I used to in London ballrooms, and Alvean cried out with pleasure, "Go on, Miss Leigh! Don't stop!"

So I went on dancing with an imaginary partner, with the moon smiling in at me. And when I reached the end of the room a figure moved toward me. "You're exquisite," said a voice, and there was Peter Nansellock. He took me in his arms and my feet faltered. He said, "No, no!" and we went on dancing.

I said, "This is most unorthodox."

"It is most delightful."

"You should be with the guests."

"I much prefer to be with you."

"You forget . . ."

"That you are the governess? I could, if you would allow me to. How beautifully you dance!"

A voice startled me. "So here he is!"

To my horror I saw that several people had come into the solarium, and my apprehension did not lessen when I recognized the flame-colored gown of Lady Treslyn, for where she was, Connan TreMellyn would be. "The Blue Danube" ended, and I put my hand up to my hair in acute embarrassment. I knew that dancing had loosened the pins. I thought, I shall be dismissed tomorrow for my irresponsibility, and perhaps I deserve it.

"What an excellent idea," said someone. "Dancing in moonlight. And one can hear the music quite well up here."

Someone else said, "This is a splendid ballroom, Connan."

"Then let us use it for that purpose," he answered. He went to the peep and called, "Once more—'The Blue Danube.' "

I gripped Alvean and Gilly by the hand. People were already beginning to dance and I overheard two of them talking.

"Alvean's governess, you know. Forward creature! Another of Peter's light ladies, I suppose."

"The last one had to be dismissed, I believe."

"And this one's turn will come."

I blushed hotly, feeling both furious and a little frightened. Connan came over, looking at me, I feared, with disapproval. How unbecoming my lavender cotton gown seemed, with its high neck and lace collar and cuffs, compared with the dresses of his guests!

"Alvean," he said, "go to your room and take Gilly with you."

I said as coolly as I could, "Yes, let us go." But as I was about to follow the children I found my arm held by Connan.

He said, "You dance extremely well, Miss Leigh. I am sure that 'The Blue Danube' is a favorite of yours. You looked . . . enraptured." And with that he swung me into his arms and I found that I was dancing with him among his guests. . . . I in my lavender cotton and my turquoise brooch, they in their chiffons and velvets, their emeralds and diamonds. I was glad of the softness of the moonlight, for I was overcome with shame. I believed that he was angry and that his intention was to shame me even further.

My feet caught the rhythm, and I thought to myself, Always in the future "The Blue Danube" will mean to me a fantastic dance in the solarium with Connan TreMellyn as my partner.

"I apologize," he said, "for my guests' bad manners."

"It is what I must expect and no doubt what I deserve."

"What nonsense," he said, and I told myself that I was dreaming, for his voice, close to my ear, sounded tender.

We had come to the end of the room and he whirled me out through the arched doorway. We were on a small landing between two flights of stone stairs. We stopped dancing, but he still kept his arms about me. On the wall a paraffin lamp burned; its light was only enough to show me his face. It looked a little brutal, I thought. "Miss Leigh," he said, "you are charming when you abandon your severity." I caught my breath with dismay, for he was forcing me against the wall and kissing me.

I was horrified as much by my own emotions as by what was happening. I knew what that kiss meant: You are not averse to a mild flirtation with Peter Nansellock; why not with me? With all my might I pushed him from me, lifted my skirts and ran as fast as I could down the stairs. I did not know where I was, but I went on running blindly until I found the gallery which led to my own room. There I threw myself on my bed.

There was only one thing to do: I must leave this house in the morning. He had made his intentions clear, and I had no doubt at all that Miss Jansen was dismissed because she refused him. I was more desperately unhappy than I had ever been in my life. I would not face the truth, but I really cared deeply that he should have regarded me with such contempt.

I rose to start packing. I went to the clothes cupboard and pulled open the door. For a moment I thought someone was standing there, and I cried out in alarm. Then I saw what it was: the riding habit Alvean had procured for me. I had forgotten about it.

When I had finished packing, I heard the sound of voices below and went to my window. Some of the guests had come out onto the lawn, and I saw them dancing down there in the moonlight. Connan was dancing with Lady Treslyn, his head close to hers.

I turned angrily away from the window, undressed and went to bed, and when I finally slept I had jumbled dreams. Sometime later I awoke with a start. In the moonlit room I seemed to see the dark shape of a woman. I knew it was Alice. She did not speak, yet she was telling me something. "You must not go from here. You must stay. You can help us all."

Trembling all over, I sat up. Now I saw what had startled me. I had left the door of the cupboard open, and what appeared to be the ghost of Alice was only her riding habit.

I ROSE LATE next morning and was only half clothed when Kitty knocked and I let her in. "Wasn't it lovely, miss?" she said. "They danced on the lawn in the moonlight. You look tired, miss. Did they keep you awake?"

"Yes," I said, "they did."

"Well, it's all over now, and Master be asking to see you in the punch room. He said, 'Tell Miss Leigh it is most urgent.' "

I finished dressing. I guessed what this meant. Well, I would be first. I would tell him my decision to leave before he had a chance to dismiss me. I went down to the punch room.

He was wearing a blue riding jacket and did not look at all as though he had been up half the night. "Good morning, Miss Leigh," he said, and to my astonishment he smiled.

I did not return the smile. "Good morning," I said. "I have already packed and would like to leave as soon as possible."

"Miss Leigh!"

His voice was reproachful, and I felt an absurd joy rising within me. I thought, He doesn't want me to go. I heard myself say in a high, prim voice, "I consider it the only course open to me after—"

"After my outrageous, my depraved conduct of last night. Miss Leigh, I fear the excitement of the moment overcame me. I ask you to say generously that you will draw a veil over that unpleasant incident, forget it and go on as we were before."

I had a notion he was mocking me, but I was suddenly so happy that I did not care. I inclined my head and said, "I accept your apology, Mr. Tre-Mellyn. We will forget the incident."

I left the room, and my feet were almost dancing as they had danced last night in the solarium. So I was going to stay. The whole house seemed to warm to me, and I knew in that moment that if I had to leave this place I should be quite desolate. Perhaps had I been wise I should have recognized the danger signals. But I was not wise. Women in my position rarely are.

THAT DAY, WHEN Alvean and I took our riding lesson, I wore the new habit—a lightweight, tight-fitting dress with a tailored jacket. Alvean showed no signs of fear after her small mishap of the day before, and I said that in a few days' time we might attempt a little jumping.

We arrived back at the house, and I went to my room to change before tea. I was about to hang up the riding habit when I felt something beneath the jacket lining. Surprised, I laid the jacket on the bed and, examining it, discovered a concealed pocket. In it was a small diary. I could not resist looking inside. On the flyleaf was written in a rather childish hand "Alice TreMellyn." I looked at the date. It was the previous year, the last year of her life.

I turned the leaves. If I had expected a revelation of character I was soon disappointed. Alice had merely used this as a record of her appointments: "To tea at Mount Widden." "C. to Penzance." "C. due back." Under the fourteenth of July was written: "Treslyns and Trelanders to dine. See dressmaker about blue satin. . . . Speak to Polgrey about flowers. . . . If jeweler has not sent brooch by sixteenth, see him to remind him it is needed for T. dinner party on eighteenth." And then, on the sixteenth: "Brooch not returned; must see jeweler tomorrow."

It all sounded very trivial. I put the book back. Then a thought struck me. Her death must have come soon after this; how odd that she should have made those entries when she was planning to leave her husband and daughter for another man! It suddenly became imperative to know the exact date of her death.

Alvean was with her father, so I was free to go out alone. I made my way down into the valley, to Mellyn village. Its few stone houses nestled about an old church, whose gray tower was half covered in ivy. I went through the lych-gate and into the churchyard. I felt surrounded by the stillness of death and I almost wished I had brought Alvean with me to point out her mother's grave. Then I thought, The TreMellyns would no doubt own a splendid vault. I saw a huge one not far off, and as I turned toward it I saw Celestine Nansellock approaching me.

"Miss Leigh," she cried, "I thought it was you."

I felt myself flush because I remembered seeing her last night among the guests in the solarium, and I wondered what she was thinking of me now. "I strolled down to the village," I answered, "and found myself here."

"I come often to bring a few flowers for Alice. Have you seen the Tre-Mellyn vault? It's over here."

I followed her across the long grass to the vault. At the entrance was a vase of Michaelmas daisies—perfect blooms that looked like mauve stars. "I've just put them here," she said. "They were her favorite flowers." Her lips trembled and I thought she was going to burst into tears.

I looked at the names inscribed on the marble and saw that Alice had died on the seventeenth of July.

I said, "I shall have to go back now."

She nodded, apparently too moved to speak.

I hurried back to the house and took out the diary. So on the sixteenth

of July last year—the day before Alice was supposed to have eloped—she had written in her diary that she must see the jeweler the next day, as she needed her brooch for a party on the eighteenth!

That entry had not been made by a woman who was planning to elope. I felt that I had almost certain proof in my hands that the body which had been found with Geoffry Nansellock's on the wrecked train was not Alice's.

Then what had happened to Alice? If she was not lying inside the family vault, where was she?

CHAPTER FIVE

I WONDERED WHETHER I should go to Connan TreMellyn and tell him about his wife's diary. But I did not quite trust him. I had already begun to ask myself, Suppose Alice was not on the train and something else had happened to her. Who would be most likely to know what that was? Could it be Connan TreMellyn?

It was impossible to discuss this matter with Peter; he was too frivolous; he turned every conversation into a flirtation. But his sister had been fond of Alice; she was clearly the one in whom I could best confide. And yet I hesitated. Celestine belonged to the world into which I, as Alvean's governess, had no right to intrude.

The other person in whom I might confide was Mrs. Polgrey, but again I shrank, remembering her spoonfuls of whiskey.

So I decided that for the time being I would keep my suspicions to myself. October was upon us, and I found the changing seasons delightful in this part of the world. The blustering southwest wind was warm and damp, and when the sun came out it was almost as warm as June. "Summer do go on a long time in Cornwall," Tapperty told me. And in the humid climate the hydrangeas continued to flower—blue, pink and white—in enormous masses of bloom.

In the village one day I saw a notice that the horse-show date was fixed for the first of November. I went back and told Alvean, "We have only three weeks to practice. Perhaps we should ride in the mornings too." She agreed eagerly.

Connan TreMellyn had gone to Penzance, Kitty told me when she brought in my hot water one evening. " 'Tis thought he'll be away for a week or more," she said.

I was annoyed with the man. Not that I expected him to tell me he was going; but I did feel he might have had the grace to say good-by to his daughter. I promised myself that while he was away there was no need to think of him, and that would be a relief.

There would be two jumping contests for children at the horse show, and we decided that Alvean would enter the elementary one, for I felt she had a good chance of winning a prize in that.

"Look, Miss Leigh!" said Alvean, reading from a list of events. "Here's one for the grown-ups. Why don't you enter it?"

"My dear child, I am not here to enter competitions."

A mischievous look came into her eyes. "*I'm* going to enter you. Nobody here can ride as well as you do."

I fell back on my stock phrase for ending an embarrassing discussion. "We'll see," I said.

ONE AFTERNOON WE were riding close to Mount Widden and met Peter Nansellock. He was mounted on a beautiful bay mare, the sight of which made my eyes glisten with envy. "Well met, dear ladies," he cried. "Were you coming to call on us?"

"We were not, Mr. Nansellock," I answered.

"How unkind! But now you are here, you must come in for tea."

Alvean cried, "Oh, do let's! *Please.*"

Peter turned his mare, and we walked our horses side by side. He saw my gaze fixed on his mare. "You like her?" he said.

"Indeed I do. She's a beauty."

"You're a real beauty, are you not, Jacinth my pet?"

"Jacinth. So that's her name."

"Pretty name for a pretty creature. She'll go like the wind. She's worth four of that lumbering old cart horse you're riding, Miss Leigh."

"Lumbering old cart horse? Dion is a very fine horse."

"*Was*, Miss Leigh. *Was!* Do you not think that the creature has seen better days? Jacinth could quickly show you what it feels like to be on a good mount again."

"Oh," I said lightly, "we're satisfied with what we have."

"We're practicing for the horse show," Alvean told him. "I'm going to be in it, but don't tell Papa; it's a surprise. And Miss Leigh is entering one of the events too."

"She'll be victorious," he cried. "I'll make a bet on it."

I said curtly, "It is only an idea of Alvean's."

"But you must!" cried Alvean. "I insist."

"We both insist," said Peter.

We had reached Mount Widden and a groom took our horses. As we went into the house, I saw that it was not so well cared for as Mount Mellyn. The hall floor was tessellated, and a wide staircase led to a gallery lined with oil paintings. But everything had an air of neglect—almost of decay.

Peter rang for tea and took us into the library, a huge, dusty room. "Sit down, dear ladies," he said. "I hope tea will not long be delayed, but I must warn you that we are not served here with the precision enjoyed by our rival across the cove."

"Rival?" I said in surprise.

"Well, how could there fail to be a little rivalry? Here we stand, side by side. But the advantages are all with them. They have the grander house and the servants to deal with it. Your father, dear Alvean, is a man of property. We Nansellocks are his poor relations."

"You are not our relations," Alvean reminded him.

"Now is that not strange? One would have thought that, living side by side for generations, the two families would have mingled and become one. There must have been charming TreMellyn girls and handsome Nansellock men. How odd that they did not intermarry. And now there is the fair Alvean, and we have no boy of her age. There is nothing for it; *I* shall have to wait for her."

Alvean laughed delightedly. She was quite fascinated by him, and I thought, Perhaps he is more serious about this than he seems.

When tea was brought, Peter said, "Miss Leigh, will you honor us by pouring?" He watched me as I placed myself at the tea table. "How glad I am that we met today," he went on. "There is not much more time left to us. I am going away in the new year."

"Where, Uncle Peter?" demanded Alvean.

"Far away, my child, to the other side of the world. I have heard from a friend in Australia. He has made a fortune. Gold! Think of it, Alvean. All one has to do is pluck it out of the ground."

"Many go in the hope of making fortunes," I said, "but are they all successful?"

"There speaks the practical woman. No, Miss Leigh, they are not all successful; but there is something named Hope which, I believe, springs eternal in the human breast. I shall come back a rich man. In years to come people will say it was Peter Nansellock who saved the family fortunes. For, my dear young ladies, someone has to save them . . . soon. And I shall then build a new wing on Mount Widden."

He began planning how he would rebuild the house, and we both joined in. It was a pleasant game, and I felt exhilarated by his company. Afterward he took us out to the stables and insisted on my trying Jacinth. She was a delicious creature and I envied him.

"Why," he said, "she has taken to you, Miss Leigh."

We then mounted our horses, and Peter came with us to the gates of Mount Mellyn. As we went up to our rooms Alvean said, "Uncle Peter admires you, I think, as he did Miss Jansen."

"Did Miss Jansen go to tea at Mount Widden?"

"Oh yes. When he bought his mare, he changed her name to Jacinth because it was Miss Jansen's name."

I felt foolishly deflated. Then I said, "He must have been sorry when she left so suddenly."

"Yes, I think he was. But he soon forgot about her."

I knew why. She was only the governess, after all.

LATER THAT DAY Kitty came to my room to tell me there was a message for me. "And something more too, miss," she added, giggling. "In the stables. Come and see."

When I arrived at the stables, I found the mare Jacinth with a stableboy from Mount Widden. He handed me a note, and I read it while Daisy, old Tapperty and Billy Trehay, standing nearby, watched with amused and knowing eyes.

Dear Miss Leigh,
   You could not hide from me your admiration for Jacinth. I believe she reciprocates your feelings. Pray accept her as a gift.
                         Your admiring neighbor, Peter Nansellock

I felt the hot color rising to my face. How could Peter be so foolish? How could I possibly accept such a gift?

"Is there an answer, miss?" asked the stableboy.

"Yes," I said. "I will write a note at once." I went with as much dignity as I could muster back to my room and wrote:

Dear Mr. Nansellock,
   Thank you for your magnificent gift which I am, of course, quite unable to accept. I have no means of keeping a horse, and could not possibly afford the upkeep of Jacinth.
                         Yours truly, Martha Leigh

I went straight back to the stables. "Please take this note to your master, with Jacinth," I said to the stableboy. I saw Tapperty watching me slyly. "Mr. Nansellock," I said, "is fond of playing jokes." And I went back to the house.

THE NEXT DAY was a Saturday, and Alvean asked if we could take a holiday and go to the moor. Her great-aunt Clara had a house there and would be pleased to see us.

We set out after breakfast. It was a beautiful day for riding, with a mild October sun and a soft southwest wind. Alvean was in high spirits, and the great tracts of moor fitted my mood. I was enchanted by the low stone walls, the gray boulders, and the gay little streams which trickled over them.

At length we reached the picturesque House on the Moor, as Great-aunt Clara's house was called. And a charming place it was, set on the outskirts of a moorland village. When we arrived unexpectedly, there was great excitement.

"Why, bless my soul if it baint Miss Alvean!" cried the elderly housekeeper. "And who be this you have brought with 'ee, my dear?"

"It is Miss Leigh, my governess," said Alvean.

I wondered then whether I had been wrong in acceding to Alvean's wishes and imposing myself on her great-aunt without first asking permission. But I was soon reassured. We were taken into a drawing room, and there was Great-aunt Clara, a charming old lady seated in an armchair, white-haired, pink-cheeked, with bright, friendly eyes. There was an ebony stick beside her.

Alvean ran to her and was warmly embraced. Then the lively blue eyes were on me. "So you are Alvean's governess, my dear. How thoughtful of you to bring her to see me. Particularly since I have my grandson staying with me and I fear he grows weary of having no playmate of his own age."

Then tea was brought, and the grandson appeared—a handsome boy a little younger than Alvean—and the pair of them went off to play. As soon as Alvean left, I saw that Great-aunt Clara was eager for a gossip, perhaps because she lived a somewhat lonely life. "Tell me," she said, "is everything quite as it should be at Mount Mellyn?"

I raised my eyebrows as though I did not fully comprehend her meaning. She went on. "It was such a shock when poor Alice died. Such a tragic thing to happen to a young girl—for she was little more than a girl. I think of them—Alice and Geoffry—quite often, in the dead of the night. And then I blame myself."

I was astonished. I did not understand how this gentle, talkative old lady could blame herself for Alice's infidelity.

"One should never interfere in other people's lives," she said. "But if one can be helpful . . ."

"Yes," I said firmly, "if one can be helpful I think one should be forgiven for interference."

"But how is one to *know* whether one is being helpful? I think of her so much, my poor little niece. She was a sweet creature, but not equipped to face the cruelties of fate. I can see that you, Miss Leigh, are good for her poor child. Alice would be so happy if she could see what you have done for her."

"I'm glad of that." I was loath to interrupt the flow of talk from which I might extract some fresh evidence about Alice. "And I am sure you have nothing with which to reproach yourself."

"I wish I could believe that. I shouldn't weary you with this, but you seem so sympathetic, and you are looking after little Alvean like . . . like a mother. I feel very grateful to you, my dear. . . ." She paused a moment, then went on. "Alice stayed with me here before her marriage. It was only a few hours' ride from Mount Mellyn, so it gave the engaged pair a chance to know each other."

"Did they not know each other then?"

"The marriage had been arranged when they were in their cradles. She brought him substantial property. Connan's father was alive then, and Connan was a wild boy with a will of his own."

"He allowed the marriage to be arranged for him?"

"They both took it as a matter of course. Well, she stayed with me for several months before the wedding. I loved her dearly."

I thought of little Gilly and said, "I think a great many people loved her dearly."

Great-aunt Clara nodded, and at that moment Alvean and the grandson came in.

I felt disappointed. I was sure that Great-aunt Clara had been on the point of confiding something to me which was of the utmost importance.

WHEN I WAS in the village one day, I passed a little jeweler's shop. There were no valuable gems in the window; a few silver brooches and gold rings, some studded with semiprecious stones. I concluded that the villagers bought their wedding rings here and that the jeweler made a living by doing repairs.

In the window was a silver brooch in the form of a whip. It was quite tasteful, I decided, although by no means expensive. I wanted to buy it for Alvean and give it to her before the horse show to bring her luck. I opened the door and went down three steps into the shop. Seated behind the counter was an old man wearing steel-rimmed spectacles. "I want to see the brooch in the window," I said. "The one in the form of a whip."

"Oh yes, miss," he said, "I'll show it to you with pleasure." He handed it to me, and as I was looking at it I noticed a tray of ornaments with little tickets attached, clearly jewelry which he had received for repair. This must be the jeweler to whom Alice had brought her brooch last July.

I smiled encouragingly. "I want to give the brooch to my pupil at Mount Mellyn," I said.

"Ah," he said, "poor motherless little girl. It's heartening to think she has a kind lady like you to look after her." He produced a box for the brooch from under the counter. "Don't see much of them from Mount Mellyn these days. Mrs. TreMellyn, she was often in. See a little trinket in the window and she'd buy it, sometimes for herself, sometimes for others. Why, she was in here the day she died."

I felt excitement grip me. "Really?" I said.

He laid the brooch on some cotton wool. "I thought 'twas a little odd at the time. She said to me, 'Is the brooch ready, Mr. Pastern? I'm going to a dinner at Lady Treslyn's tomorrow.' " His eyes were puzzled as they looked into mine. "I couldn't believe my ears when I heard she'd left home that very evening."

"No," I said, "it was certainly very strange."

"You see, miss, there was no need for her to mention the dinner to me. If she'd said it to some, it might seem as though she was trying to pull the wool over their eyes. But why should she say such a thing to me? That's what I've wondered."

"Perhaps you misunderstood her," I said.

He shook his head. He did not believe that he had misunderstood. Nor did I. I had seen the entry in her diary.

CELESTINE RODE OVER next day to see Alvean. We were about to go for our riding lesson, and she came with us.

"Now, Alvean," I said, "let's have a little rehearsal. See if you can surprise Miss Nansellock as you hope to surprise your father."

We were going to practice jumping, and we rode down through Mellyn village and beyond. Celestine was astonished by Alvean's progress. "But you've done wonders with her, Miss Leigh!"

We watched Alvean canter round the field. "I hope her father will be pleased. She is appearing in the horse show."

"He'll be very grateful to you, I'm sure, Miss Leigh." I was conscious of her eyes upon me as she smiled benignly. Then she said suddenly, "Oh, Miss Leigh, about my brother, Peter; I did want to speak to you confidentially about Jacinth." I flushed. "I know he gave you the horse and you returned it as too valuable a gift. He's afraid he has offended you."

"Please tell him I'm not offended."

"He admires you very much, Miss Leigh, but there was an ulterior motive behind the gift. He wanted to find a good home for Jacinth before he leaves England. He is very fond of that mare and thinks you'd be a worthy mistress for her. Suppose I asked Connan if she could be taken into his stables and kept there for you to ride?"

I replied emphatically, "It is most kind of you, Miss Nansellock. But I do not wish to ask Mr. TreMellyn for any special favors."

She leaned forward and touched my hand in a friendly manner. There was a faint mist of tears in her eyes. She was touched by my position, and understood how desperately I clung to my pride. I could understand why Alice had been her friend. One day, I thought, I'll tell her what I've discovered about Alice. But not just yet.

CONNAN TREMELLYN CAME back the day before the horse show. I was glad he had not returned before, because I was afraid that Alvean might betray her excitement.

I had finally decided to enter what was called a mixed event, in which men and women competed together. Tapperty wouldn't hear of my riding Dion for this. "Why, miss," he said, "old Dion, he's a good old fellow, but he ain't no prizewinner. How'd you say to taking Royal Rover?"

"What if Mr. TreMellyn objected?"

Tapperty winked. "Nay, he'd not object. He'll be riding May Morning, so old Royal 'ull be free. And nothing 'ud please Master more than for to see his horse win a prize."

I was anxious to show off before Connan TreMellyn and I agreed to Tapperty's suggestion. After all, he was head stableman.

The night before the horse show I presented Alvean with the brooch. "To bring you luck," I said.

She was delighted. "It will! I know it will!"

"Well, remember luck comes only to those who deserve it." I quoted an old rhyme Father used to repeat to us:

> *"Your head and your heart keep boldly up,*
> *Your hands and your heels keep down."*

I went on. "And when you take your jump, remember . . . go with Prince."

"I'll remember!"

She was too excited to sleep that night, so I sat by her bed and read to her from Longfellow's *Hiawatha*, for I knew no narrative so able to turn the mind to peace. The words flowed from my lips, conjuring up visions of primeval forests for Alvean. She forgot the horse show, her fears and her hopes. She was with the little Hiawatha sitting at the feet of the good Nokomis, and she slept.

I WOKE UP on the day of the horse show to find that mist had penetrated my room. I went to the window. Little wisps of it encircled the trees. All through the morning it persisted, and there was anxiety throughout the house. Most of the servants were going to the horse show. They always did, Kitty told me, because the master was one of the judges and some of the stableboys were competing.

Immediately after luncheon Alvean and I set out, she on Black Prince and I on Royal Rover. It was exhilarating to be riding a good horse, and I felt as excited as Alvean. The show was being held in a big field near the church, and when we arrived the crowds were already gathering. The mist had lifted slightly, but it was a leaden day. Alvean and I parted company when we reached the field, and I discovered that the event in which I was competing was one of the first.

Connan, riding May Morning, arrived with the other judges. The village band struck up a traditional air, and everyone stood and sang:

"And shall they scorn Tre, Pol, and Pen?
And shall Trelawny die?
Here's twenty thousand Cornish men
Will know the reason why!"

A proud song, I thought, for a proud people. I noticed little Gillyflower standing there with Daisy and singing with the rest.

A voice said, "Well, if it is not Miss Leigh!"

I turned and saw Peter mounted on Jacinth. "Good afternoon," I said.

I was wearing a placard with a number on my back. "Don't tell me," said Peter, "that you and I are competitors in this first event!"

"Then I haven't a hope," I said. "Not against Jacinth."

"Miss Leigh, you could have been riding her."

"You must have been mad to do what you did. You must know it set the stables talking."

"Who cares for stableboys?"

"I do. A governess has to care for the opinions of all."

"You are not being your usual sensible self," he said, "for you are not an ordinary governess."

"Do you know, Mr. Nansellock," I said lightly, "I believe that *none* of the governesses in your life were ordinary." And I moved away from him.

In the first event Peter went before I did. He and Jacinth seemed like one animal, a centaur. "Oh, perfect," I exclaimed aloud as I watched him take the jumps. A round of applause followed him as he completed his turn.

I saw Connan in the judges' stand and I whispered, "Royal Rover, help me. I want you to beat Jacinth. I want to show Connan TreMellyn that there is one thing I can do. Come on, Rover!"

And we went round as faultlessly, I hoped, as Jacinth had. I heard the applause burst out as I finished and left the field.

When the rest of the competitors had performed, the results were announced. "This one is a tie," Connan called out. "Two competitors scored full marks, a lady and a gentleman: Miss Martha Leigh on Royal Rover, and Mr. Peter Nansellock on Jacinth."

We trotted up to take our prizes. Connan said, "The prize is a silver rose bowl. Obviously we cannot split it, so the lady gets the bowl and the gentleman a silver spoon—consolation for having tied with a lady." We accepted our prizes, and Connan smiled as he gave me mine. "Good show, Miss Leigh," he said.

I wanted to be near the judges' stand when Alvean appeared, and watch Connan's face as his daughter won her prize—which I was sure she would, for she had worked hard.

The beginners' jumping contest for small children began, and I waited feverishly for Alvean's turn. But there was no Alvean. The contest ended and the results were announced. I felt sick with disappointment. So she had panicked at the last moment!

While the prizes were being awarded I went in search of Alvean, but I could not find her; and as the more advanced jumping contest for children began, it occurred to me that she must have gone back to the house. I pictured her abject misery because her courage had failed her at the critical moment. I wanted to find her quickly, to comfort her, so I rode back to Mount Mellyn, gave Royal Rover a quick rubdown and went into the house. It was very quiet, for everyone except Mrs. Polgrey had gone to the horse show. I went up to my room, calling Alvean as I went.

There was no answer, so I hurried through the schoolroom to her bedroom, which was deserted. I went back to my room and stood uncertainly at the window, wondering if I should go back to the horse show. And as I stood there I realized that someone was in Alice's dressing room. I was not sure how I knew. It might have been only a shadow across the windowpane. But I was certain that someone was there.

Without thinking, I ran from my room through the gallery to the dressing room. I threw the door open and shouted, "Who is here?"

No one was in the room, but in that fleeting second I saw the door to the bedroom close. I had a feeling that it might be Alvean and that she needed me. I ran across the dressing room and opened the bedroom door. There was no one there. I ran to the far door and opened it. Immediately I knew that I was in Connan's bedroom, for I saw his cravat flung on the dressing table, his dressing gown and slippers. I realized that I was trespassing, but someone other than Connan had been there before me. Who was it?

I went swiftly across the bedroom, opened the door and found myself in the gallery. There was no sign of anyone.

Who had been in Alice's room? Who was it who haunted the place? "Alice," I called aloud. "Is it you, Alice?"

Finally I went down to the stables. I wanted to get back to the horse show and find Alvean. I had saddled Royal Rover and was riding out of the stable yard when I saw Billy Trehay hurrying toward the house. "Oh, miss," he said, "there's been an accident. A terrible accident! It's Miss Alvean. She took a toss in the jumping."

"But she wasn't in the jumping!" I cried.

"Yes, she were. In the advanced class. It was the high jump. Prince stumbled and fell and they rolled over and . . ."

For a moment I lost control; I covered my face with my hands and cried out my protest.

"They were looking for you, miss. I saw you leave so I came after you. She's lying down there in the field. They'm afraid to move her. They'm waiting for Dr. Pengelly. They think she may have broken some bones."

I rode as fast as I dared down to the village, and as I rode I both prayed and scolded: Oh God, let her be all right. Oh Alvean, you little fool! It would have been enough to take the beginners' jumps. That would have pleased him enough! And then: It's *his* fault! If he had been a more loving parent, this wouldn't have happened.

And so I came to the field. I shall never forget what I saw there: Alvean lying unconscious on the grass, and the group around her. There would be no more competition that day.

Connan's face was stern. "Miss Leigh," he said, "I'm glad you've come. Alvean—"

I ignored him and knelt beside her. "Alvean, my dear . . ."

She opened her eyes. She was not my arrogant little pupil now but a lost and bewildered child. "Don't go away," she said.

"No, I'll stay here."

"You did go . . . before," she murmured, and I had to bend low to catch her words.

And then I knew. She was not speaking to Martha Leigh, the governess. She was speaking to Alice.

CHAPTER SIX

DR. PENGELLY ARRIVED on the field and diagnosed a broken tibia, but he could not say whether any further damage had been done. He set the bone and drove Alvean back to Mount Mellyn in his carriage while Connan and I rode back together in silence.

After the doctor had given Alvean a sedative he rejoined us. "I'll come back in a few hours," he said. "The child is suffering acute shock; keep her warm and let her sleep."

When the doctor had left, Connan said to me, "Come to the punch room, will you, please?" I followed him there, and we sat down. "Miss Leigh," he went on, "we must try to be calm."

Impulsively I said, "I find it hard to be as calm about my charge as you are about your daughter, Mr. TreMellyn."

"Whatever made the child attempt such a thing?" he demanded.

"You made her," I retorted. "*You!*"

"I! But I had no idea that her riding was so advanced."

I was now on the verge of hysteria. I believed that Alvean might have done herself some terrible injury. I had been wrong to try to overcome her fear of horses, to try to win my way into her affections by showing her the way to win those of her father. Yet I couldn't blame myself entirely. Connan also was to blame.

"No," I cried out, "of course you had no idea she was so advanced.

How *could* you when you had never shown the slightest interest in her? That poor motherless child was breaking her heart through your neglect. It was for that reason that she attempted something of which she was not capable."

"I see," he said. Then he took his handkerchief and wiped my eyes. "Miss Leigh," he went on almost tenderly, "there are tears on your cheeks."

I took the handkerchief from him and angrily wiped my tears away. "They are tears of anger," I said.

"And of sorrow. Dear Miss Leigh, I think you care very much for Alvean. And I think that I have been behaving in a very reprehensible manner toward her." Then he said a surprising thing. "Miss Leigh, you came here to teach Alvean, but I think you have taught me a great deal too."

I looked at him in astonishment, and at that moment Celestine came in. She burst out, "What is this terrible thing I've heard?"

"There's been an accident," said Connan. "Alvean was thrown."

"Oh no!" Celestine uttered a piteous cry.

"She's in her room now," Connan explained. "Pengelly's set the leg. He's coming again in a few hours' time. I think she'll be all right."

I was not sure whether he meant that or whether he was trying to soothe Celestine. I felt drawn toward her; I thought, She loves Alvean as her own child.

"Poor Miss Leigh is very distressed," said Connan. "I think she fancies it is her fault. I want to assure her that I don't think that at all."

My fault! I said with defiance, "Alvean was so anxious to impress her father that she undertook more than she could do."

Celestine sat down and covered her face with her hands. I rose and said, "I will go to my room." I looked down at my riding habit—Alice's riding habit. "I think I should change."

Connan said, "Come back afterward, Miss Leigh. We can comfort each other, and I want you here when the doctor returns."

So I went to my room and took off Alice's riding habit and put on my own severe dress. It made me feel like a governess once more and helped to restore my equilibrium. The mirror showed me a face ravaged by grief and anxiety, and a mouth tremulous with fear. I bathed my face, and when I had done so I went down to the punch room and rejoined Connan and Celestine.

MRS. POLGREY MADE a pot of strong tea, and Connan, Celestine and I sat drinking it. Connan seemed to have forgotten my outburst and treated me with courtly consideration and a new gentleness.

"Alvean will get over this," he said. "And she'll want to ride again. Why, when I was little older than she I had a worse accident, and I could scarcely wait to get back on a horse."

Celestine shivered. "I shall never have a moment's peace if she rides again."

"Celeste, one must not coddle children too much. Does not the expert agree?"

He looked at me. I knew he was trying to keep up our spirits. I said, "One shouldn't coddle. But if children are really set against something, I don't think they should be forced to do it. For instance, Alvean's talents may lie in another direction than horsemanship. I think she has artistic ability: she has done some good drawings. Mr. TreMellyn, I have been going to ask you for some time whether you would consider letting her have drawing lessons."

There was a tense silence in the room, and I wondered why they both looked so startled.

Connan said slowly, "But, Miss Leigh, you are here to teach my daughter. Why should it be necessary to engage other teachers?"

"Because," I replied boldly, "she has a special talent. I'm merely a governess, Mr. TreMellyn. I am not an artist as well."

He said gruffly, "Well, we will go into this at some other time."

Shortly afterward the doctor arrived, and I waited in the corridor with Celestine while Connan went in to see Alvean. A hundred images of disaster crowded into my mind. I imagined that she died of her injuries. Then I thought of her maimed for life. . . .

"This waiting is frightful," Celestine said. "If anything should happen to her . . ." She was biting her lips in her anguish, and I wanted to put my arm about her and comfort her.

Then a smiling Dr. Pengelly came out. "Beyond the fractured tibia," he said, "there's very little wrong."

"Oh, thank God!" cried Celestine, and I echoed her words.

"A day or so and she'll be feeling better. Children's bones mend easily. There's nothing for you two ladies to worry about."

"Can we see her?" asked Celestine eagerly.

"Yes. She's awake now and asking for Miss Leigh."

We went into the room, where Connan was standing at the foot of the bed. Alvean looked very ill, poor child, but she gave us a wan smile. "Hello, Miss Leigh," she said. "Hello, Aunt Celestine." Celestine knelt by the bed, took her hand and kissed it.

I said, "Your father was proud of you."

"He must think I was silly," she said.

"No, he doesn't. He told me it didn't matter that you fell. He said all that mattered was that you tried; and you'd do it next time."

"Did he? Did he?"

"Yes, he did." There was an angry note in my voice because he still said nothing.

Then he spoke. "You did splendidly, Alvean. I *was* proud of you."

A faint smile touched her lips. She murmured, "Miss Leigh, *please* don't go away. Don't *you* go away."

I sank down on my knees then and took her hand. Tears were on my cheeks again. I cried, "I'll stay, Alvean. I'll stay with you always." I looked up and saw Celestine and Connan watching me. I amended the words. "I'll stay as long as I'm wanted," I said firmly.

Alvean was satisfied.

WHEN SHE WAS sleeping again, we left her and went into the library with the doctor to discuss her nursing. Celestine said, "I shall come over every day. In fact I wonder, Connan, whether I shouldn't stay here while she's ill. It might make things easier."

"You ladies must settle that," answered Dr. Pengelly. "Keep the child amused while that bone is knitting."

He finished his instructions, and then Connan assured Celestine that there was no need for her to stay at the house; he was sure Miss Leigh would manage.

"Well," said Celestine, "perhaps it's as well. If I stayed here . . . oh, people are so ridiculous. But they are always ready to gossip."

Connan laughed and said, "How did you come over, Celeste?"

"I rode over on Speller."

"I'll ride back with you." He turned to me. "As for you, Miss Leigh, you look exhausted. I advise you to go to bed."

I was sure I could not rest, and my expression must have implied this, for the doctor said, "I'll give you a draft, Miss Leigh. I think I can promise you a good night's sleep."

"Thank you," I said appreciatively, for I suddenly realized how very tired I was.

I went to my room, where I found a supper tray waiting for me, but I had no appetite. I was about to take the sleeping draft and retire for the night when there was a knock on my door. "Come in," I called, and Mrs. Polgrey entered.

She looked distraught. "It's terrible—" she began.

I cut in quickly. "The doctor says she'll be all right."

"Oh yes. But it's Gilly I'm worried about. She didn't come back from the show, miss. I haven't seen her since this afternoon."

"Oh, she's wandering about somewhere, I expect."

"I can't understand her being at the show, miss. She's afeared of going near the horses. And now . . . she's not come in."

"Has the house been searched?"

"Yes, miss. We've looked everywhere."

I said, "I'll come and help look."

So instead of going to bed, I joined in the search for Gilly. I had seen her often in the woods and I made my way there, calling, "Gilly! Gilly!" The mist, which was rising again with the coming of evening, seemed to catch my voice and muffle it in cotton wool. I searched those woods thoroughly because something told me that she was there and that she was not lost but hiding.

I was right. I came across her lying in a clearing surrounded by small firs. "Gilly!" I called. As soon as she heard my voice she sprang to her feet, poised to run; but she hesitated when I called to her, "Gilly, it's all right. I'm here all alone and I won't hurt you."

She looked like a wild fairy child, her extraordinary white hair hanging damply about her shoulders.

"Why, Gilly," I said, "you'll catch cold, lying on that damp grass." Her big eyes watched my face, and I knew that it was fear of something which had driven her to this refuge in the woods. If only she would talk to me. "Gilly, you know I'm your friend—as Madam was."

She nodded and the fear slipped from her face. I put my arm about her; her dress was damp and I could see the mist on her pale brows and lashes. I said, "Come on, Gilly, we're going back. Your grandmama is very anxious about you."

She allowed me to lead her from the clearing, and I said, "You were at the horse show this afternoon."

She turned to me and as she buried her face against me, trembling, her little hands gripped the cloth of my dress. In a flash of understanding I began to see what had happened. This child, like Alvean, was terrified of horses. Had she not been almost trampled to death by one? And this afternoon she had seen Alvean beneath a horse's hoofs as she herself had been only four years ago. I put my arms firmly about her.

At that moment I heard the sound of a rider approaching. I shouted, "Hello, I've found her."

"Coming, Miss Leigh." I was exhilarated—almost unbearably so— because that was Connan's voice. He must have discovered that Gilly was lost and joined the search party. When he came into sight on May Morning, Gilly shrank closer to me.

"She's here," I called. He came close to us and I went on. "She is exhausted, poor child. Take her up with you."

He leaned forward to take her, but she cried, "No! No!"

I said, "Gilly, go up there with the master. I'll walk beside you and hold your hand. Look! This is May Morning. She wants to carry you because she knows you're tired."

Gilly's eyes turned to look at May Morning, and in the fear I saw there my ideas were confirmed. "Take her," I said to Connan, holding her up, and he took her in his arms and set her in front of him. I kept talking to her

soothingly. "You're safe there. And we'll get back more quickly to your warm cozy bed." She no longer struggled but kept her hand in mine.

So ended that strange day, with Connan and myself bringing in the lost child. When Gilly was lifted from the horse and handed to her grandmother, Connan gave me a smile of infinite charm. It held none of the mockery I had seen hitherto, and I went up to my room with exultation wrapped about me like the mist about the house.

I knew, of course, what had happened to me. Today had made it very clear. I had done the most foolish thing I had ever done in my life. I had fallen in love, and with someone who was quite out of my world. I was in love with the master of Mount Mellyn, and I had an uneasy feeling that he might be aware of it.

I locked my door, undressed and drank Dr. Pengelly's draft. But before I got into bed I looked at myself in my prim flannelette nightdress. Then I laughed at my own thoughts and said aloud in my best governess tones, "In the morning, after a good night's rest, you will come to your senses."

THE NEXT FEW weeks were the happiest I had so far spent in Mount Mellyn. It soon became clear that Alvean had suffered no great harm. She had lost none of her keenness for riding and asked eager questions about Black Prince's slight injuries, taking it for granted that she would soon ride him again.

We resumed school after the first week, and she was pleased to do so. I also taught her to play chess, and she picked up the game with astonishing speed; if I handicapped myself by playing without my queen, she was even able to checkmate me. But it was not only Alvean's progress which made me so happy. It was the fact that Connan was in the house; and although he made no reference to my outburst on the day of the accident, he had clearly noted it and would appear in Alvean's room with books and puzzles for her.

I said to him, "There is one thing that pleases her more than all the presents you bring: that is your company."

"What an odd child, to prefer me to a book or a game!"

I smiled and he returned my smile, and again I was aware of that change in his expression. Sometimes he would sit down and watch our game of chess. Then he would range himself on Alvean's side against me. "Look, Alvean," he would say, "we'll put our bishop there, and that'll make our dear Miss Leigh look to her defenses!" Alvean would giggle, and I would be so happy that I would grow careless and nearly lose the game. But not quite. I never forgot that between Connan and me there was a certain battle in progress.

He said one day, "When Alvean can be moved, we'll drive over to Fowey and have a picnic."

"Why go to Fowey when we have a picnic beach here?"

"My dear Miss Leigh"—he had acquired a habit of calling me his dear Miss Leigh—"do you not know that other people's beaches are more exciting than one's own?"

Alvean was so eager to get well for the picnic that she ate all the food brought to her. Dr. Pengelly was delighted with her progress. "But," I said to Connan one day, "you are the real cure. You have made her happy because at last you let her see that you are aware of her existence."

Then he did a surprising thing. He took my hand and lightly kissed my cheek. It was very different from that kiss which he had given me on the night of the ball. This was swift, friendly, passionless yet affectionate. "No," he said, "it is you who are the real cure, my dear Miss Leigh." And he left me abruptly.

I did not forget Gilly. I determined to fight for her as I had for Alvean, and decided to speak to Connan about it while he was in his present mood. I boldly went to the punch room when he was there one morning and came straight to the point. "I want to do something for Gilly. I do not believe she is half-witted. I have heard about her accident. Before that, I understand, she was quite an ordinary little girl. Might it not be possible to make her like other children again?"

I saw a return of that mockery to his eyes. "I believe that, as with God, so with Miss Leigh—all things are possible."

I ignored the flippancy. "I am asking permission to give her lessons. I would be ready to teach Gilly in my own time, providing of course you do not forbid it."

"If I forbade you, you would find some way of doing it; so I think it would be simpler to say yes. I wish you all success."

"Thank you," I said, and turned to go.

"Miss Leigh," he called, "let us go on that picnic soon. I could carry Alvean, if necessary, to and from the carriage."

"That would be excellent, Mr. TreMellyn. I'll tell her at once. I know it will delight her."

"And you, Miss Leigh, does it delight you?"

For a moment I thought he was coming toward me. I was suddenly afraid that he would place his hands on my shoulders and that at his touch I might betray myself. I said coolly, "Anything which does Alvean good delights me, Mr. TreMellyn."

So THE WEEKS passed—pleasurable, wonderful weeks.

I had taken Gilly to the schoolroom and had managed to teach her a few letters. She delighted in pictures and quickly became absorbed in them. She would present herself at the schoolroom each day at the appointed time, and the whole household was watching the experiment with interest. But I knew that when Alvean was well enough to return to the schoolroom, I would have to be prepared for opposition. Alvean's aversion to Gilly was apparent.

There were plenty of visitors for Alvean. Celestine was there every day. Peter came, gallant and teasing, and she was always pleased to see him. Lady Treslyn also called, with expensive books and flowers, but Alvean received her sullenly. "She is an invalid still, Lady Treslyn," I explained, and the smile which was flashed upon me took my breath away, so beautiful was it.

"Of course I understand," Lady Treslyn said. "Poor child! Mr. Tre-Mellyn tells me that you have been wonderful. I tell him how lucky he is to have found such a treasure. 'They are not easy to come by,' I said. I reminded him of how my last cook walked out in the middle of a dinner party. She was not such a treasure."

I bowed my head and hated her—not because she had linked me in her mind with her cook, but because Connan seemed different when she was in the house. I felt that he scarcely saw me. I heard the sounds of their laughter and I wondered sadly what they said to each other. Then I realized what a fool I had been, for I had been harboring thoughts which I would not dare express, even to myself.

One morning Celestine suggested that she take Alvean over to Mount Widden for the day. "Connan," she added, "come to dinner; then you can bring her back afterward."

He agreed to do so. I was disappointed not to be included in the invitation, which showed what a false picture I had allowed myself to make of the situation during these past weeks. It was like waking up to a chilly morning after weeks of sunshine so brilliant that you thought it was going to last forever.

CONNAN DROVE ALVEAN over in the carriage, and I was left alone without any definite duties. An idea struck me. I would go for a long ride on the moor. Immediately I remembered Alvean's great-aunt Clara, and I began to feel a sense of excitement, thinking of the mystery of Alice's death, which I had forgotten during these halcyon weeks. Great-aunt Clara would want to hear how Alvean was getting on. Besides, she had treated me with the utmost friendliness and had made it clear that I would be welcome anytime I called.

I went to Mrs. Polgrey and said, "Alvean will be away all day. I propose to take a day's holiday."

"And none deserves a holiday more," she said. "Where are you going?"

"I think I'll go out to the moor."

"Do you think you should, miss, by yourself? There be bogs on the moor and mists—and the little people, some say."

"Little people indeed!"

"Ah, don't 'ee laugh at 'em, miss. If 'ee do that, they'll lead 'ee astray with their fairy lanterns."

"I'll be careful, Mrs. Polgrey, and if I meet any little people I'll be very polite. Don't have any fears about me."

I went to the stables and asked Tapperty which horse I could have, adding that I was going out on the moor.

"There's May Morning. She be free. You be going with a companion, miss?" He laughed slyly.

I said I was going alone, but I could see he did not believe me. I felt angry because I guessed that his thoughts were on Peter Nansellock. I wondered too if my growing friendship with Connan had been noted. I was horrified at the possibility. Oddly enough I could bear to contemplate their sly remarks about Peter and me; it would be different if they talked of me and Connan.

I walked May Morning until I had left the village well behind me and came to the first gray wall and boulders of the moor. It was a sparkling December morning and golden patches of gorse were dotted over the moor. I could smell the peaty soil, and the wind was fresh and exhilarating.

I wanted to gallop across the moor with the wind in my face and I did so, imagining that Connan was riding beside me. In this moorland country it was possible to dream fantastic dreams. Some told themselves that the little people dwelt here; I told myself that it was not impossible that Connan would fall in love with me.

At midday I arrived at the House on the Moor. The housekeeper welcomed me and I was taken into Great-aunt Clara's sitting room. "Goodday to you, Miss Leigh!" she said. "All alone today?"

I told her about Alvean's accident and she looked concerned; I hastily added that Alvean would soon be about again.

"You must be in need of refreshment, Miss Leigh," she said. "A glass of my elderberry wine; and then will you stay to luncheon?"

I said it was most kind of her to invite me. I enjoyed my luncheon, which consisted of mutton with caper sauce, exceedingly well cooked. Afterward we retired to the drawing room for what she called a little chat. This was what I had been hoping for.

"Tell me," she said, "how is dear Alvean? Is she happier now?"

"Why, yes, I think she is. Her father has been attentive since the accident, and she is very fond of him."

"Ah," said Great-aunt Clara, "her father . . ."

Her bright blue eyes showed her excitement. I knew she found talking an irresistible temptation, and I was determined to make the temptation even more irresistible. I said tentatively, "There is not the usual relationship between them, I fancy."

There was a slight pause, and then she said quickly, "No. I suppose it is inevitable." I waited breathlessly as she hovered on the edge of confidences. "I sometimes blame myself," she went on, while her eyes looked beyond me as though she were looking back over the years. "Alice was with me after the engagement, you remember. Everything could have changed then. But I persuaded her. I thought *he* was the better man."

I was afraid to ask her to elucidate lest I break the spell.

"I wonder what would have happened if she had chosen differently. Do you ever play that game, Miss Leigh? Do you ever say: Now if at a certain point I had done such and such . . . the whole tenor of my life would have changed?"

"Oh yes," I said. "Everybody does. You think that things would have been different for your niece?"

"For Alice, more than most. She had come to a crossroads. If she had turned to the right instead of the left, as it were, she might be here today. After all, if she had married Geoffry, there would not have been any need to run away with him, would there?"

"You loved your niece very much, did you not?"

"Very much. Alice used to come and play with my family. My children were boys, you see, and I'd always wanted a girl. We lived in Penzance then, and Alice's parents had a big estate a few miles inland. That's her husband's now of course. Her father was dead, and her mother—she was my sister—had always been very fond of Connan TreMellyn, the elder one, I mean. There have been Connans in that family for centuries. I think my sister wanted to marry the present Connan's father, but other marriages were arranged for them, so they planned to have their children marry. They were officially betrothed when Connan was twenty and Alice eighteen. The marriage was to take place a year later. Meantime they thought she should stay with me, as I was within riding distance of Mount Mellyn."

"And I suppose Mr. TreMellyn rode over to see her often."

"Yes. But not as often as I would have expected. I began to suspect that they were not as well matched as their fortunes were."

"Tell me about Alice. What sort of girl was she?"

"How can I explain? She was lighthearted, light-minded. I do not mean she was light in her morals. Although, of course, after what happened . . . But who shall judge? You see, he came over here to paint. He did some beautiful pictures of the moors."

"Who? Connan TreMellyn?"

"Oh, dear me, no! Geoffry. Geoffry Nansellock. He was an artist of some reputation. Did you know that?"

"I know nothing of him except that he was killed with Alice."

"He came over here often while she was with me. In fact he came more often than Connan did. They would go off together and he'd have his painting things with him. She used to say she was going to watch him at work. But of course it was not painting they did together."

"They were . . . in love?" I asked.

"I was rather frightened when she told me. You see, there was going to be a child."

I caught my breath in surprise. Alvean, I thought. No wonder Connan could not bring himself to love her. No wonder my statement that she possessed artistic talent upset him and Celestine.

"She told me two weeks before her wedding day. She said, 'What shall I do, Aunt Clara? Shall I marry Geoffry?'

"I said, 'Does Geoffry want to marry you, my dear?' And she answered, 'He would have to, would he not, if I told him?'

"I know now that she should have told him. But her marriage was already arranged. Alice was an heiress, and the Nansellocks had very little. Geoffry had a certain reputation too. There had been others who had found themselves in Alice's condition. I did not think she would be happy with him." She was silent a moment. Then she continued. "It's been on my conscience ever since she died. I keep remembering that she said to me, 'What shall I do, Aunt Clara? Help me! Tell me what to do!'

"And I said, 'Go on with your marriage to Connan. You're betrothed to him. Forget what happened with Geoffry.' She said, 'How can I forget? There'll be a living reminder.' Then I did this dreadful thing. I said to her, 'You must marry Connan. Your child will be born prematurely.' Alice threw back her head and laughed hysterically. Poor dear, she was near breaking point."

Great-aunt Clara sat back in her chair; she looked as though she had just come out of a trance. I said nothing. I was picturing it all: the wedding; the death of Alice's mother almost immediately afterward; and Connan's father's death the following year. The marriage had been arranged to please them and they had not lived long to enjoy it. And Alice was left with Connan—my Connan—and Alvean, the child of another man, whom she had vainly tried to pass off as his. He had kept up the pretense that Alvean was his daughter, but inwardly he had never accepted her.

"Oh dear," sighed Great-aunt Clara, "how I talk! It is like living it all again. I have wearied you." A little fear crept into her voice. "Miss Leigh, I trust you will keep what I have said to yourself."

"You may trust me to do so," I assured her. "And you must not blame yourself. You did your best for Alice."

She came to the door to wave me on when I left, and waving back, I rode off. I was very thoughtful on the way home. I realized now that Gilly was Alvean's half sister; I remembered the drawings I had seen which had something in them of both Gilly and Alvean. So Alvean knew. Or did she merely *fear* that Gilly was her half sister?

CHAPTER SEVEN

CHRISTMAS WAS RAPIDLY approaching, with all the excitement I remembered so well from the old days in my father's vicarage.

I began to think about Christmas presents. I had a little money to spend, since I had saved most of what I had earned. So one day I went into Plymouth and did my Christmas shopping. I bought books for my sister, Phillida, and her family and a scarf for Aunt Adelaide, and had them forwarded. Then I spent a long time choosing what I would give the Mellyn household. Finally I decided on scarves for Kitty, Daisy and Gilly; and for Mrs. Polgrey, a bottle of whiskey, which I was sure would delight her. For Alvean I bought handkerchiefs with *A* embroidered on them.

I was pleased with my purchases and began to grow as excited about Christmas as Daisy and Kitty. On Christmas Eve I helped decorate the great hall. The men brought in ivy, holly, box and bay, and the pillars were entwined with these leaves. Then Daisy and Kitty taught me how to make Christmas bushes. We took two wooden hoops, inserted one into the other, and this ball-like framework we decorated with evergreen leaves and furze; then we added oranges and apples. These Christmas bushes we hung in the windows. Huge logs were carried in for the fireplaces; then the servants' hall was decorated like the great hall.

"We do have our ball here while the family be having theirs," Daisy told me, and I wondered to which ball I should go. Perhaps to neither. A governess' position was somewhere in between.

"My life!" cried Daisy. "I can scarcely wait for the day. Last Christmas was such a quiet one, with the house in mourning."

All through Christmas Eve the smell of baking filled the kitchen. The usually calm and dignified Mrs. Polgrey bustled about, her face flushed, purring, stirring, and talking ecstatically of pies which bore the odd names of lammy, muggety and herby. I was called in to help. "Do 'ee keep your eye on that saucepan, miss," said Mrs. Polgrey, "and should it come to the boil tell me quickly."

I was taking a batch of golden-brown pasties out of the oven, when Kitty came in shouting, "Ma'am, the curl singers be here."

"Well, bring 'em in, ye daftie," cried Mrs. Polgrey, wiping her sweating brow. "It be bad luck to keep curl singers waiting!"

I followed her into the great hall, where a company of village youths and girls were already singing. I then understood that curl singers were carol singers. They rendered "The Twelve Days of Christmas," "The Seven Joys of Mary" and "The Holly and the Ivy." Then they began to sing:

> *"Come let me taste your Christmas beer*
> *That is so very strong,*
> *And I do wish that Christmas time,*
> *With all its mirth and song,*
> *Was twenty times as long."*

Mrs. Polgrey signed to Daisy and Kitty to bring refreshments. Blackberry and elderberry wine were served to the singers, and great meat pasties as well. When they had finished they handed Mrs. Polgrey a bowl tied with red ribbons and decorated with furze. Majestically she placed some coins in it.

When they had gone Daisy said, "Oh, miss, I forgot to tell 'ee, there be a parcel in your room. I took it up just afore them come."

I hurried up to my room and found a large parcel from Phillida. I took out a black silk shawl embroidered in green and amber, and an amber Spanish comb. When I stuck the comb in my hair, wrapped the shawl about me and looked in the mirror, I was startled by my reflection. I looked exotic, more like a Spanish dancer than an English governess.

There was something else in the parcel. It was a dress of green silk, one of Phillida's which I had admired. A letter fell out of it:

Dear Marty,

How do you find your position? I fear your Alvean is a little horror; but since you've been at Mount Mellyn you've become so uncommunicative that I cannot tell.

The shawl and comb are my Christmas gift. Are they too frivolous? Would you rather have had a set of woolen underwear or some improving book? But I heard from Aunt Adelaide that she is sending you the former.

I am wondering whether you'll be sitting down to dine with the family this Christmas. Perhaps there will be one of those dinner parties at which a guest is missing and they say, "Send for the governess. We cannot be thirteen." Then my Marty will dine in my old green and her new scarf and comb, and attract a local landowner and live happily ever after.

To be more serious, Marty, the green gown is a gift. Do not think of it as a castoff. I love it and I am giving it to you, not because I am tired of it, but because it always suited you better than me.

Happy Christmas, dear Marty; do send me your news. The children and William send their love. Mine to you also.

Phillida

CHRISTMAS DAY WAS a day to remember all my life.

I awoke in the morning to the sound of the servants laughing and talking below my window. When Daisy brought my hot water, she was full of excitement. "You'd better hurry, miss, or you'll not be in time to see the wassail!"

Hastily I washed and dressed and took out my parcels; I had put Alvean's by her bed the previous night. I went to the window. The air was balmy. I drew deep breaths and listened to the gentle rhythm of the waves. They said nothing this morning; they merely swished contentedly, for this was Christmas.

Alvean came to my room, carrying her handkerchiefs rather shyly. She said, "Thank you, Miss Leigh. A happy Christmas!" I put my arms about her and kissed her, and although she seemed a little embarrassed by this demonstration, she returned my kiss.

She had brought a brooch very like the silver whip I had given her. "I got it in the village," she said. "I wanted one as near mine as possible, but not too near, so that we wouldn't get them mixed up. Now we'll each have one when we go riding."

I was delighted. She had not ridden since her accident. She could not have shown me more clearly that she was ready to start again. I said, "You could not have given me anything I would have liked better, Alvean."

My presents proved to be a great success. Mrs. Polgrey's eyes glistened at the sight of the whiskey. Daisy and Kitty were pleased with their scarves and, as for Gilly, she kept stroking and staring at hers in wonder.

Mrs. Polgrey gave me a set of doilies with a coy whisper, "For your hope chest, me dear."

Soon the wassail singers arrived and I heard their voices at the door.

> "O Mistress, at your door our Wassail begin,
> Pray open the door, and let us come in,
> With our Wassail, Wassail, Wassail, Wassail,
> And joy come to our jolly Wassail."

They came into the hall, and they also carried a bowl into which coins were dropped; all the servants crowded in and, as Connan entered, the singing grew louder and a new verse was begun.

> "O Mistress and Master . . ."

I thought, Two years ago Alice would have stood there with him. Did he remember? He showed no sign. He sang with them and ordered that the stirrup cups, the dash-an-darras, be brought out with the saffron cake and pasties which had been made for the occasion. He moved nearer to me. "Miss Leigh," he said under cover of the singing, "what do you think of a Cornish Christmas?"

"What I have seen is very interesting."

"There is much more in prospect. You should rest this afternoon for the feasting this evening and the Christmas ball."

"But I . . ."

"Of course you will join the family. Where else would you spend Christmas? With the Polgreys? With the Tappertys? By the way, I have something here . . . a little Christmas gift. A token of my gratitude, if you like. You have been so good to Alvean."

He pressed a small object into my hand, and I was so overcome with pleasure that I felt it must show in my eyes and betray my feelings to him. "You are very good to me," I said.

He smiled and moved away. I noticed Tapperty's eyes on us, and I wondered whether he had seen Connan hand me the gift.

I wanted to be alone. The small case Connan had pressed into my hand demanded to be opened, and I could not do so here. I slipped out of the hall and ran up to my room.

It was a small, blue plush case. Inside, on oyster-colored satin, lay a brooch in the form of a horseshoe, studded with diamonds.

I stared at it in dismay. I could not possibly accept such a valuable object. I must return it, of course.

Why did he do it? If it had been some small token, I should have been so happy. I wanted to throw myself on my bed and weep.

Then I heard Alvean calling. "Miss Leigh, it's time for church!"

I hastily put the brooch into its box and put on my cape and bonnet as Alvean came into the room.

AFTER CHURCH, AS Connan was going to the stables, I called after him. He stopped, smiling, and I ran up to him. "Mr. TreMellyn, it is very kind of you," I said, "but this gift is far too valuable for me to accept."

He put his head on one side and regarded me in the old mocking manner. "My *dear* Miss Leigh," he said lightly. "I am an ignorant man, I fear. I have no notion how little value a gift must have before it is acceptable." I flushed hotly and he went on. "I thought it suitable. A horseshoe means luck, you know. And you have a way with horses."

"I . . . I have no occasion to wear such a valuable piece of jewelry."

"I thought you might wear it to the ball tonight."

For a moment I had a picture of myself dancing with him. I should be wearing Phillida's dress, and the brooch would be proudly flaunted on the green silk because I treasured it so much.

"I feel I have no right."

"Oh," he said, "I begin to understand. You feel that I give the brooch in the same spirit that Peter Nansellock offered Jacinth. You returned the horse. Very proper and what I would expect of you. Now the brooch is given in a different spirit. You have been good to Alvean, not only as a governess but as a woman. The brooch belonged to her mother. Look upon it as a gift of appreciation from us both. Does that make it all right?"

I was silent. Then I said, "Yes . . . that is different. I accept the brooch. Thank you very much, Mr. TreMellyn."

He smiled at me. It was a smile I did not fully understand because it seemed to hold in it many meanings.

I murmured "Thank you" again and hurried back to the house. In my room I took out the brooch and pinned it on, and immediately my high-necked cotton took on a new look.

So on this strange Christmas Day I had a gift from Alice.

I DINED IN the middle of the day with Connan and Alvean, on turkey and plum pudding, and the conversation was animated as the three of us discussed the Cornish Christmas customs. I imagined Alice sitting in the chair I now occupied. I wondered what the conversation had been like then. I wondered if now, seeing me there, he was thinking of Alice. I kept reminding myself that it was merely because it was Christmas that I was sitting here; that after the festivities were over I would revert to my old place.

But I was not going to think of that now. Tonight I was going to the ball. Miraculously I had a dress worthy of the occasion, a comb of amber and a brooch of diamonds.

I took Connan's advice about resting, and much to my surprise I slept. As so often in this house, I dreamed of Alice. I thought that she came to the ball, a shadowy wraith, and whispered to me as I danced with Connan, "This is what I want, Marty. I like to see this. I like to see your hand in that of Connan. You . . . Marty . . . you . . . not another. . . ."

I awoke with reluctance. It was a pleasant dream.

Daisy brought me tea at five. "I've brought 'ee a piece of Mrs. Polgrey's fuggan to take with it, miss," she said, indicating a slice of raisin cake. "And I'll bring 'ee hot water at six. That'll give 'ee plenty of time to dress for the ball. The master 'ull be receiving the guests at eight. Supper's at nine, so there's a long time to go before you get more to eat."

She stood at the door a moment, her head on one side, watching me. Was she regarding me with a new interest? I pictured them in the servants' hall, Tapperty leading the conversation. Were they always wondering what new relationship had begun—or was about to begin—between the master of the house and the governess?

I WAITED UNTIL the ballroom was full before I went in, my brooch pinned to the green silk with its low-cut bodice and billowing skirt. I had been there only a few minutes when Peter was at my elbow. "You look dazzling," he said.

"Thank you. I am glad to surprise you."

"I'm not in the least surprised. I see Connan is about to open the ball. Will you partner me?"

"Thank you, yes."

"It's the traditional Cornish dance, you know, but it's easy. You have only to follow me."

The music began, and Connan walked into the center of the hall holding Celestine by the hand. To my horror I realized that Peter and I would have to join them and dance those first bars with them.

Celestine seemed surprised to see me join them, but if Connan was, he gave no sign. I imagined that Celestine reasoned: It is all very well to ask the governess, but should she thrust herself into such a prominent position? However, after that first start of surprise, she gave me a warm smile.

I said, "I shouldn't be here. I didn't realize—"

"Follow us," said Connan.

"We'll look after you," echoed Peter.

And in a few seconds the others were falling in behind us, and round the hall we went to the tune of the "Furry Dance."

"You're doing excellently," said Connan with a smile as our hands touched.

"You will soon be a Cornishwoman," added Celestine.

"I am becoming most interested in Cornwall," I said.

"And in the inhabitants, I hope," whispered Peter.

We danced on, and as the music ended I heard someone say, "Who is the striking-looking woman with Peter Nansellock?"

I waited for the answer to be: Oh, that's the governess. But it was different. "I've no idea. She seems quite . . . unusual."

I was exultant. I was not only at the ball, I was a success at the ball. I did not lack partners; and even when, in response to their questions, I admitted that I was Alvean's governess, I continued to receive the homage due an attractive woman. Why couldn't I have been like this at Aunt Adelaide's parties? But I knew what had happened to change me. It was not only the dress, the comb, the diamond brooch; I was ridiculously, hopelessly in love, and love was the greatest beautifier of all. Like Cinderella, I was determined to enjoy myself until the stroke of twelve.

One strange thing happened. I had been dancing with Sir Thomas Treslyn, who turned out to be a courteous old gentleman, a little wheezy during the dance. I suggested that he might prefer to sit out the rest of it and he was very grateful.

He said, "I'm getting a little too old for the dance, Miss . . . er . . ."

"Miss Leigh," I said. "I'm the governess here, Sir Thomas."

"Indeed. I was going to say, Miss Leigh, it is extremely kind of you to think of my comfort when you must be longing to dance."

"I'm quite happy to sit for a while."

"You are most kind." He leaned toward me confidentially. "It is my wife who likes these affairs. She has such high spirits."

I said, "She is very beautiful." I had noticed her, of course, exquisite in mauve chiffon over an underskirt of green.

He nodded, a little sadly, I thought, and as we went on talking my eyes wandered to the peep high in the wall, the concealed opening from which Alvean and I had watched another ball. Someone was watching now, but it was impossible to see who it was.

I thought, Of course it is Alvean. Then I was startled, for, turning to watch the dancers, I saw Alvean. I had forgotten that this was a special occasion and that she too had come to the ball. She was wearing a white muslin dress with a wide blue sash. I noticed this with half my attention, then looked swiftly back to the peep. The face, unrecognizable, indefinable, was still there.

SUPPER WAS LAID in both the dining room and the punch room. The guests served themselves, for, according to custom, the servants on this day of days were having their own ball in their own hall.

Peter Nansellock, with whom I had had the supper dance, led me into the punch room. Sir Thomas Treslyn was already there at a table with Celestine, and Peter led me to them.

"Leave it to me," he said. "I'll feed you all." He turned to me. "Our Cornish food seems odd to you foreigners from across the Tamar. Which sort of pie will you have? Giblet, squab, nattling or muggety? There'll be taddage too, and fair maids. I recommend squab pie: young pigeon with apple, bacon, onions and mutton."

"I'm ready to try it," I said.

At that moment Connan came up to us with Lady Treslyn.

"I am enlightening Miss Leigh about our Cornish food," Peter said. "She seems not to know what a fair maid is. Is that not odd, Con, seeing that she is one herself?"

Connan's eyes smiling into mine were warm. He said, "Fair maid, Miss Leigh, is another name for smoked pilchard, served with oil and lemon. It's a corruption of the old Spanish *fumado*. We say here that it is food fit for a Spanish don."

"A relic, Miss Leigh," interrupted Peter, "of those days when the Spaniards raided our shores and took too great an interest in another kind of fair maid."

Alvean had come in. She looked tired. "You should be in bed," I said.

And Celestine chimed in, "Indeed she should, poor child."

"I'm hungry," Alvean said.

"After supper we'll go up."

She nodded, and thanked Peter with sleepy pleasure when he brought her a plate. And so we sat around the table, Alvean, Peter, Celestine, Sir Thomas, Connan, Lady Treslyn and I. It seemed like a dream that I should be there with them. Alice's brooch glittered on my dress, and I thought, Thus, two years ago, she would have sat . . . as I am sitting now.

I remembered the face I had seen at the peep and what Alvean had said on the night of that other ball: something about her mother's love of dancing and how, if she came back, she would come to a ball. Then Alvean had half hoped to see her among the dancers. . . . What if she watched from another place? I thought.

My attention came back to the table. Connan was leaning close to Lady Treslyn, and I thought how distinguished they looked—she the most beautiful woman at the ball, and he surely the most distinguished of the men. I heard them laughing over something together, and their intimacy wounded me deeply. I said to myself coldly, It is time you retired.

I noticed that there were smudges of shadow under Alvean's eyes, and I said, "Alvean, you look tired. I will take you to bed now." She was half asleep already and made no protest.

"Au revoir, Miss Leigh," Peter said as he rose, and the others echoed the words. I left the punch room, holding Alvean by the hand and feeling as Cinderella must have felt with the striking of the midnight hour.

ALVEAN WAS ASLEEP before I left her room. I tried not to think of Connan and Lady Treslyn while I went to my own room and lighted the candles on my dressing table. The diamonds winked back at me from the mirror, and I was immediately reminded of the face I had seen at the peep.

On impulse I went down to the landing below my own. I could hear shouts of merrymaking from the servants' hall. The door to Gilly's room was ajar, and I went in. Moonlight showed the child was sitting up in her bed. "Gilly!" I said.

"Madam!" she cried, and her voice was joyful. "I knew you'd come to see me tonight."

"I'm going to light your candle," I said, and I did so.

Her eyes regarded my face with that blank blue stare. I sat on the edge of the bed. I knew that when I had first come in she had thought I was someone else. She was contented though, which showed the confidence she was beginning to feel in me. I touched the brooch and said, "Once it was Mrs. TreMellyn's."

She smiled and nodded.

I said, "You spoke when I came in. Why do you not speak now?"

She merely smiled.

"Gilly," I said, "were you at the peep tonight? Were you watching the dancers?" She nodded. "Gilly, don't just nod. Say yes."

"Yes," said Gilly.

"You went up there all alone? You weren't afraid?"

She shook her head and smiled, but I could get her to say no more. After a while I kissed her and she returned my kiss. She was fond of me, I knew, though I believed that she still confused me with Alice.

Back in my room I did not want to take off my dress. I sat by the window for an hour or so. It was a warm night and I was comfortable with my shawl about me. Some of the guests were coming out to their carriages and I could hear the exchange of good-bys.

And then I heard Lady Treslyn's voice. It was low, but she spoke with such intensity that I caught every syllable.

She said, "Connan, it will not be long . . . now."

NEXT MORNING, WHEN Kitty brought my bathwater, Daisy came with her. "Morning, miss. . . ." "Morning, miss. . . ." They had exciting news and were both speaking together. "Last night . . . no, this morning . . ." Then Kitty rushed on ahead of her sister. "Sir Thomas was taken bad on the way home. He were dead when they got to Treslyn Hall."

I sat up in bed, looking from one to the other, deeply shocked. This was no ordinary death. I realized, no less than Kitty and Daisy, what it could mean to Mount Mellyn.

CHAPTER EIGHT

SIR THOMAS TRESLYN was buried on New Year's Day.

During the preceding week gloom lay on the house, all the more noticeable because it followed on the heels of the Christmas festivities. The decorations had been left in place, and there was divided opinion as to which was more unlucky—to remove them before Twelfth Night or to leave them up and thereby show a lack of respect. The servants felt that the death touched us closely. Sir Thomas had died between our house and his own; our table was the last at which he had sat, and the Cornish are very superstitious, constantly alert for omens, eager to placate supernatural powers.

I saw very little of Connan, and when I did he seemed scarcely aware of my presence. I imagined he was considering all that this meant to him. If he and Lady Treslyn had been lovers, there was no obstacle now to their regularizing their union. I knew that this thought was in the minds of many, but no one spoke of it.

Mrs. Polgrey called me to her room and we had a cup of tea, Earl Grey, laced with a spoonful of the whiskey I had given her.

"This is a shocking thing," she said. "Sir Thomas to die on Christmas Day. Although 'tweren't Christmas Day but Boxing Day morning," she added, as though this somehow made it less shocking. "The funeral is a bit soon, do you not think, miss?"

I counted the days on my fingers. "Seven days," I said.

"They could have kept him longer, seeing it's winter. You hear tales of people being buried alive."

"There is surely no doubt that Sir Thomas is *dead*."

"Some seem dead and are not, after all. . . . You'll come to the funeral with me, miss?"

"I have no mourning clothes."

"I'll find a bonnet and a black band for 'ee."

So I was present when Sir Thomas' body was lowered into the tomb. The widow, in flowing black draperies, looked as beautiful as she ever had. She moved with grace and she looked even more slender and appealing in her black than in the brilliant colors I had seen her wear—intensely feminine. I tried to fathom the expression on Connan's face, but he seemed determined to hide his feelings from the world.

The winter sun shone brightly on the gilt of the coffin as it was lowered into the grave. There was a deep silence in the churchyard, broken only by the sudden cry of gulls. Then it was over, and the mourners went back to their waiting carriages.

SIR THOMAS WAS not forgotten. I heard his name mentioned often during the next weeks. When Daisy and Kitty brought my water in the mornings, they would linger.

"I saw Lady Treslyn yesterday," Daisy told me one morning. "Her didn't look like a widow, in spite of the weeds. Something in her face . . . if you do get my meaning."

"I'm afraid I don't."

"Kit were with me. She said the same. Like as though she were waiting, and content because she wouldn't have to wait long. A year though. Seems a long time to *me*."

"A year? What for?" I asked, although I knew the answer.

Daisy looked at me and giggled. " 'Twont do for them to be seeing too much of each other for a bit, will it, miss? After all, him dying here . . . almost on our doorstep, as though they'd willed him to it."

The conversation was getting dangerous, and I dismissed her.

When she had gone I thought, So there is talk. They are saying Sir Thomas was willed to die. Well, as long as that's all they say, it won't do much harm.

Later that day, strolling in the woods, I heard horses walking nearby, and then I heard Lady Treslyn say, "Connan. Oh Connan!"

In the woods their voices carried. The trees hid me, but snatches of their conversation came to me.

"Linda! You shouldn't have come."

"I know . . ." Her voice fell and I could not hear the rest.

281

"To send that message . . ." That was Connan. "The boy will have been seen by some of the servants. You know how they gossip."

"I know, but—"

"When did this come?"

"This morning. I had to show it to you right away."

"It's the first?"

"No, there was one two days ago. That's why I had to see you, Connan. I'm frightened."

"It's mischief," he said. "Ignore it."

"Read it," she cried.

There was a short silence. Then Connan spoke. "I see. There's only one thing to be done. . . ."

The horses moved away and I heard no more. That day Connan left Mount Mellyn.

"Called away to Penzance," Mrs. Polgrey told me.

SEVERAL DAYS PASSED. Alvean and I resumed our lessons, and Gilly too came to the schoolroom. While I worked with Alvean, I would give Gilly some small task, like trying to make letters in a tray of sand or counting beads on an abacus. She was content to do this and seemed happy in my company. She had trusted Alice and she was transferring that trust to me. Alvean rebelled at first, but I pointed out the need to be kind to those less fortunate than ourselves, and at length so worked on her sympathy that she accepted Gilly's presence, although a little sullenly.

Connan had been away a week, and it was a cold February morning when Mrs. Polgrey came into the schoolroom. I was very surprised to see her, for she rarely interrupted lessons; she was holding two letters in her hand and I could see that she was excited. "I have heard from the master," she said. "He wants you to take Miss Alvean down to Penzance. Here is a letter for you."

She handed me the letter and I was afraid she would see that my hand shook a little as I read it:

My dear Miss Leigh,
I shall be here for a few weeks, and I am sure you will agree that it would be desirable for Alvean to join me. I do not think she should miss her lessons, so I am asking you to bring her to stay for a week or so. Perhaps you could be ready to leave tomorrow on the 2:30 train.
Connan TreMellyn

The color rushed to my face. I hoped I had not betrayed the extreme joy which took possession of me. I said, "Alvean, we are to join your father tomorrow."

Alvean leaped up and threw herself into my arms, a most unusual display. It moved me deeply and helped me regain my own composure. I said, "That is tomorrow. Today we will continue our lessons."

I asked Mrs. Polgrey to arrange to have Billy Trehay take us to the train, and when she had gone I sat there in a daze. I could not concentrate any more than Alvean could. It was some time before I remembered Gilly. She was looking at me with that blank expression in her eyes. She knew that we were going away and that she would be left behind.

AFTER LUNCH ALVEAN and I went to our rooms to pack. I had very little to do. My two cotton dresses were clean, and I would wear my brown merino. I took the green silk dress from the cupboard. Why not take it? I had rarely possessed anything so becoming, and there might be an occasion when I could wear it.

I had not heard Gilly come in, and I was startled to see her standing there watching me solemnly. She looked at the bag on my bed and the folded clothes beside it, and immediately my pleasure left me, for I understood that she was going to be very unhappy. I stooped down and put my arms about her. "It'll only be for a little while, Gilly."

She screwed her eyes up tightly and would not look at me.

"Gilly," I said, "listen. We'll soon be back, you know."

She shook her head and I saw tears squeeze themselves out of her eyes. Then she ran to the bed and began pulling the things out of my bag.

"No, Gilly, no," I said. I lifted her in my arms and went to a chair, where I sat for a while rocking her. I went on. "I'm coming back, you know, Gilly. In less than no time."

She spoke. "You won't come back. She . . . she . . . went."

I was certain now that Gilly knew something, and what she knew might throw some light on the mystery of Alice.

"Gilly," I said, "did she say good-by to you before she went?" Gilly shook her head vehemently.

"Gilly," I pleaded, "try to tell me. . . . Did you see her go?"

Gilly lifted her little face to mine, and all the blankness had gone from the eyes; they were tragic. I realized in that moment how much my care had meant to her, and that it was impossible to make her understand that if I went away, it was not forever. Alice had been kind to her and Alice had gone. A few days would be like a year to her. I knew then that I could not leave her behind.

I asked myself what Connan would say if I arrived with both children. I believed I could adequately explain my reasons. As for Mrs. Polgrey, she would be pleased; she trusted Gilly with me.

"Gilly," I said. "Both you and Alvean are coming with me." I kissed her upturned face. It was some seconds before she understood, and then she shut her eyes, lowered her head and smiled.

WHEN WE SET OUT NEXT day, the whole household turned out to see us go. I sat in the carriage with a child on either side, and Billy Trehay, in TreMellyn livery, sat jauntily in the driver's seat. I felt so lighthearted it was all I could do not to break into song. The children were in high spirits; Alvean chattered a good deal, and Gilly sat contentedly beside me, clutching my skirt with one hand.

We finally reached the Liskeard station, took our train and were met at Penzance by a carriage. Then began the journey to Penlandstow Manor. It was growing dark when we turned into a drive and I saw a house loom up before us. A man on the porch with a lantern called out, "They be here. Run tell Master. He did say to let him know the minute they did come."

We were a little stiff and both children were half asleep. I helped them down, and as I turned I saw Connan standing beside me. He took my hand and pressed it warmly. Then he said an astonishing thing. "I've been anxious. I visualized all sorts of mishaps." I thought, He is thinking of Alvean, of course. But he was facing me, and smiling; and I had never been so happy in the whole of my life.

He laid a hand on Alvean's shoulder. "I'm glad you've come, Alvean," he said. Then he noticed Gilly. "What . . . ?" he began.

"We couldn't leave Gilly behind," I said. "You know you gave me permission to teach her."

He hesitated. Then he smiled at me, and I knew that he was so pleased to see me—me, not the others—that he would not have cared whom I brought with me as long as I came myself.

DURING THE NEXT two weeks I seemed to have left behind me the cold world of reality and stepped into one where everything I desired was to be mine. At Penlandstow Manor I was treated not as a governess but as a guest, and I became again the high-spirited girl of my youth. The house had been built in the Elizabethan era. It was almost as large as Mount Mellyn and as easy to lose oneself in. My room was large, with window seats upholstered in red velvet, and dark red curtains. My bed was a four-poster hung with silk embroidered curtains. The carpet was of the same deep red, and a log fire burned in the open grate.

A maid unpacked for me when I arrived and then curtsied as she asked if I would care to wash. Kind and friendly as Daisy and Kitty had been, they had not waited on me like this. "There be a little bathroom at the end of the landing, miss," the maid said. "Shall I show it to 'ee and bring 'ee hot water there?"

I was taken along to the room in which there stood a big bath and also a hip bath. "Miss Alice had the room done afore her married," I was told; and with a little shock I remembered that I was in Alice's old home.

When I had washed and changed my dress, I went to see Alvean. She had fallen asleep on her bed, so I left her. Gilly was also asleep in her room. When I returned to my own, the maid who had shown me the bathroom came in and said that Mr. TreMellyn had asked that I join him in the library. She took me to him.

"It is pleasant to see you here, Miss Leigh," he said.

I flushed. "That is kind of you. I have brought the children's lesson books along. . . ."

"Let us give them a little holiday, shall we? Lessons there must be, if you say so, but may we curtail the hours?"

"I think we might do so on an occasion like this."

He came and stood close to me. "Miss Leigh," he said with a smile, "you are delightful. I'm glad you came so promptly."

"Those were your orders."

"I did not mean to order, Miss Leigh. Merely to request."

"But . . ." I began, and I was apprehensive because he seemed different from the man I had known. He was almost like a stranger who fascinated me no less than that other Connan TreMellyn, a stranger who frightened me a little, for I was unsure of myself, unsure of my own emotions.

"I thought you would be glad to escape from Mellyn," he said.

"Escape . . . from what?"

"From the gloom of death."

"You mean Sir Thomas. But—"

"Oh, I know. A neighbor merely. But still—it did depress me and I wanted to get away. I am so glad you have joined me . . . with Alvean and the other child."

I said on impulse, "I hope you did not think it was presumptuous of me to bring Gillyflower. She would have been heartbroken if I had not brought her."

Then he said a thing which set my senses swimming. "I can understand her being heartbroken if she had to part from you."

I said quickly, "I suppose the children need some refreshment."

He waved a hand. "Order what you wish for them, Miss Leigh. When you have seen to them, you and I will dine alone together."

So I ordered for the children, and joined Connan in the winter parlor. It was a strange, exhilarating experience to dine with him in the candlelight. He told me about the house; that it had been built in the shape of an E as a compliment to Queen Elizabeth, then reigning. He drew it to show me. "Two three-sided courtyards," he said, "and a projecting center block. The main feature of it is the hall; then there is a gallery, and smaller rooms like this winter parlor."

When we had eaten we went into the library, and he suggested a game of chess. We played in silence—a deep, contented silence, or so it seemed to me. I knew I should never forget the flickering firelight and the ticking of the gilded French clock as I watched Connan's strong lean fingers on the ivory chessmen.

Once, as I frowned in concentration, I was conscious of his eyes fixed on me and, lifting mine suddenly, I met his gaze. It was a look of amusement and yet of speculation. In that moment I thought, He has asked me here for a purpose. What is it? I felt a shiver.

I moved my piece and he said, "Ah!" And then, "Miss Leigh, oh my dear Miss Leigh, you have, I think, walked straight into the trap I have set for you."

"Oh no!" I cried.

He had moved a knight which I had momentarily forgotten.

"Check, Miss Leigh," he said, "but not checkmate."

I had allowed my attention to wander. I sought to save myself, but could not. With every move the inevitable end was more obvious. His voice was gentle, full of laughter. "Checkmate, Miss Leigh. I took unfair advantage. You were tired after the journey."

"Oh no," I said quickly. "I suspect you are the better player."

"I suspect," he replied, "that we are very well matched."

THE NEXT DAY was as pleasant and unpredictable as the first. I did a few lessons with the children in the morning, and in the afternoon Connan took us for a drive to the coast, where we saw Saint Michael's Mount rising out of the water. "In the spring," he said, "I'll take you out there and you can see Saint Michael's chair."

"Can we sit in it, Papa?" asked Alvean.

"You can if you are prepared to risk a fall. You'll find your feet dangling over a drop of seventy feet or so. Nevertheless, many of your sex think it worthwhile."

"Why, Papa, why?" demanded Alvean, who was always delighted when she had his undivided attention.

"Because," he went on, "there is an old saying that if a woman can sit in Saint Michael's chair before her husband, then she will be the master of the house."

Alvean laughed with pleasure, and Gilly, whom I had brought with us, stood smiling. Connan looked at me. "And you, Miss Leigh," he said, "would you think it worthwhile to try?"

I hesitated for a second, and then met his gaze boldly. "No, Mr. Tre-Mellyn, I don't think I should."

"Then you would not desire to be the master in the house?"

"I do not think that either a husband or his wife should be the master in that sense."

"Miss Leigh," said Connan, "your wisdom puts our foolish folklore to shame." And we drove back in the winter sunshine.

I HAD BEEN IN PENLANDSTOW a week, and I was wondering how much longer this idyllic interlude could last, when Connan spoke to me of what was in his mind. The children were in bed, and he had asked me if I would join him in a game of chess in the library. There I found him, the pieces set out on the board, and a fire burning cheerfully in the great fireplace. He rose as I entered, and I quickly slipped into my place opposite him.

I was about to move king's pawn when he said, "Miss Leigh, I did not ask you here to play. I have something to say to you."

"Yes, Mr. TreMellyn?"

"I feel I have known you a very long time. You have made such a difference to us both—Alvean and myself. We both, I am certain, want to ensure that you do not leave us." I could not look at him lest he would read the hopes and fears in my eyes. "Miss Leigh," he went on, "will you stay with us . . . always?"

"I . . . I don't understand."

"I am asking you to marry me."

"But . . . but that is impossible."

"Why so, Miss Leigh? Do you find me . . . repulsive?"

"Oh no! But it is inappropriate; I am the governess here."

"Precisely. That is what alarms me. Governesses sometimes leave their employment. It would be intolerable for me if you went away."

I could hardly speak. "I—I am so surprised."

"Should I have prepared you for the shock?" His lips twitched slightly. "I am sorry, Miss Leigh. I thought I had managed to convey to you something of my feelings."

I tried to picture it all in those few seconds—going back to Mount Mellyn as the wife of the master, slipping from the role of governess to that of mistress of the house. Of course I would do it, and in a few months they would forget that I had once been the governess. Whatever else I lacked I had my dignity. But I thought that a proposal should have been made in a different way. He did not take my hand; he did not touch me; he merely sat watching me coolly.

He went on. "My dear Miss Leigh, Alvean needs a mother. You would supply that need . . . admirably."

"Should two people marry for the sake of a child?"

"I am a most selfish man. I never would." He leaned forward across the table. "Three people, my dear Miss Leigh, would profit from this marriage. Alvean needs you. I . . . I need you. And what will *you* do if you do not marry? You will go from post to post, and that is not a very pleasant life. When one is young and full of spirit it is tolerable . . . but sprightly governesses become aging ones."

I said acidly, "Do you suggest that I should enter into this marriage as an insurance against old age?"

"I suggest only that you do what your feelings dictate, my dear Miss Leigh."

There was a short silence during which I felt an absurd desire to burst into tears. "You put it on such a practical basis," I stammered. "I had not thought of marriage in that way."

His eyebrows lifted and he laughed, looking suddenly very gay. "How glad I am. I thought of you as so practical, I was trying to put it in the manner that would appeal to you most. What is your answer?"

I said I must have time to consider.

"You will tell me tomorrow?"

"Yes," I said. "I will tell you tomorrow."

I rose and went to the door. He was there before me. I waited for him to open it. But he stood with his back to the door and caught me up in his arms. He kissed me as I had never been kissed, so that I knew there was a life of the emotions of which I was totally ignorant. He kissed my eyelids, my cheeks, my mouth and my throat until he was breathless and I was too.

Then he laughed. "Tell me tomorrow!" he mocked. "Do I look the sort of man who would wait till tomorrow? The sort of man who would marry for the sake of his daughter? No, my dear, *dear* Miss Leigh, I want to marry you because since you came I have thought of little else but you, and I know I shall go on thinking of you all my life."

"Is this true?" I whispered. "Can this be true?"

"Martha, Martha!" he said tenderly. "What a stern name for such an adorable creature! And yet, how it fits!"

I said, "My sister calls me Marty. My father did too."

"Marty," he said. "That sounds helpless . . . feminine. You can be a Marty sometimes. For me you will be all three: Marty, Martha and my dear Miss Leigh. But my dearest Marty will always betray Miss Leigh. I knew from Marty that you were far more interested in me than Miss Leigh would think proper."

"Have I been so blatant?"

"Adorably so."

I knew that it was foolish to pretend. I gave myself up to his embrace, and it was wonderful beyond my imaginings. At length he put his hands on my shoulders and looked long into my face. He said, "We'll be happier, my darling, than either you or I ever dreamed possible."

My feelings were almost too much for me to bear. I tried to remember that the emotion which carries one so high is in continual danger of falling, and the higher the delight the more tragic the fall.

"We must make our plans," he said. "Let us go home at once and there announce our engagement. A month after that we can set out on our honeymoon. I suggest Italy." I sat with my hands clasped. I must have looked like an ecstatic schoolgirl. "You like the idea of Italy?"

"I would like the idea of the North Pole in some company."

"By which, my darling, I hope you mean mine."

"That was my intention. But what will they think at Mount Mellyn?"

"The servants and the countryside? Who cares? Do you? I long to tell Peter Nansellock that you are to be my wife. To tell the truth, I have been somewhat jealous of that young man."

"There was no need to be."

"Still, I was anxious. I had visions of his persuading you to go to Australia with him. So I need not fear him?"

"You need never fear anyone," I told him.

Then once more I was in his embrace, oblivious of all but the fact that I had discovered love, and believed, like hosts of lovers before, that there was never such love as ours.

At length he said, "We'll go home the day after tomorrow, put up the banns at once and give a ball to announce our engagement."

"I suppose it must be done in this way?"

"Tradition, my darling. You're not nervous?"

"Of your country neighbors, no."

Then, as if reminded, he began to talk of Alice. "I have never told you of my first marriage," he said. "It was arranged. This time I shall marry my own choice. Only one who has suffered the first can realize the joy of the second. Dearest, I have not lived the life of a monk, I fear. But Alice and I were . . . most unsuited."

"Tell me about her."

"She was a gentle creature, quiet, anxious to please. She seemed to have little spirit. I learned why. She was in love with someone else when she married me."

"The man she ran away with?" I asked.

He nodded. "Poor Alice! She chose not only the wrong husband but the wrong lover. There was little to choose between myself and Geoffry Nansellock. We were of a kind."

"You are telling me that you have enjoyed many love affairs."

"I am going to say that I *was* a philanderer, because from this moment I shall be faithful to one woman for the rest of my life." He took my hands and kissed them, looking deeply serious. "I love you," he said. "Remember that; always remember it. You may hear gossip."

"One does hear gossip," I admitted.

"You have heard that Alvean is not my daughter? Oh, darling, it is true. I could never love the child. She was a reminder of much that I wished to forget. But you have become a mother to Alvean; so I must be her father. And promise me not to be hurt if you hear other gossip about me?"

"You are thinking of Lady Treslyn, I know. She has been your mistress." The words seemed to come from my lips involuntarily. I was astonished that I could speak of such matters. Yet I had to know the truth. He nodded. I said, "But that is all over?"

He kissed my hand. "Have I not sworn eternal fidelity?"

"But she is so beautiful and she will still be there."

"But I am in love, for the first time in my life. Passion sometimes wears the guise of love, but when one meets true love one recognizes it for what it is. Dearest, let us bury all that is past. Let us start afresh from this day forth—you and I—for better, for worse. . . ."

It was late when I went to my room in a haze of happiness.

IN THE MORNING I told Alvean the news. For a few seconds a satisfied smile appeared at the corners of her mouth; then she assumed indifference, but it was too late. I knew that she was pleased. "You'll stay with us all the time now?" she said.

"Yes," I assured her.

"What shall I call you? You'll be my stepmother, won't you? I expect I shall have to call you Mama." Her mouth hardened.

"If you do not like that, you could call me Martha in private. Or Marty. That's what my father and sister always called me."

"Marty," she repeated. "I like that. It sounds like a horse."

"What could be better praise?" I cried.

I went to Gilly's room.

"Gilly," I said, "I'm going to be Mrs. TreMellyn."

The blankness left the blue eyes and her smile was dazzling. She ran to me and buried her head in my bodice. I could never be quite sure what was going on among all the shadows of Gilly's mind, but I knew she was contented. She had bracketed me with Alice in her mind, and to her it was the most natural thing in the world that I should take Alice's place. I believe that, from that moment, for Gilly I became Alice.

IT WAS A merry journey home. We sang all the way from the station to Mount Mellyn, and I had never seen Connan so happy. When we sang, *"On the first day of Christmas my true love sent to me A partridge in a pear tree,"* Alvean said, "He didn't give her very sensible things. I think he was pretending he loved her more than he really did."

"But he was her true love," I protested.

"How could she be sure?" asked Alvean.

"Because he told her so," answered Connan. "And you must always believe a lover."

I was astonished when we reached the house. Connan must have sent a message ahead, for the servants were all in the hall, lined up ceremoniously: the Polgrey and Tapperty families and others from the gardens and stables. Connan took my arm as we entered.

290

"As you know," he said, "Miss Leigh has consented to be my wife. In a few weeks' time she will be your mistress."

The men bowed and the women curtsied, but I was conscious, as I smiled at them and walked along the line with Connan, that there was a certain wariness in their eyes. They were not ready to accept me as mistress of the house . . . yet.

I dined with Connan and Alvean and afterward went upstairs with Alvean; when I had said good night to her, I joined Connan in the library. He asked me if I had written to my family and I told him that I had not yet done so. I still could not quite believe this was happening to me.

"Perhaps this token will help you to remember," he said. Then he took a jewel case from a drawer and showed me a beautiful square-cut emerald set in diamonds. He took my left hand and put the ring on the third finger. I held it out and stared at it. "It's the beginning of all the beautiful things I shall bring to you, my darling," he said.

Then he kissed my hand, and I told myself that whenever I doubted the truth of all that was happening to me I could look at my emerald and know I was not dreaming.

NEXT DAY MRS. Polgrey came up to me. "Miss Leigh," she said, "I have the kettle on. Could you come to my room for a cup of tea?"

I said I would like that. I was anxious that there should be no change in our pleasant yet dignified relationship.

This time there was no suggestion of whiskey in the tea, and this secretly amused me. I would be mistress of the house now, and I could not officially know of the tea-tippling. Mrs. Polgrey told me how delighted everyone was about my engagement. She asked if I intended to make changes, and I answered that while the household was so efficiently run by herself I would make none at all.

This was a relief to her, I could see, and she settled down to come to the point. "While you've been away, Miss Leigh, there's been a bit of excitement, along of the sudden death of Sir Thomas."

My heart had begun to leap in a disconcerting manner. "But," I said, "he is buried now."

"Yes, yes. But that need not be the end, Miss Leigh. There's been rumors, nasty rumors, and letters have been sent."

"To . . . to whom?"

"To the widow—and, it seems, to others. So they're going to dig him up. There's going to be an examination."

"You mean . . . they suspect someone poisoned him?"

"Well, there's been these letters. And him dying so sudden . . ." She was looking at me oddly. I wanted to shut from my mind all the unpleasant thoughts which kept coming to me.

I saw Connan and Lady Treslyn in the punch room, laughing together. Had he loved me then? I thought of the words she had spoken when the party was over: "It will not be long . . . now." And then there was the conversation I had partly overheard in the woods. A question hammered in my brain, but I would not let my mind dwell on it. I dared not. I could not bear to see all my hopes of happiness shattered.

I looked expressionlessly into Mrs. Polgrey's face.

"I thought you'd want to know," she said.

CHAPTER NINE

I WAS MORE afraid than I had ever been since I came to this house. Sir Thomas' wife had wanted him out of the way; it was known that Connan and she were lovers. There had been two obstacles to their union—Alice and Sir Thomas. Both had died suddenly. A terrible thought struck me. Had Connan known there would be an exhumation? Was I being used by a cynic? Why did I not use the harsher word? Was I being used by a *murderer?*

I would not believe it. I loved Connan. How could I believe the worst of him at the first crisis?

Then I thought, Martha Leigh, do you really believe that a man like Connan TreMellyn could fall in love with *you?*

Yes, I do. I do, I retorted hotly.

But I was a frightened woman.

I ASKED CONNAN what he thought of the Treslyn affair.

"Mischief-makers," he said. "They'll have an autopsy and find he died a natural death. Why, his doctor always told him that he must expect to go off like that."

"It must be very worrying for Lady Treslyn."

"She will not worry unduly. Indeed, since she has been pestered by letter writers she may well be relieved to have the matter brought to a head."

I pictured the legal minds at work. With Connan betrothed to me—and he was very eager to spread the news—might they approach the matter in a different spirit from that in which they would if they believed Lady Treslyn was hoping to marry him?

The invitations for the ball had gone out hastily—too hastily, I thought. It was to take place only four days after our return. Lady Treslyn, being in mourning, would of course not be there.

Celestine and Peter rode over the day before the ball. Celestine kissed me. "My dear," she said, "how happy I am. I have watched you with Al-

vean and I know what this is going to mean to her." There were tears in her eyes. "Alice would be so happy."

I thanked her. "You have been a good friend to me," I said.

Peter took my hand and kissed it lightly, and Connan's look of displeasure made my heart beat with happiness. "Fortunate Connan," Peter said. "No need to tell you I envy him. I've brought over Jacinth. I told you I'd make you a present of her, didn't I? Well, she's my wedding present. You can't object to that, can you?"

I looked at Connan. "A present for us both," I said. "Thank you, Peter. It's generous of you."

He shook his head. "I want a good home for her." He drew me aside. "I'm going at the end of next week. There's no point in delaying—now." He looked at me significantly. "Well, you'll keep Con in order, Miss Leigh. I'm sure of that. I thought Alvean seemed not displeased; I suspect that you're an even greater favorite than Miss Jansen was."

"Poor Miss Jansen! I wonder what became of her."

"Celeste helped her to find another job, with the Merrivales, who have a place, Hoodfield Manor, near Tavistock."

"I'm glad. It was kind of Celestine to help her."

"Well, that's Celestine all over. I wish you happiness, Miss Leigh. And if you should change your mind, there'll be a little homestead waiting for you in Australia. You'll find me ever faithful."

I laughed. "And whenever I ride Jacinth I shall think of her namesake, Miss Jansen—and of you."

THE BALL WAS a great success, and I was surprised how ready the neighborhood was to accept me. I felt they were reminding each other that I was an educated young woman and that my family background was passably good. Perhaps those who were fond of Connan were relieved because he was engaged to be married, for they would not wish him to be involved in the Treslyn scandal.

The day after the ball Connan had to go away again on business. "I neglected a great deal during our stay at Penlandstow," he said. "My mind was on other matters. I shall be away a week, I think, and when I come back it will be but a fortnight to our wedding. You'll be getting on with your preparations; if there's anything you wish to change in the house, do so. It mightn't be a bad idea to ask Celestine's advice. She's an expert on old houses."

I said I would, because it would please her, and I wanted to please her. "She was kind to me from the first," I said. "I shall always have a tender feeling for her."

He said good-by and drove off while I stood waving.

When I turned I found Gilly standing there. Since I had told her that I was to be Mrs. TreMellyn she had taken to following me around. Alice TreMellyn had disappeared; she was going to make sure that I did not.

"Hello, Gilly," I said.

She dropped her head in that characteristic way of hers and put her hand in mine.

"Gilly," I said, "in three weeks I am going to be married, and I am the happiest woman in the world."

I thought of what Connan had said about altering anything I wished to in the house, and I remembered that there were some parts of it which I had not even seen yet. I suddenly thought of Miss Jansen and remembered she had had a different room from the one I occupied. I had never seen hers and I decided to have a look at it. I need have no qualms now about going to any part of the house, for soon I should be mistress of it.

"Come, Gilly," I said, "let's go see Miss Jansen's room."

She trotted along contentedly by my side, and I thought how much more she understood than people realized, for it was she who led me to the room. There was nothing unusual about it except for a rather striking mural. Gilly tugged at my arm and drew me close to it. Then I understood. There, hidden in the mural, was a peep. I looked through it and saw the chapel from the side opposite the peep in the solarium.

Gilly seemed delighted to have shown me the peep. Then she followed me back to my room, clearly determined to keep an eye on me.

ALL THROUGH THE night and the next day a southwest gale blew in from the sea. Rain drove horizontally against our windows, and even the solid foundations of Mount Mellyn seemed to shake. But by the following morning the skies had cleared a little, and the heavy rain gave way to a light drizzle.

At lunchtime Mrs. Polgrey told me that Lady Treslyn had stopped by to see Connan. "She seemed very distressed," said Mrs. Polgrey. "She'll not rest until this terrible business is over."

In the afternoon Alvean and I went down to the stables.

"Jacinth be frisky today," Billy warned me.

"It's because she had no exercise yesterday." I stroked her muzzle, and she rubbed against my hand affectionately.

We rode down the slope, past the cove and Mount Widden, then along the cliff path. We made a habit of using this path, for the view here was particularly beautiful, with the jagged coast stretched out before us. Sometimes the path took us almost down to the sea; again it climbed up, narrow and high. It was not easy going, for the rain had whipped up the mud, and I began to feel a little anxious about Alvean. She sat firmly in her saddle— no novice now—but I was conscious of the horses' moods. At times I had to rein Jacinth in firmly; a gallop would have been more to her taste than this slow, careful walk along paths which were a good deal more dangerous than usual.

There was one especially narrow spot on the path. Above it loomed the cliff face, dotted with gorse and brambles; below it the cliff fell steeply to the sea. The path was safe enough ordinarily, but today I noticed that in places some of the cliff had fallen. When we came to the danger spot, I was walking Jacinth single file in front of Alvean. I pulled up and looked over my shoulder, saying, "We'll go very slowly along here." Then I heard it. I turned quickly as a huge boulder came tumbling down, bringing smaller stones, turf and bushes in its wake. It passed just a few inches in front of Jacinth, and went hurtling down.

Jacinth reared, terrified and ready to plunge anywhere—over the cliff, down to the sea, to escape. It was fortunate for me that I was an experienced rider. Within seconds I had her under control, talking to her in a voice meant to be soothing, but which shook a little.

I glanced nervously up at the top of the cliff. I don't know what I expected to see, but I found myself staring at some thickset bushes. Did I see a movement there, or did I imagine it? It would be easy for someone to hide up there. What an excellent opportunity, if someone wanted to be rid of me! If a boulder were dislodged by the rains, it would be easy to roll it down at the moment when I was riding below. And it was no secret that Alvean and I often took this path. I shivered. "Let's get on," I said. "We'll go home on the upper road."

In a few minutes we were safely up on the road, and not until we were back in the house did I fully realize how alarmed I was. A terrifying pattern was being formed. Alice had died; Sir Thomas Treslyn had died; and now I, who was to be Connan's wife, might easily have met my death this day. I was a sensible, practical woman. Was I going to refuse to look facts in the face because of what I might see there if I did so?

Suppose Connan had not really gone away. Suppose he had wanted an accident to happen to me while he was believed to be away. I thought of Lady Treslyn and her sensuous, voluptuous beauty. Connan had admitted that she had been his mistress. *Had* been? Was it possible that anyone, knowing her, could want me?

The proposal had been so sudden. It had come at a time when the body of his mistress' husband was about to be exhumed.

I was badly frightened. But to whom could I go for help?

There was Peter or Celestine. . . . No, I could not betray these terrible suspicions of Connan to them.

I thought of the house, vast and full of secrets, a house in which it was possible to peep from certain rooms into others. There might be peeps I had not yet discovered. Perhaps someone was watching me now. I thought of the peep in Miss Jansen's room and of her sudden dismissal. Then I said to myself, Hoodfield Manor, near Tavistock. Why not talk to Miss Jansen? She might have some light to throw on the secrets of this house.

I felt better when I had written a note:

Dear Miss Jansen: I am the governess at Mount Mellyn and I have heard much of you. I wonder if it would be possible to meet you—as soon as you can manage it.

I signed my name and posted the letter. Then I tried to forget it.

I longed for a message from Connan. There was none. The devilish scheme I suspected seemed more and more credible to me. I said to myself, Perhaps Alice died by accident, and that gave Connan and Lady Treslyn the idea of ridding themselves of Sir Thomas. Perhaps they slipped something into his drink that night. Then Connan became engaged to the governess to divert suspicion. But the governess was now an obstacle in her turn. So she could have an accident on her newly acquired mare, to which she had not yet grown accustomed; and thus the road would be clear for the guilty lovers.

How could I imagine such things of the man I loved? For I did love him. So much that I would rather meet death at his hands than leave him and endure an empty life without him.

THREE DAYS LATER there was a letter from Miss Jansen, who said she was eager to meet me. She would be in Plymouth the following day and we might meet at the White Hart for luncheon.

I told Mrs. Polgrey that I was going into Plymouth to shop, and I made straight for the White Hart. Miss Jansen was already there—an extremely pretty, fair-haired girl. She greeted me with pleasure, and the innkeeper's wife conducted us to a small private room.

When the food had been brought and we were alone, Miss Jansen said, "Mount Mellyn is a wonderful old place, and I was sorry to leave it. You have heard why I went?"

"Y-yes," I said hesitantly.

"It was a very distressing affair. I was furious to be unjustly accused." She seemed so frank and sincere that I believed her, and said so. She looked pleased, and as we sat eating she told me the story.

"The Treslyns and the Nansellocks had been having tea at the house. You know them, of course?"

"Indeed, yes."

"I had been treated rather specially." She flushed slightly, and I thought, Yes, you are pretty. Connan would have thought so. "They had called me in to tea because Miss Nansellock wanted to ask about Alvean. She does dote on that child. So I was called down to talk to her, had tea and chatted

297

with them as though I were a guest. I think that Lady Treslyn resented my presence. Perhaps they were a little too attentive to me—I mean Mr. Nansellock and Mr. TreMellyn. Lady Treslyn has a hot temper, I am sure. In any case I believe she arranged the whole thing."

"She couldn't be so vile!"

"Oh, I am sure she could, and she was. You see, she was wearing a diamond bracelet and the safety chain broke. She said, 'I'll take it to the village to get it repaired as soon as we leave.' She took it off and put it on the table. I left them and went to the schoolroom to do some work with Alvean. While we were sitting there the door was thrown open and there they all stood, looking at me.

"Lady Treslyn said truculently that she wanted a search made because her bracelet was missing, and Mr. TreMellyn added, in a kindly voice, that he hoped I would not object. I was very angry. I said, 'Search my room. Nothing will satisfy me but that you should.' So we all went there, and in a drawer, hidden under some of my things, was the diamond bracelet.

"Lady Treslyn said I was caught red-handed, and she was going to have me sent to prison. The others all pleaded with her not to make a scandal. Finally they agreed that if I went at once, the matter would be forgotten. I was furious. I wanted an inquiry. But what could I do? They had found the thing there."

"It must have been frightful for you." I shivered.

She smiled in a kindly way at me. "You are afraid that they may do something similar to you. Lady Treslyn is determined to marry Mr. Tre-Mellyn. He is, after all, a widower and not the sort of man to live without women."

I said, "I suppose he made advances to you?"

She shrugged. "At least Lady Treslyn imagined that I might be a threat to her, and I am sure chose that way to get rid of me."

"What a dreadful creature! But Miss Nansellock was kind?"

"Very kind. When I was packing she came to my room and said, 'I'm very distressed, Miss Jansen. You didn't put that bracelet in your drawer, did you?' I said, 'Miss Nansellock, I swear I didn't.' She said, 'I know the Merrivales need a governess. I am going to see that you get the position.' She lent me some money, which I have now paid back, and wrote to the Merrivales for me."

"Thank goodness there was someone to help."

"Heaven knows what would have become of me if she had not been there. Ours is a precarious profession, Miss Leigh. We are at the mercy of our employers." She brightened. "I try to forget all that. In six months' time I shall be married to the doctor who looks after the Merrivales."

"May I felicitate you, Miss Jansen? As a matter of fact, I too am engaged. I am to be married to Connan TreMellyn."

She stared at me in astonishment. "Why . . ." she stammered, "I wish you the best of luck." I could see that she was a little embarrassed and trying to remember what she had said about Connan. "I wonder," she said after a pause, "why you wanted to see me."

"There are things I want to know about the house, and I hear you are an expert on old houses."

"Oh no! But I've seen many and I've read a great deal about them."

"There is a peep in your old room. Did you know?"

"I lived in that room three weeks before I discovered that it was there. Do you know those in the solarium?"

"Oh yes," I said.

"Overlooking the hall and the chapel. The hall and the chapel would have been the most important rooms in the house when it was built. It's late Elizabethan, you know. At that time people had to keep the presence of priests in their houses secret. I think that's why they had all those peeps and things."

"How interesting."

"Miss Nansellock is an authority on old houses," she said. "That was something we had in common. Does she know we're meeting?"

"No one knows."

"You came here without telling even your future husband?"

Confidences trembled on my lips, but how could I say to a stranger: I suspect the man I am engaged to marry of being involved in a plot to murder me?

"He is away on business," I said. "I wanted to meet you because I believed you had been falsely accused. Many people at the house think that. When Mr. TreMellyn returns I shall tell him that I have seen you, and ask if something can be done."

"It is of little consequence now. Dr. Luscombe knows what happened. He is very indignant. But I have made him see that no good purpose could be served by bringing up the matter again."

"What a wicked woman Lady Treslyn is! But for the kindness of Miss Nansellock . . ."

"I know. Will you tell her that I am engaged to Dr. Luscombe? She will be pleased. And there's something else I would like her to know. I've been making a little study of Elizabethan houses, and my fiancé arranged for me to see Mount Edgcumbe, on the Cornish peninsula. It's very like Mount Mellyn. The chapel is almost identical, even to the lepers' squint. But the squint at Mount Mellyn is much bigger, and the construction of the walls is different. As a matter of fact, I've never seen a squint like that at Mount Mellyn. Do tell Miss Nansellock. She would be interested."

"I will," I said.

We parted, and on my journey home I felt that I had obtained from Miss

Jansen some fresh light on my problem. There was no doubt now that Lady Treslyn had arranged for Miss Jansen's dismissal. Miss Jansen was very pretty indeed. Connan admired her, and Lady Treslyn, possessive as a tigress, was not going to allow him to marry anyone but herself.

I believed now that Lady Treslyn was planning to remove me as she had removed Miss Jansen, but because I was already engaged to Connan she would have to use more drastic methods.

I had made up my mind. When Connan came back I was going to tell him everything—all I had discovered, all I feared. The decision brought me great comfort.

Two MORE DAYS passed and still Connan had not returned.

Peter Nansellock came over with Celestine to say good-by; he was leaving late that night on the London train. They thought Connan would have returned by now, and, as a matter of fact, while they were there a letter arrived from Connan saying that he would be back late that night or early the next day.

I felt tremendously happy.

As I gave them tea I told them of my meeting with Miss Jansen. They were both startled.

"But how did this happen?" asked Peter.

"I wrote and asked her to meet me. She had lived here, and I was curious about her; so, as I was going to Plymouth . . ."

"A charming creature," mused Peter.

"Yes. You'll be pleased to hear that she is engaged to be married to the local doctor."

"I'm delighted!" Celestine cried.

"She is so grateful to you," I said. "You were truly kind to her."

"It was nothing. I could not let that woman do what she did and stand by doing nothing."

"You think Lady Treslyn hid the bracelet in the drawer?"

"There is not a doubt of it," said Celestine firmly.

"Well, Miss Jansen is happy now. By the way, I have a special message for you. Miss Jansen has been to Mount Edgcumbe and has been comparing the squint in its chapel with ours. She says ours is unique—much bigger; and there's something about the construction of the walls. . . ."

"Really? That's very interesting. We'll look at it together sometime. You're going to be the mistress of the house, so you ought to take an interest in it."

"I'm going to ask you to teach me a great deal about it."

She smiled at me warmly. "I'll be glad to do so."

I asked Peter what train he was catching, and he answered that it would be the ten o'clock. "I'll ride to the station," he said, "and stable the horse there. I shall go alone. I don't want any fond farewells. But, Miss Leigh," he went on, his eyes mischievous, "if you feel like coming with me . . . it's not too late even now."

I went down to the porch to say my last farewells to him. The servants were there, for Peter was a great favorite. I guessed that he had bestowed many a sly kiss on Daisy and Kitty, and they were sorry to see him go.

His last words were: "Don't forget, Miss Leigh, if you should change your mind . . . !"

I laughed, but I felt quite sad that he was going.

AS WE WENT back into the house Mrs. Polgrey said to me, "Miss Leigh, could I have a word with you?"

"Certainly," I said, and we went to her room.

"I've just had word," she said. "The result of the autopsy. Death through natural causes."

Relief swept over me. "Oh, I'm so pleased!"

"So are we all. I didn't like the things that were being said."

"It must be a great relief to Lady Treslyn."

She looked embarrassed, and I suspected that she was wondering what she had said to me in the past about Connan and Lady Treslyn. To sweep aside her embarrassment forever, I said, "I hoped you were going to offer me a cup of your special Earl Grey."

She was delighted. We talked of household affairs while tea was made; then she tentatively brought out the whiskey. When I nodded, a teaspoonful was put into each cup. I felt that we had indeed resumed the old, friendly relationship.

I was glad, because I could see this made her happy, and I wanted everyone to be as happy as I was. If Lady Treslyn had really attempted to kill me, Connan obviously knew nothing of it. Sir Thomas had died a natural death, so there was nothing to hide. Connan had no reason to ask me to marry him except the one he gave me: that he loved me.

IT WAS NINE o'clock and the children were in bed. I wondered what time Connan would arrive. I imagined I heard a horse's hoofs in the distance, and I went to the door to look for him.

I waited. The night was still and the house very quiet. The servants were in their own quarters. Then I saw someone coming toward me. It was Celestine, and she had come by way of the woods, not along the drive as usual. She was rather breathless. "Why, hello," she said. "I came to see you. I felt so lonely with Peter gone. Connan's not back, I suppose?"

"No. I don't think he can possibly be here before midnight."

"Do you know, I rather hoped you'd be alone. I wanted to have a look at that squint in the chapel. Ever since you gave me Miss Jansen's message

I've been eager to see it again. I have a theory that there may be a door in the paneling which leads to another part of the house. Wouldn't it be fun if you and I could discover it and tell Connan about it when he arrives?"

"Yes," I agreed, "it would." We went through the hall, and as we did so I glanced up at the peep, because I had an uncanny feeling that we were being watched. I thought I saw a movement up there, but I said nothing. We went on through the far door and down the stone steps to the chapel. It smelled damp. I said, "It smells as though it hasn't been used for years." My voice echoed weirdly.

Celestine did not answer. She had lighted one of the candles that stood on the altar. I watched the long shadow which the flickering light threw against the wall.

"Let's get into the squint," she said. "Through this door. There is another door in it which opens onto the walled garden. That was the way the lepers used to come in."

She carried the candle high, and I followed her into a small chamber.

She began pressing different parts of the wall. Suddenly she turned and smiled at me. "I'll swear that somewhere in this house there is a priest's hole—you know, the hidey-hole of the resident priest into which he scuttled when the queen's men arrived. Connan would be delighted if I found it. It would be the best wedding present I could give him. After all, what can you give people who have all they want?"

She hesitated, and her voice was high with excitement. "Just a minute. There's something here." I came close to her, and caught my breath with amazement, for the panel she was pressing had moved inward and shown itself as a long narrow door.

She turned toward me and she looked quite unlike herself. Her eyes were brilliant with excitement. She put her head inside the aperture and was about to go forward when she said, "No, you first. It will be your house. You should be the first to enter."

I had caught her excitement. I stepped ahead of her and was aware of an unrecognizable, pungent odor.

She said, "Have a quick look. Careful. There are probably steps." She held the candle high, and I saw there were two of them. I went down the steps, and as I did so the door shut behind me.

"Celestine!" I cried in terror. But there was no answer. "Open that door," I screamed. But my voice was imprisoned in the darkness, and I knew that I was a prisoner too—Celestine's prisoner.

The darkness shut me in. It was cold and eerie—foul, evil. Panic seized me. I had been a fool. I had been trapped. Fear numbed my body as it did my brain, but I managed to mount the two steps and beat my fists against the wall. "Let me out! Let me out!" I cried. But I knew that my voice would not be heard beyond the lepers' squint. And how often did people go to the chapel? She would slip away. . . . No one would know she had even been in the house.

I heard my own voice sobbing out my terror, and it frightened me afresh because, for the moment, I did not recognize it as my own. I knew that one could not live for long in this dark, damp place. I pulled at the wall until I tore my nails and I felt the blood on my hands.

I began to look about me because my eyes were becoming accustomed to the gloom. Then I saw that I was not alone. . . . What was left of Alice lay there. At last I had found her.

"Alice!" I screamed. "So you were here all the time?"

But Alice's lips had been silent for more than a year.

I covered my face with my hands. There was the smell of death and decay everywhere. I wondered, How long did Alice live after the door had closed on *her?* So long might I expect to live.

I think I must have fainted. And I was delirious when I finally revived. I heard a voice babbling—my own voice, I realized at last. For a time I was not sure who I was. Was I Martha? Was I Alice?

Our stories were so much alike. They said she ran away with Geoffry. They would say I had run away with Peter. Our departures had been cleverly timed.

I realized now whose shadow I had seen on the blind. It was hers . . . Celestine's. She had known of the existence of the little diary I had discovered, and she was searching for it because she knew it might provide a clue which would lead to discovery. She did not love Alvean; she had tricked us all with her gentle demeanor. I knew now that she was incapable of loving anyone. It was the house that she loved. I pictured her looking from Mount Widden across the cove—coveting a house as fiercely as woman ever coveted man.

"Alice," I said out loud. "We were her victims, you and I."

And I fancied Alice talked to me . . . told me of the day Geoffry had caught the London train and how Celestine had come to the house and told her of the great discovery in the chapel. I saw Alice . . . pale, pretty, fragile Alice crying out in pleasure at the discovery, taking those fatal steps forward to death. I felt that she was with me. I had found her at last, and now we had comfort to offer each other as I waited to enter the shadowy world which had been hers since she was led by Celestine Nansellock into the lepers' squint.

THERE WAS A blinding light in my eyes. I was being carried.

I said, "Am I dead, Alice?"

And a voice answered, "My darling . . . my darling . . . you are safe." It was Connan's voice, and it was his arms which held me. I felt myself laid upon a bed, and many people stood about me.

I saw light glinting on hair which looked almost white. "Alice, there is an angel."

But the angel said, "It's Gilly. Gilly brought them to you. Gilly watched and Gilly saw."

And so it was Gilly who brought me back to the world. I was not dead; it was in truth Connan's arms which I felt about me.

I was in my own bedroom, from the window of which I could see the lawns and the palm trees and the room which had once been Alice's, on the blind of which I had seen the shadow of Alice's murderer, who sought to kill me too.

I called out in terror. But Connan was beside me.

I heard his voice, tender, soothing. "It's all right, my love . . . my only love. I'm here . . . I'm with you forevermore."

THIS IS THE story I tell my great-grandchildren. They ask for it again and again. They come in from play in the park or bring me flowers from the gardens, a tribute to the old lady who can always charm them with the story of how she married their great-grandfather.

The years with Connan have often been stormy ones, for we are both too strong-willed to live in perpetual peace; but they have been years in which I have lived life richly, and what more could one ask? We have had five sons and five daughters, and three more Connan TreMellyns have been born since the day we married in Mellyn church—our son, grandson and great-grandson.

When the children hear my story, they want everything explained. Why was it believed that the woman who died in the train was Alice? Because of the locket she wore. But it was Celestine who identified the locket as one which, she said, she had given Alice. Of course she had never seen it before in her life.

She had been eager that I should accept Jacinth when Peter had first offered the mare to me—I suppose because she feared it was just possible that Connan might become interested in me and therefore she was ready to encourage the friendship between myself and Peter. And it was she who later, discovering the loosened boulder on the cliff, had lain in wait and attempted to kill or maim me.

She was the sender of the anonymous letters to Lady Treslyn and the public prosecutor, commenting on the suspicious circumstances of Sir Thomas' death, for she believed that if there was a big enough scandal, marriage between Connan and Lady Treslyn would be impossible for years. But she had reckoned without Connan's feelings for me; thus, when she learned that I was engaged to marry him, she immediately began her plans to remove me. It was Celestine too who had put the bracelet in Miss Jansen's drawer. The governess was learning too much about the house, and the knowledge would inevitably lead her to the lepers' squint and Alice's body.

Celestine was in love—passionately in love with Mount Mellyn. She wanted to marry Connan only in order to be mistress of the house. After discovering the secret of the squint, she had kept it to herself, and waited for her opportunity to murder Alice—and then me.

But she had reckoned without Gilly. Gilly had known Alice was in the house that night, for Alice had made a habit of coming to say good night to her, as she did to Alvean. Because she had never forgotten, Gilly did not believe she had forgotten this time. Gilly therefore continued to believe that Alice had never left the house, and had gone on looking for her. It was Gilly's face which I had seen at the peep. She knew all the peeps and used them frequently, because she was always watching for Alice.

Watching from the peep in the solarium, she had seen Celestine and me enter the hall. Then she crossed the room and, looking through the peep on the other side, saw us enter the chapel. We crossed to the lepers' squint; it could not easily be seen from the solarium, so Gilly sped to Miss Jansen's room; from that peep she had a good view of the squint. She saw us disappear through the door and waited for us to come out. . . . She waited and waited, for Celestine naturally left by the lepers' door to the walled garden and slipped away home. Thus, while I lived through that period of horror in Alice's death chamber, Gilly was standing on her stool in Miss Jansen's room, watching the door to the lepers' squint.

Connan returned at eleven and expected the household to give him a welcome. He rang for Mrs. Polgrey. "Tell Miss Leigh that I am here," he said. He must have been a little piqued because he was and still is—the sort of man who demands the utmost affection and attention, and the fact that I could be sleeping when he came home was inconceivable to him.

I pictured the scene: Mrs. Polgrey reporting that I was not in my room, the search for me, that terrible moment when Connan believed what Celestine had intended he should believe. . . . "Mr. Nansellock came over this afternoon to say good-by. He caught the ten-o'clock train. . . ."

I have wondered often how long it would have been before they discovered that I had not run away with Peter. Celestine might already have found some way of making herself mistress of Mount Mellyn; insidiously she would have made herself necessary to Alvean and to Connan; meantime, there would have been two skeletons behind the walls of the lepers' squint. But a simple child, born in sorrow, living in shadow, led the way to the truth.

Connan has told me often of the uproar in the house as they searched for me. He told me of the child who came and stood patiently beside him, waiting to be heard; how she tugged at his coat and sought for the words to explain.

"God forgive us," he says, "it was some time before we would listen to her, and so we delayed bringing you out of that hellish place."

But finally she had led them there . . . through the door into the lepers' squint. She had seen us, she said.

It was dusty in the squint, and in the dust on the wall was the mark of a hand. When Connan saw it he began to take Gilly seriously. But it was not easy to find the secret spring to the door. There was an agonizing search of ten minutes while Connan was ready to tear the walls down.

Then they found it and they found me. They found Alice too.

THEY TOOK CELESTINE to Bodmin to be tried for the murder of Alice, but before the trial could take place she was a raving lunatic. She did not die until twenty years after, and all that time she spent locked away from the world.

Alice's remains were buried in the vault where those of an unknown woman lay, and Connan and I were married three months after he had brought me out of the darkness; Phillida and her family came to the wedding and so did Aunt Adelaide.

I dream over the past after I have repeated this story to the children. Alvean is happily married to a Devonshire squire; and, as for Gilly, she has never left me. At any moment now she will appear with the eleven-o'clock coffee, which on warm days we take in that rose arbor where I first saw Lady Treslyn and Connan together.

I must confess that Lady Treslyn continued to plague me during the first years of my married life. I discovered that I could be a jealous as well as a passionate woman. But Lady Treslyn went to London after a few years, and we heard that she remarried there.

Peter came back some fifteen years after he left. He had acquired a wife and two children but no fortune; he was, however, as gay and full of vitality as ever. In the meantime Mount Widden had been sold; and later one of my daughters married the owner, so the place has become almost as much home to me as Mount Mellyn.

The years have passed and now, as I sit here thinking of it all, Connan is coming down the path from the gardens. In a moment—because we are alone—he will say, "Ah, my *dear* Miss Leigh!" as he often does in his most tender moments. There will be a smile on his lips which tells me that he is seeing me not as I am now but as I was then: the governess somewhat resentful of her fate, desperately clinging to her pride and her dignity—falling in love in spite of herself—his dear Miss Leigh.

The High Valley

The High Valley

A CONDENSATION OF THE NOVEL BY

JESSICA NORTH

ILLUSTRATED BY SANJULIAN

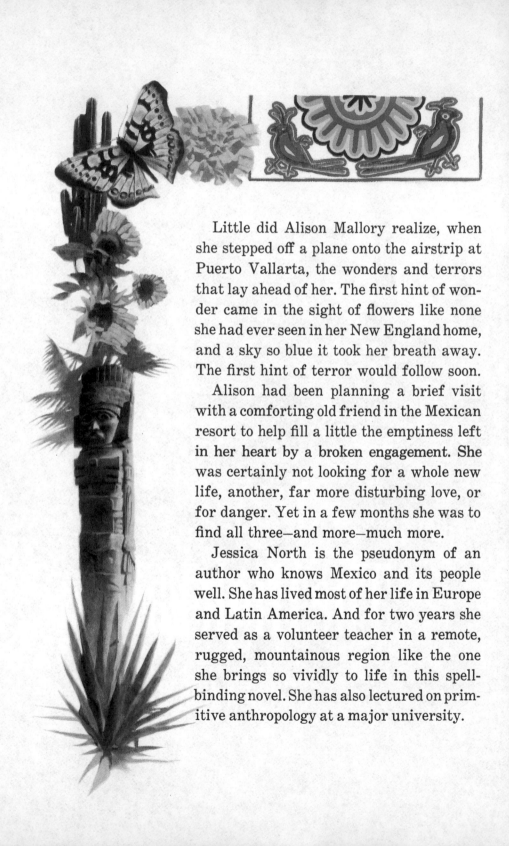

Little did Alison Mallory realize, when she stepped off a plane onto the airstrip at Puerto Vallarta, the wonders and terrors that lay ahead of her. The first hint of wonder came in the sight of flowers like none she had ever seen in her New England home, and a sky so blue it took her breath away. The first hint of terror would follow soon.

Alison had been planning a brief visit with a comforting old friend in the Mexican resort to help fill a little the emptiness left in her heart by a broken engagement. She was certainly not looking for a whole new life, another, far more disturbing love, or for danger. Yet in a few months she was to find all three—and more—much more.

Jessica North is the pseudonym of an author who knows Mexico and its people well. She has lived most of her life in Europe and Latin America. And for two years she served as a volunteer teacher in a remote, rugged, mountainous region like the one she brings so vividly to life in this spellbinding novel. She has also lectured on primitive anthropology at a major university.

CHAPTER ONE

YESTERDAY THE FIRST snow fell, great feathery flakes that vanished as they touched the ground. We watched, standing together at the window of this rented cabin, while the glass in front of us, silver-framed by frost, mirrored the blaze of pine logs on the hearth.

"Winter is almost here," I said.

"Yes." His hand touched mine, but his thoughts, I knew, wandered toward a faraway country. "We must go home soon. We've been away long enough." He spoke as much to himself as to me.

"I think so, too. We should be ready now." But my voice carried an assurance I did not really feel.

Just then the overcast sky brightened, pale sunlight struck the surface of the northern lake where we are staying. Puerto Vallarta came suddenly to my mind, as beautiful in memory as in life. I saw a flash of azure—the incredible blue of the bay—and beyond it rolled the Pacific, whitecapped by the wind. I am not yet ready to return there. We have had more than our share of violence, and the scars of it have not yet healed in our minds.

I still cannot think of Veronica without a quickening of my blood, but her ghost no longer haunts me. Her gray eyes do not watch me now, nor does she control and move my hands as she did one night only a year ago. Yet Veronica returns when the chiming of a country church bell reminds me of Puerto Vallarta, where it all began.

I wonder if he, too, thinks of her often. One day last week I almost asked him. He was standing alone, gazing toward the west, and I said, "What are you thinking?"

"Look, Alison," he told me, pointing to the sky. "The mallards are going home." Then I saw the V-shaped squadron flying southward.

"Home?" For a moment the word surprised me. I am a New Englander, born sixty miles from this lake, and to me the country of pine forests and cold streams is where the mallards live. Their home is here, and the autumn flight is only a sojourn. But he sees it differently, of course.

"Remember the mallards in the High Valley?" he asked. "Some years they come back late." He smiled quietly. "They have a Mexican disregard for time."

The High Valley. He spoke the name I'd temporarily forced from my mind. I had allowed myself to think of Puerto Vallarta, but the High Valley, that cup of land hidden in the mountains far above the town, was the setting for the violence and malice that changed our lives.

Soon we will return there; the High Valley is now home. And our homecoming must not be marred by the past. I realized the only way to forget was by remembering. I would relive all that happened one last time, and then have done with the past forever. . . .

"PLEASE FASTEN YOUR seat belts and observe the no-smoking rule. We are now approaching Puerto Vallarta."

When the stewardess spoke, I involuntarily braced myself, a little nervous. I was twenty-five years old, a child of the space age, but I'd seldom traveled by plane and still felt uncertain of the takeoffs and landings.

My mother, Helene, was exactly the opposite, forever dashing to catch a flight for New York or Hollywood—anywhere her overoptimistic theatrical agent chose to send her in futile search of a role. She never took me with her, of course. I didn't board planes, I *met* them—helping Helene with her hatboxes and makeup case, getting quickly out of the way if an airline publicity man chose to photograph her voluptuous figure and kittenish face.

The plane began its swift descent, but the rushing sensation in my ears did not drown out the memory of Helene's lilting voice. "Poor Alison's nothing but bones, eyes, and elbows. I'd make her drink malteds to gain weight, but I'm afraid she'd slip through the straw and fall in!" Always "Poor Alison!" Ironic that it was not Helene but poor Alison who in a moment would be set down in a tropical paradise. A place whose list of celebrated visitors sounded like roll call at an Academy Awards ceremony. How Helene would have loved to be near them!

The beautiful people. What was it like to be a beautiful person? After hours of buffeting in a bus and two planes, I felt a good deal less than beautiful. In fact, I barely qualified as a person. I was Miss Nobody going nowhere alone because she had no other place to go and no one to go with her. And furthermore, Miss Nobody didn't care. If no one needed me, well, I didn't need anyone either.

My decision to quit my job on one day's notice, give up my apartment, close my small savings account, and fly off to Mexico had been so impulsive and everything had happened so fast that somehow I had left my own identity behind. My passport claimed that I was Alison Mallory, born in Old Bridge, Massachusetts. I was five feet seven inches tall. The passport alleged that my eyes were gray, although my driver's license insisted they were blue. At any rate, they were extraordinarily large, and besides, who cared? The surprised-looking girl in the photograph, with full lips and long, brushed-back hair so pale that it blended into the light background, was certainly me.

The other passengers, chattering and laughing, were going toward something, but I was running away. Running from things I couldn't bear to think about. Gripping the seat belt, I blinked hard, vowing to myself that there would be no more tears.

Margaret Webber, widow of a physician, lived in Puerto Vallarta in retirement. Every Christmas her card said, "Please come for a visit." Now I was doing it—but not a visit, an escape. And because I needed Margaret badly.

The Webbers had first visited Puerto Vallarta a dozen years ago, and had returned for several vacations. Then Dr. Webber and my father, who were close friends, were drowned in a boating accident. It was a terrible blow to Margaret, yet she found strength to comfort me, while Helene alternated between hysterical grief and enthusiastic plans for enlarging the Old Bridge Summer Theater, of which she was owner and female star. Margaret then moved to Puerto Vallarta, returning to Old Bridge only once—when Helene died suddenly and I again needed Margaret's motherly strength.

Now, in the last seconds before landing, I wondered what adventures might await me in this Mexican village Margaret loved so much. I decided to play The Game, a secret left over from childhood. I closed my eyes and listened intently, pretending that the first thing I heard would tell me what lay ahead. There was silence except for the rush of air breaking against the plane like surf; then the man across the aisle spoke clearly to the woman beside him. "Journey's end, darling."

Journey's end. I remembered the Old Bridge Summer Theater production of *Twelfth Night,* Helene poised and pretty waiting to enter as Olivia, and myself sitting in the wings, a teenage prompter. The boy playing the clown role sang onstage:

> *"Trip no further, pretty sweeting;*
> *Journeys end in lovers' meeting,*
> *Every wise man's son doth know."*

As the plane rolled to a halt, I opened my eyes, glancing at my hand which for more than a month had seemed unfamiliar without the engagement ring I'd worn so long. *"Journeys end in lovers' meeting."* Not likely.

When the aircraft was almost empty, I started toward the exit, sure that everything I had done in the last few days was madness. I made my way down a short flight of steel steps, felt the sun strike me. Then I looked up and found I had entered a new world.

Color. A sky so blue that I caught my breath. Huge pearl clouds heaped upon each other, and below them shone the green of tropical forest. And flowers—vermilion, purple, orange flowers that seemed not to bloom but to blaze. And there was music. Guitars and a marimba and a dark young man in a flowered shirt singing "La Golondrina."

Inside, the terminal was cool and uncrowded except for the pushing group at the luggage counter. I did not join them. I was in no hurry and no one waited to meet me, since I hadn't known my arrival time when I'd sent the telegram to Margaret. Sitting on a comfortable leather couch, I relaxed, my eyes wandering toward souvenir shops displaying gay shawls and gossamer mantillas. Then I saw the two beautiful people approaching.

The woman was a golden blonde, her burnished hair cascading naturally over bare shoulders. She moved like a queen, proud and confident, tall even in flat sandals. Her sleeveless white shift was skillfully cut to reveal the curves of a slender figure and skin glowingly tanned by tropic sun. A film star? A television personality? She commanded every eye—and she knew it. But the man escorting her was even more dramatic than she was. His long, easy strides were accented by the clinking of silver spurs. The tightly fitted suede trousers gleamed with two rows of silver buttons, and more silver shone from the handle of a pistol strapped to his hip, while the short jacket over his linen shirt flashed with braid and embroidery.

His sombrero gave the impression of a Mexican highwayman, and one might have expected a swarthy face and bristling mustachios. He did have a mustache, but it was pencil-thin and light brown, the same color as the forelock showing under the sombrero. He couldn't be Mexican, I thought. Yet never, except in antique Spanish portraits, had I seen such sharply chiseled features. His thin, aquiline nose gave him a patrician appearance but somehow suggested coldness—perhaps even cruelty. A long, narrow scar was deeply etched on his left cheek.

The couple paused a few yards from me, and I realized that the woman's face was flushed with anger. "I want to know just one thing!" Her throaty voice rang out. "How much longer?"

His face tightened, but he spoke softly in Spanish, words I couldn't hear. If the reply was meant to soothe her, it failed. Her green eyes widened, her cheeks flared with rage. "Damn you!" She spat the words. "Veronica should have poisoned you." Suddenly she swung her arm.

He saw the slap coming and caught her wrist. "Enough of that!" He spoke in slightly accented English, and his tone was razorlike. "I told you not to say her name."

He released her, and the arm fell limply to her side. "Good-by," she said coldly.

"Not good-by, Karen." Sweeping off his sombrero, he bowed formally, tauntingly. *"Hasta la vista."*

Turning away, she moved toward the exit for departing passengers, the proud head high, her steps slow and controlled.

For only an instant I saw his face stripped of insolence, its features stricken—a naked look of longing so private that I, an intruder, lowered my eyes. He strode past me, then hesitated and suddenly glanced my way, startled. For less than a second his look held mine, then he murmured, *"Buenas tardes,"* went swiftly toward the terminal doors, and was gone.

As I claimed my suitcase, I realized that the vivid scene had stamped itself on my memory. I would never forget the man's insolent smile or the woman's taut, lovely face. Karen. That was her name. Only later would I remember that another name had been spoken. A name that would mean far more to me. Veronica. . . .

I STRETCHED MYSELF comfortably in a woven chair in Margaret Webber's sunny patio. I'd showered, unpacked, and now my feet were propped on a rattan footstool. A tall limeade, the glass frosty, stood at my elbow.

Margaret lay in a hammock that was suspended between two flowering pepper trees. Her gray-flecked hair, cropped short and tightly curling to frame a scrubbed New England face, was dearly familiar, and her warm laughter remained as motherly as it had seemed in my childhood.

"You're sure you wouldn't like some gin in that drink?"

"No, thanks. After all that's happened today, it would go straight to my head. I feel as though I've landed on another planet. You're wondering why I came so suddenly, aren't you, Margaret?"

"Well, yes. The last time you wrote, it was about setting a date for a wedding."

"Donald broke our engagement last month," I said, as lightly as I could. "The two years with him are just so much lost time. That's all."

I knew how hollow the lie sounded. Those years could not so easily be erased from my life. But we had faced a problem few young lovers had to solve. Donald Nelson had been in an auto accident that left him completely sightless. He had been in his last year of law school, and he felt he'd lost his future. We'd met because I was a teaching assistant at Bradford Center for the Blind, a private school for adults not far from New York City. Alternately defiant and despairing, he came to Bradford, and like several other "emotional cases" he became my responsibility, one of a group nicknamed "Alison's barbarians" by staff members.

I was not a trained psychologist. My knowledge was instinctive and practical, learned on the job and during long evenings of study. Maybe the "barbarians" sensed my insecurity, my struggle to learn along with them, and sympathized with me. One of the first things Donald said to me was, "Miss Mallory, you don't really know what you're doing half the time, do you?"

"Less than half," I answered sharply. "But I'm trying hard. And that's more than I can say for you, Mr. Nelson."

Suddenly he laughed, the first time he'd done this at Bradford. "Thanks for snapping at me. At least there's one person who doesn't smother me with sympathy."

He had summed up the hardest problem: how to be sympathetic but not smothering. Adults who suddenly find themselves sightless face many problems, but such mechanical tasks as learning braille are the least of their difficulties. The great challenge is the battle to regain confidence and self-respect, to overcome fear of being an object of pity. Somehow, inexperienced though I was, I seemed able to help them in this battle.

It had been this way with Donald—but during the process we had fallen in love. Not a wild, desperate love, not the secret Romeo and Juliet dreams of my childhood. But we had other things: the mutual need of two lonely people, respect, affection, and tenderness.

Then one night Donald took my hand and tried to tell me as tactfully as possible that there would be no marriage, no future for us. I suppose I should have behaved like one of the "civilized" heroines in the brittle comedies Helene loved to appear in. But I couldn't. "Why are you doing this?" I demanded, my voice breaking as I fought to hold back tears. "Why?"

"Because you don't want to be my wife, Alison. You want me to be a child, forever dependent on you. You feel safe with me, but love has to mean more than safety. If I could see you, you'd run away, hide yourself." The stare behind the dark glasses was fixed on my face, and I felt that the sightless eyes behind them were looking into the very depths of my self. "I have my blindness, Alison. And you have yours, too."

Now I pushed the bitter memory of that scene from my mind and struggled to concentrate on what Margaret was saying. Something about a wonderful vacation and a good long rest.

Not as long as I'd like it to be, I thought, remembering the thinness of my checkbook.

JUANA, MARGARET'S DARK Indian maid, served us supper at eight o'clock. The house clung to a steep hillside, no two rooms on exactly the same level, and the small dining room overlooked the walled patio to command a magnificent view of the Pacific, now shimmering in cool moonlight. The tall windows had screens and louvered shutters, but no glass. A giant philodendron gave a jungle effect to one corner of the room, and vines climbed to the rough-hewn beams supporting the roof.

At the end of the meal, Juana served spicy coffee flavored with Kahlúa and orange peel. Margaret switched off the light, leaving only the two small candles on the table burning. "Not very romantic with no males present, but I like to look at the moonlight on the bay."

We sat in the dimness, feeling the peace of the quiet ocean, while a gentle offshore breeze freshened the warm night.

"Your mentioning romance reminds me of something I saw today." I described the couple at the airport. "Do you know them?"

"A woman named Karen? No. She sounds like a tourist. How old was the man?"

"Maybe thirty-five." I described him in greater detail.

"Oh, that must have been Carlos Romano. He has a huge ranch back in the mountains. I've met him, and we have some mutual acquaintances. We're not friends, of course. He's more interested in lovely young blondes than in elderly widows."

"The blonde at the airport today was glamorous enough."

Margaret looked thoughtful. "I wonder if it could have been his wife. Maybe she has come back. She deserted him a few years ago. There was a lot of talk at the time. The Mexicans said you should expect that from an American wife. I don't know much about it. Gossip's a poisonous thing in a small town. It's best not to hear it."

"Of course." But at the moment a little gossip was exactly what I wanted.

I WENT TO MY ROOM early, thinking I'd fall asleep at once. And I did, only to awaken an hour later, my mind still filled with the speed of the trip and the newness of my surroundings. Putting on a robe, I went to the balcony outside the window. The house stood on the edge of the old town, near the cluster of tile-and-thatch buildings that had comprised the fishing village before it became famous. From the balcony I looked at the dome of a church silhouetted against a clear sky, and I heard the sound of a dance band at a hotel farther down the beach. Going inside, I tried to concentrate on the only book I had with me, *Advanced Conversational Spanish*, but felt too restless to follow a complicated dialogue in the future perfect tense.

The house was silent as I tiptoed downstairs to search the bookcase for a cheerful, undemanding novel. Moonlight streamed through every window, giving an aura of unreality to such common objects as tables and chairs. Fumbling in the dimness, I switched on the tiny desk lamp in the living room. Margaret was apparently not a reader of fiction, so I selected Madame Calderón de la Barca's *Life in Mexico*. Hesitating, I listened to the unfamiliar sounds of the night. In the patio a nocturnal bird repeated a lonely cry, and it seemed to ask, "Who are you? Who are you?"

317

As I reached to turn off the lamp, I saw Margaret's engagement diary lying on the desk, open to today's date.

I have never considered myself superstitious, but long afterward, when I knew so much more, I would remember the words I saw on that page; no matter how stubbornly I have told myself that it was only an uncanny coincidence, I have never been sure. It was my own name that caught my eye. Margaret had scrawled in capital letters, ALISON COMES TODAY. Then I glanced at the bottom of the page, where small black type announced in Spanish that this was February 4, the saint's day of Veronica.

The airport flashed into my mind, the furious face of the woman called Karen, and then her words, "Veronica should have poisoned you." Veronica. Who could she be and why had she inspired that taunt about poison?

CHAPTER TWO

THE NEXT DAYS passed swiftly. I joined Margaret in her morning swims and lost my northern pallor. She gave me a straw hat with a sewn-on scarf that formed a snood to hold my hair. "Don't ever venture out without a hat and good sunglasses," she warned me. "The breeze makes the sun deceptive. It's powerful!"

I explored the winding streets and gay native market. Before I realized, a week had passed—a week of church bells and guitars, of yellow sunshine and vermilion sunsets.

"How I love it all," I said to Margaret as we finished breakfast in the patio. "Every minute!"

"You should have come long ago!" Then her expression became serious. "I'm worried, Alison. You've been in every shop in town, admired everything, and hardly bought a picture postcard. Are you short of money?"

"I'm not short, because I haven't spent anything. But soon I should think about the matter of earning my living."

She frowned at me, puzzled. "Why, I thought you worked just because you wanted to. I mean, your father's money must—"

"What money? Have you any idea what Helene spent even when Dad was alive? Those useless trips to Hollywood! Subsidizing that summer theater so she could play the leading roles. And after Dad died she tried to buy her way onto Broadway. There was nothing I could do to stop her. By the time *she* died, everything was gone."

We sat in silence for a moment while her wise, kind eyes studied me. Then she said, "I think you ought to stay in Mexico awhile. The pace is slow here and you need time."

"I can't live off you, Margaret. You know that."

"Swallow that foolish Mallory pride for once, Alison! It's not easy to find work in this country. There are legal problems and—" She stopped, midsentence, and looked thoughtful.

"What is it?"

"Probably nothing at all. But I just remembered . . ." She said no more except that she had an idea, a possibility so remote that there was no point in raising false hopes.

Later we had some easy work to do. Margaret owned a charming house near the town plaza, and the rent from it formed an important part of her income. New tenants, a couple from Mexico City, were arriving today, and we spent an hour taking inventory, counting dishes, glasses, and linens. "They'll be here at least three months," she said. "I hope the house will still be standing. I've never rented to people with children before."

As we were leaving, a sleek white Cadillac halted in front of the house. In it were the new tenants, a square-jawed German businessman named Heiden and his thin, aristocratic-looking wife, plus a uniformed nanny shepherding two small boys. Margaret explained something about the air conditioning, wished them a happy sojourn, and then we walked to the plaza.

"Those boys look like destructive little devils," she said gloomily. "Mexican women are loving mothers, but they do spoil their children."

"Mexican?" I was startled. "I thought she was German, too."

Margaret chuckled. "There you go again, fooled by a light complexion! Of course she's Mexican." As we approached the taxi stand she said, "You go do what you like. I have an errand." She climbed into an ancient taxi, and after two or three tubercular coughs it finally wheezed away.

That evening she said casually, "I met some old acquaintances and we're invited to a cocktail party tomorrow. Very high society and I suppose it'll be deadly dull. But we'll survive."

Something in her tone aroused my suspicions. Could she be playing Cupid, wangling an invitation to a party where I'd meet what she'd call "a nice young man your own age"? I wondered again the next day when she made a careful inspection of the way I dressed. Before we left she added, "Don't forget your hat and scarf. The Millers entertain on the sun deck. They seem to have no qualms about broiling their guests alive."

The taxi we took from the plaza struggled up a road that seemed almost perpendicular. Palms and blossoming trees screened the anonymous walls of houses on both sides. We stopped at a wildly modern house jutting over the edge of a sheer cliff.

A gardener in a white cotton shirt and bloomerlike trousers opened the gate for us, and we followed a flagstone walk past a swimming pool to the house. A maid ushered us through a vast living room and down a hall to a sun deck the size of a tennis court. The view was breathtaking—a panorama of sky, mountains, and ocean. The guests, people of all ages dressed in chic sport clothes, paid no attention to the playing of a mariachi band in one corner. Waiters circulated with trays of drinks and canapés.

"Maggie, my darlin'!" A huge bear of a man clasped Margaret in an enthusiastic embrace, then, without waiting to learn my name, hugged me the same way. It proved to be our host, Harry Miller, an oilman from Texas. His wife, who seemed to have no name but Sweetie, shouted an overhearty "Howdy, y'all."

"Oh, Alison," said Margaret, pulling me. "Come over here. There's someone you have to meet." She led me to a small table that had a sun umbrella planted in its middle. And sure enough, there was the "nice young man your own age." He sat alone, a sandy-haired American wearing khaki shorts and a plain shirt.

"Roger!" exclaimed Margaret. "So you're back in Puerto Vallarta. How good to see you." The performance was so skillful that if I hadn't already decided she was engineering something, I would have thought her surprise genuine.

He rose, smiling, and shook her outstretched hand.

"Roger, this is my niece, Alison. Well, not really my niece, but she should have been. Alison, this is Dr. Blair, a veterinarian with the Alliance for Progress."

He invited us to join him, but no sooner were we seated than Margaret was up and away, tossing off the improbable excuse that she wanted the cook's recipe for mango chutney.

We made a few unsuccessful stabs at conversation, but Dr. Blair was naturally shy and I felt reticent after having been shanghaied to the table. We had somehow arrived at the subject of hoof-and-mouth disease when I glanced toward the entrance to the sun deck. The man from the airport was standing there.

He was wearing a white linen suit whose severe, almost formal cut made most of the other male guests in their flowered and striped casuals look like popinjays. Our host and hostess rushed to greet him, obviously aflutter.

Roger Blair's voice penetrated my consciousness. "Look. Don Carlos is here. A red-letter day for the Millers."

"So that *is* Don Carlos," I said. "Margaret mentioned him."

"Yes, that's the great man. The Conde Romano."

"A count? I didn't think Mexico had nobility."

"The title's Spanish, not Mexican. The family's been in this country about four hundred years. Don Carlos doesn't use the title; he calls himself Senor Romano. But he is more than a count. He was once a fairly famous bullfighter, and he's the best horseman I've ever watched. He's also part owner of the High Valley."

"What's the High Valley?"

"El Valle Alto. It's a ranch in the mountains about sixty miles from here. A ranch so beautiful I'd give my right arm to own one-tenth of it. There's a stone aqueduct that brings water down the mountainside. And two houses, almost castles. They even have a bell tower, the only real carillon I know of in Mexico."

A waiter came with fresh drinks, and then, to my amazement, Margaret appeared at my side escorted by Don Carlos.

"Mucho gusto, señorita," he murmured as he touched my hand.

My memory of him was so vivid that I almost said, We've met before. Don Carlos and Roger Blair exchanged greetings in Spanish, but were quickly interrupted by Margaret. "Roger, I hate putting you to work," she said brightly, "but Sweetie Miller's poodle has tossed its chopped sirloin twice today, and the poor dear's frantic. Would you be an angel and come with me?"

Before Roger knew what had happened, he was being led away, and I was alone with Carlos Romano. There was an awkward silence, made even more uncomfortable by the fact that he seemed to be studying me. Vaguely indicating the musicians and the horde of waiters, I said, "It's an elaborate party, isn't it?"

"A boring party given by dull people for other dull people."

"Then why did you come?"

"To meet you, Miss Mallory."

"To meet *me?*"

"Senor Miller telephoned me yesterday and told me about you. So I came to talk with you." He smiled at my confusion. "But we cannot speak here, we will be interrupted. Come. I know a quieter place." He rose abruptly, took my arm, and propelled me across the deck to a flight of steps. A moment later I found myself in a shady garden with stone benches and a tiny waterfall. "Sit down, please. We will talk here." He spoke courteously, but I realized that Carlos Romano was accustomed to giving commands. "Finding you in Puerto Vallarta is most fortunate. Senora Webber tells me you are not returning to the school where you taught in the United States."

"No, I'm not."

"Good. Then I am hiring you. You are the person I need." His firmness implied that everything was settled.

"Hiring me for what?"

"As a teacher for the blind. Did not Senora Webber tell you about my mother?"

"No one told me anything," I answered, completely bewildered.

"Forgive me, I thought you knew." He spoke quietly, but there was controlled tension in his voice. "Last year was an unlucky time for my family.

There was an accident. My small son, Luis, was trapped in a burning barn. My mother, a woman of great courage, rushed in and saved the boy. His burns were painful, but after a long time in a hospital he has recovered. My mother was not so fortunate. Her sight is lost. The doctors say it is hopeless."

I had never seen grief curbed by so tight a checkrein. His face, for all it revealed, might have been carved from flint.

"Please don't be offended," I said, "but you are mistaken."

"Mistaken?" His eyes widened in surprise.

"Blindness is a handicap. It isn't the end of life, and it needn't be the end of happiness. Your mother needs help and sympathy, but you must stop thinking of her as a tragic figure. It helps no one. Least of all, her."

"I understand," he said slowly. Then a smile played at the corners of his mouth. "Tell me, senorita," he said, leaning close to me. "Do you think I am a man given to too much pity?"

For a moment I couldn't answer. I looked into his face—the hawklike nose, the slightly mocking smile that did not reach his eyes, and the harsh, cruel line of the scar on his left cheek. Pity? Not a shred of it! Involuntarily I drew back a little, and as I did, his sardonic smile broadened.

"*Está bien.* When can you begin? I do not know what is a fair salary. We will find out, and I will pay it."

"Please! You decide things so fast, Don Carlos." I felt dismay, as though I had somehow been kidnapped. "Your mother should go to a good institution."

"She will not do that. The senora is a stubborn lady."

Although I had studied Spanish and had recently worked with both Cuban and Puerto Rican students, I found myself saying, "Besides, there's the problem of Spanish. Your mother needs help in her native language."

"My own opinion exactly. My mother is a native of Pennsylvania."

"Pennsylvania? Then you must be—"

"Half gringo?" He chuckled. "No. The senora is my stepmother. But she is the only mother I ever knew."

"But, I . . ." Why was I stumbling this way? Groping for reasons to refuse what seemed an ideal position? A good salary, living in a beautiful and exotic place. Still I resisted. "There wouldn't be enough for me to do. At first your mother could work only a few hours a week. I wouldn't earn a full-time salary."

"Ah, the Yankee conscience," he said with irritating solemnity. "To make you feel less guilty, you might help my son with his English. How soon can you come to the High Valley?"

"But I haven't agreed."

He checked his watch. "I am flying back this afternoon as soon as the mechanic has my plane ready. That does not give you enough time. But a jeep from the ranch will be in Puerto Vallarta day after tomorrow. The driver will call for you at Senora Webber's. About noon. You have all day tomorrow to decide. If the answer is no, then tell the driver you are not coming."

Never had I seen anything so self-confident as his smile. He was positive I would accept. The whole world apparently found Carlos Romano attractive and admirable, but he somehow frightened me.

"I'll think about it," I said, rising. "I can't promise."

We started toward the sun deck, and had reached the top step when I saw him tense, then halt abruptly. I tried to follow his gaze, but in the shifting crowd could not tell at whom he was looking. "Pardon me, Senorita Mallory," he said. "Too many people. I do not like mobs, so I will leave without thanking my host. He will not be surprised. My rudeness is well known." He went quickly down the steps, but paused midway to say in a different tone, "Please come, senorita. You are needed at the High Valley."

"I promise to think about it. And now good-by."

His smile came again, confident and winning. At that second I was ready to say yes, but what he said next made me hesitate. For I had heard both the tone and the words before, when they were spoken in the airport to the woman called Karen.

"Not good-by, senorita. *Hasta la vista.*"

CHAPTER THREE

THE GNOMELIKE INDIAN driver, who bore the incredible name Primitivo, arrived at Margaret's more than two hours late. The ancient jeep groaned under bags of cement, salt blocks for cows, and coils of barbed wire. In a woven cage an evil-eyed falcon perched, staring angrily at us. My luggage was added to the collection, and after a quick good-by to Margaret we were rattling and bumping through town.

Toward what destination? A beautiful hidden valley—that much I knew. But Margaret's friends, despite a slight acquaintance with Don Carlos, had provided scant information. Years ago he had made a youthful marriage to "some woman from Mexico City" and it had ended unhappily. His second wife, an American woman none of Margaret's friends had met, had caused a scandal, "hushed up, of course," by abandoning both her husband and young son, presumably for another man. Not a pretty story.

My hope that Primitivo would tell me about the people at the High Valley proved futile. He understood my questions, but I could make little of his answers, which were machine-gun fire in a language half Spanish, half some Indian dialect. The supplies in the jeep, I learned, had been ordered by Senor Jaime Romano, Don Carlos' half brother, who managed the ranch. The falcon was being taken to "the old one," Don Carlos' grandmother.

As we climbed from tropical jungle into high, rugged country, we left Puerto Vallarta's perpetual summer behind and found springtime. I took off Margaret's sun hat and scarf and removed the tinted glasses. A fresh breeze felt gloriously cool as I shook my hair loose, letting it tumble over my shoulders.

When Primitivo saw me, he gasped in astonishment. *"Dios!"* Then, after a second's hesitation, he smiled and nodded. *"Ay! La cuñada!"* In my pocket dictionary I found that *cuñada* meant exactly what I thought it meant: sister-in-law. He had mistaken me for someone else, and seemed not to understand my attempts to correct him, for now he chattered full speed. Whatever resemblance I bore to some unknown woman had to lie in the pale color of my hair and perhaps my eyes, for he had noticed nothing until I took off my glasses, hat, and scarf.

We drove on through the fading afternoon, the road now so tortuous that Primitivo had to slacken our pace. Then he pointed straight ahead, exclaiming. The shoulder of a mountain blocked the way completely. I saw an ancient, deeply rutted road climbing toward the crest. But Primitivo, ignoring this trail, went confidently forward, driving us through a tangle of oaks and underbrush, then wheeled sharply to the left. A huge hole gaped in the side of the mountain, and we plunged into its pitch-darkness. When he flicked on the headlights, I realized we had entered an abandoned mine tunnel. *"Via corta al valle!"* he exclaimed, and this time I understood his words. We were taking a shortcut to the valley, not going over the mountain but through it. This huge worn-out mine had been put to practical use.

I heard water dripping, and the chill dampness raised gooseflesh on my arms. At times black passages jutted off to one side, and there were several great chambers with pillars of rock left standing to hold up the tons of earth and stone above us. An army could vanish into this labyrinth and never be found.

When we emerged from the long tunnel, Primitivo stopped a moment, and I caught my breath. The High Valley, emblazoned by sunset, stretched before us. "Wait," I told him, and stepped from the jeep to stand gazing at the vast panorama below. Mountain palisades walled the valley on every side, cliffs of green, pink, and ebony rock broken by sloping mountain meadows. The valley floor rolled gently, crisscrossed by two streams and wandering stone fences. To the east were orchards and forest, and beyond them rose the yellow tile dome of an ancient church surrounded by a village.

My eyes widened then as, looking northward, I saw an incongruous building: a huge early nineteenth-century house with gables, mansard roofs, and two fanciful square towers, one taller than the other, rising to sharp peaks. Even in New England it would have been a curiosity. Here it was astounding.

"La casa grande," said Primitivo proudly.

Beyond the main house stood a Moorish-style castle-fortress with high windows and pointed battlements. It conveyed a forbidding reminder that even this serene valley had over the centuries seen pillage and revolution.

"The old one's house, the Villa Plata," Primitivo said. This stone stronghold, then, was the home of Don Carlos' grandmother.

As I got back in the jeep, I knew why Roger Blair had spoken of this valley with such love and envy. Don Carlos called it a ranch, but it was a hidden kingdom, a secret and beautiful world.

We drove down an incline, the road running beside a great aqueduct whose arches had been hewn from the mountain. Then we entered a cobblestone drive lined with eucalyptus trees. When we halted in front of the main house, the overwhelming sense of loveliness I'd felt only a few moments before vanished. *La casa grande* loomed before us, even more enormous than I had thought. And far more somber. Although sunset was fading rapidly, not a welcoming light glowed behind the slitted shutters.

As I climbed reluctantly from the jeep I heard a horse approaching at a brisk trot. Turning toward the sound, I saw a rider on a roan stallion, his back toward the diminished light, his face obscured by the broad brim of a sombrero. Even though he was wearing leather work clothes, it was easy to recognize the proud posture of Don Carlos.

He swung down from the saddle, and I moved forward, saying, "Good evening."

When the rider turned to me, I realized my mistake. Not Don Carlos, but a darker man who resembled him physically, yet not facially. For a second he stared at me as though frozen, thunderstruck. Then, "My God, you've come back!"

"Come back? I don't understand."

With swift strides he advanced upon me and seized my arm in a hard grip. The look of astonishment had changed to naked anger. "What kind of game is this?" he demanded. "Who are you?"

For a second I was so startled and frightened that I couldn't speak. Then outrage overcame all other feelings. "Let go of my arm, please. This is insufferable!"

I could hardly believe that the cold, contemptuous voice was my own. It was sheer acting, to cover my alarm and confusion. Releasing me, he stepped back, and we stood glaring at each other.

I realized this was Jaime Romano, the younger half brother of Don Carlos. The rugged face, bronzed by sun and wind, might have been slashed from the mountain rock. A fall of jet-black hair brushed the high forehead above heavy brows arching deep-set eyes—arresting eyes, cold blue in the dark face.

Turning away, he exchanged rapid words with Primitivo. I understood *cuñada* and "Senora Margarita . . . Puerto Vallarta." Jaime Romano glanced at me, his lips twisted in a scornful smile. "So you are being passed off as Carlos' sister-in-law. A childish and quite unnecessary deception."

"I have no idea what you're talking about. Primitivo is mistaken," I answered. "Will you kindly inform Don Carlos that Miss Mallory has arrived? He is expecting me."

"His lordship Don Carlos, the Conde Romano, has flown off on some mission of vast importance. Perhaps an elegant little riding exhibition." The initial rage had now become sarcastic courtesy. "I will have Primitivo show you to Carlos' rooms. I hope you will not find the night too lonely."

"His rooms!" I blazed with anger. "Of all the rude insolence! Are you suggesting that I am here to—" I stopped short as I saw he enjoyed my fury and had deliberately baited me. Brushing past him, I mounted the steps of the veranda, chin high, although my hands trembled. There must be someone in this enormous house who was at least civil, if not welcoming. I searched in vain for a bell or knocker, and then Jaime Romano was beside me, flinging open the door, removing his sombrero in an ironic salute. "My house is your house, senorita."

Ignoring him, I entered a huge, shadowy hall, where a curving staircase wound upward on my right. A chandelier flashed on and the hall was illuminated. A wispy gray-haired woman in a drab cotton housedress leaned over the banister at the top of the stairs.

Jaime Romano called to her. "Miss Evans, will you come down, please? We have an unexpected guest, a friend of Carlos'."

"Oh, I thought I heard someone." Miss Evans fluttered down the stairs, sparrowlike.

"Good evening. I'm Alison Mallory. Don Carlos Romano was expecting me today. I'm a teacher for the blind." I glanced toward Jaime Romano. "Don Carlos hired me to help his mother. That information doesn't seem to be known here yet."

"Carlos told us this morning, but he wasn't quite certain you'd come." A vague smile touched her colorless lips but did not affect the mistrustful eyes behind steel-rimmed glasses. Miss Evans appeared a good deal less than delighted by my arrival.

"Teacher for the blind?" Jaime Romano's tone was doubting. "He told you this after I'd left for the dam, Miss Evans?"

"He could hardly have told us before, Jaime. You were gone by dawn." Miss Evans was on the defensive, afraid of this man. And who could blame her? To me, she said nervously, "I told the housekeeper to change the

bed in the room Senora Castro had. It's small, but I hope you'll like it."

Jaime Romano interrupted her. "She *should* like it. After all, I now realize she drove Senora Castro out."

"I've driven no one out," I retorted. "I was asked to come here. Persuaded, in fact."

He paid no attention. A sudden gleam had come into the cold blue eyes. "You are right, Miss Evans. That room is too small. The Octagon is more appropriate for Carlos' friend."

"The Octagon?" Miss Evans seemed alarmed. "But it's been closed so long. There are personal things in it."

"At last count, Miss Evans, five maids worked in this house. We can spare a few to get it ready at once." He jerked a bell cord, went to the archway, and shouted orders toward the rear of the house. Within seconds, three girls in embroidered blouses and long cotton skirts covered by big aprons had rushed into the hall.

"If you'll excuse me," Miss Evans murmured. She faded up the stairs, pausing once to peer furtively back at me, a brief, sharp glance that blended hostility with suspicion.

"This way, senorita." Primitivo, the three maids, and I followed Jaime Romano through sliding wooden doors. One weak, unshaded light bulb did little to combat the gloom of the baronial living room. There was an immense stone fireplace, the hearth heaped not with logs but with withered flowers in a brass bowl. A life-size portrait hung above the mantel.

"My late father, Don Victor," said Jaime in a flat voice.

He took a candle from the mantel, lighted it, and handed it to Primitivo, who now led us down a long corridor. The floor, beneath the worn carpet, creaked as we moved through the deep shadows. At last we reached a narrow arched door, where Primitivo halted, drawing a ring with many oversize keys from his pocket.

"The electrical generator for the Octagon no longer serves," said Jaime Romano. "But I believe women find candlelight flattering."

I set my lips in a tight line and made no reply.

The air was stale in the apartment they called the Octagon, yet I caught a subtle fragrance of lingering perfume. The maids scurried about, opening windows and shutters to let in a flood of moonlight and the freshness of a mountain breeze. Oil lamps soon gave a flickering yellow light that mixed with the pale rose tones of a Coleman lantern disguised with a cranberry-glass shade. I found I was in a spacious, pleasantly cluttered bedroom, divided from a sitting room by a colonnade and an arch of lacy wrought iron.

The four-poster bed had a gaily striped canopy and a butterfly quilt. Near it stood an old-fashioned china cabinet with etched-glass doors, now used as a bookcase. I realized that the apartment's personality derived from the fact that someone *lived* here—framed photographs and prints, pressed flowers under the glass on the bedside table, stationery and pens in the pigeonholes of a drop-front desk. The maids removed zippered clothing bags from a big wardrobe chest.

I felt Jaime Romano's watchful eyes on me, scrutinizing my reactions. Glancing at my watch, I said, "Perhaps I should meet Senora Romano, since it's still early."

"My mother does not choose to receive you tonight."

And just how, I wanted to ask, had he acquired this information? But his tone forbade contradiction.

I went to the sitting room, hoping my back conveyed lofty disdain but afraid I was flouncing out like a furious child. I sat stiffly in a chair and waited until I heard the hall door open and close twice. Then I rose and went to the colonnade. A maid was still there, fluffing pillows as she finished the bedmaking, and to my surprise Jaime Romano lingered, standing near the door in profile to me, gazing at a picture that was hidden from me by its deep frame of gold leaf. There was such intensity in his face that I thought for a second he was about to smash the glass.

Then he did a bewildering thing. He made the sign of the cross with the gentleness of a benediction. Unaware of my having seen him, he left the room, vanishing into the blackness of the corridor. In my surprise at this unexpected gesture, I hardly heard the maid as she told me in Spanish that my room was ready and she would soon bring my supper.

"Gracias," I said. "What is your name?" The girl was small and doll-like. Her braided hair, tied in big loops with pink yarn, framed a sweetly innocent round face.

She curtsied, giving a shy smile. "I am called Ramona."

Together we moved toward the door, and I paused to look at the painting that had so deeply moved Jaime Romano. But it was not a painting. The heavy gilt frame held a square of linen yellowed by time and edged in fine lace. Somehow imprinted on it was a blurred image of the face of Christ in agony, crowned by thorns, bloodstained. Perhaps if hung in some ancient church, it might have had sacred meaning and even a savage beauty. But not here, not in this cheerful, soft room. "What is it?" I asked Ramona, who was standing beside me. My voice seemed a whisper.

"Oh, my lady," she said in a tone of awe. "That is the handkerchief of Veronica. When our Lord was dragging his cross toward Calvary, a beautiful woman named Veronica stepped from the crowd and knelt beside Him. She wiped our Lord's brow with her handkerchief. And then a miracle happened! His face appeared on the cloth." Ramona stepped close to me. "The old Conde gave that handkerchief to Luis' mother. Sometimes she would stand looking at it. And I think"—Ramona's voice fell to a whisper—"I think she was afraid."

HALF AN HOUR LATER Ramona returned with my supper tray, placing it on a marble table in the sitting room. I was famished, and the steaming avocado soup, pungent tamales, and frothy hot chocolate could not have been more welcome. A yellow rose nodded in a silver vase—Ramona's thoughtful touch. I seemed to have found at least one friend in this hostile house.

"I want to talk with you, Ramona," I said. "Please sit down."

"Thank you, my lady." But she appeared shocked at this extraordinary suggestion and remained standing.

"Who is the North American lady, the Senorita Evans?"

"I am not sure. She came only two months ago when Doña Leonora returned from the hospital. I believe she is an old friend, and she reads aloud and talks to the Senora Romano in English."

Miss Evans, I decided, was a paid companion, not too sure of her position. But an old acquaintance, too, for she referred to both the Romano sons by their first names.

"Tell me, Ramona, who lived in these rooms before?"

She looked astonished. "But you must know, my lady! These were the rooms of your sister."

"My sister?" I was dumbfounded. The cup of chocolate, halfway to my lips, nearly splashed over.

"Your sister. Doña Veronica."

"I have no sister! What gave you such a notion?"

"Primitivo. He said he did not recognize you in Puerto Vallarta. Then, on the mountain, he thought he saw a ghost. We laughed at him, because you do not really resemble Doña Veronica except as a sister. You have her eyes and her beautiful hair. But otherwise . . ." She stopped speaking and, lowering her eyes, blushed deeply. Ramona, not accustomed to such conversations with her employers or their guests, found this an ordeal.

"Only one thing more. What happened to Senora Veronica?"

"She went away almost three years ago. No one knows where. It was just a few months before the old Conde, Don Victor, died. She left letters saying she would not come back, but the Conde did not believe this. He ordered these rooms to be kept for her."

"Please tell the others here that I am not her sister. I am a teacher, come to help the Senora Romano."

She nodded, a little sadly, I thought, then moved quickly across the room. "Shall I draw the curtains?"

"Not yet, thank you. The mist and the moonlight are lovely against the glass."

She curtsied again and said, *"Hasta mañana,"* then was gone.

I sat down at the table, bewildered by the events of the day. But some mysteries were now solved. I resembled Veronica, Carlos Romano's wife, who "went away," but the resemblance was superficial. At the Puerto

Vallarta airport, Carlos Romano had turned back in surprise when he saw me, clearly because I reminded him of his wife. But during our interview at the party he noticed no resemblance. The reason was simple: a pair of dark glasses, a sun hat, and a scarf which covered my hair. Exactly the same thing happened to Primitivo. Jaime Romano had believed for a second that I was Veronica, but this had been in twilight, standing several yards away, and he had quickly realized his mistake.

Could so slight a resemblance, a complete coincidence, have caused his resentment of me? He seemed to feel that I was part of some plot against him—a preposterous notion. Yet why had he lodged me in Veronica's rooms? It was a taunt, a challenge of some sort, directed both at his brother and at me.

I pushed aside the supper tray and rose abruptly from my chair, then gasped as I caught a glimpse of a face outside the nearest window. It vanished instantly into the whiteness of the mist. For a second I was paralyzed by alarm; then I rushed to the window, quickly closing the heavy draperies.

To my dismay there was no means to lock the door to the corridor. Primitivo must have taken the key with him. There had once been a bolt, but the broken wood near the screw holes showed it had been torn from the door violently. When? Who had once forced his way into this room?

I improvised with a chair under the doorknob, then sat on the edge of the bed, forcing myself to be calm. The face could have been that of a curious servant, one who wanted to see "Veronica's sister." It was even possible that Jaime Romano had sent someone to my window deliberately to frighten me. Well, he would not succeed with such a childish trick.

Later, when the bell of the clock in the village softly chimed ten, I was in bed, propped by pillows, studying a passage in *Advanced Conversational Spanish*. I soon dozed over the book and at last fell asleep.

I am not sure how long I slept, nor do I know what awakened me. Surely it could not have been the thin, terrified cry I heard a few seconds after I opened my eyes. The scream was so faint that I was not certain I had really heard it, until it was repeated. I hurriedly put on my robe and slippers. I had noticed in the sitting room that one section of wall did not quite match the rest. I had supposed it was a sealed-up door and thought no more of it. Now I realized that the sound, which had changed to a muffled sobbing, came from whatever room had once been connected to this one.

The sobbing rose to a wail. "Mama, Mama!"

Heedless of anything except that terrified cry for help, I unlocked the tall French window and stepped onto a narrow porch, part of the veranda. Blinded by enveloping mist, I groped my way along the wall. The window of the next room was not locked, and as I pushed it open the sobbing seemed to engulf me.

I entered a broad, lofty chamber, with almost no furniture except a tall wooden wardrobe, a bureau, and a bed on which a small body writhed in a nightmare. A dim night-light burned on the bureau and, thankfully, it was electric. I found a wall switch, and a chandelier filled the room with light. Hurrying to the bed, I shook the shoulder of a tormented little boy as gently as I could. Two large almond eyes snapped open, bewildered. For a moment he gazed at me fearfully, then flung himself into my arms. I held the frail body close. "There, dear! It's all right. Only a dream. *Está bien, mi niño. Un sueño malo, nada más.*"

At last the thin shoulders ceased their trembling. The child lay back on the pillow, gazing at me gravely as I brushed the light brown hair back from his white forehead. He was, I supposed, about nine years old, but his eyes had a strange, adult wisdom.

"Tía?" he asked, both fear and hope in his voice. *"Mi tía?"*

I was not his aunt, his *tía*, of course, and I realized now that this child was Don Carlos' son—and Veronica's. The mother, I thought bitterly, who went away.

"Why do you think I'm your aunt?"

It took him a moment to understand my Spanish, then he said, "Primitivo told the servants that my mama's sister had arrived. I wondered why you did not come to see me. So I listened outside your window. You told Ramona you were not my mother's sister." His hands gripped mine tightly as he silently pleaded with me to deny my words to Ramona.

"Would you like me to be your aunt?"

"Oh, yes! Now that Senora Castro is gone, I need someone. I liked the senora well enough, but an aunt would be much better. Promise you'll stay."

Now it was my turn to hold back tears. I, too, as a child had awakened alone in the night, terrified, crying for a mother who was so seldom with me. I had often pretended that Margaret was my aunt, and I had even told neighbors this story.

"What are you called, nephew?" I asked, smiling.

"Luis. But I am really Victor Luis Carlos Romano y Landón," he said proudly. "My great-grandmother says the Landón is not important. It was only my mother's name and I am supposed to forget it." A stubborn note crept into his voice. "I think I will not forget, but you must not tell my great-grandmother."

"I promise not to."

"Did I cry loudly in my sleep? Is that why you came?"

"Oh, very loudly," I told him, making a joke of it. "I thought you'd wake everyone in the house."

"Please, Tía—" He was fearful again. "You must not say this to my uncle Jaime. Please!"

"Very well. It is our secret. But why not tell him?"

"He would make fun of me. He would say I was not macho. Someday I will be *conde*, like my father, so my uncle must not laugh at me. You understand, Tía?"

"Yes," I answered grimly. "I understand." Although I knew little about Mexico, I'd already learned to detest the word macho and the mentality it implied: the kind of swaggering supermale toughness that is the mark of a bully. Jaime Romano would one day hear from me about the concealed shame that haunted this child.

More than an hour passed before I left Luis sleeping peacefully. I was exhausted, but still I lay awake, thinking about this sad and beautiful child, and turning over in my mind one of the last things he had said before sleep came to him. "Ramona told you a lie," he whispered. "She told you my mother went away. My mother is . . . dead."

"Luis, how do you know this?"

"I know." The future Conde Romano set his determined little jaw and would say nothing more. Nor did he shed more tears.

Now I turned uneasily in the big four-poster bed, once shared, I supposed, by Carlos Romano and the wife who went away. Or had she? I gazed into the dimness at the dark square on the wall, at the handkerchief of Veronica. But it gave no answer, and all was silent except the creaking of the old house and the sigh of the wind swirling the mountain mist of the High Valley.

CHAPTER FOUR

AT A QUARTER TO seven the pealing of bells awakened me—daily reveille in the High Valley, a folk song rung from a bell tower. Slipping into my robe, I swished back the draperies and let morning brilliance pour into the rooms. The mist had vanished, leaving behind dew to sparkle on the broad lawns. Half a dozen horsemen, Mexican vaqueros, rode along a trail beyond a low stone fence.

Hearing a soft tap at the door, I almost called Come in, before I realized that a chair still barricaded the entrance. I removed it, embarrassed by my fears of last night.

Ramona, a fresh ruffly apron over her blue cotton skirt, bobbed into the room, wishing me a good-morning. "From the Senorita Evans," she said, handing me a note. Miss Evans asked if I would breakfast with her, and half an hour later Ramona, bearing a tray, led me along the corridor we had followed last night.

Miss Evans greeted me in her second-floor room. "Dear Miss Mallory! How *nice* of you to join me." The smile, like the enthusiasm in her voice,

333

was a bit overacted. She was still fluttery, but had changed radically in appearance. She wore an exquisite robe of brocaded Thai silk, gorgeous, except the sleeves were too long and the hem was not quite even. The effect was further flawed by cheap felt slippers. The room was no less surprising than the expensive robe. It was a hodgepodge of Oriental, French Empire, and Italian furniture combined with Mexican silver bowls and very old Dresden figurines. Every piece was lovely in itself, but in concert they gave the impression of an overstocked antique shop.

"Do sit down, Miss Mallory. Isn't the view lovely?" She sighed then, her face clouding. "But sometimes looking at so much beauty saddens me a little when I think that poor Leonora will never see any of this again. She and I have known each other almost all our lives. So when I learned about this tragedy, I came at once. Poor Leonora's completely helpless now. Pathetic. I try to make things a little easier, but there's not much one *can* do, is there?"

"Quite the contrary, Miss Evans," I said rather sharply. "Three years ago in my own apartment I learned to cook a complete dinner blindfolded. Yes, it was slow, difficult, frustrating, and I had some burns on my hands. But I learned."

"Such determination," she said. "How very unusual."

Anyone who worked with Leonora Romano would obviously find an opponent in Miss Evans, who was bent upon making Leonora forever dependent. I changed the subject. "Will Don Carlos return today?"

"I wouldn't know. He left in a rush, just time to mention you and to make sure all of Senora Castro's things were cleared out of the house."

"Who is Senora Castro?"

"A dreadful woman from some institution in Mexico City."

"Do you mean there was a teacher here until night before last?" I could hardly believe what I had heard.

"Yes. But not teaching. Snooping and interfering. She thought she was going to manage the whole place. Trying to make Leonora do things the poor creature couldn't possibly do, and she took to pampering little Luis. A fine way to turn a weak boy into a sissy! Then, my dear, she turned out to be a thief."

"A thief?"

"Leonora had a cameo locket set with tiny rubies. Last week she asked for it, and it was gone from her jewel box! Well, a few days later it was found in Senora Castro's room. She'd tucked it under her handkerchiefs! Don Carlos behaved like a perfect gentleman. He didn't openly accuse her. Just sent her away. We didn't tell Leonora about the theft. Much too upsetting! I said Senora Castro was suddenly called back to the city, and pretended to find the locket caught in a shawl." The diffident voice carried a threat. Silently she was saying, Don't *you* tell Senora Romano, if you know what's good for you! In fact, the entire conversation now struck me as nothing except veiled threats: Don't interfere. . . . Don't come between me and my dear Leonora. . . . Stay away from Luis, or you'll be sorry!

I rose abruptly. "I've imposed on you too long, Miss Evans. When will I meet Senora Romano?"

"Leonora? I'll send a note to your room. But if she's in one of her solitary moods, don't be disappointed. This is a difficult household, and terribly isolated. A talented girl like you must have so many opportunities."

"Thank you. Please send word soon."

As I descended the broad stairs I wondered what sort of game Miss Evans was playing. Her objective was to make me leave as soon as possible. But why? And was there any truth in her story of the stolen locket? No. The blind are constant victims of petty thieves. But hiding precious jewelry under a few handkerchiefs was utterly improbable. The maids who did personal laundry would open Senora Castro's bureau two or three times a week. Besides, the accused thief had to be a professional woman of excellent character, or no institution would have sent her here. Miss Evans' report was a malicious lie. I had no doubt of it.

On the veranda the sunlight was now a golden yellow, and a falcon sailed across the cloudless sky.

I followed the veranda around the house, coming to my own rooms and, around a corner, the windows of Luis' room. Then I turned another corner and came to a short flight of steps leading to a Mexican patio. In the center a fountain was shaded by lime trees. On my right and left stone walls stood, weighted by bougainvillea, and enclosing the far side of the patio was a one-story pink stone and adobe structure with a long, shady roofed porch—a charming, earth-warm building. Was it the servants' quarters? If so, the servants lived more gracefully than their masters.

I heard a shout beside me, and a pair of thin arms encircled my waist. "Tía Alison!" cried Luis. I longed to take him in my arms and promise I would not leave. But I could give him no promise. A decision had to be made at once. This child must not form a strong attachment to me only to be disillusioned by my leaving him. At the same time, I knew I *wanted* to stay. Not only because Luis had touched me deeply. It was the magnificence of the High Valley itself. One could draw strength from these mountains, warmth from this land.

"Who lives there?" I asked, indicating the house across the patio.

"Uncle Jaime. Come, Tía. I'll show you his ivory-handled pistol. He isn't there now."

"Then we can't go in, Luis."

"Why not? It's my house, too." He saw my doubtful look. "All the High Valley is mine. Uncle Jaime helps me take care of it until I'm bigger. But my grandfather told me everything is mine."

"Just the same, we don't go into people's rooms without asking."

I didn't understand what he meant by "mine," and I had no chance to ask him, for now Luis stepped back and with great effort said in English, " 'Mary 'ad a leetle lamb, Eets fleece was wyte ez snow.' "

"Very good! Who taught you that?" I asked in clear English.

He answered in Spanish, "My grandmother. She speaks to me in English. I have learned some, but it is hard."

"I hope to meet your grandmother soon, Luis," I said.

"Do you? I'll take you to her now, if you like."

As he led me up the hall staircase, I imagined Miss Evans' consternation. Alone, she might delay me forever, but she could hardly keep out Leonora Romano's grandson. We crossed a gallery, then another passage, more steps. Slowly it dawned on me that we were going to the tower. Odd that a blind woman would choose to live in the highest, most inaccessible part of the house. We reached the entrance, and before I could knock, Luis had darted into the room beyond. "Abuelita! Abuelita!" he shouted.

"Say 'Grandmother,' Luis." A weary voice spoke the words to the boy automatically.

The tower room was far larger than I had supposed, and sunshine flooded through Gothic windows. Leonora Romano was slumped in a big upholstered chair, her head crowned by a mane of short, thick white hair. Behind her, comb and hairbrush in hand, hovered Miss Evans, gaping at me in astonishment. Senora Romano leaned forward, offering her cheek for Luis' kiss.

"Grandmother, I 'av brung—"

"Brought, Luis."

"Brought a mans—no, a ladies who—" In despair he reverted to chattering in Spanish.

The senora listened a moment, then interrupted him sharply. "Miss Mallory?" Her head lifted, and the tired, drooping woman in the chair became Leonora Romano, queen mother of the High Valley, shoulders erect, chin high, a figure of force and dominance. Her left eye was covered by a black patch. The right eye, sightless but clear and unscarred, seemed to search the room, and it reflected the same cold blue of her son Jaime's eyes.

"Good morning. I'm Alison Mallory." I moved closer to her. "I hope I'm not interrupting."

"The housekeeper told me you arrived early yesterday evening. I wondered why you hadn't introduced yourself. I sat up late." A querulous note stole into the commanding voice, the plaint of neglect, a symptom I knew so well in my students.

My confidence rose as I felt professional, sure of my ground. "You're almost inaccessible, Senora Romano. I've been trying to meet you since seven o'clock last night."

"Don't call me senora," she said impatiently. "We're speaking English. I am Mrs. Romano. Fancy titles are better for my mother-in-law. I don't need them." Easy to see where Jaime Romano acquired his bluntness. But I liked this woman's lack of nonsense. Ungracious, perhaps. Yet direct and honest.

Miss Evans launched into rambling excuses why I had not been brought here earlier, until Leonora Romano cut her off. "Sometimes I think your tongue should be hinged in the middle so both ends could flap at once," she said with a sigh.

"Will you ask me to sit down, please?" I inquired. "It's rather awkward standing here like this."

"And how am I supposed to know you're standing, Miss Mallory?"

"Oh, but you *do* know. You're very perceptive. When you speak to Luis, you lower your head. When you speak to me, you lift it."

"Maybe two perceptive women are present," she said grudgingly. "Sit down, Miss Mallory. And Ethel and Luis, go somewhere. I'll speak with Miss Mallory alone."

Luis again brushed her cheek with a kiss, then skipped out. Ethel Evans departed without a glance in my direction.

When Leonora Romano had first become aware of my presence, she had assumed an air of majesty. On closer view, this did not change. But the components were different—she was still a queen, but the queen of some sturdy nomad tribe. Her face and hands were those of a woman who had not lived a pampered life.

"Carlos didn't tell me much about you," she said. "No one tells me anything these days. Who are you?"

I gave a brief biography, concentrating on my professional qualifications. When I had finished, she smiled faintly. "You omitted some things. For instance, you have blond hair and your eyes are large and blue gray. In an unusual way, you're a very attractive woman."

"Miss Evans flattered me far too much," I replied, startled.

"Not Ethel. Candelaria, who's been my housekeeper for twenty years. Also, you look rather like Veronica. Is that why Carlos hired you? Do you know each other well?"

I answered calmly, although my cheeks flared with anger. "I met him once, a professional interview, and I'm positive he's unaware of any fancied resemblance to Luis' mother. But the coincidence has already caused unpleasantness. If you have any doubts about me, ask a driver to take me back to Puerto Vallarta at once."

"Let's not have a foolish misunderstanding, Miss Mallory," she said. "Senora Castro—I'm sure you've heard of her—is mysteriously summoned to Mexico City. We didn't much like each other, but I'm astonished she didn't say good-by to me or give any explanation. Then, yesterday morning,

Carlos tells me he has miraculously found a qualified woman to replace Senora Castro. As if people with such training were as common as chili peppers! You arrive and turn out to be a type that he, by two unlucky marriages, has shown himself attracted to. Now what am I to think, Miss Mallory?" A thin, bitter smile came to her lips. "You might say I am out of my sight, but not quite out of my mind."

"I had better begin at the beginning," I said. Then I told her of my interview with Don Carlos, of Primitivo's surprise on the mountain, and the hostile reception from Jaime Romano. I reported it unemotionally, omitting only Ethel Evans' trumped-up story of the theft. Leonora Romano was shrewd enough to learn about that in her own good time. "Don Carlos did not miraculously find a replacement for Senora Castro. I must have been the immediate cause of her"—I hesitated—"being sent away. He hired me while she was still here. But, of course, I didn't know this at the time."

She nodded thoughtfully, then smiled. "How good to hear the truth for a change! Neither of us understands all this, but someday we will. We're going to get along famously, Miss Mallory. I want you to stay, but on one condition: that you are to be employed by me. Not by Carlos or Jaime. You are responsible to no one but myself. You need give no reports about my progress. Is that acceptable?"

"It is. In fact, it's the only way I would continue here."

We had *desayuno,* the midmorning meal, together, and Leonora began to tell me about herself. She had come to the High Valley thirty-seven years ago, she said, the wife of an American mining engineer. Smallpox had ravaged the valley that year, and a hundred people perished, among them the Conde Victor's wife and Leonora's husband. The Conde's baby, Carlos, contracted the disease and had a close brush with death, but Leonora nursed him through it.

"The next year Victor married me—in spite of his mother. She would have killed me to prevent it and maybe she even tried. I've never been sure. But I was beautiful in those days, and I knew how to use the brains God gave me. The Romanos, for all their pride, were land-poor. The silver mines had run out. I studied my first husband's books, and I learned that where there's silver, there's sometimes mercury. I started the mines working and made the High Valley rich again."

The Romanos, I thought, were not the only proud ones. Leonora held her head high as she recalled her triumph. "I gave Victor a fortune, and with Jaime, I gave him a second strong son. Sons are important in this country, Miss Mallory. So important that when Carlos' first wife proved barren, he divorced her with my husband's blessing. And that's why Victor thought the earth centered around Carlos' second wife, Veronica. She bore him what he wanted most in the world—a grandson. Luis."

She ceased speaking, as though some forbidden subject had been mentioned, and turned her head slightly away. "Are you satisfied with your rooms in the Octagon?" she asked.

"Yes. But I wonder what Don Carlos will think."

She laughed dryly. "Whatever he thinks, he'll say nothing. I suppose Jaime put you there as some sort of sour joke on Carlos. But if you're contented, you might as well stay there."

"Could something be done to provide it with electricity?"

"Electricity? Oh, yes. Jaime said something about the generator. I'll see it's taken care of, Miss Mallory. Heaven knows it's a problem keeping up this preposterous house."

"Preposterous?"

"Of course. Look on the wall above the desk."

I saw a picture of a house resembling this one but much smaller. "That's Dove Cote," she told me. "Where I lived as a child in Pennsylvania. How I wish that photo had never been taken! This expensive museum was built because of it. We were spending a year in Europe, and before we left, Victor secretly gave that picture to an architect and told him to create the same thing but five times as large. A surprise for me! When we returned, I pretended to be pleased, and over the years I've become used to the place." Her features softened as she thought of the Conde Victor's colossal but misguided gesture for the new wife who had restored his fortune.

"A grand present," I said. "A house like your family's home."

Again her laughter came dry and mirthless. "Dove Cote was never my family's home. My father was an artist, and he died young and poor. My mother became housekeeper at Dove Cote to make a living for herself and me. Victor never knew that. He took it for granted my people had once been rich. A housekeeper's daughter, La Condesa de Romano! Cattle, mines, land, and a house that could swallow the place where my mother worked for Ethel Evans' family! Life plays strange jokes, doesn't it?"

Ethel Evans' family. The joke was not strange; it was cruel. I could neither like nor trust Miss Evans, but now I pitied her. How could she help resenting the shift of fortunes? She always said, "Poor Leonora." Now I knew it was "Poor Ethel" as well.

Before leaving, I suggested that Leonora needed exercise and the two of us should go riding tomorrow morning. The idea confounded her only for a second, then she said, "Do you really think I could?"

"With the right horse you could win a steeplechase," I assured her. Riding, because she would be accompanied and mounted on a well-trained horse, would be an easy beginning for her reentry into the outside world.

AT NOON I SAT ON the veranda outside the Octagon writing to Margaret, telling her how beautiful the High Valley was and that I planned to stay indefinitely. Although I wrote nothing of the strangeness of the household

I had joined, my pen halted several times while I considered the peculiar world around me.

Riches and near poverty. Don Carlos flew his own plane, but the carpets in his home were shabby with age. A dozen servants, yet part of the house lacked electricity because of a burned-out generator. Handsome blooded horses, but I'd seen no motor vehicles except the ancient jeep Primitivo drove. And it was a household rife with smoldering antagonism—Jaime Romano's unconcealed resentment of Don Carlos, Leonora's bitterness about her mother-in-law. The covert malice of Ethel Evans. What hatreds had forced Veronica to go away?

I heard the tread of boots on the veranda. Jaime Romano, followed by a workman carrying a coil of electric wire and a tool kit, approached, his bronzed face hostile as ever.

"Good morning," I said, determined to be civil.

He ignored the greeting. "My mother tells me you are to stay for a while. She wants electricity in the Octagon. I am making temporary arrangements." He placed just enough stress on "temporary" to assure me that I would be out of this house soon.

Far away I caught the faint drone of an airplane. Was Don Carlos returning? It would be a relief to have someone to control the insolent character now giving instructions to the workman.

"Tía Alison!" a voice called. "Look at me!" Luis was about fifty yards away astride the big roan stallion his uncle had ridden the night before. The child looked so tiny and proud in the man-size saddle that I clapped my hands and shouted, "Bravo, Luis!"

At that second Don Carlos' airplane zoomed low. The horse reared, and I was suddenly knocked against the railing when Jaime Romano plunged past me, vaulting it, shouting, "Yaqui! *Alto!*"

He was too late. The frightened roan was already charging away, Luis screaming, clinging wildly to its neck. Another horse and rider raced from behind the patio wall, streaking to head off the runaway before he reached a grove of live oaks at the edge of the meadow. The branches, I thought in panic, imagining Luis swept from the roan's back, hurled against the tree trunks.

Then the bolting roan changed direction, began to circle back, and a moment later the second horseman was beside him, seizing the dangling reins. The roan broke his stride, slowed, and permitted himself to be led back to the house.

Luis, quaking, was lifted down by his uncle. "Good work, Marcos," said Jaime Romano. "Now take Yaqui to the stable. Dry him well."

Jaime carried the trembling Luis to the veranda and sat him down roughly in a chair. "Why did you do this foolish thing, nephew?" he demanded. "Answer me!"

"You said I could ride Yaqui." Luis gasped out the words.

"In the corral. Only in the corral!"

"The gate was open," the boy sobbed. "And I wanted to show Tía Alison." Springing from the chair, Luis ran to me and buried his face in my skirt, trying to stifle the sound of weeping.

"So it's Aunt Alison already?" Jaime Romano's hard hands were clenched. "You work fast, senorita."

I knelt beside Luis, holding him tightly. Jaime towered above us, saying nothing until Luis had become quiet; then he took command. "Luis, you are forbidden to mount Yaqui ever again. Now go to the stable and have Marcos saddle a horse for you. Not your pony. Then ride to the airstrip to meet your father."

I started to protest, but the boy was already moving away. Slowly I rose and faced Jaime Romano. "Is this necessary? Must you punish that frightened boy so?"

"This is a country of horsemen. Luis must ride again at once, and have no time to think of fear or to remember it."

"At least I hope the horse is less skittish than that roan!"

"Yaqui is not skittish. But the sound of the plane makes him nervous. Even I have trouble controlling him when my brother treats us to an aerial display. Do not complain to me. Speak to Luis' father about flying so low."

I still thought he was too harsh with Luis, but would have held my temper if he had not added, "Miss Mallory, all of this is none of your business."

Then my anger flashed. "A frightened, neglected child is *everyone's* business! Luis is sensitive, something quite beyond your understanding, I gather. No one gives him any love or attention."

"Perhaps you think he needs a kind stepmother."

"Maybe," I snapped back, "he needs an uncle he's not afraid of."

A look of doubt crossed his dark face, and the blue eyes studied me keenly, as though he could peer into my mind to confirm or deny some suspicion. "Was there something more you wished to say to me, senorita?" The question, asked in a surprisingly gentle tone, disconcerted me.

"No. . . ." I started to leave; then, trying to regain lost dignity, I said, "I need a key for my door. The bolt is broken."

I squared my shoulders, prepared to answer some taunt about whom I wished to lock in or out. Instead, he merely nodded. Stepping close to me, he looked down into my face. "If you are the good, sincere woman you seemed just now, the woman my mother seems to believe you are, I advise you to leave this place. For your own sake." He paused, and his voice hardened. "But if you are what I think you may be, then stay. You will deserve what will happen to you. Adios, senorita."

Then he was gone, moving rapidly down the veranda toward the patio with long, confident strides.

I DID NOT SEE DON CARLOS that day. Ramona told me that after landing he had gone directly to see his grandmother, the Excelentísima. That afternoon I was sent an invitation, a royal command, for Luis and me to lunch with her the following day at the Villa Plata.

Meanwhile, we had a picnic under the eucalyptus trees in front of the house. A cloud of gold and black butterflies fluttered near us, and somewhere a guitar was strummed while a man sang in a high, youthful tenor.

"That is Marcos," Luis said. "He is the one who helped me today when Yaqui misbehaved."

"What's he singing about?" I asked, unable to catch the words.

"About love. I'll tell you a secret, Tía." He lowered his voice. "Marcos is in love with Ramona. It makes him silly sometimes. I will never be in love—except with my grandmother and you and Senorita Gomez. She was my nurse when I broke my ankle."

"You broke your ankle?"

"Yes. I had this big swing. Oh, very big. One day the rope snapped. Lucky I wasn't swinging very high. Grandmother said I might have broken my foolish neck."

His young life seemed replete with accidents. A broken swing, the fire, and just today the narrow escape with Yaqui. I could almost have believed him marked for ill luck, but none of these mishaps, except the fire, had serious consequences.

Luis stood up, saying, "Excuse me, Tía. I must go now to Padre Olivera's house in the village for my lessons."

"Padre Olivera? Is it a catechism class?"

"No. Arithmetic and history and things. My great-grandmother teaches me about religion."

THE BELLS HAD CHIMED rosary more than an hour before, and now the valley lay bathed in cloudy moonlight. Two bright electric lamps burned in the Octagon, connected to Luis' room by extension cords run through the wall, and Jaime Romano had kept his word about a key. Not only had the bolt been replaced, but a modern spring lock gleamed on the door and its key lay on my bedside table.

As I went to the desk to finish a list of reminders—children's books in English for Luis; did Leonora have a cane?—my glance fell upon my passport, visa, and a few other personal papers. I considered locking them in my suitcase, then noticed that a small mahogany cabinet in the corner had a key emerging from its lock. Inside were three shelves, the bottom one empty, the upper two containing some albums and notebooks.

Taking one of the albums near a lamp, I opened it idly. A large color photograph filled the first page, a pretty young woman holding a child in her arms. This must be Veronica. The child, perhaps two years old, was

Luis. Why did anyone think I resembled her? Yes, her hair was almost the color of mine and she, too, wore it brushed back and loose. Our eyes were alike. But her features were much softer than mine, and there was an ethereal quality about her, a combination of sweetness and fragility.

Yet everyone seized upon our similarities and not our differences. Slowly the answer dawned on me. Veronica, gone three years, remained in the thoughts of all those in the High Valley. Although we were really so different, my coming here had kindled recollections. In the photo, she smiled down at Luis, a look of love and tenderness, so beautiful and so painful in the light of what had happened that I quickly turned the page.

Scores of pictures of the High Valley and its inhabitants. Leonora, Jaime, Carlos, the Conde Victor. I knew these faces, but not these expressions, for the album brimmed with happiness and love. How these people and this house had changed. . . . Quickly I returned the album to its place, feeling I had intruded upon other people's lives. I put my own papers on the bottom shelf, locked the cabinet, and slipped the key into the pocket of my robe.

Tired, yet not at all sleepy, I searched the bookshelves for something to read. Most of the volumes were in English, only a few in Spanish. I turned off the sitting-room lamp and moved the other lamp to the bedside table, noticing again Veronica's collection of pressed flowers under the glass, a quaint display of fading blossoms. I wondered if she and Luis, very small then, had searched the meadows together for these.

An hour later my eyes wandered over the pages of *Selected Poems of Robert Browning*. And with a sharp intake of breath, I read the lines:

> Beautiful Evelyn Hope is dead!
>   Sit and watch by her side an hour.
> That is her book-shelf, this is her bed;
>   She plucked that piece of geranium-flower,
>   Beginning to die, too, in the glass . . .

The book slipped from my hands. Trembling, I sat straight and stiff in the bed—Veronica's bed—near her bookshelves, beside her fading flowers. Softly in the quiet room, I spoke the truth aloud: "Veronica, you are dead."

Luis had told me last night, but I had not believed him, since he gave no reason. Now the reason shouted in my mind. He knew his mother had not gone away, because he knew she loved him. Only six years old when she vanished, yet he was sure—just as I was certain that the woman in the album whose soft face glowed with mother love would never have left her child behind. Didn't Leonora realize this? Didn't Don Carlos and Jaime? Of course they did! Yet they pretended ignorance of her death. And even as I decided this, some instinct warned me that I, too, must pretend.

CHAPTER FIVE

SPRING-FRESH MORNING flooded the meadows and cliffs of the High Valley with light, and when I awoke, the Octagon, swept clean of shadows, seemed outwardly not to have changed. But for me the two rooms would not be the same again. I felt close to the woman who had lived here before me. It was as though Veronica and I had made an unspoken pact. We are friends, I thought, united by something I do not understand. And I knew I would learn more.

After Ramona had taken my breakfast tray there came a soft tap at the door, and Nacho, Don Carlos' tall, stocky, pockmarked servant, came gliding silently into the room bearing a brief note from his master. Would I give Don Carlos the "inestimable pleasure" of speaking with him at eleven o'clock in his apartment?

"I will come here and guide you, senorita," he said, bowing. Then he departed, his soft sandals making no sound.

If I saw Don Carlos at eleven, I would still have time to devote to Leonora's first attempt at riding. I was on my way to the stable to select horses when Ethel Evans intercepted me.

"I have bad news, Miss Mallory," she said smugly. "Poor Leonora has a migraine. She asked me to tell you she'll have to postpone any try at riding until tomorrow at least."

I was not surprised. It is not unusual for the blind, during the first steps toward reeducation, to become "ill" when facing a new challenge. "I'm so sorry," I said. "Give her my sympathy. I'll talk with her later today when she feels better."

Miss Evans appeared annoyed when I took the delay in stride. But I went on to the stable to make arrangements for tomorrow.

Inside the big whitewashed building, I gazed in bewilderment at all the horses. The stableboy looked at me blankly when I said in careful Spanish, "I will need a very gentle horse for the Senora Romano tomorrow morning."

His reply spurted out in an incomprehensible language. I repeated my request; he gargled another answer. I tried sign language and gestures. Nothing worked.

"Good morning, Senorita Mallory," said a voice behind me. "Are you taking lessons in the Tarascan Indian tongue?"

I had not heard Jaime Romano enter the stable. He was leaning lazily against a doorpost, and I supposed he had spent several minutes enjoying my frustration.

"No. I'm looking for an interpreter," I said stiffly. "I imagine you'll do very well."

"Have no worry, senorita. I have already selected a horse for my mother, another for yourself."

"And just how did you know about my plans?"

"I make it my business to keep track of what you're doing, senorita." He smiled, but there was some implied warning in his tone. "By the way, you will stay within sight of the house. When you and my mother wish to ride farther away, tell me a day ahead. I will go with you, or Marcos will go. If we are both busy, you will not go. Am I clear?"

"Perfectly."

"When riding alone, go anywhere you like. It is nothing to me." Dismissing this matter, he strode to one of the stalls. "This is Estrella," he said, letting a beautiful black filly nuzzle his hand. "She is for my mother. Well trained but with a proud spirit."

I gazed at Estrella with misgivings. She was far bigger and younger than the horse I had hoped to find. And her "proud spirit" didn't encourage me. "I think not," I told him. "Isn't there an older mare? A more gentle horse?"

"I have chosen this one."

For a moment we stared at each other. His blue eyes were unyielding, and I spoke quickly, afraid I would give way. "This plan for riding is my responsibility. If there should be an accident, I would—"

"I have considered the chance of accidents." The strength of his voice silenced me. "When I heard of this riding idea last night, I thought it was crazy, loco. I was going to forbid it. Then I realized I was mistaken. Now you, senorita, are going to admit you are wrong." He moved closer to me. "I want the riding to succeed because it will give my mother confidence. I begin to believe your intentions are good. But you do not know my mother! She was a great horsewoman, senorita. What would she say if we mount her on such an animal as you suggest? She would call it a plow horse. She would sense we were afraid for her, know we thought she was capable of nothing better. I will see her thrown from the horse before I will let her pride be hurt, senorita."

I looked away, unable to meet his gaze. I remembered Dr. Thatcher, an elderly teacher at Bradford Center, who once told me, "There are no special cases among the blind, because *every* case is special." Jaime Romano had just retaught me this lesson.

At last I managed to look at him squarely. "I was completely wrong. I apologize for questioning your choice."

An expression of astonishment came over his face. "How strange that you and I should agree on something." Then, moving toward Estrella's stall, he said, "At what time?"

"Not today," I said. "Let's hope for nine o'clock tomorrow morning."

I told him about Leonora's sudden migraine, explaining that it was nothing to worry about. "I'll see her later. After Luis and I have lunch with your grandmother."

"My grandmother? The dowager empress has summoned you to her exalted presence?" His voice was laden with the same bitter irony he used when he spoke of his half brother, Don Carlos. "Watch your step, senorita. My grandmother devours young women like you. Chews them up, bones and all. Enjoy your lunch." He turned, and a moment later I heard Yaqui's hoofs on the cobbles of the drive as he rode away.

AT ELEVEN O'CLOCK SHARP Nacho ushered me into the suite Carlos Romano occupied on the second floor of the east wing. He was, I realized, the only servant I had met here that I did not like. There was oiliness in his perfect courtesy, and the hooded eyes studied me too keenly.

"Don Carlos will be with you in a moment," he said, and left me to wait in a baronial room which seemed to be a personal hall of fame dedicated to its occupant. Framed bullfight posters were mixed with enlarged photographs, some of Carlos Romano, others of Latin matadors and celebrities who had scrawled admiring autographs to "Carlos" and "El Conde."

I inspected two pairs of mounted horns, razor-sharp, reminiscent of bloody victories, I supposed. French windows opened to a balcony, and below it, oddly near the house, I saw the smoke-blackened ruins of a roofless stone building that I assumed was the burned barn.

"Yes, Miss Mallory," said Don Carlos, who had entered without my hearing him. "That is where our tragedy took place."

"It's so near the house, I'm surprised the fire didn't spread."

"The stone walls contained it. The building was intended as a chapel but was never finished. My half brother had a roof put on it and used it for storage. Do sit down, Miss Mallory."

As I moved toward a chair beside a large desk, he noticed my glance at one pair of the menacing horns, and said, "A rough fellow, that one. I have him to thank for this." He ran a finger down the scar on his cheek. He was, as always, impeccably dressed, the velvet jacket perfectly tailored for his broad shoulders and slender hips, the silk ascot exactly right for a gentleman enjoying a leisurely morning.

How different the brothers were! Jaime, half American, so darkly Latin, no trace of his northern heritage except the surprising blue of his eyes. While Carlos, the pure-blooded Spaniard, was brown-haired and hazel-eyed. Both had been born and reared in the High Valley, yet they were of different worlds. Bluntness contrasted to suavity, roughness to polish.

"I spoke with my mother about you last night," Carlos said, smiling faintly. "You made a most favorable impression."

"I think we'll do well together."

"Then I congratulate myself on my choice." The compliment, nicely emphasized by his nod and smile, remained formal and distant. "I understand that Jaime has housed you in the Octagon. Would you prefer to change? We have many unoccupied rooms."

"Thank you. I'm very happy where I am."

"I see," he murmured thoughtfully. "Very well. You know by now that Luis' mother lived there. It is still cluttered with personal possessions. Nacho will remove those promptly." Then, suddenly, came the flashing smile I remembered from Puerto Vallarta. "I am a wretched employer, Senorita Mallory. I really know nothing about you except your profession. You must have a family. Tell me about them."

Twenty minutes later, when I finally escaped from Don Carlos, I felt as though I had just been skillfully cross-examined by a wily attorney. He had learned the entire outline of my life, while I knew nothing more about him. Except how carefully he chose his words. Veronica was never called by name, nor mentioned as "my wife" or "my former wife." She was always "Luis' mother."

I hurried to the Octagon, locked its door behind me, drew the draperies, and began a quick search, determined to learn whatever possible about Veronica before her possessions were removed. Now I felt I was neither prying nor intruding. Anything I found could prove important, perhaps not to me, but to Luis and Leonora.

The photo albums had no more to tell me. I had hoped the notebooks and loose papers might be diaries, but the first page I read, crowded with Veronica's writing, began, *"Ser o no ser? Esta es la pregunta!"* Hamlet's famous *To be, or not to be* translated into Spanish as an exercise. I found the "All the world is a stage" speech and Portia's plea for mercy. None of the papers revealed anything except that Veronica had struggled very hard to master Spanish and she was a sensitive young woman who loved literature.

A cardboard letter file proved equally disappointing. No one, except a few shopkeepers in Mexico City and Puerto Vallarta, ever wrote to Veronica; or at least she kept no personal letters. There were several receipted bills, quite ordinary, although one from a silver shop caught my eye. "One man's belt buckle, monogrammed J.R." Jaime Romano, no doubt. A gift she had given her brother-in-law just before she went away. Nothing more. When Nacho knocked at my door, I gave him the albums and papers. Yet I could not banish the idea that they contained a message for me. Someday I would know, I told myself. Someday I would understand.

AN HOUR LATER I went to find Luis. Our formal summons to lunch at the Villa Plata had included the message from his great-grandmother that Luis was not to appear in her presence, as he had the previous week, looking like a "disgraceful ruffian." I found him dressed unhappily in a sort of Lord Fauntleroy suit he had long outgrown.

The path we followed, a shortcut, was deserted, and we were concealed on both sides by masses of poppies and shoulder-high sunflowers. Emerging from the field of flowers, we crossed an ancient stone bridge, passed through great gates of wrought iron, and found ourselves in a flagstone courtyard. There, sitting rigidly upright in a lacquered wheelchair, was the Excelentísima Ana Luisa. She was staring at something in the treetops and did not observe our arrival. Suddenly extending an arm encased in a leather gauntlet, she whistled shrilly. With a rush of wings a great peregrine falcon swooped from the jacarandas and glided to the old lady's wrist.

"Buenas tardes," said Luis timidly.

The woman and the hawk slowly turned their heads, and I felt myself pierced by two pairs of beady eyes. When I greeted her in Spanish, she stared at me disapprovingly. "Let us speak English," she said. "A barbarous tongue, but less grating than badly accented Castilian." The thin, scarlet-smeared lips twisted into a smile to show that the insult was merely a joke. But her eyes glittered coldly. "Welcome to the Villa Plata, Miss Mallory."

Although I knew the Excelentísima had to be well past eighty, it would have been impossible to guess her age. Nothing about her was real: a dreadful orange wig, mascara slashes for eyebrows, and impossibly long, curling lashes glued on unevenly. The sharp teeth gleamed as white and patently false as the heavy collar of department-store pearls supporting her chin. The black silk dress was a seamstress' nightmare of tucks, ruffles, and pleats. Dotted with jet beads, it fell to her ankles. Still, she was in no way a comic figure. Rapier-thin and rapier-strong, she held her large head high, and it occurred to me that some of the most venomous serpents are also the most gaily colored. The falcon stirred on her arm.

"What a powerful bird," I said. "He's a peregrine, isn't he?"

"She is a peregrine. The males are smaller, good only for bringing down grouse or ducks. This beauty can tear a heron out of the sky!" Her right hand formed itself into a claw, and the long, false fingernails, lacquered blood red, became uncannily like the talons of the hawk that gripped the leather gauntlet.

"Does she have a name?"

"Ah, yes. I call her Leonora. And you should see her seize upon a lark, senorita."

Silence followed. Luis looked wretched, and the old lady did nothing to ease our discomfort. She gently placed the hawk on a wooden perch, and said, "Luis, go into the house and study your catechism. And tell the boy to bring Coca-Cola for the senorita and myself. Make sure the idiot puts straws in the bottles. Clean straws!" She turned to me and added, with no hint of apology, "Forgive my limited hospitality. Nowadays I am permitted only two servants. That peso-pinching Leonora keeps me on a pauper's allowance. La Gringa, blind or not, is a scheming vulture. Of course, they pretend it is my grandson Jaime who forces me to live like a peon. Legally he controls the money here. But Jaime is only La Gringa's cat's-paw. I am not fooled!"

"Jaime?" I exclaimed in surprise. "How does he control the money? The High Valley belongs to Don Carlos, doesn't it?"

"No," she said. "My grandson Don Carlos was too wild. For one thing, he had a weakness for exotic females. Blond females like yourself, senorita."

I started to protest the malice in her voice, then wisely held my tongue. This was a time to listen, not argue.

"Carlos was sent abroad for his education. Who knows how many schools expelled him? I made novenas to implore the saints that he marry young, before some outraged husband hired a *pistolero* to shoot him. Well, he *did* marry young."

"He married Veronica?"

"No, no! This was years before he met that wretched woman. He married a girl from Mexico City. She was of a good enough Spanish family, but she was a bore, and Carlos soon behaved more recklessly than ever. No wonder! Three years went by and she gave him no children. When Carlos decided to divorce her, my son, the Conde Victor, was happy to pay the costs."

"Then he met Veronica?" I was determined to steer the conversation toward Luis' mother.

"Years later. While he was in exile."

"Exile?"

She waved her jeweled hand. "Exile, banishment—call it what you will. Carlos was always wild. From the time he could walk he loved the bulls and the corrida more than anything on earth. We admired his courage, but then—" She paused and almost shuddered. "He went away to fight in the public rings!"

Apparently to be a magnificent amateur was laudable, but when the son of twenty generations of Spanish nobility became a professional, he disgraced his heritage.

Ana Luisa continued. "My son, the Conde Victor, looked upon Carlos as one dead. All communication between them ceased. It was during these years he met Veronica."

"Where was she from?" I asked.

"From nowhere. She was nobody. Another *gringa*, nothing more. One day a letter came from Carlos. He said he had been married for some time and had an infant son named Victor Luis, after the Conde. He longed to return and live the life he was bred for. The Conde Victor was not a forgiving man. But Carlos had enclosed a photograph of Veronica holding little Luis in her arms. That made the difference. The Conde could not deny his own grandson, his own blood."

The Excelentísima leaned back in her chair, and her rouged cheeks burned an even deeper scarlet. "But the Conde Victor had really forgiven nothing. When he died, he bequeathed the High Valley and everything in it to Luis!" She spoke his name with bitter contempt. "Don Jaime is executor until Luis is of age. Is it not immoral? The eldest son *always* inherited the High Valley. For centuries!" Her hatred of Luis was frighteningly apparent. She thought of him as a usurper, a child of mixed blood who had stolen his father's birthright.

"And Veronica simply went away?" I ventured.

"Not alone, I'm sure," snapped the Excelentísima. "She had been slipping off to see some man. One of the maids reported as much to me. I knew from the beginning that—"

But I was never to learn what she had known. The servant boy approached carrying a bottle of Coca-Cola in each hand. Seeing him, she turned violently in her chair. "You have taken all day, idiot!" Spanish curses and imprecations spewed out while the boy quailed. Exhausted at last, she glanced at the sun to determine the hour. "Lunchtime," she informed me. "Kindly push my chair to the *entrada*."

I wheeled the squeaking chair over the flagstones. Inside the great arch of the entry, two malacca canes hung on a hook. The Excelentísima took them and slowly rose. Although a bit arthritic, she walked quite well, her large head held high and her spine straight as a steel lance. Even the broad flight of stairs leading to the dining room did not daunt her, and I realized that the wheelchair was a complete affectation. Ana Luisa could walk when she wanted to. She paused at a landing near the top, and I stepped into a patch of sunlight entering through a heavily barred window. Outside, I saw another patio, not stone but brick, and in the center stood an upright post with a crossbar at its top.

"The punishment stake," said the Excelentísima behind me. "Flogging was done on Saturdays so the punished men could recover enough to work again on Monday. My husband used to stand at this very window to count the lashes. You see that fire pit over there? That's where irons were heated to brand thieves. My husband had the power of life and death here—and he used it!" Her eyes dilated and her breathing was rapid.

A feeling of horror made me shudder. "Thank God, times have changed," I said.

The pitiless eyes held my gaze hypnotically. "Times may change, but the Romano men are as they always were. Falcons who bring down larks! It is in their blood. . . . Shall we go to the dining room, Miss Mallory? Our lunch awaits us."

THE ORDEAL OF THE next hour and a half seemed endless. At one point in the meal the Excelentísima said, "Carlos paid his respects to me yesterday afternoon after his journey and told me he had hired a new teacher for that woman Leonora."

"I find Senora Romano an intelligent and capable woman," I said. "She has all the qualities that in Spanish you call *honorable*. Apparently you hate her. Why?"

"Why would I *not* hate her? La Gringa came here as a woman beneath my notice and somehow tricked my son into marrying her. She poisoned the Conde's mind against Carlos, hoping that her own half-breed son would someday own the High Valley."

Our exchange had taken place in English much too rapid and complicated for Luis to understand. But he had caught at least one name, for he said, "Leonora Romano is my grandmother's name."

"I've told you a hundred times!" The Excelentísima seemed about to seize his shoulders and shake him. "Your real grandmother died years ago when plague came to the valley. La Gringa is no relative of yours."

What she said was literally true. But if there were no bonds of blood kinship between Luis and Leonora, they had other ties even stronger. I would explain this to Luis, make sure that Ana Luisa did no more to damage the child's fragile sense of security. Then I saw no explanation was necessary. Though he said nothing, Luis lifted his head defiantly. The outthrust lip, the set of his small shoulders said positively, My grandmother is my grandmother!

Both Luis and I were grateful when lunch was over. Walking back to the *casa grande*, I looked at him with new understanding. When he had said, "Everything here is mine," he had spoken exact truth. And Jaime Romano, not Don Carlos, was the temporary ruler here. But before Luis was born, when the old Conde disowned his elder son, Jaime must have expected to be master of the High Valley after his father's death. What a bitter turn of fortune Luis' birth had been for his uncle. A dream of power shattered. Could such a broken dream turn to hate? Hatred toward Veronica and even toward her son?

Just then Luis cried, "Look, Tía Alison! A falcon!"

Above our heads a peregrine hawk sailed in a slow circle, as though the Excelentísima had sent forth a spirit to follow us.

"Listen," whispered Luis.

The soft cooing of a dove came faintly to my ears. I saw the falcon soar in a wider, higher circle. Then it plunged from the sky, swooping to strike. I did not see it fall upon the dove, yet somehow I felt the talons stabbing and clenching. The Excelentísima's hateful smile came back to me, then her words: "The Romano men are as they always were. Falcons who bring down larks! It is in their blood."

CHAPTER SIX

OUR "MIRACLE" BEGAN the following morning. At least the servants called what happened a miracle. Its prelude was Leonora Romano's being led downstairs—awkward, hesitant, and trying to conceal her dread of failure. She had dressed herself, with help from Miss Evans, in beautiful tooled-leather boots and a split riding skirt, russet, with thong embroidery.

"I might as well fall off in my finery," she muttered as we crossed the veranda.

"You look wonderful," I told her.

"My hands are cold," she said. "I thought people got cold feet at times like this. But it's my hands."

"Now, you're not really afraid."

"A lot you know about it!"

Marcos waited near the front steps with our horses and Luis' pony. Jaime, who had provided me with the sort of spiritless old mare I had first requested for Leonora, sat mounted on Yaqui, and remained a little way off, silent and watchful. Leonora stroked Estrella a moment, then said, "Let's get it over with."

With Marcos' help she swung into the saddle. For a second the blind woman seemed to freeze; then she relaxed her grip on the reins, and she, Luis, and I rode down the path.

"We're going west," said Leonora. "I can feel sun on my back." Her face brightened, radiating a smile that said, Look, I'm outdoors again. I'm riding. I'm not afraid.

Entering the corral, we rode in a circle and within minutes were surrounded by silent, smiling people—servants from the house, workers from the stable and nearby orchards. They made no noise that might startle a horse, but their beaming faces rang with applause, and I realized that the people of the High Valley loved Leonora.

A dozen times around the corral, then back to the *casa grande*. So little, and yet so much for the first day. On the way back, there occurred one of those moments a teacher dreams of. Leonora suddenly halted Estrella and breathed deeply. "The *copa de oro* is in bloom," she said. "We must be near the veranda where the Octagon juts out. I planted that vine myself. I always loved the fragrance."

"It's climbed all the way up to the roof."

"So high? We'll have to put in guide wires for it, otherwise it'll block the eaves trough. I'll tell the gardeners."

Leonora Romano had come down from the seclusion of her tower, and I knew she would not return to that voluntary prison again.

In the next two weeks she astonished everyone. Having succeeded at one thing, she became convinced that there was nothing she could not master. Soon the tap-tapping of her cane was heard all over the house, and often her boldness was maddening.

The servants, for all their good intentions, were careless. Mops, pails, and brooms were left on stairways and in passages. Despite my pleadings, furniture in Leonora's room was not always returned to the exact places I had marked. I suppose she tripped over something at least twice a day, but she was never discouraged. Sometimes I had nightmarish visions of Leonora, in her overconfidence, plunging headlong down some flight of stairs. Yet there was no holding her back.

Leonora and Luis demanded every minute of my time and energy, but a sense of Veronica's presence never left me for long. Sometimes, looking at Luis, I would remember a photograph, and realize that he had inherited his mother's smile, her small hands, her large, clear eyes. And sometimes I would awaken suddenly in the darkness when a bird in the trees sounded the soft, clear call that to me would always be Veronica's name.

At least three mornings a week found Leonora, Luis, and me on horseback, venturing a little farther each time. Most days I joined Leonora for the midmorning breakfast, helping her relearn the skills of using a knife, fork, and spoon. Then another hour of work with her in the morning, and two hours in the late afternoon, sandwiching in time for Luis' English lessons.

Miss Evans saw that Leonora's new housekeeping projects were carried out. Rooms untouched for a year were soon put in order. A tall, dramatic statue of Saint Michael that stood on a landing of Leonora's staircase was relieved of its dust.

Jaime and Carlos Romano moved near the edge of our lives but were not part of them. They lived by the rules of an unspoken truce. I never saw them alone together in a room, never heard more than a formal greeting when by accident they met in the patio or the stable. Carlos spent much of his time away from the valley, flying off to distant places to participate in *charreadas,* the riding exhibitions he loved, and frequently he visited the capital, where he kept an apartment. To see a tall, lovely woman called Karen? I supposed so. When he returned from these trips his step was always jaunty, the air of a conqueror.

His greetings and brief remarks to me were unfailingly friendly and casual, but I never felt at ease in his presence.

ONE DAY WHEN I went to Leonora's room for an extra practice session, I found her nervous and upset. "Alison, I've just had word that Enrique Vargas and his wife and some friends from Puerto Vallarta are arriving this afternoon to spend the night. Enrique's father was attorney for my husband,

and now Enrique does legal work for Carlos. Why couldn't they come later? When I could have dinner with them and show off my new table manners!"

"You can join them at the table and say you're on a diet," I said. "Just take fruit juice. You're good with a drinking glass now."

She chuckled. "You mean I seldom knock one over. We can invite Padre Olivera—he was a friend of Enrique's father. And hire musicians from the village. Someone should take word up to the dam for Eric to come, too."

"Eric?"

"Eric Vanderlyn. He's working on the construction of the dam up at the far end of the valley. You'll probably meet him tonight."

A dinner party, I thought happily, with no suspicion of the violent consequences the evening would bring.

WHEN OUR VISITORS arrived, it fell to me to greet them. A long black car rolled into the drive, and I saw a chauffeur and five passengers. The chauffeur, the first to emerge from the car, was a stocky, powerful-looking man with an automatic pistol tucked in his broad belt.

Enrique Vargas, the young attorney, came next. A tall, stoop-shouldered man with close-set eyes, he was not a type to inspire much confidence. The black hair was so heavily oiled that it adhered to his scalp like a skullcap. I watched his reaction carefully. He must have met Veronica often. Would there be a startled second glance, perhaps a question?

"Good afternoon," he said, with no unusual stare. "May I present my wife, Raquel." A pretty, round-faced girl still in her teens smiled shyly at me. "And my mother, Doña Antonia."

Doña Antonia's plump, jolly appearance belied the black mourning dress and mantilla she wore. " 'Appy to meets you!" she exclaimed. "I learn speaking the *inglés* from my son and phonograph *discos. Qué bueno!*" .

Then a tall, middle-aged couple got out of the car. "Dr. George Hardy and Miss Alice Hardy," Señor Vargas said.

"Pleased to meet a fellow American," the doctor growled.

He was enormous. A great wattle of skin hung below a double chin. Tufts of gray sideburns jutted in front of reddish ears, and his eyebrows, stiff and wiry as brushes, gave him a look of perpetual hostility. His sister, Alice, except for her unusual height, bore no resemblance to him. Thin, angular, and long-necked, she had an arresting quality that compelled attention, an intensity that one sensed rather than saw.

They were vacationing in Mexico, and Enrique Vargas told me that he had lived with them for a year when he was an exchange student in the United States.

In the entrance hall, I explained that the servants would show them to their rooms and we would gather in the patio at seven o'clock for cocktails.

At six thirty I left the Octagon to make a last check on arrangements for the evening. The servants, with extra help recruited from the village, had taken care of everything. Tall vases filled with lilies and roses of Castile perfumed the rooms. In the patio Nacho, uniformed in a maroon jacket with gold embroidery, was inspecting torches and Japanese lanterns.

Wandering back to the house, I hesitated, hearing an unfamiliar sound, a piano being played softly and skillfully. It was the haunting melody of a Chopin nocturne. Moving toward the music, I entered a small parlor near the main living room. An elderly priest wearing the brown robes and white knotted belt of the Dominican Order sat at a spinet. He was balding, and the fringe of white hair above his ears gave the impression of a tonsured monk—a priest in Chaucer, or from a medieval tale. "Good evening," he said, smiling. "You must be Miss Mallory."

"Yes. And you have to be Padre Olivera," I replied. "Luis talks of you so often."

"As he talks of you, too." The brown eyes in his weathered but almost unwrinkled face regarded me gravely. Then he smiled again. "I meant to call on you before, to welcome you to our valley. Something has always interfered." Padre Olivera's features radiated innocent goodwill, yet I felt he was studying me, and behind the cherub face there was profound shrewdness.

"Now that we meet, I can ask a question that has troubled me," he said. "Luis calls you Tía Alison, but you are not, I believe, Doña Veronica's sister?"

"Luis has chosen me to be his aunt because he's a lonely child," I said. "He feels the loss of his mother deeply."

"I understand."

Padre Olivera's hands lay folded in the dusty lap of his cassock. Callused hands of a workman, not those of a fine pianist. The hem of his robe was frayed and there were traces of mud on it, revealing his walk from the village. Here was a priest who followed his vow of poverty with dedication, and, I felt, was a man I could trust completely.

"I wonder if you can tell me some things I need to know, Padre," I said. "I want to learn about Luis' mother."

"Doña Veronica?" For a moment he was silent, thoughtful. "I did not really know her for a long time. She was not a Catholic, but in the last few weeks before she left here, she came to see me several times. She had no family, she spent her childhood in foster homes and institutions. I think the High Valley offered her the first security she had ever known. And that security proved fragile in the end." He bowed his head, sighing, then continued. "I saw her last on the afternoon before the fiesta of San Miguel. She drove to the village that day in the small car the Conde Victor had given her. I shall never forget it. The car was white, she wore a white dress, and brought a great sheaf of red roses for the church. Just before she left me, she asked a surprising question."

"What was it, Padre?" I leaned forward attentively.

"She said, 'Father, is it possible to tell a terrible lie by keeping silent?' I explained that some of the worst lies in history have been told without one word being said. And she answered that she had always known this, she had not really needed to ask. Then she drove away, back toward the *casa grande*."

Lifting his head, Padre Olivera gazed at me, the brown eyes filled with sadness. "I should have taken more time with her, but I was so busy that day. The fiesta of San Miguel is the greatest celebration of the year. Everyone in the valley is at the church or in the plaza most of the night. It was one of the few times when she could leave with no one seeing her."

I straightened in my chair, astonished. "Are you saying that no one actually saw her go? Not one single person?"

"No one."

"But, Padre, she might never have left at all!" I protested. "There could have been an accident."

He shook his head. "No. Her car was gone, and some clothing. Not much clothing, but she left a note for Don Carlos saying she would take nothing that belonged to him. A few days later she sent another note to the Conde Victor. It was mailed from Mexico City."

"Wasn't there a search? An investigation? Surely the police were told."

"The Conde's attorney arranged a private investigation. I believe his son, Enrique, actually handled it. A wife running away is hardly a matter for the police."

"This is hard for me to accept," I told him, rising, moving restlessly across the room. "How could she leave a child she loved? And afterward she would have sent Luis a Christmas present from somewhere, or at least remembered his birthdays."

"It is difficult to understand. The Scriptures tell us that the human heart is utterly deceitful, so we should not be surprised by wickedness. Yet I am always taken unawares."

Ethel Evans scurried into the room, exclaiming, "So here you are! Leonora is asking for you, Miss Mallory. The guests are in the patio. Good evening, Father Olivera."

Outside, the beauty of the night was breathtaking. On Jaime's porch a group of guitarists strummed softly, and for the first time I heard the haunting voice of a shepherd's harp.

We were the last to arrive. Our visitors were talking animatedly with Don Carlos, and Luis stood beside his grandmother's chair, a bit awed at attending a fiesta for grown-ups.

"Good evening, Padre, Senorita Mallory," said Jaime Romano. He alone had not dressed for the party, but wore his everyday riding clothes. I knew his failure to change was deliberate, some gesture of protest or defiance. "Senorita," he said, "may I present my friend Eric Vanderlyn."

A flaxen-haired Dutchman in his mid-twenties clasped my hand lightly. "How do you do? You are the young lady who performs miracles for the Senora Romano?"

I colored slightly at the enthusiasm of his praise. "No, Leonora is performing the miracles. I only try to keep her from breaking her bones in the process."

"That is not what I am told."

Jaime Romano said, "I must speak with Padre Olivera about a matter. Talk with Eric, senorita. You have much in common."

"How is that?"

"He is the most stubborn man I know."

Eric Vanderlyn and I stood in silence while Nacho, gliding among the guests, served me a tall lime-flavored drink.

"Have you been in the High Valley long?" I asked.

"Most of my twenty-six years. I was born here. My father was an engineer and mineralogist. He was also something of a mad inventor. He rigged a device with mirrors and lenses which was supposed to concentrate the sun's rays. It looked rather like a telescope. One day he left it near a sunny window and it burned a hole in the carpet. Doña Leonora was furious, but my father was delighted. He kept shouting, 'It works! It works!' and danced around the room."

"What happened to his invention?" I asked.

"I think Don Carlos has it," Eric replied, "along with some of my father's telescopes. Don Carlos was interested in astronomy for a while. Anyway, my father was more successful with minerals than optics. He and Doña Leonora discovered the Hidden Treasure."

"The hidden treasure?"

He chuckled. "Not Montezuma's buried gold. The Hidden Treasure is the name of a mine. I should have said they rediscovered it, for it's very old. Silver came out of it for centuries. When there was no more silver, they abandoned it. Doña Leonora thought mercury might be there. My father proved she was right. It was a great mine. The last for the High Valley."

"No more mines? Can you be sure?"

"Every possibility has been exhausted. Don Carlos still has hopes, but Jaime knows the future is in cattle and crops, once we have irrigation. That's his dream. He'll make it come true, too, if he doesn't kill himself and all of us with work in the meantime. When Jaime wants something, it's like the devil was driving him."

I glanced at Jaime Romano, who was listening intently as Padre Olivera explained something about repairing the church roof. I saw the steely set of his jaw, the disturbing eyes as hard as blue flint, and said to myself, Yes, he'd stop at nothing.

"Tía Alison! Senor Vanderlyn!" Luis called us. "Come see what my grandmother is doing."

We went to Leonora, who sat with a handful of small stones in her lap. "Good evening, Alison. Is that Eric?"

"Yes, senora."

"Grandmother knows the names of all these stones I gathered," exclaimed Luis. "Don't you?"

"Well, some of them. Tell me if I'm right, Eric." Picking one up, she rubbed it gently with her fingers. "Obsidian?"

"Correct."

"This one must be green *cantera*."

"Right again." He looked puzzled. "Now how could you know that?"

She laughed. "A guess. Most of the soft *cantera* in the valley is green, although there's some pink and gray. I played the odds. It's just as Alison's been telling me. You can see a lot with your fingers once you learn how to look."

"I'm going to learn all the names, too," said Luis. "In English!"

"Good," Eric told him, ruffling his hair. "I'll give you a present to help you. A magnifying glass so you can see the fine veins in the rocks."

"Oh, thank you, Don Eric!"

Carlos Romano, debonair and laughing, joined us. "I heard you talking of rocks. No more of that! Tonight we celebrate." He shouted to the musicians. "*El jarabe!* Come, Senorita Alison. I will teach you one of our dances."

His arm around my waist, he swept me toward the porch. The music burst forth, loud and rhythmic, and I felt myself whirled this way and that, while Carlos stamped his boots to the beat of a drum, snapping his fingers like castanets. He moved with the grace and strength of a tiger, balanced and poised.

When the music ended with a flourish, the guests applauded, and Carlos said, "Now another!" But Doña Antonia, her black dress with its great flounces emphasizing her stoutness, pushed her way between us. "Mine ees dance next!" she cried.

I stepped aside and found Jaime Romano next to me. "We will dance," he said. This was not an invitation. It was a flat command.

Before I could answer, we were dancing. His eyes were fixed on mine, the dark face unsmiling. A feeling like panic caused my blood to pound. I was hardly aware of the stumbling awkwardness of my movements, knowing only that I was fighting against something like hypnosis, a fascination that blotted out all else.

The music slowed and he drew me close to him. My cheek brushed the coarsely woven wool shirt, and suddenly the light but strong touch of Jaime's arm around my waist felt warm and protective. I could lean against it, sure of its security, and not fall but always be held safe. Then, in confusion, I realized he had stopped dancing, was standing still, and at that same instant his arms dropped to his sides, letting me go. He strode away without a word or a backward glance, moving swiftly to the patio gate and vanishing into the darkness beyond.

NEARLY AN HOUR passed before we were called to dinner, and only then did Jaime Romano, his face taut and drawn, reappear. In the dining room a hundred candles gleamed on the drops of crystal chandeliers and sparkled on antique silver. Don Carlos sat at the head of the long refectory table. I found myself with Eric Vanderlyn on my left and Alice Hardy on my right.

Eric proved an easy dinner companion, but Alice Hardy was difficult, almost as silent as Jaime Romano, who ate practically nothing and spoke not a word. Despite myself, I glanced once in his direction. Head slightly bowed, he stared at the tablecloth, his features set in an unmoving mask that could not quite hide the turmoil inside him. Grief was there, I knew. What had happened to him while we were dancing? Suddenly I felt that he had not meant to be rude, not meant to hurt me. If only he would tell me! I would understand.

Stop this dreaming! I told myself sharply. I looked away, but still could not force his image from my mind, no matter how hard I tried to concentrate on what Eric Vanderlyn was saying.

"You see, I'll go back to the National University in the late fall. I'm in the graduate school of engineering there—"

Alice Hardy interrupted. "I've just realized what's been bothering me. We're thirteen at dinner. Not a lucky number!"

"Maybe we could count Luis as only a half," Eric said blithely. "Would that make it right?"

Enrique Vargas, across the table, said, "Miss Hardy is a profound student of—what is the English word?"

"The occult." Dr. Hardy supplied the word.

"The occult? Superstitions?" Senor Vargas asked.

"Not at all." Miss Hardy spoke severely, as to a rude child. "My studies involve matters beyond conventional science. I have a keen sense of atmospheres. This house, for instance, is filled with odd currents."

Luis turned to Leonora. "What is the lady talking about, Grandmother?" The English words were beyond him.

Leonora replied in Spanish. "She's talking a lot of nonsense. In a moment she'll go on about ghosts, I expect."

"Ghosts!" exclaimed Luis, delighted. This was a word he knew in

English. "We have ghosts," he informed Miss Hardy. "In the Hidden Treasure."

"Luis is talking about an abandoned mine that the villagers claim is haunted," Eric told Alice Hardy. "At one time it was infamous for cave-ins and avalanches. Many men died there, so a legend has sprung up about the ghosts of buried miners."

"Ridiculous, of course," Don Carlos added. "But we encourage the belief that it is haunted. The mine is dangerous, and the legend keeps people from entering."

"Bricking it up might do better," grumbled the doctor.

"The mountain Indians would knock down the bricks and carry them off in no time," said Eric. "It happens to fences, it happens to gates. I've wondered if that might have caused that last big cave-in at the Hidden Treasure—Indians pulling down the shoring posts for firewood."

"You had a cave-in recently?" Dr. Hardy asked.

"Not recently," said Leonora. "More than two and a half years ago."

"At the time we thought it was an earthquake shock," said Enrique Vargas. "I remember the ground shaking under my feet."

"You were here when it happened, Senor Vargas?" I asked.

"Yes, senorita. I had come to enjoy the San Miguel fiesta."

"The night of the fiesta!" I exclaimed without thinking. "Then that was the night when—" I caught myself just before saying, When Veronica disappeared.

I was thankful that Eric Vanderlyn finished the remark for me. "Exactly! A night when no one would have been watching. The perfect night for the mountain people to come foraging. That's why I wondered if any of them might have been trapped in the mine."

"Not likely," Leonora remarked. "I think we would have heard from their relatives. Now shall we go to the *sala* for coffee and brandy?"

Dinner had been very late. Luis was sent to bed, and the elderly Doña Antonia excused herself. Don Carlos dismissed all the servants except Nacho, and after coffee was served, poured the brandy and Kahlúa himself, offering it with elaborate compliments to the women, causing young Senora Vargas to titter and blush.

I sat on a small couch, and Enrique Vargas joined me, moving much too close. An odor of rose oil assailed my nostrils from the overscented brilliantine on his hair. "I enjoy much talking English with the North American women," he confided. "They are so adventurous, no?"

"I'm sure you find many who are," I said coolly, edging against the arm of the couch. "Is that why your chauffeur is armed? To protect you against them?"

"A man in my profession is bound to have enemies. And life is cheap in this country."

"I am afraid that is true," said Padre Olivera, who, seeing my situation, joined us. "How much does a *pistolero* cost these days, Enrique?"

The attorney chuckled. "Are you thinking of hiring a gunman, Padre? I can get you one from Mexico City at a bargain rate. Five thousand pesos for an amateur. Ten thousand for a real professional like my driver."

"What's this?" asked Dr. Hardy, settling his bulk into an antique chair, which creaked an unheeded warning. "You mean you can have a man shot for around four hundred dollars?"

"Oh, yes. Plus my commission, naturally." Enrique Vargas winked at me and let his arm rest on the back of the couch, so that it just touched my shoulders and neck.

"This is a rather tasteless joke," I said. I rose quickly. "Excuse me. I'm curious about what Don Carlos is saying."

He was on the opposite side of the room, talking with Alice Hardy. "I find your interest in the occult fascinating, senorita."

Across the room Hardy quoted ponderously, " '*If you can look into the seeds of time, And say which grain will grow and which will not, Speak, then, to me . . .' "*

Smiling, I picked up the cue and said in a witchlike voice, " '*All hail, Macbeth! hail to thee, thane of Glamis!' "*

"The young lady knows her Shakespeare!" Dr. Hardy exclaimed, hauling himself to his feet. "You've been an actress, of course. I wondered when I first saw you."

"Not an actress," I told him, laughing. "Just a prompter. My mother did the acting. But I memorized so many plays that later I sailed through college drama courses hardly opening a book."

"What did your mother play besides Shakespeare?"

"Well, she was the star of a not very successful Ibsen festival. Hedda in *Hedda Gabler*, and Nora in *A Doll's House*."

"Really? I was Helmer in that play years ago. Little theater."

"Forgive me, Doctor," said Don Carlos. "I wish to return to the matter of foretelling the future. Your sister impresses me."

Leonora said, "Years ago we used to experiment with a Ouija board. Nothing much happened. It was like a parlor game."

"Do you still have the board?" asked Miss Hardy. "I'd be happy to demonstrate its proper use."

Ethel Evans, who knew where the Ouija board was stored, hurried to fetch it. A few minutes later it was placed on a small marble table, and two chairs were drawn up beside it. I had seen such boards on novelty counters but had never really examined one before. The letters of the alphabet were painted in a semicircle, and on one side of the board was the word "yes," while "no" was at the opposite. A small wooden triangle stood on tiny ball bearings so it could glide easily over the surface of the board.

"Too much light for concentration," said Miss Hardy.

"Blow out some candles, Nacho," commanded Don Carlos.

"Dark enough," Miss Hardy said, when more than half the candles had been extinguished and the room had become a murky cavern, its somber shadows relieved only by tiny pools of wavering yellow light. "Rest your fingers lightly on the triangle," she explained to Don Carlos and Ethel Evans, who were the first to try. "Minds blank and receptive. Never move the triangle consciously, but when it wishes to move by itself, make no resistance."

To the others in the room she said, "Concentrate hard on a particular subject. What shall the subject be?"

"Shakespeare," said Dr. Hardy, after we'd all thought for a moment.

"Very well," agreed Miss Hardy. "All of you except the two at the board, think of a play or character by Shakespeare. Try to convey your thought to the minds of Miss Evans and Senor Romano."

I tried unsuccessfully to think about Hamlet. What had begun as a game now seemed serious, even eerie. Perhaps it was the tall, gaunt figure of Alice Hardy hovering near the table, pen and paper in hand to record letters the triangular pointer might single out. Her face was taut and ashen. My thoughts, refusing to stay in place, retraced the conversation at dinner. Why had there been a cave-in of a mine on the same night Veronica disappeared?

"Carlos, I think you are cheating." Eric's voice brought me back to the room. "Why would the Ouija call King Richard the Third *El Rey Ricardo Tercero*—in Spanish?"

Carlos Romano laughed. "No, not cheating. It was my subconscious moving the pointer. I was thinking of that play, the letters seemed to spell themselves. Uncanny, no?"

"Come on, Alison," said Leonora. "It's getting late, so this will be the last attempt. Alison and I. I'm sure she won't cheat, and since I can't see the letters, it should be a good test."

"Really, I don't think I—" My objection was brushed aside by the others, and I found myself sitting opposite Leonora at the board.

"Fingertips touching lightly," said Miss Hardy. "Minds open and receptive." She lifted her arms, bare, starkly white against her dark dress, and ran long fingers through her hair. "Now we will think of someone who has crossed to the other side."

"The dead?" whispered Miss Evans, frightened.

"Come to us now, we await you. . . ." Alice Hardy swayed, the white arms inscribing a great circle; her eyes were glassy and enormous. "Come now from the night. . . . Come now. . . ."

For a moment my hands seemed frozen on the wooden triangle. I heard the wind whisper in the vines, a shutter creaking, and the harsh, regular breathing of Alice Hardy. The others had moved close to us. Jaime Romano stared at me in a strange, probing way. Carlos leaned forward, intent, and behind him, lurking in the shadows, stood Nacho, his pockmarked features no longer impassive, but alert and wary.

"Try. Try, try." Miss Hardy's hands fluttered near me like two white birds as she whispered insistently, "One who will speak from the grave . . . Try. . . . Try. . . ."

A feeling of numbness pervaded me, my eyelids felt heavy as a slow, funereal procession moved through my mind, images, pictures beclouded in mist. A white car, a girl in a white dress, and a sheaf of roses. There were roses near me now, a vase on the mantel, and their fragrance grew overpowering, narcotic. Luis' voice repeating softly, "My mother is dead. . . . My mother is dead. . . . My mother . . ." My hands moved, some force, not my own, commanding them.

"V-E-R-O-N-I—" Shuddering, I jerked my fingers from the pointer. The trancelike hypnosis had vanished. I felt the eyes of the Romano brothers bore into me, Nacho's hands were clenched, and when I saw Padre Olivera cross himself, two words flashed through my mind: *He knows.*

"V-E-R-O-N-I—" Miss Hardy repeated hollowly. "Who has passed to the other side called—"

"Verona!" I exclaimed, my voice unsteady and too loud. "I was still thinking of Shakespeare. *Two Gentlemen of Verona.* I must have given the board involuntary help. Just as Don Carlos did." My laughter rang shrill and false.

Jaime Romano suddenly turned away, but Carlos continued studying me silently, his features fixed and expressionless.

"I'm exhausted," Leonora remarked abruptly, rising from her chair. "Alison, would you walk up to my room with me?"

"I must be going, too," said Padre Olivera. The old priest made his farewells quickly. When he came to me, he took my hand and a long look passed between us, an expression of silent understanding and, I thought, a warning.

As I led Leonora up the dim stairway, her hand resting lightly on my arm, she seemed remote and puzzled. "I would have enjoyed the party tonight except for that last business with the Ouija board," she said. "Miss Hardy is too peculiar for my liking. What does she look like?"

I described Alice Hardy briefly, and Leonora nodded. "That's how I pictured her. So strange just before we stopped! I felt something like a cold draft. Was a window open?"

"No. I don't think so," I said. "Careful. Don't bump into Saint Michael." The tall statue of the warrior saint guarded the last flight of steps leading to Leonora's room. I had never liked the sharpness of the iron sword he brandished.

At the top of the stairs she said, "I'm exhausted, but not sleepy. Too much excitement."

"I'm not sleepy either." In fact, I was much too wrought up to think of sleep yet. Only now were the full implications of what had happened dawning on me. Weeks ago an inner voice had warned me not to betray too much interest in Veronica. Yet tonight, against my own will, I had announced to everyone that Veronica was not only in my thoughts, but that I believed her dead. Would anyone believe I had been thinking of a Shakespearean comedy? No. My whole manner had given me away. I had read my own detection in Nacho's eyes, in the keen stare of Don Carlos, in Jaime Romano's abrupt turning away.

"The wind's coming up again," Leonora said. "Listen to that gale! Would you fasten the shutters, Alison?"

"Of course." But when I opened the east window, Leonora, standing beside me, said softly, "The coolness is beautiful. Let the wind come in. Tell me about the night."

"The clouds are moving west. There's moonlight now. It's a deserted world outside. The lawn and the road are silver."

"I always loved the view from this room," she said.

We talked for nearly half an hour, Leonora telling me of the old days, days when the valley was often a violent and even bloodstained land. But fascinating though her stories were, my mind kept returning to the séance, the helplessness of my hands spelling out a dead woman's name.

After saying good-night, I hesitated a moment in front of Leonora's closed door, reluctant to descend the dim stairs. I started downward, moving carefully, thankful for the small bulb burning faintly on the landing. Then, just as I thought this, the light was extinguished, the stairwell lay in blackness.

Still I felt no alarm. Temporary blackouts were not unusual in the electrified parts of the house, and from working with Leonora, I knew the stairs very well, just as she did. Nine more steps to the turn, then the longest flight, sixteen steps more. Wind whistled around the gables and a sudden, icy gust swept upward, as though someone had just opened a door or a window. I moved cautiously across the landing, passing the dark open door of the linen room. Next to it the life-size statue of Saint Michael towered on a pedestal, looming grotesquely human in the dimness, with his heavy sword held high to strike. I took the next step down, my hand resting lightly on the banister.

I will never be sure what happened next. I know there was the loud, sharp slam of the linen-room door behind me, and as I jerked toward the sound I realized the statue was moving, leaning forward. With a cry I spun away from the descending sword and plunged headlong down the stairs. I heard a crash, my head struck something hard—and then blackness.

CHAPTER SEVEN

"A TWISTED ANKLE, SOME bruises, and a nasty bump that causes your headache," said Dr. Hardy the following afternoon. "No concussion. Considering how steep those stairs are, I'd say you were a lucky young woman indeed!"

"Lucky that you were here when it happened," I told him. Dr. Hardy, bearlike and gruff the night before, had turned out to be astonishingly gentle and kind.

"We leave for Puerto Vallarta in a few minutes," he said. "All you need now is rest. One last thing," he added, smiling. "Don't go groping in the dark and upset another statue that's bigger than you are. Especially on dangerous stairways."

"I won't." So that was what had been decided. Somehow, fumbling, I had tipped the Saint Michael over and then had fallen. "Thank you for everything," I said.

After he had gone, I lay against the pillows, wishing the dull throbbing in my head and ankle would miraculously vanish. I knew I had not touched the statue, not been within a yard of it.

Leonora, the doctor had told me, was the heroine of the accident. Hearing the crash and my scream, she had tried to ring for the servants, and when no one answered, she had at last realized that the electricity must not be working, so no bells rang in the servants' quarters. She had then descended the stairs with her cane, making her way over the fragmented statue, to find me unconscious on the second landing. When she finally reached the main hallway, her shouts had aroused the servants.

The sedatives the doctor had given me were strong, for now I slipped from wakefulness into deep sleep. When I awoke late the next morning, there was a tender, swollen bruise on my head, but the throbbing ache had vanished. A tight bandage around my ankle enabled me to hobble about the room.

At noon Luis bounded into the Octagon, displaying a small magnifying glass Eric had given him. "Look, Tía, it makes everything so big! I can see lines and flecks in the rocks that I didn't know were there." Because I was not in bed, he seemed to feel that my recovery was complete. "Will we ride tomorrow?"

"Not tomorrow. But very soon."

Three mornings later we were able to resume our routine. But I could not banish from my memory the terrifying moment when the statue had seemed to move by itself. After I escorted Leonora to her room, I looked down the stairs where I had fallen. The second landing, which had broken my fall, was just a narrow triangle where the steps curved—how easy to have continued plunging downward, another long flight.

The shattered Saint Michael had been removed, but the smooth-topped pedestal remained. I stared at it now, a cold feeling growing inside me. Only a whole series of the most unlikely circumstances could have caused the statue's falling at that particular moment. Ten seconds earlier or later I would have been far enough above or below it to have been quite surprised and startled, but nothing more.

The explanation everyone seemed to accept was that a servant, for reasons impossible to imagine, had moved the Saint Michael to the very edge of the pedestal while cleaning. It had stood there, almost teetering, until my brushing against it, or perhaps the slam of the linen-room door, sent it crashing forward. This was possible, but I had noticed nothing odd about its placement when I warned Leonora not to stumble against it only half an hour before my fall.

My hand was unsteady on the knob when I opened the linen-room door and looked inside. It was large enough for a servant to sleep here near the tower. The sashes and shutters of the single window were now closed and bolted. They must have been open that night for the wind to have swept through, slamming the heavy door.

No moonlight, I thought suddenly. The linen room had been shrouded in utter blackness. If the window had been open, some illumination, however faint, would have shown through it. I started down the stairs. There must be some other explanation. Yet why had the lights failed at the exact moment when I left Leonora? I was unable to force from my imagination a picture of someone waiting unseen in the linen room, the statue already edged forward, hands touching the back of the door ready to thrust against it full strength.

But why would anyone do such a thing?

I knew no answer. But I thought again of the séance and remembered jerking my hands away from the board, staring at the faces around me. At that moment I had felt a current, a force in the room—an indefinable sense of some rage that was almost palpable.

AS THE DAYS PASSED, everything around me seemed to belie my fear and suspicion. Afternoons were warmer now, the fields a golden brown as they awaited the coming of the great rains. Leonora, steadily gaining confidence, no longer pushed herself at such a desperate pace. Both Romano brothers were busy, Jaime pressing to complete the new dam before the rainy season, Carlos organizing an exhibition and sale of horses which was to take place in the summer.

One lazy afternoon during the siesta hours I sat in the patio writing a note to Margaret to say I would soon spend a weekend with her in Puerto Vallarta. Lulled by the warmth, the drone of bees in the honeysuckle, and the quiet ripple of the fountain, I let my heavy eyelids close and drowsed a moment.

A small, fierce voice shouted, "Hands up!"

I found myself staring at a dwarf bandit, Luis, with a bandanna masking his face as he pointed a pistol at me.

"Don't shoot!" I exclaimed, starting to lift my hands. Then I realized it was a real gun. "Luis, don't point that at me," I said sharply. "Where did you get that pistol?"

"It's one of Uncle Jaime's." He looked uncomfortable.

"Give it to me! You must never play with such a thing."

He handed it over, and I took it carefully, distrustfully. "Now we'll return this to your uncle."

"Do we have to? He's at the dam now. Couldn't we just put it back in the case?"

The pleading tone was too much to resist. "All right. We'll put it back and not say anything, on one condition. You must promise never to take this or any other gun without permission."

"I promise." He said it so reluctantly that I knew his word was important to him and he would keep it.

The door of Jaime Romano's quarters stood open to catch any afternoon breeze. Entering the large whitewashed room I felt like an intruder, but told myself it was in a good cause. Unlike Don Carlos' ornate apartment, this room had no mementos, no personal objects at all except an old, much enlarged photograph of Leonora, young, happy, and dramatically mounted on a tall palomino stallion.

There was a single bed, an Indian rug on the floor beside it, an antique desk with a plain chair, an old-fashioned wardrobe closet, and the gun case protected by a steel screen.

"Luis, the gun case is padlocked," I said.

Blushing, he opened the wardrobe and took out a tooled-leather boot. When he turned it upside down, a small key fell out.

I returned the pistol to the case, then set the boot containing the key back in the wardrobe. I was not really listening to Luis when he said, "This desk is just like the one in the library. I wonder if this has a secret compartment, too." I turned just as he pulled out a concealed drawer high in the upper paneling. Luckily, he had to reach above his head to remove it, and I took it from him before he could examine its contents.

"Luis, we don't look at other people's things without asking."

"I only wanted to see if it was like the other desk," he protested, and I found myself relenting. A secret compartment was really much too great a temptation for a little boy.

"Luis! Luis!" Ethel Evans' voice called from outside. Then I heard her speak to an unseen servant. "Have you seen Luis? His grandmother wants to speak to him."

I felt panic at the thought of discovery. Nothing could please Miss Evans more than catching us here apparently ransacking Jaime's private papers. I tried to slip the drawer back in place, but it was too close-fitting—there was some trick to inserting it. "Go on, Luis," I said, hoping to gain a little time. He slipped out the door, then shouted that he was coming.

Setting the drawer on the desk, I studied the open panel, soon discovering the catch that had to be pressed for release and replacement. Then, as I started to pick up the drawer, I stopped, my eyes widening. I stared down at a photograph of Veronica seated by the patio fountain. She was smiling dreamily, a white mantilla falling over her bare shoulders. In none of the other photos had she looked so beautiful.

A picture a lover would keep.

There were two other objects in the drawer. I saw a silver buckle with the monogram J.R., and remembered the receipt in Veronica's letter file. Next to it lay a sheet of notepaper with Veronica's distinctive writing. At first I did not identify the familiar poem, because she had translated it into Spanish and it no longer rhymed. Then it came to me. *"How do I love thee? Let me count the ways."*

I read no more. I knew this sonnet by heart, and with trembling hands I replaced the compartment, then hurried into the patio.

I paused near the fountain where Veronica had sat smiling. Had Jaime held the camera that day? Had he inspired her look of soft loveliness? The sunlight seemed cold as I recalled the last lines of the sonnet she had translated so carefully for him. They rang in my memory: *". . . And, if God choose, I shall but love thee better after death."*

LATER THAT AFTERNOON I took the mare Rosanante and followed a trail cutting across the valley toward the northern slopes and mountains. I needed to be away from the house, needed time to sort my thoughts and feelings. Above all, I felt guilty. I had been a trespasser who had violated Jaime Romano's deepest privacy and, in a way, Veronica's. I could only console myself in the knowledge that a deadly game was being played in the High Valley, and usual rules did not apply.

Orchards and fields behind us now, Rosanante plodded along a scratched-out trail, slowly climbing, passing between great boulders, cacti, and stands of scrub timber. She circled the open pit of a mine shaft fenced off with a makeshift barrier of thorns and mesquite branches, then passed another and yet another. The trail turned sharply, and a moment later we were in a beautiful tiny valley where willow fronds brushed the white water of a bubbling stream. The trail now joined a rutted road, and I followed it several hundred yards to a place where the valley ended in a narrow cul-de-sac. There the stream flowed from a mine entrance, splashing over rocks to find its bed below. Two signs dangled above the tunnel's mouth; one said THE HIDDEN TREASURE and the other DO NOT ENTER!

This, then, was the haunted place frequented by ghosts of miners entombed alive a generation ago. And the place where an avalanche had cascaded down the night Veronica went away.

The phantoms, if they emerged from the dark tunnel, would find themselves in the most beautiful spot in the High Valley. A place of ferns and drooping bell-like flowers I had never seen before. Wild orchids blazed in an oak whose branches shaded a clump of calla lilies. Dismounting, I let Rosanante drink from the stream and happily graze in the rich grass. "Perfect," I said aloud. Did young lovers from the village find their way to this spot? Did Marcos and Ramona? Did Veronica?

Veronica and Jaime. I could not accustom myself to the idea that they had been lovers. I remembered the Excelentísima's malicious words: "She had been meeting some man." I had dismissed this as the gossip of a spiteful old woman, but now I realized it had been true. What could be more natural? Veronica's marriage had failed, and during the last year or more she had lived apart from her husband in the Octagon. Don Carlos spent little time in the High Valley, but Jaime was always here, and he, like Veronica, was alone. Now alone again. Haunted by grief? Or was it something more sinister than that—remorse? Perhaps Veronica had decided to end their affair. No one could know what Jaime Romano might do if enraged by injured pride and rejected love.

The light was fading, almost sunset. Mounting Rosanante, I started back, wondering if Carlos Romano had known about Veronica and his half brother. No, I decided. The old Conde had been alive then, and Carlos would have caused a public scandal that would drive an unwanted wife and the unwanted Jaime from the valley forever. No, he had not known, yet he might have suspected.

I left Rosanante at the stable and went to the Octagon, where a note awaited me, a note I read with a rising sense of desperation. It said only, "I want to see you, Senorita Alison. Jaime R."

So my prying had been discovered already. There was nothing to do but tell exactly what had happened. Across the patio the office was dark, but lights burned in the bedroom, and through the open window I saw Jaime Romano seated at the antique desk, working with a large ledger. "Come in, senorita," he said, hardly glancing up. "A moment. I am almost finished."

The two or three minutes of waiting seemed the longest of my life. I stood awkwardly near the door, hoping not to look like the guilty schoolgirl I felt myself to be.

Closing the ledger, he rose. "Sit down." He pushed the chair toward me and seated himself on the desk. "Senorita, how busy are you these days?" he asked.

"Not overworked," I said carefully. "Your mother doesn't demand as much of herself as she did for a while, and Luis has other studies besides English."

"Good. I want to ask some favors of you. Favors for which you will be paid extra, naturally."

My sigh of relief was almost audible. Apparently I had not been found out. "I'll be happy to do anything possible."

"Carlos and I are now arranging for the summer sale of horses. I send letters and invitations to possible buyers. Short letters, but each different from the others and many are in English. After I have written them, will you correct any mistakes in English?"

"Mistakes in English?" I was surprised. "Your English is excellent. I'm happy to help, but I don't think you need me."

"I speak well enough and my accent is passable. But English spelling is insanity, and these letters must be perfect. I hope you will also help with arrangements for our guests at the sale of the horses. My mother used to manage these things and now thinks she can do it again this year. She will need much help."

"That's part of my work."

"Good. You may find the horse sale interesting. There are exhibitions of riding and roping. It is very colorful." The interview seemed to be over, but as I started to rise, he asked, "Where did you go today? I saw Rosanante was not in her stall."

"To the Hidden Treasure mine. Not inside it, of course."

"Then you saw the little valley?"

"Yes. I think heaven must look rather like that spot."

"I have not been there in a long time," he said thoughtfully. "All the High Valley is beautiful, but there it is the most—what is the English for *precioso?*"

"Precious is rather close."

"That is it. When I was a boy it was precious for mercury and some silver. Now it is precious for other things." The rugged face softened for a moment. "The grass near the stream is matted and thick. With enough water, all the valley could be like that. Sometimes I look at the barren fields past the Villa Plata and I see a garden! Green as far as my eye can travel. I will make that garden real one day."

He spoke more to himself than to me, and although he talked of a dream, I felt the strength of steel behind the words. He loved this land with his whole being, yet it was not his, would never be his. The High Valley belonged to Luis alone. Surely Jaime Romano realized he was but a temporary steward! Was this part of what had embittered him?

Suddenly he ceased speaking, as though deliberately checking himself. "I have kept you too long. Thank you for your help."

"I'm happy to give it."

Just as I reached the door his voice halted me. "Senorita, another matter. I recall that on the night of your accident we danced together."

"Rather briefly," I replied.

"May we agree that I suddenly became ill that night? What soldiers call the flare-up of an old wound?" His words and tone were edged with self-mockery, and only this morning I would have taken this odd apology as an attempt at an ironic joke. Now I knew better, and with effort I kept my eyes from moving to the hidden compartment in the desk.

"We'll agree on that," I said.

"Also, I promise you that the next time my health will be better. Good night . . . Alison." Speaking my name seemed to be difficult for him, as though he had been forced to push through some self-imposed barrier to allow the smallest crack to appear in the wall with which he surrounded himself.

Returning to the Octagon, I sealed and addressed my note to Margaret. In two weeks I would see her, and I looked forward to her honest warmth, her candor that concealed nothing.

Standing up, I walked the length of the two rooms and back again, restless, troubled. Veronica and Jaime. The two names, newly coupled, would not leave my mind. My thoughts wandered to the buckle and then to the receipt in her letter file. Suddenly my pacing ceased, and I exclaimed aloud, "She *kept* things!"

Veronica had hoarded photos of the High Valley and its people. She even saved her notes as she struggled to improve her Spanish, and kept scores of pages of handwritten translations. But not one personal letter, not one contact with any friend outside the valley, not one souvenir of her life before she came here. This was terribly wrong. Even if her early life had been unhappy, she would surely have preserved some record of it. I remembered the Excelentísima's words, but now they had a new meaning. "She was nobody. She came from nowhere."

CHAPTER EIGHT

TWO WEEKS LATER, as Margaret and I strolled toward the old plaza in Puerto Vallarta, the unanswered questions in the High Valley seemed a world away. I had enjoyed three beautiful days—swimming in the clear, warm ocean, relaxing on the powdery beaches that framed the town. Now we were going to Margaret's rental house, because the tenants, the Mexico

City couple and their children, were leaving and Margaret was stopping by to refund a breakage deposit.

"When I checked the inventory, there wasn't so much as a glass broken," said Margaret. "Either those boys are born angels, or Epifania watches them day and night."

"Epifania?"

"Epifania Heiden, their mother. I think her nickname is Fani, but I don't know her that well."

Crossing the plaza, Margaret paused near the quaint bandstand. "Let's sit on a bench for a moment. I want to find out something." A moment later she gave me a twinkling smile. "Uh-huh! You have an admirer, Alison."

"An admirer?"

"Don't look! A man has been following us for blocks. Now he's sitting on a bench, pretending to read a newspaper."

I glanced casually over my shoulder. Not far away a tall, middle-aged Mexican studied a folded copy of *Excélsior*. He was dressed in the sheer white sport shirt and light trousers which were almost a Puerto Vallarta uniform. A black sombrero with a red band and brass buckle was pulled so low on his forehead that it almost met the rims of mirrorlike sunglasses.

"I wouldn't usually pay attention to a thing like this," said Margaret. "But he's been remarkably persistent. I noticed him on the beach yesterday, too. Let's move on and see what he does." She glanced at me, then frowned. "Oh, for heaven's sake, Alison! It's usually just a game. Don't look so worried."

"I'm not. It's just that his glasses and that black sombrero make him look like a film gangster."

We reached our destination and Margaret rang the bell. Senor Black Sombrero now leaned against a shady wall near a corner.

The maid ushered us to the living room, where Epifania Heiden stood surrounded by suitcases and boxes. Her freckled, tow-headed boys were struggling to find space for fishing equipment and scuba gear.

"Thank you, Mrs. Webber," she said, accepting Margaret's check. "You have been the ideal landlady." Her careful English had a charming lilt. An unusually attractive woman, I thought, with fine bones and a slender figure that was still youthful.

Wishing them a safe journey to Mexico City, we left. Outside, there was no sign of Black Sombrero, but within a block he had picked up our trail again, always staying about fifty yards behind.

"True devotion," said Margaret.

I doubted it. What was the point in following me if I remained unaware of it? We lost Black Sombrero when we took a taxi to Margaret's house, but his presence stayed in my mind, arousing suspicions I had suppressed and diminishing the pleasure of my last night at Margaret's. When Primitivo arrived to pick me up the next morning, there was no sign of Black Sombrero. I tried to tell myself that Margaret had been right, that he had been nothing more than an idle man playing a game that was harmless, if annoying.

BACK IN THE OCTAGON, Luis never left my side while I unpacked my bag. "Look what I picked for you!" he exclaimed proudly. The bud vase was crammed with wild strawflowers from the fields.

"What a beautiful bouquet, Luis!"

"Tonight we are all going to have supper in the dining room," he said. "Grandmother said that at least once we must eat together like a civilized family."

Ramona came to welcome me, and to remind Luis that he still had studying to do. He went to his room, muttering complaints about arithmetic.

"How sweet of him to have picked these flowers for me," I said, touching the small, graceful vase. "By the way, Ramona, when did you change the vase?"

"I changed nothing, my lady. It has always been here."

"No, the other one was silver. This looks very much like it, the same size and shape, but is made of . . ." I did not know the Spanish word for pewter, and had to say, "a different metal. Has another girl been cleaning the room?"

"No, my lady. And the vase has never been taken from here." Then she broke off, smiling. "Ah, how stupid I am! The Senorita Evans polished all the silver things. I had forgotten."

I vaguely remembered Miss Evans complaining about the way the servants cleaned silver. And yes, she had said she was going to polish everything herself. The vase formerly in this room, I felt sure, was now incorporated into Miss Evans' decor. I did not care; the two objects, although different in value, were equally beautiful. Nevertheless, I remembered too well that Senora Castro, my predecessor, had been accused of theft, and I was determined to set the record straight as soon as possible. I pictured Jaime Romano, an inventory list in hand, demanding, "Where is that silver vase, Senorita Mallory?"

At suppertime we gathered in the dining room for Leonora's "civilized" dinner. It was not very successful. There were long conversational vacuums, and the Romano brothers reminded me of two crouching lions ready to spring. Over coffee, Leonora kept all talk confined to business. Luis began to yawn, but Jaime said, "You must listen, Luis. This will be your work someday."

While the others discussed horses, cattle, and prices, Miss Evans and I sat a little apart. "By the way, Miss Evans," I said, keeping my voice low, "when you polished the silver some weeks ago, you returned a different vase to the Octagon."

For an instant her face blanched, but she concealed her alarm quickly. "Different? I'm sure not."

"The first one was silver; the one I have now is polished pewter."

"I hate to contradict you, Miss Mallory," she answered stiffly. "But the Octagon vase was always pewter. I recall thinking how remarkable it was that the vase hadn't been scratched. Pewter is so soft, and these servants use scouring powder on it."

Leonora interrupted us. "What's this? What vase?"

"We were talking about a pewter vase I mistakenly thought was silver," I said.

"A large bud vase with a leaf design?" she asked.

"Yes."

"There are two such vases. I was so fond of the pewter one that my husband had it copied in silver. Does that settle the mystery?"

"I think it does." I avoided looking at Ethel Evans. She had done just what I suspected: switched vases to add the more expensive one to her already cluttered room.

"Bedtime for Luis and me," Leonora announced.

"I'll walk Grandmother to her room," Luis said.

I went to the Octagon. There were still no electric lights in the rooms and corridors leading to it, but I had solved the difficulty by always carrying a small pocket flashlight attached to my key ring. My fall on the stairs had taught me to be prepared for darkness anywhere in the house.

After preparing for the night and changing into a warm robe and slippers, I stepped onto the veranda going toward Luis' room. I wanted to say goodnight to him and perhaps read aloud a page or two of *The Wind in the Willows*, our current bedtime book.

I drew up a chair and was opening the book when he said, quite casually, "The Senorita Evans is very angry. When I went past her door, I heard her speaking fast English with somebody. Tía, what does the word geridov mean?"

After several false starts, I realized he was saying "get rid of."

"It means to make something or someone go away."

He nodded. "I thought maybe it was that. Maybe Senorita Evans was talking about a servant she does not like. She said, 'Geridov her.'" Luis frowned, trying to puzzle something out. "Does not the English word medals mean *medallas?*"

"Yes."

"And I know a prize is a *premio*. Why would a servant have medals and prizes?"

"Medals and prizes?" I asked. "Who was the senorita talking to?"

"I do not know. But please, Tía, read before it is too late."

I managed three pages, but my mind was not on Mr. Toad of Toad Hall. I thought of the silver vase, of how the blood had drained from Miss Evans' face when I mentioned it. And I knew that she had not been speaking of a servant when she said to an unknown listener, "Get rid of her. She meddles and pries!"

I LEARNED NO MORE about Miss Evans and the unknown person she had spoken to, nor did she make any apparent attempt to force me from the High Valley. Yet I knew that if wishing could make a thing happen, I would have been sent packing long ago. As Leonora's accomplishments grew, Ethel Evans was no longer essential, and I read bitterness in every look she gave me.

Yet I had little reason to think about her until one morning when we were having a lesson in braille. Leonora had small interest in it and seized any excuse to avoid work. This particular morning the diversionary tactic was to talk about her jewelry.

"You haven't noticed my necklace." Unclasping it, she held it out for inspection. "Colombian emeralds. They were a wildly extravagant gift to me. And I'm not very fond of jewelry. I haven't taken this out of its case for ages. Today it was a whim."

The necklace was made of finely wrought silver links with seven large stones. "Magnificent," I said.

Leonora smiled. "What a tactful way of saying ostentatious. The stone in the center is beautiful, though. Hold it up to the light. It has real fire."

"Yes, I see." But I didn't. The stone was attractive, yet the inner prisms had no light at all. Glass, I thought suddenly. Or paste. Imitations. Yet I could say nothing now. For I was not positive.

"I've often thought I should sell it," she said. "There are certainly enough things to spend the money on."

"Well, if you don't really like the necklace, and never wear it . . ." This was the way to find out, I thought. An appraiser could give the answer. I looked at my watch. "Time's up. You avoided work very subtly today. But don't think I've given up. You'll be literate one of these days."

Confused and troubled, I left her. The emeralds had changed everything. Now the substitution of a pewter vase seemed no longer based on the harmless pride in objects that led Ethel Evans to furnish her room as a museum. What eventually became of all those objects she collected? The house was huge. Could the servants keep track of all the thousands of things stored here? Would they know which things were valuable? Don Carlos and Jaime had no interest. There was only Leonora—and she was blind. What could I do about it? Nothing but be alert and, for the time being, keep suspicions to myself.

I WALKED TOWARD THE village early that afternoon, Padre Olivera having invited me to lunch. I was only a few hundred yards from the house when Luis came running to overtake me, dressed in the absurd Fauntleroy attire the Excelentísima demanded.

"You're supposed to go to the Villa Plata today," I said. "Won't you be late?"

"It does not matter. She will be cross anyway." Luis seemed quite undisturbed by this. He pointed ahead, toward the carillon which rose majestically tall and slender. "Barn swallows have built nests at the very top. Have you been in the tower, Tía?"

"No."

"Then I will show it to you."

"We must look quickly or we'll both be late," I warned him.

We entered through a door so low that I had to duck my head. Inside was a round room with stone walls and floors. Dust motes danced in beams of sunshine that shone through slitlike windows. The great shaft soared above us, empty except for thick beams supporting bells of all shapes and sizes. In one corner dangled more than a dozen heavy ropes.

"When you pull those," said Luis, "iron hammers strike the bells. You can play a tune if you know which ones to pull." He started up the stairs circling the inside of the tower. They were dangerously steep and had no railings.

I followed slowly, glancing down once and promptly regretting it. The height made my head spin, and I dreaded going back down.

We were almost at the top, where a huge bell dominated the tower. "It is called Saint Michael and came from Spain," Luis shouted back to me. "Four hundred years old, my grandmother says."

I rounded a corner of the stairs and gasped. The stone steps ended abruptly where a platform must have crumbled and fallen long ago. Now there was only a narrow, rotted-looking plank spanning a gap to a balcony, where Luis stood. Another bell, not so large as Saint Michael, but huge and heavy, hung above the break in the stairs, where it could be rung from either side.

"That bell is rung only when there is danger," Luis told me. "It means a brushfire has broken out, or other terrible news. Everyone comes running when it rings."

"Luis, did you just walk across that plank?" My voice trembled a little.

"Yes, Tía. There is no other way to get to the nests. It is very strong. See?" Before I could stop him, he moved across it again, coming quickly toward me. The plank was nearly three yards long, and I held my breath as he passed the center, where with a faint creak it sagged under his weight. Then he was beside me. "It is safe. I have gone over it many times."

Well, this was the last time, I thought grimly. "Luis, the wood is very old and you're growing bigger and heavier all the time. Don't walk across it again until we can have it changed!"

Our descent seemed interminable, and every step of the way I kept thinking of Luis hurtling from the broken plank to the stone floor below. Before we parted, I made him promise solemnly not to visit the tower until it was made safe. Made safe? As I walked on toward the village, I realized this was impossible. No railings, the precipitous steps uneven and winding. Exactly the place for an accident. . . .

Too many accidents. A fire, a broken swing, a runaway horse, my fall the night of the séance. Yet everything around me seemed to contradict my own fears. The High Valley breathed tranquil beauty. Irises and primavera fringed the road, and hidden birds warbled in the trees. Nothing, it seemed, could mar this landscape.

Then I became aware that the birds had suddenly fallen silent. A tiny shadow flashed past me, and looking up I saw one of the Excelentísima's hawks describe a circle in the sky. The steel-taloned predator always nearby, always waiting and watching. . . .

WITH THE COMING of summer, mornings remained clear and sunny, but in the late afternoon, almost daily, clouds spilled across the sky, watering and nourishing the land, transforming the High Valley. The slopes, as by a miracle, were suddenly green; cactus flowers, violet, blue, and magenta, burst into bloom. Now I understood why Jaime Romano at times spoke so desperately of water.

Leonora made one further attempt at a family dinner, and this time she invited Padre Olivera, whose benevolent presence she hoped would have a calming effect.

I met him at the door that night, and he entered loaded down with earthen pots he had brought from the village. "For Senorita Evans," he told me. "The potter had promised them to her, but is ill. Tonight I am his delivery boy."

"Miss Evans bought these?"

"Yes. I understand she sends them to friends as gifts."

Incredible, I thought. She had never praised any Mexican crafts. On the contrary, she was contemptuous of the earth-warm Mexican pitchers and plates I found lovely.

Luis was excused from the late meal and sent to bed to recover from a summer cold. Dinner conversation moved along easily, until Leonora suddenly said, "I've decided to sell my Colombian emeralds. Money from that necklace can be put to good use."

She spoke to Jaime and Carlos, but Miss Evans instantly protested. "Oh, you couldn't part with anything so beautiful!"

"It would pay for finishing the new dam and more," said Jaime.

Miss Evans started to chatter about "sentimental reasons," when Carlos interrupted her and spoke to Leonora, his voice cold. "The necklace was a gift to you from my father."

"That's why this decision has been difficult," she replied.

"Not difficult—ill advised," he answered, shooting an accusing look at Jaime. "The necklace belongs to all the family. One day Luis' wife will wear it, and later his son's wife."

"Finish the dam and build more catch basins," Jaime said, "and Luis can one day buy this unknown bride half a dozen emerald baubles, if he's that foolish."

Carlos' eyes flashed, color blazed in his cheeks. "You would use your father's gift to make my son into a farmer?"

Both men were halfway out of their chairs when Padre Olivera interrupted, a surprising note of command in his quiet voice. "May I propose a better gift for Luis' future wife? I suggest you give her an educated husband. Luis cannot continue studying with me much longer." He turned to Don Carlos. "It would not insult your father's memory if the money were set aside for Luis' education. In the fall he must go to a good school, nearby perhaps. Later he must go abroad, just as you yourself did, Carlos."

Leonora said wryly, "With less disturbing results, I trust."

To my astonishment, Carlos chuckled. "Luis is to follow my orders, not my example."

Jaime leaned back in his chair. I saw a fleeting expression of calculation, then a suppressed smile. As executor of the estate, he had no doubt already planned the financing of Luis' education. Now that money could go into the High Valley. He had won an unexpected victory.

"Very well, Padre," said Carlos. "It will be a gift to Luis from his grandfather. That is honorable, I think. Tomorrow I go to Mexico City to bring back three guests for the stock show this weekend. I will also make arrangements about the necklace."

"Why not let Senor Ramos in Puerto Vallarta take care of that?" Jaime asked.

Again Carlos' eyes flashed. "I will not have a small-town jeweler gossiping about our affairs!"

Jaime shrugged. Town talk was obviously beneath his contempt.

I studied Ethel Evans' face. If there had been a substitution of the emeralds, it would be exposed tomorrow. But her expression was not one of fright. Strangely, it was more like triumph.

ON FRIDAY EVENING the house had a gala atmosphere of anticipation. Tomorrow would see the culmination of weeks of work and planning. A chartered bus would meet prospective livestock buyers at the Puerto Vallarta airport, and others, Leonora told me, would arrive by car, truck, and jeep.

Carlos with his three guests arrived in the plane about eight o'clock. The newcomers appeared to be a trio of unsociable and doubtlessly rich businessmen who, despite their swagger, felt ill at ease in the home of Spanish aristocrats. They quickly retreated upstairs to play poker and dominoes.

The moment they left the living room, I braced myself for an explosion over the emerald necklace. None came. Smiling, Carlos said something to Leonora, and she nodded happily, exclaiming, "Good! You got a better price than I thought. And putting it into telephone stock is exactly right."

So I had been mistaken. Yet, curiously, my misjudging the emeralds did not change my mind about Ethel Evans. I knew she was up to mischief and my suspicions remained unshaken.

Jaime Romano and Eric Vanderlyn arrived a few minutes later, having completed arrangements at the exhibition ring near the Villa Plata.

Suddenly we all caught the noise of horses and motors, and Carlos moved to a window. "*Dios!* It is the army! At least a hundred federal troops."

"What the devil!" exclaimed Jaime, starting toward the hall and the front door. A moment later he returned, accompanied by a tall Mexican officer in a dusty uniform.

Smiling, Carlos extended his hand. "Captain Montez, I believe? We met months ago in Puerto Vallarta."

"Yes, of course. Good evening."

"You seem to have brought a rather large escort."

The captain glanced around the room, surprise on his rough face. "Has no one heard the news? Don Ramón Santos has been kidnapped."

The room was instantly filled with excited, shocked voices.

"Who's been kidnapped?" I asked Eric.

"Ramón Santos. One of the most prominent men in this state."

The captain gave us the facts briefly. The millionaire's car had been halted by two men disguised in the blue uniforms of policemen. Then he had been abducted at pistol point, a chauffeur left behind, bound and gagged.

"It follows the pattern of earlier crimes by terrorists," the captain said. "This time, however, we have a witness—the chauffeur. He described the three kidnappers—the two men in uniform, and a third, who followed in a station wagon and wore a red checkered shirt. They covered their faces with scarves.

Leonora had been listening intently, and now she spoke. "We are all shocked by this terrible thing, Captain. But I do not understand why you have come here. Surely not to tell us the news!"

"We are searching, senora. And I have heard the area is dotted with abandoned mines. Perfect hiding places, no?"

"Not at all," said Jaime. "You would have to enter and leave a mine. You would be seen. Besides, most of the tunnels are too dangerous. There are avalanches, and now, in the rainy season, flash floods. These criminals are not such fools, Captain Montez."

The officer stood up. "I have my orders. We will bivouac near the village tonight. At dawn we begin combing the hills."

"We cannot accommodate all your men, Captain," said Leonora, "but for yourself and your officers, our house is yours."

"You are gracious, senora. I must stay with my men."

After he had gone, there was a moment of silence as each of us considered the news. Then Leonora said, "Kidnappers hiding in the High Valley? Rubbish!" Turning to Ramona, she said, "Please bring two cups of chocolate to my room. Will you see me upstairs and chat a moment, Alison? I have a surprise for you."

Once in her own room, Leonora moved with no hesitation, going to a carved chest, opening the top drawer, and producing a large package gaily wrapped. "For you, my dear!"

"Leonora!" I exclaimed when I opened it. "How beautiful!"

"It's a china poblana costume I ordered from Mexico City. Traditional for women riders," she told me.

The blue-green skirt with its gay red band was cut from fine cotton flannel and fell long and richly full. A white shirt had been decorated with delicate embroidery and its sleeves were clasped by four silver cuff links.

"Boots and a sombrero are in the closet," she said. "And to be traditional, wear a red ribbon in your hair. Don't tell me I shouldn't have done it. It's a present because of an anniversary I forgot."

"What anniversary?"

"Losing my sight," she told me quietly. "I used to wonder how I'd ever get through the first year. Jaime kept insisting we hire a teacher for me, but it seemed useless."

"Jaime insisted on a teacher?" I asked.

"Oh, yes. He hired Senora Castro and brought her here. She tried hard. I think I was just too discouraged to make an effort. I wanted to let her go, but Jaime kept saying if I discharged one, he'd simply hire another. He said I'd give up before he did!"

Don Carlos had told me nothing of this in Puerto Vallarta. Helping Leonora had been presented as entirely *his* plan.

"Anyway, I kept believing that if I could survive the first year of blindness, the second one would be easy. I looked forward to that anniversary. Well, the important day came and went weeks ago, but I was so busy that I forgot it completely until days afterward. That's because of you, Alison."

There was a tap on the door, then Ramona entered with our chocolate. Putting it down, she said, "Will that be all, my lady?"

"Yes, thank you, Ramona," Leonora replied, then tilted her head. "Something's wrong. I can tell by your voice."

"Only a small matter in the kitchen," Ramona said, swallowing hard. "Nacho used some harsh words." Her eyes were red-rimmed and I was sure she had been crying.

Sighing, Leonora murmured, "Nacho again!"

"It is not important, my lady," Ramona added quickly. "Nacho becomes angry because he is such an unhappy man. How can a man be contented when he has no children, no sons? We all understand this and are patient, but tonight everyone is nervous because of the people coming tomorrow. It is natural."

"You are a kind girl, Ramona," said Leonora. "If there is more trouble, I will speak to him. Now good night." When Ramona had closed the door, Leonora remarked, "Unhappiness doesn't excuse everything."

"I've never felt easy when Nacho was near," I said to her. "Yet I don't know why."

"He slithers!" snapped Leonora. Then her voice softened. "He was born the year the plague swept through the valley. We thought he recovered completely, but long afterward, when he was grown and married, he asked my husband to send him to doctors in Mexico City. You see, he fathered no children. That's a shameful thing here, a disgrace for a man. The doctors took tests, and the news must have been a terrible blow to Nacho. There would never be children. Most of the people in the valley pity him; others make sour jokes about it. Probably that's turned Nacho into what he is—bitter, solitary. He cares for no one except Carlos. Of course, Nacho grew up with Carlos. That may explain some blind worship. As boys they were inseparable, but it was always the master and the slave."

It was late, and we finished our chocolate quickly. Leaving Leonora's room, I started downstairs, automatically checking to make sure the small flashlight on my key ring worked and, as always, moving cautiously past the door of the linen room.

A lamp burned in the entrance hall and the front door stood ajar. I was about to close it when a voice said, "Alison?"

"Yes." I stepped onto the veranda. Jaime Romano sat on the steps, his back resting against one of the tall wooden pillars.

"You are awake late," he said.

"So are you."

"I know. But such a night as this, all of it should not be slept away. Sit down, Alison." The warm darkness was drowsy with jasmine fragrance. Crickets and cicadas trilled in the *copa de oro* vines, and toward the village fires burned where Captain Montez and his men had pitched their tents.

"The soldiers are not sleeping either," he said. "Listen."

Faintly I heard a guitar, and voices singing softly. "The melody is lovely, haunting," I said. "I can't hear the words."

He whispered, " '*Oh, dear one, if I should die o'er the ocean's foam, softly a white dove on a fair eve would come . . . Open thy casement, dearest, for it shall be . . . My faithful spirit that loving comes back to thee. . . .' "*

Jaime smiled quietly. "No doves will come tonight. Only the owl who has been calling in the orchard. He is lonely, I think. Are you ever lonely, Alison?"

I looked away from him. "Lonely? I have so many things to do. No hours for loneliness."

"You do not need to find such hours. Loneliness comes of itself. Is it not true, Alison?"

"Yes. It is true too often." I thought of my own life, and I imagined his, realizing for the first time that there was a bond between us: loneliness.

He gazed upward to the great stars, incredibly brilliant in the thin air. " 'The silence of space frightens me . . . I am engulfed in infinity and afraid . . .' "

"Are those also the words of a song?"

"No. Words from a book by the Frenchman Pascal."

I looked at his strong face, the dark forelock, eyes that even in the night were a cold, hard blue. "I can't imagine your being afraid," I said. "Not even frightened by space or silence."

He smiled, the rocky features softening. "No? Then you do not yet know me as well as I thought you did. Let us say that at times I am afraid of myself." He rose quickly, seeming to tower over me. "Also, sometimes I am afraid of you."

"Of me!" I exclaimed. "Why should you be?"

"Why not?" The smile altered, became faintly mocking. "For me you are a dangerous woman. Good night, Alison."

CHAPTER NINE

I AWOKE EARLY, BUT others were up and stirring long before me. I had hardly finished dressing in my new costume when Luis skipped in, aglow with excitement. He wore a new embroidered shirt and fancy trousers with silver buttons—a miniature of his father's riding outfit. "My grandmother gave me this. And look! A present from Uncle Jaime!"

Proudly he pointed to a silver buckle much too large for him. "It has my initials on it. L.R."

I looked at the buckle in astonishment. It was, I thought, an exact duplicate of the one in Jaime Romano's desk.

"How handsome, Luis," I said, kneeling down to examine it. No, this was not a duplicate, but the same buckle. A silversmith, in changing the

J to an *L,* had worked carefully, but one could see where something had been ground and polished away.

"Uncle Jaime says this is the most valuable buckle I will ever own, and I must always keep it."

"He is right, Luis." Rising, I touched his thin shoulder. How could Jaime Romano part with this gift after keeping it so long? It was a beautiful thing he had done, a present to Luis from his mother, even though he might never know. "Take good care of it. Be proud of it."

"Oh, I am!"

Cars began to arrive after breakfast. Guests were greeted at the *casa grande,* where a mariachi group played lively folk tunes and servants presented orchids to female guests. They were an exuberant, happy crowd looking forward to a day's entertainment, yet at times the good cheer died at mention of the kidnapping. Some were friends of the victim, and they buzzed with rumors and vague reports.

Leonora remained poised and patient, even with some old acquaintances who went on and on with commiserations, as well-meaning but insensitive people will. The chartered bus from the airport brought a chattering throng dressed in everything from glittering *charro* outfits and Puerto Vallarta sportswear to dark business suits. Several women wore costumes like mine.

When the crowd started for the exhibition rings, Luis tugged at my arm, demanding we ride together.

The bullring behind the Villa Plata resembled a miniature of the Colosseum in Rome. It was an extravagant family toy constructed long ago for the Romanos and their friends.

Nearby, spectators watched equestrian events. Luis sat beside me in the stands, and he astonished me with all he knew about riding. The festivities began with a beautiful parade of horses ridden by Marcos and other valley boys. The animals wore flowers and pompons in their manes and almost danced when the village band played a gay polka. Two pretty, flashing-eyed girls gave an exciting demonstration of sidesaddle riding, and the crowd cheered them.

Then men hurried in front of the stands, carrying two tall posts with a crossbar lashed between them at the top. "The ribbon race!" cried Luis. "Tía, they are going to run the rings!"

Just then someone tapped my shoulder, and turning, I saw an old man, a horse trainer on the ranch, smiling at me.

"Senorita, will you give us a ribbon for the race?"

"You have to, Tía!" exclaimed Luis. "That makes you a queen of the fiesta. One of its godmothers!"

I untied the long red ribbon, letting my hair fall loose. "Here you are."

The two girl riders were also giving ribbons, and below on the track a wire was strung between the two posts near the crossbar.

"What are they going to do?" I asked.

"The ribbons go over the wire and a small ring is tied to each one," Luis explained. "The riders will try to do something very difficult."

When the first attempt was made, I understood what running the rings meant. A young rider, his horse racing at full speed, charged toward the three dangling rings, a machete in his hand. The goal was to spear one of the rings with the tip of the machete and carry it off with the attached ribbon. Hard to do at any time, and especially so today when a breeze moved the rings.

The first three riders failed. The fourth succeeded, but won little applause because his mount had not raced fast enough. Still, he displayed the ribbon boastfully, and the band struck up a lusty tune as he rode to the old man who seemed to be the judge. Some words were exchanged between them; then the victor rode to where the two pretty girls sat. Doffing his sombrero grandly, he knelt before one of them. He gave her the ribbon, and she returned it as a gift. Now everyone cheered while the girl blushed, turning her face away.

After four more unsuccessful tries, the second ring was retrieved and the presentation performance repeated.

"Tía," said Luis, "only your ribbon is left! Who will win it?"

Then scattered applause rippled through the crowd. At the edge of the field I saw Carlos Romano mounted on a superb gray horse with markings like charcoal streaks.

The rider and his mount seemed to be a single being as they charged forward. I saw the machete slowly lifting, pointing like a sword. But at the last instant the wind fluttered the ribbon, and Don Carlos missed it by a hairsbreadth.

Although he had failed to gain the prize, the crowd had not forgotten the dramatic beauty of his charge. Shouts of "Bravo!" rang in the stands. The noise around me drowned the pounding hoofs of another horse, and I did not realize what was happening until Luis shouted, "Look! My uncle!"

Jaime Romano's great roan stallion, Yaqui, was flying past the stands, his rider crouched low. A sudden silence fell. Then, as the speeding horse neared the posts, Jaime Romano rose in the saddle, standing upright in the stirrups, lifting not a machete but a simple stick as the horse plunged on.

"He took it! He took it!" The shout was everywhere, and the band burst into *dianas*, the music of applause.

Returning slowly, Jaime held the ring high in the air, letting the ribbon float gaily in the breeze. He was not in *charro* dress, but wore whipcord trousers and a white shirt open at the throat. "No spurs," whispered Luis in awe. "He did not intend to ride today!"

Without bothering to ask the judge whose ribbon had been won, he approached Luis and me and removed his sombrero. "I return your ribbon, senorita," he said, dropping to one knee. His dark face was grave and the startling eyes, gazing into mine, were intent and serious.

"It is yours, senor," I said, awkward, unsure of myself.

"Mil gracias." He rose, lifting the ribbon and displaying it to the crowd in a strangely solemn manner. They were still cheering when he rode away.

AFTER AN ELABORATE picnic lunch, most people moved to the bullring to see men work with what Luis called "the brave herd."

"Will a bull be killed?" I asked, holding back a little.

"No, no. This is a demonstration only. And they will not be bulls," Luis explained. "Only cows are used."

"A cow fight?" It seemed ridiculous.

"A bull must never fight twice. He becomes too wise and dangerous. The cows will show the bravery of the herd today."

The black beasts I soon saw bore no resemblance to any cow I had been near in New England! Snorting, ill-tempered, and razor-horned, they pawed the ground, charging this way and that.

Don Carlos showed his skill for only a few minutes, but no more was needed to prove his ability and cool nerve. The other men had merely moved. Carlos glided, danced, spun the cape with dexterity beautiful to watch. Anticipating every move of his animal opponent, he toyed with it, working so close to the horns that I found myself gasping. Incredibly brave—or incredibly foolhardy. When he was near enough for me to see his face, it was transformed, ecstatic in the joy of battle, eyes enormous, a muscle in his cheek twitching, making the jagged scar move.

"My father is brave, no?" asked Luis.

I agreed, but studying the boy's expression, I felt he was more frightened than admiring.

Even though Don Carlos had dressed himself in the traditional "suit of lights" that flashed in the sun, he did not bother to remain long in the ring. His saunter, the tilt of his head as he left, suggested that he was above such poor competition, and he hardly acknowledged the applause. One shrill, harsh voice kept screaming, "Olé, olé!" and I glanced across the ring just as Luis said, "My great-grandmother is here, Tía."

The Excelentísima's outrageous wig and black dress were unchanged, but she had added a billowing red mantilla with sequin embroidery. "She wants me to join her," said Luis glumly, when she gestured toward him. "I will come back in a moment."

I was happy enough not to go with him, having no wish for another encounter with the Excelentísima.

Over a loudspeaker someone announced, "Magnificent brave bulls, typical of this herd! Exhibition only." Static drowned out the rest. Then the gate on the far side of the arena swung open and a huge black bull thundered into the circle, head lowered, nostrils distended as he snorted in fury. He was alone in the ring, to be seen, not fought.

Glancing toward Luis, who was listening intently to Ana Luisa, I saw Ramona standing just behind them. Smiling, I waved to her, but she shook her head and made a beckoning gesture. I made my way through the crowd and a moment later was standing beside her. "The Excelentísima," she whispered. "Listen to her, senorita."

Kneeling quietly, so neither Luis nor the old lady became aware of my presence, I heard her speaking in a tense, almost hypnotic voice: "And sometimes boys, even small ones, jump over the barrier to work with the bulls. A brave thing, no? Your father once did that when even younger than you are, Luis."

The child seemed spellbound. "Did he have a cape? A sword?"

"No, nothing! Only a woman's mantilla, red, like the one I am wearing now." She slowly removed the shawl from her shoulders and pressed it toward him.

Below in the ring, the bull, horns still lowered, paced angrily, searching for an opponent, the black tail slashing back and forth. "See, Luis! The bull is on the other side now. The barrier is not very high. Luis . . ." The Excelentísima's eyes burned with frenzy and her painted features contorted.

Just as the boy's hands touched the low railing in front of him, I seized his shoulders. "Luis! Give back the mantilla. We have to go home at once!"

For a second his expression was trancelike; then he seemed to awaken. "Yes," he murmured. "I want to go."

"Luis will remain with me! Leave at once, Senorita Mallory!" Ana Luisa seethed with fury, her great head trembling.

"Luis and I are leaving," I told her, an anger as fierce as her own blazing up in me. "I listened, I know what you were trying to do. And don't think you've heard the last of this!"

She rose to face me, fists clenched as though to strike at my face. "I will have you out of the High Valley before sunset!"

She spat then, but I did not flinch. "Come, Luis," I said, holding his arm firmly. "Your great-grandmother is ill. We must ignore her behavior."

I led him quickly away, through the whispering, murmuring people who had witnessed the scene. Behind us Ana Luisa screamed curses and imprecations, but I paid no attention. Outside, Luis, his lips quivering, said, "Tía, I did not know what to do. I was afraid of the bull."

"You should have been, Luis. I'm proud of your good sense."

Primitivo stood leaning against the jeep, waiting for passengers. "Have someone bring our horses back to the stable," I told him. "We will ride home with you."

Rain pattered lightly on the jeep as it halted at the *casa grande*. I took Luis straight to his room. There was no need for us to talk about what had happened. He knew his great-grandmother had tried to goad him into doing a dangerous thing. That he could not understand why did not matter. Luis had no ties of affection with her. Except physically, he was beyond her reach, she could not hurt him. We talked for a few minutes about the horses, about the magnificent riding of both his father and his uncle, and before long he became sleepy, ready for a nap.

THAT EVENING, RESTING in the Octagon, I heard a quick stride on the veranda. Jaime Romano knocked, then entered without waiting for me to admit him. Flinging himself into a chair, he said, "Ramona just told me what my saintly grandmother tried to do today. Thank God you were there!"

"It was horrible!" I answered. "Impossible to believe she could have said such things. Yet she did!"

"I know. She grows worse each year. And what can I do?"

"Keep Luis away from her, for one thing!"

"Luis is not my son. How far can I interfere? Yet I must do whatever is possible." He smiled ruefully. "At any moment we shall receive a royal order for your banishment."

"And what will you do?"

"I think my mother will answer any such requests. And I think she will express herself quite clearly."

Broodingly he stared at the floor, his hands clenched. "I must tell you something that is not easy for me to say. If you had been with Luis a few months ago and he had leaped into the ring, I would have thought you had caused it."

My eyes widened. "You thought I'd endanger a child? Why should you think that of me?"

"I did not know what to believe when you first came here!" Rising, he strode to the window and stood gazing into the night. "I could not understand why Senora Castro had been sent away when I was not here, or why Carlos had arranged for you to replace her. Maybe he was your lover. And if so, you might find the presence of a son by a former marriage inconvenient. Or Carlos might have brought you here to torment me with memories of Veronica."

"Memories of Veronica?" I asked.

He turned toward me, his body taut. "I have never spoken of this before. I thought I never would. Veronica and I loved each other. We did not intend that this should happen, but she was very much alone, and I—I, too, was lonely. We could not help it. Yet we felt guilty. And that is why she left. For my sake."

"She left—for you?"

"Yes. One night I told her I could endure this no longer. The High Valley is my home, but it was unbearable for me. I remember how she looked at me that night, looked at me with eyes like yours. She said she had done me a terrible wrong, she could not forgive herself for it. But this was not true! She never tried to make me love her. I told her this, but she would not listen. She said I must wait a few days before going away. So I waited through the fiesta of San Miguel. And then it was too late." He sank into the chair, his strong shoulders suddenly weak.

After a moment he continued, his voice far away, as though he spoke of events that had happened to a stranger. "I stayed on here, hoping she would return. Then my father died, and I found myself trapped, responsible for the valley."

"You didn't expect this?" I asked softly.

He shook his head. "No. The High Valley has always gone to the eldest son. But my father had not forgiven Carlos. Besides, he knew I would protect the valley, that it is in my body and my blood. How Carlos must hate him for it!"

Jaime gazed at me, his stare hard and penetrating. In the silence the clock on the bedside table ticked with unnatural loudness. "Yes, Carlos hates," he said at last. "Just as I hated him for bringing you here to replace Veronica—I thought. And I hated you for reminding me of things I had to forget. I watched you, the way you suddenly lifted your head, how you let the wind ruffle your hair. For a time I believed I was seeing Veronica again. Then, slowly, I knew I was not. It was you I watched, Alison.

"The night we danced together, I felt I was hurting Veronica, letting her memory die. And I felt in danger. It was better to be lonely than to risk suffering again. Nor could I fall in love with an illusion, as Veronica once did. When she met Carlos she had been desperate and lonely. She married an illusion—a promise of love and security she had never known."

I hesitated, then said what I had to say, dreading the answer. "You still love Veronica, don't you?"

"No. I remember her with affection. She deserves no less from me. But it is over, finished."

He was close, so close that my pulse was pounding, and I gazed into his face, longing to believe what he said, yet frightened. His hands clasped my arms. "I think I love you, Alison," he said softly. "I think it so often that I have become sure."

"Love . . . me?" My breath seemed to choke me. I knew so little of him, yet I wanted him to hold me closer, wanted to lose myself in his strength. Afraid and bewildered, I drew back.

His hands fell from my arms. "You are afraid. You do not trust me."

"No, not that. I—I'm not ready for this," I stammered. "I hadn't imagined that you felt this way." Yet, while not admitting it to myself, I must have hoped he might care for me.

He shook his head. "We must wait until you have no fear, until you are sure of me and of yourself." Reaching into his pocket, he drew forth the red ribbon I had given him that afternoon. "Senorita Alison," he said, his lips but not his eyes smiling. "I return this. One day it will again be mine. It will be your gift to me when you are ready."

Numbly I accepted the long, bright strip of grosgrain.

"I have waited long," he said. "I can wait longer." Then, leaning close to me, he whispered, "Good night now. Sleep well, *querida!*"

As he left, words from the past seemed to clamor inside me. Donald's words: "If I could see you, you'd run away, hide yourself." I could not hide from Jaime Romano. To say that I loved him would be to commit my life to Jaime, to the High Valley. I knew from the way he had spoken of Veronica that this was a man who, touched by love, would give himself completely, demanding all in return, my whole being, my whole life.

I felt my lips silently forming the words "I love you." Yet I was still unready and afraid.

CHAPTER TEN

THREE DAYS LATER the soldiers left the valley, their search unfinished, for word arrived that the kidnapped millionaire had been ransomed and released. He had been blindfolded and held captive in mountainous country, he told police and reporters.

"Why not in these mountains?" asked Don Carlos gloomily. "Perhaps in our own valley."

"Nonsense," said Leonora, no longer sounding so positive.

Such a worry was quickly forgotten in the atmosphere of new security the valley suddenly enjoyed. The sale of horses had been highly successful, and now trucks loaded with cement and steel rolled toward the construction site of the dam.

I saw little of Jaime Romano. When we met, there were always others present, and each time he gave me a quizzical smile that seemed to ask, Do you have something to say to me, Alison?

I could not help wondering if the story of himself and Veronica had ended exactly as he claimed. Could a love so fierce have changed into consuming hatred? I did not want to believe this—desperately I did not. Jaime, I was sure, was a man of profound goodness. He wore his outward gruffness like armor against a world which had made him suffer. Inconceivable that he could have harmed Veronica. Yet sometimes when I saw him riding toward the orchards, determined and proud, the doubt assailed me against my will. Could he have somehow been driven beyond control? No, I told myself. Not Jaime!

SEVERAL DAYS LATER, LEONORA called a family council to decide about Luis' schooling, and I was asked to give an opinion.

"Margaret Webber mentioned a small school in Puerto Vallarta," I said. "Luis could come home every weekend."

"Good," said Carlos. "But let him enter a few days late, after the fiesta. I remember how I was shipped away every year just before San Miguel Day. Missing the fiesta was one of the worst things about growing up."

"I recall one fiesta you didn't miss," said Leonora grimly. She turned to me. "He ran away from a school in Mexico City one year and came back for San Miguel Day. He hid in the bell tower."

"How beautiful it was!" said Carlos. "I watched the Roman candles and star showers from high in the tower. Glorious!"

"It must have been," I exclaimed, imagining the panorama of the valley illuminated by green, red, and yellow flares ablaze in the sky. "I'd love to see that."

"You know, Carlos," Leonora remarked, "I never thought the fiestas were important to you."

"Many things were important that no one thought about!" he replied with unexpected anger. His aristocratic features had never before struck me as so sharp, so hawklike. Yes, a hawk. As though some ghost conjured up by the Excelentísima had stolen into the room and taken possession of her grandson.

To DISTRACT LUIS FROM his worries about school, I planned a picnic. "A special one," I told him. "You, your grandmother, and I will go to the most beautiful place in the valley, the bank of the stream near the Hidden Treasure."

"Oh, yes! And I could find new rocks for my collection."

When I mentioned the idea to Leonora, she was enthusiastic. "That would be a real outing! What day shall it be?"

"I thought next Saturday." I hesitated, then added, "Does Luis visit the Excelentísima that day?"

"He now goes to the Villa Plata only when accompanied by his father," she said. "And Carlos is quite busy these days."

It was unnecessary for her to explain. The flat tone of her voice told everything. She knew what had happened at the bullring, and she was taking no risks. I was also sure that whatever complaints Ana Luisa had made about me, Leonora had answered.

Jaime must have learned of our plans from Luis, who was bubbling with excitement and told everyone in the house. On Friday morning, when Leonora and I were working with a page of braille, he entered the tower room. "I have come to invite myself to a picnic," he said.

"You'll go with us?" Leonora was astonished.

"Why not? I look forward to escorting two lovely ladies to such a lovely place."

Leonora laughed. "Wonderful, Jaime! Like the old days!"

Smiling with unusual gentleness, he said, "No, *Madre mía*. Better than that. *Hasta mañana*, Alison."

When he was gone, Leonora said, "I wouldn't have believed it!" She pursed her lips thoughtfully and her sightless eyes seemed to study me. Then she nodded, but made no comment.

THAT AFTERNOON I FOUND myself humming, almost singing aloud the words of a Mexican song. Tomorrow would be beautiful—a day I had planned for Luis and Leonora suddenly belonged to me. I would be with Jaime in a place that was clean and open, away from the shadows of the *casa grande*. It was like a new beginning.

Don Carlos had said he was flying to Puerto Vallarta that evening, so I wrote Margaret a note telling her to expect me in a week, that I would accompany Luis the day he enrolled in school. Outgoing mail was always left on a table in the entrance hall, and I had just placed my letter there when Ethel Evans' voice cried out at the head of the stairs, "Be careful with those things! Don't carry them by the cord, it might snap!"

Startled, I looked up to see Primitivo midway on the steps, a large paper-wrapped parcel in each hand. Miss Evans, standing above him, repeated shrilly, "Not by the cord!" Then she started forward so rapidly that Primitivo must have thought she was falling, for he reached out to help her, dropping one of the packages. I heard a crash of shattering earthenware, and rushing to it, I retrieved the parcel, which had rolled down several steps.

"No, I'll get it!" shouted Miss Evans.

But she was too late. The strings had loosened and the paper gaped open. As I lifted it, smashed fragments of a native jar fell at my feet, along with several small figures of beautifully carved ivory and ebony—an antique set of chessmen had been concealed inside the pottery.

Ethel Evans halted a few steps above me, petrified. Minutes seemed to pass before she recovered the power of speech. "I was sending to town some pottery and a little imitation ivory chess set I'd bought."

"It won't do, Miss Evans," I said quietly. Kneeling, I gathered the chessmen. "Give me the other parcel," I told Primitivo in Spanish. "Then we won't need you anymore."

We went in silence to Miss Evans' room, and her lips were a thin slashed line as I unwrapped the second package. A cheap earthen bowl, worth only a few pesos. Inside it, concealed by newspapers, I found a small book bound in calfskin, a hand-illuminated edition of the poems of Sor Juana Inés de La Cruz.

"Prove it!" she said, the sharp chin jutting out defiantly. "*You* put those things there! You or that filthy servant."

"Stop this nonsense, Miss Evans," I said sharply. "There's no difficulty at all in proving it. My only concern is for Leonora. I want to spare her as much pain as possible. Don Jaime is executor of the estate you've been robbing. I shall tell him."

"Yes, tell him! And when Leonora knows what I've found out about you, how you've behaved with both Jaime and Carlos . . ."

"Cheap lies won't work, Miss Evans. Don't bother trying them!" I strode angrily from the room, carrying the ceramic bowl with both the book and the chess set in it.

Jaime, I was told, would not return to the *casa grande* until late that night. There was nothing to do but wait until tomorrow and then talk privately with him after our picnic. Miss Evans was not going to flee the country, and I saw no point in ruining our outing. Time enough afterward. I gave the chessmen and the poems to Ramona, telling her to put them in a safe place.

A few minutes later, as I walked through the patio on my way to the Octagon, I heard the engine of Carlos Romano's plane. Pausing, I watched it disappear, not in the direction of the coast and Puerto Vallarta but inland toward Mexico City.

IN THE MORNING Ramona came to my door earlier than usual. "I have bad news, my lady," she said. "There has been an accident at the dam. Some sort of door—is it called a floodgate?—came open in the night. No one was hurt, but Don Jaime had to go there before dawn. He said he was sorry, but you must have your picnic another day."

"No one was hurt," I said. "That's the important thing."

But it did not prove to be the only important thing to Luis and Leonora.

"Why not have *two* picnics?" Luis demanded. "Our own today and another with Uncle Jaime?"

"I knew something would prevent his going," said Leonora. "We'll go without him."

I felt unsure. "He said we should go another day."

Her head inclined. "I'm quite capable of deciding what I want to do. Luis, tell the boy to saddle our horses."

Half an hour later the three of us, with a heaped basket, rode slowly toward the Hidden Treasure. I tried to put aside my disappointment that Jaime was not with us and thoughts of what I had learned about Ethel Evans. I would have the burden of this unshared knowledge longer than I had hoped.

We were less than a mile from the *casa grande* when I heard someone shouting, and looking back, I saw Ramona, mounted on a burro, frantically pursuing us. "What is it?" I asked anxiously when she was within earshot. "News from the dam?"

"No, my lady." Ramona panted from her struggle with the burro and her battle to straighten her long, full skirts that bunched around her thighs. "I came to help. See? I have brought my own tortillas." Her uneasiness gave her away. She had come, I decided, to watch over us, since no one else was available. It was sweet of her, even though unnecessary.

On such a glorious morning as this the notion of harm or danger seemed impossible. The sky was a cloudless cobalt blue, while fields and orchards, washed by the night rain, gleamed in the sun, the long, lazy leaves of pepper trees shining.

Luis began to sing, and soon Leonora joined in, then Ramona:

> *"I gave my love two apples*
> *I gave two ears of corn,*
> *I gave my love a ribbon*
> *To deck his saddle horn."*

Laughing, I touched the ribbon that tied back my own hair. Not a red one—this was black to match my sombrero and dotted shirt. A pretty ribbon, but on a saddle horn it would have been the color of mourning.

"LUIS, WHERE ARE YOU?" Leonora called sharply.

"Right here. I am inspecting rocks with my magnifying glass."

"Good. You were so quiet I thought you had gone inside the mine."

It was midafternoon now. We sat on the ground only a few yards from the dark mouth of the mine. The brook I had discovered only a few months before had turned into a foaming torrent fed by the rains.

"I love the sound of flowing water," said Leonora. "You know this stream disappeared for months the night of the cave-in. The whole north wing of the mine collapsed. It was the night Veronica—" She checked herself, conscious of Luis.

Looking down the road we'd followed, I tried to imagine that night. Everyone at the village fiesta, shouting and bells and fireworks. I pictured Veronica's small white car moving quietly in the darkness without headlights. She had not been its driver. Living or dead, Veronica had been only a helpless passenger being transported to a final place. Of that I now felt sure. The car would have rolled past the spot where we were now sitting and entered the mine. Later, rain would have washed away all trace of its tire marks. Was it still there inside the mine? Buried forever beneath tons upon tons of stone and shale?

Jaime had told me that Veronica left the High Valley for his sake. Perhaps that had been her intention, but even so, it left every question unanswered. Why did she not take Luis with her? There had been a note for Carlos; later a note for her father-in-law. But not a word to Jaime himself.

"Cave-ins are strange," Leonora mused. "The miners say you can bring down a mountain with a whistle. It's almost true. A shout, maybe just one small stone falling. Then an avalanche."

"You said the stream vanished, then came back. How? Did the village men dig in the mine?"

"No! No one was fool enough to try that. Other parts of the mine would have fallen in at the first stroke of a pickaxe. The stream found its own way out."

Luis slipped his magnifying glass into its case, put it in his pocket, and came over to us. "A rain cloud," he said, pointing to the northeastern sky.

"I suppose it's time to go home," I said. "Where's Ramona?"

"Gathering mint."

I thought I caught sight of someone moving among the willows a little more than a hundred yards away, where our horses and Ramona's burro were tethered. Luis' sharp eyes had seen the same thing, but he said in a low tone, "That is not Ramona."

"Someone from the village, then." I began to pack leftovers in the basket, covertly watching the place where I had noticed the figure concealed among the trees. Estrella, the most sensitive of the horses, suddenly whinnied and moved aside. A man in a black sombrero stepped quickly backward, vanishing behind the trunk of a tree. I had only a glimpse of him—an impression of the black hat, a red checkered shirt, and something cradled in his arms. A stick? Surely it couldn't have been a rifle!

Luis, also pretending not to watch, had noticed something else. "His neckerchief is tied around his face, Tía," he whispered. "Like a bandit's."

"What's that?" asked Leonora.

"A man is hiding near the horses," I told her quietly. "I think he has a rifle. Luis says his face is masked."

"Are you sure, Luis?" She was uneasy but not alarmed. "With all this wild talk about kidnappers, one might imagine anything."

A soft whistle came, so like the call of a cardinal that I would have mistaken it, had not Luis said, "Ramona."

I saw her then on the cliff above, kneeling behind a pinnacle of rock, hidden from any watcher in the trees. She must have climbed the far slope and circled back. She raised her hand, holding out three fingers, then pointed in the direction of the willows. When she repeated the gesture, I understood its meaning: not one man but three were lurking there. She indicated a rifle, another rifle, then put her hands to her face, showing masks. Then she slipped away—going for help, I supposed.

I reported the pantomimed conversation to Leonora, trying to keep my voice from betraying fear.

"If they mean trouble, they won't wait until Ramona gets back with men," she said flatly. "Can you and Luis scramble up the cliffs? Maybe pretend you're playing a game?"

"No. There's no way out except to go toward them."

"The mine." Luis, white-faced, struggled not to tremble. "We could hide in the mine."

Leonora rose, stretching her arms, the most careless and natural gesture possible, revealing no sign of knowledge or alarm to the watchers. But the faint breeze freshened, a gust of wind swept through the willow fronds. Three men stood there, and when I saw the blue uniform coats two of them wore, my heart hammered. Two uniforms, one red checkered shirt. Exactly as Captain Montez had described the kidnappers of Don Santos.

They knew I had seen them, there could be no more pretending. As they stepped boldly from cover, I saw a glint of sun on a buckle worn on a dark hat. It flashed through my mind that I had encountered this man before. He had followed me in Puerto Vallarta, and I had called him Black Sombrero.

I heard the sharp crack of his rifle, then the whine of a bullet as it hit the granite cliff inches from Luis and ricocheted, plowing into the ground near my feet.

"Grandmother!" Luis screamed. "Run!"

He seized Leonora's hand, and she stumbled after him into the yawning entrance of the mine. As I raced to follow them, splinters struck my cheek when another bullet hit the wooden post of the entry. Dimly I saw Luis and Leonora just ahead of me, and in a few steps I caught up with them. Before we plunged into the utter darkness beyond, I glanced back and saw three figures silhouetted against the flooding light of the entrance.

"Slowly," Leonora whispered. She was the leader now, and as we inched along, her fingers read the walls like braille.

A guttural voice shouted in Spanish, "Halt or we'll fire!" And a hundred echoes cried, "Fire . . . fire . . . fire. . . ."

"Low, narrow door near us." Leonora spoke no louder than breathing. "Somewhere . . . yes."

Stooping low, we moved through an arch, framed, my fingers told me, with blocks of cut stone. Once inside the next passage, she said, "Now we wait." And pray, I thought.

Another shouted threat rang through the darkness—nearer, I believed— and the echoes answered. Then rifle shots, ringing in every direction, multiplied as they resounded in the stony hollowness of the mountain. "The fools!" whispered Leonora. "They'll bring the roof down on themselves!"

And on us? I felt Luis shudder, and I held him close to me.

Now heavy, confident steps rang in a nearby corridor. A flashlight, I thought desperately. One of the men carried a flashlight. Only a matter of time and they would find us. A few minutes more. And then what? These men were not ordinary kidnappers. The shots fired first at Luis, then at me, had been meant not to frighten but to kill.

"Halt!" a man yelled. "I see you!"

He must have fired then at some shadow, for the echoes were farther away. But before they died another sound had begun, a low, grinding rumble like faraway thunder. Slowly it grew, increased, became a deafening roar. The men searching for us screamed, then the screams were blotted out by the avalanche.

The rock wall trembled against my back and I choked on dust as Luis clung to me. The floor shook, and beyond the narrow door of our refuge iron girders shrieked as they were twisted and crushed. Then the crashing slowly died away. "Don't move," whispered Leonora. "Don't speak!"

An eternity seemed to pass while we waited, silent and motionless, terrified that the least sound might bring the ceilings above us tumbling down. At last she said, "I think we're as safe as we will be. We'll try to go back."

"The men!" said Luis. "The men with rifles!"

"I don't think they can hurt us now, dear," she said gently.

Fumbling in my pocket, I found the key ring with its tiny light. When I pressed the switch, I gasped to see the figure of a woman in white standing near us, her arms outstretched.

"The Blessed Virgin," Luis murmured. Leonora had led us to a small chapel built long ago by the men who labored and often perished in these tunnels. Here a vaulted roof was mortared and braced with hand-hewn pillars of stone.

"I'll go first," I said. "I can see a little with this light. You two hold hands and follow me."

Outside the low door, the corridor lay strewn with rubble. We moved cautiously ahead; then, when we reached the main entrance passage, I gasped to see huge blocks of stone sealing the tunnel.

"Closed off, I suppose?" Leonora spoke wearily. She had expected this. "Any opening at all?"

"None." I forced despair out of my tone.

"Ramona will bring help," said Luis, making a show of confidence. "She wouldn't let anything happen to us."

"Of course not," Leonora agreed. "But we'd better not wait for Ramona. Do you hear the water? We'll find a drier place."

Listening, I caught a faint, gurgling sound of the stream. Leonora then spoke to me in rapid English, so fast that Luis could not understand. "This passage must have collapsed all the way to the entrance. The stream's blocked. It'll flood in a few minutes. We have to go on!"

"Speak Spanish, Abuela!" Luis cried out, his taut nerves breaking at last. "Please speak Spanish!"

As if in answer, a faraway voice shouted, "José? Juan? *Dónde están, por Dios?*"

I switched off the flashlight and the three of us waited, hardly breathing. Farther down the main tunnel a strong white beam appeared, moving slowly. I could not distinguish anything about the approaching man until he lowered his flashlight, and a second later a match flared as he lighted a cigarette.

"It is one of them," I whispered to Leonora. I did not tell her Black Sombrero still carried a rifle. He must have been deep enough in the mine, searching for us, to have escaped the avalanche.

There was a sudden rushing of water as somewhere nearby a hidden pool overflowed. Using the noise to conceal our stumbling footsteps, we made our way slowly, deeper into the mountain, turning and circling, winding through an endless maze of corridors and galleries, where the air was dank and water dripped from the ceilings. I tried to keep the tiny flashlight shielded, but we were forced to use it, even though its faint ray might guide Black Sombrero to us.

"Do these corridors connect?" I asked Leonora softly.

"Yes. They crisscross everywhere."

"Then we might meet him," whispered Luis. "He might even be ahead of us."

Ahead—behind us—moving swiftly through a parallel passage, his way speeded by the powerful light he carried. Against this we posed the small advantage that Leonora had once known the mine well. A map of the Hidden Treasure seemed to be implanted in her mind.

Passing through a narrow entrance, we came into a vast, cavernous gallery whose broken floor was strewn with split boulders and rubble. There was a sudden fluttering, swishing sound in the air above us, and when I shone the beam upward, Luis stifled a cry of terror. Bats swarmed against the ceiling. Aroused by the light or the sound of our steps, they swirled in clouds, hundreds upon hundreds, swooping and flapping across the ray of light.

"Keep going, Alison," said Leonora quietly. "Hurry. Straight ahead. Cave bats, Luis. Don't be afraid."

Shuddering, I pressed on as quickly as I dared. Then Luis let go of my hand and, crying out, struck this way and that, flailing his arms, trying to ward off the creatures skimming around him in the darkness. "Give me your hand!" I said sharply. "Luis!"

Moments later I heard wild shouts and rifle shots. Black Sombrero had trailed us to the bat-infested gallery. But how? We had passed a dozen intersecting passages, yet he had known our route. Then I realized our muddy footprints marked the way clearly.

"Leonora," I said. "We're leaving a trail. Footprints."

"Oh, Lord," she breathed. "I didn't think of that." She hesitated only a second. "Then we'll have to detour. Watch for a corridor to the left, one that slopes down."

A moment later I found it, and as we descended the slope, clinging together, the roar of an underground torrent raged nearby. Then cold brown water swirled around our ankles. We turned twice, staying always in flooded passages, shivering, and I thanked God for Leonora, who kept saying, "Only a little farther. Only a little way . . ."

IT WAS PERHAPS an hour later when we halted for rest. I had suffered the only serious mishap so far, losing my footing at a slippery spot and falling into a shallow but icy pool. Now, soaked to the skin, my teeth chattered and I trembled with cold.

The corridor we were now in was broad and dry. Luis curled up on the floor while Leonora and I sat near him. I turned off the flashlight, whose beam was becoming weaker and weaker.

In a few minutes, as soon as Luis' regular breathing revealed he was sleeping, I asked, "Where are we going?"

"Toward an old air shaft, I hope. *If* I've remembered the way, *if* it's still there. Alison, I'm going to describe the way to get there, as well as I can remember it. I want you to memorize the directions."

"Why? If you know the way?"

"I hope we've lost the man who was following us, but there's no counting on it. If he finds us, we part company. You take Luis and follow the way to the air shaft. I'll turn another way and shout and make enough noise to draw him away."

"Leave you behind?" I exclaimed. "I couldn't do that."

"That is exactly what I am ordering you to do, Alison! I don't matter. Luis must survive, not just for his own sake but for the valley. Three hundred families live in the village. Their future depends on the ranch. I don't trust that future to Carlos."

"To Carlos? I don't understand."

"If anything happened to Luis, his father would inherit the High Valley. There are no other heirs. I know Carlos very well. In a year the ranch would be bankrupt. He'd sell it piece by piece to live in Mexico City or Madrid or Paris. What about the people who were born here—as their fathers and grandfathers were? This is their land, too."

A monstrous notion crossed my mind. Don Carlos had everything to gain if one of Luis' accidents proved fatal. Surely no man could be so cruel and unnatural as to destroy his own son! I could picture the Excelentísima, Medea-like, acting in cold blood. But she was a madwoman.

"Tell me about the men hiding in the willows," said Leonora. "How were they dressed?"

"Two wore uniforms. They were exactly as Captain Montez described the kidnappers."

"Strange, isn't it?" she murmured thoughtfully. "Here in the valley, uniforms would attract attention."

"Leonora, I saw the third man, the one not in uniform, before. He followed me in Puerto Vallarta."

"Are you certain?"

"Yes." An alarming certainty formed like ice in my mind. I had known from the closeness of the shots outside the mine that these were not usual kidnappers. Now another fact was added. These men had *wanted* to be identified by distinctive clothing, had *wanted* to be connected with the abduction of the millionaire. These were not kidnappers at all, but hired gunmen such as Padre Olivera had mentioned, paid killers of the sort Carlos' attorney had practically boasted of knowing.

Leonora carefully explained the route to the air shaft, then said, "Now wake up Luis, Alison. We have to go on."

MURKY, LABYRINTHINE PASSAGES wound on and on, as gradually my flashlight began to waver and fade. Twice we found ourselves at dead ends, and painfully retraced our steps, always listening, straining to hear the man who stalked us.

Then Leonora, with quiet excitement, said, "Air! I can smell fresh air! I can feel it!"

At the same instant Luis whispered, "A light. I see light."

Ahead of us in the blackness was a faint, ghostly luminescence—dim moonlight shining through an opening in the rock above. Stumbling over shale heaps and for a moment too joyful to be silent, we made our way to the shaft. As I stepped into the pale radiance, my heart hammered and my head spun giddily with relief.

Then, as I gazed upward, despair overcame me. The shaft was broad, more than a dozen feet across, and even in the dimness I knew the walls were smooth and slick as wet marble. The remains of an old ladder, broken and rotted, lay in pieces at my feet.

"Where are we?" I asked Leonora.

"Far up the valley. It's an out-of-the-way place, but someone in the village must remember this opening. They'll come for us."

Luis soon slept again while Leonora and I kept watch. "He has to come through this safely," she said. "He's had too much tragedy. Life has been cruel to Luis."

"I know. Leonora, how could his mother have deserted him?"

"I've lain awake nights wondering. I think something happened to her soon after she left here. A fatal accident and no one identified the body, maybe. Or"—Leonora hesitated—"she might have taken her own life. The note she mailed to my husband almost suggested it. She told him it was better that he forget her and smile than remember her with sadness."

"Did she write the same kind of note to Carlos?"

"No. It was an unforgiving note, and in both of them, words and even sentences were scratched out. I think she wrote it under terrible strain. There were more mistakes in Spanish than she usually made. She said, *'Tengo que estar absolutamente sóla, si voy a me entender . . .'*"

As she went on quoting the Spanish words, I translated them in my mind. Veronica had told Carlos that she must be absolutely alone if she was going to understand herself. She said she could not stay with him any longer and was leaving immediately.

"Carlos hasn't been very fortunate in his marriages, and it's probably his own fault," Leonora said. "Veronica. Before that, Fani."

"Fani? Was that his first wife's name?"

"Yes. That's the nickname for Epifania. I felt sorry for her. Childless marriages are usually unhappy here. There's so much social pressure."

"Epifania," I repeated. "What became of her later?" Even before Leonora replied, I guessed the answer.

"I heard she remarried. A German in Mexico City." A moment later Leonora sank into a fitful sleep.

I sat staring upward through the long shaft at the cloudy stars, thoughts racing in my mind, as I remembered the first day I met Carlos Romano. The party Margaret's friends had given and Carlos halting at the head of the steps, then turning back, avoiding a meeting with someone. Epifania Heiden, now wife of a German businessman in Mexico City. Carlos' wife long ago. He had wanted no connection to be made between them. But why? And suddenly I knew the answer.

CHAPTER ELEVEN

"WHAT TIME IS IT?" Leonora whispered the question.

"Just after eleven." My throat and my head throbbed, my voice was nearly gone. The effects of my falling in the pool of icy water had now shown themselves. During the night I had alternately felt myself burning and freezing.

For hours, ever since dawn, we had stared at that taunting patch of sky, an empty, bright symbol of unattainable freedom. And each hour that passed gave more time for the hunter in the black sombrero to find his way through the maze of passages.

"I dreamed they were ringing the alarm bell in the tower," said Luis faintly. "I dreamed everyone came to find us."

"If we had some matches, we could build a fire," Leonora said. "Someone might see the smoke."

Matches, I thought numbly. Fire. There was the wood of the broken ladder, pieces of fallen shoring. I looked up where the globe of the sun had reached the rim of the shaft, and then turned to Luis. "Do you have your magnifying glass?" Even whispering was painful.

"Yes, Tía." He drew it from his pocket.

"We'll gather wood. I'll show you how to start a fire."

In a moment we had collected the driest splinters we could find and placed them in a pile. I managed to show Luis how to hold the glass to catch the sun's rays and focus them into a sharp, hot beam. There was so little time. The direct sun would shine into the shaft only for minutes.

Luis said, "Look! A little smoke. It's starting."

No longer able to help, I watched dully, my breath coming heavily. I lay back, letting my eyes close, and a fevered dream took possession of me. I sat on the prompter's stool in the wings of the Old Bridge playhouse. Helene, in a dress of maroon velvet, stood onstage only a few steps from me, bathed in the spotlights. She spoke, but I could hear no words. Her slender figure shimmered, then the features dissolved, changed, and Veronica stood in her place, uttering the same lines, but still soundlessly.

"Tía, Tía! Wake up!" Luis was shaking my shoulder. When I forced my eyes open, I saw he was smiling.

"Has Jaime come?" I asked, the words forming themselves painfully.

"Not Uncle Jaime. An old man who saw the smoke. He has gone to bring help."

I sank once more into a half-conscious state and lost all sense of time. Then I heard voices, felt strong hands lifting me from the ground. My eyes opened and I found myself gazing into Jaime's face. He carried me in his arms, gently, as easily as if I had been a child. When I tried to speak, he said, "Hush, *querida*. You are safe now."

I knew there was something terribly important I must do, and I knew tears ran down my cheeks. "Jaime," I whispered. "I want . . . I . . . ."

"What do you want, little one?"

"To give you . . ." Weakly I struggled to loosen the ribbon that bound my hair, and he held me closer.

I knew daylight and I knew when darkness came. I knew I lay in my own bed in the Octagon, and the nightmare of Veronica dressed in Helene's costume returned often. Once, half awakened, I realized that Jaime was sitting quietly beside my bed, and at other times there was a strange man, who I thought must be a doctor.

My first real awakening, after the fever and delirium had passed, came suddenly. Explosions and gunfire penetrated my sleep, and I sat up quickly in bed and said aloud, "What is it? What's happening?"

"You are awake, senorita?" said a soft voice. "You called?" Marcos had entered from the hall and stood near me.

"I heard explosions. There—again."

"It is fireworks in the village, senorita. This is the night of San Miguel."

"San Miguel? Then I have slept . . ."

"Two days and two nights. You were very ill. Don Jaime brought a doctor from Puerto Vallarta. He said you would be well as soon as the fever ended. And it has ended, no?"

"I think so." My voice was hoarse, I felt weak and tired, but my throat no longer pained me, and for the first time my mind was clear of ghosts and delirium. Marcos switched on a lamp on the bedside table.

"Where is Don Jaime?" I asked. "I want to speak with him."

"Everyone is at the fiesta. He wanted to stay with you, but is expected at the church. The *patrón* must attend the celebration and the Mass. All people from the *casa grande* are there except Doña Leonora, who is in her room sleeping. Shall I awaken her?"

"No. What I must say is for Don Jaime." A chilling memory swept through me. "Marcos, what of the man who pursued us in the mine?"

"Forget him, senorita. The shaft was guarded until last night, when another avalanche closed it forever. No one who was in the mine could have survived."

He indicated a saucer with four red capsules. "If you are sleepless, the doctor left these for you. Take only one. We will watch over you until Don Jaime returns. I am just outside the door if you call."

He started to leave, then turned back, his smile now mischievous. "Don Jaime asked me to tell you two things if you awakened. He now has the correct ribbon, the red one, and it decorates his saddle tonight. Also, please do not worry about anything taken from your doll's house." When I looked puzzled, he said, "In your fever they say you kept repeating in English that something was taken from the doll's house. Don Jaime said you must have dreamed you were a little girl again. Whatever has been taken, he promises to replace. Rest well, senorita."

Apparently during my fever I had spoken my dream aloud—shouted it, perhaps. No one had understood what I was trying to say. To the people in the High Valley, a doll's house was a toy, not the name of a drama by Henrik Ibsen, the story of a wife who leaves her husband. I rose from the bed, a little dizzy. Moving slowly, I went to the closet and found my warm robe and slippers.

A familiar book had been removed from the bookcase—*Six Plays by Henrik Ibsen*. I remembered seeing it there only a week before. Yet I did not really need to examine *A Doll's House* again. Now that my memory had been stirred, the lines of Nora, the wife, came back to me as clearly as if I could again hear Helene speaking them as she swept across the stage.

"I must stand quite alone if I am to understand myself and everything about me. It is for that reason that I cannot remain with you any longer. . . . I am going away from here now, at once. . . ."

These were the words of one of the plays Veronica had struggled to translate into Spanish. For she had never written a letter of farewell to Don Carlos. The note that disguised her real fate had been nothing more than one of the scores of translations she had done, bits of poetry, speeches from Shakespeare, and for Jaime a famous sonnet. Leonora had said that words and phrases had been scratched out of the letter. Of course. Things in Nora's scene with her husband that did not quite fit—replies, names—would be obliterated.

I thought of the note the Conde Victor later received from Mexico City—a message about forgetting her. Some poem I could not quite remember, but it, too, was surely a stolen exercise.

How simple it had been! How easy! Veronica had handwritten passages to apply to almost anything, and there was little chance anyone would identify the original. Veronica was not a very accurate or inspired translator, and no one here, not even Leonora, knew literature in English. Spanish would have been another matter. Jaime and probably his father would instantly have recognized a passage from *Don Quixote* or *One Hundred Years of Solitude*—

"The fire!" I said aloud. We had talked about that novel, even mentioned the character who, like Eric Vanderlyn's father, had invented a powerful burning glass. Luis' tiny magnifying glass had set wood aflame in only a few minutes in the cave. I pictured the device Eric's father had built, with its double lenses and powerful reflectors, standing on the balcony of Don Carlos' apartment, harmless-looking, probably mistaken for a telescope if anyone happened to notice it. Its beam did not have to ignite wood, but dry, almost explosive straw in the nearby barn.

I could not bear to think about it longer. I needed rest now, sleep, until Jaime returned after the midnight Mass. Then I would tell him all I knew, rid myself of this burden.

Lying down, I covered myself with the sheet. As I reached to turn off the lamp, my hand brushed the saucer of sleeping pills and two of them rolled across the table, falling to the floor. I felt too weary to pick them up. Drifting into sleep, I heard Marcos speaking softly to someone in the hall outside. He had said, "We will watch over you." I supposed he meant himself and Ramona, and felt grateful and secure knowing they were nearby.

THE FAR-OFF CLANGING of village church bells awakened me again. I lay still, refreshed and much stronger. Lights burned cheerfully in the sitting room. I heard footsteps beyond the colonnaded partition, and was about to call to Ramona when a pacing figure crossed the archway. It was not

Ramona—it was Ethel Evans. I stifled a gasp. How could they have left me with her? Surely they knew . . .

But they did *not* know. There had been no chance to talk with Jaime, and I had deliberately not spoken to Leonora about her old acquaintance. If Miss Evans volunteered to miss the fiesta to keep watch with Marcos, it would seem an act of kindness. I quietly put on my slippers and stood beside the bed, apprehensive.

A heavier step sounded on the veranda, a man passed my closed draperies, then entered the sitting room.

"You're here at last!" exclaimed Miss Evans, tense and whispery.

"I was delayed. It does not matter."

My heart seemed to stop beating. Carlos Romano had returned.

"She is still sleeping?" he asked.

"Yes. Even the bells didn't awaken her. I counted the capsules. She'd taken two."

"So much the better. If she is groggy it will be easier to—"

"I don't want to know!" Ethel Evans verged on hysteria.

"Naturally," he said, soothing her. "You were kind enough to forgo the fiesta for Miss Mallory's sake. Now you are afraid of falling asleep, so you will go to the kitchen to make a cup of tea. When you return, you sit in this chair and read a magazine. There is no reason to look in on Miss Mallory. You know she is sleeping peacefully." Then the gentle, persuasive tone shifted to a threat. "You understand? You will make no mistakes!"

"I understand," she answered weakly.

"I think you know that a Mexican prison is a most uncomfortable place for such a lady as yourself."

"You're a fine one to talk!" Her attempt to sound defiant gave way to trembling. "I've never touched anything really valuable. I kept still about the necklace when I knew you'd changed the stones."

So the emeralds had been substituted, and later, when threatened with discovery, Carlos had carried the imitations to Mexico City. Not to sell—there was no need for that. Luis, according to the plan, would not survive to have an education. And who would question the records of the new master of the High Valley?

"Now go to the kitchen," he said. "Hot tea will cheer you up."

I heard the sound of the veranda window opening, then closing. For a moment I stood paralyzed, unable to stir. Surely Don Carlos did not know that Marcos was just outside. The boy's strength was no match for Carlos, but Marcos would be a witness. His presence alone would prevent Carlos from harming me.

I had to be nearer the hall door when I faced him, nearer Marcos and safety. Rubbing my eyes as though I had only that moment awakened, I moved to the archway, calling sleepily, "Hello? Is someone here?"

We almost collided. "Don Carlos! I thought I heard someone."

"You are awake, Alison. Good!" He stepped aside to let me pass. "I hope you are feeling better?"

"Much. I'm practically myself again." I forced myself to meet his eyes, and managed a smile. He was dressed in dark leather and wore black riding gloves, which, with a pistol strapped to his hip, gave him the appearance of an executioner.

"I have a message from Doña Leonora," he said. "She would like you to join the family for a special celebration after the Mass."

"How thoughtful of her," I murmured. "But I thought she was still here, sleeping."

"She felt better after a rest and went to the village." He had lied so successfully and so often that now he felt anything he said, no matter how preposterous, would be believed.

"She wants me to come to the village?"

"No. We gather each year at the bell tower. The bells are blessed by Padre Olivera. You will find it interesting."

The bell tower. I thought of those steep, winding stairs spiraling floor after floor. The bell tower at night—deserted, isolated.

"You're trembling," he said. "A chill?"

"Yes. I don't think I'm able to go out. Please tell Leonora." I moved nearer the door.

He stepped toward me, his face darkening. "We cannot disappoint her."

"Very well, then. But I must tell Marcos." Whirling, I flung open the door, then gasped. Marcos lay on a straw mat, sleeping heavily, a half-empty bottle of tequila beside him.

As I knelt to shake him, a powerful hand gripped my shoulder. "No, senorita. He will not awaken for hours. Earlier he accepted a small drink from Nacho. Why not? It is the night of the fiesta."

Drugged, I thought. Tomorrow no one would believe Marcos' protests. The bottle, the odor of tequila spilled on the mat, would tell against him.

Carlos pulled me to my feet. "We waste time, Alison."

Time . . . if only I could delay him. How long did the High Mass go on? An hour? "I'll change to something warmer," I said.

"No need. Your robe is warm enough. And do not worry about its informality. This will be a very small, intimate gathering." He was toying with me now, mocking me. Taking my arm, he propelled me toward the veranda. "We can walk there in a few minutes. The moonlight is lovely. Perfect for a stroll. You will enjoy it."

How had he discovered what I knew? I wondered dully. Then I remembered the words I had repeated over and over in my delirium: *"Taken from a doll's house."* Even Marcos had learned of it. But Carlos was the only one who would understand the meaning. He was mad—the madness so apparent in the Excelentísima lay concealed in her grandson. It was useless to attempt flight. I knew how easily he could overtake me. There had to be a way—some way.

Stopping abruptly, I looked up at him. "You still have a chance, you know," I said as calmly as I could. "Everyone's at the fiesta. With your plane you could be in South America before anyone can prove what you've done." The words came too rapidly, too jerkily, but I raced ahead, improvising frantically. "It may take weeks for Margaret Webber to get answers from the attorneys who are checking the records of Luis' birth."

"What do you mean, Alison?" He leaned close to me.

"It was so obvious to Margaret and me after we spoke to Mrs. Heiden. Your father believed you divorced her because she gave you no children. Now she has two fine sons. So the lack was yours, not hers, wasn't it? I suppose it all happened because of the plague that swept through the valley at the time you were born. A terrible, tragic thing for you as well as for Nacho."

"Go on, Alison," he said, his eyes narrow.

I knew I had hit upon the truth, but had touched a matter so dangerous I could not pursue it. Something else, I thought desperately, another tactic. "Eric Vanderlyn and I talked about the fire," I said quickly. "We were quite sure how it started, but couldn't believe the truth, because we still thought Luis was your son. But he isn't, of course. Veronica's child, yes. Not yours. Soon everyone will know."

"How will they know, Alison?" He rested his hand on my shoulder, gently this time but too near my throat.

"Margaret's attorney will find out." Silently I prayed for strength not to panic. "When you wrote that you had a wife and a baby boy, everyone here accepted it. You *had* to have a son. That was the only reason your father welcomed you back. Veronica joined in the pretense. She must have loved you very much, or else Jaime is right and she was desperate for security for herself and her baby."

He frowned, uncertain for the first time. "So you've talked with Jaime, too?" he asked.

"Of course. And with Padre Olivera. He thinks Veronica felt guilty because she helped deceive your father. She really cheated Jaime of his inheritance and was going to confess it. You couldn't let that happen. So you had to get rid of her."

"You interest me, Alison, but we must not be late for the celebration," he said. "We can talk on the way. Come, now. Arm in arm. More friendly, no?"

In the brilliance of the moon, the lane stretched deserted. Had it been this way when Veronica . . . ? I didn't dare let myself finish the thought.

"You are a very imaginative woman, Alison," he said. "I misjudged you when we met. I thought you were a rather stupid girl—shy, easy for me to manage. A great improvement over Senora Castro. That's why I hired you. I thought it best that I myself make the selection." He laughed, a dry, mirthless chuckle. "I could not have done worse."

The bell tower loomed ahead of us, tall and stark against the sky. I felt my throat constricting with fear.

"You're intelligent enough to know when the game is over," I said. "No one can prove any serious crime yet. Fraud, of course. Miss Evans is bound to talk about the theft of the emeralds. But no one can prove that you"—I forced out the words—"that you killed Veronica." His grip on my arm tightened. "Why not get away now?"

"You are the one who fails to know when the game ends," he said sharply. "The Senora Webber has contacted no attorney. I have had a man watching her."

"Yes, she's been aware of that. The man in the black sombrero. One of the three you hired to ambush us on our picnic. Did you arrange the accident at the dam to make sure Jaime wouldn't be with us?" I asked without thinking, although I knew I must not put questions to him, that I must pretend I had learned everything and told others of it. We were approaching the tower now. I had two, three minutes more. What had he planned for me? Another accident? That I had wandered out, delirious with fever, climbed the steps of the bell tower, and fallen? I stifled a gasp as I remembered the day when we had talked about seeing the fireworks from the bell tower. "How beautiful!" I'd said. "I'd love to see that." Carlos had heard me; so had Jaime and Leonora. I had innocently provided evidence to cover up my own murder! I was not sure anyone would believe the story of another accident—but what would that matter? Carlos, in his madness, must now feel that my death in the bell tower would be accepted just as Veronica's disappearance had been.

"You are lagging!" He jerked me forward. "Senora Webber knows nothing. I have opened and read every letter you have exchanged. Useless lies, Alison. You condemned yourself the night Dr. Hardy and his sister came to the house."

"At the séance?" I asked. "When I spelled Veronica's name to test you? Others saw your reaction, you know."

His lips twisted in something like a smile. "You understand nothing! What do I care for such nonsense as spirits talking through boards? But what you told Dr. Hardy that night made me realize I had to get rid of you, one way or another."

"Dr. Hardy?"

"The daughter of an actress, who helped her mother learn by heart the plays of Ibsen! In time someone would tell you the words of Veronica's letter, and you would recognize them. I had to act, and I did. It was simple to arrange your fall on the stairs. I will destroy whatever stands between me and what is rightfully mine!"

I made myself look into the insane eyes, the features contorted by a terrifying madness. "A child! A helpless child!" The words choked me.

"What is this child to me? The spawn of a half-breed torero who died on the horns in Buenos Aires. His son—not mine! And the child of a stupid, passionless woman who aroused contempt in me. I used her as I needed, and the fool thought I loved her. Then she tried to defy me. But the valley is mine! Mine! And I will win it back as the first Romanos did— not by weakness but by blood."

His eyes blazed and the steel fingers bit into my arms as I clenched my teeth, holding back a cry of pain. For a moment his breath came heavily, in gasps, then he was in control of himself again. I struggled against him, but he held me easily with one arm, while his other hand moved suddenly to his side and drew the pistol from its holster. "You will walk ahead quietly."

Now we were on the path to the door of the tower. He no longer bothered to hold me, and I stumbled a few steps ahead of him, knowing the pistol was trained on my back. The door stood agape, as though awaiting me. Just as I reached the threshold, it flashed through my mind that Carlos would not fire the pistol. Maddened though he might be, my fate was to appear accidental. Lunging forward, I slammed the door behind me, searching frantically for a bolt or bar. Finding none, I threw my body against the door, trying to hold it shut against the relentless pressure of his strength.

Moonlight streamed through the windows above. I saw the stairs clearly, and spurred by terror, I let the door give way and darted toward the steps, panting, choking for breath as I climbed wildly on. I heard him following me, slowly, inexorably. For him there was no hurry. For me, no escape except to throw myself from the high windows.

The plank Luis had once crossed gleamed in the dimness. I did not hesitate, did not pause to consider whether it would bear my weight, but fled across it, feeling it buckle beneath my feet. Then I was on the other side, the top of the tower, the end of all retreat. Far below, Don Carlos followed without haste.

Kneeling, I tore at the plank. If I could pull it loose, send it crashing down . . . Splinters pierced my fingers, but the heavy nails held fast. Only a moment left now, as I reached above my head and pushed the huge bell that hung from the highest beam, the alarm bell. It swung only a little, and summoning all my strength, I tried once more. The bell moved. A long, tolling note rang through the tower, across the fields and orchards. Then a second stroke, deafening, a booming voice in the night.

Cursing, Don Carlos charged forward, up the last flight of stairs, as I threw my weight against the bell once more, and it responded, telling the village, the *casa grande*, the vast valley that there was danger and that someone was in the tower.

Carlos loomed before me, a dark silhouette against the arches. He had to stop me. Perhaps he, like Luis, had crossed this same plank a hundred times in childhood, for now, with no thought except reaching me, he rushed forward. A sudden cracking of wood, sharp and loud as a rifle report, then a long scream that ebbed in the darkness as he plummeted through empty space, his fall unbroken until he struck the floor at the foot of the stairs.

I sank to my knees, sobbing, holding my head in my hands, weeping for myself, for Veronica—and for the demented man whose body lay far below. At last able to stand, I staggered to the window that overlooked the road, clinging to its bars, waiting.

I heard hoofbeats approaching at a gallop, saw a cloud of dust in the road, and a moment later Jaime and three other riders reined their horses at the tower.

"Who's there? What is it?" he shouted.

"Jaime!" I called. "Jaime, I'm here!"

"Alison?" He swung from the horse and ran toward the tower door. I did not let go the bars, did not look down into the darkness when I heard him exclaim, "Carlos! *Madre de Dios!*" He was on the stairs now. "Alison! Are you all right?"

"I am . . . all right."

I could not turn from the window. I stood still, my eyes moving from the panorama of the High Valley to the courtyard of the tower where Yaqui awaited his master, a long red ribbon fluttering from his saddle horn.

Jaime was shouting to the men below. "*Una reata!* Or cut the bell rope. I must cross!"

I could not understand their answers or the sounds behind me. I understood nothing until I felt Jaime lifting me gently to my feet, holding me close in his arms. "*Querida!*" he whispered. "Thank God. Oh, thank God!"

"He is gone, Jaime. No more fear, no more shadows." I looked into his face, gentle, caring. "I love you."

"We love each other. We will go away, we will forget this. Then we will come home."

I clung to him, drawing strength from his strength, love from his love, knowing that I would not again hide myself, not run away, and that home was where Jaime was.

Thunder Heights

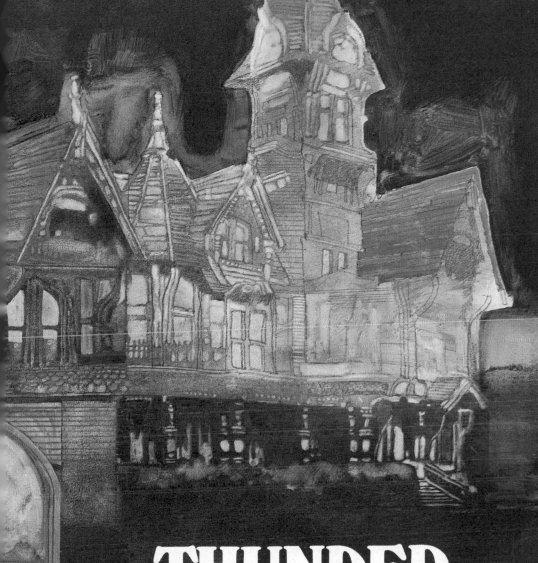

THUNDER HEIGHTS

A CONDENSATION OF THE NOVEL BY

Phyllis A. Whitney

ILLUSTRATED BY JIM CAMPBELL

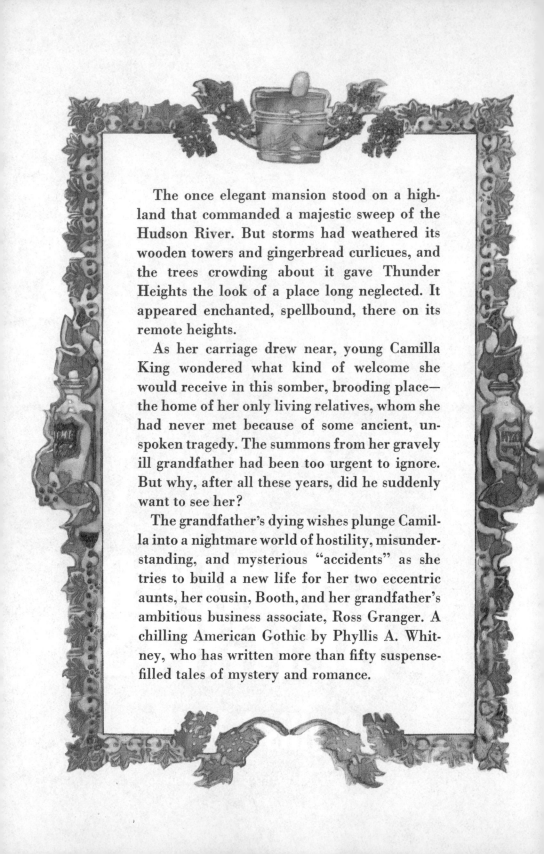

The once elegant mansion stood on a highland that commanded a majestic sweep of the Hudson River. But storms had weathered its wooden towers and gingerbread curlicues, and the trees crowding about it gave Thunder Heights the look of a place long neglected. It appeared enchanted, spellbound, there on its remote heights.

As her carriage drew near, young Camilla King wondered what kind of welcome she would receive in this somber, brooding place—the home of her only living relatives, whom she had never met because of some ancient, unspoken tragedy. The summons from her gravely ill grandfather had been too urgent to ignore. But why, after all these years, did he suddenly want to see her?

The grandfather's dying wishes plunge Camilla into a nightmare world of hostility, misunderstanding, and mysterious "accidents" as she tries to build a new life for her two eccentric aunts, her cousin, Booth, and her grandfather's ambitious business associate, Ross Granger. A chilling American Gothic by Phyllis A. Whitney, who has written more than fifty suspense-filled tales of mystery and romance.

CHAPTER ONE

CAMILLA KING STOOD at the window of her small third-floor room overlooking Gramercy Park and watched the last windy day of March blow itself out through the streets of New York. A gusty breeze rumpled treetops in the park, tossed the mane of a horse drawing a hackney cab along Twenty-first Street, and sent an unguarded bowler hat tumbling across the sidewalk.

Ordinarily she loved wind and storm. But how bleak and discouraging everything could look on a gray day in New York. The sky was as gray and as overcast as her life seemed at this moment.

Behind her in the little room Nettie was packing Camilla's trunk. This was a labor of love. A departing governess had no business using up the parlormaid's time. But the Hodgeses had gone out and there was no one about to complain.

"You'll find a better place than this, Miss Camilla," Nettie said tearfully. "You being so pretty and clever and all."

Camilla smiled wryly without turning. "And with such an outspoken way about me that it has lost me my second position? But I was thinking of the children. They're darlings and I had to speak up against their father's harshness. Mr. Hodges said I was too easy with them and perhaps he should employ an older woman as governess."

"Never you mind," Nettie said. "It's a good husband you need, Miss Camilla, and babes of your own."

Again Camilla smiled, but did not answer. Sometimes she lingered all too readily over such thoughts. But on a gray day like this, when she had just lost a position she needed badly, despair seemed ready to seize her if she let down her guard for a moment.

From the window she saw that the hackney cab she had noticed earlier was stopping before the Hodgeses' door. A man got out, holding his hat against a sudden gust.

"Someone's coming up the steps, Nettie," Camilla said.

Nettie hurried for the stairs and Camilla stayed at the window, trying not to droop with dejection. If she was pretty and clever, as Nettie said, it was of no advantage. What good did it do when it brought too easy an interest from men who could never matter to her? At the place before this, the man of the house had been altogether too kind, and had wanted to be kinder. Camilla had spoken her mind and left precipitately.

Was she pretty? she wondered absently. She put a hand to the dark, glossy waves of hair drawn loosely into a coil at the top of her head and puffed at the sides in the style of this last decade of the century. Her pink-striped shirtwaist and her gored gray skirt fitted a well-proportioned figure. And she supposed that wide brown eyes were a good feature. But what did it matter? At twenty-three she lived an almost cloistered life as a governess, with little opportunity to know young men her own age.

Nettie returned shortly, her eyes wide with excitement. "It's a caller for you!" she cried. "Maybe he's come to offer you a new position. Quick now—run down and see what he wants."

Camilla did not run, but she could not help a faint rising of curiosity. At the parlor door she paused so that she might enter without unseemly haste. Her visitor sat in a shadowy corner where she could not see him clearly at first. He rose and came toward her—a balding man in his fifties, with eyes a cool, wary gray.

"My name is Alexander Pompton," he said. "The name will mean nothing to you, Miss King. But I have come to ask a favor of you."

She gestured him to the sofa and sat down opposite.

"You are a governess here, I believe," he said. "Are your ties in this household very strong?"

The soreness of her last interview with Mr. Hodges was too recent for caution.

"I have no ties here at all," she said quickly. "Or anywhere else, for that matter. I was dismissed from my position this morning."

"In that case," he said, "it should be possible for you to take the boat tomorrow afternoon. I have gone to the liberty of procuring your passage to Westcliff." He leaned toward her earnestly. "I have been attorney for your grandfather Orrin Judd for many years. He is seriously ill—he may be dying. I have come here to ask you to go to his sickbed at Thunder Heights."

She was startled and dismayed. "But—he disowned my mother long ago. Even when she was alive he had nothing to do with us."

"That is not quite true. Mr. Judd kept good account of his daughter

Althea over the years. Had she been in need, he would have stepped in at once, even though he and your father had little liking for each other."

"My father detested him," Camilla said. "He didn't want my mother to return to Thunder Heights when Orrin Judd finally sent for her."

Mr. Pompton sighed. "What happened was a great tragedy. But your father was mistaken in blaming Orrin Judd."

Camilla's fingers twisted together in her lap. "They sent for Papa after Mother died. He went to Thunder Heights for her funeral, and he came home ill with grief. He said her family was wholly to blame for the accident. He would never talk about it, and I've never known how she died. He said I was never to have anything to do with my grandfather or the others at Thunder Heights."

"Your father has been dead for several years," Mr. Pompton reminded her. "You are a grown woman. It is up to you to make your own decisions. When a man is dying, there may be many things he regrets. Orrin Judd wishes to see his only grandchild."

A queer, unexpected surge of excitement leaped within Camilla. The name of Judd was a magic one to be spoken almost in the same breath as Vanderbilt, Astor, or Morgan. She remembered once when she had been very young and her mother had pointed out a tall structure that towered over Broadway. "Your grandfather created that building," her mother had said, with pride in her voice.

"You would need to stay only a day or two at this time," Mr. Pompton said. "You would bring your grandfather a last happiness. But you may not be altogether welcome at Thunder Heights."

Her mother's tales of the family sprang into Camilla's mind. "You mean because of my aunt Hortense?"

"I'm afraid your aunt never forgave your mother for marrying John King. But no matter—you must go and not let anything she says disturb you. Your aunt Letty lives there too, and she is a gentle soul who will welcome your coming. Then there is Booth Hendricks, whom your aunt Hortense adopted when he was ten. He must be about thirty-six now. There is another young man as well—an engineer who has been a trusted associate of your grandfather's for several years. A Mr. Ross Granger. Miss Camilla—will you give your grandfather this last pleasure?"

Camilla had never thought of getting in touch with her relatives, not after the way her grandfather had treated her mother, nor in the face of her father's bitter hatred of him. Nevertheless, there they were—in that great house up the Hudson called Thunder Heights. The emptiness of all the years when she had longed for a family crowded back upon her. Perhaps there were matters her father had never fully understood.

She smiled at her visitor in sudden bright acceptance. "There's no reason why I can't catch tomorrow's boat as you suggest."

Mr. Pompton looked relieved. He rose and put an envelope into Camilla's hands. "I will wire ahead so that you will be met."

She saw him to the door. The day was still gray and gusty, but now there seemed an excitement in the blustering wind. Camilla had her supper in her room that night. Later she went to sleep with a smile on her lips, a warm current of eagerness flowing in her, an eagerness to please her aunts and her grandfather, to love them and be loved by them.

THE FOLLOWING AFTERNOON she bade Mrs. Hodges a polite good-by, kissed the weeping children she had grown to love, and went out to her cab, carrying her suitcase.

She had never taken a trip up the Hudson River before, yet the river had always been a part of her memory of her mother. Althea King had known the Hudson in its every mood—when its banks glowed brilliant with autumn foliage, when ice encrusted its inlets, when spring laid a tender hand upon its shores, and when summer thunderstorms set the cliffs reverberating. Now Camilla felt eager and alive, ready to embrace the new life that was her heritage from her mother, with the river a vibrant part of it.

The boat that awaited her was four decks high, gleaming with white paint and gold trim. But there were storm-threatening clouds in the sky, and the day was cold for the first of April. A cutting wind sent most of the passengers scuttling for the comfort of the saloons.

As soon as Camilla had checked her suitcase, she tied a gray veil over her hat, knotting it in a bow under her chin, and went out on deck. With a great tootling of whistles the boat was drawing away from the pier.

As Camilla watched, she breathed the fresh, tangy odor of salt air and let the gale whip color into her face.

Only one other passenger had dared the cold. Ahead of Camilla a man leaned against the rail. He wore a sandy tweed jacket and a cap pulled over his forehead.

Suddenly a little girl darted out of a doorway and ran across the deck. Camilla looked about for her mother, saw no one, and hurried after the child. The man at the rail heard the footsteps, turned, and caught the little girl. Then he saw Camilla approaching.

"An open deck is a dangerous place for a child," he said curtly.

His misunderstanding was natural, and she did not take offense. She took the child and walked back toward the doorway just as the frantic mother rushed out and looked around.

"Here she is," Camilla said. The woman thanked her and hurried the little girl inside.

The man was watching. He took off his cap and the wind ruffled hair that had the glossy sheen of a red-brown chestnut. "I'm sorry," he said.

"I thought she was yours, and it's a wonder I didn't read you a lecture."

She nodded and went to stand next to him at the rail. She was glad he had spoken to her. Now she might ask him questions about the river. "Do you know the Hudson well?"

"Well enough. I've lived along its banks all my life."

"And I've lived all my life in New York City," she said. "But I've never sailed up the Hudson before."

He stared off into the wind without comment, and she hoped he wasn't shutting her out. For a moment she studied the strong line of his jaw, his straight nose and jutting brows. It was difficult to judge his age—probably he was in his mid-thirties. There was a certain ruggedness about him. This interested her, made her a little curious.

"I'm going upriver to Westcliff," she said tentatively.

He looked at her more directly than before, and she saw that his eyes were as gray as the river that flowed past the boat, and set widely beneath the heavy chestnut brows.

"Westcliff happens to be my destination too," he said.

"Then I'll at least have an acquaintance in the vicinity. I don't know a soul where I'm going. Do you know the place called Thunder Heights?"

She sensed that he was startled. The set of his mouth was unsmiling, his eyes guarded as he looked away. "Why are you going there?" he asked.

"My grandfather Orrin Judd is very ill," she said. "I—I may be going to his deathbed."

He studied her face now, clearly without liking. "So you're still more of the family?" he said. But before she could reply, a torrent of rain swept down on them, and she fled into the main saloon. He did not follow her there, but disappeared along the deck to another entrance.

She found a seat near a window where rain slashed the glass, obscuring all vision. She felt disappointed. She had been ready to like this man and accept him as a new acquaintance who might well become a friend. But the name Judd had turned him abruptly from her, and the realization brought with it a vague uneasiness.

In late afternoon the storm rolled away, and Camilla went outside onto the drenched deck to watch the steep shores of the Hudson glide by. The river had curved sharply and seemed now to be enclosed on all sides by rocky cliffs, as if the boat had steered into some great inland lake. Ahead on the west bank loomed a great hulking mass of mountain, its stony head cutting a profile into the sky.

"That is Thunder Mountain," a quiet voice said in her ear.

She turned quickly to find her recent companion beside her.

"I should have identified myself," he told her. "My name is Ross Granger. For the last ten years I have worked as a close associate of Orrin Judd's. Your sudden news about his illness came as a shock, since he seemed no worse than usual when I left him last week." He turned back to the river. "You can see the house now. Up there below the mass of the mountain—there's your Thunder Heights."

The boat was slipping past the mountain, and Camilla could see that its far slope gentled, opening into a wide, tree-grown level high above the Hudson. She forgot that the rail was sopping wet and clung to it tightly with her gloved hands. The house stood on a prominence which commanded a sweep of the river. It was a fantastic conglomeration of wooden towers and gingerbread curlicues, of jutting gables and turrets. A wide veranda, arched and bracketed beneath its eaves, gave upon the river. But storms had weathered the house to a dingy gray, left too long unpainted, and the trees crowding about gave it the look of a place uninhabited. It appeared enchanted, spellbound, there on its remote heights.

"What a wonderful place," Camilla murmured. "It's strange to think that my mother grew up there."

"How did she escape?" Ross Granger asked dryly.

"My father came to teach in Westcliff, and my mother fell in love with him. But Grandfather didn't think much of a poor schoolteacher as a husband for his daughter. So they ran away to New York and were married there. Grandfather never forgave her, and she only returned once— just before her death."

"I've heard several versions of that story," he said. "She must have been a bit frivolous and reckless—your mother."

She sensed disapproval in his tone, and resentment prickled through her. "I remember her as gay and happy," she said.

Ross Granger looked up at the house. "Gaiety seems out of place at Thunder Heights. Its happy times are long past, I'd say. You're frowned upon if you so much as laugh out loud these days. I prefer Blue Beeches, coming up there."

Blue Beeches was beyond and below the Judd heights and closer to the water. It shone in bright yellow contrast to its more somber neighbor. A woman sat rocking on the broad veranda while three children of varying ages ran down to a small landing at the water's edge, waving eagerly as the boat went past. Ross raised an arm and returned their salute, and the children shouted and waved all the harder.

Then he drew Camilla's hands from the wet rail and turned them over to reveal the gloves soaked and stained. "Better go change your gloves before we dock. That's Westcliff ahead of us."

It was exasperating to be given directions like a child, but she hurried below, retrieved her suitcase, and put on a fresh pair of gloves. When she returned carrying her bag, Ross Granger was there ahead of her, his own large suitcase at his feet. Westcliff was clearly visible now, with its clustered houses and white, steepled church. On the small dock townspeople had gathered to watch the boat come in. Her companion looked down at them with interest.

"There's your cousin, Booth Hendricks," Ross said.

"Cousin? Oh, you mean Aunt Hortense's adopted son?"

"Yes—he has kept his own name. He's the tall fellow down there in the gray derby."

Camilla studied the figure of the man Ross Granger indicated. He was lean and dark, with a melancholy face. Even at this distance she could see that he was handsome. The knot of his cravat, the loop of gold watch chain across his well-cut vest, the gray derby on his head, all were fashionable to a surprising degree. Booth Hendricks seemed out of place in Westcliff. Perhaps, like her, he was an outsider. She felt sympathy quicken for this cousin by adoption, and she went down the gangplank to meet him.

CHAPTER TWO

BOOTH HENDRICKS CAME forward to greet her. He had only a careless nod for Ross, but he held out his hand to Camilla and flashed her a quick smile in which a certain astonishment was evident.

"Cousin Camilla!" he said, his dark face glowing with an unexpected warmth. Then he turned coolly to Ross. "So you're back? Can we give you a ride out to the house?"

Ross Granger shook his head. "Thanks, no," he said, his tone equally cool. "I've business in the village first. I'll walk out as usual." He touched his cap to Camilla and walked away.

Booth stared after him for a moment. "Did Pompton arrange for you to come upriver with Granger?" he asked.

"No. I met him by chance on the boat."

"No matter. Your coming is the important thing. Though I may as well warn you that you're going to be something of a shock to the family. Do you know how much you look like your mother?"

The frank admiration in his eyes was pleasant after Ross Granger's prickly attitude. "I'm glad," she said.

Booth hailed a rig waiting on the narrow dirt road. The driver drew up before them. Booth handed her suitcase to him and helped Camilla into the carriage, then climbed in beside her. The driver flapped the reins, and they started off along the main street of the village.

"It's one of our little economies at Thunder Heights to keep no horses." Booth spoke lightly, but there was a sting in his voice. "Westcliff has little choice to offer in the way of hired rigs. I'm afraid you'll find us backward in a good many ways. Hardly like the gay city you've come from."

"I didn't lead a very good life there," she confessed. "How is Grandfather's health?"

Booth Hendricks shrugged. "I gather he survives. Amazingly, considering his years. You should be good for him."

"I hope so," Camilla said. "I can hardly wait to meet my grandfather and my aunts. And to see my mother's home. I want to know all about her. I want to ask a thousand questions and—"

The man beside her put one gloved hand upon her own, stemming her outburst. "I know how you must feel. But perhaps a word of warning at this point is a good idea. Thunder Heights isn't a particularly happy house. It's a house in which it is better not to ask too many questions. Will you take my advice, Cousin, and move softly?"

She felt a little dashed, but she could only nod agreement.

They were climbing now, the horse moving at a walk. In a few moments their carriage pulled up before an entrance in the thick, untrimmed privet hedge that shielded the property from the road. The driver got down to open a once handsome iron gate, badly in need of fresh black paint. Stone gateposts rose on either side, and on each crouched a mournful stone lion. Just inside the gate was a large coach house, deserted now, with empty stables below. The driveway was overrun with weeds, and the forest crowded in, dark and forbidding. Camilla felt the last of her eagerness melt away as the house loomed out of the dusk. Rain had begun to fall again. The driver pulled up, and Booth sprang down upon the carriage block and held out his hands to Camilla.

She left the carriage and waited at the foot of the steps, looking up at the house, while Booth paid the driver and took down her suitcase. Light shone in upstairs windows and through an arched fanlight above the heavy door of glass and wrought iron. But no one came to greet her, and as the clopping echo of the horse's hoofs disappeared among the trees, she was aware of an eerie silence.

Booth led her up the steps, and a grating of metal shattered the silence as he pushed the heavy front door open. The antehall was large and square, with a parquetry floor, and ornate plaster rosettes in the ceiling. Except for a small rug or two, the room was completely bare of furnishings, with a door opening on either side and a wide arch straight ahead. From the sides of the arched doorway and from the walls on either side, curious marble hands protruded, each grasping a torch whose flame was a burning candle behind a glass shield.

"I see you're to be given a rousing welcome," Booth said to the silence. "Ah well, come along—I've warned you."

Beyond the arch was an octagon staircase with panels of intricately carved teak. From some unseen source above, light fell upon the steps. As Camilla followed Booth, a girl in a maid's uniform came running down.

"This is Miss Camilla, Grace," Booth said to her. "Will you show her upstairs to her room, please."

He gave the girl Camilla's suitcase. "I'll see you at dinner, Cousin Camilla," he said.

She was suddenly reluctant to leave his company and go off into the unknown reaches of the house. But when he turned away to a door opening off the antehall, there was nothing to do but follow Grace.

At the second floor Grace waited for her, and as Camilla climbed the stairs she saw that the light on the steps came from an oil lamp in a carved cinnabar bowl hanging from the ceiling of the stairwell.

The octagon shaft of the stairs was set in the heart of the house, and two halls rayed out from it on each side at the second and third levels.

"Mr. Judd has given orders you're to have Miss Althea's old room," Grace told her. "Miss Hortense don't like that much, but she don't dare say no when Mr. Judd sets his mind on something. It's a real pretty room, mum. Hasn't been opened for years, so we had to rush to get it ready for you today."

Near the end of the second-floor hall leading to the river wing Grace turned and opened the door on a room alive with firelight, gracious and inviting in the cold, rainy dusk. She put the suitcase down, then nodded toward a water pitcher and basin set on a marble-topped stand.

"The water's still hot, mum. I thought you'd want a good wash after your trip. Dinner is at seven thirty. Prompt, mum. Miss Hortense don't like to be kept waiting."

Once the girl was gone, Camilla could look about the lovely room that had once belonged to her mother. The pink marble mantelpiece above the lively fire was carved with a rose-leaf design, and a small French clock of gilt and enamel ticked away upon it. The carpet was pale gold and soft-piled, the wallpaper light gray, with a gold fleur-de-lis pattern. There was a small gray and gilt French desk with a little chair to match—a desk from which her mother, who had loved parties, must have sent out many an invitation. Heavy gold brocade draperies, faded and a little shabby, had been drawn across the room's tall windows and French doors.

Camilla went to one of the doors and opened it upon a small balcony that fronted the river. It was raining harder now. She stood for a moment trying to make out the river far below, but the rain and the failing light obscured her vision. She closed the door, returned to the warmth of the fire, and then gave herself up to the refreshing comfort of bathing.

When she had put on a clean shirtwaist and had changed to a fresh blue skirt, she lay down on a chaise longue before the fire. As she was relaxing, she heard a light tap on the door. She went quickly to open it. A slight, gray figure stood in the doorway. "It's—Aunt Letty, isn't it?" Camilla guessed.

The woman's face, pale and fine-skinned as eggshell china, seemed to crumple into tiny lines, as if she were about to burst into tears. In her hands she held a small, lacquered tray with a teapot and cups upon it. She held the tray out wordlessly.

Gently Camilla drew her into the room and closed the door.

MISS LETITIA JUDD was somewhat less than fifty. She was of medium height but small-boned. She wore her gray hair bound about her head in a coronet of braids that gave her a certain dignity and presence. Her dress was made of a light gray material that floated when she moved, and she wore a coral brooch. She looked immaculately neat.

A small, gray tabby cat came into the room with her. "This is my friend, Mignonette," Letty said, smiling tremulously at Camilla. "See— I've brought you some hot peppermint tea."

She set the tray on a marble-topped table near the fire, and when she had reached out to put it down, Camilla had noted that her right arm was twisted and crooked. "My little sister Althea's daughter," Letty murmured. "You are *so* much like her."

She seated herself in a rocking chair, her hands clasped in her lap. Camilla saw there was a strong, muscular look to them, and the skin was tanned and freckled. As she poured a cupful of the tangy tea, her crooked arm seemed to hamper her little. The gray tabby looked up expectantly.

"Not now, dear," Letty said to the cat. "We're only going to stay a minute." She smiled at Camilla, as if apologizing for the bad manners of a child. "Mignonette loves all my herb teas. She joins me by having a saucerful every afternoon." She held out a cup and saucer to Camilla. "There you are—and do flavor it with a bit of clover honey. It gives you strength and courage."

Camilla spooned a little golden honey into the tea and sipped it gratefully. "How is my grandfather? When will I see him?"

At her words Letty's tears brimmed over, and she drew a lacy bit of lavender-scented handkerchief from her sleeve. "He is very weak today. Hortense won't let me go near him, for fear I'll upset him." Her dark eyes lifted to Camilla's with intense pleading.

"What is it, Aunt Letty? If there's anything I can do—"

Letty shook her head. "No, no—nothing." Her manner became faintly agitated, and her hands clasped and unclasped nervously in her lap. "You must believe that what happened wasn't my fault—you must believe that I didn't intend—"

She was upsetting herself to such an extent that Camilla dropped to a velvet ottoman beside her and took the small, weathered hands into hers. She let the strength of her own youth flow into the clasp of her hands, and her aunt looked hopefully into her eyes.

"Perhaps you've come in time. I think Papa is sorry for a good many things. It's wonderful that he has sent for you. You belong here with your family, my dear."

Unexpectedly, tears stung Camilla's eyes. Such words made up a little for the lonely years behind her.

"Booth is delighted with you," Letty said. "He came to tell me how pretty you are and how lucky we are that you've come. Booth is a dear boy. A bit moody perhaps, at times, but brilliant and talented. It will be good for him to have someone young in the house."

She would have gone on, but a peremptory knock sounded at the door. She sat back quickly, withdrawing her hands from Camilla's clasp. "That's my sister, Hortense," she whispered.

Smiling and eager, Camilla went to the door and opened it to the over-whelming presence of the woman who stood there.

Camilla's imagination had pictured nothing like this tall, handsome, red-haired woman in elaborate dinner dress. She might have been beautiful had her expression been less petulant and sharp. Certainly her red hair, untarnished by the years, was spectacular, with its pompadour of high-piled rolls and waves. Her emerald-green gown was perhaps less than the latest fashion, but she wore it like a duchess, as she did the diamonds in her ears. One had the feeling that there was little her darting eyes missed.

She noted her sister's presence without pleasure, and Letty left as she came into the room, the little cat darting into the hall with her. Camilla braced herself, the eager smile a little stiff on her lips.

"I hope your room has been cleaned satisfactorily," Hortense said. "We had so little warning of your coming. And we don't have the servants we used to have. I never could understand why Papa wanted this room left exactly as it was when Althea was alive. It's a better room than mine—I'd have liked it for myself."

Camilla was uncertain how to meet this outburst. Indifferent to her niece's gaze, Hortense paused before the tea tray. She sniffed the peppermint odor and wrinkled her nose.

"Don't let my sister dose you with her brews. She uses little sense in such matters and they don't agree with everyone." Then she turned her scrutiny upon Camilla and there was open antipathy in her eyes. "So you are Althea's girl? It has been a shock to us to learn that you were coming."

Vainly Camilla tried to think of something to say.

"Papa did the same thing that time years ago when he took a notion that he was going to die and he had to see your mother. It was Althea who died, and he's been hale and hearty all the years since, until now. Let's hope history won't entirely repeat itself."

"About my mother—" Camilla began, seizing the opening.

"The less said about your mother, the better," Hortense told her. "When she married and left this house, your grandfather gave orders that her name was never to be mentioned to him again. Even after he remanded that order and invited her here, her death upset us all so badly that by mutual agreement we have avoided the subject of Althea King. You understand? The memories are too painful."

"Yes, of course, Aunt Hortense," she said mildly, reminding herself that she must placate this woman.

"Good. Come along now and I'll take you to your grandfather. But don't stay long—his strength is fading."

Hortense led the way to the opposite wing of the house. Before a door near the corridor's end she knocked. A nurse in a blue-striped uniform looked out at them, nodded, and led the way into a large, dim bedroom. The fire on the hearth had burned to embers, and what light there was came from a lamp set on a table near the great, canopied bed. It was a handsome room, with fine mahogany furniture of vast, baronial proportions.

The old man in the bed lay propped against a stack of pillows, his hair and beard streaked with gray. His eyes, sunken above a great beak of a nose, were still vitally alive.

"Your granddaughter, Camilla, is here, Papa," Hortense said. "You mustn't talk to her for long, or you'll tire yourself."

"Get out," said the old man in a surprisingly strong voice. "Get out, both of you, so I can have a look at the girl."

Hortense and the nurse left, and Camilla approached the bed to stand within the radius of lamplight. For a few moments old man and young woman studied each other gravely.

"You're like your mother as I remember her," he said at last, and now there was a quaver of weakness in his voice. "You're my lovely Althea come back when I need her most."

"I'm glad I could come, Grandfather," Camilla said gently.

He sighed long and gustily. "I should have got around to seeing Althea's girl before this. I've let too much go these last years. Bring over a chair and sit where I can look at you. I need to talk to you quickly, before it's too late."

The nearest chair was a massive piece, but she dragged it over to the bed and sat down on its velvet seat. He breathed heavily for a while before he spoke again.

"The vultures out there are waiting for me to die. But it doesn't matter, now that you're here. We'll fool them all, won't we, girl? Will you stay here, Camilla, and help me?"

"I'll stay if you want me to, Grandfather," she said softly.

He turned and reached to a table on the far side of the bed, groping

428

for a framed oblong of cardboard. "This is the way we looked in the days before Althea married that schoolteacher."

Camilla took the picture and held it to the light. Orrin Judd sat in a carved chair, with his daughters about him. The youngest, Althea, stood straight and lovely within the circle of her father's arm, smiling warmly at the camera. On his other side Hortense leaned against him, a hand upon his shoulder, as if she strove to draw his attention back to herself. Letty stood beside Althea, a thin, frail girl with a sad smile. Her right arm hung at her side with no evidence of deformity.

"My three girls," Orrin said. "Their mother and I planned so much for them. But she wasn't here long enough to see them grown, and somehow it all went wrong."

He was silent for a moment, and then sudden anger stirred in his voice. "I should have forbidden the house to John King! What could *he* do for Althea?"

"She had everything she wanted most," Camilla said gently. "If you had really known my father, you might have loved him."

The old man stared at her for a moment. Then he said, "I like spirit, girl. At least you stand up to me honestly. You don't talk simpering nonsense." He took the picture back. Suddenly he seemed to have lost the focus of his thoughts.

"Perhaps you'd better rest now, Grandfather," Camilla murmured.

"No, no! Don't leave me, girl. There's something I had to tell you. Something that happened—" He reached out and grasped her hand in a grip that was crushingly strong. "Trouble," he gasped. "Trouble in this house. You must watch for it, girl. When I'm well I'll get to the bottom of it. But for now"—he struggled hoarsely to speak—"watch—Letty." His grip loosened, fell away. "Tired," he whispered weakly. "Althea's home is your home—you must help me save it."

"Of course, Grandfather," she assured him hurriedly.

He seemed to hear her words and gain reassurance from them, but he lay spent, and she went quietly away.

In the hall outside, the nurse sat dozing on a carved chest.

"You'd better go to him now," Camilla said.

She went back to her room and sat quietly before the fire. In those few moments of interchange she and her grandfather had given each other their love and trust. The antipathy she had seen in the eyes of Hortense Judd still troubled her. But the important thing was to help this despairing old man who was her grandfather.

THE FRENCH CLOCK on the mantel marked seven thirty as a deep-voiced Chinese gong sounded from the depths of the house.

A thought came to Camilla, and she went to her suitcase and took from it a green velvet jewel case. She had nothing in which to dress for dinner, as Hortense chose to dress, but at least she might wear a gold medallion bracelet of her mother's. Althea had kept only a few favorite pieces of the jewelry Orrin had given her, and now her daughter had them for her own.

Camilla fastened the bangle about her wrist, feeling that it dressed her up for the occasion and that, wearing it, she would take something of her mother with her.

She went downstairs and, not knowing where the dining room lay, opened a door toward the land side of the house. She found that she had guessed right. The others were not there and she hesitated, looking around the long, wide room. Dark wainscoting ran halfway up the walls, and above it pictured wallpaper presented a busy, raspberry and cream country scene. The darker red carpet was faded and worn threadbare. The sideboard and china closet were of vast proportions to fit the size of the room. The dining table had been set with linen and Spode china, with candles alight in branched silver candelabra.

Booth Hendricks came in first, wearing informal dinner dress. The lapels of his jacket were of satin, his shirtfront stiff, with pearl buttons studding it. At sight of Camilla his eyes brightened. "What a pleasure to see someone young and pretty in this house. Are you rested from your trip, Cousin?"

"I wasn't tired, really," she told him. "I've been too excited to be tired. And now that I've seen Grandfather, I'm not so worried as I was. I didn't know how he would receive me."

"And how did he receive you?" Booth asked dryly.

"With affection," she said, and explained no further.

Letty came in, still wearing the floating gray dress that became her so well, and her eyes turned to Camilla questioningly. Camilla smiled and nodded in reassurance. When Hortense entered the room, Camilla gave her the same warm smile, but her aunt paid little heed to her. All her attention was for Booth. She took his arm and let him lead her to her place at one end of the table.

"Have you had a good day, dear?" she asked him.

He seated her with a gallant flourish in which there was a hint of mockery. "What do you mean by a good day, Mother? Can any of us remember such a thing in this house?"

Hortense made a small *moue*. "At least we've been rid of Mr. Granger's dour company for a few days."

Camilla had hardly given Ross Granger a thought since she had entered the house, but now she wondered about his place in this group.

Booth seated Camilla at Hortense's left, while Letty slipped quietly into her own place across the table. He sat down at Hortense's right.

Grace, young and inexpert, brought in a silver soup tureen and placed it before Hortense. Then she scuttled back to the kitchen as though she could hardly wait to escape.

"Grace is new," Hortense informed Camilla. "Our maids are always new. The village girls these days have notions above themselves, and they don't last long with me. Only Toby and Matilda have stayed with us from the old days, and they are getting old."

The monogrammed silver service, indeed the very room, spoke of luxury long past, and the gradual decay of fine possessions. How shining and rich everything must have been in its heyday—and could be again, if only someone cared.

"Our mother always liked to dress for dinner," Hortense went on. "So I try to continue the custom. Of course, since you have only a suitcase, Camilla, I don't expect you to comply while you're here."

Camilla thanked her for her consideration and began to eat. The cream of potato soup was good, and she had a healthy appetite.

"How long may we expect to enjoy your company, Cousin Camilla?" Booth asked.

"That depends on Grandfather," Camilla said. "I promised that I would stay as long as he wanted me here."

Letty gasped softly, and Camilla saw that she was staring at the dining-room door. Ross Granger stood in the doorway, his expression unsmiling, an angry light in his gray eyes.

"You're late for dinner," Hortense said. "You know how Papa abhors any lack of punctuality."

Ross did not answer. His bright chestnut hair shone in the candle-light as he took his place at the table beside Letty. Camilla waited for some greeting from him, some sign of recognition, but he gave her none. He began to eat without paying attention to the others.

Letty coughed in gentle embarrassment and turned to Camilla, seeking to break the uncomfortable silence. "How have you been keeping yourself since your father's death?" she asked.

"I've been working as a governess for the last four years."

"Do you enjoy the work?" Letty asked with interest.

"How could she?" Hortense broke in at once. "A governess is hardly more than a genteel domestic servant."

"That isn't quite true, Aunt Hortense," Camilla said, her tone carefully restrained. "The role of governess is an important one in any household. If the parents realize it, a governess can do a great deal for their children. I've always regarded the work as important and interesting."

"Good for you, Miss King!" Ross said unexpectedly. "Don't let them patronize you."

"At least it's a good thing you have some sort of work to return to," Hortense said. "I suppose it's respectable enough work for an impoverished gentlewoman—which seems to be the condition brought upon you by your parents."

Booth flashed his mother a quick, ironic smile. "Oh, come now! Surely Grandfather Orrin will leave her a bit of a legacy? Perhaps she has that small hope to look forward to." He nodded kindly at Camilla. "There is still time for him to include you in his will."

Ross turned grimly to Hortense. "Yes, there's always time to change a will. I suppose that's why you wanted me out of the way for the last few days? So you could keep me from him?"

Hortense turned a furious red. Grace cleared away the soup plates and returned with the meat course while Letty chatted nervously about how much good today's rain had done her garden. No one paid much attention to her, and Camilla was aware of a mounting tension.

When Grace left the room again and Hortense was serving the roast beef, Ross said, "I'd like to know just why you sent me off on this wild-goose chase to New York. You wanted more than to get me away. What have you been up to in my absence?"

"You are insufferable!" Hortense cried.

Letty put her hands to her temples. "Oh, please, please! Let's have peace during dinnertime at least."

She looked as if she might burst into tears, and Booth turned to her and quietly began to speak of the gardens. It was a relief when the meal finally ended. By that time Camilla would have preferred to go upstairs to the seclusion of her mother's room. But Booth guided her across the hall to the parlor, and there was no easy way to escape.

CHAPTER THREE

SEVERAL LAMPS HAD been lighted in the great parlor that ran along the river side of the house, and a wood fire crackled in the grate. The room was crowded with treasures from the Orient. There were Chinese screens and Oriental rugs, and on every table and shelf and whatnot stand were objects of jade or coral or brass. Flames danced in miniature across the gleaming silver of a coffee service as the family drew about in stiff, uncomfortable chairs. Only Ross had absented himself. Mignonette, the cat, awaited them by the fire.

"The evening ritual," Booth said, as he brought Camilla her cup. "For an hour or so every night we sit here enjoying one another's brilliant company and sipping coffee in cups that are exquisite, but too small."

Hortense laughed. "Booth loves to tease," she said. "Papa always liked this hour when we were girls, and we've kept it up." She ran on, as if silence were something never to be suffered for too long. Waving a beringed hand, she pointed out various objects around the room, relating incidents connected with their purchase when she had gone abroad with her parents as a child.

"Did you go with them too on these trips, Aunt Letty?" Camilla asked, when Hortense paused for breath.

"I went to England and Scotland once after I was grown up," Letty said, reaching for a basket of crocheting at her side. "But I was never strong enough for much traveling."

"I was always the one with endurance," Hortense said.

As they talked, Camilla glanced at Booth, who had taken a chair well back in the shadows. When footsteps sounded on the stairs, he leaned forward, his eyes upon the door, and Aunt Letty jumped uneasily.

Ross came in with a strong, vigorous step. "Mr. Judd was too weak to talk to me," he said. "The nurse told me she had been ordered to keep me out of the room. By whom, may I ask?"

Hortense answered quickly. "Dr. Wheeler said Papa was not to be disturbed or worried. We all know that you irritate him lately. It was I who said you were not to see him."

"An order you knew I would disregard. I'm not the one who disturbs him—"

Booth stood up and leaned an arm along the mantel, his features somberly handsome in the flickering light. "Look here, Granger, we've stood a good many of your insinuations because of your former usefulness to Grandfather Orrin. But you upset him badly the last time you saw him. From what the nurse has told us, we gather that it's you who wants his will changed for some purpose of your own."

Letty's crochet hook moved in and out of her work with quick, silver flashes, and she spoke in a small, breathless voice.

"How can you blame Ross for trying to persuade Papa to change his will? Haven't we all been concerned about the same thing?"

"So you *did* want me out of the way, just as I thought. And what was this change to be?"

Hortense said, "It's none of your business! This family's affairs do not concern you, Ross."

"They concern me," Letty said. "What would I do with half my father's fortune if it were left to me, as the will reads now? I should hate the responsibility."

"So you'd let your sister take your birthright away?" Ross said impatiently. "At least I can prevent *that* move—when he's well enough to listen to me. Even if he won't follow a plan I think wiser."

"Even if he won't cut you in as repayment for your years of—ah— faithful service?" Booth asked quietly.

Listening, Camilla shrank from this heartless talk of wills while Orrin Judd lay upstairs desperately ill.

Once more Ross addressed himself to Hortense. "When I left for New York, Mr. Judd was no worse than he had been for months. What happened after I left?"

The room was so still that a bit of charred wood falling in the grate made an explosive sound. Then Hortense found her voice. "Booth was in the village at the time, and I was in the cellar. Letty was with him. I'm sure we'd all like to know a little more than she told us about what really happened."

Letty's work dropped into the basket and she covered her face with her hands. "It's true—I was there. But I didn't intend—"

"What was it you said to him, dear?" Hortense pressed her. "Or is it something that you did?"

Letty turned her head wildly from side to side. "No—I can't talk about it. You must believe that I meant well."

Ross crossed the room and put a hand forcefully on her shoulder. "Try to tell us, Miss Letty. It may be important."

Letty began to weep into her lavender-scented handkerchief. Booth came to her aid. "Let her alone, Granger. You can't believe Letty meant him any harm. Come along, Aunt Letty—I'll take you up to your room."

Camilla saw affection in the look Letty turned upon him, and his every movement was kind as he led her away.

Ross watched them go and glanced at Camilla. "An interesting family you've acquired, isn't it?" he said, and went out.

Hortense began to rub her brow with her fingers. "Headache," she murmured. "You had no business coming here . . . most regrettable. If you'll excuse me?" She left the parlor.

Camilla sat on alone for a little while before the orange-red embers, thinking about the tense, uncomfortable scene she had just witnessed and about the conflicts and antagonisms that had played back and forth.

Before she went to her room she paused at her grandfather's door, to see if she might bid him good night. But the nurse said he was sleeping.

Overcome by weariness, Camilla hurried down the hall to her room, only to find the hearth cold, its comforting warmth dispelled, so that she had to undress shivering, and get quickly into bed.

She fully expected to lie awake for a long while, thinking over the events of the day. But the bed was warm and soft with comforters and her body was utterly weary. So she soon drowsed off to sleep.

It was sometime after midnight that the sound of music roused her. Someone was playing a harp, plucking the strings so that plaintive trills and chords stole through the house like a voice crying. The sound seemed to drift downward from the floor above. On Camilla's floor a door opened and closed, and after a little while there was silence. But the music, while it lasted, had made as lonely a sound as Camilla had ever heard. Even after the harp was still, she felt the echo of it along her very nerves, pleading, bewailing. But for what, or for why, she could not tell.

Suddenly there were more sounds. Someone went past her door, and there was the sound of hurrying footsteps on the stairs. Had her grandfather taken a turn for the worse? She drew on a warm flannel wrapper, opened her door, and heard the sound of someone weeping. Her own wing of the house was empty, but a lamp still burned above the stairwell, and a candle flickered in a holder on the hall table beyond the stairs. It was from that direction the sound of weeping came. Camilla followed the hall to its far end. There, on the carved chest outside Orrin's door, sat Letty, crying bitterly, with her hands over her face.

"Is Grandfather worse?" Camilla asked.

"He's dying," Letty said sorrowfully, "and they won't let me in."

Even as she spoke, Hortense came to the door. Her face was twisted in a grimace. "It's over," she said. "Papa is gone."

Letty stood up to face her sister. "You had no right to shut me out. I should have been with him when he died."

Hortense made a futile effort to thrust back her sliding pompadour. "The sight of you would have upset him. Besides, he died in his sleep quite peacefully. He saw no one."

Across the hall a door opened, and Booth came out of his room, wearing a handsome dressing gown of maroon brocade. "What's happened?" he asked.

Hortense had difficulty controlling her voice. "Your—your grandfather is dead, Booth dear," she said. "I fear Camilla's coming . . ."

"Don't blame Camilla," Booth said. "I'll go downstairs and send for the doctor." He turned and strode toward the stairs.

"Shouldn't someone call Mr. Granger?" Camilla asked.

"Go to bed." Hortense spoke to Letty, but her look included Camilla. "There's nothing you can do."

Letty rose stiffly, like a wooden doll. "I want to see him," she told her sister. "Come with me, Camilla."

Reluctantly, Hortense let them by. Within the room the nurse was busying herself about the bed, but she drew down the sheet so that they could see Orrin Judd's face. To Camilla's eyes he looked younger now and somehow happier.

Letty bent to kiss his cheek. "Good-by, Papa," she whispered, and went sadly out of the room.

Camilla studied the proud, strong face. Only a little while ago he had spoken to her. He had wanted something of her and had said they would talk again. But now he was beyond reach.

"Good night, Grandfather. Sleep well," she told him softly, and turned away from the bed.

An unexpected movement across the room caught her eye, and Ross Granger stepped out of the shadows. Camilla stared at him in surprise. "How long have you been here?" she whispered.

He took her arm and led her out of the room. "I've been here all night," Ross said flatly. "It was the least I could do for him. Though I don't think he knew I was there. Get yourself some sleep now."

Her throat felt choked with grief, and she could not speak. She nodded and slipped away down the hall.

In her room the little clock on the mantel told her, surprisingly, that it was almost five o'clock. Moving automatically, she lighted the kindling in the grate and watched until the larger sticks crackled with blue and orange light. Then she dropped down upon the hearthrug, warming herself and thinking. She would stay for her grandfather's funeral and then take leave of his family. In spite of Aunt Letty, whom she was ready to love, she could not stay on under the same roof with Hortense.

Dawn was brightening the windows when at length she left the fire and went to one of the French doors, opening it once more on the little balcony. The early morning air was fresh with the wet scent of earth and new-growing things. She stepped out and stood at the balcony rail, watching the sunrise fling streams of rose and aquamarine across the sky.

How still the waters of the Hudson seemed now, as if they scarcely moved. Had her mother stood on this very balcony in some long ago dawn, watching the river come to life with a new day? A gull swooped down toward a spit of land, and she heard its shrill cry. It was as if the river called to her. Yet she must go from it, and she felt suddenly regretful. She could almost hear her grandfather saying, Don't run away, girl. Stay and fight. But what was she to fight? And why?

AFTER BREAKFAST THAT morning Camilla put on a jacket and went out onto the wide veranda. There were steps on the river side, and she walked down them and across the lawn. She followed a narrow brown path that wound down from the heights, crossed railroad tracks that were hidden from the house, and wandered beneath the bare trees that edged the river.

The thought of her mother had been with her often since she had come here. But now a sense of her father's presence returned as well. He had worked in Westcliff for a time as a teacher, though his real home was in New York. Where and how had they met? Had they walked together along this very path?

By now Thunder Heights was hidden by the trees, and as she walked on she came suddenly upon a noisy, tumbling brook. A little wooden bridge offered a crossing, and she went on along the path. Only a little

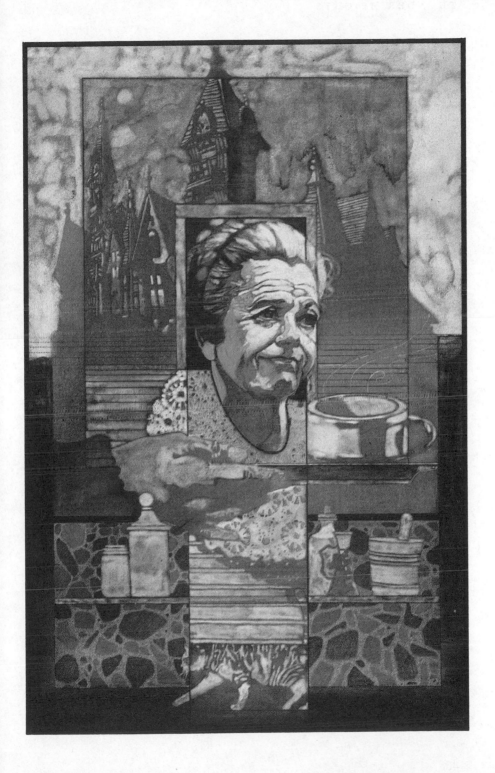

farther ahead, she came upon Ross Granger sitting on a rock above the path. He was dressed in a corduroy jacket and trousers, his chestnut head bare to the sun. He had not seen her, and his face in unguarded repose was troubled. She did not know whether to go or stay, hesitating to break in upon this solitary moment. Then he looked about and saw her.

"You're out early," he said, standing up.

"I couldn't sleep."

"Nor I," he said.

"Why did you stay all night in my grandfather's room?" she asked him, feeling that there were matters she must understand before she went away.

"I didn't want to see him bullied about a new will," he said. "I trust none of them."

"And they don't seem to trust you," she said.

His smile was wry. "Hortense took care of that. She spent the night in the room too, with Letty posted as a watchdog outside, except when she went off to play her harp."

"It seems dreadfully cold-blooded for you all to be thinking about wills while Grandfather lay dying," Camilla told him frankly.

"A man is dead for a very long time," Ross said. "The stipulations he leaves behind may affect their lives for generations. This was not a moment to be squeamish about such matters."

A dalmatian, young and awkward, came bounding suddenly out of the woods and ran to Ross with joyful exuberance. Ross pulled his ears affectionately.

"Down, fellow, I prefer to wash my own face. Champion is from Blue Beeches," he explained. "He's Nora Redfern's dog."

The dog gamboled off on an exploratory expedition. Ross removed his jacket and spread it on the rock beside him.

"Come sit down a moment," he said. "I want to talk to you."

He offered a hand to pull her up the face of the boulder, and she seated herself on his jacket. "How much do you know about your grandfather?" he asked, when she was comfortable.

"Not a great deal. My father never talked about Thunder Heights."

Ross nodded gravely. "Orrin Judd had so very little in the beginning. He was born in Westcliff, you know. His father was a country doctor. Orrin worked in lumber camps hereabout, but he had a genius for managing men and running large affairs. So before many years were up he owned a lumber business of his own. From that it was only a step into the building trade. Though that's a feeble term for what he wanted to do. He had no training himself as an engineer or an architect, but he learned from the men who worked for him and he was better than any of us. He was more an empire builder than a builder of bridges and buildings and roads. When he retired to Thunder Heights, the business world came to him. He wouldn't go to New York after your mother died, but he made it come to him—often through me."

"I've wondered about your place here," Camilla said.

"Sometimes I've wondered myself. My father was an engineer and his good friend, though many years younger. After he died, Orrin Judd kept an eye on me and sent me to engineering school. When I graduated, he put me to work on some of his projects. Before I knew what had happened I was doing a sort of liaison job for him. I suppose I've helped him keep the threads in his hands, though I never planned on playing aide-de-camp to a general."

"You've given up years of your life for this?" Camilla said.

"I don't count them as lost. He gave me a chance to learn, and there were things he intended me to do later. When he felt I was ready. Besides, I loved him."

Off in the brush they could hear the dog chasing some small wild thing. The sound of rushing water, the twitter of birds was all about them. But the two on the boulder were silent.

"Thank you for telling me these things," Camilla said finally. "I can see how much you've meant to my grandfather. What was the change you wanted to see him make in his will?"

He stood up abruptly. "There's no point in discussing that with you. You're a Judd too."

His words stung, and she stood up beside him indignantly.

"I expect nothing," she said. "The Judds owe me nothing and I want nothing from them. I came only to see my grandfather."

"Then why did you wait till he was dying before you came running? To get your hands on some of the Judd fortune?"

Camilla felt completely outraged. If this was what he thought of her, then she did not mean to stay in his company another moment. She turned her back on him and managed to get down the steep face of the rock without his help.

But he would not let her go alone. He jumped down from the rock, and the spotted dog bounded along beside him as they turned uphill and back in the direction of Thunder Heights. She walked quickly, ignoring him, though now and then he pointed out landmarks by which she could find her direction if she chose to come this way again.

For example, he said, there was that weeping beech on ahead, from which she would be within sight of the Judds' house. It grew to a considerable height, and all its boughs trailed downward toward the earth, making a blue-black canopy around the tree.

When they reached it, her companion whistled for the dog and turned back. "I'll leave you here," he said curtly. "I'm not going in yet. You'll have no trouble the rest of the way."

For a moment she stood looking after him in bewilderment. What a strange, unpredictable person he was. Then she looked more closely about the hillside. Back a little farther it rose steeply into an overgrown cliff, with a break in the brush at one point, as if a path might open there. She climbed up and came out upon a bare, craggy place from where she could glimpse Blue Beeches. The sunny yellow of the house shone fresh and clean, where Thunder Heights was drab and dingy.

As she watched, she saw the dalmatian go loping across a wide lawn. A woman came down the steps, laughing and calling to him. Camilla could not see her clearly enough to know whether she was plain or pretty, young or old. But she had a friendly greeting for Ross Granger as he came out of the woods and joined her. Linking arms, they went up the steps and into the house.

Wondering, Camilla went back down the path from the rocky outcropping to the Judd house. She was now approaching it from the rear, and saw that here a space of earth had been cleared of weeds, and there were paths leading among beds where planting had begun.

As Grace opened the back door for her, voices reached Camilla from the parlor, and she knew that the sad rites connected with her grandfather's death had already begun. Before she could slip past, Mr. Pompton appeared in the doorway.

He held out his hand to her gravely. "It is sad to meet again under such circumstances, Miss King. But I'm glad you were able to reach your grandfather before his death."

"He wanted me here," she said. "Thank you for coming for me."

"You will be staying on for a time now?" he asked.

She shook her head. "No longer than the funeral. With my grandfather gone, I am not wanted here."

He did not deny this, but made a stiff bow and returned to the parlor. As she started up the stairs, Booth came out to join her. "You've been for a walk?" he asked. "Did you get no more sleep at all last night?"

"I didn't feel like sleeping," she said.

As they reached the second floor, Hortense came down the hall carrying a tray with a tea service. She wore voluminous black today, with a fringe of formidable jet twinkling across the bodice.

"I knew Letty would make herself ill last night," she said impatiently. "And now she has run away to the nursery again. As if I didn't have enough to do!"

Booth took the tray out of her hands. "Let me take it up to her, Mother. Camilla will help me with Aunt Letty."

Hortense gave up the tray gladly, and Camilla followed Booth up the stairs to the third floor, where he led the way to the door of the old nursery. Camilla opened it for him.

The nursery was a bare, cold room—far from the cheerful room of her mother's stories and her own imagination. No fire had been lighted in its grate, and on this northern exposure of the house, sunshine had not reached the windows. At the far end Letty huddled on a couch beneath a quilt. Her face was swollen from crying, and as Booth approached with the tray she murmured, "You shouldn't bother about me, my dears."

Booth set the tray down on a small table. "You know I'll always bother about you, Aunt Letty," he said. "The funeral is tomorrow, and I want to see you strong and well for that."

At Letty's feet Mignonette lay curled in a warm, tight ball. She stretched herself, yawned, and regarded them with interest.

"Would you like me to light a fire for you?" Camilla asked.

Booth answered for her. "Don't bother, Cousin. As soon as Aunt Letty drinks some tea, I'm going to take her downstairs."

Letty managed a tremulous smile, and there was affection in the look she gave him. "I like it up here. There are always memories to comfort me. Camilla, your mother used to play with Hortense and me in this very room."

Booth poured a cupful of tea and brought it to her.

"What tea did Hortense fix for me, Booth?" she asked.

"I've no idea," he said. "Your herb mixtures confuse me."

Letty sniffed the aromatic steam. "Mother-of-thyme, with a bit of hyssop. Just the thing. You know what David says in the Bible—*Purge me with hyssop, and I shall be clean.*"

She drank deeply, and Mignonette mewed and climbed daintily over the hump of bedding made by Letty's outstretched legs.

"Give her a saucerful, Camilla—there's a dear," Letty said. "She doesn't want to be left out."

Camilla took Letty's saucer, poured tea into it, and set it on the floor. Mignonette leaped lightly from the bed and lapped the hot liquid.

Booth watched, shaking his head. "I've never seen such a cat. Don't those mixtures ever upset her?"

"Of course not!" Letty's tone seemed overly vehement. "They don't upset me, why should they upset her?"

As Letty drank the tea, Camilla told of her walk and of her glimpse of Blue Beeches.

"If I were you, my dear, I wouldn't go too near Blue Beeches," Letty said. "Not that I have anything against Nora Redfern. Her mother and yours were good friends in their girlhoods. Mrs. Landry, Nora's mother, lives upriver now, and we haven't seen her for years—which is just as well. Nora is a widow with three children. Personally I think she is a young woman of considerable courage, but Hortense doesn't approve of her."

441

"Or her mother's sharp tongue," Booth added. "If you're through with your tea, I'll carry you down to your room, Aunt Letty. Sad memories won't make you feel any better up here."

"They're not sad memories—they're the happiest of my life," Letty insisted. But she raised her arms to Booth.

He lifted her as if she weighed nothing. Camilla picked up the tray and followed, with Mignonette springing along at her heels. Just before she reached the door, Camilla saw something she had not noticed earlier. In a shadowy corner stood a harp, a stool drawn before it. So it was from this room that the harp music had issued in the dead of night.

At noontime Letty remained in her room, Booth had gone to the village, Mr. Pompton had left, and Ross did not appear; so Camilla and Hortense ate alone in the big dining room.

"What will your plans be now, Aunt Hortense?" Camilla asked.

"We'll get rid of the house, of course. Whether we sell it, give it away, burn it down, doesn't matter."

"It seems a wonderful place to me," Camilla said gently. "Isn't it rather a shame to let it go out of the family?"

Hortense snorted. "You haven't been tied to it against your will for most of your life. When Mama was alive we had houses everywhere, including a splendid town house in New York. I can still remember the parties and balls, the fun and gaiety, the trips abroad. Even after she died, Papa didn't give up, as he did when Althea married and went away. He wouldn't go anywhere then, or let us go anywhere. He sold all the houses except this one. It has been like living in a prison all these years."

Camilla felt moved by a certain pity for her. If a gay social life was what Aunt Hortense had been brought up to expect, it must have seemed a cruelty to have it taken away so arbitrarily.

"Does Aunt Letty feel this way too?" Camilla asked.

"Letty!" Hortense waved a scornful hand. "She can be happy with her harp and her garden and her cat. If Papa has left money in her hands, she will never know what to do with it. But *I* will know. I have plans for myself and for Booth. There's so much I can do for him that Papa would never permit."

Her fatuous pride in Booth was evident. "Booth is a very talented artist, you know," Hortense assured her. "But Papa always hated his painting and opposed him at every step."

"I'd like to see some of his paintings," Camilla said.

"I have one in my room. I'll show it to you."

Her aunt's room was on the second floor, across the hall from Camilla's. It was a big, dim room, heavily curtained. Camilla could feel the prickle of dust in her nostrils as she stepped into it. Hortense's love of the sumptuous had been given full play, and she had used a lavish hand when it came to velvet, satin, and brocade—dusty materials, gone too long undisturbed. She moved about lighting lamps, then waved a hand toward the end wall. "What do you think of it?"

The painting was a large one of two mountain wildcats fighting on the rim of a cliff. A storm was breaking, and the artist had painted in tawny yellows and smoky greens and grays. "Papa detested this painting," Hortense said.

Camilla could well understand that her grandfather would not want to live with such a disturbing picture. That Booth had painted it was significant. Camilla had sensed that there was a depth of passion in him that he did not reveal to the casual eye. It had spilled out in this picture, betraying him.

Hortense ran on eagerly. "When we sell this house, we'll move to New York. I'll arrange for a gallery showing of his pictures. I've promised him that for a long time."

As she left her aunt, Camilla thought that there was far more relief than sorrow in Hortense over her father's death. Indeed, it seemed to have brought all her suppressed longings seething to the surface.

CHAPTER FOUR

THE SUNLIGHT OF early afternoon rayed through the stained-glass window of the church as the organist played a solemn hymn. The mourners sat in the family pew with their heads bowed. Ross had not been invited to join them, but when Camilla turned her head, she saw him a row or two back, sitting beside a pretty, brown-eyed woman— probably Nora Redfern. When the ceremony was over, the family followed the casket down the aisle and out of the church. Camilla took her place in one of the carriages that would drive them to the cemetery. Only a few of those at the church service attended the burial.

As the casket was placed beside the grave, Letty burst into tears. Hortense bowed her head, the conventional figure of a daughter mourning her father. Booth had been a pallbearer, along with Orrin's doctor, the lawyer Mr. Pompton, and others, and he looked solemn, if not deeply grieved. Camilla saw Ross standing a little apart, with Mrs. Redfern at his side. His expression was guarded, betraying little.

Camilla stood in silence, studying the names on gravestones nearby. There, with a tall granite shaft guarding it, was her grandmother's grave. Next to that was the headstone for Althea Judd King. It was the first time Camilla had seen her mother's grave, and the tears she could not shed for her grandfather sprang into her eyes. How much her father had wanted to keep his Althea from being buried here. But Orrin Judd had had his way. Now he would sleep near his daughter in all the time ahead.

After the burial service Mrs. Redfern approached Camilla and held out her hand. "I'm Nora Redfern, Miss King. If you are going to be here for a while, do come over to see me. We ought to know each other—our mothers were best friends."

Nora was tall, with soft brown hair curling beneath her tilted hat. She looked like a woman who enjoyed the outdoors, and the clasp of her hand was strong and direct.

Camilla thanked her and explained that she would be leaving tomorrow. She could understand why Ross spent so much time with this woman, and she watched with regret as he helped her into her carriage.

When Hortense and Booth and Mr. Pompton were settled in one carriage, and Letty and Camilla in another, Ross came over to join them, to Camilla's surprise.

On the drive home Letty still needed to pour out thoughts that were troubling her. "Papa was so unhappy these last years," she said. "And so much of it was my fault."

"I think you blame yourself needlessly," Ross told her. "How could you be responsible for his unhappiness?"

Letty dabbed at her eyes with a handkerchief. "There are so many things you don't know," she said darkly.

Ross did not seem to take this seriously. "Perhaps it will comfort you a little, Miss Letty, if you realize that nothing could ever have made him happy again."

"That is true," Letty said wonderingly. "His life was really over, no matter what anyone did. In fact, it has been over for a long, long time, hasn't it?"

She seemed to take cheer from this thought.

"At least," Ross said, "it will be better if you don't express the way you feel to any reporters who may try to talk to you."

"Reporters?" Letty echoed in dismay.

"Of course. You don't think a man like Orrin Judd can die without causing a stir, do you?"

When they reached the house, they found that he was right. A group had already gathered near the front door. Mr. Pompton left the carriage to speak to them, while Booth and Ross hurried the ladies into the house.

Camilla would have left the others to go upstairs, but Hortense stopped her. "You're to come to the library, please. Mr. Pompton has agreed to read us Papa's will at once."

Such haste seemed to lack decorum, but Camilla followed her aunts to the library, where a fire burned against the misty chill of the day. She took a chair in a far corner, withdrawn from the main family gathering, feeling herself a spectator at a play, remote and untouched by whatever happened. Ross had come into the room, and he too set himself apart from the others. He walked to one of the bookcases that lined two walls and began to study titles as though he had no other interest there.

Mr. Pompton cleared his throat, looking at Hortense. "You understand, Miss Hortense, that it is only because I wish the whole family to be present that we are moving with such unseemly haste."

"Yes, yes, we understand that," Hortense said.

"As you know," Mr. Pompton continued, "Mr. Judd sent me to New York a few days ago to find Miss King and ask her to come to Thunder Heights. While I was away on this mission, and without my knowledge or advice, he drew up a new will."

Camilla sensed the quickened attention of the room.

"The new will," Mr. Pompton said, "has been legally drawn and witnessed." He began to read aloud.

" 'To my eldest daughter, Hortense Judd, I leave the family Bible, with the hope that she will learn from its wisdom.' "

Hortense sniffed. "If Papa has doled out everything stick by stick, this is going to take us all day."

"Believe me, madam, it will not take very long," Mr. Pompton said, and continued.

To his second daughter, Letitia Judd, he left the treasured photograph taken of himself and his three daughters. Letty nodded in pleasure. "I shall treasure it too," she murmured.

Several small sums had been left to Toby and Matilda, and to others who had worked for Orrin in the past.

His bequest to Ross was a strange one. " 'In view of the years of trusted service given me, I wish Ross Granger to be permitted the occupancy of the rooms above the coach house for as long as he cares to use them.' "

What an odd thing for Grandfather to do, Camilla thought. Surely Ross's quarters in this house must be more comfortable than such an arrangement would be. Besides, if his work for Orrin was finished, he would be leaving soon.

Mr. Pompton paused, and Booth looked quickly at Ross. Hortense put a hand on her son's arm, as if to restrain him.

Mr. Pompton continued. " 'To Camilla King, daughter of my youngest daughter, Althea Judd King, I bequeath this house of Thunder Heights and all the property therein.' "

Camilla was aware of Hortense's gasp and the startled silence of the others, but she was so astonished that she did not hear what followed. Mr. Pompton had to repeat the fact that Orrin Judd had left not only Thunder Heights but his entire fortune and business holdings to Camilla, who was herself named sole executrix of the will. With an effort she forced herself to listen and to understand the stipulations Mr. Pompton was reading.

In order to inherit the house and fortune, Camilla King would have to live at Thunder Heights, preserve it in good state, and continue to care for the rest of the family as long as they chose to live in the house. They were to live on their present allowances, and if anyone chose to leave Thunder Heights, he was to receive nothing at all thereafter. Nor was Camilla to receive anything if she chose to leave.

The full meaning of the burden her grandfather had placed upon her was becoming clear. Camilla rose uncertainly to her feet. "I don't understand why Grandfather did this. He must have made this will before I came here—"

"He was insane when he made it!" Hortense cried hoarsely. "We will fight this in court. The whole thing is preposterous."

"If you will allow me a word—" Mr. Pompton bent his disapproving gaze upon her. "The main body of the will is sound. Mr. Judd left everything he owns to Miss King, and I doubt that you could touch that in a court. The inheritance is hers."

Hortense had begun to breathe harshly. Letty watched in bewilderment, and there was a sardonic look in Booth's eyes. Ross was regarding Camilla sharply, his arms folded across his body.

"What happens if I refuse the legacy?" Camilla asked. A small sum of money she would have received gratefully. But not this, when so clearly the true rights to it lay elsewhere.

"Since there is no other legatee," Mr. Pompton said, "the same thing would happen as in the event of your decease. The money and property would revert to the next of kin."

"To Aunt Hortense and Aunt Letty?" Camilla asked.

"Exactly," said Mr. Pompton.

"Then I'll refuse it!" Camilla said. "I have no right to it. And I don't want the burden and responsibility of it."

"Bravo!" Booth cried. "We have a heroine in our midst."

Mr. Pompton crossed the room to Camilla and held out an envelope. "This letter is from your grandfather," he told her. "I do not know its contents. It was to be given you only in the event of his death. Perhaps you would like to take it away and read it, Miss King? It is not necessary to do so here, under our eyes."

She accepted the offer quickly. "Yes—yes, please." She left the library and crossed the hall to the parlor. Someone had placed a cloak over a chair, and she flung it about her shoulders and hurried toward a veranda door.

There had been rain since the funeral, and the air was heavy with moisture as Camilla leaned upon the railing, looking out over the lawn.

446

Beyond and below lay the river, wreathed in fog, with misty swirls drifting among nearby trees. She steadied herself with one hand upon the damp rail, holding in the other the sealed envelope she dreaded to open. Then, with a resolute gesture, she broke the seal of the envelope.

My Dear Granddaughter,

You do not know that I have long watched you from a distance. I am aware that you have been a loyal daughter to your father, and that since his death you have conducted yourself with good sense and courage. You are able to work with pride for your living, and this is a trait I admire.

Recently I have had a severe shock, and it may be that I shall not recover. Those who live under this roof with me I do not trust. The things I have built and worked for must not go into their hands, to be wasted and flung aside. What I have built is sound and good. I want it to remain with someone of my own blood who will be loyal to me.

You are the only answer. For this reason I am changing my will. Thunder Heights will be yours. Restore it, my dear. Make it what it was in your mother's day.

We will talk about all these matters, and I will explain my hopes and my fears to you. By the time you read this, I hope we will have long been good and trusted friends. I will be able to go in peace, knowing that what I leave behind rests in responsible hands. Do not fail me, Granddaughter.

Your loving grandfather,
Orrin Judd

Camilla read with sadness and an increasing sense of being trapped. The will she might put aside and refuse to consider. This letter—the last wishes of a man whom she had learned, even in so short a time, to love and respect—must be considered solemnly.

Folding the letter, she went down the steps and across the brown grass below, turning about so that she could look up at the house and at the dark mountain towering behind. How grim the structure looked—as grim and forbidding as the stony cliff above. The weed-choked clumps of thin grass added to the picture of woeful neglect. How could her grandfather, who loved the house, have let it go like this? He must indeed have been driven far along a road of despair and hopelessness.

An odd, unexpected excitement ran through her. What if she accepted her grandfather's trust? What if she set about bringing the house back into such glory as it had once known? Might this not be a splendid and satisfying thing to do?

Someone came out of the house and stood upon the veranda, watching her. It was Letty. Her injured arm was held tight across her body. Standing there at the head of the steps, she seemed strangely of a piece with the house—a part of its mystery. Letty Judd was a woman filled with secrets.

Camilla ran back to the house, her face glowing and eager.

Letty saw the look and held out her hands in pleading. "Don't stay here at Thunder Heights. Let the house go. Let all of us go. That's the wise choice, the only safe choice."

Camilla went up the steps and took Letty's hands in hers. "This is your home, Aunt Letty, and you shall live in it as long as you like, and with everything you need or want. Help me to make something good out of Grandfather's wishes."

Letty regarded her sadly. "You're going to stay, aren't you? I was afraid you might. It won't be easy for you."

"Come back to the library with me," Camilla said, and drew Letty into the house.

No one had stirred in the walnut-dark room. "I've made my decision," she told Mr. Pompton. "I accept my grandfather's legacy and his stipulations. I shall remain at Thunder Heights."

A LOG ON THE fire crumbled into ash, throwing up sparks as it fell. For a moment there was no other sound in the room.

Then Mr. Pompton began to gather up his papers. "Exactly," he said, as if he had expected her to make no other choice.

Hortense stood up, looking pale and stricken. "Help me to my room," she said to Booth, and he gave her his arm and led her to Letty, who watched from the doorway.

"Aunt Letty will take you upstairs, Mother," he said, and came back into the room.

He turned to Camilla. "Forgive us, Cousin, if we don't seem altogether happy. It's rather a shock to my mother to find herself dependent upon a niece she hardly knows." He smiled wryly. "As a matter of fact, you'll probably do better justice to the handling of Grandfather's fortune than any of us would. So, for whatever it's worth, you have my support." He held out his hand and she put her own into it, surprised that he should react like this.

"This is all very touching," Ross Granger said. "But you must admit that the situation is ridiculous."

"You might explain that remark, Granger," Booth said.

Ross threw him an irritable look. "Do you mean you don't find it ridiculous that all of this"—he waved a hand to encompass the Judd fortune—"has been left unequivocally in the control of an inexperienced girl of twenty-three?"

"You can always resign, you know," Booth said, his eyes brightening as though he enjoyed this moment of clash.

For an instant Ross stared at the other man wrathfully. Then Booth shrugged, smiled at Camilla, and went out of the room.

"If you are willing," Mr. Pompton said to Camilla, "I'll come to see you as soon as I have things in order. There are various legal matters we must go over together. In the meantime I'll say good day. If you wish, I can make a statement to the press on my way out."

She thanked him, and when he had gone she looked uncomfortably at Ross. He appeared to be thoroughly angry.

"I'll make no pretty speeches," he said curtly. "You have my resignation, of course. I'm sure you'll have other advisers who will work for you more cheerfully than I would. I'll try to be out of your way in a week or two."

"I didn't ask for any of this—" she began, but he walked out of the room, as though he dared not trust his temper, and closed the door behind him.

Camilla went to her room and lay down on the bed, trying to command her thoughts, to formulate some sensible plan of action. These first days would be the most difficult. Once the family grew accustomed to the idea of having her here, it should not be so hard. Surely they would be pleased when she made plans for the house. Hortense had longed for a gay life. Why couldn't it be gay enough for her right here at Thunder Heights? If Booth wished it, why couldn't he arrange for a New York showing of his paintings? She could do so much for all of them, once they began to trust her. Her immediate task was to win them.

At the moment, though, she had no desire to face them. And when Grace came tapping at her door to leave a supper tray, she was relieved. "Miss Letty fixed it herself," Grace said, setting the tray on the marble-topped table before the hearth.

Camilla found a brief note propped against a cup on the tray.

Don't come down to dinner, dear. Let us talk this out among ourselves. Everything will be better tomorrow.

Lovingly,
Aunt Letty

She was grateful to have her meal quietly here in her room. She went to bed early and fell asleep at once, waking now and then to the sound of foghorns on the river, only to fall quickly asleep again.

IN THE MORNING she awakened to find sunlight glowing beyond window draperies, and she sprang out of bed to let it in. When she had washed and dressed, she hurried downstairs, eager to begin the day. The dining room was empty, and she was glad to be alone so that she could marshal her plans. She had brought paper and pencil with her, and she began to jot down reminders to herself. Unobtrusively, if possible, she must learn to know the entire house. She must inquire into the possibility of hiring gardeners, carpenters, painters, so that the work might be started as soon as possible. She must draw Aunt Hortense into her plans and move gently with the others.

When she had finished her second cup of coffee, she took her newly jotted list and went down to the cellar. The large main room at the foot of the stairs was lighted by high windows that rose aboveground. Beyond it, Camilla followed a corridor that ran the length of the cellar, off which were storerooms of various kinds, and finally a room with high stone walls and an air of chill that indicated a larder.

Its door opened in and stood ajar. These days butter and cream were kept in the ice chest upstairs, serviced from the village, so another use had apparently been found for this room. Along the wall facing the door were shelves lined with small, glass-stoppered jars and corked bottles. A marble slab had been set into a work shelf at waist height, and a mortar and pestle rested upon it.

All these things Camilla saw at a glance as she stood sheltered by the door, unaware until she moved into the room that she was not alone. At her right, standing before another row of shelves, was Aunt Hortense. This morning she wore a voluminous green negligee trimmed with yellowing lace. She had not heard Camilla's quiet step in the doorway, and as Camilla hesitated, she reached up to a shelf and took down one of the labeled bottles.

"Good morning, Aunt Hortense," Camilla said, and her aunt whirled about, nearly dropping the bottle.

"Don't startle me like that!" she cried.

"I'm sorry," Camilla said. "I didn't see you till I stepped around the door."

She moved toward the shelves and looked up at them with interest, reading the labels. Here were Letty's cooking herbs: thyme, chives, basil, marjoram, summer savory—dried and pulverized, or left in leaf form. On another shelf were the medicinal herbs: angelica, chamomile, hyssop, and many more. As Camilla studied them, Hortense replaced the bottle of tansy she had taken from its place.

"My sister Letty's hobby," Hortense said. "But she indulges in too much experiment. I prefer to pick my own mixtures. I came down for something for my stomach and nerves. I hardly slept a wink all night. Is there anything you're looking for down here?" Her eyes had a look of cold resentment in them.

"I just thought I'd start at the cellar and begin to know the house. I hope you don't mind. When you feel up to it, Aunt Hortense, I'd like to consult you about so many things."

Hortense sniffed. "I'm certainly not up to it now. Not after the shocks

I've had to endure in the last few days. And after a miserable night. How did *you* sleep?"

"Soundly," Camilla said. "I hardly stirred till morning."

"She didn't bother you, then? She didn't come to your door?"

"What do you mean?" Camilla asked. "No one came to my door."

"A good thing. She might have frightened you. I've always wanted to lock her in at night, but Papa wouldn't hear of it."

"What are you talking about?" Camilla asked in bewilderment.

"When Letty is disturbed she often walks in her sleep. And we never know what she may do. I found her climbing the attic stairs last night and had a time getting her back to bed."

Hortense reached for a jar of peppermint tea leaves, lifted out the glass stopper, and dropped a spoonful of the leaves into the teapot she had brought downstairs. She added another spoonful from a jar of rose hips, and picked up the pot. As she reached the doorway, she paused.

"I should think you would be *afraid* to stay on in this house."

"Afraid? Why should I be afraid?"

Hortense shrugged. "You might ask Letty sometime just what it was she gave Papa to drink the night he had his attack." She walked out of the larder, leaving Camilla to ponder her words.

CHAPTER FIVE

IN THE DAYS that followed, spring began to move brightly up the Hudson valley. Forsythia spilled its yellow spray, and enterprising crocuses and jonquils poked their heads through the bare earth of winter. About the house there were changes as well.

Camilla went vigorously to work on her plans for renewal and repair. Booth helped her find carpenters and set them to work. Old Toby obtained help in the village for work about the grounds and went at it with a will. He planted with a lavish hand—grass, and flower beds, and new young trees to replace those that were dead.

With Letty's help, Camilla checked slowly through every room in the house to make sure of all that must be done. Letty was sweet and co-operative, but Camilla had the uneasy feeling that she did not believe in what they were doing. Hortense alone remained hostile to all plans and would take no part in them.

CAMILLA'S FIRST CONSULTATION with Mr. Pompton took place more than a week after the funeral. When she received the lawyer in the library, he droned on about investments, holdings, interest, and other affairs of a similar nature, until her head spun. Then he relented and let her know that there was little she need do about any of these matters except to sign a few papers. Mr. Granger, he said, understood all the larger business affairs, which were not Mr. Pompton's province. She could inform herself about these matters through him.

"But Mr. Granger resigned from this work right after the funeral. He is leaving tomorrow," she said.

The attorney stared at her as if he did not believe his ears. "You must not accept Granger's resignation, Miss Camilla. Later, perhaps, but at the moment you cannot do without him."

As Camilla listened, he made very plain the reasons why she could not let Ross Granger drop her grandfather's affairs, and she felt faintly relieved. Even though Ross had avoided her lately, his presence in the house had been reassuring. The fact of his being here had more than once bolstered her courage. She did not know quite why this was so, since she and Ross seemed seldom to be together without conflict or irritation. Nevertheless, at the moment she felt glad to hear that his continued presence was necessary.

When Mr. Pompton finished, Camilla rang for Grace and sent her upstairs to summon Mr. Granger from his room. He left his sorting and packing and came down to the library.

"Please sit down," she said, and plunged in before she could frighten herself by thinking what might happen if he refused. "Mr. Pompton has just made me understand how indispensable you are in Judd affairs. Must you really leave us, Mr. Granger?"

"Your cousin, Booth, and your aunt Hortense don't want me here. And I certainly haven't meant to force my services on you."

Mr. Pompton coughed impatiently. "Stop playacting, Granger. You know she can't move a finger without you."

Ross's straight mouth relaxed into a smile. "Miss King has been moving very fast in a number of directions without me."

"Women's matters," Mr. Pompton scoffed. "What does she know about the Judd projects that are in the making? These can't be dropped."

"I'd like to learn," Camilla said quickly.

"You must stay, Granger. You owe it to Orrin Judd," Mr. Pompton said.

Ross hesitated for a moment, then gave in. "All right—I'll stay. But not under this roof. I'd have moved out long ago, if Mr. Judd hadn't insisted that I be where he could call me the instant he wanted me."

"He left you the use of the rooms over the coach house in his will," Pompton said. "That was a bribe, wasn't it? To give you what you wanted, so you'd stay on and assist Miss Camilla?"

"Perhaps." Ross smiled wryly. "Or else it was meant to infuriate Hendricks."

Camilla considered the matter. Booth used the rooms over the coach house for his painting, and she did not want to antagonize him by putting him out. At the same time she did not dare to lose Ross, and he was clearly firm about getting out of this house. "There's no immediate hurry, is there?" she asked. "If you'll give me a little time, I'll talk to Booth and persuade him to work somewhere else."

Ross quirked a doubtful eyebrow but did not object. Mr. Pompton gathered up his papers and went off.

On impulse Camilla held out her hand to Ross. "Thank you for staying. I know you didn't want to."

He took her hand, bowed over it remotely, and went out of the room without further comment. Left alone, Camilla wondered about the best way to approach Booth. Perhaps Letty could help her on this, since she and Booth seemed on affectionate terms.

Camilla found her in the rear garden. Her aunt knelt at her work, the sleeves of her gray dress rolled up and her hands gloveless as she handled the soft, brown earth. So this was why Letty's hands were not the pale, protected hands of a lady. Much of her work seemed to be done with her left hand, but she used her right hand frequently by bending her body forward to accommodate the stiff arm. Her rolled-up sleeve revealed the thin, twisted shape of the right arm, and as Camilla drew near she saw an ugly, welted scar on the inner flesh of the arm.

At that moment Letty heard her. She looked up, and her smile was warm. "Spring is the exciting time of year," she said, sounding as exuberant as a girl. "I can almost feel things beginning to grow."

Camilla sat down on a flat rock at the edge of the garden. "There's green everywhere you look today. Are you planting flowers, Aunt Letty?"

"No, it's my little friends the herbs I like best. Look at coltsfoot there— already blooming. He's a bold one. Bright and yellow, with his thick leaves close to the ground. They're all so different, these herb people. Sage has leaves like velvet, while some herbs have leaves shiny as satin, or prickly, or smooth. And the garden looks gay as a carnival when they're in bloom. You'll see." Her bright, intense gaze lifted to meet Camilla's look frankly. "I'm glad you're going to stay with us, my dear. At first I thought the only answer for you was to go. But I was wrong."

"I hope so," Camilla said soberly.

"You mustn't live the way we've lived." Letty prodded the earth with her trowel. "I mean shut in with each other, turning our backs on all our neighbors. You could open the house—make it like it was in the days when we were young."

Camilla drew her knees up, clasping her hands about them. "That sounds like fun, but there's so much to be done, and it's still hard to believe in what has happened to me. I haven't begun to get used to it yet.

Yesterday, when I was going through my trunk after it arrived from New York, I found myself wondering how I could remake some of my clothes, so they would last another season."

She laughed out loud, remembering her own foolish behavior. Suddenly, as she puzzled over the problem, it had come to her that she might have all the new clothes she wanted. Whereupon she had rolled up a bundle of her old things, rejoicing in an outburst of reckless abandon, and packed them off for charity. A gesture which left her with hardly a stitch to her back until the matter was corrected.

Letty laughed with her gently, as she told the story. "Perhaps you'll let Hortense help you with your planning of new gowns."

"Of course," Camilla promised readily. "Let's plan a new wardrobe for all three of us."

Letty nodded a little absently. There was a long silence while she dropped seeds into the earth and patted them down. After a time Camilla began to speak of Booth's studio over the coach house and of the fact that Ross, if he stayed, must have the use of those rooms.

Letty listened thoughtfully. "Of course we can't afford to lose Ross if he is willing to stay. Booth will have to give up his studio. But he won't want to. And he can be difficult when he chooses. Perhaps I had better speak to him."

For just a moment Camilla was ready to accept Letty's offer. But if she was to make her home at Thunder Heights, she could not sidestep the difficult tasks. She must solve this herself.

"I'll speak to him," she said.

There was approval in Letty's look. "You're right, of course, dear. Perhaps you might offer him some other place. Why not the nursery? It's big enough and the light is good."

"Thank you, Aunt Letty," Camilla said. "I'll do that." But she did not at once go in search of Booth. "I saw your herb collection in the cellar the other day," she went on. "You must have given a great deal of study to the subject."

"Yes. I love to mix my tisanes and infusions. I used to treat the villagers in the old days, whenever they got sick. Of course I don't do that anymore."

Camilla studied her aunt's face. "Why did you stop, if you helped people and if you enjoyed nursing them?"

Letty pressed earth over seeds she had dropped and smiled down at them fondly. "Hortense didn't like what I was doing. She didn't think it was a fitting occupation for a Judd."

"Why not start again, Aunt Letty?" Camilla asked.

"It's too late," Letty admitted sadly. "Too late for so many things." She bent her head, so that only her silvery braids were visible.

Camilla stood up. "Do you know where Booth is now?"

"I saw him going out toward the coach house this morning," Letty told her. "He's probably still there. If he's angry with you at first, don't mind. I'll get him to come around."

"I'll get him to come around myself," Camilla said, with a resolution she did not entirely feel. She walked around the house and took the driveway in the direction of the stable.

THE COACH HOUSE, with its own turrets and gables, looked almost like a miniature of the main house. Camilla found its barnlike door ajar, and from the open doorway she could see a steep flight of stairs to the floor above. She did not approach them at once, but moved among the stalls and examined the big room where a carriage had once been kept. Dust and cobwebs lay over everything. Only the stairs had been swept clean. An old harness hanging from a nail rattled as she struck it in passing, and Booth's voice challenged her from above.

"Who's down there?"

She went quickly to the foot of the stairs. "It's I—Camilla."

He came to the head of the stairs and looked down. "A pleasant surprise! Come up, Cousin, and see my workshop."

Holding to a rickety handrail, she mounted the steps and took Booth's extended hand. He drew her up the last step, and she stood blinking in the bright, spacious upper room.

"You're just in time for coffee," Booth told her. He brought an armchair for her, dusting it before she seated herself. "My housekeeping here is not of the best."

While he busied himself with the coffee, she studied a nearly finished painting on an easel in the center of the room. This view was one of the Hudson, with an exaggerated Thunder Mountain rising from the bank. Black storm clouds boiled into the sky above, and the whole was a moment suspended in a flash of lightning. At the foot of the precipice Hudson waters churned to an angry yellow in the sulfurous light, and a tiny boat was caught in the instant of capsizing and spilling its occupants into the water. Booth had endowed the painting with a terror that made her scalp prickle.

"Are your pictures always so violent?" Camilla asked.

"So you see what I've tried to catch? The moment of danger! The very knife-edge, where there is life one moment and possible death the next."

She could sense the fascination such a moment might have for him as an artist. But there seemed a dark elation in him that was disturbing. She sipped the coffee he brought to her, and moved about the room, pausing to study the scene of a fierce cockfight, in which the feathers of the birds were bright with blood. The next picture was an unfinished painting of a woman who struggled to hold a rearing horse, its hoofs flailing not far from her head. Her face had not been completed, but the wild eyes of the horse, its distended nostrils and bared teeth, had all been carefully depicted.

Booth noted Camilla's arrested interest and crossed the room to turn the picture against the wall. "I don't put my unfinished work on view," he said. There was almost a rebuff in his manner, and she glanced at him, puzzled. Then she returned to her chair, moving it so that she need not stare at the painting of the capsizing boat.

"Your model has courage," she remarked. When he said nothing, she went on. "I've always loved to ride. Do you suppose I could buy a horse and ride at Thunder Heights?"

Booth sat down upon a high stool, hooking his heels over the rungs. "Why not? Grandfather Orrin's not here to forbid it."

"Why wouldn't he keep horses when he had a coach house built?"

Booth swallowed some coffee, hot and black. "We hardly needed them, since we had few places to go. The world came to Orrin Judd when it had to, and it could hire its own hacks."

She knew he was evading her question, but she could not bring herself to challenge him.

"If you're seriously interested, I'll keep an eye open for a horse that's been trained to the sidesaddle. I think I can find you a good one."

"I'll appreciate that." She finished her coffee and forced herself to the topic in hand. "Did you know that Mr. Granger has agreed to stay on for a time? Mr. Pompton says we need him."

Booth stiffened. "I was afraid we wouldn't be easily rid of him. I suppose you've come to tell me that I'm to move out of here and let Granger take over his inheritance. Is that it?"

She could feel herself flushing. "Perhaps we could fix up the old nursery as a studio for you. The light there should be better than you have here, and it might be more convenient to do your painting inside the house."

"I suppose this is a plan Aunt Letty has suggested? But what if I tell you I don't choose to move?"

She saw the rising anger in his eyes. "I don't blame you, when this place has been yours for so long."

His look softened unexpectedly and he smiled. "I believe you mean that, my dear. Don't worry, I'll cause you no embarrassment. But I'm doing it for you, not for Granger."

"Thank you," she said, and started to leave.

He came with her toward the house. As they followed the driveway, he slipped her hand into the crook of his arm. Camilla was sharply aware of him close at her side, moving as though the dark power that flowed through him was held for the moment in check.

"Tell me, Cousin," he said, "how does it happen that a young woman as attractive as you are has gone unmarried?"

"I have never known very many men," she admitted.

"We must mend this lack in your life," he said. "Unless you know a variety of men, you're likely to be too vulnerable to attention from any one man."

He went too far, but she did not know how to reprove him, was not even sure that she wanted to. Booth Hendricks filled her with a sense of— was it attraction or alarm? Perhaps a mingling of both, for it might be dangerous to grow too interested in this man.

When they neared the house, the sound of carpenters working on a scaffolding above the front door reached them, and Camilla looked up at the new repairs in satisfaction. "The house looks better already. I'm eager to see it painted."

Booth's look followed hers with indifference. "I'm afraid I agree with Mother that it's a waste of money. But if it makes you happy, Camilla, I suppose it serves a purpose."

He left her at the foot of the steps, and she went into the house troubled by a curious mixture of emotions.

Letty met her in the upstairs hall. "Did you see Booth? How did he react when you suggested a change of studios?"

"He didn't like it," Camilla said, "but he tried to be kind."

Letty was studying her with quick understanding. "You look upset, dear. Why don't you lie down in your room for a while and let me bring you a tisane to make you feel better?"

It was easier to allow Aunt Letty to minister to her than to resist. But when she was in her room she could not lie quietly on a bed. Her visit to Booth's studio had been upsetting in more ways than one. She had sensed in him a bitter anger that might one day explode. When it did, she hoped it would not be directed against herself. Or did she hope for just that? Did she want to be involved with Booth at whatever cost to herself?

She was still walking restlessly about the room when Letty tapped at the door. As Camilla opened it, Mignonette streaked in first, leaving Letty to follow with a tray in her hands. "Here you are, dear," Letty said. "There's hot toast in that napkin and a bit of rose-petal jam. Let the tea steep a minute, and it will be just right."

"Thank you, Aunt Letty," Camilla said, grateful for her consideration and affection.

Letty patted her arm lovingly and hurried away. For once Mignonette did not follow her mistress. She sat before the small table that held the tray, looking up at it expectantly.

Camilla laughed. "You're staying for your saucerful, aren't you?" The little cat mewed in plaintive agreement.

"All right," Camilla said, "I'll pour some for you."

She filled the saucer and set it on the hearth. Then she poured a cupful for herself and stirred it, waiting for it to cool, sniffing the sharp aroma. Mignonette lapped daintily around the cooling edges of the liquid, and Camilla watched her in amusement.

As Camilla raised her cup, the cat made a choking sound, and she looked down to see Mignonette writhing in pain. Then the little cat contorted her body and rid herself of the tea.

Camilla set her teacup down and ran to the door, calling for Letty. It was Hortense, however, who came along the hallway.

"Letty's not here. What is it?"

"Mignonette is sick. I just gave her a saucer of tea and she's throwing it up."

An odd expression crossed Hortense's face. She cast a single look at the cat and then picked up the untouched cupful of tea. She sniffed it and shook her head.

"I'll take care of this," she said, and picked up the teapot as well to carry away. "You mustn't let my sister dose you with these things. What if you had drunk what was in that cup?"

She went off without waiting for an answer, and Camilla regarded the cat. Mignonette was trying weakly to clean herself, and Camilla picked her up and carried her downstairs in search of Letty.

Grace said Miss Letty was in the cellar, and Camilla went down the lower stairs. She found Letty cleaning shelves, with Booth assisting her. Camilla held out the cat.

"Mignonette drank some of my tea just now and it made her painfully sick for a few moments. She really frightened me."

The color drained from Letty's face. She snatched the cat from Camilla and held her close, stroking the small body tenderly. "No one gives Mignonette anything without my orders," she cried indignantly. "Never, never do such a thing again!"

Camilla heard her in astonishment and found no answer.

"Perhaps," Booth said quietly, "we had better think of Camilla. Did you drink any of the mixture, Cousin?"

"No." Camilla shook her head. "Aunt Hortense came in, and when I told her the cat was sick, she took the pot and cup away. I hadn't even tasted the tea."

Letty gave Camilla an apologetic smile. "I'm sorry, dear. Mignonette means so much to me. I was inconsiderate."

Booth was watching her, his gaze alert and questioning. "What was in the tea, Aunt Letty?"

Letty hurried to the row of shelves and took down an empty jar. "It was just my usual marjoram and mint mixture. See? I used the last of it."

Booth took the jar from her and removed the cover, sniffing. "Are you sure? Sometimes I wonder how you tell all these leaves and powders apart."

"I know the appearance and scent of each one as well as I know the faces of those about me," Letty said with dignity.

She put the empty jar back on the shelf, and Camilla noted idly a vacant place on the same shelf a little farther along, where a bottle had been removed from between two others.

"Tell me, Aunt Letty," Booth said, "did anyone else know you were going to fix this pot of tea for Camilla?"

For just an instant Letty's gaze wavered. It was nothing more than a flicker, yet a shock of distrust flashed through Camilla. Then Letty was herself again. Had she thought in that instant to conceal blame, or to place the blame elsewhere? In any case, she did neither. "I'm sure it wasn't my tea that upset Mignonette," she said. "I tell you what—I'll fix you some fresh tea, dear. It won't take a minute."

Camilla started to refuse, but Booth broke in smoothly. "Make some for me too, Aunt Letty. I've had a bad morning." He glanced at Camilla, his look faintly mocking.

Letty made a mint tea, heating water on the stove out in the main room of the cellar. There were several straight chairs about a round table in the big room, and as they sat down, Hortense came downstairs.

"Do join us," Letty said almost gaily, but her sister refused.

Booth slanted an oblique look at his mother. "You shouldn't have thrown out that pot of tea so quickly. It might have borne looking into. Could you tell whether anything was wrong?"

"They all smell vile to me," Hortense said. "That cat was at death's door. What affected the cat might have killed Camilla."

It seemed to Camilla as though some duel went on below the surface among these three—as though each knew something she did not know, and each suspected the other two.

THAT AFTERNOON, AT Ross's request, Camilla had a talk with him in the library. His manner was correct and impersonal.

"Did you have any trouble getting Hendricks to agree to move out of the coach house?" he began.

"None at all," Camilla said. "But why are you so anxious to move out of the house?"

"Frankly, I don't want to be under the same roof with your aunt Hortense or her son. But that isn't why I wanted to see you. If I'm to stay, I need to know your wishes in various matters."

Camilla nodded. She had no idea what he expected of her.

"If you choose," he went on, "you can make final decisions from here, just as your grandfather used to do. Even though he remained at Thunder Heights, he never let the reins go slack. It's to be hoped that you'll follow in his footsteps."

His face was expressionless, but Camilla could hardly believe that he meant what he was saying.

"How could I possibly—"

He broke in at once. "Or you can go down to New York yourself and meet the directors of his business holdings and discuss problems with them whenever you like."

"I can't make decisions concerning matters I know nothing of."

"I agree. A few days ago you said you wanted to learn. If you like, we can meet for a time every day so that we can go into your grandfather's affairs together."

She could imagine him as a stern, remote tutor, and herself as his humble student. The prospect did not please her. "You'd have to begin at the very beginning," she said with a sigh.

"Shall we start tomorrow morning at nine, then?" he said.

When she nodded, he stood up, as if only too eager to escape her presence.

CHAPTER SIX

Now A TIDAL foam of cherry, pear, and apple blossoms surged north along the Hudson, and Camilla reveled in the pink and white beauty. She found a favorite spot beneath the plumes of a flowering pear, where she could sit overlooking the river, escaping the house and its submerged antagonisms.

With Ross's occasional help, she was learning to identify by name some of the boats that passed. She knew the cargoes of the flat barges, and the freighters that plied their way up and down the Hudson. But her business conferences with him were less amiable than her river discussions. He tried to make clear the complicated details of the Judd building empire. But she had no natural flair for figures and blueprints. When she tried to talk to him about her own eager plans for the house and the grounds, he shrugged them aside, which infuriated her. Why should he expect of her talents that she did not have, and ignore her real gifts?

When the outdoor painting was finished, she could regard the old house with new pride. Silver gray seemed to suit its seasoned quality, and now its turrets gleamed a clean, pale gray against the surrounding green of the woods. There was still a somber air about it, but at least it was handsome again. Ross ignored this, as though she were a child playing with toys. He

thought it a waste of time and money to trouble about the house when there were matters of moment at stake. The real quarrel between them, however, came about over the bridge.

She and Ross had been particularly at odds with each other that day over the improvements for the coach house. So far, Booth had not located a saddle horse for her, but Camilla wanted a stable ready for one when it was found. The invasion of his premises with pounding and sawing had irritated Ross. As a consequence he was shorter than usual at their morning business sessions. When he mentioned the bridge out of a clear sky one morning and said they must soon go seriously to work on this, she asked flatly why they should consider the enormous expense and complication of building a bridge across the Hudson.

Ross tried to be patient. "For miles up and down the river, Camilla, there is no way for people and commerce to cross except by ferry. Can't you see what a bridge would mean to the entire Hudson valley? And can't you imagine how it would look?" His hands moved in a wide gesture, as if he built before her eyes a great span of steel and concrete.

She had not thought of him as a man who could dream, and the realization surprised her. "Did Grandfather think such a plan practical?" she challenged.

"He was certainly for the idea in the beginning. I'll admit he lost interest in a great many things in the last few years, and perhaps he was no longer as keen on the bridge, but I'm sure he never gave up the idea completely. The legislature in Albany is interested. I've appeared before committees more than once."

He reached into a briefcase and drew out a sheaf of engineering drawings. "Here—you might as well see what I'm talking about," he said, spreading before her on the library table the detailed drawings for a suspension bridge across the Hudson.

None of them had any meaning for Camilla, but she could recognize the gigantic nature of the project. Perhaps her grandfather would have taken to the task eagerly in his younger days, but she could well imagine his shrinking from its complexities in his last years.

"I don't see why such a bridge hasn't been built before, if it's really needed," she said, trying to sound reasonable. "Would it be justified by the amount of traffic it would handle?"

"We've looked into that, of course," Ross said, "and I've convinced the legislature that the bridge is needed. You don't think traffic will remain at the horse-and-wagon stage with the motorcar coming into use, do you? Roads and more roads will be needed. And bridges to connect them, as we've never needed bridges before!"

The picture he was painting was one to stir the imagination. Yet her grandfather, who knew a great deal about such things, had held back.

His reasons had probably been good ones, and not merely the reasons of a man grown fearful and tired. She could not know. And since she didn't know, she could not take so reckless an action as to let Ross go ahead on this. She rubbed her temples wearily with her fingertips.

"If such a bridge needs to be built, let someone else build it," she said. "With Grandfather gone, it's not for us."

Ross stared at her for a moment. Then he scooped up his papers and went out of the room without another word. Camilla knew how angry he was. For a long while she sat on at the library table wondering despairingly what to do. Then a slow, resentful anger began to grow in her as well. Somehow Ross Granger always managed to put her in the wrong, and she would not have it. He was not going to involve her in the frightening responsibility of building bridges.

After that, the morning lessons became painfully formal, and finally ended altogether. Camilla had a feeling that Ross might resign again at any moment, and she was resolved to let him go.

It was a good thing there were other satisfactions for her. Letty had found a skillful seamstress and Camilla had sent for dress goods and household materials from New York, throwing herself into an orgy of sewing. A whole new wardrobe was being prepared for her, as well as a new wardrobe for the house.

ONE LATE AFTERNOON in May, Camilla sat on the marble bench in the rear garden, savoring the fragrant company of Aunt Letty's "herb people." She could always find balm for her spirits here, and she was learning to identify the herbs and liked to watch their progress. Lungwort had followed coltsfoot, with early blooming flowers of blue. Wild thyme sprouted between the stones around the sundial. Camilla loved to pinch off a leaf of bee balm and rub it between her fingers for the lemony scent. Rosemary, Letty said, belonged to warm climates and faded away in pained surprise at the first touch of winter. But she planted it anew every spring— so it was up again now, with its narrow leaves breathing more fragrance into the garden.

Camilla had worked hard inside the house today, helping the seamstress with the drapery materials that had come from New York for the dining room. The draperies were to be a rich golden color—luxurious and expensive. She could imagine their folds as they would hang at the dining-room windows, and satisfaction flowed through her over what she had accomplished.

The feeling swept her weariness away. She mustn't waste what remained of the afternoon light. Her gaze, roving possessively over the house, moved to small windows beneath the main roof. So far she had never explored the attic. Why not have a look at it now, while daylight lasted? After one last breath of the fragrant garden, she went inside and up two flights of the octagon staircase. At one end of the third floor a narrower, enclosed flight led to the attic. She found candles and matches and climbed the steep steps.

Up here the air was dusty and dim. Camilla lighted two of her candles and set one of the small holders on a shelf, retaining the other to carry about. Overhead, the ceiling beams slanted upward here, and down there, at sharp angles, to form dormers and gables.

She went through a number of large rooms, mostly empty except for old trunks, and moved on to a smaller one at the back of the house. Here she had to stoop to avoid dusty beams overhead, and a strand of cobwebs brushed across her face. Circling a post in the middle of the room, she came upon a saddle which lay across a slanting beam within easy reach. It was an elegant sidesaddle, with elaborately embossed silver trimmings and a silver horn for milady to hook her knee over. She held up her candle to examine it more closely.

A thin film of dust lay upon the leather, not so thick a layer as covered other objects in the attic. The dark leather shone richly, reflecting the light of Camilla's candle, and when she touched it she found the surface smooth as satin and uncracked. Someone had been coming up here regularly to care for this particular saddle. She searched further and found the silver-mounted bridle that matched the saddle; it too had been cared for over the years. There were other sidesaddles and bridles, stored carelessly, without attention. Only these had been treated lovingly.

Camilla took the bridle from its hook and held it, listening to the small chime of dangling metal parts. What fun if Booth could find a horse for her soon and she could use these things.

Returning the bridle to its hook, she moved toward the stairs, but on the way a wooden chest caught her eye. It was of a pale, Oriental wood, with brass handles. She raised the lid and was greeted with the pleasant scent of camphorwood. With a sense of growing excitement, Camilla lifted out a pale gray top hat that a lady might wear while riding. Beneath, carefully wrapped, was a pair of patent-leather riding boots. Finally she drew out the habit itself. It was the most beautiful ash-gray riding habit she had ever seen. The style was one of bygone years, but the draping was so graceful, so truly right, that it could surely be worn in any period. As she turned it about, she saw that on the right breast a horseshoe had been embroidered in dark gray silk against the pale ash of the material. Within the horseshoe were the letters *AJ*.

It was as if she had come unexpectedly upon the very person of her mother. Sadness and longing swept through her, and she held the gray habit to her heart as if she clung to a beloved presence.

She could not bear to leave the habit in the attic. Quickly she bundled it up, then returned to her room. There she laid the garments upon the bed, where she could examine them more carefully. To her distress, she found that a muddy stain ran down one side of the garment, with a jagged tear in the skirt. How strange that these things had been put away without being mended or cleaned. But she would care for them now. She would clean and repair the habit and try it on.

All through dinner Camilla paid little attention to the desultory conversation and waited impatiently to escape. Afterward she hurried upstairs. A full-length mirror had been set into the door of the French armoire in Althea's bedroom. When Camilla had put on the outfit—even to the boots, which were only a little tight, and the top hat that sat so debonairly on her black hair—she approached the glass with an odd hesitance. Now that she was fully dressed in these things that had belonged to her mother, she was seized by a fear that she would fall too far short of what Althea had been. She drew a quick breath and faced the mirror.

The girl who looked back at her was someone she had never seen before. The full gray skirt was caught up gracefully, hiding the ugly tear and stain in the folds. The long-sleeved jacket, with its diagonally cut closing, molded her body, outlining the full curve of her breast, the soft rounding of her shoulders, emphasizing her small waist where the jacket came to a point in front. The tall hat was bound with a gray veil that hung down in floating streamers behind. If only she had a crop to complete the picture, what a dashing figure she would make.

She moved before the mirror, stepping and turning lightly, and saw that her movements were lithe and graceful—as they told her Althea's had been. Did she really resemble her mother so much? Would she light a room when she entered it, as her father had said his Althea could?

Dressed as she was, a longing to show herself to someone seized her, and she knew that downstairs in the parlor she would find an audience. She ran lightly down and went to the parlor door, stepping into a glow of lamplight. There she waited quietly and a little breathlessly for those in the room to look up and see her.

HORTENSE, COMBS IN her red hair gleaming with green jade stones, was reading aloud. Letty listened and crocheted, while Booth sat staring at his own long-fingered hands. Ross had spread some papers on a table and was marking them with a pencil. It was he who saw her first, and there was no mistaking his astonishment, even his reluctant admiration.

Booth was the next to glance around. He sat quite still, but there was shock in his eyes. His tension made itself felt in the room, and Letty looked up and rose to her feet with a cry, dropping her crocheting. For a moment she stared at Camilla in horror. Then, without warning, she crumpled to the floor. Booth recovered himself and hurried to her side.

Hortense put down her book and stood up, frowning at Camilla. "Go upstairs," she ordered. "Go upstairs at once and take off that habit." Camilla was too surprised to move.

Aunt Letty moaned faintly as Booth held Hortense's ever-present smelling salts to her nose.

Hortense threw her sister a scornful look. "Don't be a goose, Letty. It's only Camilla dressed up in Althea's old riding habit." Then she spoke to Camilla. "My sister thought Althea's ghost had walked into this room. You had no business frightening us like that."

Camilla tried to speak, but Booth looked at her and shook his head. It was Ross who got her out of the room. He took her quietly by the arm and led her across the antehall into the library. "Sit down and catch your breath," he said. "They probably frightened you as much as you frightened them."

She turned to him in bewilderment. "I don't understand. Why should seeing me in my mother's riding habit upset everyone so?"

He sat beside her on the long couch. "I don't know all the details, but I suspect that your mother was wearing this very habit on the night she died. I know she went riding just before dusk, with a storm coming up. She rode up Thunder Mountain and must have reached the top when the storm broke. The thunder and lightning probably frightened her horse. It ran away and eventually came home with an empty saddle."

"I didn't know," Camilla said softly. She pushed her fingers against the place where a throbbing had begun at her temples. "No one would ever tell me the truth."

Ross went on in a quiet tone, with none of his usual irritation. "When your grandfather knew she was missing, he went up the mountain to look for her. He knew that was her favorite ride. She was dead when he found her. She must have struck her head against a rock when she was thrown."

Tears came into Camilla's eyes. "My father would never talk about what happened," she said. "When he came home after her funeral, he was like a different person for a long while. But why should he have blamed Grandfather Orrin for her death?"

"I don't know," Ross said. "But there was something queer about her riding out so late that afternoon, with a storm about to break."

Camilla sighed. "I can see what a shock it must have been when I walked into the room. It was a terrible thing to do. I'll go upstairs and take these things off."

"It wasn't your fault," Ross said, his tone surprisingly gentle. "You couldn't know the effect you'd have on them."

His unexpected kindness brought more tears, and she covered her face with her hands.

He touched her shoulder lightly. "You need a change from the burdens of this house. Nora Redfern has wanted me to bring you over for tea some afternoon. Will you go with me?"

Camilla looked at him in surprise. "You n-n-needn't feel sorry for me!" she choked.

There was no mockery in his smile. "Believe me," he said, "I waste no pity on you. But perhaps I sympathize more than I've let you see. You've been without a real friend in this house, and yet you haven't given up trying to crack the guard set up on all sides against you. I may not approve of your actions, but I admire your courage."

He went to the door and stood listening for a moment. Then he turned back to her. "They've taken Letty up to her room. Why don't you slip upstairs and change before Hortense sees you again?"

How unpredictable he was. He opposed her at every turn, laughed at her plans for the house, scolded her. Yet now he seemed gentle and thoughtful.

"I—I'm very grateful for—" She wanted to say more, but the words would not come, and she moved helplessly toward the door.

When she reached the second floor, Booth came to the door of his room, as if he waited for her. He had changed to a velvet smoking jacket of dark maroon. Cuffs and lapels were of a lighter red satin, and the effect was one of romantic elegance which fitted Booth so well. The look of shock had gone out of his eyes and he studied her coolly. "Althea's riding habit becomes you, Cousin. Though I must say you stirred up a nest of old ghosts tonight. You look even more like your mother than we realized." He gestured to the room behind him. "I want to show you something. Will you come in?"

Booth had a small den adjoining his bedroom, and it was into this he invited her. She stepped uncertainly into a room where lamplight shone warmly on brown and gold surfaces, a room attractively furnished with pieces that had a touch of Moorish opulence. He drew forward a Spanish chair with a velvet seat and leather back. When she was seated, he stood for a moment studying her face with a strange intensity that made her uncomfortable. If he saw the streaking of tearstains, he did not mention her weeping. Then he picked up a picture which had been set with its face against the wall and brought it to her.

"Do you remember this?"

It was the unfinished painting of a girl and a horse that she had seen in his studio. But now she could see that the faceless girl who stood struggling with the horse wore a riding habit of ash gray and a high top hat with floating gray streamers of veil.

Camilla looked from the picture to Booth's dark face, and he nodded in response.

"Your mother posed for this when she came back to Thunder Heights before her death," he said. "She loved to ride, and she was an expert horsewoman. I didn't want to paint her tamely, without action, and she thought a pose like this exciting. Though of course I had to do the horse from imagination. After what happened, I never finished it."

"I wish you had been able to finish it," Camilla said. "If you'd done her face, it would bring her back to me a little."

"Why shouldn't I finish it now?" he said. "Why shouldn't I give her your face?" He came to her quickly and put a finger beneath her chin, tilting her head. "Will you pose for me, Cousin?"

The thought gave her an intense pleasure. To help him finish her mother's picture was almost like a fulfillment.

"I'd love to pose for you, Booth," she said. The prospect of working with him so closely left her faintly excited. Perhaps this would give her an opportunity to get past the mask he so often wore and learn what the man himself was like.

"Good! We'll begin tomorrow, if you're willing. You feel better now, don't you? The tears are over?"

So he had noticed, after all. She nodded. "Ross told me how my mother died. It must have been terrible for you all that night. For Grandfather especially. What happened afterward?"

"When she didn't come home," Booth said, "I took another horse and followed the path along the river to see if she had chosen that trail. One of the stableboys had already gone after Dr. Wheeler, so he was here when Grandfather carried her in. There was nothing to be done. Later Grandfather got rid of every horse he owned. That's why we've had no carriage, no riding horses for so many years."

Camilla heard him sadly. "As if that would bring her back."

"You won't be afraid to ride, after what happened here?" Booth asked.

"Because my mother met with an accident? Of course not. It would be foolish to give up riding for that reason."

"You'd better break it gently to Mother and Aunt Letty that you mean to buy a horse. I haven't told them I was looking for one." He came with her to the door and, catching her hand, held her there a moment. "I want very much to paint you, Camilla."

There was a rising excitement in his voice, and she felt again the strength of his dark appeal striking an echo in herself. She turned hurriedly away, hoping he had not read her response.

AFTER BREAKFAST THE following morning she worked for a while on the habit, then put it on and went upstairs to the nursery, where Booth now had his studio. He had changed the room very little. Even Letty's harp was still in its place. His easel stood where the light was good, and he posed Camilla facing him.

"We'll leave the face for the last," he said. "I want to get into the mood of the picture again before I touch that. Today I'll pose you standing, so that I can do further work on the color of the habit and catch the way the folds of material hang."

His hands were light when he touched her, turning her this way and that, seeking to match the pose of the woman in the picture. Though his manner was impersonal, Camilla was sharply aware of him, and this made it difficult for her to assume the pose he wished. But when he got to work at his painting, he seemed to forget her as a woman, and some of her self-consciousness faded.

"Aren't you tired?" Booth asked after a while. "Sit down a moment and let yourself go limp." He brought a chair for her, and she sat down gratefully. Now she could watch him work. It was a shame, she thought, that a man who was so keen an artist should be buried in a place like Thunder Heights.

"Why don't you plan a trip to New York soon?" she suggested, following the trend of her thoughts along a fairly safe course. "You could take Aunt Hortense and give her a whirl in the city."

"If taking her on a trip to New York will please you, I'll do it, Camilla. Perhaps it really would do her good."

"And you too," Camilla said.

His laughter had a dry sound. "I'm content with my work. Shall we get back to it again? Do you suppose this time you can try for more life in your pose? It's the body beneath the clothes that matters. Folds of material are lifeless in themselves."

His hands were light on her shoulders again, turning her. He was so close that his touch was almost an embrace, and she had a curious desire to run, as if there were a need to save herself from the dark forces that drove this man. But she remained submissive, allowing him to turn her as he wished.

He stepped back and looked at her, clearly not pleased with the result. "No," he said, and his tone was no longer gentle. "You haven't caught it. You're merely a pretty young woman in a riding habit, posing in a studio." There was a sting to his words that brought her head up in an instinctive challenge. At once he stepped toward her and put his fingers at her throat, just under her chin. "That's it—keep your head high like that. Be angry with me, if you like. I want you to be a beautiful, angry, spirited woman, struggling furiously with a horse that must not be allowed to get out of control."

His description made her feel awkward. "But you're not painting my face today," she reminded him. "What does my expression matter?"

"Whatever is in your face will be reflected in the lines of your body," he said. "As your body comes to life, so will your garments reveal spirit.

After all, I want to paint a woman. The woman you are, if you will let yourself go. You should have seen Althea when she posed for this picture. I was only twenty-one at the time, and she was an inspiration."

With every word, Camilla felt less spirited. "I'm not my mother," she said defensively. "People are always telling me how exciting she was, but I know I'm not—"

He shook her almost roughly. "You must never talk like that! You have more than your mother had, if you'll only realize it. With confidence you can be anything." He let her go and turned back to his worktable. "We've done enough this morning," he said. "I've upset you, and I didn't mean to. Will you forgive me, Cousin, and let me try again tomorrow?"

She nodded and went quickly out of the room, feeling shaken. How foolish she had been to think posing for Booth's picture would be a simple, pleasant experience. In a strange way it had been almost like having him make love to her.

CHAPTER SEVEN

THE POSING WENT better for a few days because, Camilla felt, Booth tried harder to put her at ease. Letty soon started coming in to watch while he worked. She would sit near a window, crocheting, seldom speaking, offering little distraction.

One morning when Booth stopped the posing session early, Letty invited Camilla to her room. "Perhaps you'd like to help me with a task that may interest you," she said.

Ever since the day when the saucer of tea had made Mignonette sick, Camilla had experienced a constraint when she was with Letty. She reproached herself for this feeling, yet what had happened remained as a bar to the friendship she had previously felt for her. There was no excuse to avoid her, however, and it might even be possible to return to more comfortable ground with her aunt if they could have a good talk.

She looked about Aunt Letty's private retreat with interest. In one corner a second-floor tower bulged into a circular addition to the room, with windows all around and a padded window seat. The wall over the bed sloped beneath a slanting roof, and the entire expanse of the angled wall was covered with pictures.

While Letty knelt to pull a box from under the bed, Camilla studied the pictures. Some of them were Hudson River sketches and engravings, but there were also scenes from abroad, glimpses of castles, mountains, glens, and lochs.

"This looks like Walter Scott country," she said to Letty.

Her aunt was lifting folders and envelopes from the box and piling them on the bed. "It is. Just a few memories of a lovely year I spent in Scotland when I was a young girl."

"And did you meet a young man in the Highlands and give your heart away in the proper romantic fashion?" Camilla asked.

There was a flush in Letty's cheeks. "Oh, I met several, and perhaps I did give my heart away for a little while. But Papa didn't approve, and it was nothing serious."

Camilla curled herself up comfortably on Letty's bed, wanting now to pursue this topic. "What about Aunt Hortense? Why has she never married? Did no young men ever come to Westcliff?"

"Oh, they came," Letty said. "But Hortense had an unfortunate faculty for wanting only what someone else had."

"What do you mean?" Camilla asked.

Letty's gaze seemed far away. "There was one—I remember him as if it were yesterday. He looked as I imagine a poet might look. And he could quote poetry too—in a voice that sounded like one of our mountain streams, sometimes whispering, sometimes thundering."

The tone of her voice startled Camilla. "This was the man Hortense fell in love with?"

There was sad assent in Letty's sigh.

"Was he a schoolteacher?"

"Yes, dear," Letty said. "I see you've guessed. It was your father Hortense loved, and she would have no one else."

"So that's it." Camilla was thoughtful. "Did my mother know?"

"Hortense let everyone know. She always claimed that he would have married her, if Althea hadn't stolen him from her. Of course that wasn't true. He never looked at anyone but Althea. She was always the lovely one, the lucky one. They fell in love at their first meeting, and since Papa wanted someone else for Althea, there was nothing to do but run off. I helped her get away. Papa never forgave me for that." There were tears in Letty's eyes.

"I never knew," Camilla said. "Poor Aunt Hortense."

"It has been difficult for her. When she looks at you she sees two people who hurt her, two people she has never forgiven."

Camilla leaned back against a poster of the bed. For the first time she understood the intense dislike she had seen in Hortense's eyes. "Was it because Aunt Hortense knew she would never marry that she wanted to adopt a child?"

"I suppose she must have felt there would be an emptiness in her life without a child. We needed someone young in this house. I was glad to see Booth come. He was ten when she brought him here, and already quite talented as an artist."

"What an odd thing to do," Camilla said. "Surely if a woman wanted a child, she would want one from babyhood on."

Letty seemed agitated. "There's been enough talk about the past. That isn't why I asked you here. I thought you might like to help me sort my collection of herb recipes." She gathered up a handful of loose sheets on which clippings had been pasted in long yellowing columns, and dropped them in Camilla's lap. "I'd like to separate the medicinal information from the cooking recipes and catalogue them both so that when I want one I don't have to hunt through a mixture like this."

Camilla set to work with interest. She read through a recipe for Turkish rose-petal jam, and one for marigold custard. There were directions for making saffron cake, for rose and caraway cookies, and tansy pudding. "I should think," she said, "that you would have enough material here for a book about herbs. You've worked with them for years and you're a real authority."

"Do you really think I might do something with all this?" Letty's eyes brightened.

"Oh, I do!" Camilla warmed to the idea. "I'll help you sort it out and make a plan for presenting it."

There was a knock at the door and Grace looked into the room. "If you please, mum, here's a note for you," she said.

When she had gone, Camilla opened the note and read it. It was from Nora Redfern. Would Miss King permit Mr. Granger to bring her to tea at Blue Beeches one afternoon next week?

Camilla held out the note to Letty. "How very nice—I'd love to go."

Letty read the note doubtfully. "I don't know. We aren't on speaking terms with Blue Beeches. Mrs. Landry, Nora's mother, and your grandfather had a quarrel years ago. Naturally we took Papa's side, and we haven't been friendly with that family since."

"But all that can't be Nora's fault. Ross seems to like her." Sometimes, indeed, Camilla had wondered just how much Ross liked the attractive young widow.

"We've all regretted that," Letty said. "Papa never approved of the way Ross made friends with the Redferns. Under the circumstances, it was inexcusable."

Never before had Camilla heard Letty sound so uncharitable. Her attitude seemed more like what might be expected from Hortense. "I'll be sorry to go against your wishes," Camilla said gently, "but I'd like very much to accept this invitation."

Letty sighed and began to gather up her papers.

"Wait," Camilla said. "We must talk about your book."

Letty shook her head. "I'm not in the mood now, dear. Some other time, perhaps." She looked increasingly troubled.

"Why have you changed your mind?" Camilla asked. "Surely not because I'm going to see Nora Redfern?"

Letty pushed the last batch of clippings into the box and fastened the lid. Then she looked up at Camilla. "You know what they whisper about me, don't you? They say I've tried to poison people. If I were to do a book on the subject of herbs, all the whispers would spring up again."

She looked so forlorn that pity thrust doubt from Camilla's mind. "I think we must pay no attention to such gossip," she said. "It's too ridiculous to heed."

Letty's smile was tremulous. "Thank you, my dear." But she refused to discuss the subject further.

When she returned to her room, Camilla sat down at her mother's desk to answer Nora Redfern's note. But her mind would not relinquish the thought of Letty. One part of her wanted to trust in her wholeheartedly. That day when Camilla had talked to her grandfather, he had said, "Watch Letty." Surely he had meant to take care of Letty, to watch out for her. But something more questioning in Camilla reserved judgment.

Resolutely she put these disturbing thoughts aside and picked up her pen to write to Nora Redfern. It would be good to escape from Thunder Heights and visit Blue Beeches next week.

THAT EVENING BOOTH told her that it was hopeless to continue with his painting. Something had thrown him off his course, he said, and it would be better to stop for a while; if Camilla were still agreeable, he would accept her offer of a trip to New York for himself and his mother. Camilla readily encouraged them.

A day later, on the morning they were to leave, Grace tapped on Camilla's door. Mr. Booth, she said, requested a moment of her time in the library.

Camilla hurried downstairs and found him pacing restlessly about the room. He turned when she entered, stepped to the door, and closed it after her. "It isn't just because I'm out of the mood for painting that I'm making this trip," he said. "It's because of my mother. She's going to try to upset Grandfather Orrin's will. I thought you ought to know. She means to see a lawyer of greater eminence than Mr. Pompton and learn what steps she might be able to take."

Camilla nodded gravely. "I really can't blame her. But thank you for telling me."

He held out his hand, and when she put her own into it, he did not release her at once. It was a relief when Hortense came sailing into the room, gowned for travel. Her skirt was of mauve broadcloth, and she wore an elbow-length cape of black broadcloth, with a high, satin-trimmed collar and huge buttons. The straw hat tilted over her forehead was wreathed in violets and bound in violet ribbon that clashed with her red hair.

"I hope you'll have a fine time in New York," Camilla told this impressive figure.

"This is your chance to prove what a housekeeper you are," Hortense said. "Matilda and Toby are going upriver to visit Matilda's sister. The scullery maid has the day off, and Letty is turning out the linen shelves upstairs, with Grace's help. So you may do exactly what you like."

Camilla could only stare at her in bewilderment. She well knew now that it was Letty who quietly kept things running, in spite of Hortense's highhanded gestures. Certainly she had no intention of trying to take these duties out of Letty's competent hands. "I don't want to interfere with the regular routine," she said mildly.

"I've thought from the first that your household education has been neglected," Hortense said, sniffing. "I doubt if you can bake a decent loaf of bread. However, the house is yours for the moment—if you choose to take advantage of the opportunity."

"Thank you, Aunt Hortense," Camilla said, suppressing a smile.

Her aunt swept toward the front door, and Booth followed her without comment. Camilla looked thoughtfully after them as Booth helped his mother into the hired rig. It was ironic that she was paying for this trip to New York so that they might seek legal advice on taking everything away from her. Not that the fact disturbed her. If she lost all this, she would only be back where she was before she came here. She would have lost nothing.

She went into the antehall. As usual the marble hands reached out to her, but now their gesture seemed almost a welcome—as if the house was ready at last to give itself to her. Today was truly her own to use as she pleased. Why shouldn't she prove that she could bake a loaf as well as the next woman?

She got the starter dough from the ice chest. Then she collected her ingredients, and the bowls and utensils she would need. She decided to work in the larder, where Letty kept her herbs. It was a cool and pleasant room, and there was a ledge with a marble slab that made a good working surface. Once there, she happily began to work. Into the bowl went her lump of starter dough, sifted flour, and milk. When she had stirred the whole sufficiently with a long-handled wooden spoon, she covered the yellow crockery bowl with a cloth. Now it must rise before she could have the fun of kneading it.

She wandered idly about the room, studying the neat labels Letty had lettered so carefully. On the shelf behind the door she saw that the jar which had contained a mixture of marjoram and mint leaves had been refilled, and she took it down to smell the pleasant minty scent. Farther along the shelf there had been an empty space the day when Mignonette had been made sick by Letty's tea. There was now a bottle containing a pale liquid. Its label read TANSY JUICE—a name that had a pleasantly old-fashioned ring. She took down the bottle and removed the stopper. The odor was sharp, with a faintly resinous quality, and she was reminded of the tea Letty had brought her. Perhaps Letty had added tansy to the tea that day.

Camilla put the bottle back and wandered upstairs and outside to the riverfront. At the foot of the hill, beyond the railroad tracks, a spit of land cut out into the river. She had never been down there, and she began a descent of the steep bank, holding on to tree branches to let herself down slowly. In a few moments she had crossed the tracks to the lower spit of land. Here there were the ruins of an old wooden dock and a small boathouse, its roof long ago caved in. She scrambled around, exploring. Shrubbery grew thick to the very edge of a narrow, pebbled beach, and the wild growth had almost engulfed what men had built upon the river's edge. Her foot slipped in a muddy spot, and she grabbed at a thick bush. As she pulled herself to drier ground, her eye was caught by an object deep in the forked branches. Curious, she reached in and pulled out a flexible stick a foot or so in length, with a blackened silver head attached to it.

Though the silver was tarnished, she could make out an embossing in the form of tiny chrysanthemums. The wood of the stick was black and strong, and propped there above the earth, it had resisted the effects of decay, though it had been scarred by long weathering. A rotted leather thong hung from one end.

She realized suddenly that the object she held in her hands was a woman's riding crop. How had it been lost in so odd a place? She would carry her find home, clean it up, and polish the silver. Someone at the house might know to whom it had belonged. Had it been her mother's, perhaps?

AFTER SHE HAD taken the crop to her room and tucked it into a drawer, she went downstairs to the larder. Removing the cloth from the dough, she found it a sodden, inert mass in the bottom of the bowl. By now it should have puffed considerably. In fact, it looked sticky and wet and incapable of rising. Probably it needed more flour. She scooped it out onto the marble slab and added some, kneading it in. Now the mass turned dry and crumbly. So she dribbled in a little water and kneaded again. There seemed no way to get it right.

Her confidence began to ebb. Her dream of triumphantly producing a delectable loaf at dinner was just that—a dream, and discouragement seized her. Undoubtedly, Hortense Judd was right about her household talents.

The cellar seemed suddenly a lonely and depressing place. How still it was down here. How empty. She could hear no fall of footsteps from upstairs, no sound of voices, and the chill of stone walls seemed more damp than pleasantly cool. Before her in the bowl lay the grayish lump—and for all that it had not risen, there was a great deal more of it than she had intended in the beginning.

What on earth was she to do with this mess? Camilla could imagine Hortense's scorn if she knew what had happened. There was nothing for Camilla to do but dispose of her clandestine efforts where they would not be discovered.

She put the dough in the cloth with which she had covered the bowl, and turned up the corners, wrapping it well. Then she took one of Aunt Letty's trowels from a toolroom next to the larder and went outside. Through the herb garden she ran toward the woods, following the path she had taken the day she had come upon Ross Granger. She knew the perfect hiding place for her unpleasant burden. When she reached the weeping beech tree, she knew the thick, drooping branches would hide her from view. Smiling, she slipped between them into the shadowy seclusion of the open space around the blue-black trunk of the tree.

The shelter was like a child's secret playhouse. Had her mother played here as a little girl? Camilla wondered. She knelt and began to dig with her trowel. So absorbed was she that the sudden crackling of branches being parted came as a startling sound. She looked up in dismay to see Ross Granger peering at her.

"What's wrong?" he asked. "I saw you scurrying up here like a fugitive."

What she was doing seemed suddenly ridiculous. She covered her face with her hands to stifle her laughter and sat helplessly back on her heels.

Ross stirred her bundle doubtfully with his toe, and the cloth fell back to expose the lumpish gray contents. "What is it?" he asked.

"I—I was just trying to make bread. Before Aunt Hortense left for New York she said I couldn't even bake a decent loaf of bread. So I wanted to confound her with my skill when she came home. But the only one I've confounded is myself."

He started to grin, then to laugh out loud. "I'll help you," he said. He picked up the trowel and quickly enlarged the hole. Then he dumped the sodden dough into the grave and covered it, stamping down the earth.

"I don't suppose you want a headstone?" he said cheerfully.

Camilla looked at him in bewilderment. He was regarding her with an odd tenderness that was almost like a caress.

"Don't think I don't know what a hard time you've had in that house. You've had everyone fighting you, including me, and giving you very little help in your effort to save the old place. To say nothing of the people in it. Orrin Judd would have been proud of you, Camilla. I think you're wasting your time on what can't be changed. Which makes me sorry—because I like to see the young and brave and—and foolish—succeed."

The climate between them had changed in some subtle way. There was a long, breathless moment while she looked into his eyes and time hung queerly suspended. She was aware only of their closeness in this tiny space, hidden from the world by branches all about, aware only of him. This is what I want, she thought. Something in her had known from the first moment she had spoken to him on the riverboat that someday it would be like this. She had fought him and resented him. But now nothing mattered except that his strong, fine head with the bright chestnut hair was bending close, and there was a question in his eyes.

She raised her own head without hesitation and went quite simply into his arms. His mouth was hard upon her lips, so that they felt bruised beneath its touch. Her body ached under the pressure of his arms, but she did not want the pain lessened. When he raised his head, she would have put her arms about his neck and risen on her toes to rest her cheek against his own, admitting everything—all the wild feeling that surged through her, all the wanting so long held in check because there was no one to want. But he took her by the shoulders and held her suddenly away, his eyes grave, his mouth unsmiling.

"You *are* something of a surprise," he said.

The words were like an unexpected slap, and the blood rose in her cheeks as though the blow had been a physical one. She stared at him in dismay. Then she turned and would have run straight away from him, but he caught her hand.

"Come along," he said calmly, as though nothing had happened. "We've work to do."

She could not struggle against him without indignity, so she went with him down the path toward Thunder Heights. When they reached the back door, he did not release her hand, but led her up the steps and into the kitchen. There he looked about confidently, while she watched him, completely at a loss.

"With your permission, I'll wash my hands," he said. "You still want to bake bread, don't you?"

To Camilla's astonishment, that was exactly what they did. Spellbound, she obeyed him, afraid to wake up and face what had happened, afraid to acknowledge the emotion that had swept through her there beneath the beech tree. Under his skillful instruction, she began the process of bread-making all over again. He was as matter-of-fact, when he asked her to scald the milk, as though that exultant moment between them had never been.

"To be good," he told her, "a batch of bread should be made with a large portion of love and cheer mixed in. At least that's what my aunt Otis used to say. She had the cheeriest kitchen I've ever seen. There were yellow curtains and yellow tea towels all around, so that if the sun wasn't really shining, it would seem to be in her kitchen. Aunt Otis raised me, and she always used to say there was no reason why a man shouldn't know how to bake bread, when bread baking was good for the soul. She was right too."

Camilla listened in wonder, lulled by his words and his companionable presence. She did as he told her, and the dough seemed to come to life under her hands.

"Where is your home?" she asked him, curious now to know all there was to know about this man.

"It's on the river—but down along the Jersey bank," he said.

It was easy now to ask him questions. "Did you grow up there? What of your mother and father?"

"My mother died when I was born, and my father was mostly away in his work as an engineer. As I've told you, he was Orrin Judd's good friend and worked on many a project for him. But Aunt Otis had me in hand while I was growing up."

Camilla thought silently that Aunt Otis had done a good job.

"Now," he said, "you'll need to put this in a warm place to rise, leave it alone for a couple of hours and—"

She clapped a hand to her mouth. "That's it! I left it to rise in the cellar, where it's cool. Of course the yeast never started to grow."

He nodded at her, grinning. "Think you can carry on now? Knead it after it rises—and let it rise again. Another kneading and it's ready for baking. Can you fire the stove all right?"

"If I can't, I'll get Grace to help me," she said.

Plainly he was going to leave her now, with so much that was still unexplained between them. Yet you could not say to a man, Why did you kiss me, if you didn't mean it? Why did you invite me into your arms if you didn't want me there?

"I'll go back to my work now," he told her, "and you needn't admit you've had any help. You're entitled to the credit."

She could only nod in silence. He put out a hand and touched her shoulder lightly. Then he was gone by way of the back door. She heard him whistling as he rounded the house, returning to the new rooms. The sound was cheerful, but she did not know whether to laugh or to weep.

To CAMILLA'S RELIEF, Ross did not appear at dinner that night, sending word that he was going to the village, so Camilla and Letty dined alone. With Hortense's restraining presence removed, Letty was ready to chatter, but Camilla felt subdued and pensive. There were a few moments of excitement over the bread. Matilda, coming home from her visit, had found the fresh loaves and admired them generously, and Letty said this was the best bread she had tasted in a long while, and Camilla must certainly show Hortense what she could do when she returned from her trip.

Camilla accepted their compliments in a preoccupied state and kept her secret. The thought of Ross was never far away, and she did not want to be alone lest she give herself wholly to dreaming about what had happened.

After dinner they avoided the parlor ritual, and Camilla followed Letty and Mignonette upstairs.

"Something's troubling you, isn't it, dear?" Letty said when they reached the door of her room. "Would you like to come in and keep me company for a while?"

Grateful for the invitation, Camilla seated herself on a window cushion in the circular tower. There, high among green branches that pressed against the windows, she felt like a bird suspended in a swinging cage. She could glimpse the river shining far below in the twilight. It was a peaceful spot, and she tried to let her feelings wash away in the quiet green light.

Letty made no attempt to draw her out, but went to work on her collection of recipes. "I've decided to think about your suggestion for a book," she said. "Whether I try to have it published or not, it will give me satisfaction to compile it."

"I'm glad," Camilla told her. She picked up a book that was lying on the window seat. It was a fat volume and seemed to be a medical dictionary of herbs. The pages fell open and she read at random.

Sage tea was good for sore throats, it appeared, summer savory for intestinal disorders. The action of thyme was antiseptic. Tansy . . . Her interest quickened at the name. Tansy could be rubbed over raw meat to keep the flies away, and its leaves were useful in destroying fleas and ants. It was a violent irritant to the stomach, and many deaths had been caused by it.

Camilla looked up from the pages. "You have a bottle of tansy juice with your herb collection in the cellar," she said. "But this book says that it's poisonous."

"It is if one uses too much," Letty replied. "The Pennsylvania Dutch make poultices of the sap, and they used the leaves in tea in stomach treatments. It's all in the quantity used."

The bottle of tansy juice had been there on the shelf and available, Camilla thought, and a jar with tansy leaves.

Letty went on evenly, not looking up. "It's easy to pick up a few facts and put them together in the wrong pattern. I avoid doing that, my dear."

Camilla glanced at her, startled. "Sometimes I think you're a little fey. Sometimes you almost read my mind."

"It's my Scottish blood, I suppose. Sometimes I have a queer feeling of knowing when something is about to happen. As I did the night Papa died. And there have been other occasions too. The night your mother rode out to her death was one—" She stopped and shook her head. "I mustn't think about these things. I don't want to be queer and—and fey."

Camilla left the window seat and went to sit beside her.

"If there's anything queer about you, Aunt Letty, then it's a nice sort of queerness to have," she assured her aunt.

She began to help Letty with her sorting, and the green light faded at the windows as night came down. The sky to the west might still be bright, but the shadow of Thunder Mountain had fallen upon the house, and here night had already begun.

As the evening wore quietly on, Camilla began to feel lulled and peaceful. Letty was right, Camilla felt—she mustn't allow suspicion to grow in her mind. She must live in this house and accept the people in it, or she would find no peace.

She did not remember the riding crop until she returned to her room. She got it out and carried it back to Letty.

"Look what I found in the shrubbery today," she said.

Letty rose from her work and came to take it from Camilla's hand. The color went out of her face, and she sat down abruptly.

"Where did you find this?" she demanded.

Camilla explained how she had found it. "Do you know whom the crop belonged to?" she asked.

"Of course," Letty said. "It belonged to my sister Althea. Papa had it made for her when she first started riding."

"I saw the saddle in the attic," Camilla said. "Was that hers too?"

"Yes. Papa brought the saddle and bridle from Mexico."

"Someone has been going up to the attic to care for the leather."

"Papa did that." Letty spoke in a low voice. "After Althea ran away, he used to go upstairs and sit with those riding things she loved. Once when I went looking for him, I heard him talking to them. He was questioning and scolding—like a man who couldn't understand what had been done to him. He wouldn't let us mention her name, but he used to steal up there and take care of her things. Even after her death, he went on caring for them. I think it brought him some sort of comfort."

"Perhaps I can bring my mother's saddle down from the attic and use it again," Camilla said. "Perhaps she would like to have me wear her habit and use her things."

Letty started to speak and then fell silent.

"Why were you startled when I showed you the crop, Aunt Letty?" Camilla asked. "Was my mother carrying it that evening when she went out to ride for the last time?"

"I don't remember," Letty said. "I'm not sure."

"No, of course she couldn't have carried it," Camilla mused. "Not if she rode up Thunder Mountain. Not when I've just found the crop down near the water's edge."

Letty nodded as if relieved. "You're right, naturally. I can't imagine how it got there."

Camilla took the crop back to her room, but she felt restless and not at all ready for sleep. Perhaps a walk would quiet her thoughts. Softly she slipped down the stairs and went outside. The night was soft and cool, and moonlight flooded the world.

She drifted across the grass, running in the direction of the gate, and she did not pause until she saw the lights of Ross's rooms above the stable. Then she came to a halt, shrinking back into the shadow of an oak tree, watching the patches of light. Memory swept back on a flood of warmth, to engulf her being. She could feel Ross's arms about her, his kiss hard upon her mouth.

A shadow moved across a square of light, and Camilla came to herself abruptly. What foolish thing was she doing—spying on him out of the shadows! Eager as a schoolgirl for the sight of her love. *Her love.*

She had not asked to love this man, but there it was. She turned and ran back through the trees, letting herself quietly into the house, scurrying upstairs to the retreat of her own room. There was an exultance in her, and a torment as well.

CHAPTER EIGHT

IN THE MORNING the exultance was gone. Camilla awakened feeling tired, as though she had not slept, but her eyes were clear, her thoughts were sharp with self-judgment. How could she have been so trapped by gentle dreams last night? Love? There were times when she had been equally attracted to Booth.

Today there were other things to think of. And she had to face the possibility that someone in this house had added poison to her tea. Since it was unlikely to be one of the servants, or Ross, who was an outsider, the tamperer must be Hortense, Letty, or Booth. She must get to the bottom of what had happened. Yet when she met Letty that day, she could not bring herself to question her directly.

In the days before Hortense and Booth came home, Ross was completely matter-of-fact. He placed business matters before her once more, and did not hesitate to show his disapproval when she seemed unenthusiastic about projects that absorbed his attention.

On the afternoon when Hortense and Booth were to return, Ross reminded her of the invitation to tea at Nora Redfern's tomorrow. She had a feeling that he regretted his original impulse in urging such a visit. But she was looking forward to it.

It was with a sense of disappointment that she heard the sound of the carriage bringing Booth and his mother back to Thunder Heights. Now the quiet, friendly hours she had spent with Letty would come to an end, and disquieting influences would be at work in the house again.

Nevertheless, she went to the door to greet them. Her first look at the travelers told her that as far as Aunt Hortense was concerned, the trip had been a failure. She was clearly angry and frustrated, impatient even with Booth, and hardly civil to Letty and Camilla.

Booth appeared to have enjoyed himself thoroughly. He was ready to take up his painting again, and at the sitting next morning all went well. Letty joined them, and once Booth paused as he worked to ask Camilla a question. "What has happened to you, Cousin, since I've been away?"

Camilla was startled. "Happened? Why, nothing much. I've baked bread and helped Aunt Letty with her recipes."

Booth flashed the smile that always seemed so unexpected in his dark, sardonic face. "It was not those things I meant, Camilla. Even though you're quiet today, there's something that was lacking before. I see more than Althea in you this morning."

"I don't know what you mean," she told him.

Letty glanced up at Camilla in mild surprise, and Camilla was afraid that her aunt might add some comment of her own. "Why don't you play for us while I'm posing, Aunt Letty?" she said hurriedly. "I've never really heard you play your harp."

Perhaps Letty sensed a plea behind her words, for she put her work aside. "Very well—if Booth doesn't mind."

"I've always enjoyed your playing, Aunt Letty," he said gallantly, but his eyes were still on his model, and Camilla sensed a quickened interest and curiosity in his look.

Letty went to the harp and drew off its cover. The fingers of her left hand moved easily on the strings, but she had to bend her body forward to reach them with her crooked right arm. She began to play, and the music had a wailing, melancholy sound, as if the contented, busy Letty Judd of everyday vanished when she sat down to her harp. In her place was a woman lost and tragic. The music seemed to sing of longing and of wasted, empty years with a frightening intensity.

Booth looked up from his painting somberly. "You're hearing the music of Thunder Heights, Cousin. It speaks for us all. Trapped and damned and without hope. That's why Mother hates to hear Aunt Letty play. The music tells too much about the things we try to hide from one another."

Letty's fingers stopped. She rose to cover the instrument and without a word slipped from the room.

When Booth spoke again, it was of another matter. "As you've probably guessed, Mother found little encouragement on her mission to New York. It's possible that the will might be broken. At least the lawyer she consulted didn't try to discourage her as a client. But it seems that it would cost a fine penny—and where is the money to come from? She can hardly ask you to finance her effort to take a fortune away from you, can she, Cousin?"

Camilla watched him guardedly. "You don't seem to mind."

He shrugged. "Why should I mind? I live a more comfortable life under the new regime."

He worked on for a while longer and then laid aside his brush. "That's enough for today. It's going well. A change of scene has done me good. And I shan't give up wondering what caused the change in you, Camilla. Also, I haven't forgotten your wish to find a good saddle horse. I shopped around a bit in New York. But so far I haven't found what I think you might like."

She was glad when the posing was over. On and off during the last half hour she had been thinking about the tea at Blue Beeches this afternoon, and she was eager to get away and look through the frocks she might wear. She wanted to seem beautiful and remote and self-contained to Ross Granger. He must be made to forget that Camilla King had ever moved in so headlong a fashion into his arms.

The dress she decided upon was of pale blue Chinese silk, trimmed with touches of ivory lace. It was a thin, delicate dress, and she found it satisfying to appear in something that was far from serviceable, and not at all suited to a governess. She put on her mother's bracelet of medallions and turned before the mirror a few times. She was ready.

Letty came in to admire her just before she went downstairs. "I haven't seen anyone looking so pretty and appealing since Althea lived in this house. You'll do us credit, my dear."

Camilla gave her a quick, loving hug, wondering at her own perversity in holding anyone so endearing as Aunt Letty under suspicion. She ran down the octagon staircase, listening pleasurably to her own silken froufrou.

Ross was waiting for her outside, and as she came out he stared at her. Though his startled look was gratifying, he made no comment on her appearance. As they followed the path that led to the lower level, however, and walked along the riverbank, she found that he held branches back and helped her up and down steep places as if she were really as fragile as she wanted to believe herself today. Sometimes she wondered if he were laughing at her just a little behind his rather elaborate gestures, but she was too happy and confident to mind.

Once they stopped to watch a fleet of little sailboats gliding past on the surface of the smooth blue Hudson, and Camilla followed them out of sight, feeling that they added to the carefree aspect of the day.

The first glimpse of Blue Beeches was reassuring. It sat foursquare upon its high basement, its generous veranda open toward the river. Nora's two older children were playing croquet on the lawn at one side of the house while their nurse sat watching with the youngest. The spotted dog, Champion, came bounding across the grass toward the visitors. Ross accepted his effusive greeting with affection and held him away from Camilla.

"He misses his master," Ross said. "As we all do. Nora's husband died just over a year ago. Ted Redfern was one of my good friends. I've been trying to help Nora with some of her business problems ever since. She has a lot of courage. I hope you'll be friends." There was a note of affection in his tone that made Camilla glance at him quickly. Was his feeling for Ted Redfern's widow more than that of a friend? She did not like the pang that stabbed through her at his words.

A maid showed them into a huge parlor with moss-green wallpaper and softly cushioned furniture. Nora joined them after a brief interval, flushed and breathless. Her brown hair had been swept back from her forehead without any vestige of a pompadour, and tied with a black velvet ribbon at the nape of her neck.

"Do forgive me for keeping you waiting," she said, holding out a hand first to Camilla and then to Ross. "I had Diamond out for a ride and I lost track of time. Ted used to say it was no use buying me watches because I'd always forget to look at them."

Nora was engaging and friendly, but Camilla found herself a little watchful, a little too much aware of every glance that passed between Nora and Ross.

The maid brought tea in a handsome Sèvres service, with watercress sandwiches and frosted cakes on a three-tiered stand, and Nora settled down comfortably for conversation.

"I remember your mother well," she told Camilla. "When I was quite small she used to come here often to visit my mother. Mama lives upriver now. I wrote her that I was going to invite you over, and she wants me to tell her all about you. When you have the house fully refurbished, you must give a party and bring back the old days. How gay it used to be! I can remember coming home across the river late one night with my parents and seeing Thunder Heights lighted from top to bottom, with Japanese lanterns strung across the veranda and all about the lawn. Often here at Blue Beeches there were nights when we could catch the sound of music and laughter."

Letty too had urged her to give a party, Camilla remembered. "I'd like to," she said, her interest rising. "Perhaps we could invite people who used to know the family. Would you come, Mrs. Redfern? And your mother?"

Nora hesitated. "Mother would come in a moment—though I'm not sure that would be a good idea. She is pretty outspoken, you know, and besides, your aunts would be angry."

"But why?" Camilla asked. "What happened to break up the friendship your mother had with my family at Thunder Heights?"

"Let's not spoil the afternoon with old quarrels," Nora said. "Perhaps your coming will make the difference and we can all be friends again."

"If we give a party, we'll want you both," Camilla insisted. "I should think Aunt Hortense would love one. And I know Aunt Letty would like to see the house opened up for our sakes, though I'm not sure she would really enjoy it herself."

"She gave up that sort of thing after her arm was injured," Nora said. "She wouldn't wear evening dress after that."

"No one ever mentions her injury," said Camilla. "What happened?"

"She was thrown from a horse," Ross said. "Just as your mother was. It occurred before I came to Thunder Heights."

Nora nodded. "It was after Althea had married and gone away. Hortense and Letty used to ride a good deal in those days. Orrin gave Letty a mare that had a maverick streak they weren't aware of. Letty was thrown and dragged. The mare went half crazy, and Letty's arm was stepped on and broken. She might have been killed if Hortense hadn't been riding with her that day. Hortense rescued her and got her home. But the arm never set properly, and the hoof left a scar she has carried ever since."

"Where do you ride?" Camilla asked as Nora refilled her cup.

"Today I followed the river," Nora said. "But my favorite rides are back in the hills. I think I'm happiest when I can ride up through the woods and come out on top of Thunder Mountain."

"I've been thinking of getting a horse," Camilla said. "I loved riding as a child in the parks in New York."

"You're not afraid of the Thunder Heights jinx when it comes to horses?" Nora asked.

"I don't believe in jinxes," Camilla said.

"In that case, you needn't wait. I'd be glad to loan you Diamond. He was Ted's horse, but I've trained him to the sidesaddle. You may have him tomorrow, if you like. I'm leaving with the children to visit Mother for a few days. Ross can take one of the other horses and go with you."

Unable to hide her sudden pleasure at the thought of riding with Ross, Camilla glanced at him and saw clear reluctance in his eyes. She rushed into words to hide her hurt.

"Surely it's not necessary for me to have an escort!"

"Indeed it is," Nora assured her. "We can't have you going out in the hills alone until you know your way. You can lose yourself easily. You'll take her, won't you, Ross?"

"I'm going down to New York in a day or two," he said. "But perhaps I could manage it tomorrow."

His lack of enthusiasm was obvious, and Camilla felt relieved when it was time to go. She did not want to remain in Ross's company a moment longer than she had to, now that she felt sure where his interest really lay. On the way back to Thunder Heights, he was preoccupied, almost as if he had forgotten her presence, and she felt piqued into calling him back.

"Did you know," she asked, "that Aunt Hortense's purpose in going to New York was to try to break Grandfather's will?"

"I'm not surprised," Ross said. "If I were you, I'd break it myself and pack Hortense and Booth out of the house."

She was indignant. "Even if no one else cares, *I* feel bound by what Grandfather wanted me to do."

"You're being sentimental," Ross said. "Why not give those two the money and let them go? You'd be better off. Orrin Judd was trying to bring back the past, to undo old mistakes. You must live in the present—the future. Don't be a fool."

They were nearing the house now and she began to hurry. "If I'm a fool, I'll be one in my own way. And—you needn't trouble to ride with me tomorrow. Perhaps I can ask Booth—"

He surprised her by reaching out to catch her wrist. The medallions of her bracelet pressed into her flesh with the strength of his grasp. "I'll ride with you," he said, his gray eyes angry. Then he dropped her hand abruptly and strode away from her toward the house.

When she went up to her room, she sat down at Althea's dressing table and looked into Althea's mirror. A black-haired girl with dark eyes that were angry and a soft mouth that was all too tremulous looked back at her. "What would *you* have done?" she whispered, and her question was directed not to herself, but to a long-ago image that had appeared there.

If the shadowy face of her mother looked over her shoulder, it did not speak, or counsel her. Only Nora's words sounded again in her mind. "You must give a party."

Perhaps she would do just that. Fling open the windows and doors, open them wide to a more normal life in which gaiety had some part. A life that would bring new faces, new friends to Thunder Heights. She would tell the others about her plan right after dinner tonight.

WHEN DINNER WAS over and Ross had gone back to the coach house, the family gathered on the veranda to enjoy the evening air after a warm day—a quiet, not very companionable group. Into one of the silences Camilla spoke.

"I've decided to give a lawn party," she said.

Letty looked surprised but said nothing. Hortense murmured, "What for?" and Booth said, "Why not?" in lazy amusement.

"Today Nora Redfern was telling me about the parties Grandfather used to give. We could at least make a beginning and wake the house up. This veranda must be big enough for dancing—"

"It is," Letty said quickly. "Many's the night we used to dance out here in the summertime. Do you remember, Hortense?"

"I want to forget," Hortense said.

"But I'll need your help," Camilla pointed out. "Don't you think a party would be fun on a lovely summer evening?"

"My mother adores parties," Booth said dryly. "She's told me how she used to shine at them. And how much she missed them."

Hortense gave him a less than doting look but made no denial.

Camilla was talking about how they could set tables on the lawn and hang Japanese lanterns—just as the Judds had done in the old days—when Ross came to the veranda steps. He spoke to her directly.

"What time do you wish to go riding tomorrow?"

Silence fell upon the veranda, like a breath being held.

"Will nine o'clock in the morning be convenient for you?" Camilla asked stiffly.

"I'll have the horses here at nine," Ross said, and went away.

"What horses?" Hortense demanded when he had gone.

"Nora Redfern offered me a saddle horse to ride tomorrow, and Ross is going with me to show me some of the trails."

Letty slipped out of her chair and drifted across the veranda to Camilla's side. "I know you said you wanted to wear Althea's things, but I didn't think you really meant it. Don't go riding, dear, please. Papa said there was never to be a horse at Thunder Heights again. He made us all promise that we would give up riding forever."

She unhooked her right sleeve at the wrist and started to roll it up, but Camilla caught her hand, stopping her. "Don't, Aunt Letty. I know. But just because there have been accidents before doesn't mean there will be another one. I love to ride, and it would be foolish not to enjoy it again."

"Bravo!" Booth applauded. "I have no use for faint hearts. Althea's riding habit suits you, Cousin. I say wear it and go riding tomorrow. And give your party. If we don't have a little excitement, we may well—explode."

Letty went back to her chair without a sound. There was something unnerving about her stillness, as though she held some rush of shattering emotion in check. Hortense stood up and walked to the parlor doors. "Ride, then," she said listlessly, and went into the house.

"You've won your point, Cousin," Booth said. "I must say I find it generous of Mrs. Redfern to loan you her horse and even suggest that Granger go riding with you. She must be very sure of herself."

"A remark like that is uncalled for!" Camilla said sharply.

"Is it?" The mockery had gone out of him. "Perhaps I want to see your eyes opened in time, Camilla. A lonely, saddened woman, and a man who had a great affection for the man she loved. It's natural enough. But I would hate to see you grow too interested in Granger."

"I can take care of myself," Camilla said stiffly, and rose to go inside. Booth stopped her, his voice unexpectedly tender.

"I'm not sure you can, Cousin. But I'd like you to know that you can count me your friend."

THAT NIGHT LETTY played her harp again.

Camilla heard the eerie music stealing through the house. Was this the emotional release Letty needed—something to keep her from going to pieces when some strain became too great?

After a time Camilla fell asleep, and when she wakened some hours later, the house was as still and hushed as if no mournful harp music had ever drifted through its corridors. Then into this silence stirred a whisper of sound, as if someone moved in the hall nearby.

Camilla sat up and reached for the matches and candle beside her bed. The candle flared and smoked in a draft from the balcony's open door, then settled to a pale, steady flame. Her attention was fixed upon the corridor door to her room. With a cold washing of fear through her body, she was glad she had locked that door tonight.

As she watched, she saw the cloisonné doorknob move almost imperceptibly. An unseen hand turned it softly and carefully as far as it would go, but the lock held and the door did not open. Then the faintest sound of a sigh reached Camilla from outside the door, followed by silence. She slipped out of bed. For a long moment she stood with her ear against the panel, but there was nothing to disturb the stillness of the house. Cautiously she unlocked the door and pulled it open a crack.

No one stood in the hall outside her room, but now she heard a creaking step on the stairs above. She looked boldly into the hall and was in time to see the white of a flounced nightgown moving out of sight up the stairway. She ran barefoot toward the stairs and up them to the floor above. Letty was there, drifting smoothly ahead of her down the corridor toward the attic steps. In one hand she carried a candle, and as Camilla watched, she opened the door to the attic stairs and vanished up them. Troubled, Camilla hurried after her. Clearly, Aunt Letty was sleepwalking again. She must be brought back to her own bed, but she must not be startled awake.

Letty seemed to know exactly what she wanted in the attic, and went at once to the small rear room where Althea's saddle rested over a beam. There she set the candleholder upon a shelf and took the stirrup into her hands. Though her eyes were wide open, Letty felt blindly along the stirrup leather until she came to the saddle itself, and her hands followed it to the jutting silver horn. She was touching all these things as if her hands found some reassurance in them. Then she picked up her candle again, went past Camilla without seeing her, and started downstairs.

Softly Camilla followed, and Letty returned to her room without further explanation and closed her door. In all probability she had gone safely back to bed.

Back in her own room, Camilla locked the door and stepped out upon the balcony. The night air was cool and fresh to her hot cheeks, and there was no tinge of horror there. What hidden thoughts and sorrows roused Letty to make her walk in her sleep? And why would she go to the attic and seek out Althea's saddle? A remembrance of Grandfather Orrin's words returned to her mind. "Watch Letty," he had said.

Below the balcony Camilla heard the rustling sound of something moving. Was there someone else abroad on this strange night? But the sound, she decided, was no more than an elm branch brushing the side of the house. Starlight dusted a silver patina over Thunder Heights and shimmered on the surface of the river.

The thought of her ride tomorrow returned, and with it all the things she wanted to shut away, particularly the words Booth had spoken about Nora and Ross. She had been angry with him at first, but his words had only strengthened her own conviction of the affection that lay between those two. Booth had been right—she must not let herself be hurt. She went to bed and lay awake for a long while.

In spite of her disturbed night, she was up early the next morning. The sun rose brightly in a golden sky across the Hudson, and she felt eager to be away from the house.

A little to her surprise, Aunt Letty came down for breakfast.

"You mustn't let my foolish fears spoil your plans," Letty said, smiling. "This will be a safe day for riding." She paused to tell Grace she would have just a little toast and a cup of coffee.

"What do you mean—a safe day?" Camilla asked.

"It's not storming. You must never go riding in a storm. You're so like your mother. I hope you haven't her affinity for thunderstorms."

Camilla thought it just as well to change the subject, and asked Letty about her garden.

"The nasturtiums are thriving," Letty said, rising readily to the bait. "I love the way they brighten the garden all summer long. In the fall I use the seeds for pickling." When she talked about her garden, she was beautiful, Camilla thought. One forgot the twisted arm, the ugly scar hidden by her sleeve.

When breakfast was over, Camilla went upstairs to dress for her ride. She put on her mother's habit and boots. The gray top hat was as fetching as ever on her dark hair. She opened a drawer and took out the little black riding crop, with its polished silver head. Today she would carry it just as her mother once had.

She went into the hall to find Hortense at the top of the stairs, filling the cinnabar lamp in the stairwell with oil. She had drawn the great bowl down on its pulley, and Camilla waited until the lamp had been filled and returned to its place.

Hortense heard her and turned. "I suppose you heard Letty playing her harp last night?" she asked, in a venomous whisper.

"I heard her," Camilla said.

"I hope you realize the harp playing was your fault. She only plays at night when she's upset."

"I'm sorry," Camilla said. "Aunt Letty and I had breakfast together. She seemed quite all right then." She would have continued on her way, if Hortense had not suddenly seen the riding crop in her hands.

"Where did you get that?" she demanded. Before Camilla could answer, Hortense snatched at the crop. She only succeeded in knocking it out of Camilla's hand, and it went over the banister to fall with a clatter to the floor below. Hortense looked after it in dismay, then shrugged and went back to her own room.

Camilla ran down the stairs to find that Letty, who was standing in the hall, had picked up the crop. "Will you leave this with me, please?" she said. "I'd rather you didn't carry it."

"But—why not?" Camilla asked.

"Perhaps"—Letty hesitated—"perhaps I'm more sentimental about this little riding crop than I am about the other things."

Puzzled, Camilla gave in. Letty held the front door open for her, and she went out into the bright morning. A moment later she heard the neighing of a horse, and Ross appeared on a roan mare, leading Diamond, saddled and bridled. Nora's favorite mount was a dappled gray—a handsome, high-stepping creature, with a white diamond blaze on his forehead.

"I hope you can manage this fellow," Ross said. "Grays are supposed to be unsuitable mounts for ladies, though I'm not sure I hold with the legend. Nora handles him beautifully."

His words sounded like a challenge. She fed Diamond a lump of sugar and talked to him for a few moments. He seemed to accept her, and from the mounting block she put her left foot into the stirrup, turning her body so that she went lightly up to hook her right knee over the horn of the side-saddle. Diamond took a skittish step or two and then, sensing firmness in her hands, did as she wished him to. She smiled at Ross triumphantly.

"Where would you like to ride, Miss King?" he inquired formally, acting the role of groom.

"Let's go up Thunder Mountain," she said. "I've been wanting to get to the top. Do you know the way?"

"Of course." He went ahead along the drive toward the road. She touched Diamond with her heel to catch up, and they rode out side by side through the gate in the great privet hedge.

The air was brilliantly clear, with a bright blue sky overhead, but not too warm for comfort. Camilla loved being on a horse again. She urged Diamond into a canter and went in front of Ross. He did not take the lead again until they neared the opening to a narrow road up the mountain, when he called to her and trotted ahead.

CHAPTER NINE

AS THEY WOUND upward single file beneath the trees, Ross turned his head and spoke to her over his shoulder. "Here's something for you to see."

She followed him into a place which had once been a clearing through the woods. It dropped away in a steep slope to a rushing stream below. The stretch was overgrown with scrub now, and along the edges of the scar mountain laurel glowed in the bright pink and white blooming of spring.

Ross reined in as Camilla drew up beside him. "When your grandfather was young and worked in lumber, this was a pitching place," he said.

"Pitching place?" Camilla repeated the unfamiliar term.

"They used to snake the logs down the old road and get them started on this slope, where they could pitch them to the stream below and send them down to the river."

Camilla sat still in the saddle, breathing the spicy scent of the woods about her, listening to the noisy voice of the stream. She could almost see Orrin Judd as he must have been in his youth—a young man who belonged to the forests and the hills, reveling in this outdoor work.

The path wound back into the woods, and the climb grew steeper, emerging suddenly upon an open space at the top of the mountain. Camilla rode eagerly forward.

"Not too near the edge," Ross warned. "Sometimes Diamond has notions."

"I want to be near the edge," Camilla said, slipping out of the saddle. Ross walked the horses back toward the trees to tether them while she climbed a slope of rock and sat down on a boulder near the very lip of the cliff. Below and a little to the north lay the village, its white church steeple

492

like a toy tower on a child's house. An unknown town across the river seemed a world away, and beyond it rolled the hills clear to the blue haze of New England mountains. When she turned due north, she could see the outline of the Catskills far away on her left. At her feet the sheer face of the cliff dropped toward the river.

"It must have been near here that my mother was thrown from her horse," Camilla said softly, as Ross joined her.

"This was the place," he admitted, and said nothing more.

He climbed up to stand at the edge of the precipice, looking over the dizzy drop to the river. She studied him now, as she had done that day on the riverboat before she had ever spoken to him.

Suddenly he pointed. "Do you see the long, white boat coming down from Albany? That's the *Mary Powell*. I worked aboard her once."

"You love the river, don't you?"

"I belong to the river," he said simply. "Do you see the place downstream where opposite banks seem to reach out to each other? That's where your grandfather meant to build his bridge."

"Why do you care so much about that bridge?" she asked.

"When I was a little boy, my father took me on a trip to see Niagara Falls. But it wasn't the falls I looked at, once I was there. It was the railroad bridge John Roebling had built across the gorge. It was the most beautiful thing I'd ever seen. While I stood there staring, a locomotive pulled a train of freight cars across the span, and it stood under all that weight without a quiver. Yet it looked as though it were strung of cobwebs instead of great suspension wires. I fell in love with a bridge that day, and I've never gotten over it."

As she listened she began to understand how he felt.

"I grew up knowing I would build bridges someday," he went on. "With designs and innovations of my own. Of course John Roebling made it easier for all bridge engineers when he invented the wire rope that strings the great suspension bridges. He did what had never been done before, and we've been using his method of making wire cables ever since. He did a lot for bridgebuilding long before he designed his masterpiece— the Brooklyn Bridge."

"My grandfather knew how you felt?" Camilla asked.

"Of course. He meant to give me the job of building a bridge here. When I was ready. He set me at smaller projects in the meantime. I already have one good-sized bridge to my credit upstate, but it's not across the Hudson."

Camilla listened in growing surprise. Why hadn't he told her these things in the beginning? "Those designs you showed me," she said. "Are they of your making?"

"They are. But I shouldn't have expected you to understand them, or have the vision your grandfather had."

"Tell me something else," she went on. "In what way did you want Grandfather to change his will?"

His tone was cool as he answered her. "I wanted to see everything left in a trust, where the family couldn't get their hands on the money and tear down everything he'd built. That way the continuation of his construction empire would have been assured. I might have won him over if he hadn't begun to think sentimentally of his lost granddaughter."

"I see," she said soberly. "I won't oppose you any longer. Build your bridge. Build a dozen bridges. Do as you like about it."

He stepped down from the rock with a violent movement. "Do you know why I'm going down to New York? I'm going to find a job I can stomach. I'll be back to wind up my work here. Then I want to get away. Do you think the building of bridges is something you can toss out as a sort of largess? 'Build your bridge. Build a dozen bridges!' Because *you* have the money to pay for them? As if a bridge were a toy! As if you could buy me with a bridge. Because I was foolish enough to—" He broke off and strode back to the horses.

What had he been going to say? Because he had been foolish enough to kiss her? When he helped her into the saddle, she accepted his touch icily, but she liked it no better than he.

Diamond started at the flick of her heel and took off in a dash for home. Ross went past her on the driveway. He dismounted first and came to help her from the saddle. She dropped down into his arms, and for an instant she was as close to him as she had been that day beneath the beech tree. Her heart thudded wildly, but he let her go and stepped back as if he disliked all contact with her. Then he was gone, and Camilla walked into the house feeling keyed to a furious pitch.

Hortense came out of her room as she climbed the stairs. "I was in the village this morning," she said, "and Mr. Berton at the livery stable tells me he has a bay mare for sale. She's been trained to the sidesaddle, and I told him to send her over this afternoon for you to see."

"Thank you," Camilla said. "I'll look at her."

She hurried to her room, got out of her riding things, and flung herself upon the bed. Already her muscles were feeling the effect of this first ride, and she knew she would be stiff and sore tomorrow. But it was not the soreness of her body that troubled her now. Why must she be furious with Ross Granger when before long he would leave Thunder Heights? He would no longer be here to sting her with his scorn and criticism. Never again would she ride with him up the mountain trail, or slip from a saddle into his arms. Why was she not pleased at the prospect?

She turned her cheek and found the pillow wet with tears. That wouldn't do. She got up and bathed her eyes, put on a fresh frock, and went down to join the family for the noonday meal. She was finishing her dessert when Grace came in to say that one of Mr. Berton's stableboys had arrived with the mare. Camilla took some sugar lumps from a bowl on the table and turned to Booth.

"Will you look at this horse with me?" she said.

"Gladly," he said. "But I'm no expert, Cousin."

When they went out the front door, Letty followed them down the steps and called Camilla back. "Don't buy this horse, dear," she said. "I—I have a feeling about her. I can't explain it sensibly. I just know that she's wrong for you."

Letty would have premonitions about any horse that might be brought to Thunder Heights, Camilla thought. "I'll look at her. If she suits me, I'll buy her, Aunt Letty," she said.

When she and Booth reached the stable, they saw Berton's stableboy with the mare. She was a dainty, flirtatious creature—a smooth bay in color. Her name was Firefly.

Booth looked her over carefully, approving her lines and good health. Camilla approached the mare and held out a lump of sugar. Firefly snuffled it up with velvety lips and no unladylike snorting and blowing, and by the time saddle and bridle had been brought, she and Camilla were friends.

Camilla's stiff muscles rebelled a little as Booth helped her into the saddle, but she did not wince. She rode the mare around the drive, trying out her paces and her response to the reins. She seemed an altogether feminine creature, confident of her own charms, but she was not above taking a few skittish steps now and then. She would, Camilla felt, be spirited enough, but obedient to the touch, and friendly.

When they rode back toward the stable, she found Ross waiting. "I wouldn't buy her," he said.

"Why not?" she asked. "I like her very much."

"I'm not exactly sure," Ross said. "There's something about the way she rolls her eyes—I don't think she's to be trusted."

At another time she might have listened to him. But Ross had hurt her too often. Before she could comment, Booth spoke up. "Miss King is capable of making up her own mind, Granger."

Ross stood his ground without so much as glancing at Booth. "Don't buy her, Camilla," he repeated.

The way he spoke her name was unsettling, but she did not mean to hear the plea in his voice. "You sound as fearful as Aunt Letty," she said lightly. "I don't find Firefly frightening."

Booth laughed. "There you have it, Granger. And, after all, your advice wasn't asked."

Ross turned his back on Booth and looked up at Camilla. "I'm leaving for New York by the late afternoon boat. Is there anything you'd like me to do for you in the city?"

She shook her head mutely, and Ross left them.

The purchase of the mare was transacted that afternoon. The price was surprisingly moderate—Camilla had been prepared to pay more. A boy was hired, and the lower part of the coach house once more became a stable. She saw Ross again briefly, just as he was leaving. She had a sudden impulse to plead with him not to go, but she could not put it into words. "Have a good trip," she told him, and held out her hand.

He took it briefly and thanked her. In a moment he would be gone. "Will—will you be back in time for our party?" she asked.

"I hadn't thought about it," he admitted. "Is Nora coming?"

Camilla could only nod. If he came only because of Nora . . .

"I'm not sure I'll be there," he said, and she could not bring herself to urge him. He left quickly.

THE NEXT MORNING Camilla went for her first long ride on Firefly. The little mare was a delight, and Camilla took her up the mountain trail, feeling it familiar now.

She drew rein on the top of Thunder Mountain and sat quietly for a while, to give Firefly a breather. But today she had no sense of buoyancy as she looked out over the tremendous view, no feeling that she might shed the dark influences of Thunder Heights up here in the hills. In a little while she turned back. All the worries and problems of the house seemed to ride with her. There had been the matter of the tea, to which she had found no answer. There were the hints that something untoward had brought on her grandfather's death. There was Letty's odd behavior about the riding crop, and Hortense's open dislike, to say nothing of Booth's strange attitudes. Each segment of the puzzle remained just that—a segment. She could not glimpse the whole.

A WEEK LATER Hortense went across the river to visit friends overnight. She left for the ferry from Westcliff early on a bright and cloudless morning. As the day wore on the air grew still and stifling, with the sun burning fiercely through a haze that seemed to magnify the heat. Late that afternoon thunderheads loomed across the Hudson, bringing gusty winds to rattle the shutters and wail down the chimneys of Thunder Heights. All through dinner the noise seemed to increase. Nevertheless, the storm held back its torrents and was for a time only wind and sound.

Except for the wind noises, dinner was a quiet meal. Letty spoke not at all. Booth seemed lost in moody silence. Camilla, deep in her own thoughts, made no bid for conversation. Pleading a headache after dinner, Letty went up to bed.

Camilla slipped away from Booth and went outside to the ledge above the river. There she stood for a long while in the open, where wind whipped her skirts and buffeted her with rough fingers. Below her the river churned into choppy gray waves, and on the heights above, tree branches thrashed and moaned. Had it been on such a night that Althea had ridden to the crest? Camilla wondered.

The stinging slap of the first rain pricked through the thin stuff of her shirtwaist, and she turned back to the house. Thunder Heights looked dark and cheerless. No one had lighted the cinnabar lamp above the stairs tonight—that was Hortense's charge—and lamps had not yet been lighted in the parlor. She did not glimpse Booth in the shadows of the veranda until she reached the steps.

"Come in," he said. "Don't tempt the spirit of the mountain."

Thunder rumbled now, and lightning flashed, illuminating towers, striking brilliance from blank windows. Then darkness swept down again. As Camilla reached the door, Grace came to light lamps in the parlor. Booth followed her and locked the French doors against the storm.

How hot and close it seemed inside, hot and close and alive with rattling sound.

"Perhaps Aunt Letty would like someone with her tonight," Camilla said. "Perhaps I'd better go upstairs."

"There's no need to go to Letty," Booth said. "I've given her one of her own witch brews and she'll sleep through it all and feel better in the morning. Stay with me awhile, Cousin. It's I who don't want to be left to my own company."

She sat down in a chair from Malaya, resting her hands upon its ornately carved teak arms. And he moved restlessly about, tinkling a brass temple bell from India, picking up an ivory elephant and setting it down again. She had the feeling that he wanted to talk to her, and she watched his finely chiseled head as it moved from lamplight into shadow, drawn to him as she had been more than once in the past.

"Why do you stay here, Booth?" she asked. "Why haven't you left this house and found yourself a better life out in the world? What is there for you here?"

Her words brought him about to face her. He leaned against the mantel, one arm stretched along its marble surface. "How little you know me, Cousin! You don't even know that everything I've wanted in life is contained in this one household, and always has been. Contained, but held beyond my reach. For the moment, at least. But not forever. No, I think not forever." His eyes were bright with mirthless laughter that was troubling to see.

"What is it that you want of life?" she asked him.

He ran an appreciative hand along the graceful fluted edge of the marble. "To be a gentleman," he told her. His sardonic smile flashed for an instant and was gone as suddenly as the lightning. "To live like a gentleman, to enjoy myself as a gentleman. This has been my purpose for as long as I can remember. Does it astonish you?"

"Yes," Camilla said. "I've never thought of being a gentleman—or a lady—as an end in itself."

"That's because you never lived as a child hating your father's butcher shop, longing to get away from it. You didn't grow up watching ladies and gentlemen from a distance, having coppers tossed to you in an offhand manner, being treated as an underling." He left the mantel and flung himself into a chair, watching her face now. "What are you thinking?" he demanded. "What are you feeling about me?"

"Why, surprise, mainly, I suppose," she said.

"You mean because I've succeeded so well that you'd never have guessed my miserable origin?"

"No—only surprise that anyone should feel as you do. It must be easy enough to adopt a veneer of polish, if that's what you want. But how can that be an end in itself?"

"It can easily be an end," he said, "if it coincides with everything you wanted up to the time when you were ten years old. And if it is what you were taught from that time on."

"Aunt Letty told me you were adopted when you were ten," Camilla admitted. "Sometimes I've wondered about that. Aunt Hortense doesn't seem exactly—" She hesitated, not wanting to hurt him.

"Don't you know why Hortense brought me here? Don't you know why she snatched me out of my humble beginnings and made a gentleman out of me?" There was something hard and cold in his tone. "She had lost the man she'd set her heart on—your father. She didn't intend to marry and have children. But she wanted to make sure that a good portion of Orrin Judd's fortune came her way. She thought that presenting him with an heir of sorts would safeguard the money she wanted.

"My father was happy to be rid of me. My mother had died the year before and left the whole brood of us to him. Miss Judd had a look at me, talked to me, found that I was bright enough and eager to be part of a different world. I'd shown some talent for painting even then, and she thought me a likely boy to present to her father, who was all for humble beginnings. Unfortunately, old Orrin and I never cared for each other. Your aunt Hortense has always believed only what she wanted to believe. She imagines that she has been a doting mother. But all her doting developed after I was twenty and she found she liked a grown young man at her beck and call."

Camilla made a small gesture of disbelief. Booth laughed.

"It's not a pretty story, is it? Can you imagine Hortense mothering a boy of ten? I might have run away once or twice, if it hadn't been for Letty. It was Letty who mothered and loved me and brought me up. Of course when I was older I began to see very well which side my bread was buttered on. Sooner or later the old man would die. And whatever Hortense had would be mine. I've never lost sight of that. Everything I want is here at Thunder Heights."

Camilla felt a little sickened. "How sad and—pitiful," she said softly, more to herself than to him.

He smiled. "Scarcely pitiful, Cousin. Though you must admit that my plans and hopes went awry for a time when you appeared on the scene and inherited everything."

"I should think you would have left then," Camilla said. "I can understand why Hortense and Letty might feel they couldn't leave a security they had always depended on. But you—"

"Tell me, Cousin," he said, "have I been unkind to you? Have I made you feel that I resented and disliked you?"

"No. No, not at all. You've been far kinder to me than Hortense has been." Or than Ross Granger had, for that matter.

"Perhaps I stayed because of you," he said, and there was a gentleness, almost a tenderness, in his voice.

Camilla saw a blinding glitter of lightning. The windows shivered in an almost instantaneous crash of thunder, and she winced.

"A close one," Booth said. "That was on the mountain above us, I think." He went to one of the tall doors to peer out. Then he turned and looked at her across the room.

She was suddenly aware of how closed off they were in this room. She was aware too of a change in Booth, of a quickening in him as he watched her. Something in her own blood stirred in response to the urgency she sensed in him.

She rose uncertainly and walked from the parlor into the antehall. Candles had been lighted in the outstretched marble hands, but the octagon stairway beyond lay in shadow. Intermittently the tall window above the stairs flickered with lightning. All the dark secrets of Thunder Heights seemed to center in the heart of that weirdly illuminated stairway, and she dreaded walking up it.

In the moment that she hesitated, Booth came through the door. He moved toward her with assurance, took her into his arms, and kissed her full on the mouth. His lips were cool in the hot and stifling house, and the shock of their touch brought her to herself. In spite of the response that throbbed in her own blood, she thrust him back instinctively, lest his darkness engulf them both.

He drew her roughly against him and kissed her again. "Never fight me, Cousin," he said, as she tried to turn her head away. "Always remember that!"

There was a warning in his voice that made her cease her struggling.

She went limp in his arms, resting there inert, until he put her quietly away from him. She moved backward from him, toward the stairs. She no longer feared the darkness. She feared Booth Hendricks.

"You were drawn to me in the beginning," he insisted. "It was clear enough. What turned you away? Was it Granger?"

"No," she whispered. "Ross Granger is nothing to me."

"Do you think I haven't seen the way you look at him? Not that I mind. There's all the more satisfaction when a formidable opponent is beaten. I don't underestimate Granger, believe me. But I think you both underestimate me."

She turned and fled up the stairs through the flashing light, with the thunder drowning out any sound of pursuit. She did not look back until she reached the door of her room and flung it open. In a flash of lightning the hall behind her stretched empty and livid. Below, in the heart of the house, she heard a ringing shout of laughter.

She closed the door and locked it, stood trembling against it in the warm safety of her room. Now she was afraid in this house as she had never been afraid before. She was seized by forebodings that she could not put aside. Booth would not easily be stopped in his purpose. And his purpose was to have her. Only then would he achieve all he wanted of Thunder Heights. Had she the strength to stand against him?

CHAPTER TEN

IN THE MORNING she dreaded the moment she might come face to face with him again. When she went downstairs to the dining room Booth was there, as if waiting for her.

"Good morning, Camilla," he said cheerfully, as she paused, trying to hide her dismay. He hurried to draw out her chair, a faint mockery beneath his good manners. "You've done wonders with this room. I can remember many depressing meals in the old room, with the dark wallpaper and draperies adding to my depression. You've been good for this house."

She had nothing to say. She avoided his eyes as Grace brought coffee and oatmeal. He smiled as he took his place beside her.

"Did you sleep well?" he asked.

She nodded. How could she pretend, as he seemed to be pretending, that everything was as it had been before he had kissed her last night?

Plainly amused, he passed her cream and sugar, and she began to eat in silence. Then he picked up a knife and made a mark on the tablecloth with the rounded end of it. "Attend, my dear. I have a problem for you to consider. A theoretical problem. Do you see this line I've drawn? Let's say it represents the life span of a man. The salt cellar here is his birth, the napkin ring his death.

"At certain places in the lifeline there are forks in the road, choices a man may make. Or a woman. One road may be a pleasant one, with opportunity and safety and very little excitement. The other choice may spell danger, disaster, perhaps. Which road shall I choose, Camilla?"

She had no answer for him. When Letty came through the door, she looked up in relief.

"Good morning, children. How well I slept last night!" Letty said. "The thunder didn't disturb me at all."

"Booth gave you a sleeping draft, Aunt Letty," Camilla said.

Letty took the chair Booth pulled out for her, and the look she turned upon him was suddenly intent.

"Camilla is right, dear," he said. "I didn't want you to suffer a headache all night long. Besides, I wanted to be alone and unchaperoned for once with Cousin Camilla."

Letty glanced at Camilla and then looked away. "I see," she said. She turned her attention to breakfast.

Booth picked up a spoon and crisscrossed the lines he had made on the tablecloth, raising a dark eyebrow quizzically at Camilla as he did so. "I think I'll do no painting today," he said. "I have a feeling my model is not in the mood."

"But you've only a little more to do on the picture," Letty said. "I'll be glad when it's finished."

"You've never liked that picture, have you?" Booth asked, but Letty did not answer.

They were still at breakfast when Hortense returned from her journey across the river. Booth went to the door to help her with her bag. Camilla heard them talking in the distance, but Booth did not return.

"What happened last night?" Letty asked, when she and Camilla were alone in the dining room.

"Nothing," Camilla said. "The storm seemed to key him up. I went to bed early."

"Good," Letty approved. "Sometimes I think Booth's high moods are almost as difficult as his low ones. It's best to leave him alone until he gets over them."

After breakfast Camilla threw herself into preparations for the lawn party, putting disturbing thoughts away from her. Later that morning she went downstairs to the cellar to find brushes and paint in the room that had once been Grandfather Orrin's workshop. Some little tables that would be used on the lawn needed painting, and she wanted to do this herself.

As she came down the steep flight of cellar stairs, she saw Booth ahead of her and paused, not wanting to meet him alone. But he had not heard her and he moved with purpose toward the larder. When she saw him go into the room where Letty kept her herbs, Camilla darted toward the door of the toolroom next to it and stepped inside. She would get her things quietly and slip out before Booth emerged. But just then she heard him exclaim, "So! I thought you might be down here."

For an instant she thought he had discovered her. Then he went on angrily, "You're up to your old tricks, aren't you?"

There was a smothered cry from someone in the larder, and the crash of glass, as if a jar had been dashed to the floor.

"Tansy!" Booth said, and the word lashed like the snap of a whip. "Enough of it can kill, as you very well know. Are you such a fool that you think they wouldn't uncover so clumsy a trick? Clear up that mess and don't try it again."

The soft mumbling reply was in a voice Camilla could not identify. She shrank into the dark space behind the toolroom door as she heard Booth stride toward the stairs and spring up them. The cellar door closed sharply above, and a soft brushing sound began in the next room.

Camilla slipped out of the toolroom and fled upstairs and outside, escaping to the serenity of the herb garden. Here there was brightness and warm, perfumed air. Bees hummed around the balm, and all was quiet and peaceful. Yet not altogether so. For the very herbs in this garden had powers she did not trust.

She shivered in the warm air. How was she to live with the undercurrent of dark purpose that existed in this house? Hortense or Letty—which one? No, surely not Letty! Booth would never have spoken so roughly to the woman who had given him love and trust over the years. Or would he, if he was angered?

As THE DAY OF the lawn party approached, Hortense became almost cheerful, and began to take an interest in preparations and in the identity of the guests who had accepted. Only one name caused her displeasure. When she came upon the note from Nora Redfern's mother, she brought it indignantly to Camilla, who was outdoors on the veranda painting lawn furniture. "Do you mean that Mrs. Landry has actually accepted your invitation?" she demanded.

"Why shouldn't she?" Camilla asked. "Mrs. Redfern says her mother and mine were the best of friends when they were young. She and Mrs. Landry seem to have no wish to keep up an old feud."

"And did she tell you that Laura Landry was horribly rude to us after Althea's death and came near making a public scandal?"

"A scandal about what?" asked Camilla, concentrating on her work.

"Laura took your father's side," Hortense said. "And of course all John King wanted was to make trouble—as we very well knew. He felt he had been slighted by his wife's family, and he wanted his little revenge."

"That doesn't sound like my father." Camilla set her brush down and gave her aunt her full attention. "Just what are you talking about?"

"I've no intention of dredging up something that had no basis in fact," Hortense said, retreating hastily. "But you can take my word for it, Camilla, that Mrs. Landry was extremely rude to Papa. He told her never to set foot in his house again."

Hortense began to stride up and down the veranda. Once this woman had been in love with John King. How had it been when he had come back to Thunder Heights for Althea's funeral? Suddenly Camilla asked, "Were you still in love with my father, Aunt Hortense? I mean when he came back that last time?"

Hortense whirled about. "In love with him! I despised your father. He led me on when I first knew him, and I would have married him if it hadn't been for Althea and her sneaking ways. It's a good thing I didn't so demean myself, since his true character was revealed when he ran away with her." With that she flounced into the house.

Camilla hurried inside in search of Letty. She found her in the upstairs sitting room, working on a dress for the lawn party. Camilla asked point-blank about the trouble between Grandfather Orrin and Nora Redfern's mother.

Letty glanced up vaguely from her sewing. "That was all so long ago," she said, using her favorite retreat to shut out what she did not wish to consider. "Laura had some foolish idea about what happened to Althea. I don't recall exactly what it was— But I wish Mrs. Landry weren't coming. I—I'm afraid of what may happen. Please be careful, Camilla. Be very, very careful."

ADDITIONAL SERVANTS CAME in the day before the party to help with preparations. Hortense was in her element, giving orders right and left, while Letty quietly countermanded those that were too absurd.

Before the servants arrived, Letty had locked the door to the cellar. "If any of you need anything, come to me for the key," she told the family, thinking of her precious herbs. "I'd rather not have strangers moving around downstairs."

Hortense remarked that she was being ridiculously cautious, but the key remained in Letty's pocket.

The day of the lawn party was clear and sunny. The guests would not begin to arrive until four, and at three thirty Camilla and Letty, dressed and ready, sat down on the veranda to rest. Camilla wore a new summer frock of frilly muslin with sleeves that pushed up in soft puffs. Letty's lavender dress was soft and drifty, and the scent of lavender floated about her when she moved.

Little tables and chairs were set about on the lawn, and Japanese lanterns had been strung the length of the veranda and from tree to tree. At dusk Thunder Heights would be a beautiful sight. Letty's harp, with a stool drawn up to it, waited at one end of the veranda, so that she could sit there and play for the guests. And there were fiddlers coming later from the village.

Only one thing had disturbed this day. Mignonette had disappeared, and no amount of calling brought her to view. For a while Letty did not seem especially perturbed. "She'll turn up eventually," she said. "She's much too clever to let anything happen to her."

Only now, as they sat rocking on the veranda, did she begin to fret a little. "It's not like Mignonette to stay away so long."

"Do you think you might have shut her in the cellar when you locked it yesterday?" Camilla asked.

"No, because she was around early this morning. And I haven't been down there since I locked the door."

Hortense's voice sounded within the house, and Letty stopped rocking. "Hortense wants you, dear. I do hope she hasn't overdressed for this afternoon. She wouldn't tell me what she meant to wear."

Camilla went inside, to find her at the foot of the stairs striving ineffectively to set spikes of larkspur into a brass bowl. Her gown was elaborate. It was her favorite emerald-green color—a somewhat threadbare satin, with an old-fashioned bustle. The skirt was looped up at the side to show a panel of yellow, embroidered in black. Her pompadour was anchored soundly with the little combs studded in green jade. To Camilla her elegance of a day long past seemed a little pathetic.

"Oh, there you are!" she said, as Camilla reached her side. "No one has fixed any flowers for the stand here at the foot of the stairs. I thought this brass bowl would do, but it's not deep enough. Do run down to the cellar and get me a china vase that will be deep enough. Here—take this brass atrocity with you."

The brass bowl was large and heavy, and Camilla took it in both hands. She went out to get the key from Letty, then hurried to the landing door and pushed it open. As she stepped upon the first step, something dark leaped wildly past her up the stairs. Alarmed, Camilla jumped and dropped the bowl. The leaping creature was only the lost Mignonette, but the bowl bounced out of her hands and down the stairs with a frightful clatter.

As Camilla's eyes grew accustomed to the dim light, she saw that the bowl had done an extraordinary amount of damage in its heavy progress downward. The third step, just below where she stood, had splintered and collapsed completely. Camilla stepped carefully over the broken step and made her way to the foot of the stairs.

She was puzzled. The bowl was not so heavy as to cause such serious damage unless the step had already been rotten and ready to collapse. The stairs were of the open kind, and she walked underneath them, where she could look up at the shattered step. The board had broken in the middle. One side had fallen through and lay at her feet. The other side still hung from above.

She picked up the broken tread and studied it. The splinters of the break looked clean. Was it possible that it had been deliberately broken, then pushed back in place? If Mignonette had not come leaping out and startled her, if Camilla had not dropped the bowl, triggering what certainly looked like a trap—she would have been flung all that steep flight to the cement below.

Her knees had begun to tremble in reaction, and she found a chair and sat down. That step had been prepared for one person alone—Camilla King. Yet how could anyone know that she would be the one to step on it? Carefully she thought back over what had happened.

Yesterday Letty had locked the door. Yet she herself might have run up and down these stairs a dozen times since if she'd chosen to. So the break had been prepared when it was unlikely that Letty would be coming down them again. But how could anyone know that Camilla King would come down them?

The pattern grew clear. Hortense had waited for the prescribed moment and had conceived an errand that would send just one person down these stairs—to disaster.

"Camilla! Camilla, are you there?" That was Hortense now, on the landing before the cellar door.

She had only to be silent, Camilla thought, and see what happened. If Hortense came down cautiously, stepping over the broken stair, she would know the answer. She could see her green skirts up there now, see her foot coming down to the top step. Camilla jumped up and called to her aunt.

"Be careful, Aunt Hortense! There's a broken step. Watch out or you'll fall." She had not possessed the nerve to try the experiment, lest she risk Hortense's life.

Hortense gasped and drew back. Camilla picked up the brass bowl and went to the foot of the stairs.

"This bowl saved me from a bad fall. This and Mignonette. Someone must have shut her down here by mistake, and when she leaped out she frightened me so that I dropped the bowl and it broke the step. Odd, isn't it, that a step should break so easily?"

Hortense said nothing. She was staring at Camilla in horrified silence. Was it because of her own narrow escape—or because Camilla had discovered the trap?

"Wait there," Camilla said. "I'll get you another vase." She went to the shelf where extra vases were kept and picked one out. By the time she returned to the stairs her knees were steadier. Then she climbed the stairs, stepping carefully over the dangerous place. She put the vase into Hortense's limp hands. "I was lucky, Aunt Hortense. This is the second time Mignonette has saved my life."

Seen in the light of the landing, Hortense's face looked as though it had caught something of the reflected color of her dress.

At that moment the knocker rattled on the front door, and Camilla spoke quietly to her aunt. "The guests are arriving. Hurry and fix your larkspur. And don't worry about the step now, Aunt Hortense. We have a party to get through."

As she started for the door, her mind was busy with the three corners of a triangle. It could have been Letty, who had the key to the cellar. But access through a window was also possible. In that case it might have been Hortense. Or the entire plan, including instructions to Hortense and the fixing of the step, could have been managed easily by Booth. She could not find the answer now, for there was Nora Redfern at the door, and with her a plump, rather dowdy woman with an air of confidence and authority, whom Nora introduced as her mother, Mrs. Landry.

Laura Landry's handclasp was strong and friendly. "I insisted upon coming early," she said, "so that I could have a bit of a visit with Althea's daughter before the others arrived."

Camilla led the way through the parlor and out upon the veranda, where Letty still sat rocking peacefully. Camilla slipped the cellar key into her hand. "Be sure no one goes downstairs, Aunt Letty. There's a broken step that might injure anyone who didn't see it. It's only thanks to Mignonette that I escaped. She *was* in the cellar."

Momentary alarm flashed in Letty's eyes, and then she was rising to greet Nora Redfern and Mrs. Landry. There was no animosity in her gracious reception of the two women.

Camilla turned toward the veranda steps and saw Booth at the foot of them. "Congratulate me!" she said brightly. "I came very near killing myself on the cellar stairs a few moments ago. It was only by luck that I saw the damaged step and saved myself."

Did something flicker in his eyes? She couldn't be sure. He took her hand to draw her down to the lawn, and his manner seemed truly solicitous. "You must be careful, Camilla. I'll have a look at the bad step later on." Then he too was greeting Mrs. Landry and Nora in his usual suave manner.

Camilla walked across the lawn with Nora and Mrs. Landry for a view of the river. Mrs. Landry was more interested in her than in the river, however. "You're as pretty as your mother was," she said. "Perhaps prettier. But there's a difference. Your mother had a daredevil streak. You look more sensible."

"I'm not sure that's a compliment," she told Nora's mother. "I'm so glad you've come, Mrs. Landry. I know you and my mother were good friends, and there's so much I want to learn about her." But now other guests began to arrive, and there was no opportunity for more talk. Soon there were little clumps of ladies and gentlemen all about the lawn. Hortense and Letty and Booth moved among them, greeting old friends, meeting younger members of river families, whom they had not met before; and all three seemed at ease, slipping easily back into old ways. There was a time when this party would have seemed like wonderful fun. But that was before the shadow of Thunder Heights had crept across Camilla's spirit.

As the sun vanished behind the hill, the house stood aglow with lamps, and now servants were lighting the candles in the Japanese lanterns, so that lawn and veranda were soon rimmed in jewels of blue and green, red and yellow. Down toward the river, against the blackness of the bushes, fireflies lit small darting lanterns of their own in the warm night.

On the veranda the fiddlers from the village struck up a tune, and the young people ran up the steps to enjoy a reel. Camilla found herself handed breathlessly from partner to partner. When the musicians changed to a waltz, someone touched her arm and she turned to look into Ross Granger's face. In the happy shock of seeing him, all doubts fell away. She no longer questioned her own heart. This was her love, whether he cared for her or not. She went into his arms and made no effort to hide the joy in her eyes.

"I'm sorry I'm late," he said. "I hope I'm still welcome."

"Oh, you are, you are!" she cried.

He held her gently as they danced, and she felt that perhaps he had missed her too.

"Did you find what you wanted in New York?" she asked, and held her breath against the answer. "Are you going away again soon?"

"I'm not sure," he said. "There are some things I must finish here first. How have things gone while I was away?"

"Badly," she whispered. "I must see you where no one will watch me, or hear us."

"Wherever you say."

She thought frantically. "Can you meet me at Grandfather's grave, in the cemetery, tomorrow morning at ten?"

"Of course," he said.

The waltz had come to an end, and she went reluctantly out of his arms, feeling that she gave up all safety.

Refreshments were served at the little tables on the lawn, and Camilla went to Mrs. Landry's table, to sit with her and Nora. Up on the veranda Letty had taken her place at the harp and had begun to play the old tunes of Scotland.

"Nora tells me you're a good rider," Laura Landry said. "And that you've bought a horse of your own. I'm glad to hear it. We all rode in the old days. Althea especially."

"I know," Camilla said. "I found her gray riding habit in the attic, and I wear the whole costume—top hat, boots, and all. The older people around the countryside must think I'm her spirit come back to ride Thunder Mountain again. Mrs. Landry—were you at Blue Beeches when my mother was killed?"

"I was here when Orrin Judd brought her down from the mountain. Booth came looking for her at Blue Beeches, hoping she hadn't taken the mountain trail. So I came over and waited."

"I've heard there was some sort of scene," Camilla said.

"I made a scene. Althea was too good a rider to be thrown, no matter what that horse did. I felt there was more to the accident than met the eye. I wanted it looked into. As you know, it's practically impossible to throw a good rider from a sidesaddle unless she is taken by surprise. If your knee is over the horn and your right foot hooked behind your left calf, you're locked into the saddle and nothing is going to budge you. Althea would have secured her seat and fought her horse to a standstill. The horse didn't live who was too much for her. I said as much to Orrin Judd. But it was the wrong time."

"What do you mean?" Camilla prodded.

"He was wild with grief, and he thought I was trying to make trouble of some sort—to blame him. There wasn't anyone I could talk sensibly to until your father got here. He saw what I meant, but by that time it was impossible to get through to Orrin. I don't suppose he would have believed us anyway."

"Believed what?" Camilla asked. She felt cold.

"Believed that what happened was not wholly an accident."

"But—but why would anyone have wanted to harm my mother?"

"Your grandfather sent for her when he was ill. He was at outs with the rest of the family by that time, and he felt Althea had been treated badly. So he was going to change his will. I gather that he meant to do the same sort of thing he did in the will which left everything to you. But he tossed it in their faces. He let them know what he intended ahead of time. So two days before Althea was to leave for home, the horse threw her. Only I don't believe it."

Camilla heard her out in dismay. It all sounded so horrible. She could believe these things now because she knew what it was like to be the hunted one.

"The thing I've never understood," Nora said, "was why old Orrin waited so long before he sent for you, Camilla. If his feelings had changed toward Althea, why didn't he want to know her daughter?"

"John King took care of that," Mrs. Landry said. "I remember him as a gentle person, with great kindness and sensitivity. He won all our hearts in the old days. But when a gentle person is angered it can be a fearful thing to see. He swore Orrin Judd would never have his daughter, and that neither of them would ever set foot in Thunder Heights from that day on."

Camilla spoke softly. "And he kept his word as long as he lived. Now I understand why he would never talk about what happened, why his sickness over her death was more than ordinary grief."

Mrs. Landry reached across the little table to cover Camilla's hand with her own. "This is why I had to see you. You must never make the misstep your mother made."

Camilla nodded mutely and looked around. Across the expanse of laughing, chattering people she saw Booth on the far side of the lawn, leaning against an elm tree, the light from a lantern flickering across his dark face. She met his eyes and could not look away. It was like the exchange of a lover's gaze, she thought queerly. He was waiting for her. Waiting for the time that he would hold her in his arms. She was aware of the cold sweat upon her palms, and she reminded herself quickly that Ross had returned. She was not alone anymore. Tomorrow she would talk to him. He would know what to do.

CHAPTER ELEVEN

IT WAS WELL INTO the evening when the last guests had left and the Japanese lanterns had been extinguished. Camilla went upstairs to her room, where she found that the door she always closed stood ajar. For an instant fear swept over her. But she pushed the door open wide and found only Letty waiting there. She sat in the little rocker before the cold hearth, still dressed in her frock of misty lavender, rocking gently back and forth. Mignonette slept comfortably in the middle of the bed.

Camilla closed the door and went quickly into the room. "Did you enjoy the party, Aunt Letty?"

"I want to talk to you, dear."

"That's fine," Camilla said. "I'd like to talk to you too. Mrs. Landry told me something about my mother's death."

"That's why I must talk to you. I know what Laura Landry believed, and in part she was right. But only in part. Sit down on the ottoman, dear. Come close so I needn't speak loudly."

Camilla drew up the big footstool and sat down.

Letty closed her eyes. "Mrs. Landry doesn't know that it was I who sent Althea to her death."

Camilla waited in silence for her to continue.

"The horse that killed Althea was a mare named Folly, a beautiful little mare, good-mannered and affectionate. She was my horse, Camilla, and I loved her dearly. And then one dreadful day I learned that she had a wild streak in her that made her go crazy in a thunderstorm. I had ridden to the mountaintop and had dismounted to look at the view. There was a storm coming up, and the whole Hudson valley was a queer, livid color, with thunderheads boiling up and lightning flashing in the distance. It was frightening and very beautiful. Hortense was riding with me, but she didn't get off her horse.

"I stood on a rock to put myself into the saddle, and just as I set my foot in the stirrup there was a clap of thunder. Folly went mad. My foot was caught and she trampled on my arm, trying to get free of me, dragging me until my foot came loose from the stirrup. Folly ran away, and Hortense managed to get me home."

Letty's voice was empty of emotion, but her fingers twined together tightly. "I was ill for a long time. The doctor feared a brain injury, as well as the broken arm that never healed properly. Papa would have shot Folly, but in spite of the way I was hurt I pleaded for her. To soothe me, he promised that I could keep her as a pet, providing no one ever rode her. All this was after Althea had gone away and married."

"When my mother came here on that last visit, didn't she know that Folly wasn't supposed to be ridden?" Camilla asked.

Letty bowed her head. "She knew. Booth told her, when he tried to stop her that day."

"Booth?" Camilla repeated softly.

"He had been painting her. They didn't hit it off very well, and I think she never liked him. She posed for him, but she made fun of his painting. She was always gay and I think she only meant to tease, but she made him angry. She told him she was a better woman than the girl in the picture, because she would have had that rearing horse in hand. Booth said the horse in the picture was my Folly and that she was a dangerous animal.

"I was there, and I remember the way Althea laughed and said she would ride her. And she would do it right then. I tried to make her understand that a storm was coming up, but she said that she was a good enough rider to handle a horse under any circumstances."

Letty paused, shaking her head sadly. "She was always like that—even as a little girl. The moment anyone told her she couldn't do something, that was what she must do."

"Where was Grandfather all this while?" Camilla said.

"He had been ill—that's why he had sent for her—and he was in bed upstairs in his room at the time. Booth had been painting outside on the veranda to get the best light. Althea was wearing her habit for the picture,

and she ran down the steps and off toward the stable. Booth said he would go after her and stop her, keep her from riding."

"But he didn't, did he?" Camilla said.

Letty was silent for a moment, as though she were trying to remember something. "He tried. But after a while he returned alone, with a red slash across his face where she had struck him with her riding crop. They had quarreled out there in the stable."

Letty began to weep gently. "When Folly came home with an empty saddle, Booth caught her and put her into her stall. Then he ran to the house to let me know what had happened and that he would go out searching. I went to Papa, who got out of bed and had his own horse saddled. He rode up the mountain, where he thought she was sure to have gone. Booth was out looking too, but he chose the wrong route. He thought she might have taken the easier road along the river. He couldn't believe she would be so foolish as to go up the mountain on a crazy horse in the storm. But it was on the mountaintop Papa found her."

"Where was Hortense?" Camilla asked.

"She had a headache and had gone up to her room to lie down. She didn't know what had happened until they brought Althea home."

Letty wept softly, her handkerchief to her eyes, while Camilla sat lost in unhappy reverie. A rising wind whispered in the chimney, and Letty looked up uneasily. "Listen—it's beginning to blow again. I don't want to stay alone tonight, Camilla. I don't want to get up in the night and go walking about the house."

"You needn't," Camilla said quickly. "Stay here with me. The bed is big enough for two, and I'd like company tonight."

Letty began to speak again in a rush of words, as though she wanted to hold nothing back. "I could surely have found a way to stop Althea if I had really tried. So I am the one who is guilty. And I couldn't remain silent forever. A few months ago I tried to tell Papa exactly what had happened. I wanted to gain his forgiveness. But he was so badly upset by what I told him that it brought on his last attack. So I was responsible for his death too. And for his changing of his will—because after what I told him, he said he could never trust any of us again."

That all this unhappiness had existed behind Letty's quiet serenity was disturbing. Yet there was no real comfort Camilla could offer. Later, at a calmer time, they could talk about these things, reason them out sensibly.

"I'll go get my nightclothes and come right back." Letty rose and slipped out of the room.

LATER THAT NIGHT, when the lamp was out and the room dark except for a bar of moonlight from the balcony, Camilla lay awake quietly beside her aunt, waiting for her to fall asleep. But Letty's breathing remained ragged and uneven, and it was Camilla who slept first. Once during the night she wakened uneasily and stretched out her hand to find Letty gone. When she stirred and reached for a candle and matches, Letty spoke from the rocking chair by the hearth.

"I'm here, dear. Go to sleep. I'll keep watch. Don't worry about me. I have so much to think about."

Camilla fell asleep again and did not awaken until morning. When she sat up in bed, she found that Letty had returned to her own room.

But today she had other matters to think about. When the time came to meet Ross, she set off on the road to the village. The day was hot and still, and distant clouds in the east seemed to hang motionless. The cemetery drowsed in the humid, oppressive heat. Slowly Camilla climbed the path that led to the burial plot of the Judds. She sat on the grass beside Orrin Judd's grave and took off her big straw hat. All was still. Camilla tucked her white skirts about her, leaned her cheek against her propped-up knees, and closed her eyes.

She knew, however, the moment when Ross reached the cemetery gate, though she heard no more than his step, no more than the creaking of a hinge. She sat up eagerly.

He climbed the path and dropped down beside her, stretching out to his full length, leaning on one elbow. "A pretty picture you make," he said, "here on the grass in your white dress."

She could not bring herself to destroy the peace of the moment with the words she had to speak, and he did not ask her purpose in bringing him here. It was as if he too wanted to preserve this moment of companionship between them.

Idly he began to tell her about shad fishing at night on the Hudson, and how he had gone out one evening with Toby, and they had filled their nets with silver shad. She listened with pleasure, wishing that she might go out on the river with him.

Then, when she felt lulled and quiet, he sat up so that he could look into her face. "You were afraid of something yesterday, Camilla—what was it? Why did you want to meet me here?"

She told him what had happened—all of it. About the tea that had made Mignonette sick. About the night when Booth had kissed her and she had run away from him. About the words she had overheard in the cellar, and the broken step.

He listened grimly. "There's only one thing to do. You must get away from the house," he told her. "Break your grandfather's will and do as you please. You have no real obligation to any of these people. They'd never given a thought to you. If you must, settle something upon them so your conscience will be free. But get away from Thunder Heights and don't come back. It's the only way."

"If I couldn't live up to Grandfather's wishes, then I would have no right to any of the inheritance he left me."

There was a light in Ross's eyes she could not read. "Do you really want it? You lived without it before—you can again."

"That's not the important thing," she said helplessly. She could not put into words her feeling about all this. How could she make him hear the echo of her grandfather's sorrowful voice? How could she convey her tenderness for Letty, whom she could not abandon? Or her conviction that she must somehow pick up life in her mother's place? The ties that held her to Thunder Heights were intangible and emotional. They could not be held up to the cold light of reason.

He saw refusal in her face and sighed. "The choice is yours and I shan't try to dissuade you. But if you stay, you must safeguard yourself by making a will. Pompton's in New York now, but he'll be at his office in Westcliff tomorrow. See him then."

"What good would a will do?"

He reached out and circled her wrist with his fingers. "The will must leave everything you have to charity—with no more than a pittance for Letty and Hortense. And you must let them know the wording of the will as soon as it has been safely drawn up. Then you'll be safe. You'll be worth a good deal to them alive, and they're likely to guard you tenderly."

"They would hate me for it. At least Hortense would. And Booth. How could I go on living at Thunder Heights in an atmosphere like that?"

"How can you live there anyway?" He dropped her hand impatiently. "This is the only safe move for you to make! Unless you do as I first suggested, and give the whole thing up."

"I can't," she said. "I can't do that."

"Then think about the will and do something about it soon," he told her. "They must realize you might take such a step, so they're unlikely to wait once they're sure you're suspicious. These—accidents—may grow more deadly."

Camilla plucked a blossom of white clover, twirling it between her fingers. She felt painfully torn.

"I'd better get back," Ross said. He got up.

She stood up beside him, not wanting him to go, and he stepped toward her as if he could not help himself. She was in his arms, where she had been once before, held close to his thudding heart, clinging to him, and weeping.

"My dear," he said. His hand was on her hair, and he held her head against him for a moment before he bent and kissed her lips. There was tenderness in his touch, and a great sadness.

"Why must you go away?" she wailed.

"I can't stay any longer," he said gently, his lips against her hair. "I've given ten years to your grandfather, but they were years of preparation. Now I must get on with my work."

"Build your bridge here," she whispered. "Build it for Grandfather. Build it for me."

"And if I did?"

"Then you could stay nearby. For all the time you were building it you would be a part of my life."

"But after that I'd be gone," he said. "You're tied to Thunder Heights, Camilla. You could never come with me to all the places where I'll go. It's better to end this now. It would hurt us all the more later."

She clung to him more tightly than ever. "No, no! We mustn't ever be apart again. Ross—I'll do as you say. I'll give up the inheritance and go wherever you wish."

He put her out of his arms, as he had done once before, but this time there was pain in his eyes.

"Stay here in the cemetery a little while longer," he said. "Then we won't be seen together outside. It won't help you if the Judds think you've met me here secretly." He started away from her and then turned back for an instant. "Please be careful, Camilla," he said, and hurried off.

She stood stricken and helpless, watching him go. Then she went to stand for a little while beside the grave of Althea Judd King. How young she had been to die. Yet she had known the fullest meaning of happiness. She had lived with her love and borne him a daughter. And now that daughter stood beside the place where Althea lay. Once more her thoughts turned to that stormy night on the mountain and all the dark puzzle of what had happened there.

If Althea had been too good a rider to be thrown, how had Folly freed herself and come home with an empty saddle? And what had happened between Althea and Booth out there in the stable before she had ridden off in the storm? Why had she struck him?

She thought again of the riding crop as she reached the gateway to Thunder Heights. How could it have fallen into those bushes? And why had Aunt Letty taken the crop away, kept it out of sight, said nothing to the others about the finding of it?

LUNCHEON THAT DAY was a solemn meal, with Booth working upstairs on his picture and only Hortense and Letty to keep Camilla company. "I'll take Booth something when we finish," Letty said. "I'm glad he's working again. I'll be happy when this painting is finished. I can't look at it without seeing Folly's rearing hoofs striking at me. Just as they must have struck at Althea."

"Do talk about something else," Hortense said brusquely. "We can do without such a gloomy subject with our luncheon."

They finished the meal in silence.

Afterward, when Letty had fixed a tray for Booth, she asked Camilla to come upstairs with her to his studio. "He wants you to see the finished picture, dear," she said.

Camilla would have preferred never to look at that painting again, but she had no reasonable excuse to offer.

Up in the nursery, Booth had set his easel facing the long windows along the north wall. When they came in he was standing back studying the picture with critical eyes. "It's done," he said to Camilla. "Come and tell me what you think."

With the background completed, the violence of the scene seemed to hurl itself at the beholder. Folly was rearing, her ears were laid back, her nostrils dilated, her lip curled above vicious teeth. But the girl who stood clinging to her bridle was almost laughing, as if in satisfaction of taming this rearing beast.

Camilla, staring at the picture, could not be sure whether the exultant face she saw there was her own or her mother's.

"I don't think I've ever looked like that," she said to Booth.

"But I can imagine you like that, after seeing Althea angry."

Letty had stepped closer to study the picture's details and uttered a soft exclamation. "You've painted in Althea's riding crop!" she cried.

"It's a good touch, don't you think?" Booth said. "I needed something to fill that empty spot."

"But the crop was never found up there," Letty said softly.

Booth shrugged. "Aren't you taking this too literally? I started the painting before I knew what would happen to Althea."

Letty said, "Wait for me here a moment, Camilla."

She hurried off, and Booth smiled at Camilla. "What's the trouble, Cousin? You hardly came near me at the lawn party yesterday. I suppose Mrs. Landry filled your ears with old scandals?"

Before Camilla could answer, Letty had returned, carrying in her hands the little riding crop with its head of silver chrysanthemums. She held it out to Booth.

"Here you are," she said. Booth took it, and a queer, electric excitement kindled in his eyes. The moment of danger, Camilla thought. The crop had meaning for him—that was plain.

"Where did this turn up?" Booth asked.

"I found it when I climbed down to that spit of land that strikes out into the river, below Thunder Mountain," Camilla said. "It was caught in a crotch of brush."

"As if it had been flung there," Letty puzzled. "But where could it have been thrown from, I wonder? Not from the top of Thunder Mountain— the spit is too far out for that."

"I'm sorry there's been such a mystery about it," Booth said easily. "I can tell you what happened."

"If you knew, why didn't you tell us sooner, dear?" Letty asked. "Why didn't you tell us when Papa kept wondering about the crop and looking for it to keep with the saddle and bridle?"

"I didn't tell anyone before, because Althea struck me across the face with the crop, and that was not something I cared to tell. I took it out of her hands, and she mounted Folly and rode away. I carried the crop to the lawn above the river and flung it out as far as I could. Into the water, I thought. I intended that she would never strike anyone with it again."

Letty's sigh was a soft release, as if she had dreaded his explanation. She took the crop from him and held it out to Camilla. "You may have it now, dear. Carry it the next time you wear Althea's things. She'd want you to have it."

"I'll carry it this afternoon," Camilla said. "I've had no time for riding lately. But I've wanted to explore those queer ruins that look like a castle, over on the next hill."

"You're right about the ruins," Booth said. "They are those of a castle. But they're man-made. A few families along the Hudson got the notion years ago that some expensive castle ruins would give the river a look of the Rhine. When I was a boy we used Castle Dunder for picnics. It's a good spot for a view."

He turned his attention to the tray Letty had brought him, and Camilla slipped away from the room. There was in her a growing urgency to be out on Firefly again. She could use the entire afternoon for riding and exploring the ruins. Then there would be only dinner, the evening, and one last night to get through. In the morning she would go to Mr. Pompton's office in Westcliff and await his coming. Ever since she had looked at the finished picture of girl and horse, she had known that she must act swiftly. Booth's explanation had been glib and logical, but she did not believe it. He might fool Letty, but he could not fool her. His story about what had happened to the crop was a lie. She had seen it in the exultance in his face, in his supreme confidence that he could step to the very knife-edge of danger and back away in time to save himself.

And yet, while instinct told her that he was concealing something about the crop, she could not think what it might be. Why had he painted the crop into the picture unless it had really lain there on the ground near Althea when she had struggled with the horse? Had he done it deliberately, playing with danger? Or had he done it from memory, without thinking— with an artist's unconscious observation of every detail?

When Camilla was dressed for her ride, she went down to the larder in search of Letty. The broken step had been repaired, but she stepped cautiously as she went down the steep flight.

Letty glanced up as Camilla came in the door. "I see you're ready for your ride, dear." Camilla saw that her hands were trembling.

"Yes. But I wanted to talk to you first, Aunt Letty."

Letty sighed. "I came down here to be busy and peaceful."

"I think you ought to know that the step that might have killed me yesterday was deliberately tampered with. I'd have shown it to you if it hadn't been mended so quickly."

"Tampered with?" Letty's hands went on with their work, and she did not look at Camilla.

"I think it was intended that I should be badly hurt on that step. But I don't think you planned such a trap, Aunt Letty. Nor Aunt Hortense. It's the sort of thing a man would execute."

Letty whirled to look at her. "You're making a dangerous accusation. And without proof."

"The proof is gone," Camilla said. "But I know what I saw."

"I don't believe it," Letty said.

"What about the riding crop, then? I know that worried you when you saw that Booth had painted it into his picture. And I think I know why. You were wondering why he saw it there in his mind's eye—just as I was wondering."

Letty shook her head wildly. "Ever since Booth came to this house, everyone has been against him. I didn't expect you to turn against him too, Camilla."

"Then you don't believe, Aunt Letty, that Booth would ever make an attempt on my life? Or even, perhaps, on my mother's?"

There was a long silence in the room as Letty struggled for words. In the end she merely shook her head.

"Very well," Camilla said. "I just wanted to know where you stand in all this, Aunt Letty. I'll go out for my ride now."

As she went upstairs she felt torn and saddened. If it came to a choice between her safety and Booth's, she suspected that there would be only one decision Letty could make. She was no more to be trusted than Hortense or Booth himself. At Thunder Heights every hand was against her, and that was as it would always be. And for such emptiness she must give up her love.

She let herself out the heavy front door and started down the steps. Behind her Letty's voice called out and Camilla turned around. Letty stood on the steps, breathless.

"Don't go riding, dear," she said. "It's going to storm."

Camilla looked up at the blue sky. "There's not a sign of a storm anywhere," she said.

She would have walked on toward the stable, but Letty came after her and caught at her arm in entreaty. "Please, dear. You must believe me. It's a feeling I have about that horse. Something terrible will happen if you go riding today."

"Firefly and I understand each other," Camilla said. "I feel safer with her than I do—in this house."

Letty drew back as if Camilla had slapped her. Then she turned and went up the steps, a drooping, pitiful little figure, her crooked arm held against her body. With a mingling of impatience and sympathy, Camilla walked away toward the stable. There was nothing more she could say to Letty, and it was just as well to leave her with that last thought.

CHAPTER TWELVE

SHE HAD NOT SENT word to have Firefly saddled, so she had to wait for it to be done after she reached the stable. More than once she scanned the sky to see if there was any evidence of Letty's threatened storm, but it burned blue and empty, with no hint of a breeze.

Firefly was restless. She stood impatiently while the groom helped Camilla into the saddle. Out upon the road, Camilla gave the mare an easy run as far as the place where the winding trail led up Thunder Mountain. With the horse moving like a dancer beneath her, something of the joy of riding returned, and Camilla could put Thunder Heights away from her for a little while.

They climbed the trail up Thunder Mountain, but this time Camilla did not dismount at the top. Firefly was behaving skittishly.

"All right," Camilla said, "I'll let you have your fun, but let's get over to the next hill. There's more room there for your tricks. I don't care for them at the top of a cliff."

Camilla urged the mare along a trail that emerged on an open slope just below the ruins of Castle Dunder, which looked far less picturesque than they seemed from a distance. However, the main tower appeared solidly built.

Camilla let Firefly prance up the slope. A low wall offered an easy foot-hold for dismounting, and Camilla stepped down to it, jumped to the ground, and tethered Firefly in the shelter of a stablelike shed at the rear of the tower.

As she started toward the tower, a spate of rain struck her. She looked up in surprise and saw that Letty's threatened storm was coming—clouds were moving up the sky. She hurried toward the tower entrance, where a few stone steps led into a dark room. In the dim light she could make out stone stairs circling upward. She followed their spiraling wedges until she emerged in a bare room at the top. Here several archers' windows, deep and narrow, slit the circular stone walls, letting in slivers of gray light. A rusty iron ladder led up to a trapdoor to the roof.

Now she wanted to reach the very battlements and watch the storm clouds rise. Testing the rungs to make sure they would hold her weight, she climbed up beneath the trapdoor. She pushed it with her shoulder, and it creaked open, sending shivers of dust and rotting wood down upon her head. The air smelled sweet and clean as she stepped out. The spurt of rain was over for the moment, but the mountains were obscured by mists. Far below, the Hudson was whipped with curling threads of foam, and the entire scene was like one of Booth's wild Hudson valley paintings.

So lost was she in watching the swiftly rising clouds that she had almost forgotten Firefly; then the mare neighed. She must go down at once, she thought, and start for home. It would be raining hard before long. As she hesitated for a last long look, she heard the answering neigh of another horse.

She looked toward the shed. Firefly was there, and tethered near her was a second horse, a man's saddle upon its back. At the foot of the tower a step sounded, and she leaned over the parapet to look straight down. She was just in time to see Booth Hendricks enter the doorway below. A shiver ran through her as she shrank back from the parapet. He must have hired a horse in the village and ridden out here deliberately. She could hear him walking about below.

He came to the foot of the spiraling stairs and called up to her. "Camilla! Are you there, Camilla?"

If she did not answer, he would think she was elsewhere and go away. But almost at once she heard his footfall on the echoing stone of the steps. She was trapped, with no means of saving herself and only the riding crop in her hands to fight him with.

With deadly certainty she knew what his purpose would be. There would be no need for indirection this time. A fall from the tower could be explained easily and Booth's ends would have been met.

In a moment he would emerge in the room at the top of the tower, and then it was only a few steps to the roof. As she trembled there, her mind turning this way and that like a hunted thing, a course of action came to her. Foolish, perhaps, and hopeless. But the only chance she had.

She pulled the gray hat from her head and tossed it to the far side of the tower. Then she dropped to her hands and knees and crouched in the one hiding place the roof offered—the niche made by the trapdoor where it lay propped against the parapet. The door itself shielded her and he could not see her as he climbed the stairs. She pulled herself small in the cramped space as he came up, his feet ringing on the iron rungs.

"Camilla?" he called again—and was out upon the roof.

He saw her hat at once and went toward it. In that instant Camilla flung herself from her hiding place and down the ladder. There was no time to be quiet, and she set the echoes ringing. She was on the stone steps now, slipping, stumbling, catching herself before she pitched headlong. Above her she could hear him following—and he was unhampered by a heavy riding skirt.

At the tower door, she sprang to the ground and fled to the shed. Firefly heard her coming and pawed the earth, neighing in nervous excitement. But Booth could move more swiftly than Camilla, and his hand caught her arm and he whirled her about. She saw his face in the gray light. He knew she had guessed the truth. There was danger in his eyes.

She struck at him with the riding crop, lashing it across his face. For an instant he was blinded by pain and he drew back. She twisted free of his grasp and sped the few yards to the low stone wall beside the shed. In a second she was up on the wall, from there into the saddle, the reins in her hand.

She swerved Firefly about and made her rear, her front feet sticking out in Booth's direction. Again he fell back, and Camilla turned toward the woods trail. Crouching low over the saddle, she gave the mare her head along the narrow trail. Caught up in Camilla's own fear, Firefly hurled herself into breakneck speed, seeking only to flee the unknown terror. Camilla could not hear the other horse, and she dared not look back, but Booth would be in the saddle by now and after her.

"Hurry, hurry!" she moaned to Firefly. "Hurry!"

Suddenly they were in the open, and Camilla knew they had reached the top of Thunder Mountain, with cliffs falling away on three sides, and the downward path behind them. Camilla fought the mare to a halt and turned her about. She could hear hoofbeats now, as Booth ran his horse through the woods, and despair swept over her. Thunder Mountain, with the way down cut off, would be as bad a trap as the top of the tower.

And then, without warning, Ross Granger rode out from the lower path. She urged Firefly toward him.

"It's Booth!" she gasped, pointing. Ross understood at once. "Go home!" he shouted. "Ride for home!" Ross wheeled across the path to intercept Booth.

She had no need to urge the mare now. Firefly was tearing down the lower path. But now there was something new and frightening about her gait. She lunged against a tree in passing, and Camilla felt a crushing pain in her left leg. The mare was trying to rid herself of her rider.

Camilla ducked low beneath the next branch before it swept her from the saddle, and clamped the toe of her right boot behind her left calf. Her hands ached with their effort to bring the mare under control. The trail was steepening and danger lay in a misstep that might cause the mare to stumble and roll on her. But the fight was hard on Firefly too, and with

Camilla clinging like a burr to the saddle, and never relinquishing her struggle to get the mare's head up and under control, the horse was tiring. When the road suddenly opened on a level before them, the fight drained out of the mare and she cantered to a halt.

Camilla pushed her tumbled hair from her forehead, spoke in a low, soothing voice to the mare, and turned her toward Thunder Heights. Only then did she have time to think of what might be happening now between the two men. More than once she drew the mare in and listened for the sound of a horse on the hillside above. Thunder rumbled in the distance and there was wind in the trees, but no other sound.

At the gate of Thunder Heights Hortense stood waiting. She called for the stableboy, and came forward herself to take Firefly's bridle. "Get off," she said curtly to Camilla. "If you can. You look beaten."

Camilla's body felt sore, and her left leg was bruised, but she took her foot from the stirrup and slipped down. She swayed for an instant. Hortense gave the boy the bridle and took her arm.

"That mare has a vicious streak, hasn't she?" Hortense said. "I expect she's killed a rider or two somewhere along the line. That's why Booth had her brought to Berton's. That's why he told me to—'find' her for you. You didn't know that, did you?"

Camilla shook her head wearily. "It was my own fault. I was frightened and I frightened the mare."

"I've been a fool," Hortense said. "I believed that he only wanted to make you afraid—so you'd give everything up and leave. I wanted that myself. I thought if I made you sick with that tea . . . but the cat drank it."

Camilla could only stare at her numbly. She was more convincing and forceful than Camilla had ever seen her. "He means to kill you, Camilla. He tricked me into sending you down to the cellar on a trumped-up errand. I'd never have been a knowing party to that broken step. I've never meant you serious harm. But Booth will stop at nothing."

"Yes, I know." Camilla's lips barely formed the words. All this was something she must come to later. Now only part of her mind focused on what might be happening on Thunder Mountain. For herself, she wanted only Letty's presence, and a bed to lie upon.

"Where is Aunt Letty?" she asked.

There was a strained note in Hortense's voice. "She's locked herself in her room. She's waiting for them to bring your body down from Thunder Mountain. The way they did Althea's."

THE DRIVEWAY SEEMED endlessly long as Camilla followed it, leaning on Hortense's arm, limping a little as she walked, but bruises were nothing compared with the pressure of anxiety in her mind.

"Who sent Ross after me?" she asked.

"I did," Hortense said. "When I learned that Booth had hired a horse and was riding up the mountain, I knew he meant you harm. So I told Ross. He got a horse from Blue Beeches and went out at once."

"Aunt Letty didn't want me to ride," Camilla said. "She tried to stop me from going."

Hortense tossed her head scornfully. "You mean that nonsense about a storm? It must have surprised her as much as anyone else to have one really blow up."

Suddenly Hortense clutched Camilla's arm. "Look!"

The afternoon was growing dark, and a few lamps had been lighted inside the house. Against the light a man stood before the front door of Thunder Heights as if braced, with his legs apart, his arms akimbo. It was Booth, waiting for them.

Hortense ran toward him. "How did you get here? Where is your horse?"

As Camilla drew near, she saw a jagged tear in his jacket. His tie was gone, his hair disheveled. A cut from the riding crop marked his forehead. "I left my horse and came down the cliff by way of the shortcut."

"Where is Ross?" Camilla demanded.

"We met—if that's what you're wondering." He regarded her almost airily. "Granger managed to interfere with my seeing you home, Cousin. But where he is now I don't know or care."

"What did you do to him?"

"A better question might concern what he did to me. I've never taken to rude physical brawling. But I know the mountain better than he does. I knew it as a boy."

"You went up the cliff the night Althea died, didn't you?" Hortense said. "I always thought you were up there."

"But since you doted on me, my dear mother, you kept your suspicion to yourself? That was kind of you."

A deep, tearing anger began to stir in Camilla. "What happened that night? What did you do to my mother?"

He stepped back from the fury in her face. "I did nothing. Nothing at all. I knew she would go up there, and I tethered my horse at the foot of the cliff while I was supposed to be out searching the river path. I could get to the top easily by the cliff path while Orrin was taking the long way around by the hill. But I assure you she was already dead when I came upon her body, and she couldn't taunt me anymore."

"Is that when you found the crop?"

"Yes. I'll admit picking it up was a foolish impulse. I wanted to make sure no one would ever strike me with it again. So I carried it down the mountain and flung it into the river. Or so I thought. I didn't dream it would turn up years later to be used against me in the hands of Althea's daughter."

Before Camilla could speak, a voice called from the upstairs sitting room in the house. The three on the driveway looked up to see Letty at the open window.

"Booth?" she called. "So you're back, dear. Please come up here. I want to see you."

Booth shrugged. "I'll go see what she wants," he said.

Camilla followed him slowly into the house. The candles in the antehall had been lighted, and so had the lamp that hung above the staircase. She moved toward the arch opening upon the stairwell and watched Booth start up the stairs.

He paused, one hand on the banister, and looked upward. Apparently Letty had come to the rail above, for Camilla heard her speaking to him softly. Booth cried out in sudden warning.

"No—no, Aunt Letty! Don't!"

There was alarm in his voice and Camilla stopped, with Hortense just behind her. Even as they stared, a sheet of flaming oil streamed down from the great lamp above as Letty's hand tipped it. The flame spilled over the wooden steps, encased the octagon railing, and dripped to the floor below. It was caught at once in the strong draft of the stairwell, and in a flash the entire wooden structure was a roaring chimney of flame. Letty could escape above, but Booth, partway up the stairs, was trapped.

To her horror, Camilla saw that Letty had not moved back from the fire, but was coming down the stairs toward Booth, toward the very heart of the blaze. In the same instant Booth tore off his jacket and leaped up the stairway, to fling it over Letty's head. He picked her up in his arms and came down through the flames, his own clothes on fire, his hair burning.

Hortense rushed wildly outside, screaming "Fire!" and a man dashed through the door past Camilla. It was Ross, and he took Letty from Booth's arms, beating out the streak of flame in her skirt. Then he caught up a small rug, wrapped it around Booth, and rolled him across the floor to the door. In a moment Ross had him outside on the grass, and Camilla drew Letty down the steps, where she crumpled to her knees on the driveway.

The servants had rushed out of their quarters at the side of the house, and one of them ran off toward the village to summon help. Hortense kept up her screaming until Camilla took her by the arm and shook her. "Stop it!" she cried. "You can't help anything by screaming." Then she turned to kneel beside Letty.

A patch of Letty's gray skirt fell to ashes when Camilla touched her, but her aunt sat up dazedly and leaned against Camilla's arm. Beyond them the heart of the house was burning like an enormous torch, and the fire was spreading into both wings, even as they watched.

"Booth!" Letty cried. "Where is he?"

She flung off Camilla's restraining arm and sprang up to run to Booth, where he lay upon the grass, with Ross bending over him.

"Don't touch him," Ross warned. "He's unconscious. You'd better leave him for the doctor to tend."

Letty stood quietly, looking down at the man who lay at her feet. The extent of his burns was frightful, and Camilla turned away, faint and shaken. No matter what he had been, she would not wish this for him. But Letty did not wince.

"He won't live." She spoke softly, but her voice did not quaver. "It's better that way."

She leaned sadly upon the arm Camilla put around her, and they walked a short distance away beneath the trees.

"He saved my life," Letty said. "He came up through the flames and brought me down. I didn't mean it to be like that. I didn't want him to live, but I meant to go with him."

"Hush," Camilla said. "You mustn't say such terrible things."

Hortense had come to stand beside them. "Let her be," she said. "Let her say what she pleases."

Against the stormy darkness of the sky the great tinderbox of a house flamed with a wild brilliance. Sparks showered as a center turret collapsed. Suddenly there seemed to be many people thronging the grounds, some shouting and moving about, some watching helplessly. The volunteer firemen were here now, with the horse-drawn engine from the village. The play of the hoses made a weak hissing against the tornado of flame.

"Let it burn," Letty said. "Let it burn to the last ember." Tears had begun to stream down her cheeks and she made no effort to stop them. "I knew when I saw the riding crop that he'd painted into the picture. Even then I wouldn't believe such evil of him. I'd always remember him as a little boy. Such a sad, handsome, unloved little boy. But when I saw the riding crop in the picture I knew that he'd gone up Thunder Mountain the night Althea died, and I had to face the truth."

"He told us she was dead when he found her," Camilla said quickly. "Perhaps that was the truth."

Letty shook her head. "Only part of the truth. He sent her to her death. I made him tell me today. He taunted her and made fun of her courage until she was so angry she struck him with the crop. But he knew she would ride Folly if he made her angry enough. When the time came he saddled the horse for her and he left the girth only partly buckled, knowing it would give if Folly acted up in the storm, as she was sure to do. Althea was too angry to check the saddle when she mounted. She must have been thrown violently when it began to slip. When Folly came home with an empty saddle, Booth caught her and took her to the stable before anyone could see what had made the saddle slip.

"Afterward he went up the mountain by the shortcut to see what had happened to Althea. I—I don't know what he might have done if she had been alive then." She looked up in entreaty at Camilla and Hortense. "You see why I had to act? He couldn't be allowed to go on like that. There would be no end to it as long as he lived. Yet in spite of everything, he saved my life."

The doctor came, and when he had examined Booth, he shook his head gravely. "It will be only a little while now," he said.

Letty knelt on the grass beside Booth, her eyes tearless, her gaze never moving from his burned and blackened face. Camilla stood with Hortense, waiting. Ross had gone away to work with the firemen. Only once did Booth open his eyes, and his gaze was all for Letty.

"Thank you," he said strangely. "We'll all be free now."

His eyelids closed. This time he had stepped across the knife-edge of danger.

The fire was past its fiercest burning now, though one tower was still in flames and the ruins would smolder for a long while. Ross had left the futile struggle. He came to draw Camilla away into the deep, cool shadow of the trees.

"You're safe," she said. "I worried so. What happened between you and Booth?"

"We fought. I think I was getting the best of it, when he broke away. I don't know how he got back, and I don't much care. I had to take the long way with the horses."

Camilla looked up between high branches and saw the stars in a night-blue sky. The storm had rumbled away in the distance, and more rain had never come. She turned in the shelter of Ross's arms and looked into his face.

"Booth spoke the truth," she said softly. "We're all free now. There's nothing to tie any of us here."

He held her closely, and she put her cheek against his. "Will you take me with you, Ross? Wherever you go?"

His kiss answered her, his arm was her support.

The last burning tower crumbled and fell with a great roar and a rush of high-flung sparks. The sound echoed against the mountain above and clapped back and forth across the river. Far below, the quiet Hudson waters flowed as they had always done. But Thunder Heights was gone forever.

Tregaron's Daughter

Tregaron's Daughter

A CONDENSATION OF THE NOVEL BY
MADELEINE BRENT

ILLUSTRATED BY ROBERT McGINNIS

At her window high above a gleaming canal,
young Cadi Tregaron reflected on the
strange twists of fate that had brought her
to a sumptuous Venetian palace. Until
two years ago she had known only the wild
Cornish coast, the simple fisherfolk who
were her neighbors and the homey cottage
where she and her father lived.

Now she was in Venice, the guest—
or captive?—of an inscrutable Italian
family. Even as she marveled at the beauty
of the city spread out before her, she knew
that its ancient stones had witnessed
centuries of cruelty and evil. And she
had a chilling premonition that something
sinister was closing in around her too. . . .

Madeleine Brent is the pen name of an
established author who had never
written a Gothic until Tregaron's
Daughter. Since its publication she
has written others, including
Moonraker's Bride and
Merlin's Keep.

CHAPTER ONE

O N THAT DAY in summer, the day that Lucian Farrel came into my life,
I awoke in the morning with a strange sense of uneasiness that was
close to fear. There was no reason for it. For all I knew, this would be
just another ordinary day, and in any case it was not my nature to be
nervous, even for some cause. But as soon as I opened my eyes it seemed
that all my senses were unnaturally keen and vivid, the world was sharper,
more clear-cut than usual, yet curiously unreal.

Twice before this had happened to me: on the day that my mother and
grandmother were killed, and again when within a few hours a drifter was
wrecked on the Mogg Race rocks and an undersea shaft of the tin mine
collapsed. Mawstone, our little village, lost seven men on that black day.

Now I had the same feeling upon me. It is hard to describe, except as a
kind of special awareness that seemed to herald disaster. I heard the ticking
of the magic lantern clock that Granny Caterina had given me on my tenth
birthday, seven years ago. The blend of fishing-village smells, salt and fish,
tar and good clean air seemed as sharp and new to me as if I had lived my
life in some big town far from the coast.

I shook myself, trying to throw off the strange feeling, and then got out
of bed to wake my father. It was a joy to me that I would be able to put a
decent breakfast in front of him, eggs and ham and piping hot potato cake.
In the bad year, two years before, the year that Queen Victoria died, the
town crier had watched day in and day out for the red glint on the sea
which told of schools of pilchards in the bay. Not once could he lift his
speaking trumpet to cry out "Heva! Heva!" We Cornish fisherfolk saw
little of meat or eggs that year.

"That smells handsome, m'dear," my father said as he came into the kitchen. This morning even he seemed strange to me: my father, Donald Tregaron, forty-four years old, six years a widower, his hair as fair as mine was dark; a strong, loving man who spoke softly and not often.

"It'll be a wisht ol' job if you burn that tetty cake," he said now.

I lifted the skillet quickly and pulled myself together. "Go and sit down now, Dad," I said. "It makes me all fussed to be watched serving up."

He smiled and went to the table. "That's just what your mother always said, Cadi."

I was named after my Italian grandmother, Caterina, but I had always been Cadi to everyone in the village. It was Mr. Rees, the vicar, who first used the Welsh form of Catherine with me. Only one person ever called me Caterina now. That was Miss Rigg, the English lady who gave me lessons three afternoons a week. My father insisted on that, even in bad times. It was because of Miss Rigg and Granny Caterina that I had never really talked in the true Cornish way. Granny had always spoken to me half in her own rather strange English and half in Italian, so I had learned Italian as easily as only a child can. And then my lessons with Miss Rigg helped to prevent me having a strong Cornish accent. This made me something of a foreigner in Mawstone. And my Cornish blue eyes contrasted oddly with my Italian black hair.

While we ate breakfast I was trying to plan my housework so that I would be free to go out with the fishing boats.

"Can I come out with you this afternoon, Dad?" I asked.

"I'll be on the quay mending the nets all today, Cadi."

"You'll be home for dinner, then," I said. It was on the tip of my tongue to suggest beef with pickled samphire for our dinner. But it was that cliff-growing flower, St. Peter's herb as some call it, that had brought tragedy upon us. From the day my mother and Granny Caterina fell to their deaths while out picking samphire, we had never touched it. Luckily I bit back the words before they were spoken, but I was shocked at myself.

When my father had set off I got down to work, keeping at it busily in the hope that the strangeness would pass away, and by the time he came home at midday I had got through most of the tasks I had set myself.

"Bob Rossiter was saying there's English gentry—five Kentish folk—staying at The Anchor," my father said as I cleared away our pie dishes.

The Anchor was a little hostel in Bosney, the next village along the coast from us. "Gentry don't stay in the villages," I said. "In a big hotel up along Newquay more likely."

My father shrugged. "You can never tell what foreigners'll do next."

Foreigners. I remembered how it had always amused Granny Caterina, the way Cornish people spoke as if England were a separate country. "What else did Bob say?" I asked.

My father rubbed his head, frowning in an effort to remember, just as he used to do when my mother pestered him for details of news he thought of no importance. "Well . . . Bob said something about their hiring his brother Davey's boat to go sailing." He looked pleased with himself for having remembered so much, then got to his feet. "Well, I'll be getting back. You look fine in that blue dress, Cadi love. Proper handsome."

With the strange feeling still upon me, I wanted to be alone that afternoon. I took a book that Miss Rigg had lent me and walked up the cobbled street to the end of the village, where a track led through hard, tufty grass to the top of the cliff. This was my favorite place for reading. To the left I could look down on the village and the little bay of Mawstone. To the right was a smaller bay, hemmed by tall cliffs. This was Mogg Race Bay. Even in the calmest weather it was a dangerous stretch of water. About a hundred yards from the western arm a great round rock lifted its glistening black bulk from the sea. This was Mogg. East of Mogg all was safe, but beyond the rock a savage current would swing a boat round perhaps three or four times, always drawing it nearer to the cliffs, until at last it was dashed against the granite fangs at their foot.

I tried to read, but my mind kept wandering. "You're in a dream, Cadi," I told myself, then sat up sharply. For last night I had dreamed the dream that came to me three or four times a year. The dream was always the same—no, not quite the same, because it had two opposite endings. There was a house, a big house more like a palace. Moonlight picked out the beautiful stone carving over the great portico. Well forward of the splendid façade, massive railings rose to twice the height of a man. Strangely, the ground on which the palace was set rose up out of flat calm water. Also rising from the water were several tall striped poles, in line along the front of the railings. In my dream I came to the house in a boat, and went up broad stone steps that marched out of the water between two pillars, and on to the great doors, which stood open. Beyond them lay darkness.

I was looking for somebody who was waiting for me in the house. In my dream I knew clearly who it was, but as soon as I woke I knew only that it was a man. I made my way across gloomy halls, along broad corridors, and up a great curving staircase. The man was waiting for me in an upper room, and I was longing to find him. I was calling as I moved along an upper corridor. A crack of light showed beneath a door at the end. The door opened and I saw a figure silhouetted against the light beyond. I ran forward gladly, and when I reached the doorway I saw him clearly.

It was here that the two dreams were different, right at the end. In the good dream I saw his face, and a great happiness swept over me as I went toward him. Then I would wake up, slowly, reluctantly, a great warmth within me. But if it was the bad dream, the one I had had last night, then when I saw his face, the same face as in the good dream, I was suddenly racked by fear and turned to run from him in terror. Blackness would engulf me like a cloak, and the nightmare would end without my wakening.

I had never told anybody about the dream. It had not begun until three years after my mother and Granny Caterina died, when I was fourteen and starting to change from a girl into a young woman. From what I had heard, all sorts of odd things could afflict young girls in those growing-up years, and I thought the dream was just a part of it.

Now I wanted to turn my mind away from it. I decided to think about Granny Caterina and the story she had told me so many times, of how Robert Penwarden, the grandfather I had never known, had saved her life one day long ago in a faraway place called Naples. Granny knew hardly anything of her life before that time, not even her family name, and could only recall little dreamlike scenes of her youth. She had remembered the Italian language, her Christian name, Caterina, and that was all.

I pictured her as young and beautiful in the long white dress she was wearing when Grandfather Penwarden had found her unconscious in the waters of the Bay of Naples. Then I had to imagine Robert Penwarden, a young seaman of twenty-six, on a fine sailing ship, carrying a cargo of salted pilchards to Naples. I saw him as having a likeness to my mother, a man as powerfully handsome as she was beautiful, but with fair hair.

And now I was free to concoct my own solution of the mystery to which nobody would ever know the true answer, the mystery of what had happened to the young Caterina on that bright day in Naples.

Suddenly my daydream stopped short. I was staring down into Mogg Race Bay, and what I saw there brought me to my feet with a gasp of horror. A little sailing boat was east of the line where Mogg's Head lifted from the sea. It was safe for the moment, but it was moving gradually closer to danger. The boat was Davey Rossiter's; I knew it by the triangular blue patch on the sail. So the man in it must be an English gentleman from The Anchor. As I shaded my eyes and stared harder, I realized that the man knew of his danger, for he was trying to tack away from the invisible line where the current would take him in its grip. But the boat's rudder was evidently almost useless. Twice I saw the Englishman swing the tiller to and fro without response. He was handling the sail delicately to catch the shifting gusts, but despite his skill he was being pressed back slowly and remorselessly toward the race beyond Mogg.

I turned and began to run down the grassy slope toward the village, slithering and sliding in my haste. If my father and I could pull out round the point and into Mogg Race Bay, we might be in time to save the stranger from certain death. That he carried no oars was only too clear, and he must be unable to swim, for otherwise he would have abandoned the boat long minutes ago, to swim round the point and into Mawstone Bay.

It was a long run down to the village, and by the time I reached the twisting cobbled street, my heart was pounding and my lungs heaving.

Suddenly I heard the clip-clop of hoofs not far behind me. Glancing over my shoulder, I saw a man on a gray horse cantering down upon me. I could not see his face clearly, but I had the impression of somebody young and slim. He must have seen the distress on my face, for as I halted I heard his voice from above me say sharply, "What's the matter?" There was crisp authority in his tone.

I pointed down the street, breathing hard. "Sailing boat . . ." I panted. "Caught in Mogg Race Bay . . ."

"Here, take hold." Next moment the young man reached down under my arm and plucked me from the ground. I flung myself astride the saddle, close behind him. He spurred the horse to a gallop as I clasped him round the chest. "Hold *tight*, girl!" he said in an angry voice. It was as well I obeyed, for as we rounded the corner where the fish cellars lay, the horse's hoofs slithered and scrabbled for purchase on the shiny cobbles. Then as if by main strength he lifted the stumbling horse and we were galloping like the wind again as we clattered along the quay.

My father looked up from his nets, then came to his feet, staring. As the rider reined in fiercely, I let go of him and slid off the horse sideways.

"Sailing boat in Mogg Race," I said breathlessly. "Davey Rossiter's boat. Rudder's gone. Trying to sail her out, but . . ."

My father said softly, "Dear God." Then, "We'll have to try. You take the tiller, Cadi."

As I ran for the gig which lay moored to the quay I heard my father say, "Can you row, sir?"

The cool voice said, "Well enough. Can the girl steer?"

"Well enough." My father echoed. "Will you take the midship oars, then?"

The young man sprang down into the boat. Then my father dropped a coil of rope at my feet, settled himself on the stern thwart, and ran out the long oars. I untied the painter and pushed off from the quay. The four oars dipped as one. We were heading for the western point of Mawstone Bay, a hundred and fifty yards away.

"Shave her close, Cadi love," my father said. I nodded. I knew exactly how to use the backwash of current so that we would be carried swiftly round the point, close in.

The gig glided swiftly over the smooth water. For a second I glanced at the rowers, but I could only see my father, for the stranger was behind him. Still, I could see the working of the man's oars, and he was keeping a good rhythm, feathering them nicely.

I focused on the point again. I had never before taken it as close as I took it that day, to win every scrap of advantage from the backwash.

As we pulled into Mogg Race Bay no sail was in sight. My heart sank as I realized that Davey Rossiter's boat had capsized in the race.

"He—he's gone, Dad." My voice was shaking. "The boat's capsized and in the race—no, *wait!*" I stared as the overturned boat came swinging round in a great circle. "He's hanging on to the side! He's still alive!"

The stranger spoke, his breath rasping. "You know best what to do. Give your orders, man."

My father said, "Cadi, take us twenty yards south of Mogg's Head, and the same east." Then he spoke over his shoulder to the young man. "We'll bide steady there, short of the race, see? And get a rope to the gennelman when he comes back along past Mogg. You heave the line, sir—I'll stick wi' the oars."

Two minutes later I called, "Back oars!" and we slowed to a halt.

My father heaved on one oar to swing us round stern on to the race, and I turned my head to seek the capsized boat. There came a scramble of feet from behind me and next moment the stranger was standing up on the stern sheets astride me as I ducked down to secure the rope he held. He lifted his voice sharp and clear. "Uncle Edward! Stand by for a line!"

Uncle Edward? Now I realized for the first time that the stranger was one of the English people staying at The Anchor. I tried to look up and see his face, but all I could see were his gray-trousered legs, a stretch of white shirt, and the line of his chin.

A faint answering cry came from the sailboat. In seconds now it would be as close to us as it would ever be again. There came a grunt of effort as the man above me cast the line. I expected to see the man in the water let go of the boat at once and cling to the line so that we could tow him out of the race, but the line had caught fast between the broken rudder and the stern. Before the line ran out taut, my father began to row with a madman's strength. Then came a smooth but powerful jerk as the full weight of the wrecked boat came upon us and began to drag us toward the race.

At that sudden lurch the stranger had crouched down over me, holding the gunwale to brace himself. A second later he was up, and jumped clear over my father in one long stride to take up his oars again. Both men were pulling now with all the power they could muster.

I glanced to my left, and my heart lurched. We were within a few feet of the powerful current. If we kept the capsized boat in tow, Mogg Race would draw us slowly in, like a great fish on the end of a line.

From only thirty yards away the Englishman in the water called, breathless yet astonishingly calm. "I . . . cannot free the line. Cast off your end, please. Good-by, and thank you for trying."

They were the words of a brave man. I saw my father's brown face harden with stubbornness. "Lash the tiller, Cadi!" he gasped. "Take bow oars!"

I slipped the twin nooses over the tiller bar, eased past the rowers as they bent forward, slid the oars into the oarlocks, and took up the stroke. Then the ordeal began. After the first few minutes my eyes were blind with sweat. Through a blur I could see only the soaking white shirt of the man who sat in front of me. It had split at one shoulder under the strain. Soon I felt the side of my own precious blue linen dress tear in a great rip.

I shall never know how long we fought Mogg Race that day. Each time I swung forward I knew that I could manage only one more pull, but somehow I managed that one last pull again and yet again.

Then quite suddenly I knew that we were actually moving through the water, not just inching along. I heard a gasping shout from my father. "Easy all!" I hung forward over the looms. My limbs and back seemed to be one huge fiery ache. With a great effort I lifted my head. Astern, the line stretched out at an angle toward the capsized boat, which was twenty paces on the safe side of Mogg now, clear of the race.

We had won.

I heard my father speak, and saw the young man start to row again with easy strokes while my father hauled on the line to draw the capsized boat alongside. I made out the head and shoulders of the man who still clung to the wreck. By some chance a white, peaked sailing cap was still on his head, and I saw that he had a small pointed beard.

A sudden wave of relief swept me, for now—now of all times—the strangeness of the day had dissolved and vanished. The disaster I feared had come, I suppose, and so the spell was broken.

My father helped the Englishman as he dragged himself over the gunwale of the gig. I heard the young man say, "Good afternoon, Uncle Edward."

"Good afternoon, Lucian." The voice was breathless still, but quite calm. "I hardly expected to see you here, my dear boy."

The older man looked at my father, who was making fast the wreck. "My name is Edward Morton," he said, "and this is my nephew, Lucian Farrel." He paused, and then quietly went on, "I'm sure that better men than I have failed to find words for those who have saved their lives. I can only say that I thank you from a full heart."

My father gave a nod of his head. "Our pleasure, sir," he said in his slow Cornish burr. "I'm Donald Tregaron, and there's my daughter, Cadi. It's her you've to thank, I reckon. She was the one that turned the scales."

Mr. Morton looked past Lucian Farrel to where I sat on the bow thwart, nursing my sore hands. "She did, indeed," he said soberly. He took off his peaked cap, revealing a head almost completely bald, and gave a polite bow from his half-lying position. "Your servant, young lady," he said.

We rowed back round the point into Mawstone Bay at an easy pace. I was vaguely aware that Lucian Farrel and his uncle were talking in the odd, mock-courteous manner that they seemed to use with each other.

"You'll need dry clothes, Uncle. If you've finished sailing for the day, that is."

"I feel that the call of the sea has waned within me for the moment, my dear boy," Mr. Morton said reflectively. "As for my clothes, I'm sure they will shortly be dry in this capital sunshine."

"You will need some means of conveyance to Bosney, Uncle. It's a long four miles."

"A pleasant walk, Lucian. You'll enjoy it, my boy. I shall ride the horse, as befits the weight of my years."

I heard Lucian Farrel laugh as he leaned forward into the stroke. I looked at his back, the broad shoulders and the narrow waist, and realized that through all this adventure I still had not truly seen his face.

Word of the trouble had spread, and there were a dozen women and two old men on the quay as we drew near. "All's well, don't fuss," my father said impatiently as we climbed from the gig.

My legs would scarcely support me, so I sat down on a bollard to hide my foolishness. Mr. Morton came over to me and gently picked up my hands, turning them to look at the raw palms.

"You must have ointment and dressing for these at once," he said sharply. "Lucian! This young lady's hands must be seen to."

Lucian was crouched on the edge of the quay, staring down at the stern of the capsized boat, so absorbed that he did not hear his uncle's words.

"Will you come here a moment, Uncle Edward?" he called. Now I saw that my father was crouching alongside him.

Mr. Morton said, "Excuse me, Cadi," and turned to join them.

Tired though I was, something made me rise and follow him. I peered over my father's shoulder as he crouched on the edge of the quay. It was easy to see why the rudder had failed. The lower pintle, one of the two square iron hooks which secured the rudder to the sternpost, was missing.

Kneeling, Lucian Farrel pointed to the bright and unweathered face of the metal where the pintle had broken off. "That didn't just happen, Uncle Edward. Somebody sawed it halfway through."

I could see it clearly, and I was horrified. There was a long silence until at last Mr. Morton said in a strange, quiet voice, "The pintle was flawed, no doubt, which made it break in that curious way." He turned to my father. "I hope that you and your daughter will put all thought of it out of your minds."

My father hesitated. He had seen, as clearly as I, that what Lucian Farrel said was true. "If that's what you wish, Mr. Morton," he said at last.

Lucian Farrel stood up, wiping his hands on his grimy shirt. Then he turned, and for the first time I saw him fullface. Rather long, with a very square chin, his face held none of the usual pallor of the city dweller. There was a short white line of scar on one cheek. In contrast to the dark chestnut hair, his eyebrows were black. They were strange eyebrows, and his most noticeable feature, for they flared up slantingly above light blue eyes to give him a faintly satanic look. The cold anger in his eyes as he gazed

sightlessly through me was frightening, but it was not this that made every nerve in my body jump with shock.

Lucian Farrel's face, which I had never seen before, was the face that I knew in the dream, the face of the man who waited for me in that palatial house surrounded by water, the man whose presence brought me either intense joy or nightmare fear.

CHAPTER TWO

LUCIAN FARREL'S RAGE faded; his eyes focused slowly, and he looked at me. Strangely, stupidly, I expected him to recognize me from the dream, but his look held no emotion now except for a vague curiosity. I must have looked a sight. My face was streaked with sweat; my dress was torn; my hair hung about my face.

The sky suddenly seemed to lurch over my head, and there was a great rushing noise in my ears. As if from a long way off I heard my father's voice cry out, "*Cadi!*" An instant before darkness enclosed me, I felt strong arms catch me as I fell.

Some time later, when I came to, Mrs. Mansel, the midwife who was better than any doctor, was bandaging my hands with a cool salve. She put me to bed, clucking about menfolk being "proper buffleheads."

I slept all through the night and into the morning until the sun was three hours risen. The strangeness, the fear, the tiredness had all passed away, and there remained only the excitement of yesterday's adventure to think about. I could laugh at myself now for imagining that Lucian Farrel's face was that of the man in the dream. At that moment on the quay, I told myself, after the frightful effort of the rescue, I had been in a daze. My mind had played a trick, confusing the dream and reality. There was nothing more to it than that.

I removed my bandages and washed before I put on a clean dress, and then I went down to the kitchen. My father had made me a special breakfast. "Them gentry from Kent, they'll be calling this afternoon," he said as I ate hungrily. "We'll have to offer 'em tea, Cadi. You make a sheet of saffron buns and you'd best get the good china out."

That day I scrubbed and polished the tiny parlor until it shone. Meanwhile the saffron buns were baking, and for good measure I made some of the clotted cream that foreigners to Cornwall always marveled over. At three o'clock I put on my Sunday dress, an ivory-colored cotton with crochet work at the neck.

"Mind you keep 'em eating and drinking, Cadi," my father said. "I don't want 'em chattering on and on with their thank-yous."

"You won't be hearing much chatter from that young Mr. Farrel. He's sparing enough with talk," I said. Then, changing the subject, "Dad, it was a queer thing about that pintle, wasn't it?"

"Main queer. Half sawn through, like the young feller said."

At four o'clock we heard a rumble of wheels and a jingle of harness, and then through the window I saw a small pony phaeton draw up outside. I opened the door and Mr. Morton looked down at me with quick pleasure. "Ah, so you've recovered, Cadi. I'm so glad, my dear."

"Won't you come in please, sir?"

Lucian Farrel followed him, saying in his cool voice, "Good afternoon." As I led the way through to the parlor I decided that I did not like Mr. Farrel. It seemed to me that he thought himself much too good for our little home. But I liked Mr. Morton very much. I think I had liked him from that first moment when he lay half-drowned in our boat, yet had taken off his cap to greet me with courtesy.

He quickly put my father at ease, and in a few minutes they were discussing boats and sailing and all the tricks of the local waters, as if they had been friends for years. Lucian Farrel hardly said a word, listening instead to their talk.

When I brought in tea and set it out on the table for passing round, Mr. Morton ate heartily. He had never tasted saffron buns before, and he was very complimentary to me. Lucian Farrel ate half a split and drank one small cup of tea. Then there came an odd change in the atmosphere. The conversation became stilted and awkward. At last Mr. Morton said, with many hesitations, "Mr. Tregaron, Cadi, you saved my life at the risk of your own yesterday. I want to thank you again more fully, and yet I—I have a strong feeling that this will embarrass you—"

"It would, sir, it would," my father broke in hastily. "All's well, and we're glad you're safe, and let that be an end of it."

"There is one other thing . . ." Mr. Morton said slowly, and then stopped, as if not knowing how to go on.

"If I can speak for my uncle," Lucian Farrel broke in, "the matter which troubles him is this. You saved his life and he is in your debt. It is a debt that cannot be repaid, certainly not with money. But money has its uses, and my uncle is not a poor man. He knows that the Cornish are proud people, but it would give him very great pleasure if you would accept a gift from him."

I stole a glance at my father. To my surprise, he was smiling. "Yes, we're proud," he said. "But I'll ask one thing, for I think it'll please you." My father's smile broadened as he went on. "Cadi there ruined her best working dress with the rowing. If you've a fancy to give her a new one—just a linen dress with good wear in it—then I'll be happy to accept for her."

Mr. Morton smiled ruefully. "It's not what I had in mind, but at least I haven't offended you," he said. "You're an understanding man, Donald Tregaron." He leaned back in his chair with a sigh of relief. "Cadi, my dear, do you think I could beg a fresh cup of tea?"

When our guests rose to go Mr. Morton put his hand on my father's shoulder. "I won't thank you again, Donald, nor Cadi either." He took a card from his pocket and put it down on the little shelf by the door. "But if ever you need a friend, write to me. I'll not forget you."

Two days later the dress arrived for me, the same blue as the one I had ruined. It fitted perfectly. With the dress was a short note. "Lucian assures me that this is the right color and size," Mr. Morton wrote. "I hope we may meet again before our holiday ends."

I was astonished. "Lucian Farrel picked it out!" I said to my father as I showed him the dress. "Now would you ever believe it!"

"He took more notice of you than you reckoned, Cadi love."

I wrote a little letter of thanks, which I posted to The Anchor. I looked forward to seeing Mr. Morton again, but that was not to be. Bob Rossiter reported that Mrs. Morton had been "took bad." Next day a note arrived from Mr. Morton again, saying that he had to return home with his family and regretting that there would be no time for another visit with us.

After the excitement of those few days, life seemed rather flat for a while, but there was always work to be done, keeping the home, helping my father on the boat or the nets, lessons with Miss Rigg, books to be read. The slight feeling of emptiness soon passed, but something was left behind.

As summer gave way to autumn and the purple-pink foxglove sank into winter sleep, I often thought of Mr. Morton and of Lucian Farrel. Then winter was upon us. The sea pounded the granite cliffs. Snow sheeted the gray slate roofs of the cottages, and no boat moved out to sea.

Twice that winter I had the dream about the house that stood in water. Once it was the good dream, once the bad dream. In both, the face of the man was the face of Lucian Farrel. This seemed to make the good dream better but the bad dream worse.

THE SEASONS TURNED, and it was in the spring of the following year, as the tulips came to their best, that the blow fell. On a May night a freak gale sprang up. A drifter from Penzance was dismasted two miles off Bosney. My father was one of the crew that pulled out through thunderous waves to save what souls they could.

Hours later they returned. The first light of a gray dawn was in the sky. I stood with those who had huddled on the quay all night, waiting. The lifeboat was full, overladen with the crew from the drifter. But my father was not there.

As the men came from the lifeboat I saw their drawn, weary faces, and the way they avoided meeting my eye. Then Mrs. Warren from next door to us put her arm round my shoulders as her husband, Jack, came toward us, soaked and exhausted. "Come back home wi' us, Cadi," he said. "Your dad . . . he's gone round land."

My grief was too deep for tears. We walked back to Mr. Warren's house in silence, and I remember being given something hot to drink. I recall nothing very clearly of the next two days. Though everybody was kind to me, I knew that I was alone now. Eight years ago, my mother and Granny Caterina had been taken. And now, in the same way, suddenly and without warning, my father was gone.

On the fourth day, although it troubled the Warrens, I moved back into our own little house. That night I was able to cry for the first time. In the morning I was limp and exhausted, yet I felt better. My father would never have wanted me to mope and wail, or to be dependent on other people. I had to think of the future, and what I would do. I went to see Miss Rigg, and asked if she thought I could get a job as a governess.

"I'm sorry, Caterina," she said, looking distressed. "It won't do, my dear. For one thing you are too young, and for another you really haven't the qualifications."

"But I've kept up my lessons, and you said I was very good, Miss Rigg."

"You are far ahead of most village girls of your own age, but that is not enough, child." Even now that I was nineteen she often called me "child." "What the gentry want in a governess," she went on, "is education, experience, and *background*." She gave a sympathetic smile. "That's the trouble, really. Your background is not right, Caterina."

"You mean because my father was a fisherman, Miss Rigg?"

"Yes. I'm sorry, but that is the way things are, Caterina. The gentry want their children *brought up* in a particular way, a way that you know very little about. I'm sorry if my opinion is disappointing to you."

I wanted the truth and Miss Rigg had given it to me. "There's another idea I might try," I told her. "I thought I might rent a little piece of land and grow spring flowers. Cityfolk pay an awful lot of money for them."

"Not 'awful'—that's quite the wrong adjective," Miss Rigg said automatically. Then she stared at me in some bewilderment. "Running a flower garden? You are an extraordinary child, Caterina. Flower growing is a *business*."

"I can rent a small piece of land for a few shillings a month, Miss Rigg, and I've got green fingers, and Mr. Warren says he'll make the shipping crates for me."

Miss Rigg took off her glasses and blinked. "Quite extraordinary!" she repeated. "Such a—a *practical* attitude in a young girl!" Suddenly she smiled. "But I really think you might succeed, Caterina."

For the next two days I did nothing but work and plan for my flower-growing adventure. Then came an event which changed everything. I was sitting at the kitchen table, composing a letter to Mr. Dobson of Bosney, who owned a piece of ground that I hoped to rent, when there came the sound of a horse's hoofs in the street outside. I scarcely noticed when the hoofs clopped to a halt, but the tapping on the front door made me jump. When I went to the door I was startled to see Mr. Morton. His expression was grave as he said, "Cadi, my dear, do you remember me?"

I stammered, "Oh! Mr. Morton—please come in, sir." I led the way through to the parlor and said, "I'm afraid my father isn't here. He . . ."

"I know, Cadi," Mr. Morton said gently. "That is why I'm here. I read what had happened in the London newspaper, how the lifeboat went out and how your father saved the others but lost his own life carrying a line to the drifter. I can't tell you how distressed I am. I came down by train this morning."

This was not just the local squire riding a few miles to offer his sympathy. Mr. Morton, a gentleman I had met only twice before, had made a journey of over two hundred miles to see me.

"Yes . . . it was in the newspaper yesterday," I said, trying to collect my thoughts.

Mr. Morton moved closer and put a hand on my shoulder. "Donald Tregaron was a good man," he said simply. As he spoke, something seemed to break inside me and I began to cry desperately. Next moment Mr. Morton had put his arms about me and was holding me against him. "Weep your grief away, Cadi. It's a woman's gift to do so," he said.

Soon, because I did not try to resist, I began to feel better.

After a little while Mr. Morton made me sit down on the couch, and he sat beside me holding my hands. "Do you have any relatives, Cadi? Or are you alone now?"

"I'm alone now," I said. "But I'll be all right. You needn't worry."

"Listen, Cadi," he said quietly. "Two years ago you saved my life, you and your father. But when I ask you, as I do now, to make your home with me and with my family, it isn't simply because I wish to pay my debt to you. I also want you to come and live with us because I like and respect you very much, and it would make me happy."

It was all too much for me to take in. I could leave Mawstone, with its constant reminders of my sorrows, and travel far away to live in Kent, under the care of a man who had gained my affection by the warmth and kindness of his whole manner. The house would be a big house, no doubt, very splendid and comfortable. There would be books to read, a new world to explore and a new way of life to be learned.

"I'm sure I would be very happy to live in your home," I said at last, rather shakily. "But your wife and children might feel I was an intruder."

"At the moment," Mr. Morton said slowly, "my wife is full of enthusiasm for the idea. But . . . her enthusiasms are inclined to wax and wane."

Humor crept into his eyes and he went on. "For myself, I don't take her good moods too seriously, and then I am not disappointed when she is perhaps not at her best. You're a steady girl, Cadi, and I think you could easily do the same."

I nodded. "And your children—would they mind, Mr. Morton?"

"I have only two," he answered slowly. "My elder son, James, died a few years ago in an accident . . . a shooting accident. My other son, Richard, is twenty. My daughter, Sarah, is seventeen." He paused, thinking. "Sarah will be shy at first, but she will very soon become fond of you. As for Richard . . ." Mr. Morton smiled wryly. "I regret to say he is not a *sincere* young man. We find it very difficult to know his true feelings. But I'm sure he will not resent you, Cadi."

Mr. Morton stood up. "So there you are. There may be problems at times, as there are in all families. But you will lack for nothing, you can pursue whatever interests you wish, and . . ." He turned to stare out of the window and added after a pause, "You will be as my own daughter."

At that moment I felt a strange pang of pity for him, though it was hard to tell why. Perhaps I sensed that he yearned for something his family had been unable to give, for suddenly he seemed to me a very lonely man.

"I'm a fisherman's daughter, Mr. Morton," I said, and looked at my work-roughened hands. "If I go with you, I shall have new ways to learn, and I shall make mistakes sometimes. I'm frightened of failing you."

He remained staring out of the window, and answered in a whisper, "You did not fail me on the day when Mogg Race had me in its grip, Cadi Tregaron. With your lungs close to bursting and the skin tearing from your palms, you did not fail me then."

"You make too much of it," I said desperately.

His eyes were warm as he gazed at me. "You have courage and heart, child, and that is what matters. All the other frippery of becoming a young lady can easily be learned."

I tried to keep my voice steady. "Then I'll be happy to come with you, Mr. Morton."

"Splendid!" he cried, and I could see that he was truly delighted. "Now let me see, if we make an early start, we can catch the eight-thirty train from Plymouth. It will bring us to Paddington Station by two o'clock. But today we must see your teacher, Miss Rigg, isn't it? And also your vicar, so that they know everything is in order."

He ran a hand over his bald head. "Now, what else? Ah, yes. You must have some clothes. We shall have plenty of time to do our shopping in London before we take the train down to Sevenoaks." He went on, his eyes twinkling, "If we place ourselves in the hands of the ladies at Mr. Harrod's emporium, we can't go wrong."

My head was muzzy with excitement and nervousness. A dozen pictures flashed across my mind, and with them came as many half-formed questions. But I asked only one that I had not even realized was in my thoughts.

"Does your nephew, Mr. Farrel, live with your family?"

"Lucian?" A shadow seemed to dim Mr. Morton's pleasure. "No. He has a flat in London, and he travels quite extensively. We have an occasional visit from him, usually unheralded, but . . ." He hesitated, as if trying to decide whether to say more, then gave a little shrug and simply concluded, "But he does not live with us."

"I asked because . . . he didn't seem very friendly."

Mr. Morton nodded and looked past me with distant eyes. "There are some who reject friendship rather than suffer the risk of being rejected," he said quietly. "It is the way of the outcast, Cadi."

Outcast? Lucian Farrel? I could not imagine what Mr. Morton meant. It was on the tip of my tongue to ask, but Miss Rigg had warned me many times that to be inquisitive was a great fault, particularly in a young lady.

Next day was the most exciting I had ever known. I could not take my eyes from all the fascinating sights as we roared through the countryside in our first-class compartment. I must have asked Mr. Morton a hundred questions. He was very easy to talk to, with no trace of that stilted manner which some older folk have when they are talking to young people. At last the roar and bustle of London was all about us. The air smelled smoky, and everyone seemed to be hurrying as we rattled along the busy streets in a hansom cab.

At the big shop called Harrods, Mr. Morton put me in the care of a very pleasant lady with graying hair, and soon I was trying on so many dresses and bonnets that I became almost tearful in my confusion. The lady was very distressed that I did not want to be corseted. But Mr. Morton said, "I don't care whether it's proper or not, madam. Nature and exercise have given that child all the corseting she needs."

After two hours, one large trunk was packed with clothes to be sent by rail, and a smaller trunk containing all I should need for the next few days was carried out to a hansom cab. My old ivory-colored best dress had been placed in the large trunk, and I now wore a beautiful pale green silk dress with a bonnet to match. Mr. Morton took me to have tea at a huge new hotel called the Ritz. Then another hansom cab took us to Charing Cross, where we boarded a train for Sevenoaks.

Mr. Morton had sent a telegram to say which train should be met, and his own carriage and driver were waiting for us when we arrived. We trotted along a country lane for two or three miles and then at last turned into a drive between tall stone pillars. As we passed beyond the trees which screened the house from the road I caught my breath. I had expected a large house, but this was huge. It lay beyond a wide carpet of lawn, with the drive curving round to an apron of cobbles in front of the porch. I learned later that it had been built when Queen Victoria was young. The red bricks had mellowed over the years and were softened by ivy.

"Welcome to Meadhaven," Mr. Morton said, tucking my hand under his arm. The door was opened by a butler, the first I had ever seen. He was a rather plump man with thin gray hair and a grave manner.

"Good evening, John," said Mr. Morton, and took me into the lofty hall. "This is Miss Cadi, the new member of our family."

"Welcome, Miss Cadi," John said politely.

"How do you do?" I said, in the way Miss Rigg had taught me. I looked round the hall. A broad staircase curved up to a gallery above, and a balustrade ran round the four sides of the gallery. The hall was beautifully furnished, with sofas, carved chairs, a grandfather clock, and several statues and paintings.

John coughed quietly. "Mrs. Morton, Miss Sarah, and Master Richard are in the garden, sir."

"We'll join them out there," Mr. Morton said. "Come along, Cadi."

But I could not move, and his words came to me only faintly. I was gazing at a picture which hung above a side table, and though my head was pounding, it seemed that my heart had stopped beating. Before me was a fine, detailed painting of a house set against a starry sky, an ornate and foreign-looking house, more like a palace. Dark water lapped its walls and its stone steps. I knew every detail, every pillar of the colonnade, for I had seen this house before, not in reality but in the dream.

This was the house where joy or terror waited for me, and a man with the face of Lucian Farrel. It was a house that existed only in my dream. But somebody had painted it in detail on canvas.

CHAPTER THREE

I HEARD MR. MORTON say anxiously, "Cadi! Are you all right?"

With an enormous effort I tore my eyes away from the picture. "Yes. It's nothing, thank you. For a moment I felt dizzy, but it's passed now."

He looked at me curiously. "After all our traveling, most young ladies would have had swooning fits long ago. John, bring Miss Cadi a nice tall glass of fruit juice, if you please."

We moved into a huge drawing room and out onto a terrace. The garden before us was large and beautifully kept, with neatly trimmed hedges and long flower beds full of tulips. Beneath the surrounding trees lay a dark green quilt of periwinkle. A girl in a pink dress and a young man were playing croquet. A tall lady in a long white dress rose to her feet rather dramatically as we approached, putting one hand to her breast. Her hair was golden, her eyes were a startling violet, but on seeing her more closely, I realized that there were little lines on her face which hinted at a long-suffering nature. I judged that she was in her late forties.

Mr. Morton took her hand and kissed her on the cheek, saying, "Helen, my dear, this is Cadi."

Enfolding me in her arms, Mrs. Morton cried, "Cadi, my poor, poor child. I am so truly *happy* that we can repay the kindness you showed my husband on that dreadful occasion when the water came into his boat."

Mr. Morton gave me a slow, deliberate wink. I realized that he had given his wife some account of our first meeting, but that he had made it sound very much less dangerous than it was, to avoid distressing her.

Mrs. Morton released me from her embrace, smiling fondly. "Now you must meet your new brother and sister," she said in a voice that shook slightly with emotion. "Richard, Sarah . . . this is Cadi."

Sarah, who was pretty and blond, had been waiting timidly. I shook hands with her and said, "How do you do, Sarah?"

Then Richard was presented. He had his mother's golden hair and violet eyes, with fine delicate features and a warm sweet smile.

"We're so happy to have you with us, Cadi," he said softly, and leaned forward to touch his cheek against mine. I was strangely moved by the gesture, and my eyes were pricking when I answered, "Thank you very much, Richard. It's wonderful for me to be here."

"Now let us all sit down," said Mr. Morton, and as he spoke John appeared from the house with a tall glass on a tray. "Cadi must have a cool drink to refresh her after our long journey."

The conversation was a little stiff at first. Sarah gazed at me nervously while Richard asked about our journey. Mrs. Morton sighed and said that Mr. Morton should never have left the selection of my clothes to the Harrods lady.

"I'm sure we managed quite well, my dear," Mr. Morton replied. "And I was afraid the strain might be too much for you."

When speaking to his wife, Mr. Morton did so with much courtesy and kindliness but, it seemed to me, rather automatically. I felt that this came from long-established habit. Mrs. Morton apparently was a lady who liked to feel that the burdens of life lay heavily upon her. A wrong word and she would feel unappreciated. Tired though I was, I took note of this.

After a little while Mr. Morton said, "I think you might take Cadi up to her room now, Sarah. After she has a rest you can show her round the house before dinner."

Sarah said, "Yes, Papa."

As we went up the wide curving staircase from the hall, some of Sarah's timidity faded. "You can sail a boat, can't you?" she said rather sulkily.

"My father was a fisherman," I said, "so I've sailed since I was small."

"I can't do that." Her voice was disconsolate. "I always feel sick."

"It's only because you're not used to it," I said. "I felt sick in the hansom cab, there's a silly thing for you."

Her face brightened and she said, "I'm glad you've come, Cadi."

She opened the door of a beautiful bedroom, with pink walls and thick rugs on the floor. A maid in a frilly white apron had just finished hanging up the clothes from Harrods in a huge wardrobe. "This is Betty," said Sarah, and the maid dropped a little curtsy. "Betty, this is Miss Cadi."

I just stopped myself putting out my hand.

"Miss Cadi is going to rest for a little while," Sarah continued. "Wake her at half past seven o'clock, Betty, and bring up hot water for a bath. That will be all for now." Whether or not Sarah could sail, she had plenty of experience in speaking to servants, and I had none.

IT SEEMED ONLY minutes later that Betty was touching my shoulder. "Half past seven, Miss Cadi. Your bath'll be ready in just a minute."

I had slept soundly for two hours and now the bath was a joy, for it seemed that I washed all fatigue and sleepiness from my body. I had dressed and was just brushing my hair when Sarah tapped on the door and came in. Five minutes later we began a tour of the house.

The family had not yet come up to change for dinner, so I could see all the upstairs rooms. Mr. and Mrs. Morton had separate bedrooms on the other side of the gallery. His was simple in style, but hers was full of frills and knickknacks. I thought how much work it would be to clean and dust, but then remembered there were servants to do all this.

Sarah's room was next to mine, and Richard's lay beyond. Hers was full of souvenirs, dolls, a coronation cup, and small ornaments brought back from holidays. Richard's was very different. On the walls hung ancient pistols, African spears, a witch doctor's mask, and other strange objects. It seemed out of key with Richard's innocent, almost seraphic face.

We went down to the kitchens. Here there was a great bustle of servants preparing for dinner. John, the butler, stood watching with sharp eyes and snapping out an order every now and then. A huge fillet of beef was turning slowly on a roasting spit, and half a dozen large saucepans were steaming on the range. The door of a vast larder stood open, and when I saw all the jars and bottles, the cheeses, the dishes of cold meats and poultry, it seemed to me that Mr. Morton must be one of the richest men in the whole country. It was not until several weeks later that I realized there were many such households within a few miles of Meadhaven and that these were modest compared to the estates of the truly rich.

When we went back up to the big hall, one of the footmen was going round with a long taper, lighting the gas lamps. Holding my breath a little, I turned to look again at the painting.

"That's a lovely picture," I said to Sarah, keeping my voice casual. "Do you know who painted it? And where?"

"You like it?" Sarah said rather doubtfully. "I remember my father bought it when I was little, but it frightened me because it always seemed so . . . so mysterious. It's a Venice scene."

Venice. Of course! Why had I never thought of that? I had read of it in one of Miss Rigg's books, an ancient and fascinating city, where the roads were waterways and the carriages were gondolas. In my mind was a hazy notion of splendid palaces, of masked balls, beautiful women, and handsome men.

"Is it a real scene?" I asked slowly. "Or just from imagination?"

"Goodness, I don't know, Cadi. You'll have to ask Papa."

Sarah tapped on the door of Mr. Morton's study before entering. The room was large, with a thick carpet, and a very big desk across one corner. All along one wall were oak filing cabinets. Beyond the study lay the library, and I gasped with pleasure as I saw the rows and rows of books which lined the walls. "Do you think your father would let me borrow a book to read sometime?" I whispered.

"Of course." Sarah looked surprised. "But they aren't books you can enjoy much, Cadi. They're all about history and politics and, oh, lots of things ending in 'ology. I only like stories where they fall in love." She sighed romantically. "Have *you* ever fallen in love, Cadi?"

"No, not yet."

"Oh, dear." Sarah looked concerned for me. "I've done it three times."

"Are you in love just now?" It was hard not to smile.

She hesitated, then said shyly, "Yes, with Lucian Farrel. You met him with Papa. Oh, Cadi, I think he's so . . . so *wonderful*."

It was the strangest thing, but I felt a sharp pang of jealousy.

Just then a gong sounded somewhere in the house, and Sarah caught my hand. "That's for dinner," she said. "Come along, Cadi—and you won't tell my secret to anyone, will you?"

"I promise," I said, and we set off for the dining room.

Peeping at all the knives and forks and spoons before me as Mr. Morton said grace, I felt suddenly very nervous.

Soup was served, and nobody spoke until the footman had withdrawn. Then Mr. Morton said, "Well, Cadi—" and paused. When I looked at him he slowly picked up a big spoon from the right-hand side of his plate, giving me a quick encouraging glance. I picked up a similar spoon, and he went on, "Do you feel rested and refreshed now, my dear?"

"Very much so, thank you, Mr. Morton." My nervousness had gone. I loved him in that moment, and could hardly speak. Fortunately there was little need, for Mrs. Morton launched into an anxious monologue.

"Edward, I have been giving serious thought to a number of matters.

550

We simply must get Cadi a hat with a large brim to shield her face from the sun. The poor child is so *brown*, and a tanned face is quite unbecoming to a young lady." Without a pause she changed the subject completely. "And you will have to speak to Gertrude." She heaved a martyred sigh. "For the third time in as many weeks, Gertrude forgot to wash the small change from my purse this morning. It is hardly believable when one considers she is paid eighteen pounds a year to carry out her duties."

Mrs. Morton paused for breath, and Mr. Morton said amiably, "Helen, my dear, your soup will grow cold. Let me tell you my thoughts on the matters you have raised. First, a fashionable pallor is quite definitely unhealthy. Cadi is a picture of health, and I wish her to remain so."

Mrs. Morton made to interrupt, but her husband lifted a hand and continued mildly, "If I may finish, my dear. On the matter of Gertrude's negligence, I will indeed speak to her. I suggest it would help if you put your purse on your dressing table each night." He smiled very gently. "And now that we have settled these troublesome matters, let us take the next course." He rang a little bell which stood on the table near his plate.

That was the biggest dinner I had ever eaten. Wine was served with the beef, and Mr. Morton proposed a toast in honor of my joining the family. The meal ended with what I later learned was apricot Condé with cream, though the cream was poor compared with our Cornish cream, as Mr. Morton himself declared. After dinner he excused himself and went to his study to attend to some urgent work.

"He must constantly sacrifice his family for his work," Mrs. Morton said in a lamenting tone. "Really, he must be longing for the day when this dreadful Mr. Balfour is thrown out of office."

"It makes no difference to Father," Richard said with a smile. "As a civil servant, he has no politics."

"And a good thing too," Mrs. Morton sighed. "They cause nothing but trouble. I really don't know why your father goes on. Surely they can find somebody else to do whatever it is he does at the Foreign Office."

"Lord Lansdowne seems to think otherwise, Mama. Do you remember the letter he wrote to Father last year? It was most flattering."

"Oh, these ministers," Mrs. Morton said vaguely.

His face as serenely angelic as ever, Richard looked at me and rolled his eyes upward. I had to turn my head away or I might have giggled.

Later that evening, when Sarah had played the piano for us and Richard had given me my first lesson in chess, Mrs. Morton rose and said that it was time for me to go to bed, since I had endured a tiring day.

I was very ready to agree and went to the study to say good night to Mr. Morton. He put down his pen and sat back in his chair with a half-mournful, half-humorous smile which was becoming familiar to me now. "I won't ask you if you are happy, Cadi," he said. "It's much too early for that. But I would like to think, if I were suddenly plunged into a completely strange world, that I might do as well as you have done today."

"Everybody was so kind, Mr. Morton. You all made it easy for me. And you've only seen me on my best behavior. I'm impatient, and if I'm in a bad temper I have a spiteful tongue, and I hate it if other people can do things better than I can, and that's envy really, Miss Rigg says. . . ."

I stumbled on until he threw back his head in deep, unrestrained laughter. When he recovered he said with an attempt at gravity, "I'm very glad you've warned me, Cadi." The humor faded from his face. "Now . . . there's a question I would like to ask you. It seemed to me that when you suddenly felt faint this afternoon you were staring at the picture of Venice that hangs in the hall, as if it was familiar to you. Did you recognize it?"

I would have been ashamed to tell Mr. Morton even a white lie. "I've seen the house in a dream," I said awkwardly. "Quite often." I described the dream to him, with its two different endings.

Mr. Morton sat brooding for a full minute. "There are many recorded instances of recurring dreams," he said thoughtfully. "Mr. Freud deals at length with their significance. Have you heard of psychology, Cadi?"

"Only that it's about what happens in people's minds," I said.

"We all have our dreams, good and bad, Cadi. Don't worry about yours. If Mr. Freud is right, it simply means that there is a deep-seated desire in you for fulfillment. Time will take care of all that, I think."

He looked at me sharply. "Goodness, child, you can hardly hold your eyes open and I'm keeping you from your bed." He came forward and kissed me on the cheek. "Off you go now." I desperately wanted to thank him for all that he was doing for me, but could find no words, so I put my arms about his neck and hugged him for a moment.

"I'm so glad you are here, Cadi," he said in a rather muffled voice.

I went upstairs to my bedroom and undressed. Five minutes later I was in a deep, dreamless sleep. I had drawn back the heavy curtains because I liked to have sunlight coming into the room when I woke. But it was long before dawn when I was roused by a light that threw flickering shadows on the walls and ceiling.

Mrs. Morton stood only a pace or two from the bed, holding a candle in a big brass candlestick. She wore a long white nightdress, and her wonderful hair hung loosely down on each side of her face. The candle flame was reflected in her eyes, to give a glittering blend of gold and violet.

She neither moved nor spoke, but stared down upon me with a strange and frantic gaze, and in her eyes there was no recognition at all.

MY SKIN CRAWLED with shock.

"James?" Mrs. Morton's voice held great tenderness. "Ah, you're back from the shooting, darling. Did you get any pigeons?"

I sat up slowly in bed. "It's me, Mrs. Morton," I said in a croaky whisper. "Cadi."

"What would you like for tea, James dear? The strawberries are really at their best just now," she said with a fond smile.

The feeling of horror began to lose its edge as I realized that Mrs. Morton was sleepwalking. "Strawberries would be very nice, thank you," I whispered. My thoughts whirled as I tried to choose the right words. "But . . . but I think you should have a little nap before tea—"

I broke off as a figure appeared in the open doorway beyond her, and with a great surge of relief I saw that it was Mr. Morton. He said quietly, "Yes, a splendid idea. You look rather tired, Helen, and a nap before tea would be just the right thing." He took her arm, coaxing her toward the door. I could hear him murmuring as he led her to her bedroom.

Two or three minutes went by before he returned. I whispered, "Is she all right now?"

He nodded. "I'm sorry, Cadi. Such a shock for you." His face looked tired and strained. "James was our elder son, as I told you, and this was his room."

Now I remembered. There had been a son older than Richard, and he had died in a shooting accident.

Mr. Morton said, "Cadi . . . thank you for keeping so calm and not waking her. Poor dear soul, it would have been very distressing for her. This hasn't happened for a long time now."

"I'm so sorry. About your son, I mean. Will Mrs. Morton remember in the morning?"

He shook his head. "No. Say nothing, Cadi. And get back to sleep now. You won't be disturbed again."

I hugged the bedclothes around me, but it was a long time before I went to sleep again.

EXCEPT FOR THAT incident, the novelty of my new life carried me along as if on the crest of one of the big rollers that race into Mawstone Bay. But then the roller beneath me seemed to break, and homesickness struck hard. I knew times of great melancholy and renewed grief. Mr. Morton remained the same as always, but the rest of the family lost some of their warmth and enthusiasm. I felt alone and unwanted. It was foolish, of course. They could not continue to treat me as a newly arrived guest forever, nor could I continue to act as one. But I did not realize it then.

The Kentish countryside seemed soft and vulnerable after my native Cornwall. Sarah irritated me. She did beautiful needlework and played the piano without too many mistakes, but that was all. After the first excitement of welcoming a new member of the family, she went through a period of silently resenting me. I have no doubt I caused this myself by being unable to hide my frequent irritation with her. When at last this dawned on me, I asked myself how I would have felt if my father had introduced a sharp-tongued stranger into the house. Mrs. Morton was sometimes kindly and at other times gave the impression that I was yet another burden life had laid upon her. Richard was always pleasant, but I chose to think that his manner to me was no more than politeness.

I think I began to emerge from that unhappy settling-down period when I realized that in some ways I was more at home with Mr. Morton's family than he was himself. That seems a strange thing to say, but it was so. I soon saw Mrs. Morton's moods for what they were, simply an outward reflection of what she happened to feel at any given moment, not necessarily connected with me or with anyone else. And as growing instinct helped me to anticipate her more difficult moods, I could often prevent them with the right word of sympathy, admiration, or apology. Although I humored her, I was too stubborn to sink into a milk-and-water attitude with her, which I think made her respect me.

My irritation toward Sarah grew rapidly less. I accepted her for what she was, an honest and affectionate girl, childlike in many ways, but good-natured. Mr. Morton was always rather awkward in his manner to her and did not know what to say to her. He loved her but was at a loss with her. If he made a joke, she would look blank; if he commented on something in the newspaper, poor Sarah would get a hunted look in her eyes. I knew very well that compared with Mr. Morton I was stupid and ignorant, but I was eager to learn. With me he could chat for hours, ready to explain anything I did not understand, seeking my opinions and listening with a twinkle in his eye.

One thing I could not understand was his attitude toward Richard. I can only describe it as wary. It seemed to me unfair and unkind, which was quite out of key with Mr. Morton's character. As with father and daughter, so conversation between father and son was oddly stilted, but for a different reason and one I could not fathom.

As my homesickness and settling-down difficulties passed, I realized that Richard's quiet friendliness was genuine. I think the last barriers between us went down on the day that I visited him in the small building where he had set up a workshop. He enjoyed using his hands, and the bench was covered with springs, coils and magnets. He showed me a miniature steam engine he had made, an alarm clock, and a mousetrap which operated as a guillotine. When I made a face at this last object he only laughed and asked if I thought a mouse would prefer to be killed by a spring.

It was watching Richard in his shop which made me realize the final step needed to make me feel truly at home. The trouble was that I did not have enough to do. In Mawstone there was always work to be done. Now, most of each day was simply wasted. How did I spend my time? I went riding quite often, but I was not allowed to ride alone yet, and either Old Kemp, the stableman, or Young Kemp, the coachman, had to go along. Young Kemp, the son, was over sixty, and Old Kemp was hardly ever awake, even on a horse, so our rides were not very exciting.

There were hundreds of books for me to read in Mr. Morton's library, but I did not want to read all day. In the afternoons I would often join Sarah in the sewing room, though I had little skill in delicate needlework and quickly became impatient. More often my afternoons were spent in paying calls or receiving calls with Mrs. Morton and Sarah, and making polite conversation over cups of tea and cucumber sandwiches. I hated that, but to Mrs. Morton and to most of the ladies of our acquaintance it was the most important part of their lives.

When I decided that I must find something useful to do, I made up my mind what it would be. Old Kemp was very old indeed, and could only potter slowly about his work. The stables in his charge always looked slovenly, and the eight horses were never groomed very well. Until my arrival the horses were seldom used except for carriage work. The big carriage, a mail phacton, and a dogcart were Young Kemp's responsibility, but he seemed to begrudge whatever energy he expended on them.

I wanted to tackle the stables. With Old Kemp's help I would clean and maintain them handsomely. I would groom the horses and make them beautiful. And with Young Kemp's help I would make sure that our carriages sparkled. When I spoke to Mr. Morton about it he blinked in surprise. "But you can't become a stableboy, Cadi!"

"I wouldn't be, Mr. Morton. It means"—I watched him anxiously— "I'd have to wear breeches for working, but I want to do that anyway, for riding. And it would only be for an hour or two each day. Once I've got the stables all repaired and clean, Old Kemp can easily *keep* them clean, because I'll look after the horses."

Mr. Morton chuckled. "Can you imagine what my wife will say?"

I pressed on pleadingly. "Mrs. Morton is always saying that the carriage and horses are a disgrace."

"She is indeed," he agreed with a sigh. Then a faint gleam came into his eye. "What I simply cannot resist," he said, "is the idea of turning you loose on Young Kemp. All right, Cadi, you can be in charge of the stables. But you must only supervise the work, except for grooming. I'll let you have the gardener's boy for an hour each day to help Old Kemp."

I was so happy that I ran to hug him. I think it warmed his heart, but he always pretended that I was being a nuisance.

"Go away and don't pester me anymore, child," he said. Then he looked at me strangely for a moment. "I must stop calling you child," he said slowly. "You're a very beautiful young woman, Cadi. Now be a good girl and let me get on with my work."

IN THREE WEEKS I TRANSFORMED the stables. There were several battles with Young Kemp at first, but in the end he saw that my mind was made up, and resigned himself to working harder. Mr. Morton was delighted.

Mrs. Morton had been full of protest when Mr. Morton first told her about my new project. However, she had been diverted by his calming reassurances. Then I found another occupation which pleased Mrs. Morton. Two miles away was a small orphanage called Wealdhurst, and after talking with the vicar I began to visit there three afternoons each week to teach a dozen of the younger children their letters and numbers. This charitable work was quite acceptable in our circle of acquaintances, and it helped to make up for the peculiar behavior of "the Tregaron girl," who actually groomed horses with her own hands.

And so, as the weeks went by, the strangeness of my new life faded, and I was content. Now I could think of my mother and father, and of Granny Caterina, without the heartache becoming unbearable. I rarely spoke of them, because none of the Mortons ever asked me about the past. I think they refrained at first to avoid making me unhappy, and this became an unconscious habit which continued. I did not mind, for my memories seemed very private and precious to me.

The dream came to me only once during those early weeks at Meadhaven. Often as I passed through the hall I would stop and gaze at the picture of the palace in Venice. Was this a real palace? Or could I have dreamed the same dream as some foreign artist who perhaps had been dead for many years now?

That thought was settled when Mr. Morton called me into his study one morning. "I have been making inquiries about the painting of the Venice scene, Cadi," he said. "Apparently the picture was not painted from imagination. The house is some four hundred years old and still stands near the Grand Canal. It is called the Palazzo Chiavelli, and part of it is still occupied by descendants of Count Chiavelli. Does the name Chiavelli mean anything to you?"

I shook my head. "No . . . I've never heard of it before, Mr. Morton."

"Apparently the picture is well over a hundred years old, so you could have seen a copy of it in a book."

"Perhaps," I said doubtfully.

"If we go to Venice next year, we may be able to visit this *palazzo* of yours." He laughed and added, "But let's not worry about it just now. We have the end-of-summer ball to think of."

I had been thinking of little else, for the ball was only three days away. Preparations had been going on all week. I had spent hours in my bedroom while Betty practiced putting up my hair, and a wonderful new dress of cornflower-blue silk had been specially bought for me. I was so excited I could hardly sleep.

At last the great moment came. The huge drawing room had been cleared for dancing. A magnificent buffet supper was laid out on long tables in the garden, with white linen cloths and sparkling silver. Lanterns had been set in the trees, to cast a shimmering light over the whole magical scene. At the front of the house a long red carpet had been rolled out and an awning set up. Soon the carriages began to arrive, and from within the house came the sound of an orchestra playing "Valse Bleue" as we stood receiving our guests.

When the early formalities were over, the dancing began. For the past three weeks I had been practicing with Richard and Sarah, under Mrs. Morton's guidance. I loved dancing. I always felt as if I were floating, but Mrs. Morton's pleasure at my quick accomplishment was marred by certain doubts. "If only you could move in a rather more *ladylike* manner, Cadi," she said several times. "A little less free and exuberant, perhaps."

But I could not contain my exuberance. My program was soon filled, and I found myself dancing with one young man after another, having the happiest time of my life. I chattered furiously, and yet I hardly noticed the young men. They might all have been the same person, for all I knew. It was almost midnight, and I had just been returned to my seat beside Mrs. Morton, when I looked across the room and almost jumped out of my skin. Sarah was coming toward us, glowing with delight as she towed a reluctant man behind her.

"It's Cousin Lucian!" she called. "He's just arrived!"

Mrs. Morton seemed flustered as Lucian Farrel bent to kiss her cheek. "Why, Lucian, my dear boy. What a surprise! Have you come down from London? You must be so tired. Perhaps you . . . perhaps you would like to have a meal sent up to your room?"

Lucian said, "If you wish, Aunt Helen."

Mr. Morton had joined us. He patted Lucian on the shoulder and said, "Nonsense, my dear nephew. I'm sure you didn't arrive in evening dress to spend the time in your room. And think how disappointed all these good people would be!"

Lucian gazed round the room. I noticed glances being darted at him and whispers exchanged. "I feel they should have the opportunity to show their pleasure," he said ironically. "Do you mind, Uncle Edward?"

Mr. Morton smiled. "I think perhaps it is time you tested the atmosphere here once again. But first let me reintroduce you to the latest member of my family. I wrote to tell you about her joining us. Lucian Farrel . . . Miss Cadi Tregaron."

Lucian looked at me. "Well I'm damned," he said softly. He put out his hand to take mine. "Hello again, Cadi. Did the blue dress fit you?"

"It was perfect, thank you, Mr. Farrel."

"I was grieved to hear about your father. He was a fine man." He looked down at me. "Have you made any more rescues recently?" he asked.

"She has rescued us all from boredom," said Mr. Morton. "She gallops around in breeches, bullies Young Kemp into submission, has transformed the stables, teaches at Wealdhurst Orphanage, dances too exuberantly—"

"I must test that exuberance one day," Lucian broke in. "But it would hardly be fair to her tonight." He looked speculatively around the room. "Now, who shall the victim be? Mrs. Garner's red-nosed daughter, I imagine." He gave us a little bow. "Excuse me, ladies."

The orchestra had begun a new dance, and young David Steadman appeared, to claim me. As we danced I noticed with surprise that people were leaving the floor with grim, embarrassed faces. Soon only two couples were on the floor—ourselves, and Lucian with Dorothy Garner. My partner said anxiously, "We . . . we'd better sit this dance out, I think."

"Why?" I asked sharply.

"Well . . . you know. Because of Lucian Farrel." Then without further asking he took my arm and hurried me back to where Mrs. Morton sat.

Lucian and his partner continued. He was smiling, seemingly unaware that they were alone. I saw Dorothy's scarlet face as she whispered to Lucian and stopped dancing. He bowed to her, and she left the floor.

The orchestra played on. Lucian stood alone, looking slowly round, his face without expression. I could not think why he had been treated in this way, but sudden anger rose up inside me. Lucian Farrel was a member of the family, my family now, and I would not stand by and see him insulted. As I began to move forward I heard Mrs. Morton gasp, "No, Cadi!" Then Mr. Morton's voice, soft but decisive, saying, "Let her go."

I walked out and faced Lucian with what I hoped was a serene smile. "My partner has deserted me, Mr. Farrel. Will you take his place?"

LUCIAN FARREL WAS taken aback. Then, under the sound of the music, he said short and sharp, "Don't be a fool, Cadi."

"I shall indeed look a fool if you refuse me, Mr. Farrel."

I saw wonderment in his face, then he smiled. I jumped inwardly, as if some nerve had been touched. The smile made him a different man, yet a man I knew, for this was the face of the man in the good dream.

"Call me Lucian, please," he said. He lifted his arms to take me into the dance. "My God," he said softly, and laughed. "You seem to make a profession of rescue work, Cadi."

Mr. Morton had once spoken of him as an outcast, and now I had seen him treated as one. I wondered what lay behind it all, but at this moment I was too much taken up by the joy of dancing to ask questions, and I didn't care that we were alone on the floor. But we were not alone for long. I saw Richard cross the floor and lead Sarah out. Then Mr. Morton was dancing with his wife; her eyes were closed, her face stiff with em-

barrassment. One by one, more than a dozen other couples joined us.

Mr. Morton was waiting for us when the dance ended. "As I was remarking, Lucian," he said blandly, "she is a most unladylike minx. But she has one or two good points, perhaps."

"We are none of us all bad, Uncle Edward," Lucian replied.

Mr. Morton laughed and took my hand as I stood beside him, holding it so tightly that it almost hurt. His eyes were glistening.

Mrs. Morton said feebly, "I thought I was going to *die*, Edward, when Cadi walked out onto that empty floor."

"We are all very glad you were mistaken, my dear," Mr. Morton said soothingly. "Sarah, run and fetch your mother a glass of champagne."

That night Sarah crept into my room, as I knew she would.

"What has Lucian done, Sarah?" I asked. "Why did everybody turn their backs on him and stop dancing?"

"Oh, it was because of that thing in the war," she said. "The South African war against the Boers. Lucian was a cavalry officer."

"What did he *do?*" I asked.

"He got cashiered from his regiment," she said reluctantly.

"Cashiered?" I echoed. "That means dismissed, doesn't it?"

"Yes." Her eyes filled with tears. "It was a terrible disgrace, Cadi."

I was very shaken. "But you still haven't told me what Lucian did."

Sarah tossed her head. "He was cashiered for being a coward, they say."

I remembered Lucian in the boat that day when Mogg Race had almost taken us, and I shook my head. "They're wrong, Sarah," I said.

CHAPTER FOUR

AFTER BREAKFAST NEXT morning I changed into a shirt and breeches, plaited my hair in two pigtails, and went out to the stables. For over a fortnight now I had been allowed to take Pompey out on my own. He was a fine, spirited horse, and we were good friends.

This morning I wanted a good fast ride, with the wind buffeting my face. A bridle path ran beside the fields of Meadhaven until it reached a long grassy slope. From the crest of the hill I could look far out over the Weald of Kent. The ridge was over a mile long, and a beautiful place for a gallop. Pompey seemed to catch my mood, for when I nudged him with my heels he gathered himself and broke into a gallop that made my pigtailed hair fly out behind me.

I reined him in gradually as we reached the end of the ridge. To one side lay the slope up which I had come. On the other side, the hill descended to a stretch of woodland, where a horse entering at a downhill gallop could easily dash its rider against a tree. I was not allowed to ride down there.

I turned Pompey to face along the ridge again, and as I set him to a gallop I glimpsed from the corner of my eye a rider coming up the hillside from the direction of Meadhaven. I thought it was Lucian but had no time to stare, for Pompey was racing along joyously.

It was then that the rein in my right hand went slack, and Pompey suddenly veered to the left, flying down the forbidden slope toward the woods below. I could not see the end of the broken rein, much less reach it. So I clung to his mane and could sense that, free of guidance, he was in a panic, beyond all hope of stopping. The line of trees was very close now, no more than fifty yards away. Any root or a hollow in the ground could trip Pompey, and even if he kept his feet, I would be scraped off against the trunk of a tree or struck by a low branch.

There was another danger, even closer. In front of the woods lay a pile of half-rotted hay, almost as high as Pompey's shoulder. He was racing straight for it, and I was certain he could never clear it. I would be thrown over his head, then he would fall, somersaulting perhaps, rolling on me.

As I braced myself for the jump, Pompey swerved to miss the haystack. Instinctively I kicked my feet free of the stirrups and let myself slip sideways a little, still clinging to his mane. As we passed the stack I let go and thrust against Pompey's flank with all the strength of my left leg. Feet in the air, I landed on my shoulders in the hay. Engulfed in its dampness, I could hear the fading sound of Pompey's hoofs as he flung himself into the woods. For several moments I lay there shivering, marveling at my escape.

There came the sound of another horse thundering down the slope of the hill, and I heard Lucian's voice shouting, "*Cadi!*" I heard the slither of hoofs as he wrenched his horse to a halt. Then he dismounted. "Cadi! Are you all right?" His voice seemed more angry than concerned.

I found my feet. "I'm all right," I said as my head emerged from the hay. I had to trample a lot of it before I could stand waist-deep, picking dry wisps from my hair, my ears, my mouth.

Lucian stared. "You're not hurt?"

"Of course I'm not hurt—I just said so! Aren't you going to help, instead of just looking?"

He came forward, reached out and took me under the arms, then gave one heave which plucked me out of the hay.

I must have looked like a scarecrow, but I was too angry at knowing Lucian had seen me thrown to have any thought for my appearance. Suddenly he began to laugh, unable to help himself.

"Don't you *dare* laugh!" I said furiously. "The rein broke. It would have been the same for you if your rein had broken!"

"I wasn't laughing because you took a fall, Cadi. . . ." Another convulsion of laughter. "It was . . . look at you!"

I looked down at myself. My breeches and shirt were blotched by the rotting hay, and wisps of it were stuck all over me. I could imagine the picture I must have made. I started to giggle, and then remembered Pompey. "We have to find Pompey," I said anxiously. "He may be hurt."

Lucian's face changed, and as he turned to Adam, our big roan, he asked, "Will you rest here or come with me?"

"I'll come."

He swung up into the saddle and reached a hand down to me. "We seem fated to ride double," he said with a smile as he lifted me up. When at last we were through the belt of trees, we saw that Pompey was trotting fretfully in the pasture which lay ahead. As we drew close he stood still, poised for flight. I slipped from the saddle and edged forward, talking to him gently. Suddenly he trotted toward me and nuzzled my shoulder.

"Poor Pompey, poor old boy," I said. "Did you have an awful fright? Never mind. Let's see if you're all right."

"Hold him while I look," said Lucian, dismounting. He checked Pompey's legs carefully, one by one. "Just this graze along his right flank," he said at last. But it was more than a graze. A broken branch had made a long gash along his side. I felt cold again when I thought what would have happened to my leg if I had been in the saddle.

I heard Lucian catch his breath and turned to look at him. He held the end of the broken rein in his hand. A break in the ring connecting it to the snaffle showed clearly. I thought there might have been some hidden fault in the metal. Then I saw that at the point where it had broken, the ring was very thin and slightly rough, as if it had been filed down.

I lifted my eyes to Lucian. He was gazing past me, eyebrows flaring over the blue eyes. In his face was that same bitter fury I had seen on Mawstone quay as he gazed at the broken rudder pintle which had almost caused Mr. Morton's death. "Half sawn through . . ." he had said at the time. And now I had nearly been badly injured—perhaps killed—because the ring on Pompey's snaffle had been filed thin. I felt sick inside.

"I've known these rings to break before," Lucian said. His face was impassive again now.

"But that didn't just break!" I cried.

"Please, Cadi. Don't imagine things. If anyone wanted to harm you, this would be a foolish way to do it. And besides, who in the world would wish you ill?"

I shook my head slowly, beginning to doubt what I had been so sure of a moment ago. For a fleeting moment I thought of Young Kemp, and then was ashamed. Despite his brusque speech, that surly old man had grown to like me over the past few weeks as much as he would ever like anybody, I was sure of that.

"You must be right," I said at last, and began to pluck away wisps of hay that still stuck to me. "Have I still got any hay in my hair? If I'm seen riding in, I don't want to look like a scarecrow."

"Keep still a moment." He pulled some pieces of hay from above my brow, then turned me round and picked a few wisps from my pigtails. I felt suddenly shy at the touch of his hands. "You'll do," he said at last.

"Are we going to tell Mr. Morton that you took a fall?"

"I'll have to," I said. "Not telling him would be like telling lies."

"I see. And do you never tell lies?"

"Sometimes, I suppose. But not to Mr. Morton."

Lucian laughed softly. "You don't set limits on your loyalty, Cadi, do you?"

THAT NIGHT WHEN Sarah came to my bedroom she said with a great sigh, "Lucian is only staying for three days. I could cry. I'm sure he's *tormented*. I'd think it was because of you, but he was like that before, anyway."

"Because of me? What on earth do you mean?"

She sighed again. "Oh, if only he'd sometimes look at me the way he looks at you, I'd be in *heaven*. Richard has noticed too. Perhaps he's madly in love with you, Cadi. Perhaps he'll ask you to marry him!"

"Oh, don't be silly," I said impatiently. To change the subject I asked, "What does Lucian do all the time in London?"

Sarah rambled on about his mother, Mr. Morton's sister, who had died when he was born. His father, a well-known architect, had died only a few years ago. It had been intended that when Lucian left the army he should join his father's old partners, but after being cashiered he was unwelcome among them. For a time he had drifted; then two years ago he had set up stables near Epsom and gone in for breeding horses. He often traveled abroad, to France, Ireland, and even Turkey, buying or selling.

"Papa says he does quite well now," Sarah said. "But I don't think Lucian cares very much about money. He just enjoys working with horses—as much as he enjoys sculpting."

"Sculpting?"

"Yes. It's a hobby, really, and he makes the most beautiful sculptures in wood. Horses, of course, but people too." Sarah paused for breath and giggled. "He did a bust of an actress. We saw it when we visited his flat in London, and the bosom was so . . . *exposed!* Poor Mama was shocked, but I wasn't. It seemed to teach me something, because it was real and true," she concluded with a streak of her father's good sense.

All the next day I felt strangely unsettled. I was glad that Lucian had gone to Tunbridge Wells to look at a mare. Although Sarah's words about his interest in me were foolish, I knew that I would find myself watching to see if he was looking at me and that I would feel awkward in speaking with him. It was all quite absurd, and I felt impatient with myself, but that day marked a quiet turning point. I realized for the first time that I was at an age when a girl should begin to think of marriage, and I felt at a loss.

That night I took from my wardrobe the little box in which I kept a few precious mementos. In it were three photographs, one of my mother, one of my father and mother on their wedding day, and one of Granny Caterina and Grandpa Penwarden. I had a silver brooch and a tortoiseshell comb with a silver back, both belonging to my mother. There was a filigreed gold locket belonging to Granny Caterina; it had been on a chain round her neck when young Robert Penwarden had rescued her. It was hinged on one side, and made to take a miniature daguerreotype photograph. The silvered copper plate of the daguerreotype was still there, fixed inside the locket, but it had blurred patches—damaged by salt water, perhaps.

I put my box of treasures away and went to bed. I was in a restless sleep when I woke suddenly to the touch of a hand on my shoulder. My first thought was that Mrs. Morton had walked in her sleep again, but when I sat up I saw Sarah standing there in a pale shaft of moonlight. She put a finger to her lips and said urgently, *"Shhh!"* then bent to whisper in my ear, "Please—you *must* help me, Cadi!"

"What's wrong?" I whispered back in alarm.

Sarah's face twisted. "You've got to help, Cadi. It's Richard—he can't get into the house."

"Into the house?" I echoed dazedly. "But . . . isn't he in bed?"

She shook her head. "He went to the village tonight. He does sometimes. And then he comes in by my window, because the ivy is thick enough to climb there."

"He's been to the village tonight, you say? But why?"

"He goes to see a woman there. Some woman who does dressmaking," she said vaguely. "Young men have to sow their wild oats, you know."

My astonishment deepened. Sarah had shown that she could keep a big secret, even from me. More surprising still, she was quite unshocked by her brother's behavior.

I climbed out of bed and pulled on my blue velvet dressing gown. I whispered furiously to Sarah, "Don't you realize the terrible trouble Richard will be in if your father and mother find out?" I stopped short, puzzled. "Why can't Richard get in tonight if he's done it before?"

"I—I don't know," Sarah said tremulously. "He threw some gravel at my window to wake me, and then he whispered that he couldn't climb up. He told me to go and let him in at the front door, but I—I *daren't*, Cadi! It's so dark down there, and awfully ghostly. Besides, somebody might hear me." Her voice was rising, so I took her by the shoulders and shook her.

"Go back to your room and go to sleep," I whispered sternly. "Go on! I'll see to Richard."

Sarah left and I tiptoed across the landing.

My heart was in my mouth as I moved slowly down the stairs through the heavy darkness. I moved across the hall with my hands stretched out in front of me, dreading that I might bump into something and make a noise. Then I was fumbling with the bolts, easing them back inch by inch until the front door swung open and Richard stood silhouetted against the starlight. He was in dark clothes, and his face looked paper white.

I urged him toward the stairs and carefully bolted the door. My eyes were accustomed to the dark now, and I wanted to guide him to his room. As we crept up the stairs I moved my hand to his shoulder. He stifled a gasp. I realized then that he was hurt. I went with him into his room and closed the door behind me. "Light a candle," I whispered, and heard the faint clatter as he found the candlestick and matches.

The flame threw flickering shadows round the room. Eyes seemed to gleam behind the empty eyeholes of the African witch doctor's mask; the cheeks of an Oriental idol seemed to crease in a dreadful smile.

"I'll be all right now, Cadi," Richard said softly. "You . . . you won't tell my father?" There was a film of perspiration on his handsome face, and he stood stiffly, awkwardly, as if movement was painful.

"You're hurt. What happened to you, Richard?"

"Nothing." He moved his arms to take off his jacket, then froze rigidly and gave a muffled gasp of pain.

Without a word I began to ease the jacket very carefully over his shoulders. The back of his white shirt was torn and covered with spots of blood and smudgy dark lines. As I moved round in front of him to unbutton it, he said weakly, "No, Cadi," and sank onto the bed face down.

"I can't leave you like this!" I whispered fiercely. I put two fingers of each hand in one of the tears down the back of his shirt and jerked my hands apart. I gasped with shock as I stared down. His skin was marred by a dozen or more livid red welts. "You've been . . . flogged!" I breathed incredulously. "Only a whip could do that!"

"A riding crop." His voice was muffled against the coverlet. "I'll be all right, Cadi. Just stiff for a few days."

I poured cold water from a pitcher on the washstand into a bowl. My hands were trembling as I bathed the swollen welts with a towel. Then I found scissors on his dressing table and cut the rest of his shirt away so that I could soak pieces of it in the water. "Who did it?" I asked as I laid an oblong of the cool, damp linen on his back. "That woman's husband?"

"Sarah told you, then?" He rested his head on one forearm. "No, her husband left her long ago." Slowly he turned his head and looked at me over one shoulder. A painful smile twisted his lips. "Who?" he whispered. "Why, Lucian, of course. Who else?"

My heart pounded. "But why?" I breathed. "*Why*, Richard?"

"Sometimes Lucian does strange things," he said slowly.

"He must be mad! You'll have to tell your father."

"I can't, Cadi. Ahhh . . . that's good." A long sigh of relief escaped him as I replaced the linen with a fresh piece, cold from the water. "I can't tell Father without telling him that I was out tonight. Lucian was waiting for me as I came home through the woods."

"If you don't tell your father about this, I'll speak to Lucian myself," I said fiercely. "He can't do things like this!"

Richard lifted himself on his elbow. "Don't, Cadi," he said. "It would do no good. You see, he won't remember." Richard's smile was the smile of a sad angel. "There's a . . . weakness in his mind, Cadi. Usually the strange things he does cause no harm. Tonight was a little different, that's all."

Tiny cold fingers of horror were awakening suspicions in my mind. I thought of a broken rudder pintle, and a bridle ring that had snapped. Lucian had been there on both occasions. He had even shown his suspicions clearly, and been almost frightening in his anger. But had some twist in his mind made him forget what he himself had done?

RICHARD FELL INTO a half sleep. For the next two hours I sat by him on the edge of the bed, moistening the linen when it began to dry. At last the welts were far less swollen and angry.

"I can't do any more, Richard," I whispered.

He gave a little start and lifted his head slowly.

"Tomorrow you'd better pretend to have a feverish cold so you can stay in bed for a day or two," I went on. "But for goodness' sake stop going to see this woman. It's bound to bring trouble in the end."

He put his hand on mine. "Thank you, Cadi, for helping me. You're the most wonderful girl in the world. I love you so much." He gazed at me with a kind of wonder.

"Don't talk foolishness," I said, and went thankfully back to my room.

I still had not decided whether or not to speak to Lucian of what he had done, but when I went down to breakfast the next morning I found that there was no decision to make, for Lucian had gone from Meadhaven.

"He left last night," said Mr. Morton. "A sudden decision, characteristic of Lucian. He asked me to say good-by to you girls on his behalf."

Sarah sighed, but I felt relieved, for I had not looked forward to confronting him.

Then Mrs. Morton swept in, fluttering with alarm and saying that poor Richard was abed with a chill. "He refuses to have the doctor," she said, sinking into her chair.

Lost in my thoughts, I missed the next minute or two of the conversation.

"Would you like that, Cadi?" I suddenly heard Mr. Morton say.

I gave a start, and blinked at him in confusion.

"Bless me, you haven't been listening." He chuckled. "I was just saying that we shall be having a guest to dine with us tonight, and suggesting that you and Sarah might like to join us."

Mr. Morton sometimes brought home diplomats with whom he wished to have some quiet and unofficial talks away from the Foreign Office. On these occasions Sarah and I would have an early dinner alone before making a brief appearance in the drawing room.

"You are both growing up," Mr. Morton went on, "and I feel that a family atmosphere at dinner, with you young ladies present, might have a pleasantly relaxing effect on our guest."

CHAPTER FIVE

THAT EVENING SARAH and I came down to the drawing room half an hour after Mr. Morton and his guest had arrived. The guest was a tall man, with thick black hair brushed smoothly back. He had a quick, warm manner that matched his smiling eyes.

"These are my daughters, signore," said Mr. Morton. "Cadi, Sarah, this is Signor Vecchi, the Italian ambassador."

I dropped a little curtsy as I shook hands. It had not occurred to me that our guest might be Italian.

"I am honored to meet such charming young ladies," he said slowly, with a pleasant smile. His English was far from fluent.

I almost greeted him in Italian, but just stopped myself in time. It might seem like showing off, I felt, and also it could be taken as a criticism of the way Signor Vecchi spoke English.

"I think . . . you will be very—ah—proud of your daughters, Mr. Morton," Signor Vecchi continued. "They are much attractive, and yet so different. The one dark, the other so blond."

"Cadi is not of our family," Mr. Morton said. "I speak of her as our daughter because she is that to us in spirit."

As we reached the dessert stage of dinner I forgot myself for a moment. Signor Vecchi had been admiring a big vase of chrysanthemums, fresh cut from the garden. "In Kent is very nice now," he said, "but still more nice at April. There is much beautiful . . ." He tried to recall the word he wanted, muttering *"Germogli . . . germogli?"*

"Blossoms," I said without thinking.

"Ah, yes—" He stopped short, looking at me in surprise. *"Lei parla l'Italiano?"*

"Si, signore," I answered. *"La parlo tutta la vita. La mia nonna era un' Italiana—"* I broke off, suddenly conscious that the Mortons were all staring at me in complete astonishment.

567

"Where on earth did you learn to speak Italian, Cadi?" Mr. Morton asked.

"I've always spoken it, Mr. Morton," I explained, somewhat flustered. "That's what I was just telling Signor Vecchi. My grandmother was Italian, and I learned it from her. My mother spoke it too, of course."

"Why didn't you *say* so?" Sarah cried. "It's *ever* so clever of you, Cadi!"

"I just never thought about it," I said.

"Well, I'm glad to know it as there may well be occasions when you could help me by translating," Mr. Morton suggested.

"Why not tonight?" Signor Vecchi said. "For me it would be much help."

Mr. Morton inclined his head. "Since the idea is your own, I am happy to accept it. Cadi is to be trusted entirely, I assure you."

He looked at me with a hint of apology and sighed, shaking his head. "I realize now that we have never asked you about your family, Cadi, to avoid distressing you. Perhaps now we can repair our omission. Your grandmother was Italian, you say—would you like to tell us about her?"

I told them then what had happened when young Robert Penwarden sailed into the Bay of Naples nearly fifty years ago. On the ship's third night at anchor he was with some of the crew in a guard boat when they heard the sound of oars nearby. As they pulled through the mist to investigate, there came a heavy splash, followed by the sound of oars once again. Then they briefly glimpsed a small boat with three men pulling hard for the dockside. Drifting, suddenly they noticed air bubbles breaking the surface alongside their boat. It was Robert Penwarden who snatched up the end of a coil of rope and dived into the black water. His groping hands felt a rough, shapeless object which was sinking slowly. A canvas sack, his hands told him, tied at the neck, weighted, and carrying something soft and yielding. He managed to make fast the end of the rope to the neck of the sack. Then he clawed his way to the surface and gasped to the other sailors to haul in. When the dripping sack lay in the well of the boat, Robert Penwarden carefully cut it open with his knife.

This was his first sight of Caterina. In the light of the boat's lantern he saw that a white dress clung to her body. Her long dark hair was plastered about her face. Her hands were bound, and an ugly bruise showed on one temple. In the bottom of the sack were three heavy pieces of iron.

The sailors brought her aboard the ship believing her to be dead. It was Robert Penwarden who felt the feeble flutter of her heart. While the other seamen gathered to stare and chatter, he laid her on rough blankets and worked for half an hour to force the water from her lungs. Captain Dowding was called, a dour man who swore with rage because this affair might cause long delays. "Now hear me, Bob Penwarden," he had said, "alive or dead, that wench is not to be reported to me until after we've sailed. I've no fancy to rot here in Naples for a week or so."

Robert Penwarden felt strangely glad. There were men not far away who had tried to kill this young girl, and he had no wish for her to be taken back ashore. "She's alive, Cap'n," he said. "She'll live, given care. But if she's to have care, she'll need a cabin."

"Cabin!" cried the captain. "D'ye think I'll turn out an officer for a drowned foreign wench?" But he yielded in the end. Caterina was carried to the tiny cabin of the second mate.

Robert Penwarden had worked as an apothecary's assistant for two years, and he was called upon for any doctoring needed on board. So it was that he nursed Caterina on the voyage home.

Her fear was very great, but gradually Robert Penwarden's patience and gentleness convinced her that she was safe in his care. Within ten days she had learned enough English to hold a labored conversation with him and to make him understand that her memory was gone.

They fell in love. He knew by instinct, and by the clothes she had been wearing, that she was of gentle birth. Caterina knew it too, but this did not touch her love for the young seaman who had saved her life. When they landed in England, he brought Caterina to his home in Mawstone. His parents took her in and came to love her. He gave up the sea and took work in the mines. He asked Caterina to go to London with him and try to discover who she was, but she would have none of this. She had said in her careful English, "No, Robert, I do not want to remember. I do not wish to find out why someone wanted me dead . . . and who it was." Six months later Caterina married the young Cornishman.

The room was very quiet as I ended my tale. Sarah's eyes were swimming, and Signor Vecchi was leaning forward, listening with great concentration. Mr. Morton gazed upon me with curiosity. Mrs. Morton sat with her eyes half closed.

"I never knew my grandfather," I ended. "But Granny Caterina used to tell me that it was like an English fairy tale—they lived happily ever after."

"It's a beautiful story," Sarah said in a shaky voice.

"Both Caterina and your grandfather were people of courage, I think." Mr. Morton smiled. "But that hardly surprises me, Cadi."

One thing I had left untold, and I told it now, was the way in which Granny Caterina and my mother had died together while going along the cliff tops to gather samphire. Rain had made the grass slippery. Young David Moulton had seen my mother lose her footing on the edge of the cliff, seen my Granny snatch at her arm to save her . . . and lose her own balance. They had fallen together, down to the brutal rocks below.

When I finished speaking, there was another little silence. Then Mrs. Morton roused herself. "Did you never find out who your Granny was, Cadi?" she asked wonderingly. "Did she have nothing about her person to help identify her?"

"She was wearing a locket, which I still have, but the picture inside was spoiled by salt water."

"Would you mind letting us see it, Cadi?" Signor Vecchi asked.

"Not at all, signore."

I went up to my bedroom and returned with the locket. Signor Vecchi studied it. *"Bellissimo lavoro,"* he murmured. "Beautiful work. Your grandmother was not of poor family, that is sure." He gazed at the ruined daguerreotype inside, then passed it to Mr. Morton.

"Fascinating . . . fascinating. But there is no engraving, nothing to help solve the mystery," Mr. Morton said as he examined it. "Here, Sarah, take this and show it to your mama."

Sarah skipped eagerly round the table and then uttered a little squeak of dismay. She had dropped the locket as she handed it to her mother. It slithered off the table, fell to the floor, and seemed to break into two parts.

"Oh, Cadi, I'm sorry—" she wailed, picking up the two pieces. Then her tearful face brightened. "Wait a minute, I think it's just that the photograph has come out." She ran to her father. "Look, Papa."

He took the two pieces, then gave a little sigh of relief. "Yes, there's no damage, Cadi. We can—" He stopped short with a little exclamation, staring more closely into the locket. He raised his eyes and said softly, "Great heavens above. Come here, Cadi." I almost ran to his side. He was pointing to the inside of the locket, where the daguerreotype had rested. "Look, child. Surely that is a name engraved there!"

My voice sounded strange to me as I read out the name, "Caterina Chiavelli."

I heard Signor Vecchi murmur as if to himself, "Chiavelli of Venice, perhaps . . . ?"

Venice! I looked up with a start and saw that Mr. Morton was gazing at me as if thunderstruck. I could read the thought in his mind and knew now why the name of Chiavelli was familiar. It was the name he had been given when he had inquired about the picture that hung in the hall. The palace that for years I had seen in my dream, the *palazzo* in that painting—it was called Palazzo Chiavelli!

Dazedly I realized that this must have been the young Caterina's home—until she had been left for dead in the Bay of Naples. A shiver ran through me. It seemed that a door was opening slowly before me, opening on dark, strange secrets which had remained hidden for two generations.

THERE WAS NO doubt now that my dream was based on reality, on a fragment of hidden memory inherited from my grandmother. Granny Caterina was one of the descendants of Count Chiavelli, who had built the *palazzo* in the sixteenth century . . . and so was I.

I was afraid Mr. Morton would begin to speak of my dream. With relief

I saw him give me a tiny shake of his head in warning, as if telling me that this was not the time. "Sit down, child," he said, guiding me to my chair. "Here, take a little wine." Then, with a comforting hand on my shoulder, he asked, "What do you know of the Chiavelli family, Signor Vecchi?"

"A Venetian family of much wealth, I believe," came the slow reply. "I can tell you no more, but if you wish an Italian lawyer to look at this affair for you, I gladly recommend my own."

"That is very kind. Perhaps we could speak of this later. For the moment I think we should let the matter rest." A wail of protest came from Sarah, but Mr. Morton lifted his hand. "We have had enough excitement for one evening. That closes the subject for now. Signor Vecchi and I shall go to my study for our talks. Under the circumstances, Cadi, I think it would be an imposition for us to claim your services as an interpreter."

"I would really prefer to help if you and Signor Vecchi still wish it, Mr. Morton," I said hopefully. "It will be more useful than for me to do nothing and have this going round and round in my mind." I touched the locket.

He laughed and squeezed my shoulder. "My ever practical Cadi." For the next hour and a half I sat in the study with the two men. Although my understanding of their political conversation was vague, I found it easy enough to translate whatever was said.

At last Mr. Morton asked, "May we now spend a moment on a personal matter? You suggested I might use your own lawyer on Cadi's behalf."

"*Ah, si.*" Signor Vecchi looked at me and spoke rapidly in Italian. When he had finished I said to Mr. Morton, "He says he will give you his lawyer's name and address in Rome and will write a letter of introduction to him. If you will give him the name of your lawyer here, the two legal gentlemen can proceed with the matter together."

Mr. Morton considered for a moment, then said, "Tomorrow I shall see old Caldwell in London and explain the matter to him. Then all we can do is wait." He stood up and took my hand. "Cadi, child, you look a little tired, and no wonder."

When I wished Signor Vecchi good night he bowed over my hand. "In a few weeks I return to Rome," he said in Italian. "But if ever I can be of help, you have only to ask."

The next two days were miserable for me. Mrs. Morton and Sarah would talk of nothing but Granny Caterina and the coincidence of the picture in the hall. Mr. Morton and I had felt bound to tell them that it was a painting of the Palazzo Chiavelli, though we had said nothing about my strange dreams. Fortunately Sarah quickly reverted to her romantic daydreams and Mrs. Morton to her social calls.

Richard remained in bed for three days before I saw him going to his workshop. After a little while I followed him there. He was fiddling idly with some gadget on the bench. "Is your back all right now?" I asked.

He nodded. "Yes. I can hardly feel it. Thank you again, Cadi. You didn't tell my father, I know that. And you didn't speak to Lucian?"

"No. But I've told Sarah she'll be sorry if she helps you again."

"You needn't worry. I go back to Oxford soon, anyway." There was an awkward pause, then he went on. "Mother told me about discovering who your granny was, and that perhaps you're really a titled lady."

"She hopes so, I expect, but it's very unlikely."

He raised his eyes and looked at me. I was taken by surprise when he said simply, "You're so pretty. I meant what I said that night, Cadi. I love you."

"Well, I hope you do," I said quickly, trying to keep my voice light. "I'm one of the family now."

"I meant more than that. Much more. You needn't say anything. I'm glad if you just like me. But I do love you. You'll see one day."

I could think of nothing to say, and after a moment he went on, "Don't ever trust Lucian Farrel, will you?"

I was completely taken aback. "What on earth do you mean, Richard?"

"Only what I say. He's a master of deceit. That's not my own description. It's my father's."

"But your father likes him!"

"Perhaps. But I've heard him say that Lucian is a master of deceit."

"I like to make up my own mind about people," I said. Then I turned away and walked to the stables with strangely mixed feelings. Whatever Lucian's faults, instinct told me he did not dissemble. If my instinct was right, what Richard had said must be untrue. If my instinct was right . . .

Four days later, to my surprise, I received a short note from Lucian which said he'd had lunch with Mr. Morton. "Uncle Edward told me your startling news," he wrote. "I hope that whatever you may discover about your family will bring you much happiness."

I took the letter to show Mr. Morton. "You should be flattered, Cadi," he said. "It's rare that our Lucian can be troubled to put pen to paper."

"I find it hard to make Lucian out, Mr. Morton."

He smiled. "So do most people. I confess to being puzzled when we lunched together that he asked so many questions about you and the Chiavelli discovery. When I asked why he was so interested he said, 'If our little Cadi proves to be a wealthy heiress, naturally I would want to court her with all speed.'"

Mr. Morton spread his hands, eyes twinkling. "But that is Lucian. A shocking young man in some ways, but very amusing."

On a sudden impulse I said, "Would you call him a master of deceit?"

He stared, then said slowly, "It's my own phrase, of course, that has been repeated to you. A master of deceit. Yes, I think it well applies to Lucian."

So Richard had spoken the truth. I felt all at sea for a moment, then stammered, "But—but you *like* him, Mr. Morton!"

"Oh, very much." He gave me a little smile. "You see, it depends upon who is being deceived, and why."

THREE WEEKS PASSED, and it was during this time that I became steadily more aware of a person I came to think of as the gray-eyed stranger.

I first saw him two days after Signor Vecchi's visit, as I rode Pompey along the bridle path that ran through the woods. He was sitting at ease on a grassy bank, doing nothing in particular. I judged him to be from the city, for he wore a neat gray suit and a bowler hat. As I approached he rose to his feet, raised his hat, and gave me a polite good morning. His hair was light brown and well trimmed, his voice pleasant, his age anywhere between twenty-five and thirty-five, for though his face was youthful, it held a deep maturity. I returned his greeting and rode on. When I looked back I saw that he still stood there, gazing after me.

After that it seemed that I rarely went out riding without seeing the gray-eyed stranger. He always gave me the same polite greeting. I began to feel irritated by his constant appearance.

One day, meeting the stranger at the foot of the hill, I reined Pompey to a halt. "Good afternoon," I said a little coolly. "You seem to spend much of your time strolling in these parts."

"I hope it's causing you no annoyance, miss," he replied. I thought I detected a note of mockery.

"There's freedom for anyone to walk here," I said shortly. "You're not from Wealdhurst, are you?"

"I'm from parts greener than Kent," he said with a faint Irish lilt in his voice. "But I'm staying at the Three Tuns in Wealdhurst for a while."

"Will you be staying there long, Mr. . . . ?"

He ignored my invitation to introduce himself and said, "It depends. I'm a traveling man, as you might say, and a student of nature. But there, I mustn't keep you from your ride." He stepped back and raised the bowler hat. "I'll wish you good afternoon."

I was sure I heard mockery in his voice now, and I felt annoyed as I cantered away. But by the time I reached the stables I was puzzled and uneasy. The stranger knew more of me than I of him, I was sure of that, and I felt certain that he was in Wealdhurst for a purpose. I made up my mind that I would speak to Mr. Morton about him at the first opportunity.

This decision was driven out of my head the very next day. As I came down for breakfast, Mr. Morton was standing at the foot of the stairs, a telegram in his hands. He looked up, saw me, and said, "Cadi, my dear, as soon as we have finished breakfast I want you to go and dress for a trip to London. We're going to see Mr. Caldwell. He has news from Italy."

MR. CALDWELL, A PLUMP MAN with old-fashioned muttonchop whiskers, puffed around his office getting us comfortably settled. Then he sat down behind his big desk and opened a folder which lay in front of him.

"Well now, things have moved very quickly, Mr. Morton. Signor Vecchi had government couriers carry some of the letters from his lawyer in Rome, Avvocato Bonello." He glanced at me. "I gather you want the young girl here while I tell you about it?"

Mr. Morton waved a hand and said coolly, "Pray tell Miss Tregaron what you have to say, Caldwell. It's her affair, and I'm simply here to watch her interests."

Mr. Caldwell cleared his throat and turned his swivel chair a little to look at me. "Very well then, Miss Tregaron. First thing I did was to secure affidavits from Mawstone, declaring that it was common knowledge that your grandfather Robert Penwarden saved an Italian girl named Caterina from drowning in Naples Bay, brought her home, and married her. They had a child called Jennifer, who grew up and married Donald Tregaron. And you, Caterina Tregaron, are the issue of that marriage.

"Now the next step. Sent all this to Avvocato Bonello. Question of whether it was sufficient under Roman law to establish that Caterina, your grandmother, was in fact Caterina Chiavelli. He had inquiries made in Venice, where the present Count Chiavelli and his family still live. Learned of an amazing story. Whole thing reported in the journals of the day."

He turned some pages in the folder. "Caterina was born in 1841, the only child of the then Count Chiavelli of Venice. Her mother, the countess, died ten years later. The count became something of a recluse, and the young Caterina was brought up by his sister, Marguerita, and her husband, who was a penniless Hungarian baron." Mr. Caldwell peered down at the papers. "When Caterina was in her twentieth year her aunt Marguerita took her on a trip to Naples, where they stayed at the house of a wealthy friend of the family. And there, during the second week, Caterina disappeared."

Mr. Caldwell paused and offered a huge snuffbox to Mr. Morton. "Disappeared," he repeated impressively. "The last that anyone saw of her, she was walking in the grounds just before dusk. Marguerita is reported as saying that Caterina was a headstrong young woman, difficult to control. When she disappeared, Marguerita's theory was that she had run away with her—ahem—her lover. She was never seen or heard of again."

"Except by Robert Penwarden that same night?" Mr. Morton suggested.

"Exactly, sir!" Mr. Caldwell banged his hand on the table triumphantly. "The dates coincide. I have inquired at the shipping company, which still exists. So we know now that she was taken by force, to be drowned in Naples Bay. What we don't know is *why*."

Mr. Caldwell cleared his throat. "Now," he said, "let's go back for a moment to the Chiavelli family. Marguerita had a son and a daughter. The boy died while in childhood. The daughter was a few years older than Caterina. Count Chiavelli lived to be seventy-six, more of a recluse than ever after his daughter's disappearance. His title was such that it could continue through his heirs female, and collaterally through blood kinship. Understand that piece of legal jargon, young lady?"

"Does it mean the title could pass to a daughter if there was no son, and to a brother or sister if there were no children at all?"

Mr. Caldwell smiled, looking suddenly like a friendly frog. "Pity you can't rewrite some of our lawbooks, Miss Tregaron. Very well then, the title passed to the count's sister, Marguerita, who became the countess. She'd long been a widow. But she only survived her brother for a year, so the title passed down to her daughter, who was married to a man who doesn't concern us. They produced a son and a daughter. The daughter became a nun. The son is now forty-nine and is the present Count Chiavelli. He is married and has a son of twenty-five. The count, his wife, and their son all live in the Palazzo Chiavelli."

"Does all this have any material effect on Cadi?" Mr. Morton asked.

"I'm coming to that, sir. I'm coming to the nub of the matter now," Mr. Caldwell said. "The old count always clung to the belief that his lost daughter was alive and would one day be found. Reading between the lines, I rather think he was ashamed of having neglected her. Be that as it may," he went on, "the count made a strange provision in his will. Couldn't do anything about his title, of course—that's a matter for the courts—but he was a wealthy man, and he entailed his whole estate."

I said, "I'm not sure what that means, Mr. Caldwell."

"In simple terms it means that his estate did not pass on to his sister in this case. All she got was the income from his property and investments. But the capital of the fortune couldn't be touched. That clear now?"

"Yes. Thank you very much."

"The entailment will end in a few years. After that time the estate will go free of all encumbrances to the then heir to the title. In other words, the present Count Chiavelli. Until then, however, the estate is held in trust for Caterina Chiavelli, if she should be found alive, or otherwise for her closest living descendant on attaining the age of twenty-one."

"Do you mean that if my grandmother was alive today she would inherit the estate?" I asked.

"Quite right." Mr. Caldwell nodded. He looked at me intently. "But as she is no longer alive, and neither is your mother, the inheritance will pass to you, Miss Tregaron, when you reach the age of twenty-one."

I felt my eyes growing round with astonishment. Lucian had joked about this with Mr. Morton, and Sarah had built wild daydreams, but I had never imagined that it could happen.

Mr. Caldwell continued. "My colleague, Bonello, is also of the opinion that the courts may declare in Miss Tregaron's favor as regards the title."

Mr. Morton looked at me, smiling, but, in the shock of what I had just been told, I did not feel thrilled or happy—I felt afraid. When at last I could speak I only managed to blurt out, "I—I don't think I want to be a countess! Please, Mr. Morton!"

CHAPTER SIX

HE CAME TO ME quickly and held my hand. Then he turned to Mr. Caldwell and asked, "Is the fortune a large one?"

"Very substantial." Mr. Caldwell rummaged through his papers. "Bonello suggests that a quarter of a million sterling would be a conservative figure."

I gasped and clutched Mr. Morton's hand tightly. "A quarter of a million?" he echoed. "Oh, my little Cadi, you will be very wealthy indeed." He got up and paced thoughtfully across the room. At last he said, "The present count may lose his title then, and when Cadi becomes twenty-one he will certainly lose the fortune he otherwise expected to inherit when the entailment ends in 1911. I imagine he will fight the case."

"I thought the same," said Mr. Caldwell, "and so did Bonello. However, we've misjudged the man. Bonello visited Count Chiavelli and placed the facts before him. Had to be done sometime, and Bonello wanted to judge the fellow's reaction. It seems that after the first surprise the count was delighted to learn that the great family mystery had been cleared up at last, and that a grandchild of Caterina's existed. Warmhearted sort of chap, apparently, with a strong family feeling. He's accepted Cadi as being who she claims to be without the slightest quibble."

I said slowly, "It seems unfair, somehow . . . I mean, for me to take his fortune."

"My dear child, it is *not* his fortune," Mr. Morton said gently. "It is your great-grandfather's fortune. Neither you nor he has any justification for criticizing the manner in which the old count disposed of his estate. And the present count seems to be a gentleman of sufficient wisdom to realize this, I'm happy to say."

"Very rare," Mr. Caldwell grunted. "Seen families fight like wildcats over a piano, let alone a quarter of a million."

"Oddly enough," Mr. Morton said, "we had half planned to visit Venice next year. We shall certainly have to do so now. Well, thank you very much, Caldwell. Carry on the good work and let us know when the trustees have accepted the new position legally."

576

Mr. Caldwell got up and waddled round his desk to see us out. "By the way, remember I asked you to provide me with some good photographs of Miss Tregaron? Well, I sent a couple to Bonello. It appears there is a portrait of Caterina in the Palazzo Chiavelli. Bonello says she's the very image of Miss Tregaron. Staggering likeness between 'em. And she was wearing the locket when she sat for her portrait."

As we walked from Mr. Caldwell's office that first sensation of fright had passed, but somehow joy and excitement at the idea of being rich eluded me. I turned to Mr. Morton and cried, "Whatever am I going to *do* with the money?"

He looked down at me with his funny half-mournful smile. "Have you come to the truth of it so quickly then, Cadi? Well . . . forget the money for now. Rich or poor, just be yourself." He chuckled. "Rescue silly old gentlemen who go out sailing in boats. Dance with outcast young men when everybody else leaves the floor—" He broke off as if struck by a thought, then said, "Speaking of Lucian has given me an excellent idea. I have to go to my office for an hour or two, and I've been rather wondering what to do with you. But if we take a cab to Lucian's flat first, I can leave you with him. He has a housekeeper who will be there by this hour, so you will be properly chaperoned."

I was caught a little off-balance, but agreed. It would be the first time I had seen Lucian since the night he had beaten Richard so cruelly, and I did not know how I would feel when I saw him, but I could not tell Mr. Morton this. He hailed a cab and told the driver to take us to Half Moon Street, where Lucian's flat lay. There we climbed two flights of stairs to his front door. A gray-haired lady answered the doorbell.

"Good morning, Mrs. Redman. Is Mr. Farrel in?"

"Why, it's you, Mr. Morton, sir. Come in, please. Mr. Farrel's in the studio. I'll call him at once."

She led us through to the drawing room. I looked about me curiously. The room seemed sparsely furnished, and the walls were painted pale blue, in contrast to the dark colors and florid wallpapers that so many people favored. Yet I liked it, for the reflected sunlight on pale walls made it all seem light and airy.

We heard Lucian's voice calling. "Hello there, my aged uncle. Will you come through? I'm up to my elbows in clay."

Mr. Morton smiled, moving to the door. "May we both come?"

"Aunt Helen?" came Lucian's voice, a little doubtfully.

"No, it's Cadi."

"Ah, come along then. Aunt Helen would disapprove of my work, I'm afraid."

Lucian's studio was a big room with a huge window in one wall and a fanlight in the ceiling. Around the walls stood roughly cut blocks of wood in a variety of sizes and colors. On shelves and side tables stood a number of wood carvings. There was a life-size head of an old man; a miniature carving in relief of a naked goddess with arms lifted; the forepart of a horse, rising as if from the sea. There were two smooth hands, clasped with fingers interlocked; a bare ankle and foot, shapely, feminine.

A bust near the window caught my eye, and I knew that this was the carving Sarah had spoken of. The woman was young, yet her face seemed to hold the experience of all the ages, and the tilt of the head, the curve of the mouth, gave the effect of feminine assurance and insolence. I had the overpowering conviction that there was truth in the sculpture, and this essence lay in all the carvings. Their impact was immediate, yet there was a depth to them that held the mind and eye.

Lucian stood by a table, scooping handfuls of gray clay from a huge jar and building it round a thick rod, preparing a model, as I learned later, for a carving to be chiseled in wood. His dark face was very intent as he worked with sleeves rolled up. Then he lifted his head and smiled at us.

"Please take a seat. Forgive my rudeness, but I just wanted to finish that little job." He began to wash his hands. "What brings you here this morning?"

"Necessity, my dear nephew, necessity," said Mr. Morton. "We would hardly seek the company of a clay-smeared reprobate for pleasure."

"What necessity drove you to it?" Lucian asked.

"We've just come from old Caldwell," said Mr. Morton, dropping his bantering manner. "He had considerable news for Cadi."

"Considerable news? That sounds exciting. And yet our Cadi doesn't appear to be excited."

"She's being levelheaded, thank God," said Mr. Morton.

"Is Cadi to be a great heiress, as I suggested?" He threw the towel aside, smiling.

"We have discovered," Mr. Morton said, "that Count Chiavelli was Cadi's great-grandfather. She will inherit his estate when she reaches the age of twenty-one. She may also inherit the title."

There was a long silence. Lucian had stopped smiling. "A large fortune?" he asked.

"In the region of a quarter of a million sterling."

An even longer silence. Then, "I see . . ." said Lucian, and sat with folded arms, gazing at me broodingly. "How does the present count feel about losing his money and his title?"

"We're told he's deeply moved to hear that the old count's great-granddaughter has been found."

"Well . . . that's wonderful," Lucian said vaguely. "I suppose you'll be taking Cadi to Venice as soon as you can arrange it?"

"I imagine we shall go out there not later than the spring," Mr. Morton said. He got to his feet. "I'm inviting you to lunch, dear boy, but I have to spend what's left of the morning in Whitehall, and I'd like to leave Cadi in your care. To my astonishment she agreed to suffer your company for an hour or so."

"She has a kind heart," Lucian said absently. He was prowling now, looking at me intently, as if I were an object rather than a person. "I suggest you make it the Café Royal for lunch, Uncle Edward, to celebrate Cadi's good fortune."

When Mr. Morton had gone Lucian continued to move about, gazing at me in that strange way.

"I like your sculptures very much, Lucian," I said at last.

"Hmm? Never mind that. Take your hat and coat off, Cadi." He took my hand. "Come and sit on this upright chair, here under the fanlight."

"Do you mean you want to make a sculpture of *me?*"

"Yes, of course." He looked about the studio. "Ah, this will do." He picked up a piece of rope. "Now then, Cadi . . ." He bent to tie the ends of the rope round a leg of the table, then put the loop in my hands. "Draw it tight, as if you were holding reins, Cadi."

With quick, energetic movements he turned to the shapeless clay on the armature and tore handfuls of it away. "All right," he said impatiently. "Unbutton your sleeves and roll them back."

Somewhat in a daze, I obeyed. Lucian's aloofness had vanished. Excitement ran deep in him. "Hold the reins a little tauter . . . so! That's good. Talk if you want to, tell me all about old Caldwell. Sing if you like, but don't move your hands."

"My . . . hands? *Just* my hands?"

"What? Yes, of course!" He did not look up from his work.

"Why do you want to carve my hands?" I asked.

"Because they're beautiful," he said brusquely. "Pull harder on the rope, I want to see the effort in them."

"Beautiful?" My voice was incredulous.

"Hands aren't just ornaments," he said. "Can't be beautiful without purpose as well. Yours are beautiful. I knew it that first day, after Mogg Race, when you'd worn them raw on the oars. They're more elegant now, but they haven't lost their character."

I sat gazing down at my own hands as if seeing them for the first time. For a while I talked, telling Lucian all that had passed in Mr. Caldwell's office, but it seemed to me that he was hardly listening, for he asked no questions and made no comment. At last I stopped, but he seemed unaware of the silence. My hands and arms were beginning to ache, but I was determined not to ask if I could rest. Richard had warned me that Lucian was perhaps dangerously unbalanced, yet in his presence I simply could not believe the warning. If it was true, Mr. Morton would surely know, and he would not have been content to entrust me to Lucian. But then, why had Richard lied? And who had played that dangerous prank with the harness? There was the prowling gray-eyed stranger. Or . . .

The thought came unbidden to my mind. Could it have been Richard himself? What had Mr. Morton once said? "He is not a *sincere* young man . . . it is difficult to know his true feelings." My thoughts went round and round in circles. I watched Lucian, keeping my mind fixed on him, for I was distantly aware that my hands were on fire with the strain now.

At last there came a tap on the door, and Mrs. Redman entered carrying two letters. She stared indignantly. "Have you had the young lady sitting for you all this time? What are you thinking of, Mr. Lucian?"

"Eh? All what time?" Lucian glared at her.

"All this last hour and more!" Mrs. Redman said firmly.

"Hour?" He threw down the spatula he had just begun to use. "Sorry, Cadi. I didn't realize. Why the devil didn't you say?"

My hands were resting on my lap now, but I could not straighten my fingers after the long tension. I winced as pain shot up my arms when I tried to move my fingers.

Lucian moved toward me. "Cramp?"

"My fingers are . . . stuck!" I said helplessly.

He knelt by the chair, took my right hand, and started to massage it, gently at first but then kneading and squeezing more firmly. Almost at once the pain began to lessen. I ought to have felt flustered, but somehow it seemed quite natural. Lucian's head was turned a little, for he kept his eyes on the clay model, as if he were trying to see in it the hands that he could feel under his own. I knew that he was unaware of me, but I watched every shade of expression on his face.

As I gazed at him I felt a strange warm feeling steal over me, a great yearning and softening that I had known before only in the good dream. Slowly and irresistibly, like a rising tide, I knew that I loved Lucian Farrel. I had never believed that love came like a stroke of lightning, and I did not believe so now. This feeling toward Lucian had been growing within me since . . . when? I could not tell. Perhaps it had begun from the moment when he snatched me up onto his horse in Mawstone, or when I knew it was he who had chosen the blue linen dress for me to replace the one I had ruined in Mogg Race Bay. Whenever it had been, I knew that it was not new and sudden.

When he turned his head at last and said, "Is that better, Cadi?" I snatched my hand away and jumped up quickly. The spell of wonder was broken, and I felt only panic. It was madness to love such a man. He was an outcast, cashiered from the army, perhaps unbalanced. He was an artist, and all artists were notoriously bohemian, so I understood. The insolent, languorous face of the young woman he had sculpted seemed to mock me. I began to move about the studio, pretending to look at his work, terrified that he might read in my face the thing that had happened to me.

"You're not yourself, Cadi," Lucian said. "It must be the delayed shock of discovering that you're an heiress."

"Yes, I expect so," I said numbly, glad of any excuse as long as he did not hit upon the truth.

INSIDE THE CAFÉ ROYAL all seemed red plush, gilt, and mirrors. Mr. Morton was waiting for us at a table, a bottle of champagne standing in a silver ice bucket at his elbow. He rose as we approached. "Cadi, my dear. Come and sit here, with your back to the wall, so that you can watch the human zoo at feeding time. How are you, Lucian? How have you spent the morning?"

"I've been modeling Cadi's hands," Lucian said as the waiter handed us each a menu. "Can you bring her up to town one day next week for another sitting, Uncle Edward? Wednesday or Friday for preference."

"It's entirely up to Cadi," Mr. Morton answered blandly.

I could find no excuse, so I nodded. "If it's convenient for you, Mr. Morton."

He looked at me sharply. "You seem tired, child. Are you all right?" His gaze moved to Lucian. "Did she tell you the whole story, Lucian?"

"Most of it, I think. . . ."

I only half listened to their conversation, but I was vaguely conscious that Lucian was asking question after question in a way which made it clear that he had heard every word I had told him.

I sipped the champagne. At first it tasted like lemonade without enough sweetening, but the taste seemed to improve as the glass emptied. Soon my spirits lifted and I felt quite carefree. The meal was excellent, and I began to join in the conversation. I had the strange sensation of being two persons. One was sitting at the table, chatting gaily. The other was furtively watching Lucian Farrel and wondering why I should so dread that he might guess I loved him. I tried to persuade myself that this was natural modesty. But this was not the real truth. Deep within me I knew that I mistrusted him, and feared that if he knew that I loved him he would in some way use me to his advantage.

When we left the Café Royal Mr. Morton hailed a hansom cab and asked, "Can we give you a lift, Lucian?"

"I'm touched, Uncle mine, but after that splendid lunch I shall enjoy a walk," Lucian responded rather absently.

Halfway round Piccadilly Circus Mr. Morton tapped on the trap. The cabbie opened it and looked down. "Yes, sir?"

"Go round the Circus and up Regent Street again, will you? I forgot that I have a package to collect from my tobacconist." He turned to me. "A box of cigars."

In Regent Street Mr. Morton excused himself and went into the tobacconist's shop. I was deep in my thoughts, and perhaps a minute passed before I realized that I was gazing across the street at the façade of the Café Royal, which we had just left. Lucian stood on the steps there, his hat tilted slightly back on his head, a cane under his arm, smoking a cigarette and watching the passersby. I had the impression that he was waiting for somebody.

Suddenly I went stiff with shock. A man was approaching him, a man in a gray suit and bowler hat. It was the gray-eyed stranger who had haunted the fields around Meadhaven for several weeks past. The stranger stopped and spoke to Lucian, who turned, gave a smile of welcome, and dropped a hand on the stranger's shoulder in a gesture which spoke of close friendship. They conversed for a moment, and I saw Lucian laugh. Then they turned together and began to stroll slowly up Regent Street.

FOUR DAYS AFTER our visit to Mr. Caldwell a letter arrived for me by the first post, with a crest embossed on the envelope. It was in a beautiful hand, and written in excellent English.

> My dear Caterina,
>
> My family and myself are overjoyed. As you will know by now, Avvocato Bonello has visited us with the news that you, the great-grandchild of the seventh Count Chiavelli, are alive and in good health.
>
> I remember your great-grandfather well. He never ceased to mourn the strange loss of his daughter, Caterina, and we mourned with him, for we are a united and affectionate family.
>
> My wife, my son and I look forward most eagerly to embracing you and to receiving you among us as soon as you are able to make the journey to Venice. What is yours must be yours, and we yield it to you with gladness in our hearts.
>
> Dear Caterina, please write to us so that we may learn to know you. We send to the English gentleman, Mr. Morton, our respects and gratitude, and we hope that he and his family will come with you to Venice.
>
> To you we send our love and affection.
>
> Guido
> Count Chiavelli (pro tem)

I took the letter down with me to breakfast and gave it to Mr. Morton to read out loud.

"The count evidently accepts the situation with the utmost good grace," Mr. Morton said when he had finished. "I see he has even added pro tem to his title, and that is a very proper attitude."

Sarah said in alarm, "You won't go away to *live* there, will you, Cadi?"

"Of course not," I said.

"But you might have to!" Her voice took on a tearful note. "You can't be a Venetian countess in Meadhaven."

"Don't distress yourself over problems which have not yet arisen, Sarah," Mr. Morton said mildly. He then gave a resigned sigh and handed me back the letter. "You must answer it today, of course," he said. "Please give the count our respects, and say that we plan to visit Venice in the spring." He looked down the table at his wife. "A trip to Venice would make a very pleasant holiday for you, my dear. If we arrange it while Richard is on vacation, we can all go together."

Mrs. Morton put a hand on her breast and closed her magnificent eyes. "I should adore it, Edward," she breathed, enraptured.

That night when Sarah came to my room I told her the details of my day in London at Mr. Caldwell's office and then about sitting for Lucian. She was agog with excitement. "Isn't it wonderful that you'll be a countess, Cadi? As long as you don't have to leave Meadhaven . . ."

"For goodness' sake stop saying that, Sarah. The very idea makes me feel—I don't know—silly."

Sarah gave a long sigh. "It must be an awful responsibility. I don't suppose countesses are allowed to gallop about on horses or do any of the things *you* like. And then there's all that money when you're twenty-one. What you really need is somebody to worry about everything for you." She gave a little gasp and clasped her hands together. "*I* know! You should marry Lucian, and then *he* can look after everything."

The only light in my room was from my bedside candle, and I was thankful for this, for my face felt like fire. I pretended to yawn and said, "I thought you were madly in love with Lucian yourself."

"Oh, I was, Cadi. But it's somebody else now." She sat on the bed, gazing thoughtfully at the candle flame. "I'm really and truly in love this time."

"Who is it, Sarah?"

She shook her head. "It's a secret. I can't tell you."

"All right." I could not help admiring Sarah for the way she could keep a secret when she wished, even if it was a foolish, romantic secret.

"So you could marry Lucian, and everything would be lovely," Sarah continued. "He must be madly in love if he wants to sculpt your hands."

I smiled at her strange logic, but her words reminded me of something I was dreading—posing again for Lucian. "Oh, go to bed now, Sarah," I begged. "I've spent hours writing to the count today, and I'm tired out."

She slipped from the bed and giggled. "Good night, Countess."

Mr. Morton had arranged my next meeting with Lucian for the Friday, and I could find no good excuse for refusing to go. Sarah was to go with me for the outing. Mr. Morton would leave us with Lucian for the day, and come to collect us in the afternoon.

I was clinging to the belief that there was no reality in my sudden feeling for Lucian. How could there be? I was a practical Cornish girl, and I could not fall in love with a man unless I saw in him the kind of qualities Granny Caterina had found in Robert Penwarden, and my mother in my father. All that I knew of Lucian was obscured by mystery and suspicion, and it was against all reason that I could love him. Yet I was afraid to test myself, afraid that when I saw him next I would again feel that sweet and terrible heartache. "Little fool!" I muttered to myself. "You're as bad as Sarah with her romantic nonsense."

Friday came, and my first sight of Lucian brought me a sense of relief, for I felt nothing of the emotions I had feared. His manner was brisk and businesslike. As he posed me he told Sarah to chatter as much as she liked, but not to expect any answers from him. She was to watch the clock and tell him each time twenty minutes had passed, so that I could rest for ten minutes.

By lunchtime the clay model was finished to his satisfaction. But by then I was in despair, for as I watched Lucian at work that same feeling I had known before grew steadily within me, a yearning so powerful it almost hurt. I tried hard to concentrate on Sarah's chatter, but it was hopeless. Lucian held me fascinated. I felt my heart jump absurdly at the tiniest things, the moving sinew of a forearm as he worked the clay, the tightening of his mouth as he carefully shaped a curve with the spatula.

At lunch I was thankful for Sarah's presence. Her talk helped to hide my own lack of conversation. "When can we come to Epsom and see your stables?" she asked Lucian eagerly.

"A visit can be arranged anytime. Would you like that, Cadi?"

"It's very kind of you." I made myself look at him squarely. "But I really don't know when I'll be free."

"Well, you do surprise me!" Sarah said. "I thought you'd love to go."

"Cadi never ceases to surprise one," Lucian remarked with an ironic smile. "I hear that she is in correspondence with the count, and that you're all going to Venice in the spring."

"Yes! Isn't it wonderful?" Sarah bubbled.

"I might well be in Italy about that time," Lucian said thoughtfully. "Perhaps I could sell some horses to the count."

I looked at Lucian and said tartly, "Horses in Venice? Surely you'd do better to breed gondolas."

Lucian explained politely, "Count Chiavelli owns land near Padua, about fifty miles inland from Venice, and he has a small racing stable there. So the idea of selling him horses isn't really absurd."

I had made a fool of myself. "I'm sorry, Lucian. It was very rude of me to be sarcastic. But how do you know about the count's stables?" I was amazed to hear my own voice sounding so calm. I wanted to touch his hand, to push back the lock of hair that drooped over his forehead.

He shrugged. "It's part of my business to know who's interested in buying or selling horses. I've made inquiries about Count Chiavelli."

"You mean before you knew that I was related to him?"

Lucian hesitated for a fraction of a second before saying, "No. Since then." He smiled suddenly and with a return of the old mockery. "After all, perhaps you'll own that land of his in Padua when you're twenty-one, then we can do business together."

Somehow I knew that he had not made those inquiries idly. Perhaps he wanted to discover how large a fortune I would inherit— I hastily turned away from that line of thought, for it was too distressing.

After lunch Lucian and I returned to the studio. Sarah preferred to stay in the drawing room and watch the passersby from the window there. Lucian set a block of dark wood on a table. It had been cut very roughly to the shape he wanted. "I can work from the model now," he said, "but I may ask you to pose for a little while now and again, Cadi. There's more life in flesh and muscle than in clay."

He began to carve the wood, and at once became absorbed. Sometimes, at a brusque word from Lucian, I took up the pose for a few minutes, but mostly his attention moved from the clay to the wood as he worked silently. I watched him, that unwanted yearning growing within me. I suppose it was in desperation that at last I tried to break the spell.

"May I ask you a question, Lucian?"

"Hmm? Yes, if you want to." He spoke vaguely.

"Why did you beat Richard with a riding crop?"

He straightened up slowly. "Beat Richard with a riding crop?" he echoed. "Did he tell you that? He must have been dreaming."

"But *I* wasn't dreaming. I let him into the house that night and attended to his back. What I saw wasn't imagination."

Lucian looked down at the carving, where the curve of my wrists was beginning to emerge. "Perhaps Richard was caught by an angry husband. Did that occur to you?"

"Yes. But the woman he was . . . visiting didn't have a husband. He'd left her."

"Ah, that will be Meg Dawson, the dressmaker."

"So you know her?"

He tapped gently with a chisel. "Yes, I know her."

"Then perhaps you didn't like having Richard as a rival? Perhaps you were interested in her yourself—and so you beat him?"

He rubbed his chin with the handle of the chisel. "That's right," he said unexpectedly. "I remember now."

"You remember *now?*"

"Yes," he said. "But it's all over and best forgotten—unless you intend to raise the subject with Mr. Morton."

I shook my head dumbly.

"Good. Then that's settled." Lucian's eyes moved from the model to the wood. "Take the pose again, Cadi. I want to see how the light falls on your wrists."

CHAPTER SEVEN

DAILY LIFE AT Meadhaven went on its accustomed way. No mention was made of a further trip to Lucian's flat, and for this I was glad. I nursed the hope that the less I saw of him, the quicker my infatuation would pass. I had sometimes mocked Sarah for her absurd affairs of the heart, and it was humiliating to think that I cut no better figure myself.

I kept busy with the stables and with teaching at the orphanage. To my surprise, Sarah took to riding out with me. I felt sure she did not enjoy it, for she dismounted thankfully when we returned. But even when the days grew short and cold, she kept it up. She had also taken to going for walks by herself in the woods adjoining Meadhaven. Together with the riding it began to put color in her cheeks, somewhat to Mrs. Morton's distress.

The gray-eyed stranger had gone from the district, or so I thought, and it came as a shock to me one day when Sarah and I were trotting through the woods to see him walking toward us. I had the impression that he was as surprised as I. I drew Pompey to a halt and said, "Good morning. You're back in Wealdhurst, then?"

"I've not been away, Miss Tregaron," he said.

"Really? I haven't seen you for several weeks."

"Well now, I'm not a noticeable man, maybe. I just go about here and there, minding my own business, as you might say."

I was not quite sure whether he was being rude, and said, "Then I'd better mind *my* own business, I suppose. Good morning."

I put Pompey to a canter, and then had to wait while Sarah caught up. "You were very sharp with him, Cadi," she said.

"I used to see him about here a lot," I answered, frowning. "I had a funny feeling he was watching me. Have *you* seen him before, Sarah?"

"Me?" She gave a wide-eyed stare. "Gracious, I haven't time to notice *anyone* when I'm riding. And you know, Mama tells us never to speak to strangers."

I had the curious feeling that behind her innocent stare Sarah was gently mocking me. Although I did not see the stranger again in Wealdhurst, I never quite forgot him, for I was always half expecting to encounter him. Yet when at last that encounter came, it was to be in a far place, completely unexpected, and truly terrifying.

THE WEEKS PASSED. Christmas came and there was all the joy and bustle of preparation. Sarah and I saved from our pocket money for presents, but we also took over part of one of the greenhouses and grew potted plants there, which we later sold to a florist in Sevenoaks. Sarah had a knack of making the plants grow beautifully by talking to them and coaxing them. I was the one who sold them when they were ready.

Lucian stayed with us for two days at Christmas. I was depressed to find that my feelings for him had not faded. Instead of being natural with him I was either surly or overgay. He brought with him the finished wood carving of my hands, as a present for Mr. Morton. Mr. Morton was delighted and made a place for it in his study. "A reminder," he said to me when we were alone there. "A reminder that but for those hands I would not be here today, Cadi, my dear."

It should have been a wonderful Christmas, but for me it was something of an ordeal, partly because of my awkwardness with Lucian and partly because my thoughts often turned to Mawstone and my father at this time, the first Christmas since his death.

Richard was with us for the vacation. He and Lucian seemed as friendly as they had ever been. But when I saw that Richard's present for Lucian was a new riding crop, I held my breath, watching them both.

"I'm rarely heavy-handed with a crop," Lucian responded pleasantly, "but my old one is rather worn, and I'll be glad to throw it away." He examined the crop. "This is splendid. Thank you very much, Richard."

The moment of tension passed, and I heaved a silent sigh of relief.

With Christmas over I settled down once again to put Lucian out of my mind. Sarah's birthday came in January, and my own, my twentieth birthday, five weeks later. We each had a party, with many young people from the district as guests. Lucian sent his greetings and a present on each occasion—a fob watch for Sarah, and for me a pair of earrings brought back from one of his trips abroad. They were of silver set with green peridots. The first time I put them on, Sarah gave a little awed gasp.

"Cadi! With your black hair and nice long neck they make you look . . . *queenly!*"

"They are certainly very dramatic on you, Cadi," Mrs. Morton said doubtfully. "But a little old, perhaps?"

Wearing those earrings from Lucian brought him so close that I felt thoroughly uneasy. "Yes," I said quickly, staring at myself in the looking glass. "I'll keep them till I'm older, I think, Mrs. Morton."

About twice in each month I received an affectionate letter from Count

Chiavelli. I always answered promptly and tried to respond in the same vein. On only one occasion did his letter contain anything concerning the matter of my inheritance, and that was when he wrote:

> Please do not think that the passing of your great-grandfather's fortune into your hands will be an embarrassment to me or to my family. I am a person of considerable substance in my own right, and we shall not be in any way deprived by the happy circumstance that brings you to your birthright, dear Caterina. . . .

I felt very much easier in my mind after this, for it was something which had troubled me.

In the middle of February, Mr. Morton called me to his study. He had received a long report from Mr. Caldwell, and the gist of it was that I had been legally acknowledged under Italian law as being the sole contingent beneficiary of the old count's estate.

"The word contingent is used," Mr. Morton said, "because your inheritance is contingent upon your reaching the age of twenty-one. However, under the terms of the will, you are entitled to the income from the estate until that time. I think you should draw a reasonable allowance from the income." His eyes twinkled suddenly. "At least you will no longer have to sell potted plants to augment your pocket money. And since the count has been so kind, it's only right that we should take you to visit him as soon as possible. April seems a good time."

He got to his feet and paced slowly about the study, his hands behind his back. I sat waiting, wondering what was pressing on his mind. Finally he halted in front of me, frowning, then went on abruptly, "I spoke with Lucian a few days ago. In fact, he sought me out, asking if he might pay his attentions to you."

"His . . . attentions?" I said incredulously.

"Yes, Cadi. It seems he wishes you to be his wife." Mr. Morton smiled. "Perhaps out of respect for his aged uncle, Lucian has asked my permission before speaking to you."

A hundred questions whirled in my head, and of course I chose to ask the most stupid of them all. "But how can he pay his attentions to me when we hardly ever meet?"

"Why, he had in mind to stay here at Meadhaven—but, my dear Cadi, that is hardly the point. I want to know how you *feel* about this."

"But—it's absurd, Mr. Morton," I stammered. "Lucian has never treated me as anything but . . . well, a child."

"Presumably he has realized you are no longer a child and has fallen in love with you, my dear."

I shook my head. Pangs of longing stabbed through me, making it difficult to collect my tumbled thoughts. It was very tempting to forget all else and to drift in a rosy dream of believing what a part of me so desperately wanted to believe. But I would not yield to that sort of self-deception. If Lucian loved me, he had never shown it by so much as a word or a gesture.

"I don't believe Lucian has fallen in love with me," I said in a strange-sounding voice. "Do you, Mr. Morton?"

He made a troubled gesture. "I wish I knew, Cadi. I've always been very close to Lucian, but I must confess he has puzzled me of late. I find him less frank, less communicative."

There was a long silence. "Do you think," I said at last, reluctant to utter the words, "do you think that he wants to marry me because I'm an heiress now?"

"If you had asked me that a few months ago, I would have laughed at the suggestion. I believe I still ought to laugh at it . . . but I am uneasy." Mr. Morton came to me and put his arm about me for a moment. "Do you know, Cadi, I once had a little secret dream. It was after the night of that first ball, when you defied them all and danced with Lucian. It stole into my mind that one day you and he might be drawn to each other. That was my dream." He wrinkled his brow and sighed. "Yet when Lucian spoke to me the other day," he went on, "I felt anxiety rather than pleasure. I'm not sure why. There is something very much on his mind. When Lucian has a purpose, he keeps it to himself and follows it through to the end. I sense a purpose in him now, not simply to marry you, but a purpose behind that. And I cannot decipher what it is." He gave a shrug and spread his hands. "But just now, Cadi, you have only to tell me whether or not you wish Lucian to pay court to you."

My heart was a leaden weight within me as I formed in my mind the painful words I would speak. "I want Lucian to leave me alone, Mr. Morton," I said tiredly.

"Very well." It was as if he did not know whether to be glad or sorry. "I shall inform Lucian."

"Does he know that you were going to speak to me?"

"No, and I won't mention it. It will soften any blow to his pride somewhat if I present the decision as my own. I may well suggest that I consider the time is not yet right."

Toward the end of March, when preparations for our trip to Venice were well advanced, Mrs. Morton was taken ill with influenza. It was three weeks before she could leave her bed. Dr. Bailey prescribed a sea voyage to help her convalesce, and so Mr. Morton arranged for Mrs. Morton, Richard, and a nurse-companion to go by ship to Venice at the end of April. The three-week voyage meant that Richard would be absent from the university for part of the term, but this did not seem to disturb him.

Mr. Morton could not be away from his office for too long, so Sarah and I would keep him company at Meadhaven and leave with him only two days before the ship was due in Venice, crossing to France by the Channel ferry and traveling through France and Switzerland to Italy by train. This would bring us to Venice only a few hours after the ship was due to arrive there.

One thing troubled me. Mr. Morton had decided that he could not impose the whole family upon Count Chiavelli, so he booked rooms at a comfortable hotel in Venice, and the Mortons would stay there while I stayed at the *palazzo*. "I know it will be an ordeal for you at first, Cadi," he told me gently, "but we shall be seeing you very frequently, no doubt."

The day Mrs. Morton was to depart I found myself alone in the garden with Richard. He looked very handsome in the dark blazer he wore, and his violet eyes were almost startling against the gold of his hair. He seemed to have grown from a boy to a man since the turn of the year.

"You'll take good care of your mother, won't you?" I said. "She really has been ill, Richard, so don't do anything to—"

He smiled. "I won't get into any mischief. I'm taking some lawbooks with me and I'm going to study hard."

"That's a change," I said, teasing him a little.

"I know, but it's different now. I want to do well." He took my hand. "Will you kiss me good-by, Cadi?" he asked.

I pretended to misunderstand and said, "Of course I'll kiss you good-by. I always do when you go away."

"I didn't mean in front of the family, Cadi. I meant now."

I did not know how to refuse without being unkind, so I tried to take the matter lightly, and smiled as I put my arms round his neck to touch my lips to his.

He drew me close, kissing me hard. "You're not my sister, Cadi," he said. "I love you."

I wanted to say that nothing had changed, that I did not feel love for him in the way he wanted. "But—" I began.

"But you don't feel the same?" he prompted. "I know, Cadi. Perhaps you never will. I'm content to wait and hope." He took my arm and we strolled on across the lawn, as if nothing had taken place between us.

SOON THE DAY arrived when our own trunks were packed for the holiday, and we caught the boat train for the Channel crossing. Landing in Calais, Sarah and I were fascinated by the strangeness all about us, the Frenchmen in their blue working clothes, the signs and advertisements, the cries of the porters, and the chatter of the French passengers as we moved through the train to our reserved compartment.

We settled down to the long journey ahead, first through the flat plains of northern France and then the more wooded and hilly country as we approached Châlons at the end of the day. We were to stay in that town on the Marne River, threaded by canals and small streams, before continuing our journey at the same time the next evening.

Our hotel was in a pleasant square off rue Jean Jaurès, and the room I shared with Sarah looked out on it. Mr. Morton had told us to join him in the lounge when we had washed and tidied ourselves, and then we would have dinner. Since we left the train Sarah had seemed rather nervous and flustered, and as soon as she was ready she went downstairs without waiting for me. I was a little puzzled by her manner, but put it down to the fact that this was a foreign country and all very new to her. Five minutes later I found Mr. Morton alone in the lounge. "Where's Sarah?" I asked.

His eyebrows shot up. "I thought she was following you down."

"No, she came down before me."

He stood up, frowning. "Then where has she got to?" We went into the reception hall, but there was no sign of Sarah. Mr. Morton marched up to the desk and began to question the clerk there, but at that moment Sarah came in through the open doors which led to the street.

"Sarah!" her father said in astonishment. "What on earth were you doing outside?"

Sarah looked blank. "It's such a warm, close evening, Papa. I walked up and down for a few minutes to get a breath of air."

Mr. Morton let out a gusty sigh. "Well, don't go wandering out on your own again. Now come along and let's have dinner."

In the restaurant Mr. Morton gave us some of the history of Châlons. "Attila the Hun fought the Romans here. That was fifteen centuries ago. I don't think there can be much left from that day, but we shall have time to look at some beautiful things tomorrow."

We dined well, perhaps too well, for next morning both Mr. Morton and Sarah were pale and drawn, with upset stomachs. I felt well enough myself, and ate a good breakfast while they watched with a touch of envy.

"I should have remembered," Mr. Morton said sadly, "that though French cuisine is excellent, the English stomach needs to adjust to such differences gradually. Sarah, my dear, you and I will have to rest and take only a light diet today, or we shall be in a poor state to continue our journey this evening." He gave me a look of apology. "I'm sorry, Cadi, but we shall have to cancel our exploration of Châlons."

So it was a dull day for me, even though the weather was brilliant. I spent the morning in our bedroom with Sarah, reading to her and playing pencil-and-paper games. I had a good lunch in the hotel restaurant, all by myself, and an hour later I went to see Mr. Morton in his room. He was sitting up in bed reading a book, and looked a little better now.

"May I go out for an hour, Mr. Morton?" I asked. "I've been looking at a map, and I thought I could walk to the market and come straight back."

He hesitated. "On your own?"

"You wouldn't mind if I walked round the market in Sevenoaks on my own. I won't talk to anybody, and I promise I won't get lost."

"Well . . ." he said slowly, "I don't see that any harm can come to you. But keep to the main streets, and just go to the market and back."

It took me only ten minutes to reach the market. There must have been fifty stalls in the square, but they were all closed. Their wooden doors, flaked with weathered paint, were fast secured by hasps with padlocks. I had hoped to find all the bustle of a market, with the sellers of meat and fish, vegetables and groceries, candles and cloth and trinkets, all plying their trade. But there was only the almost empty square lying silent under the hot sun. Evidently the afternoon was a time for resting.

Unwilling to return to the hotel yet, I walked slowly round the square, past the church of Notre-Dame, then sat down on a wooden bench under the shade of a tree and watched a bowlslike game going on a stone's throw away. I suppose it was a very peaceful scene, but I wanted to be moving about and seeing new things here in this strange land.

Two minutes later I had no cause to complain about the quietness. From one of the roads leading off the square there came the sound of marching feet, faint at first but growing steadily louder. There must have been forty soldiers marching in the column, all wearing smart blue uniforms and carrying drums, horns, flutes, cornets, bassoons, trombones, and every variety of wind and reed instrument. It was a military band. I remembered Mr. Morton telling us that there had been a large army troop-training center to the north of the town since the days of Napoleon III.

When the band reached the middle of the square, there was a minute or two of tuning up; then the music crashed forth in a great blare, pigeons took wing, and the bowls players lifted their eyes to heaven. Here and there windows and shutters banged to. It was clear that the band had been ordered to play in the square, but it was playing for an audience of one, Cadi Tregaron. Within minutes I decided that if I sat there any longer I would have a splitting headache. I got up and moved quietly away, intending to walk round the edge of the square and on back to the hotel.

As I passed the church I saw a man coming toward me, moving quickly, his head turning from side to side as if looking for somebody. He wore a gray suit and bowler hat, and I saw his face clearly as he stared about him. It was the gray-eyed stranger from Wealdhurst. I knew that in another second or two he must see me, and I was seized by a chill of alarm. This could be no coincidence. He was here in a foreign country because I was here. He must have known our plans and taken the same journey, been on the same train, no doubt. In his face was a grimness and purpose I had never seen there before, and I had a keen sense of imminent danger.

I turned aside into a narrow street which ran alongside the church, quickening my pace until I was almost running. Glancing back, I saw him pass across the end of the shadowed side street and out of my view.

Within a few seconds I began to feel rather foolish for giving way to fear, but all the same I did not intend to let the gray-eyed stranger find me. I decided that if I walked on to the end of this little side street, I would come out in the main road which lay between the square and the hotel.

But I was not sure of my route, and soon I found myself in an alley rather than a street, with high windowless walls on each side. Even here the sound of the band filled the air. As I started to turn back, a big, slouch-shouldered man wearing the white jacket of a hotel porter entered the alley by the way I had come. To my surprise he lifted a hand as he approached, and made a gesture, as if urging me to go back. "M'sieu Morton," he said.

"What is it?" I asked. "What about Mr. Morton?"

He pointed again, moved past me, and said, "Come!" He beckoned urgently, and set off along the alley. I followed, full of anxiety as I tried to think what could have happened to make the hotel send a porter to find me. When we passed round the curve of the alley, he stopped and turned. Beyond him a blank wall stretched across the alley. The band music seemed very close, and I think that only a small, high-walled garden separated us from the square. But there was no exit. The alley was blind.

The man put a hand under his jacket, and when he withdrew it he was gripping a piece of iron bar almost a foot long. He darted one quick glance beyond me, then lunged toward me quickly. There was no doubting his intention, and terror exploded within me as I turned to run, struggling to lift the skirt that hampered my legs. I came to the bend of the alley, running with all my strength, praying that I could reach the street beside the church before he caught me, for there I had the hope of help. It was a slender hope indeed, for even if I found breath to scream, I would never be heard above the noise of the military band. But I thrust on desperately.

Then, twenty paces ahead of me, at the entrance to the alley, the gray-eyed stranger stepped into view, and those gray eyes were as cold as the bitter sea fog of winter. The man with the iron bar was close behind. I was trapped between the two of them, and my terror gave way before a crushing despair that seemed to drain all strength from my body.

EXPECTING AT ANY instant to be struck down from behind, I threw myself to one side and turned with my back against the wall of the building. Then I saw that the man with the iron bar had hesitated. His glance darted past me to the gray-eyed stranger, who was moving quickly forward. As he moved he spoke, and in that instant the music stopped, leaving only the echoes of a final crashing chord. I heard again that soft voice with its underlying Irish brogue, "It's all right, Miss Tregaron, don't you be worrying."

Next moment he had passed in front of me and was standing between me and the big, sallow-faced hotel porter. I sobbed with relief as I realized that he was not attacking me but guarding me from attack. Then came new alarm as I saw the Frenchman take a firmer grip on the iron bar and lunge toward him. Calmly the gray-eyed stranger spun his bowler into the Frenchman's face, so that the hard brim struck him across the bridge of the nose. The iron bar missed its intended mark by inches. For a moment the men were at close quarters. I heard two soft-sounding blows, a whistling gasp, a sharper blow of bone on bone; then the porter lurched against the far wall and slithered to the ground, the iron bar clattering as it fell from his limp hand.

The gray-eyed stranger picked up his hat, brushed the dust from it, and turned to me. His smile was full of mischief. "That was closer than I'd wish for you," he said almost apologetically.

He squatted down and began to go quickly through the pockets of the unconscious man. I saw now that the porter's jacket was far too small. He must have stolen it for his purpose. With an effort I tried to gather my scattered wits. I was still shivering, but no longer felt close to tears. "I . . . I don't understand," I said. "Did you *know* this would happen?"

"If I'd known, I'd not have let things run so damn close, Miss Tregaron."

"But who is this man? Why did he try to harm me?"

"Ah, now. If we could answer that, we'd be much wiser than we are." He stood up empty-handed. "There's nothing in his pockets to tell us."

"But . . . who *are* you? And how did you come to be here?"

"Didn't I once tell you I'm a traveling man?" Again he gave me that quick, mischievous smile. "Will you hurry back to the hotel now, please, Miss Tregaron? We want to be away from here."

I nodded, too confused to press any further questions. As I reached the entrance of the narrow alley I turned and looked back. "Please come and meet my family," I said. "Mr. Morton will want to thank you."

He shook his head. "Best not trouble him with this. The wheels turn slowly in France, and you'll find yourselves having to spend a week or more in Châlons before you know where you are. Besides, you have Miss Morton with you and she might be much alarmed, d'you not think?"

I said, "Then won't you at least tell me your name, please?"

For a moment he hesitated. Then, "Call me Flynn. But away with you now, Miss Tregaron, and a pleasant journey to you."

"Thank you, Mr. Flynn. Thank you again."

Along the road to the hotel I looked round once. There was no sign of Flynn, but I felt strangely sure that he was not far away. I could feel my hands trembling again, and I felt sick. Luckily I had been away from the hotel for only half an hour, and so I was able to sit quietly in the little courtyard garden for a while as I tried to decide whether I should tell Mr. Morton what had happened. It seemed the right and sensible thing to do,

but I found myself shrinking from it. I would tell Mr. Morton later, when he and I were alone, and when I felt calmer.

That night, in the sleeping compartment I shared with Sarah, I lay awake for a long time as the train rattled rhythmically across France and into Switzerland. Over the past few months I had been close to death twice, once when Pompey bolted and again today behind the square at Châlons. Somebody wished me ill. The man who had tried to strike me down with an iron bar was surely a hireling, but who was his master?

Richard said he loved me. Lucian had spoken to Mr. Morton of marrying me. Could there be somebody else, an unknown enemy? For a moment I wondered if Count Chiavelli wished me dead. But he had acknowledged my rights with gladness and affection. And he had not known of my existence when Pompey's reins were tampered with. I found no answers to the questions that danced in my head, or to the mystery of Flynn. I felt sure that he had traveled from England with us, and this gave me a sense of comfort, for I knew now that he was not my enemy.

My thoughts turned suddenly. Did I really have an enemy at all? The broken rein could easily have been an accident. Could the man at Châlons have simply been a poor deranged creature? No, I thought reluctantly. He had spoken Mr. Morton's name to lure me into the blind alley. For one frightful moment my brain staggered under the thought that Mr. Morton himself might have known what was to happen.

I closed my mind and started to recite in my head all the Shakespeare speeches that Miss Rigg had had me learn. If I could even begin to think such a thing of Mr. Morton, my weary brain had gone beyond all reason. I must stop thinking and wait until time had given me a true perspective.

I slept at last as the train sped on its way toward Venice. When morning came, my imaginings of the night seemed foolish beyond words. But I did not speak to Mr. Morton of what had happened to me in the alley behind the market square.

PORTERS WITH CARTS were everywhere, and there was a great bustle and shouting as luggage was unloaded from the train and trundled away to waiting gondolas and big rowboats. I felt tears come to my eyes, for the Italian accent I could hear all round me was not that of Signor Vecchi, who was a Roman, but the same accent I had learned from my mother and Granny Caterina. Even without any other proof, I would have known in this minute that Granny Caterina had come from Venice.

We saw Richard edging his way through the throng, his usually pale face lightly tanned now from the sea voyage. We greeted him excitedly and with a flurry of questions.

"Mother's very well," he said, smiling. "We arrived this morning and the count himself was there to meet us—"

"What is he like?" Sarah broke in. "Is he nice?"

"Very nice indeed. Mother's quite overwhelmed. He took us to our hotel, and an hour ago he called for me in one of his private gondolas so that we could come to meet you."

Richard gave me a warm glance, then turned to his father. "There's a gondola waiting to take us to the hotel, with a rowboat for the luggage. Cadi will go with the count, straight to the Palazzo Chiavelli."

Everything was happening too quickly for me. "Couldn't I stay at the hotel with the rest of you just for tonight, Mr. Morton?"

He slipped his hand through my arm. "You are the count's guest and you are of his family. I think it would be discourteous to delay your arrival at his home. Now Richard, where is the count?"

"Waiting by the jetty, Father. It's only a few steps. He sent me on to meet you so that I could explain what had been arranged."

My first sight of Count Chiavelli did much to ease my nervousness. Hat in hand, he stood waiting for us beside two beautiful gondolas painted in red and gold. Four gondoliers in matching uniform waited on the steps. The count's hair was thick and dark, his eyes wide-set. His features were strong, sharply defined, hinting at a powerful character. His smile went straight to my heart, it was so like Granny Caterina's.

"Caterina!" he said softly, and came forward to kiss me on each cheek, then looked at me and shook his head in smiling wonder. "How very much like her you are!" he said in English.

"I'm very happy to make your acquaintance, sir," I said clumsily.

He laughed and gripped my hands. "No formalities, please, Caterina. We are some sort of cousins, but in view of my age, perhaps you will call me Uncle Guido." Then he turned to Mr. Morton. "Forgive me, sir. You will be Mr. Edward Morton, and this is your daughter, Sarah. Yes?"

There was handshaking and a friendly and informal exchange of greetings. "You will be tired now," said the count, "and so will Caterina. I shall see you safely on your way to the hotel, and I hope that tomorrow you will bring your family to dine with us, Mr. Morton. I will send a gondola for you at seven o'clock, if that will be convenient?"

"We shall look forward to it, sir."

Mr. Morton put his hands on my shoulders and kissed my cheek. Then all three Mortons were moving away from the steps in their gondola, with the rowboat following. I waved, feeling a little lost.

When I turned, the count took my arm and guided me down into our own gondola. A gondolier took up his position in the stern, and then we were moving quietly over water that gleamed with the rose tints reflected from the mackerel clouds left glowing by the setting sun. "This is your first sight of Venice," said the count in a soft voice. "I will not spoil it by talking. Just look, Caterina, with your eyes and with your heart."

We were in the Grand Canal, and at this moment it was like fairyland. Already the lamps along the banks were being lit. The water shimmered, pink and gold. All about us were moving craft, gondolas, cargo barges, the little rowboats called *sandali*. I saw that the tide was falling, for a ribbon of damp green showed at water level along the base of the weathered stone buildings. It was a very little tide compared with the tides of the English Channel.

On either side of us, smaller canals wound away from the Grand Canal, and people were crossing the arched bridges which spanned them. As we passed under the Rialto Bridge a man in a small rowboat pulled up to the steps. A dog waited there, a big, slow-moving old dog. With the ease of long practice, it jumped lazily into the boat and settled down. I laughed aloud in delight, realizing that every creature in Venice was born to the canals.

I fell in love with Venice as we glided slowly down the Grand Canal. The atmosphere that gripped me came from many things—the soft quality of the light, the sense of slow, dreamy movement, the very texture of the ancient stone. At some deep level of my being I had inherited fragments of Granny Caterina's memories. I knew this, from my dreams in which I had seen the *palazzo*. Now it seemed that time slipped backward, and I was seeing with my granny's eyes and feeling with her heart. My own life seemed far distant. Mawstone was a vague blur, Meadhaven scarcely seemed to exist. Even Lucian held no part of me.

I was so deep in the spell that it came almost as a shock when the count said quietly, "We have arrived, Caterina."

"Oh! I'm sorry, you must think me so ill mannered."

"Not at all. It would have been rudeness on my part to intrude upon your first meeting with the Queen of the Adriatic."

"Thank you for being so understanding." I hesitated, then added, "Uncle Guido."

He looked pleased, then pointed as the gondola slid into a canal leading off the Grand Canal. "There is your home, Caterina."

When I turned to look, the Palazzo Chiavelli was exactly as I had always seen it in my dreams. There were the broad stone steps rising between the two great pillars. The gondolier brought the craft alongside the steps and Uncle Guido steadied me as I stepped ashore. Together we walked up the long flight to the splendid portico.

As we arrived the double doors were swung open. A dark-suited servant stood on each side of the doorway, and beyond waited a lady in a long green dress with her mahogany hair piled high on her head. Beside her was a young man in a gray suit and a deep red velvet waistcoat.

"Here is our little Caterina," said Uncle Guido. "Dear child, I present you to my wife, your aunt Isola, and my son, Bernardino."

Their words were warm and welcoming, but I think the only thing I noticed at the time was that the countess was plump and soft, and that Bernardino's cheek, when it touched mine, felt as soft as his mother's.

We began to move down a long hall hung with great portraits. "Now you shall see something," said Uncle Guido happily. "Now you shall see why we had no doubts that you were Caterina's granddaughter when we saw your photograph." He touched my arm and halted, pointing.

The picture was in a beautifully carved golden frame, and it was as if I were looking at myself. This was Granny Caterina at my age. She wore a white dress, delicately pleated, and the gold locket hung about her neck. I felt close to tears as I whispered, "Poor Granny . . ." I turned to Uncle Guido. "Do you remember her?"

"Quite well," he answered. "Though I was only a child of five when she disappeared. She was very beautiful—as are you, her namesake."

Moving on past other portraits, Uncle Guido pointed out the old count, Granny's father, a man with somber, hooded eyes. But it was another picture that suddenly caught my attention.

"Who is that?" I asked.

"That is Marguerita, the old count's sister and my own grandmother," Uncle Guido replied. "This was painted a year before she died. I remember her well. A formidable old lady."

So this was the woman who had taken the young Caterina to Naples, where she had disappeared. The face was strong-featured, like Uncle Guido's, but in contrast to his it was proud and haughty. The eyes held a hard, penetrating stare. Shapeless fears flickered through me. Without reason, unless it was the traces of my grandmother's memory, I felt such dread of this woman who stared down upon me that my body shook.

I had known fear before—in Mogg Race Bay, and only a day ago behind the square at Châlons. Then I had had good cause to be afraid. The fear I felt now was quite groundless, yet it was more intense and horrifying. I felt that I could not breathe, that I was drowning. The painted eyes looked down. They seemed to know what was happening to me, and were glad.

CHAPTER EIGHT

I HEARD UNCLE GUIDO'S voice saying with quick concern, "Are you all right, Caterina?"

His words broke the suffocating spell. "Yes . . . I was only thinking."

"Thinking that Marguerita was the last of our family to see your grandmother?" He nodded. "Yes. It was the great tragedy of her life."

I remember little else of that evening. I was shown to my room, which was large and handsomely decorated in pale blue and gold. At dinner I made such an effort to hide my weariness that I hardly tasted the food. Uncle Guido must have realized how tired I was, for as soon as we rose from dinner he suggested that I might like to retire.

When I woke the next morning I felt refreshed and excited as I looked out upon the magic of Venice. The sun was dissolving the last cobwebs of mist, clothing the spires and turrets in robes of gold. I longed to explore, and looked forward eagerly to the coming day.

At breakfast I had my first chance to gain an impression of Aunt Isola and Bernardino. Aunt Isola continually smiled at me. She did not appear to have any thoughts of her own, and simply repeated whatever Uncle Guido said but in different words. Bernardino kept paying me compliments. "You are much more beautiful than your photograph, Caterina," he would say. I wanted to laugh, particularly when he praised my "pretty little feet." Both he and his mother struck me as empty characters, but Uncle Guido made up for them both. He talked well and amusingly, and it soon became clear that he was a man of many activities, quite apart from running the stables in Padua.

After breakfast I was shown round the *palazzo*. Uncle Guido acted as guide, and Bernardino trailed along with us. Over half of the forty rooms in the *palazzo* had been closed. "We are a small family now, compared with the old days," said Uncle Guido. "I would like to see the *palazzo* as it was when I was a boy. There were three times as many servants then, and the whole place was in use. It will be costly, but I have many business interests that are prospering. So in a year or two we shall see what can be done."

We made our way through two salons and a great ballroom, a library, and a study. Sunlight gleamed through tall windows upon walls of gold brocade which rose to marvelous painted ceilings. Vast couches and chairs, intricately carved, were set widely apart. Immense Persian and Chinese carpets lay beneath glittering chandeliers. I was awed by the thought that over years and even centuries past, all this had been brought to the *palazzo* by the waterways of Venice.

As I went to tidy myself for lunch, I stopped to look again at the portrait of Marguerita, determined not to be so foolishly affected by it this time. Slowly I relaxed. An old lady gazed down at me with the same haughty stare, but she inspired no fear in me. After a while I made a very unladylike face at her and turned my back.

When we had lunched on the broad terrace, which looked out upon the canal at the back of the *palazzo*, Uncle Guido asked, "Is there something you would like to do this afternoon?"

"I'm longing to see Venice by day," I told him.

"Why, certainly!" He looked pleased. "Bernardino, you can take Ugo as gondolier and show Caterina something of our city."

My heart sank a little at the thought of Bernardino being my escort, and I was not wrong to have misgivings, for I found that I had to drag answers from him to any of the hundreds of questions I asked during our trip. Soon I gave up, and encouraged Ugo to tell me all he could as we made our way along the network of canals. Ugo was hesitant at first, but when he saw that Bernardino was relieved rather than put out, he became quite talkative and proved an excellent guide.

We passed under the Bridge of Sighs, and there we mounted steps to make our way into the very heart of Venice, the Piazza San Marco. The vast square was thronged with strolling people and fluttering pigeons, and it seemed to me that there must be hundreds of gaily painted chairs and tables set outside the cafés. Ugo told me of the day only a few years ago when the great bell tower of St. Mark had tumbled down after standing for almost a thousand years. It had been expected, he said, for the structure was failing. He had been on the perimeter of the square himself, watching with thousands of Venetians on that July morning, as the tower collapsed slowly, gracefully, into a huge mound of brick and rubble. But wonder of wonders, the great bell which had tolled for six centuries was unbroken by its fall. Now the bell tower was being rebuilt.

I came to like Ugo, with his wrinkled face and slow manner, for whatever I asked he always produced some fascinating story to go with the answer. But I tried once more to engage Bernardino in conversation.

"Which palace is that, Bernardino?" I asked.

"That?" He gazed at it with his mouth open, then said, "Contrarini-Fasan." He looked at me and seemed to be searching his mind for something more to say. Finally he added, in English, "I think you are the most lovely girl in England, Caterina."

"Thank you," I said, and turned away. "Ugo, is it a very old palace?"

"Quite old, signorina. It was built before Columbus sailed to America."

THAT EVENING, WHEN the Mortons came to the Palazzo Chiavelli for dinner, we all sat round the magnificent table in the great dining room, and the conversation had no awkward pauses. Both Mr. Morton and Uncle Guido were excellent talkers. Sarah bubbled with excitement and made everybody laugh by mixing up the places she had seen that day.

Both Richard and Mrs. Morton were clearly enthralled by Uncle Guido. When he told tales of his youth, of masked balls, romantic escapades, and duels, Richard sat drinking in every word, his eyes shining.

"I hope I do not shock you with such stories, Mrs. Morton," Uncle Guido said, smiling. "They are all a part of the historic fabric of Venice. Among the noble families here there has always existed a kind of secret wildness."

"Is it the same today, my dear Count?" Mr. Morton asked.

Uncle Guido shrugged. "Not quite. But less than three years ago I saw a young fellow from a noble but impoverished family stake everything he possessed on the turn of a card."

Mrs. Morton gasped. "But . . . what did he possess if he was impoverished?"

"The family *palazzo*. But he was unable to maintain it. And rather than sell, he gambled it against a sum of . . . let me see, now . . . forty thousand of your English pounds."

"And what happened, sir?" Richard asked for us all.

"He won," said Uncle Guido, and smiled. "With the turn of a card he reestablished his fortune." He looked at Mrs. Morton and raised a reassuring hand. "I am not commending his action. We Chiavellis stand aside from such headstrong wildness."

He lifted his glass and looked at it. "The Chiavellis are more practical people. These glasses we are using, they were made in my own glass foundry. Beautiful, are they not?" We all murmured admiringly.

"Your glass foundry is on the island of Murano?" Mr. Morton asked.

"Not quite. On a small islet a short distance from Murano."

"Can we go there?" Sarah asked eagerly. "I'd love to see glass being made. They blow it, don't they?"

"Yes." Uncle Guido smiled. "They blow it, Sarah, and they color it with chemicals, and mold it with a paddle of charred wood, just as their forefathers have done for centuries."

The evening ended all too quickly. Two days passed before I saw the Mortons again, when we met for the visit to the glass foundry. It lay only a mile away across the lagoon, and consisted of a sprawl of buildings in the center of the little island. We watched with fascination as the men drew their long blowpipes from the furnace pot, each with a blob of molten glass glowing on its end, then blew, rolled and swung the blowpipe, blew again, reheated, shaped with a charred wooden paddle, and finally cut the excess glass away with shears. What left me amazed was that a man could produce goblet after goblet all of identical size and shape.

"It is a matter of experience," Uncle Guido said when I asked him about this. "They begin as little boys, and their craft is a mystery handed down from father to son."

Every day I was taken out, either to see some new part of Venice or to visit Uncle Guido's friends. Each night when I fell asleep my head was buzzing with fresh impressions. Friends of Uncle Guido twice gave a party in my honor, and Mr. Morton and his family were invited. Though they were all enjoying their visit thoroughly, they told me that they missed having me with them. I was deeply glad, for I found more and more that I missed seeing them daily. It was the little things which affected me most. I missed Sarah tiptoeing to my bedroom to gossip when we went to bed, Mr. Morton's little dry jokes, Richard's quick affectionate smile, and even Mrs. Morton's breathless fluttering.

I enjoyed Uncle Guido's company, but Bernardino and Aunt Isola seemed to have no spirit. I found that the evenings grew irksome, for then Uncle Guido was usually elsewhere and did not return until long after the rest of us had gone to bed.

It was toward the beginning of the third week that I realized with a shock that Uncle Guido expected me to stay on at the Palazzo Chiavelli when the Morton family went home. Various remarks made it clear to me that he thought I should now look upon Venice as my true home.

Though I had lost none of my first delight in Venice, I did not want to stay. Soon, I knew, I would begin to long for the green lawns of Meadhaven, the pink clouds of flowering cherry in the spring, the riot of summer roses, and the golden fall of leaves in autumn. Above all, I realized that the ties of blood could not compare in strength with the ties of heart and mind. Though Uncle Guido was kindness itself, my love and my sense of family belonging lay with the Mortons now.

I did not wish to hurt Uncle Guido, and so from time to time I began to make little observations to indicate that I had always expected to return to England with the Mortons. Uncle Guido was quick to take notice, and one evening he said, smiling a little wistfully, "I thought you were happy here, Caterina. We have done our best to make you feel so."

"Oh, but I am," I said. "You couldn't have given me a happier time."

He looked puzzled. "But it seems you wish to leave us. I have only recently realized that you are thinking of returning with Mr. Morton and his family. Surely Venice is your true home and we are your true family?"

I felt myself going red. "I've only ever thought of this as a visit," I said, stumbling over the words. "It's hard to explain, but I've lived all my life in England, and I think of that as my country. Please don't be hurt, Uncle Guido. You've been wonderfully kind, but when my father died I was able to make a new home with the Mortons. It's not very easy, so I don't want to have to do it once again. Please understand."

He nodded his head. "I understand, Caterina. But . . ." He was silent for a long while, as if not quite knowing what to say. "I have to tell you something," he said at last. "My son, Bernardino, is in love with you. Deeply in love. Did you know that, Caterina?"

"I'm . . . I'm very honored," I faltered. It was a lie, but the truth would have been insulting. "Bernardino has my—my affection, but . . ."

"You do not reciprocate his feelings?" Uncle Guido said, and gave a wry shrug. "I know. But you do not really know him yet, Caterina." He sat brooding for a few seconds, then went on softly, as if to himself. "When I heard how he felt toward you, I felt sure that in time Bernardino

603

would overcome his shyness and awaken a response in you. I would do anything to help make that possible." He paused and looked at me.

"I'm sorry," I said helplessly. "Really, Uncle Guido, I'm very sorry."

"Could you not give him a little time, Caterina?" he said almost pleadingly. "Stay with us here for a while, just until the end of the year, perhaps. I only ask you to give him time, to give yourself time to know him better."

I was twisting a handkerchief in my fingers and had torn the lace edging in my agitation. "I can't!" I said desperately, and felt tears begin to trickle down my cheeks. "I'm sorry, but I can't!"

He stood up and came to me quickly. "There now, do not cry, my little Caterina." He took my hands and held them gently. "And do not be sorry. It is for me to apologize for upsetting you so. Dry your eyes and we will say no more. I simply ask that you will tell me if you change your mind."

I knew I would not change my mind. And I felt immense relief that it was settled that I should return to England.

Two days later Mr. Morton and his family came to tea—*my* family. I was so overjoyed to have them about me again that I kept feeling my eyes grow moist. It was clear that the holiday had refreshed the Mortons. Only Richard seemed tense, an almost feverish look in his eyes.

For a few minutes Sarah and I were alone together, walking through the little rock garden beyond the terrace. "Cadi," she whispered, and glanced furtively over her shoulder, "I don't know whether to tell you."

It was wonderful to be called Cadi again. I laughed and linked arms with her. "Who have you fallen in love with now?" I asked.

"Oh, it's not that!" She looked quite hurt. "Stop teasing and listen, Cadi. Richard has been going out at night again!"

I turned to look at her. "Here? In Venice?"

"Of course, silly! He creeps out after we've all gone to bed. The other night I saw him come back in a gondola to the side door of the hotel. What shall I do, Cadi? I daren't tell Papa!" She gave a little wail. "Oh, look. Here come Mama and the count now."

"Tell Richard that you know and you've told me. Tell him that if he . . . if he cares what I think of him, he'll stop these escapades at once."

She looked at me curiously for a moment and said, "All right. I'll do that, Cadi." Then, in a louder voice, "Aren't these little flowers pretty? Oh, do come and look, Mama."

That evening I sat pretending to read a book, while Aunt Isola busied herself with embroidery and Bernardino spent his time gazing sheepishly at me. I found it hard to believe that Richard was behaving here as he had done in Wealdhurst. But perhaps he was seeking the company of other women because I had not responded to him while Lucian Farrel still gripped the fibers of my being.

And there my thoughts took an abrupt turn, for I realized that something very strange had happened. For weeks past I had set a barrier in my mind against thinking of Lucian. I would not let myself dwell on any memories of him, for I had resentfully known that even to remember the touch of his hand could still send the blood to my head. But now something had changed.

Cautiously I let myself picture Lucian. I put my hands to my cheeks, and they felt cool. More boldly then, I recalled the moments in the studio when he had kneaded life back into my numbed fingers. No painful longing stirred within me and no fire touched my blood. I was free, and in my joy I could have taken the book that lay in my lap and tossed it into the air. I had suffered the puppy love that was a common torment of the young, and now it was over.

My main concern now was that Mr. and Mrs. Morton should not learn of Richard's escapades. I felt they were much less likely to do so when he was away in Oxford than when he was here with them in Venice or under their roof at Meadhaven. It was with this thought that I eased my anxiety and made the most of my remaining time in Venice, exploring the city with Bernardino as an almost silent companion and Ugo as my guide.

Two days before our departure, we had just finished dinner when Uncle Guido said, "Isola, my dear, I should like you and Bernardino to withdraw for a short while. There is a matter I wish to discuss with Caterina."

"Of course, Guido," Aunt Isola said, looking quite nervous as she rose quickly from her chair. "Come, Bernardino."

When they had left, Uncle Guido took a slip of paper from his pocket and passed it to me. "Will you look at that please, Caterina?"

A few words were scribbled on it in Richard's handwriting, and I felt myself go white as I read them. "It . . . it says he owes seven thousand *pounds!*" I whispered. "But he can't! It's not possible!"

Uncle Guido took the paper back and looked at it, pursing his lips. "I'm afraid it's true," he said, and shook his head regretfully. "It is what you would call an IOU in English, I believe."

"But I can't believe it! How could he owe anybody so much money?"

Uncle Guido looked surprised. "It is a gambling debt, my dear. And there is no doubt about it, I assure you. I saw him write this note out at the card table myself."

My head whirled. "*You* saw? Then *you* must have taken him gambling? At night? And without his parents knowing?" I was trembling with shock as I spoke. "Oh, how could you do such a thing?"

He looked puzzled. "What are you saying, Caterina? Here, we expect our young men to indulge in the excitements which attract all young men. But it is not for the father to encourage the son. It would be for one of the father's friends, a man of the father's own age, to be the young man's companion and preceptor." He shrugged. "In discreetly showing Richard the hidden entertainments of Venice, I have only followed our customs."

"Surely you should have protected him from himself?" I cried.

Uncle Guido sighed. "I assure you that when a rash and confident young man, befuddled by wine, keeps doubling the stakes to regain what he has lost, he can soon achieve a debt of seven thousand pounds."

I sat stunned with horror. "You should have stopped him," I whispered.

For a moment Uncle Guido's voice held a note of anger. "You speak without knowledge, Caterina. There is a limit to the advice that one gentleman may give to another without it becoming a serious insult."

Seven thousand pounds! It was a huge sum. All Meadhaven could not have cost so much. For Mr. Morton even to hear of this affair would be appalling. Something flickered in my mind. In less than a year *I* would be rich. I looked at Uncle Guido with sudden hope. "Was the money lost to one of your friends?"

"To an acquaintance, rather, one who lives by gambling."

"Would he wait for a year if he was paid extra money?"

Uncle Guido shook his head. "The note promised repayment within one month. Lazoni will not wait. That is not the way of a gambler."

My hopes slumped, then rose dizzily again as he added slowly, "But Lazoni is no longer the creditor. I paid the debt this morning."

I gasped. "You *paid* it?" I ran round the table to him, full of gratitude and relief. "Oh, thank heavens . . . I was so afraid . . . I mean, about Mr. Morton finding out and having to pay Richard's debt. I'll repay you myself, Uncle Guido, I promise I will, as soon as I'm twenty-one."

He sat twisting the note in his fingers, then slowly tore it to pieces. "It is done with. I do not want you to pay the debt, Caterina."

"But how else can I repay you for saving Richard?"

He turned to look at me, a sad smile on his lips. "I will be truthful with you, Caterina," he said. "I would never pay the boy's debt simply from kindness of heart. I paid his debt because I thought it might help me in striving for my son's happiness." He raised a hand reassuringly. "Have no fear that I would compel you in any way, Caterina. To convince you of that, I have destroyed the note. I can only hope that if you truly wish to repay me you will stay here with us until the end of the year."

Elation drained from me, and I struggled to hide my feelings. My thoughts ran round and round like little caged creatures as I sought some way of escape, some excuse for refusing, but beneath my confusion I knew with sinking heart that there was only one answer I could give.

I managed to smile and said, "I'll stay, Uncle Guido. And thank you, with all my heart."

He stood up and put a hand on my shoulder. "Thank you, dear Caterina." He made a wry grimace. "I am afraid we cannot tell Mr. Morton the reason that you are staying on with us. That would never do."

"No," I said hastily, and then it came home to me that another ordeal lay ahead. The sadness that pierced me was like a physical pain. "No . . . I can't tell him the truth," I went on heavily, "and there's no excuse I can make. I can only say . . . that I don't want to go home."

The distress I felt at having to stay on in Venice for so many months was nothing compared with the distress that came from knowing how much I should hurt Mr. Morton. On the day before their return to England the Mortons came to dine at the *palazzo*, a farewell dinner. At table, Mr. Morton and Uncle Guido were in a very happy mood. Mrs. Morton had become far less fluttery than I had ever known her. Sarah was ecstatic about the holiday but seemed excited to be returning home. Richard was withdrawn, watching Uncle Guido with a curious, wondering look. I knew Uncle Guido had taken him aside before dinner and told him that the debt had been cleared. No doubt Richard was dazed by his good fortune and wondering at Uncle Guido's generosity.

When we were all together in the drawing room later, I summoned up my courage to speak, but Uncle Guido forestalled me.

"I hope you will have a very comfortable journey home," he said, smiling at the Mortons. "Please do not worry about Caterina. She will be cared for in every way, and she will write to you frequently, of course."

A startled silence fell on the room. Then Mr. Morton said, "I don't understand. We've always assumed that Cadi would return with us."

Uncle Guido looked embarrassed. "Oh!" he exclaimed. "Please forgive me if there has been some misunderstanding. It is for Caterina to tell you what she wishes to do, as I am sure you will agree."

I saw Mr. Morton relax, and his eyes twinkled as he turned his head to gaze across the room at me. "Well, Cadi?" he asked.

I looked at Mr. Morton as I spoke, and I think this was the most difficult thing I had ever had to make myself do. "I'd like to stay for a while, Mr. Morton," I said, and was amazed that my voice sounded quite calm. "Perhaps until the end of the year."

CHAPTER NINE

ALL EYES WERE ON me now, and there was that intensity of silence which follows a thunderclap.

"You . . . wish to stay?" Mr. Morton said at last. He blinked and rubbed his brow in agitation.

I felt a traitress as I answered, "Please don't be offended, Mr. Morton, but I want to be with my real family for a while."

I had expected squeals of protest from Sarah, but she simply sat watching me with a shrewd, thoughtful look. After one startled glance Richard gripped his knees with his hands and stared down at the floor. His face was very pale. Mrs. Morton waved her hands in vague distress.

"Of course we understand," Mr. Morton said at last in an uncertain voice. "The decision is entirely yours, Cadi, my dear. I have been foolish to think—" He broke off and drew in a long breath, forcing a smile as he looked at me. Beyond the smile I saw such sadness that I could have wished for the *palazzo* walls to fall in upon me.

"So it is settled," Uncle Guido said pleasantly.

Mr. Morton nodded and everybody tried to continue chatting as before. But the atmosphere was strained to breaking point. It was a relief to me when finally Mr. Morton rose and said quietly, "I think we must take our leave. We have to rise early tomorrow."

As we stood on the steps, with the gondola waiting below, Uncle Guido said, "I shall bring Caterina to see you off tomorrow, of course."

"If you will forgive me," Mr. Morton said politely, "I should prefer to say our good-bys now."

He kissed me, then held me tightly for a moment, and I knew he was telling me that his affection was as strong as ever. I was so shaken by distress that I scarcely remember saying good-by to the others.

When the gondola was swallowed up in darkness, I could only mutter an apology before turning and running into the *palazzo* and up the great staircase to my room, where I threw myself on the bed and wept as I had not wept since my father's death.

Pride made me present myself at breakfast next morning. I was paying the price for what Uncle Guido had done to save Richard, and it would have shamed me to pay grudgingly. I had made up my mind that in the long months ahead I would try to be cheerful.

I found it hard to keep my resolution, for even in the next few days it seemed to me that a different atmosphere pervaded the *palazzo*. Slowly I began to feel that the quietness of Aunt Isola and Bernardino, and their anxiety to please Uncle Guido, arose not from timidity but from fear. It must be my imagination, I thought, for I had never seen Uncle Guido show anger or even annoyance with them. Even worse, I began to imagine that I was being watched. It seemed that except when I went to bed I was never left alone. If I walked out into the gardens, I would find Bernardino strolling behind me, or Aunt Isola, or one of the servants.

Naturally I could not leave the grounds unescorted, and one day when Bernardino could not accompany me on my explorations in Venice I asked if Ugo could serve as my guide. Regretfully Uncle Guido said that this would be a breach of convention. Two days later Ugo was dismissed from the *palazzo*, for impertinence I was told, and so I lost the one person, apart from Uncle Guido himself, with whom I felt reasonably at home.

Even outside the *palazzo*, Venice herself seemed to be changing for me. I began to see that it held much that was menacing and grotesque. In the arcade of the Doges' Palace was a carved column of beasts of prey: a griffin devouring a rat, a wolf with a mutilated bird, a whole tangle of entwined animals gorging in horrid gluttony. On the wall of Santa Maria Formosa was a hideous head, neither man nor beast, with bolting eyes and lolling tongue. I shuddered at the head of Goliath in the Church of San Rocco, and at the writhing souls of Titian's *Last Judgment*.

This was a city with a bright and glorious past, but intertwined with that past were all kinds of cruelty and evil. In Uncle Guido's library I read of the fearsome and secret Council of Ten and Council of Three, who had ruled by terror, spies, assassins, and torturers. I saw for myself the ancient dungeons of the Doges' Palace, and it seemed to me that the dank stones still echoed the groans of victims. But those days were past, I kept telling myself. This was the twentieth century. And then, one night two weeks after the Mortons had left, I came to know that I was not a victim of my own imagination but of a dreadful truth.

Uncle Guido had been away in Padua for two days and was to return late that evening. I had gone to bed early rather than spend another tedious evening with Aunt Isola and Bernardino. The familiar dream came to me, this time in a curiously muddled way. I approached the steps of the *palazzo* in a gondola. I passed along the dark hall and up the staircase. Then I found myself walking along the broad corridor.

There was the door ahead of me, as usual, with the crack of light showing beneath, but on this night it stood ajar. I had never compared my dream with what I now knew as the reality of the *palazzo*'s interior, but I was dimly aware that this was one of the spare bedrooms. I touched the door, and it opened a few inches. Confusion swept me, for now all familiarity ended. I could see, as I looked through the doorway, a dressing table with an ornate mirror. Something moved, and a reflection appeared in the mirror . . . a man, wearing dark trousers, pulling on a white shirt over his head.

In that moment I knew I was awake. My dream had merged with reality. I had walked in my sleep from my bedroom, to stand before this door in my nightdress. Shock ran through me, as if I had been touched by lightning. I could not move; I could only stare through the slightly open door at the mirror. Then the man's head emerged from the neck of the shirt, and I saw that it was Lucian. I was more than startled to see him here. I was terrified by the expression on his face. There was in it none of the mockery that I knew so well, none of the cool humor. I had never in my life seen a face so cold, so hard, so merciless.

With an effort I forced my legs to obey me and backed slowly away. Then I turned and fled on bare feet, down the long corridor to my own room. Crawling under the covers for warmth, slowly I began to seek sensible reasons for what seemed incredible.

Lucian was here. It must be because he had come to do business with Uncle Guido. Perhaps he had been in Padua with him, at the stables, and they had come here to complete their business. But why hadn't Uncle Guido mentioned Lucian's coming? Perhaps he had felt it would make a happy surprise for me to find Lucian here in the morning. But, with the instinct that goes beyond reason, I *knew* that Lucian had come secretly to the *palazzo*. I *knew* that something dark and sinister was growing up around me, and that Lucian was a part of it.

I lit a candle and looked at the little watch that lay on the table. It was well past midnight. It seemed likely that Lucian had been getting ready to join Uncle Guido, who rarely went to bed until the early hours.

Quite suddenly I knew what I was going to do. I was going to creep downstairs and listen to what they were saying. No twinge of shame touched me. Here in this ancient *palazzo* I felt completely alone. There was nobody to help me, nobody I could trust. All my senses were sounding a warning now, and I was afraid. I got out of bed, pulled on my dressing gown, and cautiously opened the door of my room. With pounding heart I went silently along the passage and crept down the stairs.

I could hear the faint sound of their voices in the library. I crouched in the darkness, with my head close to the doors. There came the sound of clinking glass as wine was poured.

"A good wine," said Uncle Guido's voice. "A damn good wine. And we're doing it justice." I could detect a very faint slurring in the words.

Lucian laughed lazily. "Did you think me a namby-pamby young fool like Richard?"

"I may have done, for I have let you outbargain me over the horses."

"Ah, come now, Chiavelli. I'm giving you a year to pay. God knows why I'm being so generous."

"Generous?" Uncle Guido chuckled. "You are a rogue, Farrel."

"We're two of a kind, my friend." Lucian's voice sounded heavy from the wine also. "You're mortgaged to the hilt, and I might never get paid."

"You will be paid," Uncle Guido said. "Never fear."

"I'd have less fear if my dear little adopted cousin wasn't going to collect the Chiavelli fortune you've been counting on. If it was my fortune," he said with a tinge of contempt, "I'd not let some girl from nowhere take it from me."

"The law is on her side, so how would you prevent her?"

"Damn the law." Lucian laughed brusquely. "I'd deal with her the same way somebody dealt with her grandmother fifty years ago."

A chill of horror, sharp as a knife, reached into the marrow of my bones. I had once suspected Lucian of trying to injure me, not deliberately perhaps, but because his mind was unsound. This cold-blooded suggestion, casually made, was something quite different.

Uncle Guido did not seem to be shocked. He said slowly, "I will tell you something, Farrel. A secret that my grandmother, Marguerita, told me on her deathbed." He gave an admiring chuckle. "Ah, she was a real Venetian, that one. Dark and dangerous."

"What secret?" Lucian did not sound much interested.

"It was Marguerita who got rid of her," Uncle Guido said dreamily, the slurring of his words very marked now. "Took her to Naples and hired footpads to kill her and drop her in the bay. Caterina would have had the fortune when her father died . . . but Marguerita wanted it for herself . . . and she got what she wanted."

I heard Lucian laugh. "Not the fortune, Chiavelli. Only the income from it. But it was a good try, and I'm not greatly surprised. It's all there in her face, in that portrait. I can always spot my own kind."

"I have told you between these four walls," Uncle Guido said with a touch of unease.

"You needn't fear I'll give away your secret," Lucian said scornfully. "Besides, I admire her, Chiavelli. She knew damn well that if you don't help yourself in this world, nobody else is going to help you."

When Uncle Guido spoke again it was as if something in Lucian's contemptuous manner had goaded him. "You think I lack Marguerita's courage?" he said in a low voice. "You think I will let that child snatch a fortune from me when I am in debt to my ears? You are wrong, Farrel. From the day I learned she was alive, I knew something had to be done—" He broke off and muttered, "I am talking too much."

Lucian grunted. "If you're afraid to talk, I'm not—so between these walls I'll say this. She means nothing to me, that girl. When I heard she was going to be rich, I tried to marry her, but my dear Uncle Edward put a stop to that. So I've nothing to gain from her . . ." He paused before adding, "Except through your plans, perhaps."

"How do you know I have any plans?"

"If you haven't, you're a fool," Lucian said with scorn. "Let's forget about it and talk of horses."

"No, wait." After a few moments Uncle Guido said, "I will tell you this. I hope to keep control of the fortune by marrying her to Bernardino."

Lucian laughed, and I heard him splutter as if he had choked on the wine. "She'll never marry *him*," he said. "I don't know the boy, but you've told me yourself that he's an empty fool. Cadi won't marry that kind."

"They are thrown together a great deal," Uncle Guido said, as if trying to convince himself, "and I have schooled Bernardino in what he must do. He has six months to make himself acceptable to her."

"He could have six years and he'd not succeed," Lucian said bluntly.

611

"But her feelings are easy to play upon," Uncle Guido said. "She wanted to go home, but agreed to stay. Do you know why?"

"No. It puzzled me."

"I worked through Richard. Took the boy out gambling and wenching— and put him seven thousand pounds in debt. Then I bought his promissory note, to save him from disgrace, and told Caterina. She agreed to stay from gratitude toward me."

"Where the devil did you raise seven thousand?"

"The note cost me only one hundred. I hired Lazoni, who is a professional cardsharper, for the task."

Lucian laughed again, but this time there was a note of respect in it. "Yes . . . I can see that would touch Cadi's loyal little heart. But all the same, she won't marry Bernardino. In six months she'll come home, and soon after that she'll be twenty-one. Then you'll lose everything."

"No," Uncle Guido said very quietly. "If I can see in a month or two that Bernardino has no chance, then . . ."

"Then what? Get rid of her?"

"You were going to suggest something after I had told you my plans, Farrel. Well?"

"I'll do it for one-fifth of the fortune," Lucian said softly. "If she has an accident while she's in your care, there'll be suspicion."

"I have provided against that. Why do you think I wrote those letters, full of affection and welcome? Morton and the lawyers believe I am the most generous of men. And here in Venice, everyone knows that I have lavished affection on the girl."

"There'll still be suspicion if anything happens to her while she's in your charge." Lucian's voice was positive. "You stand to gain too much."

My mouth was dry and there was sickness in my throat as I crouched against the door, dazed by the hideous knowledge that I was listening to these two men discussing my death. All the darkest traditions of Venice lay in their conversation.

"A little suspicion will not trouble me," Uncle Guido said, but I could hear doubt in his voice.

"It will be the second time in three generations. You don't want to have a shadow hanging over your family, Chiavelli."

A long silence, then Uncle Guido said, "There may be something in what you say. What is in your mind, Farrel?"

"Cadi doesn't know we've met. I'll be gone early, before she's awake, just as you wanted. But I'll come back openly—in a month's time, let's say."

"And when you come back openly?"

"Why, Cadi will be delighted to see me. I can take her out and about, sailing or riding. But whatever happens, she'll be under *my* care when the accident happens."

"The . . . accident?"

"Yes. We don't want another mysterious disappearance. I'll have ample time to arrange something convincing. But above all, it will happen while she's in *my* care, not yours. Then there'll be no breath of suspicion."

Uncle Guido said in a thick voice, "You're a cold-blooded rogue, Farrel. You'd have done well in Venice in the old days."

"I hope to do well in the present," Lucian said. "One-fifth of the fortune. That leaves plenty for you."

"I have not made up my mind yet," Uncle Guido said. I guessed that he knew the wine was affecting him, and wanted to have a clear head when it came to making a decision. "But in any case, your price is too high. One-tenth is enough. Twenty-five thousand sovereigns."

"Forty thousand."

"Thirty thousand, or you can go to the devil, Farrel."

I could bear no more. Strange though it may seem, this dreadful bargaining sickened me more horribly than all that had gone before. I turned blindly away and crept slowly along the passage and up the stairs.

Two minutes later I lay in bed in the darkness, my mind reeling.

I was in danger of my life. I must escape. But how? And where to? I had no friends in Venice. If I ran to a policeman in the streets and told him my uncle was planning to kill me, he would think me mad and I would be taken back to the *palazzo*.

A month, Lucian had said. *I could write to Mr. Morton!* The hope died as it was born. Uncle Guido always took my letters to post them. I could be sure he opened them carefully and read them first. I must plan to escape on my own. A boat. There was a dinghy moored with the gondolas, and it carried a sail for use out in the lagoon. Down the coast, twenty miles, thirty—as far as the wind would take me by night. And then? Find a fishing village. Yes, I was a fisherman's daughter and could talk with my own kind. Like Mawstonefolk, they would listen, and somebody would take me in. There I could stay hidden and write to Mr. Morton.

Toward dawn I must have dozed for a while, for I opened my eyes to bright sunshine as Maria, a maid, drew back my curtains.

"I think I have a chill, Maria," I said. "Will you tell the countess, please, and ask her if I may stay in bed today?"

In the days to come I would have to act a part very carefully. I needed time to prepare myself, so that when I faced Uncle Guido and his family I would appear friendly and at ease with them. I was no actress, but my life depended on this.

After dinner that evening Uncle Guido called to see me in my room with Aunt Isola. I smiled, and apologized for being a nuisance, and kept gazing straight at his face. In the end it was Uncle Guido who averted his eyes. As I had expected, nothing was said of Lucian's brief visit.

The next morning I got up, saying that my chill had passed, and began to prepare for my escape. For several days I now hoarded bread and biscuits and sweetmeats from the afternoon tea I took in my room as I sketched the view from my window. I studied the atlas in Uncle Guido's library, trying to plan where I would land on the Italian coast.

Above all, I spent much time testing how well the *palazzo* was guarded. I knew from the beginning that my escape would have to be made after dark, and so I spent an hour or two after the rest of the household had gone to bed, studying the grounds from the downstairs windows. To my dismay I found that from nightfall to sunrise there was a man patrolling the grounds with a big mastiff. I could only guess that he and his dog had been hired by Uncle Guido on the pretext of guarding the *palazzo* against thieves.

I also discovered that at night the great iron gates at the front of the *palazzo* were closed and locked. Somehow I would have to open the gate or climb the tall railings which surrounded the grounds.

In Uncle Guido's library was a paperweight of Venetian glass, with a small compass set in it. I planned to steal that on the night I escaped. I had no money of my own, so I also intended to steal anything small but of some value when the time came, so that I would not be completely penniless. I felt no shame at such plans, for each day I woke with the same sure and dreadful knowledge that I stood between Uncle Guido and a fortune he was determined to have.

I did not allow myself to think of Lucian. I knew him now for what he was. If I let myself remember the past, the day of Mogg Race, the day of the summer ball when I had danced with him, the day in the studio when I had been shaken by the sweet agony of first love, the contrast would have been too horrible to bear.

Ten days went by, and I sat one afternoon by the rock garden at the rear of the *palazzo*, sketching the houses on the far side of the narrow canal. I had little skill for this, but it served as an excuse to spend time in the grounds while I studied ways of escape.

A small wrought-iron door was set in the tall railings at the back of the *palazzo*, and I was studying it as I sketched. Alfredo, the gardener, was only thirty paces away, keeping watch on me as he worked.

I was in a mood of black despair, and gazed almost unseeingly at a small boat making its way past the *palazzo*. It carried a mast, but the sail was not raised, for the canals were far too narrow for any maneuvers. A man was at the oars, pulling slowly. He wore a shabby black hat with a floppy brim, and a worn dark jacket. Then a small stone fell close to my feet, and I saw through the railings that the boatman was resting for a moment only ten yards away from me. Nobody else could have thrown the stone. He lifted his head and removed his hat. Every fiber of my body went taut as I saw the brilliant violet eyes that were now staring at me.

It was Richard.

He put a finger quickly to his lips and darted a glance beyond me. It was clear that he knew somebody was guarding me. Next moment he made a small circular movement with his hand, then held it up with his five fingers widely splayed. He replaced the hat on his head, the floppy brim hiding his face again, and rowed slowly on along the canal.

HOPE AND EXCITEMENT raced through me like fire. Richard was here! And he must know I was in danger—his furtive manner made that clear. How he came to be here I could not guess. I struggled to thrust aside the questions that tumbled about in my head. What had his signal meant? A circular movement of the hand, then five splayed fingers.

I gathered my wits. He did not dare to approach, so he would come back after circling round the *palazzo*. The splayed fingers meant . . . at five o'clock? No, that was two hours away. Five minutes, then. That must be it. In five minutes I had to be ready to pass a message to him.

My sketch pad lay on my knees, and I tore a strip from it.

I made up my mind that I must escape tonight. And, since he did not know the exact situation in the *palazzo*, it was up to me to take the initiative. I scribbled: "At this spot tonight, two a.m. Have sail ready to hoist, and two spare oars. Take care. Very dangerous. My love to you."

I wrapped the scrap of paper round the stone and waited. Two unending minutes passed, and then I saw Richard's muffled figure again, pulling slowly down the canal. As he came level with me I threw the wrapped stone between two of the railings. It hit the water just short of the boat, but, though the stone sank, the paper floated clear. In a flash Richard had reached over and scooped it up. Then he was pulling steadily along the canal once more, hunched over the oars.

I felt weak with relief. I was no longer alone.

Now questions flooded into my mind again. How had Richard known I was in danger? Had he come back to Venice on his own? Had he never left Venice? He should have been at Oxford for the past two weeks at least. Was Mr. Morton in Venice? My heart jumped with the thought, but after a moment I reluctantly decided that this could not be so. If Mr. Morton were here, if he knew the truth, he would have marched into the *palazzo* and confronted Uncle Guido.

Only one thing was important at this moment—I had to find a way past those high stout railings, whether through them or over them. It was half an hour before I found what I thought was a solution to that problem.

For the rest of that day, I set myself out to appear happy and at ease. I must have been convincing, for after dinner Uncle Guido patted me on the shoulder and said how glad he was that I had settled down happily. He glanced at Bernardino, then back at me with a questioning smile. I returned the smile, then looked quickly down as if embarrassed, which was the best I could do in the way of response to his unspoken question.

At one o'clock in the morning I was warmly dressed, wearing my riding breeches and with woolen socks pulled on over my shoes to muffle any sound. My hair was plaited in pigtails. My little hoard of food and water, together with the paperweight compass and a silver snuffbox, were all tied in a blanket.

From a spare room which looked out over the front of the *palazzo* I saw Uncle Guido return from his evening pleasures. The night guard, dog at heel, locked the big gates after him. I stole back to my room and lay in bed, just in case he might peer in to make sure I was there.

I must have looked at my watch a hundred times before the moment came at last when I could creep down the great staircase. Every stair seemed to creak and groan, as if trying to cry out a warning to their master. Reaching the kitchen, I fumbled with the bolts of the door which opened onto the grounds at the rear of the *palazzo* and slowly opened the door. Swirling ribbons of mist hung in the night air, drifting in the gentle breeze.

I strained my eyes, watching for the guard and his mastiff to pass along the railings on their rounds. Ten minutes crept by. Then, through the shreds of mist, I saw them moving slowly past the rock gardens. I eased the door to, afraid that the dog might scent me. When I opened it again, they had gone. I drew a shaky breath and ran for the wrought-iron gate, which was locked for the night with a big padlock and heavy chain.

I set down my bundle and peered through the iron curlicues of the gate. The canal was empty. Despair rose like sickness in my throat, and I gripped the cold damp iron feverishly. A shadow moved. A boat took shape as it slid from the misty darkness of the far bank. I almost sobbed with relief. The boat touched the wall below me, and Richard's face looked up.

"An oar," I whispered urgently. "Pass me an oar."

He looked startled but obeyed, passing up the oar between the bars of the gate. I slid the oar beneath the bottom of the gate and levered upward with all my strength. The hinges groaned faintly as they began to come clear of the butts on which they turned. I could see the gate lifting. An inch . . . two inches. I thrust forward. The gate wavered. Then, with its hinges free, it fell away from me, the chain holding it on the padlock side so that it swung round to hit the railings with a great clangor that seemed to echo over all Venice.

For a frightful second I stood petrified, and then, even as the sound still rang through the darkness, I threw the oar down to Richard, snatched up my bundle, and slithered down the steep wet slope of the canal wall to fall in a heap in the boat.

I heard the deep bark of the mastiff, and a man's voice shouting. I threw myself onto the bow thwart. "Oars!" I croaked desperately. The

oars hung in the oarlocks there, and Richard was slipping the spare oars into the midship oarlocks.

"Just pull!" I whispered fiercely. "I'll steer." That was why I had taken the bow position myself, for I would have to keep looking over my shoulder to steer, and I had far more experience of boats than Richard. "Give way now," I said, and next moment we were gliding into the shifting mist. I was looking for the turn into a branch canal close by. As we made it I heard furious barking, and a man's voice raised in an urgent cry which held a note of fear. *"Chiama il conte!"*—"Call the count!"

At last we emerged from the network of minor canals I had chosen for our escape route, to strike the Grand Canal well above the Rialto Bridge. On the far side of it lay a canal which would take us into the lagoon north of Venice. Tonight the breeze was blowing gently from the southwest, and so I had chosen to head northeast, out past the islands of Murano and Torcello, to seek a fishing village on the mainland near Portegrandi.

We slid out from the canal into open water, where we shipped our oars and hoisted the sail. It flapped, then caught the faint breeze. I sat at the tiller with Richard in front of me, his hand on the mainsheet. He spoke for the first time. "Are we moving, Cadi? It feels very slow."

"It's a little quicker than it feels. Better to save our strength for the oars in case the wind drops. Besides, they don't know where to look for us." My heart went out to him suddenly, and I was close to tears as I said, "Oh, thank God you came, Richard. I'd almost lost hope."

He smiled, taking off his broad-brimmed hat, and even in the gray darkness I could see a whole world of happiness in his face. I rummaged in my blanket bundle for the paperweight compass, and passed it to him. "We have to head northeast. Can you see the needle?"

He nodded. "Just, if I hold it close."

"Keep me on course. Richard, are you on your own here? Did nobody come with you?"

"I'm on my own, Cadi. I've been staying at a back-street hotel for three days, rowing past the *palazzo* half a dozen times a day, trying to see you."

"But . . . how did you know I was in danger?"

He turned his head sharply. "I was right, then?"

"Yes." I shivered. "Uncle Guido wants me dead before I'm twenty-one, so he can have all the money." I had to force the next words out. "Lucian was going to . . . to see to it for him."

"Lucian? But that *can't* be so, Cadi."

"I heard him offer to make sure I had an accident. You were right, Richard," I went on wearily. "You once told me his mind was blemished. It's worse than that. This wasn't some wild act that he did without knowing it. This was something he offered to do for money." My voice broke. "I heard them . . . bargaining."

Richard stared down at the compass. "Port a little, Cadi," he said.

"Port," I repeated dully. My ecstasy at winning free had passed, corroded by bitter memories. "How did you know, Richard?" I asked at last.

"I didn't know about Lucian," he said in a low voice. "It was Sarah who opened my eyes to the count. She had the sense to guess there was something wrong when you decided to stay in Venice. The rest of us were troubled . . . hurt, but she knew you thought of us as your family. She knew something or somebody was *making* you stay."

Dear, wonderful Sarah, the silly one of the family, whose simple belief in me had proved wiser than all the puzzled wonderings of the others.

"She said as much on the train home," Richard went on, his head still bowed over the compass. "But we all shushed her. Then, just over a week ago, she wrote me a letter in Oxford. She said she *knew* you wanted to be with us and asked if I'd got into any scrapes in Venice, because perhaps you were doing this for *my* sake."

He raised his head and looked at me squarely. "Then I knew, Cadi. Everything fell into place." His face was stony with self-contempt. His soft speech and withdrawn manner had gone. There was strength and purpose in him, and the courage to meet my gaze. "Seven thousand pounds. I must have been mad as well as drunk. But I thought if I made a lot of money like that, I'd have been in a position to marry"—he smiled briefly, without bitterness—"if you ever came to love me, Cadi. But I lost. It was a stupid dream. I know that now. And then, on our last day in Venice, the count took me aside and said he'd paid the note for me, to save me from disgrace." Again I saw self-contempt in the twist of Richard's lips. "I was so grateful, so desperately grateful. It makes me sick to remember it."

"He cheated you," I said. "He hired a cardsharper to cheat you."

"Yes. I guessed the swine had done something like that," Richard said with harsh savagery. "When I read Sarah's letter I guessed everything. I knew that the count wasn't generous; I'd seen him at the card tables. He's greedy and ruthless. That meant somebody else had persuaded him to help me—at a price. And it could only be you, Cadi."

"Except that I didn't have to persuade him. It was all planned to make me stay here out of gratitude."

Richard muttered an oath. "I asked myself *why* he'd made you stay. And as soon as I'd asked the question I knew the answer. He wanted the estate. He'd expected it all his life. Now *you* stood in his way, and to have what he wanted he had to get rid of you." I saw his mouth set in a hard line. "I was frightened to death for you, Cadi," he said in a low fierce voice. "I remembered what had happened to your grandmother."

"So you came?"

"I came." He nodded grimly. "It was no good speaking to Father. He wouldn't have believed me. So I borrowed some money in Oxford and came here to take you away. Nobody knows yet." He shrugged. "Well, I suppose Mother and Father know I'm missing from Oxford by now, but they don't know where I am." He looked at me. "I didn't realize you knew of your own danger. There was a note wrapped round that stone I threw to you, but it came off and fell in the canal." His lips thinned in a humorless smile. "At least you're not alone now, and that's something."

"Oh, Richard . . ." I groped for words to thank him, but they all seemed too small and clumsy. Then the boat shuddered faintly, and a jar ran through her timbers.

Richard stared at me. "What was that?"

"We're aground on a mudbank, I think. The lagoon's full of shallows. See if you can push her off with an oar."

I was too optimistic. It was ten minutes later, and we were knee-deep in mud, before we managed to heave the bow free and drag ourselves into the boat again. But that was only the first of our disasters. I had not realized the true nature of the Venetian lagoon. Its shallows, mudbanks, and reedy patches made it half land rather than true water.

If I could have seen the tall stakes marking out the channels which criss-crossed the great lagoon, I might have navigated with more success, but the darkness and mist were my enemies now. Three times in an hour we found ourselves stranded on a mudbank, and on the third occasion Richard let slip the compass as we struggled to thrust the boat free. We were soaked to the thighs and caked in mud to our knees. The sail had long since been lowered, and we had taken to the oars. It seemed likely that we would grope our weary way from mudbank to mudbank until the dawn left us in full view of every boat Uncle Guido could muster to search for us.

Suddenly a shattering thought struck me. "Oh, I've done an awful thing, Richard. I drew maps of the canals and traced two routes. I had the map beside my bed tonight, studying it while I was waiting . . . *and I left it there, Richard!* Uncle Guido's bound to find it!"

Richard wiped his face on the sleeve of his jacket, leaving a smear of mud. "Let's just carry on, Cadi. If we could find one of the little islands, we might be able to hide there during the day in a patch of reeds. Then we could make for the mainland tomorrow night."

My hopes rose again. We blundered on slowly for a while, and then I felt a new coldness on my cheek. A breeze was beginning to blow. With luck it would help us. "Get the sail up, Richard," I said. "The breeze may roll this mist back long enough for us to spot one of the islands."

As soon as the sail was up I turned the boat into the wind. The mist rolled across us under the thrust of the breeze. Quite suddenly we were bathed in moonlight, and eighty yards away I glimpsed a line of stakes curving away to our starboard quarter. To one side of the line, still partly hidden by mist, I caught the shadowy outline of land rising from the water.

"Starboard oar, Richard. Bring her round."

He heaved on the oar, and the bow came round to point toward the stakes. I felt the wind take the sail. As the dinghy came alive I heard Richard say huskily, "Boats astern, Cadi!"

I threw a glance over my shoulder. Three gondolas and two big rowboats, each with several men aboard, were strung out in a line. The nearest was no more than forty paces from us. The gondolas were Chiavelli craft, and I knew that Uncle Guido had found the map I had so stupidly left.

"They're stuck," Richard said, and I saw that two men from the rowboat nearest to us were knee-deep in the water. A man in the boat stood staring in our direction. In the clear bright moonlight I recognized the figure of Uncle Guido. He appeared to be pointing at us. I heard a sharp report, as if one of his men had broken an oar in trying to free the boat. And then I saw something which brought me new hope. Beyond the line of boats, which were spread out like beaters on a hunt, a tall gray cliff of mist was rolling toward us. Already it hid the last gondola in the line. Uncle Guido's boats and men were being engulfed.

We were still moving at a good five knots and I could see the stakes jutting from the water close ahead of us. I stared ahead, trying to burn into my mind a picture of the line, knowing that in another few seconds the rolling mist would hide them from my sight.

"There's an island close by," I said in a low voice. "I think I can hold the course for it, Richard."

He muttered something I could not catch. I was busy now, watching the curving line of stakes as we crept along. If my judgment was right, it led to the island I had glimpsed.

With a faint rustling sound, the bow drove into tall reeds. "Sail down!" I whispered urgently, but Richard sat unmoving as we slithered to a halt. I left the tiller and ran the sail down. "It's one of the little islands!" I said, leaning to speak close to his ear. "I saw it when the mist cleared for those few moments just now. Come *on*, Richard, don't just sit there!"

He lifted his head, and the whiteness of his mud-smeared face in the darkness frightened me. "You go on, Cadi," he whispered hoarsely. "I'm hurt. When the count fired. He missed you . . . but hit me."

I sank to the thwart beside him. Now I remembered the sound I had thought to be the snapping of an oar. It had been a pistol shot.

"Where did it hit you?" I whispered.

He moved his head in a downward nod. "Somewhere in the side of my chest . . . the ribs."

"Richard . . ." I took his face between my hands and felt tears pouring down my cheeks.

"Don't cry, Cadi. Don't cry."

With huge effort I pulled myself together. "Can you move, Richard? Can you get ashore if I help? I've got to find shelter for you and fetch help."

He nodded, his teeth chattering. "See if you can find shelter, Cadi. But don't call out for help. If the count finds us, he'll kill us both."

With sick despair I realized that Richard spoke the truth. My instinct had been to surrender, so that he could be taken to a doctor as quickly as possible. But Uncle Guido was desperate. If he caught us, we would die.

"I'll be as quick as I can," I said. I climbed out of the boat and plodded through the soft mud. When I found dry ground beneath my feet, I took off the mud-caked socks I wore over my shoes and put them down to mark the point where I would have to reenter the reeds to find Richard again. Then I moved on slowly through a straggle of low bushes.

The mist grew thinner. Suddenly ahead of me I could see a huddle of stone buildings, and from the largest of them rose a smoking chimney. I realized then that this was the tiny island near Murano which held Uncle Guido's glass foundry. The glassworkers came daily by boat, but a watchman stayed the night to keep the furnaces stoked.

I drew back a little. I dared not risk being seen by him. Standing there in my sodden breeches, I searched my memories of that day I had spent on the island. After watching the glassworkers I had strolled round the shore with Sarah. On the eastern side, to my right now, there was an old landing stage, I recalled, and near it an abandoned stone hut.

Five minutes later I had found the hut. The ancient wooden door was unlocked. Groping about inside, I found only bare earth and a pile of old canvas which had once been sails.

Richard had not stirred when I waded back through the reeds to the boat. I took my bundle in one hand and put my free arm about his waist, so that he could lean on me as we moved slowly up the mudbank to the shore. Twice we had to stop and rest, but at last we reached the hut.

"There's some canvas somewhere," I whispered. "Yes, here. Come lie down." I had thought to bandage his wound, but with the door closed, there was not even a gleam of light in the hut.

"Cadi . . ." Richard's voice was husky. "There's a little lantern and matches from the boat's locker. I put them in your bundle while you were gone." I untied the blanket. When I had found a match dry enough to strike, I saw that the lantern was of the unspillable kind. I lit the wick, and that yellow glow of light was like a blessing.

Now I eased Richard's clothes from his body to examine his wound. It was small and not bleeding heavily, but all around it a huge bruise spread over the ribs. I was very much aware that it might be more serious than it looked. I pulled my petticoat out from the waist of my breeches and tore off some wide strips to make a pad to place over the wound. Next I had to help Richard sit up while I bound strips round his chest to hold the pad in place. Before he lay back again, I spread my topcoat beneath him, and then covered him with the blanket. After that I fed him some of the biscuits and gave him small sips of water.

Richard lay looking at the lamp for a while as I knelt beside him, then he turned his head toward me and said slowly, "Hold my hand while I tell you something, Cadi."

I gripped his cold hand. "Don't talk, Richard, dear. Try to sleep."

"I have to tell you, Cadi. I have to tell you why Lucian whipped me that night. It was because . . . because I tampered with your bridle that day when the ring snapped." Without taking his eyes from my face he went on. "Don't hate me, Cadi. I hate myself so much."

"I'll never hate you," I managed to say at last. "But *why*, Richard? Why did you do it?"

He moved his shoulders slightly and closed his eyes. "I don't know. I've done things like that before. My brother James, he died long before you came to us. It was my doing, Cadi. I did something to the safety catch of his gun, so that when the catch was on it didn't really work." Tears squeezed from beneath his eyelids. "I didn't mean to hurt him, Cadi. It was just . . . an experiment. He tripped, and when the gun went off it killed him." He opened his eyes again, and I saw pain in them. "When Father and Lucian examined the gun and found out what had been done to it, they knew it must be me. I think my mother knows, but she would never let herself believe it. And then . . . then I did another thing when we were on holiday in Bosney. The rudder pintle . . ."

I remembered the way Lucian and Mr. Morton had looked at each other on the Mawstone quay. They had known who had sawed the pintle halfway through.

"It always goes wrong," Richard said, his voice anguished. "I couldn't know James would trip and fall, or that the pintle would break." He turned his head to look at me. "Or that Pompey would be going at a gallop when the ring snapped, and that he'd bolt with you."

Reproach was useless. His need now was for comfort. "Of course you couldn't know," I said, fighting to keep the horror from my eyes.

"All those things . . . they were experiments, really," he said. He shook his head slightly. "Sometimes a strange thing comes over me, and I'm tempted. It's like gambling, Cadi, to see what will happen. I have to do these things to see . . . well, to see how they turn out. Can you understand? I don't mean to harm anyone."

I knew now why Lucian had examined the ring more closely. He had known the truth.

"That's why Lucian beat me," Richard said, as if he had been following my thoughts. "Father had talked to me before about . . . about doing things that might harm somebody. That was after James's accident. He couldn't understand that I hadn't really meant anything bad to happen. But when"

623

—his voice faltered—"but when that thing happened to *you*, Cadi, then Lucian must have decided talking was no use. He flogged me, and threatened worse if I ever made any more . . . experiments."

"He must have been afraid for himself, then," I said bitterly. "Not for me. He's the man I heard offer to kill me for money."

Richard closed his eyes again and whispered, "Will you forgive me, Cadi? I love you so much."

"Of course I forgive you," I said quickly, and bent to kiss his muddy cheek. "When this is all over, you won't make any more experiments."

He nodded feebly, and a smile touched his pallid lips. "I'm glad I've told you, Cadi. Tomorrow night we'll take the boat and—"

A gasp of dismay broke from me. "The boat!" I said desperately. "We didn't unstep the mast, Richard! It's sticking up from among the reeds for anyone to see. I've got to go back and hide it."

"You can't unstep the mast alone," he said slowly.

"I'll manage. The boat's only in a foot of water and she's very light."

He smiled faintly. "All right, Cadi. You know about these things."

I blew out the lamp and told Richard that I would be back soon. His answer was a mumble, and I saw that exhaustion was pushing him down into sleep. As I made my way toward the shore it seemed to me that the mist was thinner than before. When I reached the muddy slope I peered ahead with sudden unease. I should have been able to see the mast sticking up from where I stood, but there was no sign of it. Then I froze, as if every nerve had turned to ice. A crouched figure, only a few paces away, was moving toward me, a nightmare creature befouled with mud from shoulders to feet. In the milky moonlight, I could see him. It was Lucian.

For a long instant we stared at each other. His brows were a straight line above fierce, urgent eyes, and suddenly I saw his teeth show white against the grime on his face. Breath rushed into my lungs for a shriek. Lucian sprang, and I was thrown to the ground under his weight. The breath was knocked from my body. I knew an instant of pain, bright lights flashed before my eyes, and then darkness struck down upon me like a hammerblow.

CHAPTER TEN

WARMTH. A FAINT SMELL of burning. Something soft beneath me, not a bed, but perhaps a table with blankets spread on it. An aching bruise at the back of my head. Dried mud on my face and arms. A voice, tantalizingly familiar, with a touch of brogue. "She'll give us the edge of her tongue when she wakes. Did you have to knock the senses from her?"

Flynn! The gray-eyed stranger who had saved me in Châlons. My weary mind struggled with the impossibility. I tried to open my eyes, but they would not respond yet.

"She must have bumped her head when she fell." Lucian's voice, calm and rather thoughtful. "I had to stop her screaming out, and there was no time to be polite. Chiavelli and his cutthroats might have heard her." A pause. "How's Richard, Paddy?"

"He's sleeping again now. He'll be better here than in that hut."

A confusion of thoughts stirred in my mind. Chiavelli's *cutthroats?* Why would Lucian speak of them in such a way? And Richard was here. They had carried him from the hut and were anxious for him.

"How the devil did the boy know what was happening?" said Flynn wonderingly. "It put a year on my life when I saw her jump in the boat with him. Never dreamt it was young Morton."

I tried again to open my eyes, and this time the lids moved a fraction. Through a tiny slit I saw that we were in semidarkness and that a bright glow came from the three small open doors of a furnace. We were in the glass foundry, in one of the smaller buildings where special orders were carried out. Richard lay close to the furnace, a blanket over him, sleeping.

I could see Lucian without turning my head. He was scrubbing vigorously at his body with a strip of blanket, trying to clean off the mud, and in the red glow from the furnace I saw a puzzled frown on his face.

"Richard must have guessed somehow that Cadi was in danger," he said. "He came out to rescue her."

"Fools rush in," Flynn said. "Your way was better."

"Only as long as Cadi didn't know what Chiavelli planned for her, only as long as she wasn't frightened—and she *must* have known, Paddy. That's why she escaped. Knowing Chiavelli was out to get rid of her but not knowing there was any chance of help—that's enough to send a girl out of her mind," he added in a tight voice.

"Not this one," said Flynn. "Not Cadi Tregaron."

"I know that," Lucian said quietly. "I've known that since the first day. I told you." He threw the strip of blanket aside and came toward me. "Thank God we were on hand tonight, though." I had barely to move my lids to close my eyes. His hand touched my cheek, then moved to brush the hair gently from my brow.

"Poor little Cadi," Lucian said in the same quiet voice.

I wanted to lie there forever with his hand on my brow and with this great warm joy spreading through me. I knew now that all I had ever suspected of Lucian was wrong, and for the moment nothing else mattered. This was the most wonderful, the most glorious gift I had ever known.

Perhaps my infatuation for Lucian had indeed died in the struggle I had fought against it, for I knew now that real love can spring only from full trust and knowledge of the one who is loved. But it was from the ashes of first love that something much greater had risen, like the new day's sun over the sea. I could feel it living and pulsing within me, a glowing longing to give and to receive, a longing rooted in sure and perfect trust.

"Your jersey's dry," said Flynn. I half opened my eyes and saw Lucian lift his hands to catch a thick dark jersey Flynn had tossed to him. I felt a strange, deep happiness in simply watching the man I loved and hearing him speak. But I did not deceive myself about his feelings for me. I knew now that his conversation with Uncle Guido had been part of a deception to save me. But his manner toward me, when he thought me asleep, had been that of a man to a child, no more. Whatever risks he had taken to help me, he would have taken for anyone he counted as a friend.

"I fancy we'll have company soon," Paddy said. "You got them in a tangle with your pranks, but if Chiavelli has any sense he'll bring his bully-boys ashore to reorganize for the search."

Lucian's voice was grim. "I'll go and watch out for them. You stay here. I don't want Cadi to be frightened when she wakes."

As he turned toward the door I lifted my head and said, "Lucian . . . it's all right, I'm not frightened now." The words came slowly from my tongue. He was beside me in a moment, helping me to sit up on a big workbench.

"Ah, Cadi," he said, as he smiled into my eyes. "That's my girl."

In the glowing red light from the open furnace doors I saw Flynn standing by one of the shuttered windows. He inclined his head in that polite, half-mocking way I knew of old, but there was affection in it now. "Top of the morning to you, Miss Tregaron."

I held on to Lucian's arm to steady myself, as sitting up had made me dizzy for a moment. "Good morning to you, Mr. Flynn."

"I have to go out for a while, little one," Lucian said, and put his hand to my cheek. "But don't worry. You'll be safe with Paddy."

"I know. I know that." I could hardly get the words out. Lucian's manner to me was so gentle, so without reserve or arrogance, that I was suddenly racked by shame as I recalled all that I had believed of him. Words poured from me in a stammering wail. "Oh, Lucian, I have to tell you. I've thought such *awful* things of you. That night when you were with Uncle Guido, I—I heard everything. I thought that you were willing to—to kill me." I put my arms round his neck, laid my head on his chest, and cried silently.

"There now, there," he said, patting my shoulder as he held me. "You weren't to know, Cadi." With enormous relief I heard the note of laughter in his voice and knew that he was not angry.

Flynn chuckled. "If you overheard this feller twisting the truth from your dear uncle, and *didn't* believe him a villain, you'd be a fool, Cadi Tregaron. Dear God, I've watched Lucian at that game a time or two. . . ."

"Shut up, Paddy, or you'll have her doubting me again," Lucian said. I lay in his arms, and suddenly remembered Mr. Morton's words when he had agreed that Lucian was a master of deception: "But it depends upon who is being deceived, and why . . ." Now I began to understand what he had meant.

Lucian put a hand under my chin and tilted my face to look at him. "I've never been false with you, Cadi. I'd not know how to begin."

I could tell him with my eyes that my trust was given now, once and for all. He gave me a quick, reassuring smile, ran a hand over my tangled hair, said, "Little mud lark," then moved to the door and went out.

I got down stiffly from the table. Kneeling down beside Richard, I put a hand on his brow. He felt feverish and his breathing was a little fast, but he did not seem restless in his sleep. "Is there nothing we can do for him, Mr. Flynn?"

"Not until we can get him to a surgeon. And I'll answer to Paddy, if you'll be so kind, Miss Tregaron."

I tucked my legs under me and settled down on the floor close to Richard. "And I'll answer to Cadi, please. Will you tell me what's happening?"

"Where will I begin?"

"I first saw you at Wealdhurst. Why were you there?"

"Ah now. That was a job the captain set me to."

"The captain?"

"Captain Farrel. Lucian. We soldiered together." He looked down at me quizzically. "We were cashiered together."

"Never mind that part, Paddy. Why did he send you to Wealdhurst?"

Paddy Flynn looked down at Richard and shook his head. "He was frightened for you, Cadi. The boy here, he's a little sick in the head, sometimes, you see. It was him that nearly got you killed on Pompey."

"I know. Richard himself told me today. You mean Lucian was afraid of it happening again?"

"Or something like it. I used to watch you by day, and by night I'd prowl the boy's workroom, seeing what he was up to. I was guarding you, as you might say—as best I could."

"But . . . day and night, for all that time! Why was Lucian so concerned over me?"

Paddy smiled, but ignored the question. "It was only meant to be till the boy went back to Oxford, but by then there was something else. You'd become an heiress, Cadi. So Lucian asked me to stay on. He couldn't come and keep guard over you himself, for there'd be too many questions. I'm a man he trusts quite a bit, d'you see."

"Do you mean Lucian suspected Uncle Guido even then?"

Paddy began to fill his pipe. "We knew a little about Count Chiavelli. When buying and selling horses, we'd heard a few rumors in France, Italy, and the Levant. Not the feller we fancied doing business with at all."

"We?"

"I'm Lucian's partner at the stables at Epsom. From what we heard, this feller Chiavelli was up to his ears in money troubles, scraping along on credit because of the fortune that was to come to him in a little while. Then *you* appeared, Cadi. *That* must have been a shock for his nibs. But he didn't fight, he just smiled, and agreed, and wrote those letters. Full of sweetness and charm they were, remember? Mr. Morton was delighted. But not Lucian." Paddy's gray eyes were a little bleak. " 'Paddy,' he says to me when we met in the woods one day, 'can you imagine a Venetian nobleman not caring about losing a fortune unless he was too rich to care? I smell a rat, Paddy, and it scares me. I can't say anything to Uncle Edward, for I've no shred of proof. I've an idea in my head that might bring me to stay at Meadhaven myself to watch over Cadi, but I'm doubtful that it'll work, so she'll be in your hands, Paddy. Meanwhile I'll make a few inquiries of my own about the count.' "

Paddy struck a match and set it to his pipe. "So I stayed. And the time or two you went to town, I was on the same train with you."

"And at Châlons? You traveled with us to guard me?"

Paddy nodded. "I was on the train, prowling the corridors most of the time. And I got a bed for the night in the little café opposite the hotel." He gave me an amused glance. "You're a hard one to guard, Cadi. I never thought you'd be going out from the hotel on your own."

"Uncle Guido sent that man with the iron bar?"

"Your uncle knew you'd be stopping in Châlons. Mr. Morton had written and told him. So he hired a cutthroat there to watch for a chance at you." Paddy shook his head. "I would have been too late but for Sarah rushing across the square in a great fret to tell me you'd gone out."

I could not believe my ears. "Sarah knew you were watching over me?"

His face softened. "Sarah knew. We'd met while I was prowling around Meadhaven, d'you see." He shrugged. "After a while it wasn't by accident we met, and we used to talk quite a bit together. She has a quick enough mind behind that pretty face, and she'd heard my name as Lucian's partner. She guessed I was playing guardian angel for you."

I remembered Sarah going out of the hotel almost as soon as we arrived at Châlons, for a breath of air, so she had said. But she had met Paddy Flynn to learn where he would be staying. My debt to Sarah was becoming greater than I could ever pay.

"She never breathed a word about it, Paddy," I said wonderingly.

"She didn't know the whole of it, and I asked her not to speak. Why frighten you and the rest of the family without need? Would Mr. Morton have believed a few bits of suspicion? More important, would *you*, Cadi? You'd have thought it was some trick Lucian was up to. So I told Sarah nothing and she asked nothing, just trusted me to be doing what was best."

A thought slipped suddenly into my mind. "Paddy, I think she loves you. I know there's somebody, and it must be you. She seemed to become grown-up in such a short time—as if something *big* had happened to her."

"I hope so." Paddy nodded slowly and smiled into the glow of the fire. "It's on both sides, Cadi."

"Oh, Paddy. I'm so glad for both of you." I thought for a moment. "Now I see why Sarah was worried about me when I wouldn't come home with the family. She knew already that something was amiss. And that's why she wrote to Richard, of course!"

"Ah, so she wrote to him, did she? And that's what brought him running out to save you. Poor Sarah, she must have been fretting her heart out with neither me nor Lucian there to turn to."

"Have you been out here in Venice all the time then, Paddy?"

"I have. Pretending to be an artist. I rented a top-floor studio just across the small canal at the back of the *palazzo*."

"And Lucian was with you?"

"Not until later. He was moving around between Rome, Venice, and Padua, talking to one or two people about your uncle." He drew on his pipe, and frowned. "We thought you'd be safe enough for a while. It wasn't likely your uncle would be fool enough to get rid of you straightaway. He had to take his time and make everyone believe you were happy with him before he could make a move. And then, when the family went home, Lucian was set to go gray with worry. 'I have to get her out, Paddy,' he says to me, 'but Chiavelli's still a powerful man here in Venice, so we'll need to tread softly, for we've no law on our side.' "

Paddy grinned suddenly. "So he went to Padua and talked about some fine horses he had for sale. Next day the count was out there, keen to talk business. Lucian played the rogue for him, sly and sharp, and in two days he had your uncle convinced that Lucian Farrel was as big a scoundrel as you'd find anywhere."

We were silent for a few moments before Paddy went on. "Well, there it was. Lucian tricked the count into declaring himself, and at the same time set the scene for taking you away nice and quietly in a month's time. We decided your uncle wouldn't hurt you when he was relying on Lucian to do his dirty work." He looked down at Richard and shook his head. "Then this young feller put a spoke in our wheel."

"He couldn't know what you were doing, Paddy."

"But it's made things awkward."

"You saw us escape?"

"We did."

"But how did you keep track of us through all the canals in that mist?"

"We followed the count's string of boats in a little canoe that Lucian bought weeks ago. We were close to the search boats, though they didn't know it. Then the mist cleared just for a minute or so, and we saw you."

"So did Uncle Guido. That's when he fired and wounded Richard."

"His men might have caught up with you, but Lucian went over the side and into the water and turned over a gondola and a boat without them ever knowing how it happened. There was a rare old confusion."

"They'd have killed him if they'd seen him!"

"He's a hard man to kill," Paddy said casually. "When I picked him up again, we'd lost you, or so I thought. But Lucian knew better. 'Find that line of stakes, Paddy,' he says. 'She'll follow the stakes and go to ground on the island, sure as you're alive.' "

I saw that Paddy Flynn was looking down at me with a whimsical smile. "We came ashore, and Lucian sent me on to find the watchman." He jerked his thumb toward a small door. "He's safe in the toolroom there, tied up. Meanwhile Lucian was hunting for you. He found your boat and tipped her over on her side to hide the mast. Then a few minutes later he spotted you as you came out of the hut." Paddy gave a little laugh. "It's no wonder you were set to scream at sight of him, all plastered with mud like some creature from a swamp."

A kind of sleepiness had come upon me, partly from weariness, but partly perhaps from the mental relief of having so many mysteries answered. "Who are you, Paddy Flynn?" I asked slowly. "Why have you risked so much to help Lucian keep me safe?"

"I'm Lucian's friend. We've done many things together, and the bonds are strong."

"You were an officer with him in the army?"

"I was his troop sergeant. Did you mistake me for a gentleman?"

"I don't think I made a mistake, Paddy."

"Maybe not," he said wryly. "I've a family in Ireland that's very much out of the top drawer, as they say. But I was the black sheep, d'you see, always in trouble. So my father turned me out, and I can't say I blame him. I joined up as a trooper. A gentleman ranker, that's what they call my kind." He smiled. "I was lucky to find myself serving under Lucian."

"You said you were cashiered together. What happened, Paddy?"

He gazed with unseeing eyes for a while, as if staring into the past. "It was a bad war," he said at last. "There's thousands of fine boys lying underground today who died from the stupidity of those who gave the orders. We saw it, Lucian and I, for months. Then Lucian went home on leave and talked with Mr. Morton. They made a plan together."

"Mr. Morton?" I was bewildered.

"He's an important man in the Foreign Office, Cadi. He knew brains would do the trick quicker than guns, especially after Lucian talked to him. So after Lucian came back to the regiment we let ourselves be captured."

He gave an ironic smile. "God knows it was easy enough. We only had to obey orders instead of using our heads. So after we'd been taken we were questioned by the Boers . . . and little by little we told them our order of battle, the plans for the new attack, and where our lines of communication would lie, bargaining all the while for money after they'd won the war. They despised us for traitors to our own side, but they listened."

He stretched, and gave a sigh of satisfaction. "Lord, how they listened! We both told the same story, the story Lucian had planned with Mr. Morton and some of the military chiefs in London. A good story it was, and false as a wooden leg. They were no fools, the Boers, but Lucian, he had them believing every word." Paddy laughed with sudden pleasure at the memory, then shook his head. "With his friends he's straight as a gun barrel, but when he's dealing with enemies he can play the rogue to perfection."

"And . . . the plan worked?"

"Even better than we'd hoped. Because of what we told them, the Boer commander in that area threw everything into an attack on Lichtenburg— and lost the best part of his army. That was the beginning of the end. Lucian and I escaped that night, the night of the battle, and just as well. We'd not have lived long once the Boers found how we'd tricked them."

Words tumbled from me in a fury of indignation. "But Lucian's been an outcast ever since! And you too, I suppose! Why hasn't everything been told? Why can people treat Lucian as if he really had been a traitor? It's not fair, Paddy, it's not fair!"

"Easy now," he said amiably. "It's no more than we expected. We knew the truth wouldn't be told for a while. Rumors soon crept around. We were arrested and cashiered, and we couldn't defend ourselves with the truth, for it was what they call most secret. But we knew the price in advance, Cadi, so we can't complain."

"But you can!" I exclaimed. "The war's been over for three years!"

"It's still too soon," Paddy said gently. "The military intelligence folk hate to have their secrets told, in case they want to use them again. Oh, it'll come out one day, thanks to Mr. Morton. He's pressing hard, and he'll have his way in the end."

"I think it's horrible," I said bitterly.

"It's better than war, Cadi. Better for a couple of fellers to end up as outcasts than for a few thousand to end up dead."

Richard groaned in his sleep and stirred. I put my hand on his hot forehead, and after a few seconds he settled down again without waking.

"You and Lucian must be very great friends," I said. "But I still don't understand why he should put you both to so much trouble over all these weeks and months for somebody who's a newcomer to the family."

"Do you not, Cadi? Have you really no idea?"

I looked at him, baffled. "He knows Mr. Morton is very fond of me, that's all I can think of."

He laughed. "It's a shade more direct than that. I remember . . ." He paused. "I remember just after the war being worried about Lucian. He was drifting, doing nothing special. Then one day nearly three years ago he came to me in London and said he was setting up stables at Epsom and would I come in with him as equal partner. There was something about him . . . he suddenly seemed a different man."

"Different in what way, Paddy?"

"Well, like a man who's suddenly found something worth living for. 'Paddy,' he says, 'the damnedest thing has happened. We've lived hard, you and I, and you know I'm not some young fool whose head's easily turned. So listen, Paddy. A week ago in Mawstone I met a young girl, a child almost, not much over seventeen, and there's no girl in the world like her.' Then he tells me the story of what happened in Mogg Race Bay."

I found my hands were trembling, and linked them together in my lap. To learn that Lucian had spoken of me in such a way made me glow with joy, yet I was dumbfounded. He had given no hint that he even liked me.

Paddy went on. "When Lucian finished the story he says, kind of pleading with me to agree, 'If I wait a year or two until she's grown up a little, I could go to her and court her, couldn't I?' " Paddy shook his head and made a wry face. "I had to say it to him, Cadi. 'But you're a man disgraced, like meself, Lucian. There's that to remember.'

" 'It's that I'm thinking of,' he says. 'But if she ever came to like me and believe in me, she wouldn't care what other folk thought. She's a little thing, with little hands, but I'd trust my life in them as I would in yours, Paddy.' "

Paddy looked at me. "So we started the stables. He wanted to have something to offer you when the time came. And we've done well, more than well. I'll tell the truth and say I thought Lucian would forget you in a few months. But I was wrong. I hadn't met you then."

"He . . . he never showed what he felt," I said.

"Ah, how could he now? You had all the troubles of settling down in a new life and he wanted to give you time, Cadi. But you were quick. He was just thinking the time was right, that he could begin to show his feelings, when it came out that you were heiress to a great fortune. That hit him harder than the bullet from the Boers he took at Brandwater Basin."

"Hit him? Why, Paddy?"

He sighed. "If he'd begun paying attention to you as soon as you became an heiress, what would you have imagined?"

"But he did ask Mr. Morton if he could court me," I said.

"Ah, but that was only after we knew you were in danger from Count Chiavelli. Lucian was desperate to be with you at Meadhaven. But Mr.

Morton wouldn't allow it, so we had to manage as best we could." He stood gazing down at me curiously, as if trying to read my thoughts. "Lucian loves you, Cadi Tregaron. I wonder what you feel for him?"

I did not answer, for even as Paddy spoke I heard the door opening softly. Lucian stood staring at us with a strange, angry look. He pushed the door shut behind him.

"Damn your wagging tongue, Paddy!" he said.

Paddy returned the stare, his chin outthrust a little. "Damn it as much as you like, but I'm not sorry," he said stubbornly. Then, with a touch of anger, "Have you no sense, man? First you keep silent because she's a child, and then because she's an heiress, and you were a fool on both counts. Has it never dawned on you that if she loves a man she'll love as her grandmother did—because *this* is the man she loves and trusts? And the devil with all else!"

I said, "Be quiet, Paddy dear," and got to my feet. I walked toward Lucian and put out my hands for him to take. "The devil with all else, Lucian," I said.

He freed one hand, tilted my face, and kissed me gently on the lips. Then, with his eyes still upon me, he said, "They're here, Paddy. Chiavelli and his rogues. They've started searching."

CHAPTER ELEVEN

FOR A FEW BLISSFUL moments I had forgotten the danger that threatened us all, but the tautness in Lucian's face was a grim reminder.

Holding my hands, he was looking past me at Paddy Flynn now. "Chiavelli must have guessed Cadi's hiding somewhere on the island."

Paddy glanced down at Richard. "You'd better take Cadi in the canoe and fetch help from Venice, then. I'll stay and guard the boy."

Something stronger than fear made me say quickly, "I won't leave Richard. He came to save me, and I won't leave him."

"You have to, Cadi," Lucian said. His eyes were suddenly anxious. "You can't help Paddy protect him, so it's foolish for you to risk everything by staying."

"I don't care if it's foolish," I said desperately, "I've *got* to stay, Lucian. If he wakes up and I'm not with him, he'll feel deserted."

Paddy broke in. "Think back, Lucian. Did *you* leave me wounded that day at Magersfontein because it was the sensible thing to do?"

Lucian's thick brows drew close together. "All right, I won't argue. You take the canoe, Paddy, and I'll stay here with Richard and Cadi. You know what to do when you reach Venice."

"I know sure enough, but you're known to the people who can best give help, and I'm not."

Lucian stood very still. I could see that he was seeking a way round the truth of what Paddy had said. But there was none.

"Don't worry about us," I said quickly. "You'll be back before Uncle Guido and his men find us here."

He shook his head. "It's not long till dawn. They'll have searched every cranny within an hour—" He broke off, and from his grimy face the blue eyes shone suddenly bright. "But not if I give them something else to keep them busy," he added softly. "Yes . . . I think I can manage that." He lifted my hand and kissed it, then led me toward Paddy and put my hand in his. "For God's sake take good care of her."

At the door Lucian paused and looked back. I knew that in leaving me now he was perhaps doing the hardest thing he had ever done. "Don't look for trouble, Paddy," he said, "but remember, Chiavelli has a pistol."

"And I have me wits, Lucian. Don't be fretting now."

It was five minutes after we had barred the door behind Lucian that I first saw the flames. I was standing by a window, peering through a crack in the heavy shutters. The mist had vanished, and in the semidarkness I saw a flower of yellow flame suddenly blossom beyond the main foundry building. I could see men running, pointing and gesturing, though I could hear no sound at this distance.

"He said he'd keep 'em busy," murmured Paddy beside me.

"There's another fire," I whispered. "There, to the right."

Paddy chuckled. "There's no lack of fuel in a foundry, praise be."

"Uncle Guido's taking charge. Look, can you see him? He's getting the men to form a bucket chain."

A voice behind us croaked feebly, "Cadi . . . ?" I turned and ran to Richard. He lay staring up at me with enormous eyes. "What . . . what's happened?"

With all my heart I was thankful now that I had stayed. I knelt and smiled down at him. "Don't worry, Richard dear. Lucian's looking after us."

"Lucian?" Richard sighed and relaxed. "That's good . . . oh, that's good, Cadi." His eyes closed. "I lied when I said you shouldn't trust him, Cadi. He's a strong man, Lucian . . . I was jealous. . . ." His voice became a mumble. His breathing was quicker now, more shallow, and I felt a growing fear for him.

That was the beginning of a long vigil. Paddy stood like a statue by one or another of the windows. Now and then, through the slats of the shutters, I could see a red glow from one of the fires Lucian had started, and catch the faint sound of shouting as Uncle Guido and his men fought the flames. I lost track of time and seemed to be in a dream. Strangely, despite the danger that threatened so closely, I would have felt full of joy if it had not been for the sharp anxiety that Richard roused in me. Lucian loved me, and my whole being wanted to sing with the knowledge, but it seemed wicked to rejoice, with Richard's hot dry hand in mine, and the sound of his troubled breathing in my ears.

It was a shock when I lifted my head and saw that the gray light of dawn was showing through the shutters.

"Paddy?" I whispered. "What's happening?"

He did not turn as he answered. "They've doused the fires and they've started searching again."

"How long has Lucian been gone?"

"An hour and a half. They've wasted most of it."

"Can he bring help from Venice? Will anybody believe him?"

"It's not just anybody he'll be talking to, Cadi. There's two gentlemen should have arrived last night—" He broke off and I saw him stiffen. "They're coming this way at last, his nibs and a few of his cutthroats."

Paddy moved quickly, and the end of the furnace hid him from my view. "Be easy now," he said. "We've a trick or two up our sleeves yet."

The future was suddenly a cold reality to me. Uncle Guido and his men would break down the door in a minute or two, and then we would die. Paddy Flynn, for all his coolness and his experience, was only one unarmed man against a dozen or more.

There came a hammering on the door, then a shout. "It's barred! She is here!" I stood up so that I could see above the shoulder of the furnace.

The door was shaking under heavy blows from a sledgehammer. The wooden sockets holding the bar gave way, and the door swung open.

Uncle Guido appeared in the doorway, his face and clothes black with smoke. He held a pistol in his hand. Behind him I could see the first pink of the rising sun. From the black mask of his face, two eyes glittered feverishly as he peered slowly round the gloomy interior of the foundry.

"Caterina!" he cried in a voice that cracked with long-pent fury.

My breath hissed from my lungs.

His head jerked, seeking me. And then, incredibly, I saw a glowing spear flash through the air toward him, the tip bright red for a full twelve inches. A blowpipe! A glassblower's pipe, its end almost white with heat! From the shadows that hid him, Paddy had thrown it like a javelin.

Uncle Guido threw up his arms to ward it off, and screamed as the touch of it seared his hand. I heard his pistol clatter to the floor. A second blowpipe flashed like some monstrously long firefly through the air. Uncle Guido staggered back in panic, falling. The pipe whistled above him through the doorway as he fell. I heard a new scream as it found a target beyond. Then I saw Paddy leaping across the foundry floor, a thick beam of wood in his hand. He slammed the door, set the beam at an angle against it, scooped up the pistol, and stepped back. "Let's have ye, gossoons!" he roared in a great voice. "There's a bullet 'tween the eyes for the first face to show at door or window!"

He turned to me. "Tell 'em in Italian, Cadi," he said. "A bullet for the first man to show—tell 'em quick now."

I moved out from behind the furnace and shouted the warning at the top of my voice. Then we stood listening. We could hear a rapid scuffling of feet moving away from the foundry, and a medley of frantic Italian.

"We have 'em," Paddy said softly, and weighed the pistol in his hand. "I fancy they've no other firearm between 'em."

Hope surged high in me, and by some strange quirk of the mind I thought of the day when I would tell Sarah this story, of how Paddy Flynn, the man she loved, had outwitted our enemies at a single stroke. "That was wonderful, what you did just now," I said. "I thought we were lost."

"Ah, well, I have all me wits, but it was serving under Lucian that sharpened them. When it comes to a scrimmage, he's the master. One day I'll tell you how we escaped the twelve-man guard in De La Rey's camp with just a piece of soap." He gave a joyous chuckle at the memory, but he stopped short as from some distance beyond the door there came a shout.

Uncle Guido was calling, and there was a trembling wildness in his voice. "Caterina! Do you hear me?"

I looked at Paddy. He shook his head and I remained silent.

"Caterina!" Uncle Guido shouted again. "We have bundles of straw and dry wood here, and we shall pile them round the walls and set them blazing. If you do not come out, we shall *burn* you out! Do you hear?"

Hope turned to despair. Then Paddy touched my arm, and when I looked up into his face I almost flinched at the cold fury I saw there. "Burn us out, will they?" he breathed. "We'll see. Stand by to open the door and shut it fast again, Cadi. I'm going out. And if I can't bring him down with a shot before his pack of wolves reach me, then I'm no soldier."

Waves of sickness swept me. I was afraid for Paddy, afraid for Richard and myself, even afraid for Uncle Guido. This was the inexorable horror Lucian and Paddy had found in war, and now I could understand why they had sacrificed their reputations to shorten the span of brutality.

With an effort I lifted the beam of wood jammed against the door. Paddy stood crouched, ready to race forward, when a new sound came from outside, a sudden uproar of shouting and running feet.

Paddy darted to one of the windows and peered through the shutter, then gave a little laugh and turned to look at me with humorous eyes. "It's sunrise, Miss Tregaron," he said. "It's sunrise on a beautiful morning, and Lucian is here—with some friends."

Paddy kicked the beam aside and threw open the door. I saw men running, and being pursued by other men in uniform. Two policemen held

Uncle Guido. Lucian was coming toward us, and I gasped as I saw that beside him walked Signor Vecchi, the Italian diplomat who had been at Meadhaven on that evening when Granny Caterina's locket disclosed its secret. Behind them came a man I had not seen before.

Lucian looked dirtier than ever in the light of day. As I came out of the foundry with Paddy beside me, he ran forward and caught me in his arms, murmuring my name over and over again. Then he turned his head a little and said, "Did you have any trouble, Paddy?"

Paddy was watching the police roundup of Uncle Guido's men. He held up the pistol and said, "A little, but we managed."

Lucian took my arm. "Cadi, you already know Signor Vecchi. This other gentleman is your Italian lawyer, Signor Bonello. I've been in touch with them over the past week or two, and I managed to persuade them to come to Venice to meet me, so I could tell them exactly what I'd discovered about Count Chiavelli. I had an appointment with them this morning— which I kept rather earlier than they expected."

Signor Vecchi took my hand and bowed over it. "It is a great relief to find you safe," he said in Italian, his distress and agitation very plain. "We have Mr. Farrel to thank for that. He is very persuasive. At first, when he came to me and told me of the bargain he had pretended to strike with Count Chiavelli, I could not believe it. But my friend Bonello urged that we should come to Venice and look into the matter ourselves." His smile was full of apology. "I am sorry we did not come sooner." He looked about him, and his face became stern. "But there is no need for investigation now. Chiavelli is revealed for all to see as a scoundrel who would murder his own kin for gain."

In the last minute or two, with the knowledge that the long night of danger was past, a stupefying weariness had descended upon me. My mind seemed numb. "Richard," I said. "Richard is hurt. . . . Please, please get help to him." The ground tilted beneath my feet. I clutched at Lucian and felt him pick me up in his arms before a great wave of blackness rose to engulf me.

The next thing I remember is sinking into a soft bed while covers were drawn up about me. It was not until many hours later that I discovered that Signor Vecchi had sent two nursing nuns to look after me. I was told that as they bathed the mud and grime from my body and put a nightdress on me I had talked continually, about mudbanks and glowing spears, sea mist and boats. But always I kept returning to Richard, crying out in anxiety and saying that I must go to him, so that in the end I was made to drink a strong sedative. When at last I woke to my proper senses Sister Angelina told me that I had slept the clock round. Before I would drink the broth she brought I asked after Richard.

"A surgeon operated on him at noon yesterday, and we hope all will be well, but it is too early to know yet. Come now, eat your broth, little one." She spoke in English, for she had spent several years in an English convent, as I learned later.

"Where's Lucian—Mr. Farrel?" I asked. "And Mr. Flynn?"

"They have had much to attend to, and they also needed rest. Signor Vecchi says they will come to you as soon as they can."

For three hours I fretted because Sister Angelina would not let me go to Richard in the hospital. Then Lucian came, and when I saw his face I felt all hope go out of me. He sat on the side of the bed and took my hand.

"Be a brave girl, Cadi," he said quietly. "Richard died half an hour ago. The bullet set up an infection that struck very quickly, and he had no resistance to it after that night on the island."

I wept, thinking of Mr. and Mrs. Morton and Sarah. Lucian sat holding my hand. I was glad he did not try to utter useless words of comfort. When the spasm of weeping had passed I whispered, "How will you tell them?"

"I've already sent a telegram, and I'll write a letter to Mr. Morton today, telling him all the details. Signor Vecchi will send it by courier."

I gripped his hand. "How long must we stay here? I want to go away from Venice. I want you to take me home, Lucian. Please!"

"I will, just as soon as I can, my darling." He pushed back the hair from my brow. "Now try to sleep a little more. I'll stay with you."

To MY OVERWHELMING relief we left Venice only ten days later. This was because the powers that be wanted as little scandal as possible. Uncle Guido claimed that he had not intended to shoot Richard, but had meant to fire a warning shot because he believed that I was being kidnapped. It was a hopeless story. Both Paddy and I had heard him threaten to kill us, but I did not seek revenge against Uncle Guido. Mr. Morton, for his part, felt the same way. Nothing could bring Richard back, and to prolong the affair would only prolong the distress of us all. He could not leave Mrs. Morton, but he wrote a long letter to Lucian.

> We mourn Richard and ever shall. There was a strangeness in him, as well you know, Lucian, but I feel that in trying to save Cadi, so rashly, so gallantly, he has redeemed all faults. We grieve, but we can justly temper our grief with pride in what he did.
>
> As for pressing charges against that evil man Chiavelli, I have no heart for it. You say that if Cadi and I agree to take no action against him, then he and his family will secretly be banished from the country. Let that suffice. He will find no place in Europe, for rumors will always dog him there. Let him live with his conscience and his defeat in some far place across the world, and let us forget him.
>
> Above all, bring our Cadi home to us with all speed, Lucian. Her presence will give us comfort as nothing else could. . . .

And so, on a day in summer, I came home to Meadhaven. Richard's body had been sent by ship, and he was laid to rest in the churchyard at Wealdhurst. By Lucian's wish, Mrs. Morton was told nothing of the part he and Paddy Flynn had played in saving me, but was allowed to believe that Richard had succeeded alone, and had given his life for my sake.

Strangely, I found Mrs. Morton more calm and serene than I had ever known her before. After the first dreadful shock of losing Richard, it seemed that some deep and unconscious anxiety within her had been taken away, leaving her a kind of peace beneath the sadness.

Our time of mourning at Meadhaven was not long, for Mr. Morton disliked the outward trappings of a family's sorrow. Paddy Flynn and Lucian became constant visitors, and as the summer wore on, Sarah and I often spent a day at the stables in Epsom. We were both engaged by summer's end, I to Lucian and Sarah to Paddy Flynn. She still came to my room to chatter before going to bed, and never tired of making me tell once again the story of those terrifying moments in the foundry when Uncle Guido and his men were breaking down the door.

The day of my marriage to Lucian was arranged for early May, three months after my twenty-first birthday. I had come into the fortune, but to my relief and to Sarah's disappointment I had not inherited the title. I gathered from Mr. Morton that the authorities in Rome had decided that unless I laid claim to the title, it should be allowed to lapse.

I did not care to lay claim. I cared about two things. First, that the shadows of disgrace should be lifted from Lucian and Paddy, and second, that Lucian should not be troubled by my wealth.

For the first, I had to be patient. "Just one more year, Cadi," Mr. Morton promised. "I have the foreign secretary's firm undertaking on that."

"But will he *keep* his promise?"

Mr. Morton chuckled. "Well, I have told him plainly that if he fails, I shall resign from the Foreign Office, stand for Parliament myself, and raise the matter in the House as a scandal." His eyes were grim for a moment. "Believe me, child, they will give way rather than allow that."

My second care was resolved simply by speaking about it. We were at the stables one day soon after my twenty-first birthday, waiting for a mare to foal. I put my hand through Lucian's arm as we sat on a pile of straw, and said, "Tell me what to do about the money, Lucian. I love you so much, and I don't want it to spoil things. You know I've arranged with Signor Vecchi to put some of the money in trust, for the *palazzo* to be made into an orphanage in memory of Granny Caterina. But if you think it's better to give the rest away, just tell me."

He looked startled. "Don't be a little idiot, Cadi."

"I'm not. A month ago I had nothing and was happy; today I'm rich and happy. It makes no difference to me—the money, I mean. Do you want me as I was, Lucian, or as I am? All I long for is to come to you the way you want me."

He chewed a straw, and was silent for a long minute. Then he turned to me, smiling. "Ah, Cadi, my own little fishergirl, never stop teaching me the wisdom you were born with. Keep what's yours and do whatever you want with it. You could start by buying a beautiful motor lifeboat for the Mawstonefolk. And one for Bosney, perhaps. You could have Cadi Tregaron—Cadi Farrel—lifeboats all round the coast."

We were married at St. Mary's Church, in Wealdhurst, and for our honeymoon we took a house in Cornwall, near Truro. This was by Lucian's suggestion, and I joyously agreed. A cook-housekeeper would come in each day to look after us. We would sail and swim, we would ride and walk through the countryside of my childhood, and we would go to Mawstone so that I could renew acquaintance with my old friends there.

It was on the night of our wedding that I first told Lucian of the dream and of the strange ways in which it had gradually been fulfilled. I was standing before him as he sat on the edge of the big bed. We were both in our dressing gowns, mine a beautiful silk one that Sarah had made with her own hands. He looked troubled when I told him how I had walked in my sleep that night in the Palazzo Chiavelli, how I had seen his face in the mirror and fled from him in terror.

"Oh, Cadi, I was busy thinking myself into the part I had to play. I'm sorry."

"There's nothing to be sorry about now." I put my arms round his neck and held his head close against me. "That was the bad dream, and it's finished forever," I whispered. "Now come over to the door and wait for me, Lucian. I know it's silly, but I want the good dream to come true. Please?"

He stood up and took my hand. "It's not silly. I want it fulfilled for you too, Cadi."

I went out of the room and a little way along the passage. Lucian had closed the door, and a crack of light showed beneath it.

I began to walk slowly toward the room, and as I moved I felt the joy and longing spread from my heart to my whole body. Before me lay the end of dreaming, for Lucian was real, and I loved him.

With a happiness almost too great to bear, I lifted my hand to the door. As I did so it swung wide, and Lucian stood there smiling, his eyes warm with a world of love and his arms open to receive me.